GILLESPIE

by

J. MacDOUGALL HAY

Introduction by Bob Tait and Isobel Murray

He that is greedy of gain, troubleth
his own house.   Proverbs 15:27

CANONGATE

Edinburgh

Canongate Publishing Ltd.
17 Jeffrey Street, Edinburgh

First published 1914
First published by Canongate 1979
Canongate Paperback edition reprinted 1983

Introduction © Bob Tait & Isobel Murray 1979

ISBN 0 903937 79 4 Cased
0 903937 80 8 Canongate Paperback

*The publishers acknowledge the
financial assistance of the Scottish
Arts Council in the publication of
this volume.*

Printed in Great Britain
by Redwood Burn Limited
Trowbridge

INTRODUCTION

by BOB TAIT and ISOBEL MURRAY

A leech, a pirate, a predatory beast, anti-Christ, hell: in such terms
is Gillespie Strang described by a variety of people in the course of
this book. The fact that some of the same characters at other times
see him as a rising man, a public benefactor, the fishermen's
friend, and not a man but a god is only a further tribute to the
power of his malice and intelligence in the manipulation of his fellows. The character of Gillespie is only the most outstanding
feature in a novel of extraordinary power and range, a novel important to the Scottish consciousness and intended to be so: Hay
believed that "the growing spirit of materialism in Scotland needed
a Gillespie."

The author, John Macdougall Hay (1881–1919), was a Church
of Scotland minister, who was born and raised at Tarbert, Loch
Fyne, the fictional "Brieston". Hay's familiarity with "Brieston",
the fishing and farming and history of the place, is an inestimable
asset to this, his only important book. (He published only one other
novel, *Barnacles* before his early death.) *Gillespie* was warmly received by critics in Britain and America, but 1914 was an unfortunate year for a literary début. The book sank out of sight until, at
the instigation of the late Robert Kemp, it was reissued in 1963,
when it caused another brief sensation. In October 1972 Harry
Reid wrote a warm appreciation of the novel in *The Scotsman*, but
the difficulty of finding the book prevented all but the most determined from pursuing the subject.

Without getting bogged down in the extent to which Hay based
the book on his native Tarbert, Reid shows that he did have Tarbert and given historical and social conditions in mind. The
phantasmagorical tale has then in this sense a very real setting: and
it is the more effective for that. The chronology is another matter.
As we note below, Hay has his own ways of bending and contracting
time to suit his artistic purposes—when he isn't being, frankly,
inconsistent. However, we know that the use of ring-nets (Hay's
"trawls") was prohibited on Loch Fyne between 1860 and 1865,
and a Commission investigated many such local rules and regula-

tions. An Act in the mid '6os legalised the practice. So we can with some confidence place the action of Book II in that period.

That is the crucial moment of transition for Hay: the moment when historical forces began to incorporate such relatively stable and isolated rural and fishing communities and economies into the industrial and commercial nexus—with Glasgow not only the nearest main centre, but one Hay knew well. Kemp suggests that his experience of the city was uneasy and unhappy.

The forces of evil—both natural and man-made—are frighteningly powerful in the world Hay presents to us in *Gillespie*. Hay's preoccupation with the notion of evil is so clear and intense that it is a key factor in interpreting the book within the context of Scottish culture at the turn of the century. Here is a Scottish novelist, writing in the early years of the twentieth century about events which—all else besides—mark a crucial historical turning point for his kind of community. New technology, transport and marketing opportunities, the accumulation of capital and property (including land), all are there, factors in the transition. The straightforward dominance of gentry over tenant farmer and fisherman will be intruded upon by new kinds of entrepreneurs, merchants and capitalists. Gillespie is their prophet. These men will exploit the technical and commercial factors with the aid of those survivors of the *ancien régime*, time-serving lawyers and bankers. Gillespie is both chief protagonist and vehicle of treachery and opportunity.

However, in Hay's sombre vision of his world and its history there are forces, notably forces threatening and hostile to mankind, which are beyond the reckoning of this generation, beyond even men as "souple", tirelessly scheming and tenacious as Gillespie Strang. To complicate matters further, hardly anyone (except Morag Strang) is cast as a mere victim or innocent plaything. It is a sinister twist that Gillespie, applying the strength of his mind and will to his own affairs, *has* to be considered responsible for the malicious things he does and for the harm he brings about. He also *does* bring doom, a "curse", down on his house and on others in the community. None of it could have happened without him—except, presumably, the extraordinary sequence of natural disasters which so strangely, nonetheless, coincides with his doings. And yet the terrible things he brings about—in collaboration, wittingly and unwittingly, with others—are also inexorable, brought about in a sense unknowingly but surely.

It is striking that Hay so often associates foresight and energy

viii

with wilfulness, malice, greed, vengeance and disaster. And there is more to this than homilies on the text "God is not mocked", or sermonising about sins of selfishness or presumption. It is more interesting and significant that he is inconsistent about the source of all these compelling and fascinating evils in the world. Men and women make their own, yes. But some evil comes out of history. And some of it from beyond the confines of this world. Richard Strang feels such a baleful influence touch him the very hour his son Gillespie is born (8). "History", that is, is portentous, fascinating, dangerous—and unmasterable.

It is this fearsome, unintelligible Past dimension rather than God—or as well as God—that is mocked when such humans seek to intervene and take charge. The history of these Scots is only matter for "romance": they are apt indeed, as in the case of Mrs Galbraith's use of the Bible, to turn not only their own history but larger historical testimonies into fuel for their "superstition". This fear-tinged, magical conception of time and destiny can inspire such as Mrs Galbraith to adopt a monstrous misconception of her earthly mission. It can affect the balance of a mind such as Eoghan's. But what of Gillespie?

He is the one trained to turn his back on time past and whatever lurks therein: he is harbinger of the new era. But in effect the fear of doom that explains his upbringing creates an outlet for the darkest of forces in a scarcely human being. Gillespie is as relentless as time. His appetites are all the more threatening for being utterly cold in an almost superhumanly merciless and ruthless way. He is everything that a people unable—or afraid—to come to terms with their history might fear in historical forces personified. Here Hay seems to probe deep into a Scottish problem, its roots and ramifications: fear of the unintelligible and unmasterable in life and history producing malevolent colossi from the Kailyard.

The English novel characteristically limits itself to issues more domestic than the Scots. Where the strength of the English novel can very generally be said to reside in analysis of individual, family or group relationships, of individual psychology, or in forms of the novel of manners, *Gillespie*, like other Scots novels, has a wider scope. To find similar scope and ambition we have to go to the Russian or American novel, where matters political, social, philosophical and metaphysical are more commonly treated. In some ways the elemental drama—and the over-writing—of *Gillespie* recall most the wild, ambiguous universe of *Moby Dick*. Hay and Melville share a relentless questioning of the nature of the universe and the source and nature of evil.

The comparison with *Moby Dick* remains a useful one when we consider *Gillespie* as a literary achievement. Like Melville's novel, Hay's is vast in scale, often overpowering in its language, elemental or obsessively religious in its imagery, full of inconsistencies, dominated by a large pattern of narrative, touched with comedy, pathos and effective irony, innovatory in narrative technique.

The inconsistencies have to be acknowledged. Sometimes they are trivial: initially, Mrs Galbraith is described as "in middle age" and is attractive to both Lonend and Gillespie: at least twenty-three years later, she is still the same in looks and attraction! That is unimportant: more troubling is a certain failure on Hay's part to convey imaginatively his logical and theolgical *schema* of her life. *That* says that Mrs Galbraith went wrong when she prayed for vengeance and chose to usurp God's prerogative (76). This wrong is underlined by Dr Maclean: "Let him alone: he'll maybe find out that a man can buy gold too dear" (73). Theoretically, she continues to "retrogress" until she finds the fruits of her vengeance in Eoghan's death (439, prophesied 36), knows her responsibility for it and then suffers a dark night of the soul and regains her angelic qualities, nursing old Strang *and* Gillespie devotedly.

This is not the experience of the novel: we are not imaginatively sufficiently aware of her regeneration at the end and Hay is not always sufficiently aware of her corruption in the body of the book. So we find his admiration of her communion with nature in Book II, chapter 11, when she has a "glorified face", Lonend sees her as an "angelic guest" and she muses on the "Holy Land" of memory—and in the very next chapter she begins "to knead the clay of Mrs Strang's life", and to prepare Morag's road to prostitution.

It is easier to forgive even these more important inconsistencies and impossibilities of chronology when we realise that they do not damage the large pattern of the novel. This larger pattern is always controlled: events are prepared for and often prophesied and the plan is fulfilled. But more than that, Hay is often concerned to show the crooked or twisted ways in which prophecies, self-fulfilling or otherwise, come true.

The novel is divided into four "Books" of very unequal length, but the division shows Hay's full awareness of his strategy and its development. Book I starts with the house, the "Ghost". An atmosphere of menace, bloodshed and horror is created before the

Strangs are even mentioned and the promised horror spreads through the entire novel. Gillespie's ambition is made clear as is his insatiable rapacity, but this Book is mainly concerned with these within the ambit of family and personal relations. Although he already schemes for a "big fishing fleet of trawlers" (22), here he is concerned with Galbraith and his widow, with Lonend as present colleague and future victim, with Morag , "a creature made for love" (87), whom Gillespie can treat "only on the basis of a commercial agreement" (27). Gillespie, we are told for the first of many times, "was not a religious man; but he conceived that the stars were fighting for him"(26).

Book I then indicates Gillespie's monstrous nature, "dark, pernicious, impenetrable, without bowels of pity, immovable as granite"(102). It inculcates horror of Gillespie, alarm regarding Mrs Galbraith, pity for Morag. And it takes place mainly at the "Ghost", at Muirhead and at Lonend—in family houses and farms outside the town, with the action still centred on individuals.

Book II is the longest section of the novel and is about Gillespie's fluctuating relationship with the town of Brieston. The Book is set exclusively in the town and traces the graph of Gillespie's popularity and of his success. The legalisation of trawling, for example, makes him an idol in chapter 19; now he is the man of the new epoch; but in chapter 20, when the herring are short, he is blamed. There follow heat, drought, plague and storm, and while the people of Brieston suffer or die, praise or blame Gillespie, he goes inexorably on, emotionless and insatiable, like a big trawl himself. Only the united social attempt at punishment affects him, when his fleet is burnt—and he characteristically makes a profit out of the apparent misfortune and plans vengeance on the whole town. This Book is about his manipulation of the town for commercial ends and vengeance, what is spelt out in the final chapter as "the sin of the fallen angels" (256).

Book III might be termed the Book of the sons. Gillespie is grimly present in chapter 3, "immersed body and soul in the glittering pursuit of gain" (276). But the two boys are in the foreground. Iain is brought in for four chapters, most importantly to comfort his grandfather and love Eoghan, to hear the spey-wife's prophecy and to die bravely at sea because of his father's parsimony. Eoghan is of great importance from the start of Book III. His strange sensibility, fed on romance and starved of normal relationships, is to cast a hallucinatory aura over the action henceforth. His dreams and nightmares and experience of a "dim ancestral voice" enhance the horror of the whole situation, and his confused and gradual adolescent apprehension of his mother's alcoholism and harlotry indicate the precarious hold the Strang family now has on life and reality.

This is continued and intensified in Book IV, where Eoghan and Morag continue to be the central figures until the end. The gloom is relieved by the introduction of Barbara, and her relationship with Eoghan implies that he is with luck capable of normality. But instead dream, unreality and madness are dominant: Eoghan and Morag grow more and more self-destructive, each potentially destructive of the other, until in the end Gillespie comes back, beaten, to the "Ghost". The action has been gradually moving back to the family source since Iain's corpse was brought home (321). All that is left of the family dies there, in punishing silence. The plan is complete.

The large shape of the book also contains many other contrasts, in particular that between violence, natural or human, and the silent malevolence that marks Gillespie's crimes. So the violence stretches from storm, plague and shipwreck to such human episodes as Mrs Galbraith's symbolic destruction of her home, the dramatic rescue and cruel death of Jock o' the Patch and the final climatic blood-bath. Even more spine-chilling are Gillespie's unobtrusive crimes: he cheats Mrs Galbraith with Lonend's help and then cheats Lonend; he gets Morag pregnant to hasten his revenge on Lonend; he cheats Janet of all her possessions; he cheats Red Duncan out of his share of the boat and does the same for many more; he cheats over the Poor Rates—the list is endless. Most of his characteristics can be summed up in two crimes—his selling illegal trawl nets at inflated prices at no personal risk and then informing on the customers so that the nets will be confiscated; and his long, continuous crime, his inhuman treatment of Morag.

Silence and cunning are his trademarks. The most appropriate end to this often apocalyptic and raging book is the silence that greets him after the carnage in his house and the calm silence of his father when he goes, too late, to attempt reparation, "the judgment of unearthly silence" (444).

The characterisation is already implicit in this larger pattern. Gillespie is of course central. He is utterly cold and lacking in compassion; the most appropriate image Hay finds for him is in his courtship of Morag, where he momentarily softens. Hay compares this to the sun's rays briefly reaching "something inflammable" in the heart of an iceberg: once the "gross ice" has extinguished this brief fire, it is "gone for ever" (29, 59). The really horrible thing about this wholly callous man is his warm and hearty exterior, his "jolly, rubicund face" (85), "so big and soft-looking", as Mrs Galbraith puts it (72).

What distinguishes Gillespie from the merely amoral and greedy is the scale of his ambition: he *does* believe the stars are warring for him, and combines the over-reaching ambition of a Faustus with the money-worship of a Volpone. In this, of course, lies the seed of his downfall. Against the advice of the "Good Book" he has laid up his treasure on earth. He never stops being "a worshipper of things" (10): his idea of reparation at the end is to pay back his father's loan with interest and to bring him expensive doctors. But he finally understands that things become dust and ashes if he cannot at least have an heir. His attitude to his first son is simply commercial: "Nae use peyin' a man when I hae a son for the work" (278). Even after Iain's death he thinks: "his father had had all the profit out of Iain" (328). Then he begins to realise the importance of the only son remaining. This late development of some human feeling is necessary if Gillespie is to begin to understand, as well as suffer, his punishment.

Morag is essentially victim rather than active character and our feelings about her are largely controlled by Hay's imagery. She was potentially a "Madonna" of love and purity: she inevitably becomes a "Magdalene", drunk and degraded. Her suffering is very long drawn out. Her "*Via Dolorosa*" is her helpless return to Gillespie in Book I, chapter 18, when he has rejected her: no subsequent sins can seriously be held against her. Except, of course, by her son Eoghan, whose reaction to the domestic situation is intensely Scottish as well as adolescent. Drunkenness in a *woman*, promiscuity in a *woman*, are sins more shame-making than any manifestations of the malice of man. This is also forced on the reader, ironically enough, in the meditations of Mrs Galbraith, the exploiter of Morag, on the wrongs of her sex: "Man had taught woman bestiality and then visited her sins pitilessly upon her" (360).

After Gillespie himself, Eoghan is probably the most important character, because his sensibility contributes so much to the impact of the last two Books. He is a superbly drawn unhappy adolescent, acutely observed and recognisable, and yet more than usually unstable and fey. His dreams, nightmares, visions and emotions are

xiii

frenzied and hectic: one nightmare includes a burning sea, strangled infants, fallen stars, the army of the drowned, a burned and ruined town, himself in manacles and a redemptive Magdalene! He is the product of the romantic reading the elder Strangs did so much to protect Gillespie from, he is clearly the inheritor of his grandmother's sensibility—and he is the son of a hideous home. With all that we are assured he is not mad, that given the chance he and Barbara could have acheived something positive—even Gillespie sees that—but this only heightens the waste and horror of the murderous ending, where the only mitigation is that he *is* saved from the matricide he contemplates when he momentarily sees Morag as "incarnate evil" (393).

Lonend is useful as a foil to Gillespie and a measure of him: their backgrounds and circumstances are so similar that we measure both Gillespie's intellect and evil by Lonend's inferiority. Even Spider McAskill, wholly unpleasent though that gentleman is, is mere fluff in comparison to Gillespie. But the description of Spider (65–6) is a brilliant piece of invective, comic and yet frightening. Long introductory descriptions are a feature of the book related to other aspects of Hay's narrative method: he tells a great deal about the characters in these set-piece descriptions and prepares us, often very fully, for their subsequent actions.

Evil dominates the book, but there is a long list of quiet good characters, most importantly the doctor, Maclean. He is Gillespie's intellectual equal and solves the riddle of the moving torso, as Gillespie did, and his role of service is impressive. Other characters variously indicating life or goodness in humanity include Barbara Strang, old Richard Strang, the schoolteacher Mr Kennedy, the Fiscal, the undertaker, Topsail Janet and Iain Strang. Enough of these are left at the end to allow some faint possibility of restored order when the house of Strang has finally succumbed to the curse and been exterminated. The good, however, while able to offer strength, service and understanding born of suffering are not so obviously able to offer social reconstruction. At the end the sower sows: but the harvest is unknown.

The comparison with Melville can be sustained in Hay's language and narrative techniques. There is no doubt that Hay's use of language is heightened and his imagery extraordinary. We may often justly accuse him of over-writing, but if we submit to the flow of the book the effect is extremely powerful.

Further, there are saving ironies and passages of very effective dry humour. The description of Spider already mentioned (65–6) is one such. The irony is pervasive, in little buffeting phrases: when things went well for the fishermen, we are told that Gillespie's "ill-fame suffered euthanasia" (200). Early on the banker faced Galbraith, and "sighed the sigh of a man of sorrows" before, naturally, refusing help. A few lines later we learn that "Galbraith had passed to that Bank, where the deeds done in the body, whether they be good or whether they be evil, are husbanded till the Books are opened" (15).

As irony is used to punctuate or puncture the flow of prose, so different kinds of comedy interrupt the pitiless logic of the larger pattern. Hay uses comic interlude as carefully as Shakespeare uses the porter in *Macbeth*. The scenes in the Back Street are essentially comic, because of the language of the gossiping women, even while they can be described as approximating also to a tragic chorus. The harmless comedy of Janet's day off and journey to Dunoon lightens the desperation of the final Book.

A most important individual technique, mentioned briefly earlier, is Hay's cavalier attitude to chronology. He habitually tells us the end of a story and then goes back and relates it, not necessarily in the chronological order. The effect is a particular combination of suspense and recognition which is very powerful. An outstanding example is at the book's bloody climax. We have witnessed the deaths in book IV, chapter 16 and we know what Gillespie is coming home to. But the seven pages of chapter 17 are almost unbearable, as he comes full of expectations, of Eoghan as a partner and, with any luck, Morag's imminent death.

His gradual realisation is quite painfully slow. He finds a candle, then Eoghan's picture and then Morag's body, but imagines her drunk and harangues her as usual. After he realises she is dead, he fails to find Eoghan and fears no more until Maclean announces murder. Then he fears for his reputation. Janet is the suspected victim, but then Janet innocently appears and it is a kind of relief to the reader when the men finally discover Eoghan's mutilated body. This is a chill reversal of the technique of farce when we know delightedly in advance what will happen: Hay's success is complete.

*   *   *

It has been the concern of this introduction to focus firmly on Hay's novel, rather than to "place" it in the Scottish tradition. That is the next step. While the book has been difficult to obtain it has too often been briefly mentioned as a sort of adjunct to or variation on George Douglas Brown's *The House with the Green Shutters*. Any sweeping comparison distorts both novels. Certainly both have a domineering father, a hopeless mother, a febrile son; but, as Francis Russell Hart points out in *The Scottish Novel*, so does Stevenson's *Weir of Hermiston*, to name only one other. The other main resemblance between *Gillespie* and *The House with the Green Shutters* is that both are angry and astonishingly accomplished first novels. But while Gillespie is "souple" and endlessly cunning, John Gourlay's main qualities are brutality and stupidity. More importantly, Gillespie Strang is the agent of modernisation and capitalist enterprise in a basically peasant society, while John Gourlay falls victim to just such changes because with all his strength he fails to understand a changing society as his weaker rival Wilson does.

Both Hay's novel and Brown's fit interestingly and importantly into a Scottish tradition stemming from Hogg and Stevenson. With the re-publication of *Gillespie* it is hoped that the debate about Hay's position and importance will really begin.

Aberdeen, 1979

BOOK I

1

SOMEWHAT by east of the bay two of the Crimea cannon, each on a wooden platform, lifted to seaward dumb mouths which once had thundered at Sevastopol. A little west of the derelict guns, and almost at the end of the shore-road, stood a gaunt two-storeyed house. Its walls were harled, its gables narrow and high, and its plain windows, whitened in winter with sea-salt, gave it the appearance of an old high-browed lady, with her white hair tightly drawn back from her forehead. This house, at the root of the hills, bleached with the gales of centuries, and imminent upon a beach of gravel, had a sinister appearance. From a distance one was infected with a sense of austere majesty at first sight of the house. It came as a discovery, nearer hand, that it was the tall gables which produced this effect. Attention, however, was attracted, not to the gables, but to a sign which hung over the door. Dimly traced on this heart-shaped sign was the half-defaced head of a man, and a hand grasping a dagger. The hand stabbed down with sleuth-like malignity. The place had once been an inn and of considerable repute; but horror came to nest there in the inscrutable way in which it attaches to certain places. Two men had come up from the sea in the dusk, and put in for the night at the inn. His wife being sick, Alastair Campbell went up in the morning to rouse the men. He found one of them lying on his back on the floor as if sunk in profound meditation. A bone handle rested on his left breast.

"Clare tae Goäd," said Campbell, "I thought it was the dagger o' the sign above the door. A cold grue went doon my back." The slain man, one-eyed, with a broad black beard, was a Jew. His pockets had been rifled. The hue and cry was raised, but the tall, swarthy fellow had vanished even more completely than the dead man, where he lay nameless in the south-west corner of the graveyard.

Fear fell upon the inn. It was named the "Ghost." The painted

I

dagger seemed to grate aloft when the wind blew. Campbell took to drink, and used to wander through the house at night, candle in hand. His wife became worn, watching him, and, always ailing, died within the year on child-bed. It came to this at last that her husband sat in the bar all day drinking with every wastrel, and too sodden at nightfall to make a reckoning. He roved the rooms, shouting with terrible blasphemy on a concealed left-handed devil to come out and show himself. Fishermen sailing past said that they saw lights dancing about the rigging of the "Ghost" in the grey of dawn. Soon all the bottles in the bar were emptied. Campbell's comrades from the town dropped off, and the scavengers who remained held the pewter measure beneath the tap as Campbell tilted up each barrel in turn. Of all that he had done, of all that had happened to him in his down-fall and degradation, this was the most pitiable.

"This is the last nicht, my he'rties," he cried, tilting up the last barrel. Without the sign creaked ominously in the scuffling wind. "Hark to it!" he yelled; "the bloody dagger's speakin'. Here's to it;" and with an oath he held the tankard to his mouth. His bloodshot eyes rolled in his inflamed face. "By Goäd, boys, I'll fire the hoose ower my heid and burn oot the bloody Spaniard." The scavengers stamped out the fire, and carried him upstairs to the bed of the room where he had discovered the Jew lying on the floor, sunk in eternal meditation. He kicked and screamed in mortal terror, the veins standing out on his brow like whip-cords, and the sweat drenching his face. In the midst of a scream he clapped his hands to his head and heaved upon the bed, and the room became suddenly quiet with the dumbness that follows a thunderclap. Campbell had taken a shock. The coyotes at his bedside held the tankard to his twisted mouth; the liquid trickled impotently down over his chin, and they knew that he was done. At the turn of the night Campbell joined hands with the bearded Jew, and together they went into the Shadow to look for retribution on their maimed and scarred lives.

Through the night the creaking of the sign without was as the rattling of Death's skeleton keys.

2

RICHARD GLAMIS STRANG bought the inn. Nobody else would bid for such a nest of bad odour. Mr. Strang, untainted with the supernatural of the West Highlands, was young and about to marry. He had established himself in Duntyre. He was not a native of these parts, having sailed from the Heads of Ayr, where his folk had been ling-fishers. For a year he had lived penuriously, like a Viking, in the fo'c'sle of one of the derelict smacks heeled on the beach, and took to the herring fishing. He wore a thin silver chain twisted round his neck in a double loop. Its ends disappeared with a heavy silver watch beneath his oxter. Over his jersey he wore a waistcoat lined with red flannel, which peeped abroad at the armpits. Only in the coldest weather did he wear a jacket. A hardy, tall, weather-beaten man with a stoop, taciturn and slow of speech, whose large hands gripped like steel. His eyes, grey and keen as blades, were seated in those depths which sea-vigil digs in the head of man. He took the sea in his little boat, working his lines during the winter, and in the spring he sold her to a boat-hirer, and offered money down for a share in a fishing-boat. He told the crew he had come from Ayr to found a home in the west. He was accepted; his skill recognised; his seamanship became a matter of wonder. None in the fleet could steer as he by the weather-ear. He went upon his own ground unquestioned, till on a Saturday night at the "Shipping Box," a Macdougall, a red-haired, vitriolic man, half drunk, called him by an indecent name, saying he was a Lowland interloper. A strain of Irish blood in Mr. Strang surged up into his pale face, and his eyes glittered like swords upon the little red man, who mouthed at him.

"Come on," he spluttered. "Dae ye ken who I am? I'm the man that boiled a kettle in the lee o' a sea. Come on, ye Ayrshire bastard, I'll show ye the wy tae fush herrin'."

A plump smack sounded abroad, and the Macdougall went down under the palm of Mr. Strang. A laugh from some twenty salt-hardened throats burst boisterously on the fallen hero's ears.

"Dived like a solan, Erchie," some one cried; and the Macdougall rose, his coward heart fluttering in fear.

3

"By the jumping Jehosiphat!" he cried, "but you're a man," and put forth his hand. Mr. Strang took it and nodded.

"We're aye learnin', Erchie, to work to windward," he said with a quiet smile.

Thus was he enlarged upon the imagination of men. Thus do men found the pillars of their house upon clay, rust, and mire.

He fell in love with one of the girls of the town, a Macmillan, lissom, white as milk, red as the dawn, with an eye for mirth and an abundance of sympathy—a trusty, wise mate. He had been reared in an iron school; bred to the sea with nerves of steel informed against the chances of gales, the darkness of fogs, the welter of snow-showers. He had the sailing lore by rote; and putting no store by anything but his business in the waters, neither legend nor superstition, took the inn at an easy rate, made some alterations, but left the sign above the door, where on surly nights it swung and groaned as if lamenting the weird upon the ill-fated house. On tempestuous winter nights of the first year of their wedded life, when they sat in the stone-flagged kitchen, her tales of the countryside came upon him, not with the stuff of surprise, but of magic. She had fed on oral romance and was its herald, proclaiming to him the deeds of her ancestors of Knapdale, and their mad ploy on the playground of half the county. Outside the seas thundered and clawed the beach; the old sign of the faded head mourned and jabbered; the sea-fowl screamed over the roof; and the house shook to the hammers of the gale. To the man the Lord of Hosts was abroad upon the air, and the wings of His angel troubled the deep.

The whole thing was so different from the sordid life of an Ayrshire fishing-port, which had no leisure and little inspiration for romance in its pale flat lands, that his life became clothed upon with wonder, and he lived in a world with more in it of magic than of reality. He sat under the elusive deft hands of a seer, who wove upon him a garment rich with pearls and shone upon with a haunting light, here and here alluring and splendid; but there also stained with the shadows of what was grim, terrible, and foreboding. He could not feel himself sib to this glancing wife. This strange food of reality for her had always been to him the thinnest stuff of dreams—things he had heard of vaguely, things so improbable and intangible in a world of deep-sea lines and strife with winds, tides, and piratical dog-fish that scarcely the phantom of their ghostly presence had passed

4

upon the face of his seaboard. Now he heard them, plucked from the life of a people, and chanted as their gospel by a girl who crept close to him, shivering at the sadness of her tale. As the sea without droned the antiphon, and the homeless wind upon the hill cried the antistrophe, he thought it was a wilding elfin thing he loved who was one with the witch-wind upon the waste, and with the changeling brumous sea. At the end of the tale, as a dog that is half drowned shakes the water from its pelt, he shook himself free from an undefined sinister influence.

One evening, when dark-bluish shadows lay upon the snow, she had been telling tales of olden bickerings—how one of her race had been hanged by the Duke of Argyle from the tall mast of his galley within the harbour there at the west end of the Island; of one that had been out in the '45 and had fled the country to France, and had married there—there was a strain of French blood in her veins; of another that had come out of the foreign wars limping under the weight of a major's commission, and had found his grave in the lee of Brussels at Waterloo; and then suddenly veered to an ancient tale of a heroine of her race who had slain her son to save her lover. She ceased talking. Her husband looked at her with simple level eyes. In the silence they heard the cry of wild geese high up in the sky—the ghostly birds, instinct-driven, passing as the arrow of God through the heavens to their decreed place.

"We are driven by something deep within us that we have got from our ancestors, to do strange things that were allowed in their age, but are unlawful now," she said. "Honk! Honk!" vibrant and clear as a bell it rang out high over the snow in response—the bugling of birds borne along by the "something deep" within them—and was heard by these frigate-birds, a man and a woman, sitting facing one another in the pitiable belief that they, alone of all God's creatures, can stem the call of destiny.

She told of her who had slain her son to save her lover, and of the terrible doom that rested on the name ever since, and was not yet fulfilled, that fratricide, parricide, or matricide would yet stain their house and open the ancient scar again before the house and name perished for ever.

"Oh, my dear, dear husband, if the doom should fall on you or on our children!" She lifted a scared white face searchingly to his. Alas! that every evangel must have behind it a doom.

"I vowed again and again never to marry to escape it"—a

5

faint smile stole across her serious face—"but love for you compelled me. Oh, Dick! Dick!" she wound her arms about his neck, "you love me, don't you? tell me again that you do. Our love must keep the doom at bay."

He struggled back again to the place of reality from that twilit land to which she had led him. He was vexed with her imagined woe.

"Doom be blowed," he cried; "it's as dead as a red herring."

"Oh, Dick! Dick!" she visualised the haggard spectre riding the back of her house; "you must love me to fight it. You do, don't you?"

"As weel as I love my mother, lyin' i' the mools o' Ayr Kirkyaird," he answered solemnly.

She held up her mouth to him.

"Mary," he adjured her, "the time's gane by for ony mair nonsense o' thae olden times. Doom be hanged. Wha's tae kill either you or me? We're mairrit eighteen months lucky, an' hae nae wean yet."

"I'd like to have a baby, a wee girlie; but I'm afraid, terribly afraid."

He jumped to his feet, flushed and angry.

"Feart o' an ault wife's story."

"Hush, Dick, hush; even this house isn't canny. There's a curse on it. Do you hear it? That creaking sign scares the life out of me at nights, when you're at the fishing. I can't sleep for listening to it."

He clapped his two big hands together.

"Doon it comes noo; where's the hammer?"

He searched, but could not find it.

"Never mind, Dick," her eyes followed him through the kitchen; "you can take it down in the morning."

But in the morning the frost had frozen the wind, and Dick was gone to shoot "the big lines" ten miles away on the Nesskip banks. The sign was forgotten; and the wild geese had passed on unerringly, unquestionably, on the path of destiny.

3

Six months later Richard Strang came to face something that was elemental. His wife was pregnant. As she became heavier with child he deserted his work to comfort her, but could not drive away her fear.

"Pray God it's a girl; a girl can do no harm;" and again she harped on the ancient tale, and summoned up the black rider that rode with such sinister menace on its back.

"Mary," he cried, fumbling impotently with his hands, desirous to strangle this hideous ghost, "will ye bring the doom on yoursel'?"

"Oh, no! no!" she moaned, wringing her hands.

"You're like to," he answered bitterly. "You'll kill yoursel' an' the wean in your womb wi' fright."

She cowered, but clung despairingly to the arms of her cross.

"Oh, no! no! Dick; it won't be that way, however it comes."

He was fairly angry now.

"Let me hear nae mair o' this trash an' nonsense. Your wild ancestors is no goin' to herry my nest. If they had to labour at the oar there wad be nane o' this." His voice had a ring of pride in it. It was the first time he had referred to his people. "It may be bonny to tell; but I'm thinkin' it wad hae been better for them to hae earned an honest penny like me an' mine." He got up and strode through the kitchen, the iron of his sea-boots ringing on the flags. "They were a bonny crew wi' their ongoins. As for oor folk, they were skilly at the lines an' the oar. They werna trokin' wi' princes that hadna a penny to their name. I don't ken as ony were hangit or got a red face for being ca'ed a thievery set. We didna brag o' being rebels an' shoutherin' a gun; oor name wasna cried aboot the countryside for dirty work wi' the lassies and ploys at the inns."

She put out her two blue-veined hands to him piteously, her eyes big with fear, her breasts heaving rapidly. He pushed them away. "We didna ride hell-gallopin' on black stallions, an' leave the weemin' at hame scared o' their life."

She burst out sobbing, her face like clay. He strode up to her.

7

"Mary! Mary! my lamb, I'm no angry at ye, lassie; I'm vexed at the wy ye're vexin' yersel' wi' a' this clishmaclaiver."

"Dick! Dick! Oh! Oh!! Oh!!! don't look at me that way; don't be angry with me; you'll kill me."

He gathered her in his arms with a groan.

"Downa greet; downa greet mair; it's a lassie that's comin'."

The sobs trailed away.

"If it's a boy, leave him to me. I'll teach him hoo tae handle the tiller, no' the dirk. Just bide till you see." And he comforted her.

Five months later he made fast his boat to an iron staple beneath the guns and hurriedly leapt ashore. Last night his wife had taken a fancy for whitings. Since daybreak he had searched three banks. The white fish, strung on by the gills to his fingers, shone in the dusk as angels of mercy come up out of the sea. As Richard Strang stepped within his door and stood in the passage at the foot of the stair, he heard a wailing cry in the room above— thin, fretting, querulous. His heart stopped in its beat. Openmouthed he listened, with his massive dark head leaning forward. The sign rasped above the door; and mingling with its harsh noise was that feeble whimper. The hand of something alive, which had that moment drawn in from a far-off impenetrable deep, beyond the confines of the world, touched his heart with tender fingers. A new life from inscrutable eternity mingled with his being. Out of a vast silence it had come, away back in the ages. He gasped. Was she right after all? Did ancestry stalk Time and become reincarnate? That wail seemed to drift up from the dim spaces of a far unknown. Lugubriously overhead the sign rasped and ground out its baleful note. Once more the wail rang out, now strong and lusty. Tiny fingers creeping over his heart, set it drumming in his breast. "Good God!" he whispered, "the baby's born;" and shaking the fish from his fingers he took the stairs in three bounds, and saw the pallid face of his wife turned to the wall. The room was heavy with the dumbness and mystery which pass into the chambers of birth. Lucky Ruagh from the Back Street was bending over a long-shaped, dark-haired head. His wife turned a face of woe to him, as she stretched out a thin white arm and pulled his face down to her.

"Oh, Dick! Dick! it's a boy."

Stunned, he could answer nothing; and when he was again at the foot of the stair he was listening to a wail which, borne down upon the wind of Time out of an inimical midnight past,

8

and passing beneath the heavens like an arrow of God, struck unerringly into his heart, as he stood listening to the scurry of the wind rasping the rusty dagger overhead. With every swing of the drunken sign the dagger was plunged downwards with a snarl.

4

MAN is the blindest of God's creatures. We concert measures and cast the most sanguine of plans, and all the time are weaving a mesh for ourselves. We harness life and put a snaffle bit in its mouth, and, gathering up the reins, direct our hopeful course. All the time we are trotting down a road that has been prepared for us. Richard Strang was determined to conquer heredity by habit. The vision which he had seen of the spirit of ancestry gleaming out of the past had terrified him, and it was he who was now afraid of the doom. He had established the house of Strang and, forgetting that heredity is stronger than the bands of habit, planned a definite mode of life for his son. Purblind, he was but fashioning the dynamite that was yet to ruin his house. The son took after him. He trained the boy to the sea; gave him no books to read; took him from school at the bare age of fourteen. The tales of his romance were figures; his tradition was record catches of fish. The only doom the boy feared was loss of gear in a gale. The parents pathetically believed that if the lad got no stupid stories into his head he was safe. The son not only inherited his father's temperament; but where his father judged of the chances of the sea, the boy dreamed of them. From training as well as by nature he became close-fisted. Where the father was keen the son was greedy. The parents, dreading the very word "ancestors," secretly rejoiced; and the father even tempted fate one idle night by asking the lad if he ever read a story-book. The boy curled his lip. "Story-books 'ill no boil the pot." The parents smiled. Purblind!

Mrs. Strang had no more children. Life became fuller for her. She lay awake at night when husband and son were on the sea, not from any fear of doom but from fear of the perils of the deep. The boy grew supple, tall, broad, commonplace in mind,

9

a worshipper of things. At twenty, when his father had given him his own bank-book, he began to dominate the house. His mother, folk noticed, was failing. She was troubled with a little hacking cough, and seemed to have grown lately. She was out a good deal, by Doctor Maclean's advice. Her favourite walk was up to the town, round its curving shore street to the north road, which brought her to Galbraith's farm. She had often wondered why Mrs. Galbraith had become a farmer's wife, for this woman read books of philosophy and poetry, played the piano, and could discourse about Nature, its beauties, its secrets, and its wayward moods, to Mrs. Strang by the hour as they sat on the brae, looking down on the fishing-fleet in the harbour and on the town. Once or twice Mrs. Strang's son accompanied her on these walks.

"Gillespie," she asked him once, "what secrets have you and Mr. Galbraith got together?" There was a pleasant ring of maternal pride in her voice. It was difficult to know if Gillespie Strang ever flushed. He had his mother's high colour. It was brick-red on the nape of his bull-dog neck. Gillespie looked fixedly ahead.

"There's nae secrets. He's learnin' me to ferret an' trap rabbits for a pastime."

Times were never so good. It was a word with the elder fishermen, "When spring comes in with spring tides and a new moon the fishing is sure to be good." Each herring meant money. Gillespie was constantly on the sea. At twenty-five he had a strong name in the bank, and Lowrie the banker would cross the street, seen of men, and talk civilly to him. Every man's fortune is in a lockfast box, of which he has the key. Some men use it skilfully; some blunder and break the lock; many tell themselves they are unable, and live by assisting other men to use their key. Gillespie, a master of craft, had the wards well oiled. None was defter with the key. He looked to unlock a fortune, this wiry supple youth.

He had extended the scope of his operations from the sea to the hill. This hybrid life put him in bad odour with everybody. To be a fisherman is always a fisherman; to be a farmer always a farmer. Gillespie was despised as an idiot, who wrought clashing irons in the fire. His eye was as quick on the gun as on the line; as cunning with the snare as with the tiller. He made a bargain with Lonend, whose farm marched with Galbraith's, for the rights of fishing, shooting, and trapping over his lands. He worked like two men; his robust frame was seldom fatigued. He visited his snares at dawn, when he had returned from a night's fishing. Secretly he snared the runs in the graveyard. Superstition made him immune from detection. In the winter when he could not tempt the sea, he shot rabbits and roamed the forest for white hares. He arranged with a Glasgow merchant of the Fish Market for the disposal of his hares, rabbits, wild-duck, and trout. He was seldom in his father's house. If he was not on the sea, draining his nets of their ultimate fin, he was at Lonend. He was now on his way there with his mother; but suddenly left her in the hollow below Galbraith's farm and skirted the edge of the Fir Planting. In this sere time of the year the place looked bleached and grey, and was full of a haunting melancholy. It was empty, save for a solitary man ploughing the Laigh Park. He was a tall spare man, loosely knit, whose hair was turning grey. His face had something of the geniality and frankness of a child's. In the plum-like bloom of the winter dusk he ploughed the lea, urging his ministry of faith in a pentecost of peace. It was strange to watch him at his work of redemption, for he looked wan, haggard, spent. The fruition of autumn seemed an impossible thing to this prematurely aged man, and his worn grey and brown team. As the pallid sunset fell across the lines of resurrection which his plough turned up, the field looked a half-torn, rifled purse. At the end of the field he turned, with the gait of a man who has weariness even in his bones. In the dimness Gillespie could discern but the faint outline of a figure. He heard a dull creaking of harness, and a monotonous voice urging the drooping horses, which moved beneath a faint cloud. Patiently they drew out of the shadow of the firs and plodded down the field. A curlew cried on the moor above; a vagrant gull flitted by like a ghost with silent swoop. The trees on the east and south sides gathered the gloom about them. In the oppressive stillness they stood up like gaunt sentinels of the man's labour, screening him from the pirate eyes of Gillespie. Inexpressible sadness, and the pathos of human frailty, set their profound significance upon this altar of hope; for though the man was at the beginning of things in his labour, yet he was consumed with the modern cancer of unrest. He was up to the ears in debt to Gillespie. The money had been largely squandered in Brodie's back-room. Late and early he wrestled with the sour soil, relying upon the imperishable husbandry of earth to stop the mouth of the wolf, without perceiving that whisky would make the ground sterile.

With a faint shearing sound the plough lifted the scented fallow, but the aridity of Galbraith's heart would admit no savour of the fresh earth. The dying are not revived with eau-de-Cologne. In the upturned soil Galbraith knew no potency; in its young face felt no resurrection. Only in the doggedness of despair he caught a gleam of far-off gold in the black, shining furrows. He ploughed on mechanically, straight and silent to the end of the field. He was assisting in turning Gillespie's key in the lockfast box.

The early stars arose upon the wood. So benign it all was, and he so weary. He came to a halt in the thick shadows of the Planting. A little wind began to rustle among the skeleton boughs, like the feet of timid animals scurrying in the dark. Suddenly a light flared in the window of the farm. It spoke of the security, the tranquillity, the tenderness of the hearth across the perplexing vastness of this outland brooding night. The ploughman turned his eyes upon it in a long hungry stare. Slowly he unyoked and turned his horses home, and upon them fell the deliberate night, as the moon grew by stealth over the tree-tops and across the half-ploughed field.

Our nature is rarely prophetic of happiness: very little causes to brood over it the sable wings of omens. Thus Galbraith, harassed with vexing thoughts, was not startled on hearing Gillespie's voice as he stepped out of the shadows.

"Makin' heidway wi' the plooghin', Calum."

This was Gillespie's way—no salutation. There was something sinister in the tone. It was the voice of an overseer.

"It's a dreich job," Galbraith answered wearily. He sought for no explanation of Gillespie's appearance there at such an hour. The movement of vultures are unquestioned.

The business became rapid—so rapid that Galbraith never finished his "dreich job." Gillespie's voice was honeyed.

"I thocht it better to see ye here, no to be vexin' the missis."

Gillespie lied. He did not want his mother, who was at the farm-house, to pry further into his affairs. Galbraith was nervously plaiting the mane of the half-foundered grey. Man and beast were stooping to the earth in exhaustion.

"It's kin' o' thochtfu' o' ye," Galbraith said, with a gleam of irony.

"Weel, Calum, I dinna want to press ye, but I'm needin' the ready money ee' noo. I'm thinkin' o' buyin' a trawl."

Galbraith was puzzled. "Trawling" for herring was illegal.

"The Government 'ill no alloo trawlin'." In censorship Galbraith plucked at hope. Gillespie, on the other hand, had foresight.

"Ay! but it's comin'." His exultant voice flouted the song, "There's a good time coming, boys," in Galbraith's face. "I've ordered a couple o' trawls frae Greenock. I'm needing the ready money to pey them." As a matter of fact he had requisitioned no fewer than half-a-dozen "trawl" nets, and thereby entered upon another step in his career. He had no intention of using them: that was too risky; but he meant to sell them—secretly. They could only be bought "sub rosa." It is the ideal way of commerce for a Gillespie, who could make his own selling price

"I'm fair rookit oot," answered Galbraith, in a despondent voice. The grey nickered uneasily, and whinnied towards home.

"I'll maybe hae to foreclose then." The voice was as suave as Satan's. Galbraith's fingers suddenly ceased from teasing the horse's mane. He half raised his clenched hand to the stars.

"By Goäd, ye'll put me to the door!"

Gillespie saw the threatening gesture. He was a coward, physically and morally. Lares and penates were meaningless to him. He cut the red strings which bound these to the heart of the man as readily as he cut cheese. To save his skin he temporised.

"I'd bide off till the fall if I could, Calum," he said plausibly; "but thae merchants in Greenock 'ill no' be put off." He made a gesture implying urgent necessity, and said coaxingly, as if advising a friend:

"What's to hinder ye gettin' Lowrie to back a bill for ye?"

Galbraith regarded him moodily.

"It comes agin the grain," he answered. He pondered, stubbing the fallow with his toe; then raised his head.

"Hoo muckle will I lift?" he asked. We talk of "lifting money" out of the bank.

It did not suit Gillespie's book to be clear of Galbraith altogether. He wanted a grip on the farm.

"Let me see; let me see"—in the stillness his breath whistled sharply in his nostrils. "I'll mand, I think, wi' three hunner." Galbraith slightly staggered against the grey, which moved forward at the touch.

"Whoa, there!" he called out irascibly. "Three hunner!" As

13

a straw is more than a straw to a drowning man, so Galbraith in the depths was unable to estimate this sum at its proper value.

Gillespie twittered upon one of his rare laughs.

"Hoots, man, gie Lowrie a lien on the hairvest, an' the hunner's yours lik' the shot o' a gun."

A man will see resource in the wildest scheme when the roof is cracking over his head.

Galbraith acquiesced. He was the first of many whom Gillespie brought to dance to his pipe.

Lowrie was a withered looking man, bald, clean-shaven. The skin below his chin hung slackly, and was of the grey colour of a plucked fowl's. He nipped at it when dealing with grave matters of finance. He nipped at it now as he interrogated Galbraith. This Lowrie was a man who never went abroad, save to church. He had a beat on the pavement in front of the bank over which he lived; and there, as upon a balcony, he spied upon the town. He knew to a farthing the state of every man; and he astutely estimated their occasions.

"A large sum, if I may say so, a very large sum on a sudden notice." His small, quick, penetrating eyes searched Galbraith's face. Galbraith, a child of the piping winds and blowsy rains, was ill at ease in this musty atmosphere. The large green safe, with a screw arrangement on the top, appeared to him an ambuscade. Malevolence lurked in it, waiting for threadbare men. And this pursy little man probed him. If they had foregathered in Brodie's back-room, with glasses winking jovially at them—but here the sombre angel of want seemed to shake a mildew from its wings. Galbraith was silently reviling the foxiness of Gillespie which had driven him there.

"May I ask what you need such a large sum for at this time of year?"

Galbraith seized the chance to smite Gillespie. He would show him up.

"It's for Gillespa' Strang," he blurted out.

The banker's eyebrows went up; the tips of his fingers came evenly together. He crossed a plump leg.

"Ah! indeed, for Mr. Strang; I see, for Mr. Strang. And what call has Mr. Strang upon you?"

"I owe him risin' on five hunner, the fox."

Galbraith was warming to his task. Lowrie held up a fat preaching palm.

"No personalities, please. That does no good."

"He's brocht me to the end o' my tether," said Galbraith bitterly. The banker sighed the sigh of a man of sorrows, as who should say, "They all come to me to deliver them;" but his tones were incisive.

"Will Mr. Strang not accept a lien on your crops?"

Galbraith shook his head.

"That is unfortunate. Mr. Strang is a keen business man; and in the interests of my employers I do not feel myself justified in accepting your bond. You see, Mr. Strang has a prior claim." The banker hesitated a moment, and looked as if plunged in thought. The next he rose abruptly.

"I'm sorry to say that I cannot consider your proposal, Mr. Galbraith; extremely sorry." With his left hand he plucked at the slack beneath his chin; his right he extended in a dry official way to Galbraith.

"Mr. Grant." He raised his voice.

A tall, fair-haired man appeared, with a pen in the cleft of his ear. He had peeped over the top of the glazed glass portion of the door before entering.

"Mr. Grant, please show Mr. Galbraith out."

Galbraith, in tow of the banker's clerk, vanished from the malice which loured from the green steel safe, and its screw apparatus which ground down the lives of needy men.

The banker sat down and wrote a note to Mr. Strang, junr., at the "Ghost," desiring the favour of an interview with him at his earliest convenience. He proposed to himself to inform Mr. Strang privately of the visit of Mr. Galbraith. In this fashion the banker sought the confidence of "solid men." Gillespie came late to that interview, for in the meanwhile Galbraith had passed to that Bank, where the deeds done in the body, whether they be good or whether they be evil, are husbanded till the Books are opened.

5

THE following night Gillespie tip-toed into the kitchen of Lonend's farm. There was an apology in his sleuth-like gait. He flung down a bundle of rabbits on the floor. The soft brown fur was

here and there mottled with blood. Carefully he cleaned and
oiled his gun and hung it on two steel-racks above the dresser.
The cartridges he retained in a little canvas bag. He counted the
rabbits, and with tongue protruding in an absorbed face packed
them in a wicker basket, roped the basket, and attached to it the
label of a firm in the Glasgow Fish Market. He arose from his
stooping posture, and asked Lonend if he would send the basket
by cart in the morning to the pier. Gillespie had no need of
stable or horses just yet.

Lonend's father had made money. He had been a butler of the
old Laird's, who had left him a legacy with which he had set
up in business as a carriage-hirer, and had a shop in which he
sold harness, whips, and the like. He pottered in an ineffective
way at saddlery to keep the rust off his bones. He had financed
his son Hector in the farm of Lonend. This Hector was a small,
broad, black-a-vised man; slightly bow-legged, sturdy, with a
bright dark eye; gross in his tastes; salt in his life; a born
grumbler—no sort of weather pleased him—an excellent farmer,
but with no initiative. He worked the land scrupulously, as he had
been taught, watching his rotation of crops. He would as soon
have thought of experimenting with horticulture as of using a
new patent manure. He was as mechanical as a reaper, and drove
his men as unflinchingly as he drove that machine. A man of
substance who had no need to fire his hay-ricks for their insurance
value. Ratting was his open diversion. Everything about his
farm was slovenly and dirty. The parlour, which he rarely occu-
pied, was as musty as a vault. He was eager to push his fortune,
so far as his limited intellectual resources would allow. These
being limited, he had pushed it more by craft than by honesty.
He was ardent only by turns, becoming alert and greedy when
he stumbled on a flint which struck a spark out of him. He was, in
short, one of that sort of men who of themselves are neither good
nor bad for anything; but once instigated, and with none of the
carelessness of creative genius, will worry and gnaw at the matter
in hand till the bone is bare. Gillespie was now the flint, the
begetter of fire and guile.

Lonend nodded.

"The mear's for the Quay the morn for potato seed ony wy."
He had had a curious piece of information from Galbraith's wife,
the truth of which he wanted to test. He pondered Gillespie's
impassive face.

"Ye're doin' weel off the bit rabbits," he added.

"They're hardly worth a' the trachle." Gillespie stretched his back and walked to the pump at the kitchen door. His hands were stained with blood and soil.

"Ye winna objec' to a bit mair gr'un'."

Gillespie cut off the water to hear better, and re-entered the kitchen, his hands wrapped in a sodden dish-cloth, his massive head inclined to Lonend in interrogation.

"Calum Galbraith's ta'en a shock." Lonend kept unwavering eyes on Gillespie's face, as he knocked the dottle out of a wooden pipe on the heel of his boot.

"I didna hear." Gillespie was delicately drying his finger tips.

"He burst a blood vessel this aifternoon, and lost a sight o' blood afore Maclean got up frae the toon."

"Is he by wi' t?" asked Gillespie dispassionately.

"I met Maclean in the gloamin' comin' ower the brae. He gied me the news. He says Galbraith 'ill no see the morn."

"Ay! ay! it's surely kin' o' sudden."

Lonend's bright eyes were turned full on Gillespie.

"Maclean was bleezin' mad; he cursed an' swore you for a' the blaiggarts."

Gillespie's hand shook slightly on the dish-cloth. He showed no other sign of fear.

"Me! A didna murder the man."

"Maclean said if he was a judge he wad hang ye."

The dish-cloth shook violently. Gillespie, crossing to the pump to lay it down, said over his shoulder:

"What spite has Maclean gotten at me?"

"He said you worrit Calum tae daith. Ye thraitened to rook him."

Gillespie returned from the pump. His hands were now in his pockets.

"A bonny lik' story. Did I no' hear Maclean tell Galbraith at the Cattle Show if he didna stop the dram, the dram wad stop him. It's Brodie's wee back-room, that's worrit him to daith." Gillespie made a show of indignation; and Lonend of conviction at these words, as he answered:

"Weel! weel! he took a heavy dram, an' he's in higher hands than oors noo." The matter was shelved. They were content to leave it in those unseen Hands, which are patient so long with men, fondly imagining that their pious resignation is the winking of the Judge at their deeds. Lonend entered upon matter more immediate. He, a notable breeder of Highland cattle, was greedy of Galbraith's moorland. Gillespie felt that Lonend was about to make a serious proposal. The tentacles of these two minds reached out and played with each other warily. Gillespie, relieved at the new trend of conversation, found himself again and nursed his caution.

"She'll hae to gie up the ferm an' sell oot."

Lonend had this piece of information at first hand from Galbraith's wife. He had paid a visit to his afflicted neighbour while Gillespie was shooting down rabbits with the help of a ferret. It was upon this mission of sympathy that he had met Maclean, from whom he had taken his doleful tidings as news. As a matter of fact, he was aware of Galbraith's attack an hour before, for Mrs. Galbraith, in an extremity of grief, had sent Jock the Ploughman to Lonend to ask his assistance. Lonend had found Galbraith unconscious and breathing stertorously. His wife in her misery revealed the low financial state of the farm, and had asked Lonend's advice. He thought her best plan was to give up the farm and sell out. He had hurried home to intercept his *advocatus diaboli* Gillespie.

Gillespie's mind hovered round Lonend's piece of information as round a web.

"Are ye for takin' it ower?" he asked nonchalantly.

"Maybe ay; maybe no; it all depends."

"On what?"

Lonend had figured it all out on his way home. He stole a furtive glance at Gillespie.

"On you;" the tone was emollient.

Gillespie, himself practised in such methods of address, recoiled from the cajolery. He answered wheedling:

"I'm no hand at the fermin'; I ken mair o' a boat than a sheep."

Lonend was pleased to laugh at this deprecating humour.

"Ye're gey keen on the gun though; there's a good pickle rabbits in the Laigh Park."

"Ay," answered Gillespie. He had poached there, when he knew Galbraith was drunk in Brodie's back-room.

"Ye'll mak' a tidy bit off the rabbits alone," urged Lonend.

"Maybe ay; maybe no; it a' depends."

Lonend saw he was skirmishing fruitlessly with a strategist, and decided to table his cards. Visibly crouching, he seemed to wither into lesser bulk.

18

"Can you an' me no' mak' a bargain? it's a chance."

"Whatna bargain?" Gillespie asked softly.

"I've gaun ower't in my mind." Lonend spoke briskly now. "The Laird maun tak' ower the sheep." His look was significant. No need to explain to Gillespie about "acclimatisation value." Lonend knew the Laird and his affairs. He had had a master deal with him five years ago. His lease had expired. Lonend threw his stock on the Laird's hands. The Laird, a young jolly man with no head for business and served by a stupid factor, would not face even a valuation of the hundreds of black-faced sheep on Lonend's farm. Threatened with law proceedings, he was brought to his knees. At an easy figure Lonend bought the land outright. In seven years he made up the price in the saving of rents. The land was now his own w.thout burden. Gillespie listened to the tale with greedy face, and sunk each detail in his memory. How blind are the crafty! In five minutes Lonend had mightily enlightened his co-plotter.

"The Laird canna tak' ower Galbraith's sheep; an' Mrs. Galbraith's heid sae wrunkled wi' books an' museeck she doesna understan' their value." His little dark eyes darting about, searched Gillespie's sphinx-like face. "We'll tak' ower the ferm frae Mrs. Galbraith, an' get the stock reasonable."

Gillespie sat down in silence on a chair beside the dresser. His face was thoughtful.

"What sort o' bargain wull we mak'?" he asked, lifting an intent face and thirsty eyes.

Lonend approached the critical part of the discussion. He wanted the land in his own hands, especially the moorland. Gillespie, being no farmer, would take as his share the steading and plenishing. Lonend would control the live stock. But Lonend had been fatally fluent concerning his own dealings with the Laird. He had spoken with pride; but he had armed Gillespie.

"We'll go halves an' share an' share alike the profits."

There was a profound silence in the kitchen, broken only by the drip, drip of water from the pump at the door. The sound was like the drip, drip of the blood which had ebbed that afternoon from Galbraith's mouth on to his kitchen floor. Lonend was too plausible, Gillespie thought, and leapt at the heart of the matter.

"I'm thinkin', Lonen'," he said, bending and toying with the label on the hamper, "if it's a good thing, ye're ower neebourly offerin' me the half."

Lonend leered and winked.

"I winna gang in harness wi' ony other man leevin'."

"An' what wy me?"

Laughter purred in the kitchen. Lonend put on a jocose face. "Dae ye think I'm blin', Gillespie? Maybe I'm wrang, but I'm jaloosin' there's something atween Morag an' you."

Gillespie neither blushed nor hung his head. He had no room for sentiment. He wanted a woman, not as a wife, but for her money, and said, "Morag 'ill mak' a guid match." This direct simple statement had no effrontery in it for her father, who wagged his head.

"Ye ken whaur yeer breid's buttered; Morag kens more o' a fermhouse than ony twa." He was pleased to show her paces. Gillespie accepted them phlegmatically, and spoke with an air of finality. "Morag an' me 'ill settle a' that, if you an' me 'gree first." He was naïvely confident.

Lonend, having now the affair on the rails to his liking, disappeared into an inner room and returned with a decanter and glasses. Gillespie shook his head. He rarely drank and never smoked. More than once he had spoken in the hearing of his parents of how much he saved yearly by this abstemiousness.

"Man! man! ye'll hae a nip the nicht," cried Lonend jovially; "it's no every day ye'll speir for a wife." His eyes smiled without cunning. He filled out a measure of whisky into each glass, with that feeling of sociability which infects tipplers enhanced, because the canteen was solemnised by the presence of an austere, almost astral recluse.

"Here's to oor success, an' the prosperity o' the young couple." Lonend admired the deeply coloured whisky scintillating like liquid gold.

"Maybe ye'll tell me noo, Lonen', whatna bargain ye hae in your mind as regairds us twa." Gillespie emphasised the final words.

Lonend had no doubt about the bargain. Here was a young couple beginning life. They would be glad to step into a furnished house. That constituted their half share. The workings of Lonend's mind were not acute or subtle. Gillespie was no farmer; never would be a farmer. He would be content so long as he shared the profits, and held the plenishing and the house. Lonend would keep his grip on the stock, interrogate the markets, and himself buy and sell there. He fancied he could blind Gillespie and cook the accounts, because he knew a dealer up Barfauld's way who, for a percentage, would give him discharge receipts on the stock and wool at an arranged spurious price. Secretly he blessed that admirable institution—percentages. But he specified no details to his attentive colleague. "Share an' share alike" was the shibboleth for this Gileadite.

"Weel, it's this wy"—Lonend laid down his glass carefully on the heel of the table—"Ye'll need a bit roof ower your heid when ye mairry. We'll go halves on the profits, as I said. I'll buy ower the stock; ye'll can tak' the furniture an' plenishin'; we'll square up the hale price atween us later on. Will that suit ye?"

"Maybe ay; maybe no. Does that mean the stock's yours still an' on?"

"Huts! man! alloo me to buy the stock"—he stopped to wink —"an' alloo me to wark it. We'll go halves ower the profits. You an' Morag can tak' up hoose ready furnished."

"The lease," observed Gillespie, "is Mrs. Galbraith's."

"Come the term she'll hae to flit. Galbraith's behind han' wi' the rent."

Gillespie pondered in silence.

"Is Morag willin'?" He did not ask this for information; but to gain time for thought.

A meagre intelligence rarely sees obstacles to the specious plans which it has so laboriously hammered out. Lonend fancied that Gillespie, reduced to considerations of matrimony, was won. This vulture was no more, after all, than a grey gull. Lonend was warmed at the thought of his astuteness. A sordid plan that has become clothed upon with achievement is, to a mean nature, the attainment of an ideal. Lonend flung out a contemptuous hand.

"Huts! man! she's fair kittlin' for a lad."

This caused no sort of emotion in Gillespie's mind. It was simply another nail in the treasury lid of the agreement. Yet Gillespie was by no means finished. He had the tortuous persistence of a weasel, with a Fabian tenacity of purpose. He made no answer to Lonend's scurrilous flippancy. This had not at all been his target. He pondered on the chances of a bull's eye in life from another sort of butts, which, however, he was content to have masked till the time was ripe and his arsenal stored. A big fishing-fleet of trawlers was sure to come into being. The evolution of circumstance, whose wheels grind down tradition and pulverise effete laws, would create of necessity a new law.

21

The origin of law is not in governments that only legalise the incontrovertible wishes of the people, whose unrest is the stuff of change. The still small voice of Cabinets is but the echo of the thunder of the masses. Gillespie had scrutinised the fishermen. Chance crews were already secretly "trawling"; he saw that the revolution of to-day was the convention of tomorrow: foresaw the fishing-fleet of a hundred boats engaged, within the next few years, at their legitimate business in the seas of "trawling." At present these crews of some five hundred men were supplied with gear and provisions from impecunious small traders. His plan was to kill off those piffling merchants; build a large curing shed; a shed for "smoking" herring; another for storing salt in large quantities; a store for housing fishing gear—nets, oil, ropes, varnish, tar, and the like; a barking house; and especially to open a big shop in the Square that would supply the whole fleet. He would have stables too. He had quietly noticed the country people plodding in to Brieston at irregular periods for provisions, and hanging about the town-foot with their gawky air, shy of the little merchants, and returning home ripe with whisky. Nothing simpler than to send a bi-weekly van to "the country." In Mains-foot, twelve miles off, they largely depended on the whim of that aristocratic Jehu, Watty Foster, the driver of His Majesty's mail coach, which rolled down the west brae behind three horses at noon, for many of their necessaries; and a bulky mail meant that the long-expected jar would cool itself for a season at Brodie's.

Three things prevented the immediate operation of Gillespie's plan: the present illegality of trawling; the want of suitable premises in the Square of Brieston; and especially the lack of capital. But he had vigilantly been hoarding. If he sunk his money in a farm, this would perilously delay the working of his scheme. As he pondered now he saw in a flash an opulent way out. If he made a proper agreement with Lonend, remembering that individual's account of his transaction with the Laird, he, too, could sell out his stock and retire from the farm at the opportune time. "We'll go halves." He recalled the plausible phrase. "I thank thee, Jew, for that word." He determined that his half would also be *in land*. And he could realise his money at any time on the plenishing and furniture. He had only one fear now—that Lonend might specify that each should retain his half share of the farm as long as the other lived. But here he over-reached Lonend, who, imagining he was setting up his future son-in-law in life, did not dream of any contingency. Again it was, once a farmer, always a farmer. What was a good living for him must, Lonend judged, prove even more attractive to a man following precariously the sea. It was Gillespie, wary as a lynx, who now was anxious to close with the offer. To the surprise of Lonend he held out his glass.

"As you observed, Lonen', it's no every day a man tak's a wife." A pleased look irradiated the swarthy features of Lonend. He had been anxiously scanning the brooding, disconsolate face of his comrade, whose anxiety, Lonend remarked with relief, had nothing to do, after all, but with the problem of marriage. It was an anxious time, no doubt, for a man, and rather sudden for Gillespie. Himself a widower, he had his own loose ideas about the sex; but these were strictly private. In some things Lonend was exemplary and discreet.

He generously filled both glasses.

"Here's luck," he cried merrily, "to the first wean."

Gillespie followed his lead, interpolating, "Morag 'ill bring something wi' her."

The giver-away of daughters was generous.

"The maist o' her mither's things are hers for the liftin'— blankets an' napery."

Gillespie pushed the marriage settlement.

"I'll be gey an' dry in the bank when I've peyed my wheck o' the ferm." In point of fact he hoped to pay nothing. There was the matter of Galbraith's debt "risin' on five hunner."

"Ye're no blate, Gillespie."

"I've my wy to mak' in the world—Morag an' me."

Lonend screwed up his face in paternal solicitude.

"Huts! the lassie 'ill no' gang cauld; she's a pickle siller in her ain right. Her uncle in Isla' left her in his will."

Gillespie nodded. The agreement was concluded. He had made a gigantic stride towards respectable citizenship. For what details remained, Lonend now exercised his cunning openly for their mutual benefit.

"I'll see the Laird aboot takin' ower the ferm. He'll be at the funeral. Ye can mak' an offer tae Marget for the plenishin'. It'll save her the unctioneer."

Lonend rose and reached for the bottle. Gillespie also rose and faced him. "We'd be as weel to sign an agreement," he said.

Lonend questioned him with a look.

23

"Agreement here, agreement there; when ye're mairrit on Morag we'll a' be the wan faimly."

"It'll keep things square."

Lonend, obsessed with the idea that Gillespie would never dream of relinquishing his hold on the farm, acquiesced, lest his partner should offer any further objections. Gillespie, asking for writing materials, made out a simple bond that Hector Logan of Lonend and Gillespie Strang of the "Ghost" agreed to buy over in equal shares the stock, gear, and plenishing of the farm of Muirhead, to hold the farm equally between them, and equally to share the profits of the same.

"That's your proposeetion," said Gillespie in an even voice, as he read it, Lonend stooping at his side over the document whose tenor was "share an' share alike." He saw nothing in the phrase "to hold the farm equally between them," and omitted to notice that there was no stipulation as to the period of tenure. He offered to sign it. Gillespie put the offer by, and folding the paper put it in his pocket.

"I'd better see the Spider first; it'll maybe need a Government stamp." Sufficient to add that the Spider did his part, and a proper document was made out, and attested.

When Gillespie was on the threshold Lonend said, "I'll speak to Morag the nicht; an' ye'd be as well to speir her yersel' the morn's nicht."

Gillespie promised and said good-night.

About a dozen yards on his right there was a yellow square of light. As Gillespie passed he saw Morag Logan, seated on an upturned pail, with her dark head leaning against the flank of a cow. He heard the crooning of her voice mingling with the hiss of the milk. Gillespie quietly passed onwards into the night. He was thinking, not of the girl, but of how long he would require to hold on to the farm. Two or, at the most, three years he hoped. He walked rapidly down the cart-track and came on to the north road. A little way down the road a man passed him. The night had fallen dark and still.

"It's a fine night."

Gillespie, about to answer, suddenly clenched his teeth and passed on in silence. The voice was his father's. An hour ago he had been sent for by Mrs. Margaret Galbraith, whose husband, without regaining consciousness, had passed away. In that precise moment in which Mr. Strang passed his son on his mission of mercy to the bereaved, Lonend was informing his daughter that the days of her virginity would soon be ended. As he spoke, Jock, the ploughman at Muirhead, entered the kitchen.

"Mrs. Galbraith sent me ower for ye, Morag;" he turned his heavy gaze on Lonend. "He's by wi 't."

"Goäd help us," said Lonend; "when?"

"He died at twenty meenuts past seeven."

"Ye'd better step ower, Morag," he nodded to his daughter; then turned and reached out his hand to the bottle. His breathing was slightly rapid. After the battle, the vultures.

6

GILLESPIE, with hurried step, entered the "Ghost" by the back door. His mother was seated at the kitchen fire knitting. She was rather thin now, and getting grey. A tracery of veins could be distinguished about her sunken temples. Lately she had complained a good deal of her breathing, and her voice was noticeably weaker. Gillespie looked round the kitchen.

"Your father's away up to Calum Galbraith's." A slight fit of coughing arrested her, and she covered her mouth with her hand and bowed herself. "We heard he took a shock this afternoon. Poor Calum! he was the best man at our weddin'."

"Is he bad?" asked Gillespie.

"They're waitin' on him," his mother sighed heavily, "the old folk are all droppin' off. Poor Calum! he—" Another and longer fit of coughing took her.

Gillespie, lifting a candle from the mantelpiece, passed up the stair to the garret. He returned with a bundle of rabbit snares.

"I'll hae time to run up to Lonen' an' set a few snares." He walked to the dresser, opened the door, and took out a lantern.

"I wish ye'd bide in the night, Gillespie; I'm not feelin' very well. I'm eerie all alone."

With failing health her fear of the doom had returned.

"You mak' the supper," he answered, examining the interior of the lantern; "I'll be back in an oor."

She did not attempt to persuade him. A pathetic resigned look came into her face as she looked at the wag-at-the-wa'. "I wish your father was home. It's weary in this empty house."

He muttered that he would not be long. Her hungry eyes followed him as he went out. As he unlocked the shed at the end of the house and took out a pair of oars and rowlocks, he heard the dull sound of her coughing in the lonely house.

His punt, lying in the mouth of the burn which tumbled into the bay, was easily floated. Gillespie flung in his traps, laid down his lantern in the stern-sheets, and with oar pushed out to sea. The full beauty of the night had arisen with the moon. A winter mist wavered and bellied about the midst of the hills. Clear beneath the moon the summits seemed to be floating out of a turbulent sea. They took on a myriad shapes—now the battlements of ivory palaces; now the craters of smoking volcanoes; and again the black turrets of a giant marble castle. The moon struck through the fog and opened doors of silver upon long pavilions of snow. Gillespie saw nothing of this as he pulled noiselessly through the fog. He hoped it would not lift as he dodged his boat into the harbour through the muffled silence, crept across the east end of the Island, and shot into the shadows of the Fir Plantation below Galbraith's farm. He made the bow-rope fast to a stone. His movements had the precision of experience. With his traps and lantern he struck through some sparse whin bushes, his feet sinking noiselessly in the open soil, and gained a footpath. This he followed deftly to a dry-stone dike which he leapt with a stertorous grunt, crossed a potato field, and stumbled on the furrows which Galbraith had ploughed, fell forward. He picked himself up in silence, wallowed through the furrows, and reached the edge of the field beneath the firs. There, behind some bramble bushes, he lit his lantern. He knew every inch of the ground, and at every rabbit run he set a snare. The kindly mist concealed his piracy. Gillespie was not a religious man; but he conceived that the stars were fighting for him. He snared the Laigh Park, blew out the light in his lantern, crossed the fallow and took the cart-road to the farm. He hoped an opening would be given him for a conversation with Mrs. Galbraith on her husband's financial state, and vaguely wondered how long Galbraith "would stand it." At the farmyard gate at the foot of a wooden post he concealed his lantern. Assuming a face of solicitude he knocked at the door. For a moment he stood blinking in the light, and could not discern who had opened the door.

"Oh, it's all mist!" he heard Morag's voice. "Who's there?" The inquiring voice was guarded. She seemed to be barring him out—she, who would soon stand there, his wife, opening the door. A faint ironic smile passed over his face at the thought as he announced himself.

"Oh! is it you, Gillespie? Father said ye'd gone home." A consciousness of what her father had further said made her silent. Her eager inquisitive eyes looked out upon the loom of his figure.

"Yes, I did; but I cam' ower again to ask for Calum."

"Will you come in?" she asked him. Death is strong; passion stronger. It was he who closed the door which she had opened. At right angles to the porch a passage ran east and west. At the west side it ended in the kitchen; and opening off the passage to the right, was a small room where the family lived. With his cap on his head Gillespie followed the girl to this room. At the door she stopped.

"Have you a match, Gillespie?" she asked in a low tone.

"No," he replied. In his pocket he had the box of matches which he had used to light the lantern.

"Wait till I get some." She went into the kitchen. His mind was slightly perturbed. He had to ask this girl to marry him. Gillespie's mind was pigeon-holed. He drew out the business for the hour; and this particular business had been laid by in its pigeon-hole for to-morrow evening. Besides, able as he was to read men when he was making "a deal" with them, he was every other way at sea with character. Gillespie had had few dealings with women. He could treat Morag only on the basis of a commercial agreement. He was to discover that passion has no rules; that the elemental is a law unto itself.

Morag returned with a lamp, which she placed in the middle of a small circular table near the window. She stood in the light of the lamp at attention. She was of middle height. Her narrow, receding forehead was covered with a wave of hair. She had prominent cheek-bones and a heavy lower jaw, and was rather short in the arms. This was due probably to the fact that, save for the evening milking of the cows, for which she had a passion, her father allowed her to do no manual work on the farm. The hands were long and fragile; the feet small and narrow. She had a great abundance of dark hair like a tower on her small narrow head. There was an album on the table, and a blighted aspidistra in an earthenware pot. The mantelpiece was loaded with white,

27

red, and blue prize-tickets won at cattle shows. Over the mantel-piece, hanging on the wall, was a photograph of a ram in a carved wooden frame. Gillespie was pleased to notice that Morag appeared at home in this atmosphere of a farm. He regarded the furniture and the girl as his own.

"Will you take off your cap and sit down?" she asked, bending over the lamp, and turning higher the flame.

"I can only wait a meenut," he said, and sank down on a horse-hair sofa, which ran along the wall. He held himself stiffly upright. The girl's pale face flushed.

"Your father's just gone. Did you not meet him on the road?"

"I cam' ower in the punt," he answered evasively. Without his native cunning he appeared mulish and lethargic. As Morag kept silent he hazarded a question.

"I hope Galbraith's a wee thing better."

"He's dead." She stared at him, round-eyed.

"By wi' 't." His astonishment was genuine.

"Yes," she said in a softer voice; "he died shortly before your father came in."

"Poor Marget! I wonder what she'll do now." His voice was slightly wheedling.

"I don't know"—the girl shook her head—"she can't think of that just now."

"She'll be poorly off, I'm thinking."

Gillespie was getting on to his own ground and his figure thawed rapidly. Morag met him with a peevish tone. She had not brought him into the parlour to discuss the barren affairs of Gillespie.

"I wish you would not talk of these things just now; he is hardly cold yet."

Gillespie stooped and picked up his cap where it had fallen on the floor. When he raised his head he found Morag watching him intently, rather kindly he thought. At once he transferred his business with Morag from to-morrow's pigeon-hole to that of the immediate present. He tried to refine his mind from its cross-grained commercialism. This girl had been better bred than the village girls. Her mother had been one of the MacKenzies of Islay. She had been to school in Edinburgh when her mother was alive, and he had heard Lonend boast, when in his cups, that he had "gien a twa-hunner pun' eddication" to his girl. He knew that Lonend had a braw pride in her, and sat in the two-shilling

28

seats in the Good Templars' Hall at the Shepherds' concert when she played the piano for the singers. There was some talk at one time of her and one of the banker's clerks—the one that wrote the poetry in the *Gazette*. It was hinted that she was fell fond o' the lads. He stole a quick glance at her pale oval face and deep dark eyes. She had a curious way of looking up and leaning upon you as she spoke. These dark lustrous eyes were now fixed upon him. His own hard eyes swam in them as in wells; and something far beyond his ken, in untraversed deeps of his nature, rose to the summons of her eyes. It was as if the sun's rays had penetrated to the crystal heart of an iceberg, and touched something inflammable there to fire. It would burn fiercely till the gross ice had extinguished it. Afterwards the sun might shine on for a million years, but the fire was gone for ever. Gillespie was influenced from without inwards; while love is a flame which burns of itself internally, through to the surface of the face and eyes.

Her lustrous eyes were deepening into unfathomable wells, and changing every moment. Like a man in a dream he slowly rose from the sofa, and made a gesture towards her with his hand.

"Morag, will ye be my wife?"

Slowly she rose from the chair at the table.

"My father told me this evening, Gillespie." Her face was alight as she drew near to him. Still as in a dream, he felt her slip inside his arms. By a power that did not seem of himself they tightened around her. She was resting her cheek on his shoulder. He could not believe a woman's body was so soft and light. Like a feather he lifted her off her feet.

"Gillespie! Gillespie!" He felt her arms round his neck. They were bringing his face slowly downwards. Something soft and moist lay on his lips; her teeth met and clicked against his own. Her eyes were shining like diamonds. She was curling about him like a soft flame. He ceased to wonder at men getting married. He had never dreamt of this softness and warmth. Her hair tickled his face. She was standing on his boots, reaching upwards to his mouth. His neck was aching with her weight upon it, but he felt he could endure the strain for ever. Suddenly she flung her head back. He slipped his arm up beneath the nape of her neck. Her face was upturned to his; the eyes were closed; the mouth half open, showing the low sharp edge of the upper row of teeth.

Again he kissed her; and she began to croon his name. "How thick your hair is." Gillespie heard the turbulence of her words, but did not follow their meaning. He was bewildered at her caressing softness.

"Oh, it is so sweet!" She closed her eyes languidly. "Tell me, Gillespie, do you love me?"

She was so engrossed in her own tumultuous state that she did not notice the lack of warmth, the want of answering passion in him, or that he had scarce spoken a word since she came into his arms.

"Yes," he lied glibly.

"Oh, very, very much?" she whispered fiercely.

"Ay, Morag." Kindled by contact with it, he believed himself stung to the quick with love.

"Oh! how happy we'll be; won't we, Gillespie?"

She wriggled up from his arm and flung her two arms round his shoulders. Herein was unwomanly love, asking, not giving; desiring to be satisfied, not to satisfy.

"How tall and strong you are."

She touched his moustache with her fingers, and began teasing it gently.

"How funny it feels."

This wayward child of passion was examining her toy, blind with ecstasy of her possession, when she heard a heavy footstep in the passage without, and sprang away from Gillespie as the door opened and Mrs. Galbraith entered.

"Are you here, Morag, my dear?"

The girl's face flushed guiltily, as she bent over the lamp, and fumbled with the screw.

"The lamp has been smokin'."

Mrs. Galbraith cast a straight, piercing glance at her, which the girl did not meet.

"You'd better put it out then and come into the kitchen."

Passion had committed its first sin in a little lie, which Gillespie heard without any amazement. The tide of his mind was gradually drawing back to its normal mark, as a wave rolls down the beach from the impact of a gale. He had more important things to consider than the moral temperament of his betrothed. Immediately he took the reins into his hands; "Morag," he said, "Mrs. Galbraith an' me hev a wee bit business to transac'. We'll no' be long." He indicated the door ajar with a slight inclination of his head. The girl passed, looking at him with bright eyes, and went out. Gillespie closed the door behind her. In that moment commerce had striven with passion and got an easy mastery. In the lie which she had told, in her meek obedience, the girl had yielded all to him—morality, honour, life.

7

MRS. GALBRAITH was a woman of ideas, not of action. She had been trained at the Normal College in the Cowcaddens, Glasgow, from whose murky environment she had escaped as a bird from a cage. For a year she had been a school teacher in Paisley, and had married Galbraith to get back to the robust life of the country. She came of a landward stock, one of six daughters, who had heroically, and with cheerful semblance, taken to teaching to relieve the cramped life of their father's farm. Galbraith had to pay for her, to take her to wife, to the Education Department, because she had not served two years at teaching. This generosity opened the doors of her heart's affection. He used to say jocularly, in his cups, that he had bought her like a filly.

She was accomplished—played the piano well, had a cultured taste in poetry, read Wordsworth among the woods, was fond of philosophy and, on occasion, would enter warmly into argument with the Rev. Angus Stuart, minister of the parish, a gross, stout man, a gourmand who preferred Galbraith's bottle to his wife's incisive speculations. She was tenacious of her opinions, and Stuart hated her secretly, because she often cornered him in argument. He would wave her aside with a lordly sweep of his arm. "Gie me a dram, Galbraith; I'm sick o' thae blethers." And Galbraith's loud laugh would ring out, "Help yersel', Stuart; oil your machinery. It's her should be in the pulpit."

Every Sunday she devoutly read a portion of *The Imitation of Christ*, and of Tennyson's *In Memoriam*.

She was a capable mistress, up early at the milking, and went to bed late; humane to her servant, having a fine sense of the brotherhood of humanity. Jock, the grizzled ploughman, worshipped her. In the bothy o' nights he puzzled over her sayings.

31

"I'm as stupid as a new-calved calf when she speaks to me," he would tell his aged mother, who lived in the town in MacCalman's Lane, and was blind. She despised her husband's weakness for the bottle, and laboured zealously at her milk, butter, and eggs to keep the farm afloat. Galbraith, who had a dog-like affection for her, was secretive about his misdemeanours, and withheld from her the painful knowledge of his debts.

She was in middle age, the clear colour of health in her cheeks, her hair coal black and richly shining over heavy dark eyebrows and a fine broad forehead. An imperious woman to look at, with her clear, penetrative glance from level, fearless eyes. She had the hearty laugh of one who readily detects the humour in things. Her face in repose had the calm of one given to meditation. She pondered by the hour, as she walked slowly in the fields at sunset when her work was finished. She knew every wild flower and bush on the farm; bathed in the sea from June till the end of August, when she would sit listening to the solemn music of its ancient waters, as if deep called unto deep, and sniffing with unrestrained ecstasy the briny smells of a half-ebbed shore. Daily she fed a colony of wood birds, that she might hear their song in the trees around the north end of the house.

She turned on Gillespie a face full of quiet interrogation.

"What is it you wish to see me about?"

Gillespie found her level gaze disconcerting, and cast about for a propitious opening by the way of condolence.

"This is a sair blow for ye, Mrs. Galbraith; Morag was just tellin' me the sad news when ye cam' ben."

The woman bowed her head.

"The hand of God is always inscrutable to us poor mortals."

Gillespie was nonplussed. Hitherto men bargaining with him had broken the ice, and he had always had the pleasure of weighing his reply. He shifted ground.

"Ye'll be in a state," he said softly. He meant this to be oracular. If she took it for commiseration on her bereavement, well and good; if in reference to her affairs, all the better for him.

"I'm a childless widow," was the simple answer. This in turn was oracular to Gillespie. Did she refer to the loss of her husband or to her impecunious estate?

A sound of one loudly belching wind came from the kitchen. To gain time Gillespie pretended a look of inquiry towards the door. A faint smile appeared on the face of Mrs. Galbraith.

32

"It's Mary Bunch," she informed his small questing eyes.

Gillespie never paid attention to such frippery in the *olla-podrida* of life as the belching of wind; never made an aside, unless in some way it contributed to his main purpose. He was pleased to notice the kitchen grampus, in the hope that by such sociability Mrs. Galbraith would be disabused of the suspicion that he was a hawk. He had concluded that she was suspicious. A pirate thinks that others constantly recognise his black flag. But Mrs. Galbraith, who had often seen him in her husband's company, thought him merely an acquaintance come to sympathise with her. Her mind, more than half detached from mundane things, was only partially aware of Gillespie. Truth needs no armour; deceit an arsenal which Gillespie was laboriously furnishing for himself without a cause. How much of the effort of sin is pure wasted energy, mental or physical.

"Is she no' a fair pollute?"—Gillespie wasted some of that energy—"riftin' awa' there in the faice o' the deid; she's aye reingin' where there's a daith for the sake o' the dram."

There is that sort of man who would win the complaisance of another by defaming a third person. Mrs. Galbraith was not to be inveigled by claptrap. Her outlook was too sane and serene.

"Mary has her own point of view. If it is for the dram, as you say, yet she prefers it weeping with those who weep rather than rejoicing with those who rejoice."

Gillespie made a gesture. It meant that he cast overboard the ballast Mary Bunch, that was proving a dead-weight. He used his energy more immediately upon his business.

"When is the funeral?" he asked.

"On Thursday at three o'clock."

"Is there onything I can dae to help?"

"Your father promised his assistance; perhaps you will consult him. It is very kind of you."

"What's the use o' a neebur, if no at a time lik' this?"

"Thank you very much, Mr. Strang."

Gillespie felt himself slowly forging ahead. They were still standing, facing one another.

"Ye micht tak' a sate, Mrs. Galbraith," he said in his blunt way; "there's something else I want to talk ower wi' ye."

She sat down on the sofa, looking at him with eyes of mild surprise. He took a chair at the table.

33

"Ye'll no' be left too weel aff, Mrs. Galbraith. We a' ken the wy he was, aye tak' takin', taste tastin', easier to corn than to watter as the sayin' is."

"You dared not speak this way of the living"—her eyes flashed sudden fire on him. "If this is your business, look to the door; it opens easily from within." Wrath made her swell visibly in his eyes, which dropped from her blazing face.

"Wheest! wheest! Mrs Galbraith; I dinna mean tae insult ye," he said soothingly. "I've come to gie ye a bit o' advice."

She was instantly mollified.

"We should all be wise, for the world is full of advice,"— scorn rang in her voice—"but I shall be glad to hear you advise for my good." She smoothed down her black apron with a plump white hand.

"I suppose ye ken Galbraith was twa years ahint hand wi' the rent."

Her fine dark eyes widened seriously upon him.

"May I ask where you got your information, Mr. Strang, for it is correct?"

"Frae himsel'." he almost smirked.

"I did not know you were so deep in my husband's confidence."

"We'd oor bit saicrets thegeither, him an' me."

"Plainly." The dove was trying to outsoar the hawk. In some unaccountable way she felt nettled at Gillespie and at her husband's unwarrantable communicativeness.

He put on a sudden serious face.

"Ye ken that braks the lease. The Laird 'ill likely be wantin' the ferm aff your hands."

Mrs. Galbraith, who had not given much consideration to the matter, recognised the gravity of this statement, and at the same time divined that she was dealing with a man who had intimate knowledge of her affairs. She concluded that it would be best to let him talk. Gillespie smiled reassuringly.

"I'm thinkin' o' tryin' my hand at the fermin'." He drew his chair a little nearer to her. She quickly interpolated a question:

"Can't Jock and I manage the farm?"

He shook his head.

"It's this wy, Mrs. Galbraith. The Laird's pushed for money, an' he'll no' can buy ower the sheep"—she watched his furtive face intently, wondering by what mischance such a son came of

34

such parents—"he'll sell them to a black stranger, an' there's no mercat ee noo for beasts."

"But it wouldn't take all the stock, Mr. Strang, to pay the arrears of rent. There would surely be something left to carry on the farm with."

He looked at her solemn,—pityingly.

"Is that a' Galbraith's debt?" he asked.

The change which importunity slowly works on us was becoming visible in her face. The hawk was outsoaring the dove. The roots of her life had gone deep into the farm—the byre, the lea, the stubble, the weight of gold upon the corn, the ruddy face of autumn upon its flanking woods, the holy silence of its snowy uplands, the sacrament of eve in the glades, the solemn requiem of the sea. To tear these roots up would be to leave her bleeding—to death she thought. The cross of Calvary is always erected on a green familiar spot.

Gillespie saw alarm in her face, for very easily is the shadow of trouble seen upon the forehead of purity, like the faintest flaw of wind ruffling a glassy sea.

"I—I do not know," she faltered, and felt humiliated at the confession, and delivered into the hands of an enemy. The good cannot humiliate us.

"It's just as weel to let ye ken then that he's five hunner in debt tae another man."

Some cover their wound with a smile; the maudlin make an industry of their misfortune; the bravest cannot help but wince at a sudden stab. He heard the gasp and saw her eyes dilate with something akin to fear. This attorney pored upon her face.

"Are—are you sure of this?" She was too stunned to ask who the man was.

"Deid sure."

There was a long silence in the room. The prize ram above the mantelpiece seemed to look down in wondering innocence. She was breathing heavily as she drank her bitter cup; but, save for a quicker rise and fall of the breast, she made no other outward sign of her emotion. When she spoke it was in a steady tone.

"Then I'm a pauper."

"Hoots," said Gillespie, "ye're amang freens."

"One finds many friends, but few to till one's land."

Even yet she was more absorbed in ideas than in action. But when Gillespie spoke again it made her realise how impoverished

35

and futile are ideas when confronted with the satire of existence, and with that ruthless egoism which is the spirit of that which we call "business."

"Ye'll maybe hae to roup your furniture as weel. Ye winna lik' your things to gang that wy; the very bed he de'ed in."

"What does it signify, if it must come to that?"

"It signeefees a' things. A roup means laawers an' unctioneers; an' it's no the bottom o' the barrel they'll tak'."

"What am I to do then?"

These words were her flag of capitulation.

"Weel, ye see, Mrs. Galbraith, it's no' the thing, as I said, to sell to a wheen black strangers." She could have pointed out that their gold is as good as another's, but refrained. One whose back is to the wall has lost the art of persuasion. "That wad mean yersel' put to the door. No' a very nice thing at your time o' life."

"It would break my heart," she answered quietly. Her face was becoming immobile and strained. The voice seemed to issue from a sphinx.

"Like as no'; like as no'; an' seeck an' sorry I am for ye, Marget." She took the familiarity in her name unquestioned. What has travail to do with nicety of punctiliousness?

"Weel, no' to gang ahint your back, I cam' here to mak' a bargain wi' ye:" the hawk was ready to swoop. "I'm thinkin' o' tryin' the fermin'; it's a fine healthy life. The fushin's sair on a man wi' the rheumatics. I'll buy ower the furniture an' tak' the sheep."

Her eyes wavered and fell. A single bright tear oozed out of their corners—a feather fallen from the talons of the hawk. It was the only tear which she shed in the whole business—the only tear till that far-off day when she heard the men at the funeral of Gillespie's son slowly tramp by her little house, and she flung herself, convulsed with sobs, upon the open family Bible, seeing in letters of fire before her burning eyeballs the terrible words:

"Vengeance is Mine: I will Repay, saith the Lord."

At present a look of hesitancy and indecision, pathetic in that strong face, made her wilt. She spoke in a voice choking with the poignancy of her position—a voice burdened with the sapping fatalism which she had imbibed from her books of philosophy.

"The oldest house will have a new hand at the door; another's

36

step on the stair. The dust that lay in the old corners will be cleaned out." Her eyes had a far-off, visionary look. "Mr. Strang, we all suffer hell. To the good it is the loss of what is familiar and dear; the fading away of the things that have been precious." She seemed to rouse herself with an effort. "What is the use of troubling yourself, if I must go? Horror to the dispossessed is this, that the world is so large and wide, and yet has in it so very little room."

Gillespie looked at her in amazement. She was talking nonsense.

"Who's askin' ye to gang?"

"I—I—don't understand," she faltered.

"I daursay! I daursay," he allowed himself the luxury of contempt. "Ye canna thole leavin' the ferm;" contempt spawned irony.

"Give me my home; I'll ask no more."

This appeal would have touched any other heart. The "lares and penates" had become part of her being. To lose one's roof and bed is a greater evil to some women than to lose one's honour. Gillespie edged his chair a little nearer. "Ye see, Marget, it's this wy. I've nae wummankind to wark here." He put a tentative cajoling hand on her knee. She looked down at it from her eyelids with loathing, but did not move a muscle. "My plan is to buy over frae you, an' ye'll stay an' look aifter the kye an' the hoose. It's either that or sellin' tae a black stranger, an' oot ye'll hae to gang."

"I'll do anything rather than have to leave."

Gillespie was unconscious of the studied insolence of these words. He was too engrossed in his plans. He would consult the Laird, "an' tak' a' responseebeelity aff" her hands. Oh, yes, he would see to that, although the farm would be in her own right till Michaelmas term. She was to have no responsibility, no trouble, not even with the rabbits. He figured his profits from this source at from £4 to £5 a week. Lonend would have no finger in this pie till the term. And he had other lucrative schemes.

"It's a fell peety o' ye, Marget," he said. "My mother's greetin' ower yonder in the 'Ghost' lik' a bairn. 'Be sure, Gillespie,' she said, 'that Marget 'ill no' suffer or want.' "

She made no answer. She heard a babble of words, but grasped no meaning in them. With head bowed in sorrow, she was thinking of the grey dead man upstairs, her thoughts bent on the

37

sudden terrible upheaval which is caused in the lives of others by the death of one. One moment tranquillity; the next chaos. To-day everything hangs by a name—house and home and lands; estimation, rank, outlook, security. To-morrow, when that name is engraved upon a coffin lid, the world has fallen to pieces. Exile suddenly haunts the shadow of the coffin. At the last breath the veil of the temple of home is rent; publicity stares in; old landmarks are torn up; and an angel of reckoning sits upon the rigging of the house. The stillness of the death-chamber is intensified by contrast with the noise of a falling house around its solemnity; its awful impassivity becomes the more marmoreal because of the babblings to which its august calm has given birth; and its sanctity is desecrated by the importunate ghosts of affairs which gibber at its threshold. He was a hard drinker, careless, improvident, impecunious; but what a buckler against Fate: a roof for her head; her bread; a covert from the tempest. And now the rock was removed out of his place, and she stood in the pitiless sun, alone in a weary land.

"We'd better be steppin' ben the hoose afore Mary Bunch 'ill hae the bottle feeneshed."

He had taken her silence for acquiescence, and spoke as one with the reins already in his hands; and suddenly careful of the gear and victuals of the farm. She arose wearily, looked at him as if about to speak, then walked towards the door in silence. She turned the handle, and glanced at him over her shoulder.

"I thank you, Mr. Strang, for offering me a home. I entered this room a mistress. I leave it a servant."

Before he had time to answer she had passed swiftly out. In her wake he pocketed the box of matches which Morag had left on the table, and blew out the lamp. He had often told his mother that he hated "wastery." As he did these things he was silently comparing Morag and Mrs. Galbraith. He had the acumen to estimate the enormous interval which lay between them in capability and in character.

"If she'd a pickle siller, it's her I wad be merryin'," he muttered as he groped for the door.

Mrs. Galbraith, gazing down upon the face of her dead husband, was spared the bitterness of this avowal.

8

GILLESPIE had his own plans for establishing himself in the town, but he was in a sort already established; Mary Bunch, that frequenter of houses of mourning, being witness where she sat at the kitchen fire of Muirhead, nursing her cold feet to the sound of her belching.

"Excuse the win'," she said to her *vis-à-vis*, Mrs. Effie Tosh. How she came to be there requires a reference to the Back Street. This street had once some bigness of life when Bruce of Scotland, fleeing to Ireland, had had his boat drawn down that ancient way; and returned to build the fortress whose rags yet hang from a height over the harbour. The Way of the Boat, once royal, is now cobbled and broken; twisted like the precarious lives of its inhabitants, squirming among its thatched houses as if ashamed of its holes, and at every greater sore scampering round a corner out of sight. It is so narrow that the sun rarely comes there, being a sunset street lying to the west and the sea.

Everything that is old is there. The houses, whose lozenged windows are but a child's height from the ground, look ageless, and on its thatched roofs cats pursue sparrows. Dominating its head is the bridge, upon the corner of which is the Pump, black with age, the chiefest thing of the street, the eyrie of the town. It is the home of censure, the seat of wrangling, and the folk who live by it are all middle-aged or old.

Not a few of the bowed windows in the Back Street give upon the Pump, so that Lucky can lean out for a chat with Nan at Jock, the same who is Jock Sinclair's wife, while she draws water. Sometimes the windows do not serve; great occasions woo them to a closer intimacy at the Pump. After this fashion. In the still afternoon there is a curve of water in the air. Slap! it takes the quiescent street along its drowsy length. This humid scavenging marks one bell. Towsy heads pop out of doors and rummage at the windows.

Nan at Jock is rinsing out her stoup. Everything depends on how she is facing. If up over the bridge, the business is one of cold water; if down the street challenging the blank windows, the idol of gossip is set up at the Pump, and every needy newsmonger, with a sudden desire of water upon her, carries her importunate thirst and stoup to the place of worship. The brightly flowing curve is fast filling Nan at Jock's stoup, so that Lucky reaches the Pump just as Black Jean scurries down the wind, her shawl flying like a jib, with Mary Bunch more leisurely in her wake—more leisurely, for her house is approached from the street by a flight of three stone steps, the only stair in the street. The aristocrat is never hurried, even though she knows that Betty Heck is hard at heel.

Lucky lends a greedy ear to skim the cream of the news before the corvettes arrive.

"Good day to ye, Nan; I hope ye're weel."

"Never was he'rtier since I was craidled."

"What's ado the day, Nan?" She cast an eye askance at the troop of marauders bearing down upon them.

"Jamie's hame frae Injia." Nan's eyes gleamed; her face was transfigured. "He just cam' walkin' in, pushin' the door open as if he'd been oot for a waalk, an' cried, 'Hallo, mother'." He had never called her mother before in his life.

Here was news. But Lucky, not being one to admit an empty larder, lied deliciously, and every word was honey to the mother.

"Fine, I ken. I was telt he was seen comin' up frae the Wharf ahint a big black seegar."

What a warm palpitating world for Nan. The very cats on the roof must be carrying the news. The Pump was now ringed with hungry devotees.

"Yei! Yah! frae the land o' the neegurs an' the teegurs; ye'll be the prood ane," cried Betty Heck.

And Nan flashed, a star of pride. "What dae ye think he's brocht for me?"

They knew only of large shells with the sea droning in them, and were as ignorant of the Sack of the East as of the riches of the hanging gardens of Babylon: but Black Jean put in a hasty oar: "A monkey," she cried, making a discovery.

"A parrot," urged Mary Bunch.

Betty Heck, alarmed at the swift graduation of these students of foreign travel, spoke irascibly: "Monkey here, parrot there; a black man is liker it." Nan smiled and shook her head. "Haud yeer tongue: noathin' less than a white silk shawl the neebur o' the Queen's."

Lucky, who had been silent and vigilant, flashed her white

teeth in criticism of the childish guesses she had heard. "Monkey, guidsakes; ye'd think Jamie was an Eyetalian." She turned her swarthy face on Nan at Jock as if she had known it all. "The neebur o' the Queen's, div ye say, Nan?"

Nan at Jock nodded and suddenly whipped up her bratty. "An'—this!"

A long bottle wrapped in tissue paper was disclosed. Such silence as possesses men upon a Darien peak fell upon these women.

"What is it, Nan?" Mary Bunch's face craned forward.

"Is't something tae drink?" from Betty Heck.

"Is't thon gold-fush in watter?" from Black Jean.

Dumbly they stared at the exotic, a very nunnery of amazement and awe, each after her nature eaten up of envy or jealousy, or glowing with pride that the Back Street could send out such a riever to the high world. With flushed face and trembling fingers Nan at Jock unwrapped the tissue paper and held up a long bottle with a green label. The sun glittered on a silver stopper.

"It's scent," said Nan in an awed whisper.

Five pairs of eyes were riveted on the bottle; four pairs of hands were itching to clasp it. With a dignified movement Nan handed it to Black Jean, who sniffed at the stopper. Solemnly it was handed round.

"It cowes a'," said Betty Heck, turning it round and round in her grimy hand; "the last hand that touched it was away furrin'."

Mary Bunch, holding it aloft, spoke: "Put it on the top shelf above the dresser beside the 'nock.' Everybody 'ill notiss it there when they're lookin' at the time."

Then a strange thing happened. Out of the fount of happiness welling up in her breast Nan at Jock broke the alabaster box very precious. Swiftly she unscrewed her stopper, and before Betty Heck realised it she was sprinkled with the odours of Araby, and squealed in surprise and ecstasy. Ah! if you could have seen Nan's shining eyes at her baptismal benediction—her son's gift anointing her comrades; the riches of the East falling like ichor upon the penury of the cold West. How cunning she was, asking Mary Bunch where upon her person this dew of loving-kindness was to rest, and before Mary could open her mouth to reply, wheeling and sprinkling Black Jean.

"I never lookit for this, Mrs. Sinclair," said Betty Heck in a husky voice, with her nose in her breast; if only I'd on my Sunday dolman."

"The bonnie, bonnie smell," said Mary Bunch; "it's like the Planting in April when the primroses are oot."

"I'm feart tae draw my braith," cried Lucky, her tall form towering with pride, her white teeth flashing beneath her heavy dark eyebrows. And Nan at Jock with the glee of a girl purred, "Weel, we're big fowk for wance."

"Yei! Yah! here's wan o' the rale big fowk comin'; here's Effie Tosh," and Betty Heck danced with unashamed mirth. "I'll bate ye she's smelled it doon the burn Davie lad."

There was something of the earnest of a precursor in the gait of Mrs. Tosh, and a shadow of doubt fell on Black Jean's face. "There's mair nor scent in the win'; she's weirin' her gloves."

All eyes were bent on the scurrying lady, as Nan at Jock screwed on the stopper and made a deft movement beneath her bratty.

"Man! but she'll get the doon-fa'," said Mary Bunch; "she'll be hurryin' wi' the news o' Jamie." There was the least possible trace of acidity in Mary's voice, for Effie was inclined to be uppish. She kept a "wee shop" in the lee of the burn, and spoke of her rich relatives and her famous dead relations.

She arrived blowing, a little apple-cheeked woman, with cold grey eyes and a mass of brown hair.

"Good afternoon, leddies. I see ye're at your meeting. Hae ye heard the news?" She panted.

"We've got mair nor news, Mrs. Tosh, seein' ye ax"—Betty Heck's lips were so firmly pursed that the words appeared to be squeezed out—"we've got a praisint as weel."

"A praisint, really?"

"Ay, a praisint; where's your nose?" snapped Black Jean.

Mrs. Tosh, stupefied, touched that organ, and was greeted with a jeer.

"Really! really! where's your mainners, leddies?"

"In the portmantle wi' the seegars an' the big silk shawl—neebur o' the Queen's. Neilsac cairried it up. Where's your eyes?" Black Jean openly scoffed.

"Really, Jean, I dinna understan' your joke." Mrs. Tosh, on every possible occasion said, "really." She had overheard the Laird's wife at a Mothers' Meeting use the fatuous word, and had practised it in private.

"Ou! we heard ye were to be mairrit the morn, an' kirkit

come Sunday," said Mary Bunch, "an' we were speakin' o' praisints." Mrs. Tosh's face was now irascibly condemnatory of such unwarrantable persiflage.

"A weddin'; really, you astonish me; if ye had said a funeral noo—"

Nan at Jock took immediate umbrage. She fancied the whole town knew of Jamie's arrival, and this was spite and malice on the part of Mrs. Tosh. "I'll hae ye tae understan' that my Jamie— Jamie Sinclair o' the Clan Line has come hame frae Injia."

"Wi' a braw silk shawl, the neebur o' the Queen's," thus Mary Bunch. "An' scent ye never smelt the lik' o' since ye were craidled," thus Betty Heck—all like the spit, spit of rifle fire.

"I wish ye better o' your son, Mrs. Sinclair, than Kate the Booger has o' her yin. I hae my ain opeenion o' foreign pairts, an' it was the opeenion o' my faither afore me. Look at Kate the Booger's son, the nesty sodger fella wi' his galluses an' his black face. I had it frae Mrs. Lowrie"—she was always "having it" from the banker's wife or the minister's sister—" 'Mrs. Tosh,' says she, 'I'll tak' a skein o' silk,' an' then, leanin' ower the coonter, she said, 'Did ye hear, Mrs. Tosh, o' the scandlas way Kate the Booger's son cairried on at the Shepherds' Concert? The Laird said he was a fair disgrace to the Airmy.' Them's foreign mainners or I'm an Irishman. Him an' his galluses an' his dirty face breengin' aboot the toon. Really!"

But Mary Bunch had scented carrion at the word "funeral." Her little red face perked up and her bright eyes watched hawklike till Mrs. Tosh had shut her mouth.

"It's you that hes the news, Mrs. Tosh. Who's bereavit in the toon? I was at the whulks a' yesterday wi' the spring tides an' a'm no in the forefront o' the news."

Mary Bunch always referred to "the bereavit."

Mrs Tosh put on a prim mouth. She was the bearer of weighty tidings after all.

"Really! have ye no' heard? Well, I may say it's a far-oot freen o' my faither's that passed away last night at tea-time."

"Yei! Yah! is the Laird deid?" rapped out Nan at Jock.

The prim mouth tightened. "The Laird's well. Miss Stuart was ca'in' there last week. I had it frae her; an' my Lady—"

"Then it's the Spider," said Black Jean. This was the town lawyer—a man of ill repute.

"Really! I'm surprised at your behaviour"—she stopped a

43

moment, fishing for Mary Bunch's word—"It's Calum Galbraith that's bereavit." To the chagrin of Mrs. Tosh her news caused no flutter of astonishment in a company that was steeled against astonishment at her hands. They simply accepted the fact that Calum Galbraith was dead. Except Mary Bunch they all took this to be the meaning of the word "bereavit," and proceeded to chastise "the far-oot freen," led by Nan, who remembered the jibes about foreign pairts.

"Poor Calum! a fiddlin' kin' o' body aboot the ferm." Her tone was disparaging.

Betty Heck's head wagged slackly on her scraggy neck.

"I saw him last week at Baldy Bain's funeral. He was that scuffed lookin', I couldna keep my eye off the tie he'd on. An' noo he's awa' himsel'." Nan at Jock, who in her maiden days had wrought "at the Bleachfield oot o' Paisla," was an accredited authority on attire.

"The tie was noathin' to his lum hat. I never liked to see Calum in a lummer. Ye'd think he was sweetin' at a pleughin' match wi' the hat on the back o' his heid. I aye thocht he was gaun to fa' ower on his back. Poor Calum! there's noathin' but changes."

Mrs. Tosh saw redly. "Really! it's no wonder Miss Stuart ca's ye a set o' common people. I winna be seen wipin' my mooth on the same tooel wi' ye aifter a meal. Ye're just a wheen o' nesty back-biters"—she tossed her head, sniffing—"that's my opeenion o' ye, an' it was my faither's afore me. Ye canna let the bereavit alone—a wheen o' low black back-biters. I'm just on my wy to see Marget, an' I'll let her ken my opeenion o' ye." She swung round the Pump, down the burn in the direction of the "wee shop."

"Look at her, the wrunkled poke o' whesels," cried Nan at Jock.

"Ay," said Black Jean, lowering, "her he'rt's lik' a funeral letter, a' black roond the edge."

There was a silence in which you could feel them hastily tearing off the mask which they had worn before the illustrious Mrs. Tosh, and it was a big-hearted Nan who spoke, hiding her scent-bottle, for the hour of its glory was eclipsed by the news of affliction.

"Ach! ach! poor Calum, he'd his ain trials."

You could only understand what these meagre words meant

44

if you had heard them uttered with the world of sorrow that was in Nan's voice.

"Ah! he'd his ain sorrow"—Lucky wiped her nose with the back of her hand till it glistened like a beak—"an' it's Gillespie Strang that kens it fine. I winna be in his shoes the day for a' the gold in Californy; they're the shoes o' a deid man."

"I didna hear Gillespie was thrang wi' Calum." Mary Bunch was big-eyed with curiosity.

"No; he's that quate an' snake-lik' it's no' much ye'll can hear o' thon man. Floracs gied a run ower last nicht an' gied me a long lingo aboot Calum an' Gillespie. Ach! is't Gillespie; he'd skin a louse for the creish." Floracs was the banker's servant. The banker's wife, a loud, over-dressed woman, was a cistern running over. Thus is the world informed, and the secrets of many hearts revealed. "Poor Calum wasna the wan to compleen. He aye ca'ed me Nan Gilchrist, an' no' my mairrit name, as he gied by. 'An' hoo are ye the day, Nan Gilchrist?' an' wad wave his hand that cheery lik'."

Betty Heck sighed towards the ground.

"It's me that'll miss him noo goin' tae the Plantin' for a bit bundle o' sticks. He wasna sweert to gie ye a male o' pitaetas oot o' the pit. 'They're that dry,' sez he, 'they're chokin' my hens. Here, Betty, tak' them awa' to the waens in the Back Street, or I'll süne no' hae a hen leevin' on the ferm."

Ah! not poor Calum, but poor Mrs. Tosh! Pride hath devoured the radiance of life and hidden from thee, Mrs. Tosh, what is best and tenderest in the human heart.

Towards candlelight they left the Pump and the burn, calling mournfully on its way to the sea—the burn on whose bank, higher up, Morag and Gillespie were, that same night, to hold a lovers' tryst.

"What I was lik' tae ken," said Betty Heck, as they trooped through the dusk with a faint savour of Eastern scent about them, "is this—who's deid, Calum or his wife?"

Black Jean answered scornfully.

"Did ye no' hear thon poke o' whesels say Galbraith's bereavit? Who but poor Calum's the cauld corp this night?"

Thereupon Mary Bunch, a more consummate linguist, privately made up her mind that that night she would examine into the records of the Angel of Death at the farmhouse of Calum Galbraith.

Towards the full entry of that same night, certain men of the Back Street could be seen creeping with empty stoups to the Pump, and there heard with amazement the subdued voices of furtive fellow-beings on a like expedition. Together they held curious speech concerning this strange domestic famine of water.

"Surely tae Goäd, there's something in the win'," said Neilsac, and asked despitefully for a match. They little deemed that the causes of the water famine lay in the irruption of a man from the East, and in the visit of the angel who is called Death. And the Pump that knew all things, made a dumb guttural sound of mockery in its mouth as they filled the stoups.

9

So we discover Mary Bunch belching wind in the kitchen of Galbraith's farm, and proving to Mrs. Tosh that Gillespie, who wished to establish himself in the town, was in a sort already established there.

Mrs. Tosh appreciated Gillespie, because he was a man of means, with a growing name. But she was now to bring her private estimation to the touch-stone of public opinion. Mary Bunch, accompanied by a taciturn raw girl with beefy face, her daughter, had already found in the field Mrs. Tosh, who criticised sharply.

"Really, it's no' just very polite, riftin' awa' there in the face of the deid."

"Ach! excuse me; I'm aye fashed wi' the nervous win' at night. It's the hot tea that's bringin' it up." Mary Bunch desired to be amicable. "This is a sair come-doon for poor Marget."

"It's really a sore trial"—a phrase of the minister's purloined by Mrs. Tosh, who delivered it stiffly, remembering the episode at the Pump.

"I'm telt Calum never recovered conscience aifter he fell in the Laigh Park cryin' on the dog. Marget never got wan word oot o' him."

Mary Bunch, who was told nothing of the sort, was thirsting for more copious information. Mrs. Tosh, who had found Mrs.

46

Galbraith singularly reticent, determined to pique Mrs. Bunch in turn.

"As ye ken, I'm a far-oot freen o' Mr. Galbraith's"—Mary Bunch's wizened rosy face nodded jerkily beneath her black bonnet—" 'Really, Margaret,' I said to her before ye came in, 'you and me will take a jaunt tae Glesca for the mournin's.' There's nothin' suitable in the village, as ye know, Mrs. Bunch."

"She'll be gaun afore the coo 'ill calf," cried Mary Bunch eagerly. Mrs. Tosh was ruffled at this fresh spate of knowledge concerning the farm.

"Certainly."

Mary Bunch, conceiving herself now largely in the confidence of these ladies, became explanatory concerning her self-imposed prohibition from this venture to Glasgow.

"I'm too roosty noo for jauntin'; am I no', Effie?" Effie, her tall daughter, was seated like a sentinel at the window. Her mother flung embarrassing questions at her without expecting any answer. "It's seeven years since I was in Glesca, when your faither gied awa' wi' the Volunteers tae the Crystal Pailace tae see the Queen"—she nodded to her voluminous daughter. Mrs. Tosh had broached an ocean of garrulity. "He wasna for takin' me. Ye see it was the time I had my third, wee Erchie. He got £15 the night he was born, an' whaur is't noo? A' in the Crystal Pailace. He was born on a Sunday, an' on the Friday Jenny, my first, was beerit, an' I never saw the corp. Dr. Maclean wadna alloo them tae bring it in. That was the morn the MacLachlans was drooned—a sore day in the toon. There was a big guttin' that day." Her small face was held sideways to Mrs. Tosh like a sad bird's. "Ay! that was the first job at the guttin' that auld Strang got in Brieston. He cam frae Ayr in his boat the day afore. I mind it was the Thursday o' the Fast."

Mrs. Tosh hastened into the stream of the narrative at the chance name of Mr. Strang.

"Gillespie's in the parlour just now wi' Margaret—I'm waitin' till he's awa'."

Mary Bunch's bird-like eyes darted to the door.

"Gillespie! I wonder what he's efter. But I'd be seeck an' sorry afore I'd hae any daleins wi' him."

"Really!" Mrs. Tosh conveyed the politest scorn; "the banker has got a very good name o' Mr. Strang."

47

"Ye're a freen o' Marget's." Mary Bunch leaned with an air of confidence across the hearth.

"I sincerely hope so." Mrs. Tosh, rather pleased at this mark of respect, found herself less inimical towards her companion.

"Weel, tell Marget that Gillespie's no' the wan tae let the flies bide on his honey. It was an ill day that poor Calum ever spoke tae him."

Mrs. Tosh, with the reflected power of censorship upon her from the minister's sister, assumed a face of grave concern.

"Really, Mrs. Bunch, I never heard onything against his character."

"Wheesh! wheest! ye dinna ken ye're leevin' up in the wee shop"—she waved a chiding hand—"Is't Gillespie, wi' his eyes for ever on the ground, looking for preens?"

A raucous outburst of laughter from the Sphinx at the window interrupted Mrs. Bunch. She cast a glance of aspersion at her unseemly offspring, and plunged into the sea of her tale.

"It was Nan at Jock's man that put the hems on him. Did ye hear o' the words they had thegeither?"

Mrs. Tosh was gradually becoming alienated from Mr. Strang, since Mary Bunch had hinted that he was an interloper at the farm; and she condescended to lend her ear to the doings of Gillespie with the plebs.

"There was a big ebb, an' Jock was awfu' thirsty. Ye ken the wy poor Nan just works hersel' tae the bone for him tae gie him his minch collops an' his tobacca. She took the whittle in her thoom' an' couldna wash, an' Jock was off at the wulks wi' the big ebb. He 'manded half a bag, keepin' up his he'rt a' the lee-lang day wi' the thought o' Brodie's in the fore-night, an' brought half a bag tae Gillespie."

It falls here to be recorded that among his other activities Gillespie, in the winter time when there was no fishing, bought whelks and exported them to Glasgow. He professed the business was scarce worth the trouble, but had not the heart to see the fruits of a laborious day's toil rusting without chances of a market. If the whelk-gatherers demurred at his niggard prices, pointing out the hardship of the work on a raw shore, he invited them to try the market themselves, knowing that a man can reasonably tempt the market with a dozen to a score bags bought from all the scavengers of the shores, while a single sea-side reaper would thrust his own sickle in vain into the heart of the Glasgow Fish

Market. A single bag would scarce stand the freight. Gillespie had terms from the Steamship Company for anything over a dozen bags.

"Weel," nodded Mary Bunch, "ye see Jock's no a right fisherman; just a sort o' bent-preen wan, an' Gillespie was fu' o' his nesty dirty tricks, an' told Jock he'd only some coppers in his pocket."

" 'It's no a bite o' hard breid I'm wantin'," sez Jock.

" 'Jock! Jock! mind I'll hae a big washin' for Nan when her thoom's better. My mither's fashed wi' her breath, an' canna scoor the blankets.'

" 'It's no Nan ye're needin' for your washin',' sez Jock—ye ken Jock gets as mad as a whesel—'it's the toon's scavenger.'

" 'Hoots! hoots! dinna be sae hasty, man, an' you sae ill to please, thae hard times. Ye should be glad there's wulks to gether.'

" 'If I wasna thirsty, Gillespie, I'd send the wulks to Bannerie'—this was the town twelve miles north, which had a poorhouse and an asylum.

" 'Ah! ay! Jock, that's just it; aye thirsty; boozin' awa' a' summer, flingin' doon the siller on Brodie's bar like swells. It's a wonder the coonter doesna tak' fire. An noo' ye're at the wulks.' " To say that a man was "at the wulks" was to utter the deepest contempt of him. Nothing but abject misery would drive a man to this occupation.

"Jock got ootrageous mad. 'Are ye no at the wulks as well's me, ye scabby eel?'—Jock shut his neif in his face—'What's the differ' 'tween buyin' wulks an' getherin' them?' Jock was shootherin' the bag when a thocht struck him. Aw! ye should hear him at the story. I wis sore laughin' at him. Doon he flung the bag. 'Gie's wan an' six an' the wulks is yours.' An' Gillespie coonted oot the money tae him in coppers."

"Really, really! tinkler's money," said Mrs. Tosh.

Mary Bunch made a gesture of contempt.

"An' off whupped Jock tae the Red Tiger, an' sez he tae him, 'Tiger,' sez he, 'are ye on for a spree?' an' the Tiger had maist a fit.

" 'Suxpence worth o' beer,' sez Jock tae Brodie, 'an' a shullin's worth o' whusky.' An' Jock told the Tiger aboot the wulks. Oot they came frae Brodie's quite joco, an' got Neil Dhus's punt, an' awa' doon the hairbour they gied like creished lightnin', tae

49

where Gillespie keeps his wulks in the salt watter below the auld stores, an' off they loused the rope, an' whupped the wulks in tae the punt, an' inside half-an-oor the Tiger was doon wi' the punt ablow the 'Ghost' sellin' half a bag o' wulks tae Gillespie.

" 'Ye're throng the day,' sez he tae the Tiger. 'I'm just efter peyin' a shullin' to Nan at Jock's man for half a bag.'

" 'A shullin'!' sez the Tiger, 'an' them ten shullin's in Glesca. Poor Jock, he doesna ken the value o' wulks. He'll be wantin' tae buy snuff wi' the shullin'.'

"They argy-bargyed even-on till the Tiger got half-a-croon for the wulks."

"Really, Mrs. Bunch, I never jaloosed Mr. Strang was so near the bone."

"Ah! the kirn's aye tae churn wi' him, an' the milk's aye tae earn."

"He's the boy tae haud his grup," came a squeak from the window. The Sphinx had spoken, and cast eyes of fear on the floor at her voice. The comrades at the fire regarded in silence the figure which had emitted the voice. The face of the figure under scrutiny examined the sombre twilight without. Mary Bunch was heard to sigh gently, and took Mrs. Tosh by the eye.

"If there wasna a horo-yalleh next mornin'. Gillespie was up at the 'Shuppin' Box' lookin' for Jock and the Tiger, an' accusin' them o' stealin' his wulks.

" 'Wheest, ye dirt,' said Jock; 'I'll hae the law o' ye for spoilin' my character!' There was a wheen o' the men at the Shuppin' Box.' 'Boys,' cries Jock, 'ye're a' witnesses. Stealin' your wulks'— Jock was winkin' hard at the men—'I'd such a heavy list tae starboard wi' the coppers ye gied me that I couldna walk the length o' my shadda tae steal anything.'

"The Tiger pulled his gravat roond his throat an' turned the broad o' his back on Gillespie.

"Ye'll hae tae excuse me turnin' my back,' sez he, 'an' strappin' my gravat roond my thrapple, for I aye hae the feelin' of your knife slashin' my Adam's apple.'

"Gillespie didna say a word for a fell strucken meenut. Then he gied thon wee laugh o' his an' sez, 'You Brieston folk are the wutty boys; there's no' makin' a leevin' wi' such jokes gaun aboot.' An' off he gied, an' no' a sowl kent whether he was angry or no."

Gossip being the compass of a people's heart, you will see

that Mr. Gillespie Strang was making a definite name for himself. He was held to be grasping, a dealer in any sort of chance commerce. His sign, in the estimation of some, should be—retail trade in all sorts of villainy. Most people knew him to be a sly, sordid huckster, who crept like a pirate through the town with oiled helm; a man whose lance rested on the exposed back of the simple. They judged—and Lonend was among these—that he was no match for the open-eyed. He crept too much like a lapwing to take the high air with eagles or hawks.

So that Mrs. Bunch's verdict was a plagiarism taken from public opinion: "Gillespie's here for nae good, I'se warrant ye, Mrs. Tosh," and Mrs. Tosh, by virtue of her "far-oot freenship," assumed arms against Mr. Strang. She deemed as little as the town deemed that it was not arms so much as armour that was needed in the arena with Gillespie. In the meantime she thrust after the ancient manner of her kind.

"Really, Mrs. Bunch, I don't know what things are comin' to in the toon wi' thae incomers. That's my opeenion, an' it was the opeenion o' my faither before me that's deid an' gone. They don't ken their own place. I had it frae the banker's wife that his faither hadn't a shirt to his back when he came to Brieston. Thae incomers hae no pride when it comes tae the siller." Mrs. Tosh pursed her lips into the thin red line of gentility's scorn.

"Pride!" echoed Mary Bunch shrilly; "he heeds naebody or naethin'. He's tinkerin' awa' doon at the carpenter's shed at an auld fabric o' a boat wi' a handfu' o' roosty nails. He'll put a rotten net in her an' gie her tae the school-boys tae fush for him, an' sell the cuddies through the toon, a penny a baeshin', an' maybe droon the weans. He should be stoppit by Cammel the polishman."

From the ages unto the ages shall obscure foes, no less than Herod and Pilate, fraternise over a common enemy. Mary Bunch and Mrs. Tosh set their vanguard against Gillespie, with the Sphinx as sentinel, as do those who have passed the pipe of peace from hand to hand.

"I ken the cut o' his jib fine," cried Mrs. Bunch vaingloriously, when the acute sentinel spoke her warning from the depths of the window:

"Here he's comin'."

And two snails at the fire hurriedly sought the asylum of their shells. Gillespie appeared with a bottle in his hand. His position

51

was yet all to make on the farm; and he knew his adversaries. He was that sort of man who imposes silence at his approach. People did not take him lightly; they waited on his word as a cue, in the manner of inferiors with important persons. In addition, Gillespie, being a large full-blooded man, dominated physically such wizened mice as the ladies at the fire. Though he was by no means deaf, he had a disconcerting way of making his hand a horn at his ear; and he carefully waited on every word, and weighed the most trivial answer as he slowly replied. He put people on their mettle or made them cringe. These women had not met him personally before. There was something rugged, impervious, granite-like in his silent bulk, the thought of attacking which shrivelled them up. Mrs. Tosh conceived a sudden animosity against the wily Bunch for having alienated her from this rock-like friend of the banker's. She became emollient, subservient.

"And how are ye, Mr. Strang?" she asked with finicking air.

"Skelpin awa'," answered Gillespie.

Mary Bunch, in more characteristic fashion, took up the cry.

"Effie's weary bidin' on ye an' Marget." She always contrived to lay anything disagreeable on the broad shoulders of her mute daughter, who accepted the onus like a lamb. There were reasons for this. The daughter, a tall, dark woman, with a dull red face, thick lips, and a large, slack mouth, had been troubled in the shadow of the altar. A gentleman, somewhat light in love, had taken marriage-fright and disappeared two days before the consummation of love, leaving a tall bridescake staring in Marshall's, the baker's, window as a monument of his perfidy. Its little blue banner at the top stood like a flag of shame flying at the fore. The baker was in a dilemma. No other bride would purchase the tombstone. He could not well force it on one who had, in a manner, fulfilled her destiny, and never appeared now in public except at the tail of her mother, as her scapegoat. Meanwhile the effigy lay languishing in the baker's shop, slightly tarnished, and waiting upon love. The top-gallants of its favours had been removed.

Gillespie had no humour and scarce any bowels of sympathy. He turned his leonine head slowly to Effie.

"Ye're there, Effie; Marshall an' me wan o' thae days 'ill mak' a bargain for the bit bridescake."

Gillespie could not bear to let any such chance slip. He knew

52

the thing would keep, and some day, when he had opened his shop, the affair would have blown over, and the gee-gaw could be sold at a profit. In the meanwhile he spoke as a benefactor who would clear this stigma of shame from the girl. Effie hung her head in red-hot confusion. Mary Bunch loped in to the rescue.

"Ye'd think Marget an' you were limpets glued to a rock on your chair ben the room. Effie was wonderin' whatna libel you an' her had." Effie was seen to squirm.

Gillespie smiled blandly.

"Marget an' me were just arrangin' for the coffinin' an' the funeral."

"I just thocht that." Mrs. Bunch spoke with emphasis. "I was sayin' afore ye cam ben that it's a God's blessin' Marget has some man tae help her ee noo. She has her ain trials." Mary Bunch belched. "Och! och! my meat's yearnin' in my stomach. There's naethin' helps me lik' a wee drap. Dr. Maclean telt me aye tae hae it handy——"

Gillespie assumed government, and assisted the fireside ladies to a little from the bottle. Mary Bunch, an old practitioner at such gatherings, addressed herself to the elegancies of conversation which the hour demanded, striking a vein which she conceived would require some wetting before it was worked out.

"Ye didna tell me"—she squared her thin shoulders against the jamb—"was Calum compleenin'?"

Gillespie did not hear the siren. He was calculating the strength of the rabbits in the Laigh Park. There were some white hares on the higher ground over by the Forest.

Mrs. Tosh felt it incumbent upon her to display intimate knowledge. "He got terrible dizzy in the heid the day o' the Fast. Dr. Maclean gied him a bottle; he got half blin' wi't. He compleened it was like smoke whirlin' oot o' his eyes."

"Guidsakes! whatna strange trouble was that?" asked Mary Bunch, making silent signs towards the bottle.

Mrs. Tosh cleaved to her narrative. "The doctor said he'd a heap o' suet about his he'rt, an' might go off like the shot o' a gun."

"So I h'ard, so I h'ard." Mary Bunch nodded towards the bottle, and drained her glass. "Poor Calum! his was the kind hand wi' the dram." Gillespie, who had not been listening, lifted the bottle from the meal barrel where he had set it down, and left the kitchen.

"Ay!" narrated Mrs. Tosh, forgetting her airs in her forthright tale. "He went away that quate"—now she was indeed the "far-oot freen." A handkerchief fluttered in her hand—"he opened his eyes an' gied a wee greetin' sab, an' was gone." The handkerchief was upon her eyes. Mary Bunch leaned across the fire-place.

"Guidsakes!" she ejaculated; her hand closed over the glass of Mrs. Tosh.

"Ay, Mrs. Bunch; he never spoke wan word." She removed the handkerchief, and saw her friend tilting back her head and drinking. She was reminded of a sympathetic duty, and put out her hand in a companionable way; then stared at the top of the range.

"Where's my gless?" she asked in amazement.

A half-suppressed squeal from the Sphinx enlightened her.

"Is that my dram ye hae, Mrs. Bunch?"

"Ach wheest"—Mary Bunch waved a fluttering hand—"dinna vex me mair, Mrs. Tosh. I'm that vexed for your freen Mrs. Galbraith, that if I dinna get something noo, I'll no can help greetin'."

"Really! ye needna hae been sae smert, Mary Bunch, that's my opeenion." She rose to the dresser, but found no bottle. She gazed around like a marooned mariner.

"I'm gettin' fair stupid," she cried with vexation, "between ye a'. I thought I notissed the bottle on the dresser."

"Gillespie's taen it awa'." It was Effie who spoke from her eyrie at the window. There was a ring of triumphant vindictiveness in her voice. It is profitable at times to be a Sphinx. It makes one immune from the sordid cares and paltry troubles.

"Ay! ay!" said Mary Bunch, making a hasty gurgling noise; "that's oor Effie; aye bad news." She set down her empty glass and shook herself.

"Effie 'ill be priggin' me in a meenut tae be goin'. It'll be gey an' dark on the brae sune."

Mrs. Tosh drew beside her. There was one dark matter which she could not lay in the lap of the minister's sister or the banker's wife. She wanted genuine and secret counsel.

"Mrs. Bunch," she asked with a companionable air, "hoo much mournin's should a far-oot freen lik' me weir oot o' respec' tae the deid?" The tree of Mrs. Bunch's knowledge was ripe and profuse.

"Thae mairridges"—she glanced peevishly at her daughter—"thae mairridges an' funerals, they're aye expensive things oor

54

freends pit on us." She dolefully shook her head. In some dim way, over the accusation against her in respect of that purloined dram, she felt she owed a stab at Mrs. Tosh.

"Wad twa shullin's worth o' crape be plenty?"

Mary Bunch held up hands of horror.

"Losh! losh! the minister's sister was weir mair nor that ower her wee Pommyrenian dog. Twa shullings! and ye're gaun tae tak' a jant tae Glesca for that. Mrs. Tosh, ye'll be the fair scandal o' the hale toon. Ye'll need a new skirt, an' a black silk blouse, an' black gloves; an' maybe new boots an' an umbrella. Ye're a far-oot freen——"

Gillespie entered.

"Ye're for the road," he said.

"Whaur's Marget?" Mrs. Tosh's face was rather white. The honour of a friendship that was cataclysmic had been suddenly thrust upon her.

"Marget's no' very weel," answered Gillespie suavely. He was anxious to be rid of these females.

"There's mair nor Marget no' very weel," snapped Mary Bunch. "I'd a sair trachle up the brae. I'm no' as licht in the fut as I used tae be. Och! och! they rheumatics. I hae them in the boo o' the knee, an' the boo o' the airm, an' the shouther heid." She touched each part of the body named as she spoke. "Effie here says a wee drap's the only thing for 't." Her tone was deprecating. She was chiding her bibulous offspring.

"Effie's wrang," said Gillespie; "try sulphur inwardly an' torpety outwardly. Torpety's very searchin'."

"Maybe ye ken better than Dr. Maclean?" Mrs. Bunch replied with venom.

Gillespie smiled slowly in her face.

"Weel! weel! Mary, there's nae use threshin' watter; naethin' but bubbles reise."

Mary Bunch saw that the hunt was over and the fox dead. She now addressed herself in real earnest to going.

"Thank ye; I'm no' needin' sulphur an' torpety. Guid nicht tae ye, Mr. Strang. Ye can tell Marget I'll take a run up to the coffinin'." She turned her small irascible face on Mrs. Tosh.

"Are ye for the brae?"

Mrs. Tosh signified assent by a dumb nod, and Mary Bunch sheered across the kitchen floor with her tall daughter in her wake, like a corvette in a sea-way with a three-decker in tow.

Without the night air became full of grumblings.

"Is he no' the dour deevil? stiff as a turnip wi' the bottle."

"Really! really! thae incomers——"

"Wi' his wee eyes lik' a traivellin' rat's, an' his chin as long's a lamb's. Any man wi' thon chin can look aheid o' him." Mary Bunch was indignant, and poured out her vials to the stars. "Whuppin' off the bottle as if it was his ain when you an' me, Mrs. Tosh, could hae made a nicht o't. I'm surprised at Marget."

"Are ye no' just over the score, Mrs. Bunch, aboot the mournin's?" Mrs. Tosh's lament was cut short by a stumble in the rut of the cart-road. She lurched against Mary Bunch, who was impinged upon the paling, and recovered herself vixenishly.

"Ye may weel spend a five-pun' note on mournin's efter a' ye've cairried awa' wi' ye, staggerin' there lik' a lord."

"Dinna insult me, Mary Bunch, dinna insult me; I'll no' stand it."

"I notiss that," answered Mary Bunch, with hauteur. She gave the cold shoulder to her companion and engaged her daughter.

"The mean scart that he is, Effie. The east win's aye in his coal-bunker. I've been at sixty-fower bereavements an' coffinin's an' never saw the lik' o' thon. Whupped off the bottle under my very nose. It bates cock-fightin'."

And Effie Bunch, the Sphinx, laughed loud and vaguely to the night. Concerning the trio, Gillespie had commented to the un-blemished bottle: "Thon's no' the sort o' hoodie craws to burn guid pooder on."

10

GILLESPIE found the ploughman, Jock o' the Patch—so named from the birth-mark which he had over his right eye—asleep in the bothy with a sheep for a pillow, and bade him go to the kitchen and keep his mistress company. Jock growled at him like a dog, and slouched off round the gable-end with a surly face. Jock and Gillespie were at variance. They had met in the dimness of the dawn on Galbraith's lands, and Jock straightly charged Gillespie with trespass and theft. Gillespie took a high hand at first; then hinted that Galbraith was in his power, and that it would be to Jock's profit to subserve the interests of Gillespie. Jock incontinently swung a loyal fist upon Gillespie's jaw, relieved him of several pairs of rabbit snares, and ordered Gillespie off the land. Jock marched like a sentinel behind him, and jeered him at parting.

Jock, a squat, broad man who sang Gaelic songs half the day, had a fund of native shrewdness. He concluded that Gillespie's invasion had been by way of the sea, and, searching the shore, came on his boat. He confiscated the oars, the rowlocks, and bow-rope, and staving her in with a great stone set her adrift to founder.

As Gillespie on this night turned down the cart-road he meditated an early dismissal of Jock o' the Patch. His step was agile. He had done a good piece of business that day, and felt in a rare light mood. There are some natures for whom pleasure is the staple of life. To Gillespie it was the infrequent interest that accrued on the capital of his schemes—the meagre star which hung in the sky after the burden and heat of the day. Under its influence he was in a brisk mood. He was exalted with the wine of success, and saw himself rapidly becoming a man of substance.

The night was bland. The moss and ferns were yellow in the moon. The burn, lined with the dry trunks of thin silver birches and rowan trees, closing him in as in a chamber, babbled from its lair its ancient runes. A thin silver mist, the outer garment of moonlight, clothed the fields and veiled the crooning sea. In the south thin, bluish clouds were drawn taut across the steep sky, like the bows of an ancient army strung for battle, and the purple northern hills, expectant of the moon, loomed up black to the tiny stars.

Almost at his feet she arose out of the bracken like a fawn, brushing a wisp of hair back from her forehead. He saw her face, as it were, through a window. Though he did not observe it, she stood as one who was his possession, and waiting for his judgment on her act.

"I've been waitin' for you"—a fluttering hesitancy was in her speech. Her appearance pleased him. In the parlour of the farm-house one thought had paraded the cold doors of his heart like a sentinel: "I must play the lover; without her my plans will fall to the ground." But the sentinel had now thrown away the arms of commerce, for that fight had been waged victoriously. He was ready for dalliance. He felt grateful to her, waiting to cap the day for him with a love-draught, and was flattered that a woman should thus minister to him. The tragedy was that the woman was waiting upon herself, tending the flame of her own passion. The scents of the night drifting from hill and shore were the incense upon the altar.

Her head was bare. Her fascination aided the subtle power of the night. A spirit of youth walked the dusk. He stepped within a magic ring and, peering down into her luminous face, was drowned in the lustrous eyes.

"I expected ye," he answered, and was pleased at the sudden light which the lie evoked upon her face. This was a new power he possessed—of moving the countenance of a woman. Satisfaction that was almost a thrill seized him. He proceeded to experiment with this power. He caught her hands. The girl did not now invite him. Instinctively she was asserting her right within the most ancient empire in the world. She knew she would be wooed; and, like the female, was prepared to run that she might hear the delicious thunder of the pursuing feet of the male whom she had lured. Around them the world stood still and the stars listened. A strange new power this! It could create flame and a sea of witchery. They were being swept on a river of fire beyond the world and the things of time. She swayed as a flower in the wind in his arms. Her hair was a fragrant cloud. Beyond the world, beyond time; where the blood beat thickly in one's ears.

"Oh! oh! you're hurtin' me."

It was a sob rather than words. They were in a cloud of fire beyond the world, beyond time. Everything around was white like snow in the moonlight. Gillespie wooed her in the shadow of a whin bush.

Far across the moon-whitened bay a woman lay sleeping in the "Ghost." She stirred and moaned in her sleep, for she dreamt of the ancient doom that lay upon her house. By a burn-side, that was crying like a fretting child, the working of the doom was begun.

Feverish, a little hysterical, Morag went up the cart-road between the ruts. The burn, on her left, crooned on, visionary, impalpable, lit with the light of dreams, a grey wayfarer, eternally singing in its coldness with elfin voice. Her heart was throbbing tumultuously; and the burn sang and pulsed with its ancient lure. At the gate she stumbled on a lantern, picked it up, and moved slowly to the house.

Opposite the whin bush the burn lay dark and silent in a pool, from which it issued to go down to the sea, where death sits in the grey shadows waiting for the men who, in little boats, tempt her among the isles where the south-east wind hangs out upon the sky the battle bows of heaven. Fraught with the experience and knowledge of its long journey from the hills, past the Pump and the "wee shop" of Mrs. Tosh, it issues from its dark pool with a single note of the still small voice that is bred of the earthquake and the fire, repeating its tragic chorus—that which is shall be; sorrow, grief, and heartaches for ever springing up from the ashes of desire in clear, quenchless flame between the cherubim in the face of God.

Something had stirred within Morag, new, strange, and wild. As the bright ribbon of the burn flashed, she felt a magic light glitter on the current of her own life. She did not dream that the moon which cast the light on the burn was a cold luminary. The inflammable in the heart of her lover had taken fire; rapidly it would burn out; and the ice of greed would grip and sterilise. She hung out of her window, a yearning look on her face, and heard the plash of his oars and their roll in the rowlocks as he crossed the star-powdered bay. She saw the boat trail, a dark speck in the moon, across the east end of the island and vanish. Then silence fell upon the living and the dead in the house of Muirhead. Without the lonely burn whispered to the night in the voice of a *lorelei* spirit gloating over a foundering boat drifting through the dark to the sounding weir.

She stripped and stretched herself out upon the bed on her back, her mind moving swiftly, like a shuttle of flame upon the loom of her love.

11

GILLESPIE conceived the stars to be fighting for him in their courses. Certain accredited seamen of the port, Ned o' the Horn, Lang Jamie, and Big Finla' in especial, manned the forlorn hope, being the pick of the fleet. Big Finla' was known as the

Pilot of the Port, for he could sniff home like a terrier through the darkest snow-shower, and make a reach by the weather-ear from the recollection of old sailing-songs, and the wise sayings of dead mariners; while Ned o' the Horn, the husband of Black Jean, had seen the grey blunt cliffs of Magellan full of black stars, and the spindrift rise like the spouting of whales upon the iron cliffs there. He had lost an arm on the black thundering cape. Neilsac, husband to Betty Heck, was one of the company—a tom-tit of a man, with nerves of steel. Inasmuch as the picked men of the port were tall, reticent fellows, it was left to the alert tongue of Neilsac to inform the "Shipping Box" of how they got their beards bleached in the gale, when news came that Jock o' the Patch lay dying on the Barlaggan Hill, having by a mischance stumbled in the heather, and shot himself with the gun he carried. He had been searching for foxes. It was the dog of the Barlaggan shepherd which nosed him out; and the shepherd who bore him on his shoulders three miles across the breast of the hill to his house, then walked seven miles across the hill in a screaming gale in the heart of a pitch-black night into Brieston to inform Maclean. Even the Barlaggan shepherd could not tell how he had accomplished that herculean journey. He only knew that the fear of death was the scourge at his heels.

The picked men of the port took the sea in all its raging to carry the doctor to the dying man. He had a mother, who was living in MacCalman's Lane, and she was a widow and was blind.

"It was rainin' in sheets when we came doon tae the skift"— Neilsac told the tale—"The doctor was aboard. 'Tell the policeman we can't wait,' I heard him cry.

"An' there was the bobby rubbin' his eyes wi' the sleep. Ye'd think wi' his red hairy face he'd been caught in birdlime. He heard the doctor.

" 'By Chove!' sez he, 'I'll go, if I hev to sweem.'

"It was smooth watter oot tae the 'Ghost'; but oh! boys-a-boys, it was blowin' good O! frae the suthard—fair glens o' seas runnin' oot on the Loch. We'd four reefs in, an', being close-hauled, I got into the fo'c'sle beside the bobby for the jib. Just wi' that we opened Rudh'a' Mhail an' she got the weight o' the sea, bow under. Ye ken in the deid o' winter we werena oot at the fushin'; an' beds an' nets were lyin' aboot; an' the hale laggery fetched away tae leeward, an' the bobby wi' them. If ye ever saw a greetin' bubbly-jock it was Cammel the bobby.

His face was lik' a foozy moon in the fog. Weel, I cried tae Big Finla' tae ease her a bit till I got the jib on her—Lang Jamie was by him at the sheet; an' there was the bobby standin' at the break o' the fo'c'sle—the very worst place he could stand in. I told him tae come awa' doon aft beside the doctor, but he thought I was takin' a fiver oot o' him. So I just left him jaloosin'. Off the Fraoch Island she was staggerin' in tae't, good O! when she took wan green lump aboard an' it drenched the bobby, runnin' oot at his boots. We saw him crawlin' aft, and sez he, 'Iss it to hell we'll be goin', or tae Jock o' the Patch? my legs iss aal wet.'

" 'This is noathin' tae the time o' war,' sez I.

" 'Then, boys,' sez he, 'I don't envy ye your chob.'

" 'Weel,' sez I tae him, 'ye might gie us a wee bit more rope on a Setterday night if we go on the spree. Ye see something o' what we hae tae thole.'

" 'Dhia!' sez he, 'if I get home to the poliss-station I'll be giffin' you aal the rope you'll be wantin' to hang yerself, by Chove!'

"We managed tae get her in tae the Black Hole ablow Barlaggan. We left the bobby an' Ned o' the Horn aboard, an' took the brae up tae the shuppurd's hoose. It was black as the earl o' hell's wescuts. An' O! boys, thon was a sight. I tell ye, boys, poor Jock's veins were hingin' aboot his legs lik' a weepin' willow-tree. He was fair sweemin' in blood. I canna tell ye what Maclean did, for I hadna the he'rt tae look. By the Lord! boys, but Maclean's a man, I'm tellin' ye! We cairried poor Jock in a blanket through the heather. Och! och! boys, I can hear him groanin' yet. An' there was the job tae get him aboard. Maclean and Lang Jamie were oot tae their airm-pits, an' poor Jock was blin' wi' the spindrift. I thought I was leevin' in eternity the time we took gettin' him aboard. Och! och! the squeals o' him. 'Clare tae Goäd, I'll hear them on my daithbed. It was fair win' runnin' home, an' a' the time Maclean was on his knees beside Jock. We reached the Quay, an' off gied the bobby tae the 'Ghost' tae get Gillespie's barrow, oot o' the auld store where he hes the wulks. The mean deevil, he winna gie Cammel the key, in case he'd steal his wulks, but kept him waitin' till he'd thrown on his clothes."

Some one in the dark of the "Shipping Box" swore softly. "He'll get his belly full o' wulks some day."

"We hurled Jock up the street tae his auld blin' mither. I tell ye, boys, I couldna stey longer; my blood was lik' watter wi' thon cries o' poor Jock——"

The moment Jock o' the Patch was brought to the stair foot he ceased moaning.

"She canna see; an' she's no' goin' tae hear," he babbled. These were the only words he had spoken since the journey began.

They heard the blind woman groping about on the stair-head.

"Is that you, Jock?"

"Ay, it's me!"

"It's a wonder ye won hame a nicht lik' this."

"For Goäd's sake somebody speak tae her," moaned the dying man.

"I'm comin' up, granny, to licht the lamp," Gillespie cried, and ascended the stair. She had been sitting waiting, waiting, her own darkness within, gross darkness without.

At Gillespie's voice, Jock o' the Patch opened his eyes.

"Maclean," he whispered.

The doctor knelt down.

"Tell Marget—tae hae—nae dailin's—wi' Gillespie; he's a—damn thief—he's—rabbits," the voice trailed away; the sweat of anguish poured down his face.

Their hands were wet with blood as they bore him up the stair and laid him on the bed. A fierce gust of wind dragged the barrow down the street. At the scrunch the sick man stirred and opened his eyes, and saw the lean crooked hands of his mother wavering over him, feeling for him. He tried to signal with his eyes that they should take her away. But Gillespie had darted down the stair after the barrow; Maclean was at the dresser, writing on a slip of paper the two words "hypodermic case." He gave it to Ned o' the Horn, with a whispered injunction that he was to rouse Kyle, his chemist. The hands descended—worn tentacles of love—and touched his face.

"Where are ye hurt, Jock?"

He muttered doggedly, "I'm no' hurt."

"Ay! ye're like your faither, dour as daith."

The hands were rapidly moving over him.

"Dinna tell me ye're no' hurt."

"It's only—a bit—scratch."

"A geyan scratch: ye're no' the wan tae be cairrit hame for a scratch, ye dour deevil."

The dying man groaned.

Her voice became wheedling, "Dinna be sae thrawn, Jock, my man. A gun's no a chancy thing. Tell me noo, is that the place, Jock?" She spoke as if the benign maternal touch would draw the balm from Gilead and soothe his wounds.

"Ay,"—her hands were groping over the region of his heart. "It's there—I'm—hurt."

Ned o' the Horn entered, followed by Campbell, the policeman, and Lang Jamie, who had remained behind to help Big Finla' to moor the skiff. Ned o' the Horn handed the doctor a small Russian leather case. The doctor lifted the lamp from the dresser and placed it on the kitchen table, where there was a cup and saucer, half a loaf, and some butter on a cracked plate. The doctor asked for water, and getting it from Ned o' the Horn, stooped over the table beside the lamp, his grey beard looking white in the light. The policeman, big-eyed, watched him drawing a liquid from the saucer into a thin tube, which ended in a shining point of steel.

"Now, Jock, I'm ready." Maclean straightened himself. His voice rang cheerily through the kitchen. The policeman felt grateful to the doctor for something invigorating in the words. In some dim way the policeman felt the power of archangels to be in the thin shining steel tube.

"Is that Jock's medicine, doctor?" The hands remained, the bandage of motherhood, over the son's heart. The blind face was turned over the shoulder in interrogation. Maclean took her by the arm and gently drew her from the bedside. "I'm going to give Jock his medicine." He signed to Lang Jamie, who was towering up at the fireplace, to lead her to a chair. The blind woman refused to move.

"Aw! mo thruaigh! mo thruaigh! I felt a hand lik' a bone on me last nicht in my sleep. It wasna chancy. An' me sae blin'; I canna see ye, Jock."

Maclean had shouldered quietly past her to the bedhead. With a pair of scissors he deftly cut away the sleeve of Jock's jacket, shirt, and semmet and bared the arm. With blinking eyes and racing heart the policeman watched the point of the needle piercing the skin. There was no sound in the room but the sick man's quick breathing. The wind scurried along the street like a rout of panic-stricken animals. Jock opened his eyes and gazed once, long and deep, into the eyes of Maclean. The doctor nodded and smiled.

"You'll sleep now."

The dying man caught the note of compassion, and lifted his right hand. Maclean took it. The eyes closed. After a few moments the doctor laid the hand down on the blanket.

A step was heard on the stair. It was Gillespie's. He had secured his barrow. Just as he entered the room, Jock opened his eyes, and turned them to the door, without movement of his head.

"What o'clock is't?" he asked in a strong, clear voice. Gillespie consulted a vast mechanism of silver.

"Twenty meenuts to five."

The eyes closed again. Jock took a deep breath.

"The morphia has got him," said Maclean.

Suddenly the sick man began to babble in a whispering voice of a fox in the Laigh Park among the lambs. Twice he uttered Gillespie's name. Maclean, tugging fiercely at his grey moustache, stood looking down at him. The policeman's eyes were hungrily fixed on the doctor, as if he were some divine oracle about to speak. But it was not Maclean who spoke.

"Jock's ower quate, doctor," moaned the blind mother. Maclean was gnawing savagely at the grey moustache. When people met him in the street pulling at that moustache they left him alone. It was over that moustache he fought many a death-and-life case.

A faint, indistinct whispering came from the bed. It sounded grotesque from such a man. The blind woman pricked her ears; but a heavy gust of wind boomed in the chimney, and the rain cried on the window.

"Ower quate, doctor; ower quate. He's takin' the high road aifter his faither."

The policeman leaned tremblingly forward to gape upon Maclean's face, as if he were indeed about to summon the dread Angel.

"Ay! damn it!" cried the doctor, spitting out the end of his moustache, and the tears welling in his eyes; "but we'll send him out easy."

The breathing suddenly became laboured, and the whites of the eyes rolled upwards. Gillespie, who was watching, turned away and looked into the fire. The head jerked upwards with every breath and fell forward again. A choking gurgle rolled in the throat.

The blind woman stretched out her hands over the bed, and turned her face upwards to the ceiling.

"Behold, the Bridegroom cometh," she cried, "for you, Jock, my son."

The laboured breathing ceased: the eyes were fixed upwards in a heavy stare. The mouth hung open, with the drooping ends of the black moustache falling over the lip. A deep silence filled the room. Every eye there was upon the face of Jock o' the Patch, except Gillespie's and the blind mother's.

"Dhia! Dhia!" whispered the policeman; "iss he gone?"

No one answered.

The wind moaned in a long sough down the street and whined in the chimney.

Tick-tack! tick-tack! the wag-at-the-wa' hammered the moments upon the anvil of eternity.

Maclean stepped to the bed and stooped down to the wide-open mouth. Then he raised his tall form, turned and gazed at Gillespie.

"The Bridegroom has come," he said, in a low, solemn voice.

Thus, as the cocks were crying towards the winter dawn, Jock o' the Patch, the one man whom Gillespie feared, having died, Gillespie conceived that the stars were fighting for him in their courses. He was beginning to learn that Death is a more powerful lever than Life.

12

ANOTHER circumstance Gillespie took blithely as the result of those excellent warring stars. Morag Logan was pregnant. This would force him to marry earlier than he had anticipated, and make the dismissal of Galbraith's widow at Whitsunday easy. She was bound to see in reason that she could not remain where a young wife was coming.

He was on his way now to Nathanael McAskill to have his agreement with Lonend drawn out in proper form. This gentleman was nicknamed the Spider—a tall, one-eyed man, thin as a wire, with spindly legs, who had the appearance of bearing down upon one like a landslide. He was learned in the filthy

secrets of the town, and had the look of a lean fox as he hung in
the offing like a pirate, and came to heel at a nod. He was a suave
liar. His clean-shaven face was smoothed with perjury. He was
relied upon at certain festivities as a singer of indecent songs.
This was his popular accomplishment. He knew law, and had
been a clever student at Glasgow University in the old days, when
the University was situate in the High Street. He was especially
clever at conveyancing; had no friends or relatives; was one of
that sort of miserable men whose name was most frequently
used as a subject for a jibe; and he was so degraded that he acquiesced in the jibe. One can imagine him fawning upon the
devil when Satan gathered him by main force to the Pit. No one
believed that he could be herded there by wile.

He was bland as wine and as sparkling, when men hatched
plots with him, and the whisky was between them. His lean face
would be eagerly cocked, his single eye bright, like a pecking
bird's, and his tongue ready either for defamation, a witticism,
or a story, as it suited the humour of his client. But there was
nothing rapacious in him or venomous. He simply did sharp
things to satisfy the cunning of his nature. Altogether too silky
and sleuth-like, and a dangerous tool; but a golden solicitor;
for he was such a despised devil that retaliation was sure to fall
upon him and not upon his client. Therefore, when Gillespie
buttoned up the agreement and walked out of his dingy office,
saying it would take more than Lonend's teeth to bite through
the bargain, and that he would see the lawyer later, Nathanael
McAskill wetted his thin lips with the point of his tongue and
smiled, recognising that he had met a rogue peer to himself.

Gillespie called at the bank. This was in answer to the summons which Mr. Lowrie had sent him. But Mr. Lowrie was out,
the clerk informed him. Gillespie was pleased at the clerk's
deference, and, in good humour, went to Lonend, whom he found
threshing corn in a huge machine which perambulated the
county, and for whose hire he paid at the rate of seven-and-six
an hour.

We carry our coffins on hand-spokes to the graveyard, each
man taking turn and turn about. The chief mourners walk ahead
of the coffin; cousins, uncles, nephews, and the like behind;
after whom trails the line of the procession. Lonend had walked
with the Laird, who was present at the obsequies of one of his

farmers, and, sounding him, arranged in a fashion for the transfer of the farm. At first the Laird was averse, but, learning of Galbraith's debt to Gillespie and that the widow was bankrupt, haltingly gave his consent. He was glad to have such strong tenants as Lonend and Gillespie Strang. Lonend learned that at Whitsunday next three years' rent would be due on the Muirhead farm. The lease would be transferred to them jointly in their names. The Laird fancied it had some four or five years to run, but wasn't sure.

Lonend told all this to Gillespie as they walked slowly from the barn door to the house; but when Lonend saw the legal document spread before him on the kitchen table he hesitated.

"It's you that's in for the fat o' the ham." Lonend had had time to think. Secretly he was not without bowels of pity for his neighbour, Mrs. Galbraith. "Ye'll get a sittin' doon, an' ye're takin' Morag frae me. I'll hae to fee a servant noo to fill her place. I'm kin' o' sweert to venture it."

In point of fact the trouble was not the hiring of an additional servant. Lonend was inordinately proud of his daughter, and lavished all the affection of his nature upon her. He was doubtful if Gillespie would make her happy.

"Hoots!" cried Gillespie; "never heed lossin' the milk, if ye get the cream. What's the sense o' ye speirin' the Laird an' me peyin' for this"—he laid his forefinger on the legal document —"if it's a' goin' to end in smock? Ye'll only mak' a fule o' the hale business." Which decided the wavering Lonend. He tried to draw the sleep-hindering thorn from his conscience.

"My grandfaither used tae say when a sheep broke awa' at the clippin', 'Let her go; she'll no' leave the ferm.' "

"We'll no' be in ony hurry wi' the ewe"—and Gillespie smiled. Having placated his conscience, Lonend became pleasant to his future son-in-law.

"Ye've fa'en on your feet, Gillespie. Though ye put your hand in a ballot-box ye couldna be luckier," and he took up the pen and signed. The business being completed, he was anxious to be rid of both the document and the man. "I snowkit snaw in the west. I'll best go gether in the sheep. There was frost in the stars last nicht." Gillespie did not seek to detain him. He was in a hurry to inform Mrs. Galbraith of the state of affairs.

Lonend, on his way to the thresher, found Morag at the gate of the yard looking after Gillespie, who had met her and, saying it was gey and snell, was passing on when Morag asked him if she would see him that night. Gillespie had reluctantly promised. Lonend looked after the retreating figure, tall, sturdy and broad.

"Ay, Morag! a God-fearin', rabbit-stealin' man. He's gettin' his name up." And Lonend passed on to his hired machine.

With Mrs. Galbraith Gillespie used as little ceremony as a dog uses. He told her of the new agreement made with the Laird, and that come Whitsun the farm would change hands. She offered her furniture and plenishing in lieu of the arrears of rent. Gillespie took her squarely between the eyes. The furniture was not hers, but his.

"Won't you give me time? I'll work hard. Every penny will go to your account." She was ashamed to have to beg at his hands.

"No, Mrs. Galbraith, I'll no' chance it. It's no' every man that can sweem when it comes to a broken brig."

Her large red face took on a deeper flush.

"You know it has been a very wet harvest, Mr. Strang," she pleaded.

"That's the hand o' Goäd, no' mine," he answered softly.

She smiled grimly at him. "So I am a pauper, and must leave the farm—through the hand of God?"

"There's nae use timmin' yer ain mooth to fill ither folk's," he answered.

Gillespie felt thoroughly at his ease. He had talked the farm into his hands; yet he wanted a servant. Mrs. Galbraith's next question gave him his chance.

"Is that all you have to say, Mr. Strang?"

"Weel, Mrs. Galbraith, ye dinna expec' me to pey Galbraith's lawin' at Brodie's. That poor fugleman"—this was a common word of contempt on Gillespie's tongue—"ye see the wy he's left you wi' his ongoin's." She watched the tip of his tongue jerk backwards and forwards, gleaming inside his mouth. It reminded her of a snake's head swaying above its body preparing to strike. Maliciously he evoked the misdeeds of Galbraith's spent years out of an oblivion where most people would have left them buried. He was practised in attaching blame in other quarters— with a show of justice. "A poor fugleman," he continued, and, putting on a pitying face, added, "but ye're among freens, Marget. Nobody's axin' ye to leave the ferm. Ye're welcome to bide."

68

Mrs. Galbraith cut him off abruptly. "The farm is mine till the term."

"Maybe, Marget, maybe; but, ye see, ye're awin' me fower hunner an' saxty pun'. I'm no' pressin' ye. Bide on the ferm. It'll no' be said that Gillespie Strang turned ye to the door."

Pride, shame, mortification struggled on her face.

"I remain as your servant."

"No! no! Marget: ye'll just bide an' dae your bit turns, an' tak' the bite an' sup that's goin'. I've gotten another man for Jock's place. Dinna tak' things to he'rt. Brocken ships whiles come to land."

The shadow from the woman's tortured soul vanished off her face. Her home was still to be hers. She pressed her hand over her left breast, where a great fear had been gnawing.

"I ken ye'll keep things snog an' be carefu' o' the gear."

Mrs. Galbraith bowed her head in silence; and silently accepted the successor of Jock o' the Patch, whom Gillespie had feed at the Bannerie market—a lean-faced man with a withered red beard; a needle-looking wretch, hooked in the nose and hollow in the eye, that brazened one out; a penurious, hungry watch-dog, the descendant of a race of cattle-lifters and plunderers. His small, predatory eyes roved the farm-steading like a hawk's.

There are times when the most self-opinionated are influenced by an outside judgment. This was the case with Mrs. Galbraith, to whom Mary Bunch paid a consolatory flying visit that same evening. Expertly she platitudinised after her kind, having first of all made a sally in the direction of the bottle. "I'm that sair harashed wi' a pain in my heid. My sight's failin' me terrible, Marget. It's worse since I fell doon the stairs an' got a crack on the broo."

With a sympathetic glass in her hand she comforted. "Ye're no' tae tak' on, Marget. We must submit tae His wull. Time'll bring its ain balm." She tested the strength of the liquid and polished her nose with the back of her hand. She was finding Mrs. Galbraith preoccupied and irresponsive. Sorrow will alone cure sorrow, and so she said, "I was maist he'rtbroken when Jonsac"—this was her first husband—"when poor Jonsac was ca'ed awa'. He strained himsel' over a rope at the fushin' an' took the dropsy. It's me had the trial wi' him. We thocht he'd never win awa'. He stood stickin' five times tae let oot the watter,

69

an' him fair sclimmin' the wa's wi' pain. Deary me! thon was a
sicht. The last time he lifted up his shirt himsel' tae gie Dr.
Maclean a chance. 'Ach, doctor,' sez he, 'I think the hale Loch
o' watter's inside me.' His side was fair hacked, poor Jonsac.
An' noo Erchie's wearin' his seal-skin wescut." By this Mary
Bunch hinted that there are as good husbands in the sea as ever
came out of it.

"I am not concerned about the loss of my husband: it is the
loss of the farm which is troubling me. It belongs to Mr. Gillespie
Strang."

Gillespie, for reasons of his own, wanted to keep the matter
quiet. Mrs. Galbraith calmly announced the fact, as she would
have announced anything, from the shame of her own house to
the visit of an angel.

Mary Bunch cast a searing light upon Gillespie's character.
She spoke shrilly, decisively:

"The nyaf! I met him on the brae, an' wondered where he
was stravaigin'. He'd a lip on, the soor deevil, ye could dance the
Hielan' fling on. Dinna ax peety o' him; there's nane in the marrow o' his briest banes." The opinion of the Pump is at times not
without its value.

"I don't want pity; I want justice."

Mary Bunch assumed a face of scorn. "Justice frae a wulk-
picker. A man wi' the pack aye on his back doesna ken the name
o' justice. Ay sook, sookin' awa' lik' a leech. That's Gillespie."

Morag watched for her lover in a twilight snow. Before Gillespie reached home the snow had stilled the land, and the hills
stood white down to a black harbour.

"The snow has gruppit a' thing," Gillespie said to his mother,
as he shook himself at the back door of the "Ghost." This was an
excuse for absenting himself from Lonend.

Morag looked across the trackless fields in vain for her lover,
who had failed at the tryst.

Mrs. Galbraith was of the old-fashioned school, who keep by
them the dead-clothes. That night she solemnly dressed herself
in the sacred garments, her raven hair standing out against the
white linen. "My life is dead," she moaned, as she lay down on
the bed in which her husband had died. The angel of blight had
shaken his despair upon her from his sombre wings. The angel
of vengeance was yet to pass by her lintel.

70

13

THE people of Brieston were accustomed to send their children with jugs to one or two people in the town who kept cows, and buy milk at their doors. Gillespie ordered a brand-new milk-cart, grooved for three six-gallon barrels, and brought the milk to the doors of Brieston evening and morning, summoning the household by bell. Sandy the Fox—he soon won his name— drove the cart. Gillespie accurately measured the milk into the barrel that the Fox might not cheat. Lonend was in a rage; he had not been consulted. He was not a partner yet, and had to keep his mouth shut; but it gave him a foretaste of the man. Lonend became moody and suspicious, and would have kept his daughter from Gillespie had he not seen her grow big with child.

Mrs. Galbraith had settled down to the new conditions of life, and was disposed to forget her suspicions of Gillespie, chiefly through the friendship of his parents, for Mrs. Strang yet paid an infrequent visit to Muirhead, and would have come oftener, but the long brae tried her breathing. Mrs. Galbraith, indeed, was beginning to take her tenure as secure when, without warning, Gillespie demanded a settlement. He laid before her certain slips of paper, all signed by her husband, promising to pay divers sums, amounting in all to £458. Interest, he pointed out, was due at the rate of 5%. In this he lied, for he had yearly extorted the interest from Galbraith. The security was the furniture, plenishing, and gear of the farm. Mrs. Galbraith, numb with bewilderment, stared at Gillespie and, when she found her voice, said, "I thought it was arranged that I should stay on at the farm."

No one would be more pleased than himself, but he was to be married to Morag Logan at the term. It was in reason that Mrs. Galbraith must leave. The furniture was old, and a good deal decayed; Galbraith had not kept his farm implements up to date. It would be best to have the whole movables valued. Gillespie fancied they would not cover his debt, but he would be lenient, and write off the debt against the movables. She must, however, move at the term. There was a hint of menace in his voice. He struck his trouser-leg with a switch to drive home his sour news.

71

Mrs. Galbraith went to Lonend, and found him wrathfully impotent.

"There's naething to be done, Marget, but go hame and greet."

She held up her shapely dark head. "I'll want to see Mr. Strang's tears first," she answered.

"The damn wolf canna greet," said Lonend, turning aside in sullen mood, a miserable man who was beginning to drink the brew of his sin. He spoke frankly, telling her of his daughter's condition, and of the agreement which he had signed, wishing to God he had never put pen to paper. He advised Mrs. Galbraith to see the doctor to whom her husband had spoken of Gillespie.

"I was deceived in him, he is so big and soft-looking." Thus Mrs. Galbraith thought as she descended the brae to Dr. Maclean's house. He was at the bowling-green, Kyle, the chemist, informed her, and sent a boy for him. Maclean, a tall, broad, wiry man, was the light of the town; a skilled practitioner, with a wide parish under his hand. He grudged no service, and brooded on his cases as he walked about the parish or tried to beat Brodie on the bowling-green. He was a handsome man, whom many women loved openly or in secret; a friend of the landed gentry; a greater friend of the poor, to whom he rarely sent an account. It was said that he was somewhat rough with his patients, but Kyle asserted that he had seen a doctor "greetin' like a wean" for some young man or woman whose case was hopeless, and his driver said that on weary journeys to the country, the doctor would ask strange questions after long intervals of meditation, as "What is God? Where did God come from? What is the use of praying into space? If you answer me properly I'll give you a drink at Mainsfoot Inn." Here Pat would wink to his audience and say, "Well, doctor, I can tell you wan thing; there's some use o' me prayin' into space."

"How's that?"

"I am praying for that drink."

And the doctor's big cheery laugh would roll across the horse's head. But he was too extravagant, the minister's sister always said, with a sigh.

"If he has got money in his pocket for the day it's all he cares. It's a shame that his house is allowed to go to wreck and ruin with servants. He needs a wife."

All the Pump knew that the minister's sister would walk from the Manse to the doctor's house barefoot for his smile. "Hullo, Marget," he cried cheerily, coming into the surgery; then, seeing her face, added:

"Come away upstairs and pour out my tea; I'll give you some ham."

"Thank you, doctor, not this evening," and lifting a brave, smiling face she told him her tale. She knew that here she would get the truth from one who was without stain of cloth. He spoke no words of pity, but told her abruptly that Galbraith and Gillespie had had a scene in the Laigh Park. Gillespie taunted her husband, and threatened to roup him out of house and home. The doctor was of opinion that this had induced Galbraith's end. Maclean told also of the warning of Jock o' the Patch.

"You're in the hands of a Jew, Marget," he ended.

"A murderer and a thief," she cried.

"I'd give five hundred down to bring Calum's death home to him; but it's impossible," the doctor said sadly.

The woman's face underwent a rapid change. Light blazed in her dark eyes. "This morning I thought he only stole my home"—even that thought seemed to suffocate her—"my home; the morning and the birds in the trees; oh! I used to thank God for the light of another day when I heard them singing. And the cattle rowting on the moor. He has stolen from me summer and winter, spring and the harvest-time. What will they be to me now in the Back Street? I'll never know the spring coming there, or see the wind in the corn or the lea rig white with frost. He's robbed me—the home . . ."—her voice choked—"my man! he's killed my man——!" In her eyes he slew and then harried the slain. She leapt to her feet. "I'll never be content till the snow is his winding-sheet; till I see him without house or home or coffin."

"Let him alone, Marget," said Maclean in a hard voice. "He'll maybe find out that a man can buy gold too dear."

She laughed fiercely.

"Thanks, thanks, Mr. Gillespie Strang; I thought my life was empty, but it is not so now." . . .

"Kyle," said the doctor, as Mrs. Galbraith passed through the shop, "make up this medicine for Marget"—the doctor looked up at her from writing the prescription—"she's a bit run down."

Ah! the common people could not analyse their affection for Dr. Maclean, because they could not analyse tact. He once said to Brodie, when that individual questioned him on an obscure case which puzzled gossip, "Ah! Brodie, a doctor is a man who will have many secrets buried with him." After that Brodie, one of the few who was privileged to sit with the doctor o' nights in his smoking–room, durst ask him no more questions.

14

THAT night Mrs. Galbraith walked in the low field at the sea beneath the pine-wood, brooding. She was a woman who, by nature, found in every one something to appreciate; some gift, aptitude, or virtue. Gillespie had trailed humanity in the mire. Living so much on Thomas à Kempis, she could not conceive that a predatory beast inhabited a human frame. Her face was swollen, her thick, glossy hair blown awry in the high sea-wind. She walked in a garment of misery, as she adjusted life to a new balance, seeing more steadfastly its heaven and its hell, and how the adversity of one is the prosperity of another.

She turned and gazed at the farmhouse. It was cheap, jerry-built, and the deafening poor. It sounded like thunder in the kitchen below when one walked overhead. The windows rattled in the wind. Galbraith had fashioned wedges of wood to jam them tight. The wedges were always kept ready on the sills against a high wind. The rain leaked in on stormy nights. She understood now why her husband was averse to asking the Laird for repairs.

But for all that it was ramshackle, the roots of her life had gone deep there. She had never lived under any other roof for twenty-six years. The ancient cry of all races that are not Bedouin was born in the travail of her breast. "Home, Sweet Home." Soon she would sleep no more beneath that roof, or find her place familiar with the morning light. She recalled her home-coming with her husband. He was then a tall, supple, young man, thin-faced, with laughing grey eyes; alert, handsome.

"This is your home now, wife," he said.

She felt he was offering her his life, and had been inexpressibly touched; and now that fount of tenderness, perennial all these many years, was dried up. She was puzzled at the triumph of evil, at the suffering of the righteous.

"The sun touches your window in the morning." He had remembered her love of the dawn. Now this pirate, with his carrion eyes and expressionless face, had told her she must go. He had been deadly suave about it. She remembered a blackbird which, a fortnight ago, she had found stiff with frost. She shivered, as if the blight of frost had touched herself. She recalled Gillespie's sour smile, the leprosy of his deprecating eyes, his wolfish face, and clenched her hand till the nails sunk in her flesh. She looked at the house seated on the brae-head, grey, cold, darkling. It flashed upon her that it, too, was mourning. The desolate house and she were merged in a common grief. She had a vision of Galbraith, who would come there no more, stooping at the door, bent as tall men are, gaunt, putting down his feet slowly one after the other, as if they, too, were heavy with care and weariness, coming from the kitchen window to meet her.

"Ye bring the sea up wi' ye on your face," he used to say, on her return from her evening walk. He was filling his pipe, thrusting in the tobacco from his palm with his forefinger. It was this last touch, domestic and of a man, that filled her breast with the wild longing which surges within us for that which, precious and now lost, leaves behind a dreary emptiness. She turned away a face of inexpressible woe from beholding the house, the tears smarting in her eyes.

"Oh, dear God, I think my heart will break." The words came in dry sobs which shook her frame. She brushed her hand across her eyes, sank upon her knees, fronting the sea, and lifted her face to where a single star, high in the zenith, blinked down at her.

"Give me strength, Almighty God, to endure," and covering her face with her hands, she invoked vengeance. "I want vengeance," and, horror-stricken at the thought of plucking this prerogative from the Eternal, she arose and went towards the house to consult the oracle in which she had perfect faith. She passed into the kitchen and locked the door. If Gillespie were to come he would have to remain without; but Gillespie was at Lonend, arranging the details of his entry at the term. He did not come that night, because it is not given to mortals to behold the slow unveiling of the white throne of justice.

In times of crisis she was wont to consult the Bible, taking oracularly the first verse which her eye lit upon. One child had been born to her, which fell ill at the age of five months. She sought the Bible and read, "The child also that is born unto thee shall surely die." She watched Maclean's efforts almost with pity; and when her babe died upon her knee at eventide, she looked down at the waxen face in stony grief and acquiescence.

Her ancestors had believed in elves and fairies, and the little folk dancing in the glades in the moonlight. Her intellect was powerful; but the superstition that is the second oldest stratum of human nature was awakened, and the dominance of her intellect and her will-power were concentrated on the rite. Her mouth was a thin line of determination, and her eyes had a profound contemplative look. She closed them as if peering into the future, and opened the great Bible. A leaf fluttered out of her fingers and sagged over with a thin crinkling sound. She opened her eyes slowly, and betrayed no emotion or surprise, though the letters ran in forms of fire as she chanted aloud:

"Be not deceived; God is not mocked: for whatsoever a man soweth, that shall he also reap." Thrice she read the words, graving them on the granite of her resolution. She had been nurtured in a school of grim theology, and the mantle of prophecy fell easily upon her. She saw the sword of vengeance bared in her hand. A sinister aspect of life seized her mind as the idea of revenge fast settled there. Something of the recording angel, napoleonic in its proportions, entered her soul. She imagined herself in that moment to be standing at the bar of the Last Judgment, accusing Gillespie before the great White Throne. The justice of heaven could not exact retribution without her instrumentality. She was the vicar of the wrath of God, and the blood of her husband would cry up from the earth night and day till she had extorted the uttermost farthing in the price of her revenge. She would dog the man; track him like a sleuthhound. Life became large and terrible with purpose. Divine punishment would fall on her own head if she proved a traitor, and the dead would be washed from his grave and condemn her if she failed to keep her grim tryst with Gillespie. She sat down and bent the resources of her intellect to the task. Hour after hour passed as she sat in the dark beside the open Bible, fixed like a rock. The wind cried round the gable-end, but she heard nothing, for she had entered into the grave beside her husband, and came forth carrying his secret torture, with the grey look of the dead upon her face. Plan after plan arose like waves out of a yeasty gloom, only to fall back on the granite cliffs of her

resolve; and each time she was baulked her large dark eyes swept across the pale page where a line of fire was burning. *"God is not mocked"*—the words rang in her ears like thunder— *"for whatsoever a man soweth, that shall he also reap."* The irony of Gillespie's position struck her, and she smiled grimly.

The sudden fluting of an early bird in the trees aroused her, and she thought how the vale of crying birds, where the wild pigeons haunt the fir-wood with unfatigued wing, would be hers no more. The song died away, as if the bewildered bird were questing for the tardy dawn. It rippled in song once more; then the wind washed over the tree-tops, soughing restlessly, and there was silence. She arose, shivering with the cold, and extinguished the lamp, and saw the fresh trees swaying in the wind as if they, too, with the baffled bird and herself, were seeking, seeking eternally.

"We've drifted far before the wind, our house; we've a heavy leeway to make up," she muttered, looking at the frail dawn. And the pilot of that broken ship went back to the Big Chart lying open on the table. Bending down, she kissed the book, and then went heavily upstairs to her room.

She did not dress herself in the dead-clothes.

15

TOWARDS noon Mrs. Galbraith rose, and, as she dressed, pondered on her husband, whom lately she had ceased to love. He had become coarse, rude, blasphemous in drink; ungainly about the farm, ill-dressed, and dirty; and even more gawky on market-days and on Sundays, when he dressed in broadcloth—a grey, stooping, withered man, knock-kneed, loose-jointed. He slavered at the mouth when he was in a rage, and his temper was short and hot. But she had respected him. He had wooed her with hot ardour, riding through the night on a coal-black mare to see her. He had given her a good home, had been faithful to her, was proud of her accomplishments, of which he had boasted on market-days at the Inn. Though she had complained of the house as naked-looking, severe, with rattling windows and cold, draughty passages that had killed her only child, yet now its precious associations were poignantly remembered—the song and the dance when she played at Yuletide in the parlour, and the kitchen was loud with the thunder of dancing feet; birth, death, and friendship; these things had hallowed its walls and made sacred its chambers. "Surely I have eaten the bread of affliction," she cried as she descended the narrow stair to the kitchen.

Tick-tack, tick-tack, the pendulum of the kitchen wag-at-the-wa' answered. The big brass hand jerked spasmodically on the dial, like a dead limb that has been galvanised. These sounds in the still kitchen became sombre, measuring time with the aloofness and impartiality of a god. Tick-tack, every moment nearer the time of her departure from the farm cried aloud. In the sound she heard a silvery bell, whose echo was melting away into a great vastness where, when it died, the hour of her exodus would strike. She felt it was impossible for her to abide that moment. The minute-hand jerked again with a sudden spurt of malice. Now it seemed to sweep devouringly over a greater arc of the dial's face. Was she to go on daily watching it, her heart's blood drip, dripping away from her? For a quarter of a century she had regulated her comings and goings by that clock, and had never noticed the terror of the hand before. Jerk! jerk! it reminded her of a raven she had once seen plunging his hot beak in the carcase of a sheep and tossing it up with bloody fragment in the air. Jerk! jerk! the beak of time was picking at her life. She would go mad if she waited through the days and watched. She formed a sudden resolution. She would not wait in her condemned cell till the twelfth hour and the executioner. She opened the clock door and stopped the pendulum.

"I am finished here," she said, and went out to take farewell of the fields and the woods.

The grass was green as emerald. The pale light of primroses haunted the burn. A wild cherry-tree there was white as snow. The clay of the deeply-rutted cart-road shone like gold. Hillock and mound swelled away like waves of the sea, full of inlets, nooks, and glades right up to the Planting. She had watched that wood in all seasons. Sometimes it had appeared to her in leafless winter like an army with spears watching upon the hill over against the sea; when stiff with frost it was a giant foreland, upon whose forehead had frozen the foam of the ocean. In summer

Pan drove stallions through it, shaking multitudinous bells. In autumn it was an army bivouacked in blood. To-day it was beaten, slain, broken; the light of the babe eyes of spring had been quenched upon its face. She interpreted the wood with her own personality. She was defeated, beaten. She passed through the little wooden gate at the end of the cart-track above the burn, and sat down on the moss in the lee of the wood, pine-sheltered from the cold sea-wind. From where she sat she saw the low, rambling farmhouse, its whitewashed walls stained with the rains. A cart was uptilted at the byre-end. The shafts raised impotent arms to the sky. There was a deep silence about the place. The fields, the hills, the wood, the farm-steading were robbed of life; buried with her husband. A heavy sense of loss besieged her. It begat pain. She tried to repress the welling tears. She was amazed when she heard herself sobbing. A tramp passed along the high road, carrying a bundle in a red handker-chief. She bent her head as he went by. Her throat was hot and burning. Presently she raised it again toweringly, shaking the tear-drops from her eyelids; but at the first glance at the farm an incontinent sobbing broke forth, her breast heaving con-vulsively. Life, she knew, had missed its completion; without child, without husband, without home. "What have I done? what have I done? I have been a good woman"—the anguished thought kept ranging her mind. The hopes she had thought to realise were broken; failure, disappointment, disillusion were her portion; the locust had eaten the grey years. Last night she had been possessed with lust of vengeance. Now she recognised that malice dies, grief dies; shame, remorse, scorn die; nothing remains but profound, desolating sadness. She became afraid of this weary weight of loss and loneliness—afraid that it would unnerve her hand and leave Gillespie untouched. The anguish became so intolerable that she struggled to her feet, over-whelmed with a feeling of pusillanimity and cowardice; then sank down again, with her face turned from watching the farm. It was the desolation there which turned her blood to water. Her jewel was in the mire; she was dispossessed of something that was eternal; she saw her life in chains, hanging in the wind of fate; the delicate porcelain of life was in fragments beneath the ruthless heels of a thief and murderer. She writhed. Her body was passing in the midst of fire. She leapt up from her vigil with blood in the palms of her hand. The atrophy of anguish

79

had passed away. She had crossed the border-line of pain, and drew out of the battle with a stone where her heart had been, and her sunken eyes shining with the fires of revenge which ate into her soul.

At the whin bush on the cart-road, where Gillespie and Lonend's daughter had become betrothed, she swiftly turned aside, and went down to the pool in the burn. Stooping, she washed her hands in the dark water. The act was symbolic. She was a priestess purifying herself to lift the knife upon the altar. When she reached the farmhouse she closed and locked the door. The next hour she spent rummaging through the house. She packed her clothes and treasures—a few books, two photographs, a gold locket with the wisp of a child's hair within. She carried the bags to the barn, deposited them there, locked the door, and put the key in her pocket. She returned to the kitchen, sat down at the table, marked the verse in the Bible heavily with ink, then, with steady hand, wrote for a minute on a large sheet of paper. She took a hammer and a box of tacks from a shelf in the scullery, and tacked the paper on to the front door. She returned to the kitchen and, with the hammer-head, stopped the pendulum of the grandfather's clock. There was another clock in the parlour. This she also stopped. A smile of irony played on her face as she moved about the house. Her last act was to extinguish the kitchen fire with a pailful of water. She backed away from the cloud of dust and steam. "Dust to dust," she muttered, and flung the pail in a corner. It trailed round slowly till it rested on the handle. The hissing in the fireplace died away, and a profound silence fell on the mangled kitchen. She flung the door wide open; walked down the passage, pulled the front door open, and passed out into the dancing spring sunshine. The first act of revenge was committed. There were still three weeks to run till the term-day. She took her portmanteau from the barn, leaving the door agape, carried it down the cart-road, and hid it among the whin bushes above the burn. She never returned to the farmhouse.

On the morning of the next day old Mr. Strang called at the house of Muirhead Farm with some salt herring, which his wife had sent to Mrs. Galbraith. Having read the placard on the door, he crossed the brae and told Lonend that his neighbour's house was deserted, and the doors were banging about in the wind. The house, he said, was uncanny. He left the salt herring with Morag, went home, and kept silent before his wife. Lonend had asked him to send up Gillespie at once. Together they crossed over the brae, and through the edge of the Laigh Park at the Planting, and came up the cart-road. Lonend was silent, chewing a straw. Against his better judgment he felt himself being dragged into a scandal. A dull rage against Gillespie was smouldering in his mind. The matter of the milk-cart still rankled; and now this.

"There's something no' richt aboot the hoose," he burst out savagely, his wiry black moustache bristling, as his eye rested around its smokeless chimneys. "It's like a place o' the deid."

"It was aye a wee thing deid an' alive," answered Gillespie blithely.

"By Goäd," snarled Lonend, "ye've gien't the feenishin' touch."

"Hoots, man! I winna fly intae a pawshun because a lum's no' reekin'."

"I'd raither see't on fire," snapped Lonend, biting on the straw. The feeling of desolation in a forsaken homestead touched Lonend.

"There's somethin' gars my banes grue about thon"— he nodded towards the house—"it only wants the corbies sittin' on the riggin'."

"Nonsense," said Gillespie, breathing a little rapidly; "the hoose is a' richt. I wush everything was as weel."

Lonend strode through the wooden gate, his wiry, alert form moving as on springs.

"Look at the windas," he muttered.

"What's wrong wi' the windas; needin' cleanin'?"

"They're deid," replied Lonend sharply, "deid an' blin' lik' the eyes o' a corp."

They entered the farmyard. The silence was oppressive.

"No' even a cock-craw"—Lonend spluttered a harsh laugh—"man! but ye hae the gran' toom biggin', Gillespie."

"The cocks 'ill be reingin for guid coärn seed. Ye'll hear them cryin' brawly when their crap's filled."

"Ah! ah! the wy they cried to Peter the Apostle," and Lonend turned sharply away.

They crossed the steading. The stable and byre were empty; the barn door wide open.

"I'm dootin' I'll maybe hae to speak to Sanny," said Gillespie. His voice trembled a little.

"I'm dootin' ay!" mocked Lonend.

They went round the corner of the house in Indian file, Lonend leading, and reached the front door. It was swinging idly in the breeze. They came to a halt in their tracks, staring. Suddenly Lonend closed his right hand. He had searched for the damning placard of which Gillespie's father had told him, and recalled the old man's words:

"There's a wee bit writin' yonder on the wall. I kenna wha' the Belshazzar is."

With the stump of his thumb projecting from his fist, Lonend pointed to the paper on the door.

"The shirra's notiss," he said.

They stepped up to the door, shoulder to shoulder, and together, in silence, they read the large, clear lettering:

THIS HOUSE IS DEAD.
IT HAS BEEN MURDERED.
IT IS BURIED IN THE GRAVE OF A WOMAN'S
HEART

"BE NOT DECEIVED; GOD IS NOT MOCKED: FOR WHATSOEVER A MAN
SOWETH, THAT SHALL HE ALSO REAP."

The straw dropped from Lonend's open mouth.

"It's Goäd's shirra," he said in a low voice.

Gillespie turned pale about the lips; then the blood rushed to his face.

"A bonny lik' joke," he said; "Marget's put her learnin' to grand use."

He tore the placard from the door, crumpled it up in his hand, and threw it on the path. He entered the passage, and Lonend, swiftly stooping, picked up the ball of paper and thrust it in his pocket.

He heard Gillespie moving about on the stone-flagged kitchen floor as he stood without in the sunshine, wiping the sweat from his forehead with a red handkerchief.

"Come awa' in here," he heard Gillespie shout.

Lonend made no answer, but cast a look of hatred towards the direction of the voice. Presently Gillespie appeared, his face flushed an angry red.

"Come awa' ben," he cried; "ye never saw such damage an' destruction since ye were craidled."

82

"No," answered Lonend, stepping back and curling his lip, "I'll no' cross the door."

Gillespie stamped on the threshold.

"I'll hae the law o' that wumman."

"Wi' the Spider? A bonny feegur he'd mak' in the Coort o' Session." Lonend sneered openly.

"The kitchen's a' a laggery o' wreck wi' rain an' wun'. The grandfaither's clock's lyin' in smithereens on the flure, an' the back door's open to the tide."

Lonend flamed up.

"What richt hae ye," he cried, "to be reingin' through another wumman's hoose?"

Gillespie stared at Lonend with a stupefied look.

"Reingin'! wha's a better richt to reinge?"

"Ye've nae richt to set fut ower that door till the term." Lonend shut and opened his fists, his face black with rage.

"An' let a' thing gang tapsalteerie to the backside o' the wun' an' rain. A bonny lik' thing." It was Gillespie's turn to sneer. "A bonny lik' pickin' aff a cleaned bone."

"Pickin'! by Goäd; there's nane for Hector Logan o' the Lonen'. I aye cam' by my money dacent, an' no' plunderin' the weeda an' puttin' her oot o' hoose an' hame." Gillespie backed into the passage, for Lonend's eyes were flashing fire.

"See that?" he cried, and, whipping his hand into his jacket pocket, held aloft the paper. "It'll come on ye yet, for a' your laawers." He struck the paper sharply with his hand. "You an' me 'ill hae to pairt here, Gillespie. 'This house is deid, deid an' murdered' "—he struck the wall twice with the flat of his hand—"Ye can rob the corp gif ye hae the wull; but it'll no' be Hector Logan that 'ill face up to Goäd's shirra wi' the likes o' you. I'm done wi' ye." He crammed the placard in his pocket.

"There's another wee bit paper o' McAskill's ye'll hae to dae wi'," said Gillespie, with a grave face.

"To hell wi' ye an' the laawer!" cried Lonend, who wheeled and strode away, leaving Gillespie standing alone on the threshold of the deserted farmhouse.

16

WE follow Mrs. Galbraith to her new home in the Back Street. No asylum is congenial, and hers was far from being a place in which to ponder upon the beauties of the *Imitation*, and study Beethoven and the Jacobite songs upon the piano. There were flights; but of vastly different kind, irritating to one accustomed to the placidity of Muirhead Farm. It is true that they were of the common stuff of Back Street comedy; but the comedy was a horror to her; its levity and vulgarity she assessed as an additional debt to the black score which Gillespie owed her. He had driven her from home; he had pitchforked her into a welter of wrangling voices, sordid contumely, defiant recrimination, and the banal horse-play of life. Had she been a visitor she would have been tolerant, amused; as a resident, forced to submit to these jests of Fate, whose waves rolled upon her, fast threatening to make her a denizen of the Back Street, her resentment against the initial author of her bitterness was increased two-fold. These vulgar bickerings were vinegar to her, and threatened to draw her into the mesh of Back Street life. She saw that with repetition she would become accustomed to these sallies, and gradually would be woven into the warp and woof of such a sordid existence. Once a denizen her purpose would be fatally weakened, for such people lived only for the day. She must have a house of her own, divorced from contact with all extraneous interests. Thus it came about that Mrs. Galbraith moved into a room beneath the thatch vacated by Janet Morgan, whose husband, the plumber, had died. The room was situate near the end of the Back Street, and cost six pound a year in rent. Janet Morgan, a pawn in the game, moved to the Quay, and thence, having sold her husband's tools and remnants of tin and lead, opened a little toy shop.

17

GILLESPIE STRANG'S wife had a rage for jewels, and in the first days of their married life at Muirhead Farm loaded herself with trinkets, many of them cumbersome and old-fashioned, and, dressed in the height of fashion, kept the parlour, where, big with child as she was, she entertained her friends and visitors from the town and neighbouring farms. Fond of gossip, and full of cheap pride and vanity, she queened it, conceiving she had made a happy match. Gillespie gave her a sour, frowning look for a week. In the next she was rudely made acquainted with his harsh remedies, and trailed about the house white-faced and horrified. Her trinkets were locked away. When she asked for them he said that such baubles had no room in a farmhouse. From the hour in which she learned he had seized her jewels and personal ornaments she hated him. She considered herself disgraced by him. She hoped God would punish him for preying upon her. As for Gillespie, he told her to find more profitable occupation in the byre. With her eyes fixed upon her person, she said she was unfit for such work. Gillespie, ignorant of the danger, spoke with contempt; but, realising it at length, thought it prudent to hire a female servant till the days of his wife were accomplished. He restricted her to the absolute necessaries of life, so that, with such a frugal economy, she was ashamed to call in her friends. He denied the cravings common to women in her state, alleging them as artifice to compass her social ends. She became isolated, starved in soul; and, brooding upon her indigence, went to Lonend, asking, with tears, to be taken home. Hitherto Lonend had wavered and was irresolute with Gillespie, feeling his own guilt in the matter of Muirhead Farm; but now his mind was pierced to the quick. He saw his daughter's shame and degradation exposed to the common eye. Privately he gave her money and went, whip in hand, to Gillespie, and taunted him with cruelty. Gillespie would not be provoked to a quarrel. He turned up to Lonend a jolly, rubicund face wet with sweat from smearing the sheep with a mixture of tar and fat, and prevaricated, trumping up the colourable pretext that the time was not convenient for luxury. He had a heavy leeway to make up in his

85

share of the price of the farm. His policy was to screen his avarice behind an ebbed bank-account. Lonend, aware of his malignant heart, itched to lift the whip he held upon him, but saw that that would only abandon his daughter to perhaps greater horrors. He looked, however, he said in an aggravated tone, to more lavish treatment of his daughter. Gillespie answered that by and by he would make a lady of her, when he had got rid of his more pressing burdens; and, with a smiling face, invited Lonend into the house to consider the advisability of having some repairs done to the kitchen windows. The smile maddened Lonend. He felt himself a dupe and baffled, and that Gillespie had eluded him by an eel-like flexibility. From sullen silence he flashed to an out burst of rage, and striking his leg with his whip, cried:

"You big braxy beast, ye'll sweep your doorstep clean before I'll cross it again."

This was the beginning of open rupture, and Lonend retired, full of resentment.

Two months afterwards a son was born. Gillespie's mother in the "Ghost" pleaded for it, on the plea that she was lonely. It was in reality the old fear which urged the request. Gillespie was nothing loth. He disliked the child, for he fancied he had been lured into begetting it; while to have it reared in the "Ghost" would save expense. Morag wept her eyes out, but Gillespie, inflexible, ferried the child across the harbour. At this juncture Lonend brought down the gun from the steel-rack over the fireplace, cleaned and oiled it; but Morag dissuaded him from violence, saying that she had the promise from Gillespie of another child, that would be her own. She told this in a state of mind bordering on distraction. It was a lie; and was her dream of what she might be able to coax from her husband. Within the year she achieved her purpose. On a morning that Gillespie, yawning and stretching himself, was about to rise, his wife said:

"Are you goin' to get up?"

Gillespie yawned again and looked abroad at his clothes.

"It's time," answered Gillespie; "Sanny 'ill be stirrin'."

He would allow no servant to be beforehand with him. His wife sighed.

"Am I no' your wife any longer, Gillespie?"

There was fondness in the tone. She could not understand that this buirdly man was slipping from her grasp. Her questing hands were held out eagerly for the gifts of youth and passion. She was a creature made for love, with a heart within her breast as warm and tender as a Madonna's. As long, previous to her marriage, as the gifts of love were withheld or paid out niggardly, but with the promise always to be fulfilled, her face was beautiful, like a dark flower, with the light of dreams; and as long as her heart kindled thus in her eyes, her radiant face could attract even Gillespie. He had always found her beautiful at Lonend. But once the debt of matrimony was paid coldly enough, and the treasury, she then discovered, empty, the light perished in her eyes, and, with the vanishing of the look of youth, the last vestige of power over her husband was gone for ever. Greed grew in his soul with swift, cancerous growth. He emptied his heart to make room for his one dominant passion. With feminine tenacity she clung on to hope: "Am I not your wife?" Her eyes searching his louring face with timidity.

"Bonny wife wi' your fal-de-lals." He had restored her jewels when she had pleaded for them on child-bed—her mother's rings, gold chain, and cameo brooch.

A trembling seized her body. She shivered as with cold, and became afraid. Her eyes blinked; a clear drop oozed out of the corner of the left eye, and trembled on the lid. She held up her head to prevent it falling. The sight of tears made him malicious. Her nostrils contracted and expanded like the fluttering wings of a wounded bird.

"An' what will I do now?"—she was interrogating Fate— "I'm not fit to be a widow woman."

"Weeda wumman! wha's gaun to mak' ye a weeda wumman?"

"I can't do without you, Gillespie," she answered simply, like a child. There was a large helpless air about her which put him into a dull rage. Why could she not get up and go to the byre? She cast herself, her thriftlessness, her unprofitable fancies upon him, wasting the morning. The air whistled in his nostrils as he heard her mournful plaint. What to do, forsooth. Get up and kirn the milk an' nae mair words.

"Don't be angry with me, Gillespie; I can't bear you to be angry."

The swift access of anger, so unnatural to him, died away. He threw the blankets aside and stepped on to the floor.

"No! of coorse, no! I'm just to liesten to yeer whimsies an' no' open my mooth. P'raps ye'll no' be pleased till I gie ye the

87

mill alang wi' the meal." The housekeeping expenses, a thing new to him, were a constant source of annoyance. He never missed a chance of pushing home this grievance.

"I don't ask for anything. I only want yourself." The naïve innocence of this remark appeared to strangle Gillespie. She was back to her fancies. He could not range himself alongside this desire, for he was beginning to regard her now as cumbering his house. She was slow of her hands, laggard in business, unpunctual, stupid in house-work. Once already he had told her that her father's praise of her skill was part of the game to lure him to Muirhead.

"Ye had as muckle o' me as ever ye'll hae"; his grim sourness was unpleasant to see.

"No! no! my husband; surely you're not done with me like that." She put out her hand timidly, the hunger of affection and the desire of maternity flaring up in her eyes and quickening her haggard face. He seemed to be standing up to the neck in cold water that was rapidly freezing about him. His one desire was to be rid of her importunity, and get out to the yard. He pulled up the window-blind, and the soft light of dawn flooded the room. He stooped, searching for his socks, and muttered:

"What mair do ye want o' me?"

"Am I so old then?" Her voice was humble, pleading; sorrow was darkening her eyes.

"What mair? what mair?" he said testily.

She arose in the bed with ardent face.

"Gillespie, dear, am I not your wife? Am I so old? Oh, don't be so cruel! It's long, long since your arms were round me. Do you not love me any more?" The torment of a heart long brooding upon neglect burned in her appeal. She sat straight up in bed. "I lie wakened at your side every night hoping ye'll take me in your arms, an' every night I greet myself to sleep." A single deep sob burst from her. The clock rang the hour of five. At the end of the fifth chime a profound silence filled the room. The dawn had gathered the sob to itself; and Fate was listening with bated breath. Worlds for them were in the making. The ancient doom upon the house was spinning its thread in the silence.

An ironic smile passed over the features of the man. The only way to get to his more important affairs was to yield to her. He put on his waistcoat as he walked to the window.

88

"A fine lush morn," he said, looking out; then turned. "What's your wull wi' me, mistress?"

She crept out of bed to his side like an invited dog, her eyes dewy with hope, and deep with the cherished thought that had woven the long nights into dreams. A light not of the dawn glorified her face. She attempted to speak, and sobbed.

"Dinna waste my time, mistress"; he pressed his thumb beneath her chin. A wave of colour passed upwards, surging over her forehead.

"I'm wantin' another baby."

She looked terrified after she had uttered the words. He did not observe her confusion.

"Dhia!" he muttered, and stared heavily at the grate, like a man in a dream. A hand was plucking at his sleeve; a voice calling hollow out of a shadowy world.

"Dhia! hae ye no' a bairn already?"

She began to sob. Her fragile shoulders heaved and shook with suppressed convulsions.

"Iain's no' my baby—he's—he's—his granny's boy."

Gillespie was amazed, and could find nothing to say.

"Do—ye—no' love me—any more?" The words were punctuated with sobs. "You haven't—kissed me—since Iain was born." She had treasured up the long reckoning of bitter time and neglect.

"Kissed ye; I never thocht o't."

"No—no—ye think of—of everything—but me."

A frown settled on his face.

"Ay! if I dinna think o' a' thing wha's tae; early an' late to keep the meal in the barrel." His frown deepened.

She lifted a wet face to him.

"Oh! Gillespie, Gillespie, don't be angry; I'm only askin' for a wee bit o' love. I'm—oh! I'm wantin' a baby. I've lain late at night"—her eyes sought the floor—"listenin' for your step. I've watched you sleepin' and waited for you wakin';" reproach, condemnation were in her voice. She spoke as a martyr who has kept long vigil by the vestal flame of love. "But you slept and wakened, and never a word to me but of milking and sowing." Her eyes quickly sought his face. "Many's the night when you were sleepin' I drew your hand over on my breasts—my breasts burnin' for a wee baby girl." Her eyes suddenly shone on him. "You'll no' deny me, my man; a baby girl. I know her hair and her eyes. I see them every night as I fall asleep. I feel her mouth on my breasts." Her thin face was transfigured. "It's all I ask. Surely I'm no' an auld cloot yet."

She stood before him, her hair on her nightdress, her half-exposed breasts rising and falling in quick pants. Gillespie was stupefied. Were there human beings in this world of work and money-making who could have a passion for aught else? Such madness for a child.

"Dhia!" he said, "ye're like one that's drunk."

"I'm drunk and sick for a baby girl," she wailed; "will I go on my knees to you?"

Sandy, the ploughman, was whistling to the lush dawn. The sound sharply aroused Gillespie to the world as from a dream.

"Hoots!" he cried, swinging his jacket across his shoulder, and shoving in his arms with a jerk, "is that a' ye want?"

"It's all my hunger and my thirst," she answered.

"Then I'll speak to Dr. Maclean aboot it." His guttural laugh was acquiescence.

"Tell me! tell me!" She looked up eagerly.

"It's a bargain, mistress. Sandy's wastin' his time, whistlin' to the craws." His tone was impatient.

"Give me a kiss before you go." She snatched at his sleeve like a slave. He made a wry face and laid his mouth over her temple.

"Ye'll no' bide late the night?" she whispered.

There was silence for a moment. The echo of Sandy's footsteps died away in the direction of the stable. Fate bent her ear.

"I'll no' be very thrang the nicht, mistress."

Passionless Fate had heard. Suddenly a cock crowed loudly.

Before Gillespie left the farm a second son, Eoghan, was born.

18

GRADUALLY the farm came to be divided between Lonend and Gillespie by the burn which ran east and west, a stone's cast from the house. According to agreement Lonend sold the wool and the lambs, and at Christmas some score of Highland cattle for English consumption, to a dealer whom he knew at Bannerie;

and Gillespie the rabbits, hares, game, and trout in Glasgow; and milk and butter in the village. At the end of the year they examined their financial position in the office of Mr. McAskill, who, for the time, was banished to Brodie's. They shook hands when they met, their palms rasping.

"Ye're lookin' weel on't, Lonen'," Gillespie said cheerily.

"Nae thanks to you if I am," snapped Lonend.

"Hoots! dinna be hasty to blame a man that never blamed ye for aucht." In no time they were bickering. Gillespie suspected Lonend's handling of the market, though all receipts were duly produced.

"There's naethin' to hinder this fella in Bannerie, whaever he is, frae gein' ye a false recate for a conseederation." This suspicion had been put into Gillespie's mind by the Fox; and Gillespie had enough hardihood to make an accusation when the matter touched his pocket. He was wont to say that men learn quicker in the affairs of their purse than in any other. The random shot went home. He saw hesitancy and read confusion in the face of Lonend, who began to bluster and rapped the table with his knuckles.

"Ye'll no' come stappin' ower me the wy ye did ower Galbraith. Hae ye the richt coont o' a' the gallons o' milk an' a' the butter ye kirned an' a' the rabbits ye trapped?"

Gillespie shoved his papers across the table. "There's the frozen truth," he said, with a sneer.

"Ye can thaw it oot afore I'll tak' it."

"Tak' it or leave it." Gillespie's tone was desultory with self-righteousness, flicking aside any suspicion of underhand work.

"I'll no' be at my damn fash."

Gillespie rose to his feet and gathered up his papers.

"Very weel! I'll send ye the hauf o' thae profits"—he tapped his papers with his forefinger, and rolled up the sheaf—"an' ye'll send me my hauf o' the wheck o' that"—with the sheaf he indicated Lonend's straggling papers—"inside o' three days. Aifter that I'll chairge ye interest."

"Who are ye to order me like that? Ye damn sow, I took ye frae a fishin'-boat." Lonend's face was purple with rage; the hairs of his stubbly moustache bristled. "It's an ill day I ever had onything to do wi' the likes o' you. Ye're black to the bane, I tell ye tae your face. Ye'd rob the Apostle Peter off the cross."

Gillespie put his hand round his ear and screwed up his features in a grimace.

"Ye're on my deif ear, Lonen'."

"Deif! deif!"—raged throttled Lonend—"Goäd broke the mould He made ye in for fear He micht mak another o' your breed." He took a stride forward as he spoke. "Ye herrit Galbraith's nest; an' ye'd herry mine, wad ye? It's no' a wife ye've made o' my lassie, but a slave, a damn slave. Ye'd herry mine, wad ye, ye mildewed nyaf?" Lonend clenched his hands. "Ye——"

"Ye winna strick me, Lonen'." Gillespie backed away with upraised hands. "Ye daurna; that wad be the jyle for ye, man; it's no' the time o' year for the jyle wi' the neeps to sow."

"Ay! by Goäd! in twa shakes o' a lamb's tail. I'll gie ye a gutsfull that'll put neeps oot o' your heid for the next fortnicht." And Lonend, with a snarl, sprang at him and swung an iron fist full on Gillespie's mouth.

"That's the wy Hector Logan pays his lawin'."

In the silence that followed they heard the drip, drip of blood on the floor from Gillespie's mouth. Gillespie looked down at the bright spots on the floor, then up at the panting Lonend placidly, unwinkingly. His broad form was trembling; a slow, maddening smile crept over his face.

"Ye jeely-fish," Lonend yelped; "say't an' be done wi't. I see the dirt in your eye."

"That's the wy o' Hector Logan." Gillespie drew the back of his hand across his mouth and brought it away smeared. "It's a wy ye'll hae to pey me for yet." He stooped and picked up his scattered papers.

Rage was dying quickly in Lonend. His breathing became more regular. "Wait till ye pleugh the half o' what I harrowed afore ye try to come ower me wi' your tricks."

"Ay! man, I'll wait." Gillespie turned the handle of the door. The still sunshine streamed into the dingy room, lighting up the dust on the table and its books. Gillespie spat blood. "Ye've knocked the teeth doon my throat," he said; "I'll pull wan or twa o' yours afore I'm done wi' ye," and he passed out into the peaceful light.

"Gang an' sell your seeck hens an' coont their feathers." Lonend's taunt followed him down the brae.

Gillespie, with mouth tightly shut, walked home, pondering

92

upon his agreement with Lonend concerning the farm. He decided he would sow no neeps. He jeered at his wife, whom he found in bed. "Ye were he'rtier wance doon the burn-side."

She scrambled from the bed, all awry in her clothing, tousled in her hair, and staggering slightly on the floor. He narrowed eyes of menace upon her, regarding her condition a moment in silence.

"Like faither, like dochter," he muttered; "an' what's the meanin' o' a' this?" he said, with low incisiveness.

"I'm not well to-day, Gillespie."

"No, no' very weel"—he took a stride about the room—"a fine turn I've done to mairry you, wi' your trinkets an' your bangles an' your piano. I've come an' gone, slavin' nicht an' morn for ye to squander my hard-gotten siller. Ye'd think I was a millionaire."

"I'm no' to blame, Gillespie," she answered wearily; "Dr. Maclean ordered me to take spirits when Iain was born."

"Tak' your fill; ou ay! tak' your fill for a' I care; but let Dr. Maclean pey for 't."

She lifted a stunned face to him. There was something of the perplexity of a chidden child in her look.

"I don't want my fill."

Gillespie made no answer. He often met his wife's conversation with contemptuous silence.

"You've never a kind word for me at all now, Gillespie," she said timidly.

"I've nae mair words for ye, guid or bad. Haud your ain wy, wumman, but no' wi' my siller," and he walked out of the room. She felt she was despised. On the next day she learned that he would reveal the domestic intimacies ruthlessly to the world, for when she asked him for money for household necessities, he refused, and said that in future himself would pay all these things.

Stung to the quick, she crossed over to Lonend with a shawl about her head—a shawl, the signal of distress flown by a woman. Lonend, sore over yesterday's business, gave her little comfort.

"Naethin' like feedin' his ain gulls wi' his ain sea-guts," he said irascibly. She stayed there over the night, expecting her husband to come for her. He never came. In the morning she crept back, broken in spirit, and watching furtively that no one would see her walking the Via Dolorosa.

In the meantime Lonend had other matter for thought. Gillespie neither ploughed the Laigh Park nor sowed neeps; and neeps were important for wintering the cattle. His ploughman informed him that Gillespie had "putten on sheep as muckle's the land wad cairry, frae the Laigh Park at the slack o' the wud tae the Bull Park"—exactly one half of the farm as marked by the march of the burn. This was beyond endurance. Against the grain Lonend was forced to visit Muirhead Farm. Gillespie and Sandy the Fox were exchanging gossip and pleasantries at the door of a little outhouse, containing a boiler and heating apparatus for making mash for the cattle. The Fox had informed his master that Mrs. Galbraith was living in the plumber's house in the Back Street. The conversation turned on the piracy of the Back Street denizens. The Fox blamed Galbraith. Do what he could the Fox was unable to prevent these female plunderers from trespassing in the Laigh Park when they went to the Planting for sticks.

"There's wan o' the hungry seed that'll bother us no more. I'm telt they found Betty Heck standin' against the dike-side at the Holly Bush stone-deid, wi' a bundle o' sticks across her shouthers."

"A savin' wumman," answered Gillespie jocularly; "makin' hersel' her ain heidstane."

The Fox was tee-heeing shrilly in Gillespie's rubicund face when Lonend tramped across the yard. He had a short whip in his hand, with which he slapped his trouser-leg.

"A braw day, Lonen'," cried Gillespie suavely.

Lonend planted his feet apart, squarely facing Gillespie.

"What's this you're up tae?" he demanded surlily.

"Ye'll p'raps be a wee mair expleecit."

"What dae ye mean by puttin' sheep on the low grun'?"

The Fox moved away with reluctant step. Gillespie stayed him with a gesture.

"Ye'd better bide, Sanny," Gillespie whistled through his nose; "I'll maybe need a witness in case o' assault."

The Fox, with bleared, ferrety eyes shining evilly upon Lonend, slouched against the wall of the outhouse and picked in his red, tangled beard.

"Ye'll need mair nor this scraggy witness"—Lonend jerked the butt of his whip in contempt towards the Fox—"afore I'm done wi' ye."

"I winna gang sae fast aboot wutnesses, Lonen'; I'm jaloosin' I'm no' gettin' market-price frae your freend up by at Bannerie."

Gillespie, who had already seen this random shot go home, welcomed the chance of pushing it now in the presence of the Fox, who had suggested it. "I ken a' aboot the recates ye ha frae him—a bonny hand o' write, stampit an' a'. Imphm. P'raps noo you an' him mak' your ain price on paper. Hoo much noo is he takin' for the job, Lonen'?"

Lonend's face was white.

"What job?" he growled.

"Ou! I'm nane such a scone o' yesterday's bakin'. Did ye never hear o' the trick o' a man peyin' ye twenty-four shullin'. for a sheep, an' gein' ye a bit o' recate made oot for auchteen or twenty?"

Men have ability to sin; not every man has enough to conceal guilt. This is because man is an ethical animal. Guilt was plain on Lonend's face. He was learning that conscience is the handcuff which binds us to God.

"Gang an' sell your ain stuff," he said, frowning at Gillespie and his conscience.

"Just so, Lonen'; that's the wy I'm puttin' sheep on the low grun'. It's no' hauf the profits ony mair; it's hauf the ferm atween us to mak' a kirk or a mill o't."

"Ye've taen your time to tell 't." Lonend was exasperated.

"Ay," replied Gillespie drily; "dinna show hauf-done work to a wean or a fool—ye ken the sayin'?"

"Who's a fool?" Lonend eagerly turned the conversation to recrimination.

"I'm dootin' it's me ye were takin' for a fool."

"I'll hae the law o' ye for puttin' on sheep on the low grun' withoot my consent."

"Ca' canny!" said Gillespie, smiling. "You an' me 'greed to hae wan hauf o' the ferm; ye put your hand to paper on't. I'm mindin' that ye wanted the heather for the Hielan' beasts"— he shot a sudden keen glance at Lonend—"I'm takin' the Laigh Parks, an' I'll sell the lambs an' wool mysel'. Ye can dale wi' your freen' at Bannerie by yersel', gif ye like."

Lonend, frustrated, inwardly cursed the day he had signed the bond.

"It's no' set doon in the paper that the farm's to gang half an' half this wy."

95

"Wi' a wee bittie ower to your freen' up by," sneered Gillespie.

Lonend took a sudden step forward, his hand wrestling with his whip, his mouth twitching.

"No; ye'll no' knock ony mair teeth doon my throat. It's no' neifs noo; it's the paper ye put your hand tae."

"Ye damn thief," roared Lonend, flaming out in rage; "ye'll land on your backside yet wi' your wee bits o' paper, an' your wee per cents. Ye Jew frae Jericho! Mrs. Galbraith sweirs she'll hae the hale toon aboot your ears."

"Does Mrs. Galbraith ken wha began the ploy?" sneered Gillespie; "it's no' for you to be cairryin' sculduddery o' wee-min's clatter."

"Sculduddery!" shouted Lonend; "every wumman's scul-duddery wi' you. Morag haesna the life o' a dog wi' you, you hound. By Goäd, she'll come hame wi' me this very day."

Lonend's one affection was for his daughter. The treatment she received rankled more than his own defeat at Gillespie's hands. He imagined that this threat would daunt Gillespie.

"Tak' her an' welcome. See an' hae the jar ready. I'll be weel rid o' her."

Gillespie's measured answer fell upon Lonend like icy water. He quailed inwardly, seeing that Gillespie was in earnest. He groped for the significance of the word "jar," and feared to ask its import. He was baffled, forced to stay his hands, and wage battle with impossible argument. Gradually he recognised him-self in the presence of an adversary the like of whom he had never met—a master of craft and words. He had no stomach to suffer the shame of seeing his daughter back at Lonend. He retreated under cover of threats.

"Tak' guid care, the twa o' ye, to stick to the Laigh grun'. Dinna let me catch ye stepping north the burn or I'll gie Dr. Maclean a month's job on ye."

"Hoots! what's your hurry, Lonen'?" said Gillespie suavely; "step in an' hae a cup o' tea—if Morag's no' at the Lonen'."

"Keep your dirty whustle an' your sang. I'll step in the day o' your funeral." The whip handle was snapped in two and flung on the manure heap as Lonend disappeared round the corner of the byre.

Gillespie strolled to the manure heap, picked up the remnants of the whip, and handed them to the Fox.

"It'll stand splicin'," he said. As the Fox was examining the

96

trophy Gillespie turned on him a meditative eye. "I'm dootin', Sanny, I'll no' be keepin' the Laigh Park very lang."

Gillespie had profited by Lonend's tale of how, by his astute manoeuvre, he had "done" the Laird in the matter of the black-faced sheep. Gillespie would better the instruction. The Fox waited, eye upon the whip.

"Lonen' 'ill be gey an' gled to see me off the ferm. We'll leave him a bit praisint o' the black-faced sheep afore we'll gang. Ye ken, I never thocht muckle o' the fermin'. But, I'm thinkin', maybe the shore end wad cairry another fifty or mair."

The Fox teased his meagre beard in glee.

"Man," he purred, "but Lonen' 'ill dance"—he shuffled with his feet—"dance as if the fires o' hell were singein' the soles o' his feet."

Gillespie smiled and whistled in his nostrils. "It'll serve him right for his dirty tricks in puttin' puir Marget oot o' hoose an' hame." Gillespie pondered a moment. "Dae ye ken, Sanny, I never played my cairds weel aifter a'."

The Fox waited, toying with the whip handle.

"It's Marget," said Gillespie softly, "that I ought to hae mairrit."

"Ay," replied the Fox; "a braw wice-lik' wumman."

19

THESE matters created some talk in both the Butler's shop and in the Back Street. The talk in the shop was of no great importance, but it brings us into the presence of that forcible free fellow, the darling of the town, Lonend's father, Chrystal Logan, a large, effectual man, carrying a pliable torpedo beard, well-trimmed from a thick, red face. Nothing stiff there or about him. He carried a breeze with him and walked with a surge, as if the wind of prosperity always blew in his wake. There are men of that kidney always taking the world in tow. He would throw up his work to attend any auction sale within a radius of twelve miles, and come home suffused with liquor and burdened with impedimenta for which, at the instance of his wife, he anxiously sought purchasers on a sober to-morrow. But he had had his day. Lycurgus will always have a noble feast upon his table.

He told jocular, rather doubtful, stories to married women, and carried these off with a roaring laugh. A joyous man, who had his photograph taken every New Year day, when he made a pilgrimage to Rothesay. The walls of his shop and house were covered with these representations, faithfully dated. To the favoured he would show this gallery, going around with an inch-tape in his hand. "Here I had an inch and a half of whisker; and here three inches," and would heavily sigh, for the hirsute growth marked the scurrying feet of Time. A toward man, the friend of children, he carried the sun in his pocket. In his youth he had been in gaol for poaching, and after took service with the Laird. It was the only way of curing the itch for the gun.

He wore a famous waistcoat of sealskin, with pearl buttons up to the torpedo beard, which was dark; on occasion greyish-white. This was the lovable vanity of the man. When he had been drunk the world, on the next day, discerned a change of colour in the beard, like wakening to streets whitened with a snowfall through the night. In Brodie's he always drank "whisky hot," and wore a blue ribbon when in the service of the Laird. At need he turned up the lapel and flew the blue flag. Comrades in Brodie's made a point of asking him the secret of his youth—in allusion to his chameleon beard. "Be temperate," he would cry, with a wide-spread gesture of the hands, "like me"; the hands would swoop to the lapel; "always at the fore—the Blue Peter"; and he never failed to wink. As for the sealskin waistcoat, it was travelled. The pearl buttons came from Ceylon; the sealskin from Seattle, where one of his friends had gone. "It's in Central America; or, if you want to know more parteecularly, near Washington." In point of fact it had been one of the Laird's friends who had gone there, while the waistcoat had been a present from the old Laird, and the seal which delivered up the pelt had been caught napping by his salmon fisherman on the rocks below the castle.

Lonend found his father in specs and shirt-sleeves, bending over a piece of leather with a squat sharp-edged tool in his hand. Lonend, at the counter, brought down his fist in a rage.

"Him! the Irish scum. His folk got banished frae Ireland for lifting a rope wi' a filly at the end o't, and cam' hidin' behind the Heids o' Ayr. And when the Kyle men made it too hot for them they sneaked in here. An' noo he's stolen Galbraith's ferm, the black Irish thief."

When Lonend had ended his philippic his father delved the sharp edge of the squat knife into the leather, snipped off a paring, swept it to the floor, and lifted a preoccupied eye upon his son.

"Be calm, Hector, be calm. At all costs be a gentleman. The old Laird never got angry. It does not become us to get angry over a lobster-catcher, a wulk-gatherer." The Butler screwed up his resin-blackened fingers and made a suggestive plucking gesture. Here was the eternal distinction between farmer and fisherman. Justice would perhaps allow a barrel of herring to be equivalent to a bag of potatoes, but salt water is unstable, and commands no rent, while land is a hoary possession.

"We"—the Butler slapped the strip of leather on the counter, and his eyes gleamed—"we are the land that barred out the Romans; the land that has pride without insolence; courage without audacity; blood with condescension. Think of the Douglases and Wallace. Do not condescend upon this sea-villain who would be a farmer. Console yourself with cordials, and let him know his master when he comes to me for harness."

"Harness!" His father's pigeons on the roof scuttered away at Lonend's derisive laughter. "He'll gie ye an order for harness when the rope in the middens is done."

"Say no more, Hector, say no more; remember I sell whips; and there will always, I hope, be a length of tow left. The crab always crawls back to the sea. You shall have the farm yet."

The Butler also was among the prophets. Was it fatality, chance, or coincidence that caused both the Butler and Gillespie within the same hour to utter almost the same words? The crab would go back to the sea, but set its claws in Lonend as it scuttled.

Another scrap of conversation is more illuminating, for it gave Mrs. Galbraith her line of action. It came to be noticed in the Back Street that, while she never encouraged gossip, she always had an ear for particulars from Muirhead. So we find the waspish, rosy face of Mary Bunch at her door. She is on an errand of borrowing a frying-pan, and cannot forbear observing that Morag Logan has been living with her father for more than a week.

"The Logans aye had trouble with their faimly. Chrystal was

99

in jyle for poaching, and wan o' them died in the horrors o' drink. If Morag escapes it'll be gey and droll."

Mrs. Galbraith encouraged her with a nod. "Do you think so?" and lifted her lustrous dark eyes a moment upon the pinched face of the garrulous narrator.

"Ay, div I! She was left five hunner pounds in dry money frae an uncle in Isla'. And he was a bad, bad man. He got his money makin' whusky an' sellin't to the fishermen withoot a leeshins. His wife wad go an' cairry up the stoups o' salt watter to mek the whusky. She was never in her bed, that wumman, makin' whusky. An' that's the money Gillespie got wi' his wife. No good 'ill come o't. It'll gang wi' the whusky yet." The small head jerked violently; she lowered her voice to a whisper, and stole a look over her shoulder at the door. "They're sayin' Morag's tastin'." Mrs. Galbraith lifted calm, unwavering eyes to Mary Bunch's face, and her heart beat faster. Had the voice of Fate entered into this mean channel? "Since Eoghan was born she's aye sook, sookin'. It'll a' gang wi' the whusky yet. You wait an' see." She compressed her lips into a thin, prophetic line. "See the wy Morag Shaw went an' Morag at Donal' Graham. Dae ye ken? It's my belief a' the Morags are the same." Her puckered face had a bewildered look as if she were puzzled by the thought of a disastrous name. "Let Gillespie reinge an' scrape an' milk the coo as he likes; she's on the whusky; an' the ebb-tide 'ill tek away more than the flood 'ill bring in." The biographical titbit had its own effect on Mrs. Galbraith, who wanted leisure for thought. With an imperious uplift of the head, well known to the Back Street, she dismissed Mary Bunch. "That will do, Mary," she said; "there is the frying-pan in the sink cupboard."

"Drat her," Mary Bunch apostrophised the cat's without on the thatch in the sun, "that's her high-an'-mighty wy—'that'll do.'" With spleen Mary Bunch thought, not so much of the words of dismissal, as of the imperious sweep of the head, which none in the Back Street could either withstand or combat. "That's a' the thanks I get for my news." Yet so magnetic a woman was Mrs. Galbraith that Mary Bunch would be prepared on the morrow to furnish anew a banquet of gossip. She had forgotten that she had had some sort of thanks in the loan of a frying-pan.

20

WE allow the years of wrangling between the partners to pass with their infamy, and come to the exodus of Gillespie. He had held his half of the farm for three years, steadily covering it with sheep, during which time Lonend never lost an opportunity of sneering at the fisherman farmer—"wha never saw neeps shawed" in his life. All Brieston knew that they were at variance; and believed that Gillespie was making a muddle of the business. Lonend even hinted that it was he who had broken away from Gillespie, for he had "mair to do than throw awa' his siller on the experiments o' a man wha kens mair o' a lobster creel nor a pleugh stilt." Lonend made capital out of the fact that Gillespie had converted his share of the farmlands into sheep pasturage. "He's only fit for herdin' kye an' sellin' milk wi' a bell to a wheen weemin."

Old Mr. Strang was perturbed at these rumours, and warning his son of the risks which an amateur ran in farming, urged him to return to the sea.

"I'm no' forgettin' a'thegeither the saut watter," answered Gillespie; "but it's saut enough to keep. I'm no' just makin' a fortune here"—he swept his arm around the compass of his land—"but I'm layin' the foundation o' ane."

His father imagined him to be suffering from delusion, and urged him to give up the business. "I hear naethin' else but you an' your ferm frae the Bairracks to the 'Shipping Box.' Lonen's makin' a mock o' ye; he says he'll no' foregaither wi' ye at the end o' the lease. Either you or him maun hae the hale o' the ferm."

"I'm dootin' he's findin' me gey kittly to run in harness wi'."

"Give it up," said the old man shortly. He was grieved at the common talk of his son's incompetence. His wife was ailing more than usual ot late. Her cough racked her at night and harried her in the morning. She rarely left the house now, and her voice had become husky and weak. Maclean had ordered her inland, but, for some unaccountable reason, she refused to leave the "Ghost" unless Gillespie accompanied her. At night, in dreams, she mourned over her only-begotten son; by day pleaded for his release from the purgatory of Muirhead. "Can you not give him a helping hand, Richard? we've more money in the bank than we need." There was a deposit receipt for £835 in the kist.

Gillespie, listening to this account of his mother's state of health with a face of solicitude, flashed a look of cunning at his father.

"I dinna see my wy clear to move intae the toon."

"What's to hinder ye? your mother an' me 'ill no' see ye stuck."

"If I'd a wee thing mair capital, I'd mak' a move. I'm gettin' seeck o' the fermin'." He spoke as if a vast, dreary world were oppressing him.

The old man sighed heavily. It was difficult for him, in a land of strangers, to withstand their taunts. "I've a pickle siller in the bank," he hazarded.

"No, no!" Gillespie interrupted; "ye'll need a' ye hae."

"Your mother's gettin' sore failed," was the pathetic answer; "we've mair than 'ill cairry us to the grave. If five hunner wad gie ye a stairt ye're welcome tae 't."

"Are you sure it'll no' leave ye bare?"—with beautiful filial reluctance. Yet he drained the deposit receipt to the amount of £500, callously stripping the slates off the roof which sheltered grey hairs. He gave no bond or IOU, and his father asked for none. Instead he hinted that his father should sound Lonend about that farmer's willingness to let his partner go. The old man stayed to tea, dandled Eoghan, said he must come to the "Ghost" to see his granny, and left half a sovereign with Morag for the boy. She concealed the money, and said nothing to her husband of the gift.

Old Mr. Strang, with whom Lonend was friendly, asked that his son be relieved of his half of the farm-lands. "He's makin' naething o't, an' it's killin' the auld woman." Lonend wavered. The guilt of his crime towards Mrs. Galbraith was pricking him. This would increase its burden. He compromised with his conscience by determining that he would invite her back to Muirhead. Several circumstances induced him to close with Mr. Strang's request. He was weary of brawling with Gillespie, who, he admitted to himself, was more than a match for him, disarmed as he was in the contest by his affection for his daughter. Gillespie he found dark, pernicious, impenetrable, without bowels of pity, immovable as granite. Lonend's suspicions harboured the

gloomiest fears. At the expiry of the lease he was persuaded that
Gillespie would find means of getting the whole farm into his
hands. The Laird was no friend of his since he had wrested
Lonend from the estate. He could not brook the loss of Muirhead,
being greedy for land, especially after his public jibes about the
lobster-catcher. Morag, who should have made their relations
tender, alienated them. Lonend suspected that Gillespie studi-
ously harassed her to vex him. Removed out of his immediate
neighbourhood Gillespie might give over this guerilla warfare
upon his girl. Besides, he hated being partner with a man who
was pursuing a separate interest. Do what he might, Lonend
could not take off his guard one who was armoured in duplicity,
who spoke no word of censure, who uttered no asperity. "A
damn black frost, that's what he is," Lonend said to the Butler.

"But who, my son, proposed the plan? was it not you? Never
consort with a rascal. He will make your cheek burn at last."
Thus early was Lonend taken in the caprice of Fate, which
turns our foresight to an ironic jest, and cherishes the most
unexpected things in obscurity, to make of them, in the end, the
master of our life.

It was not without a sense of relief that Lonend saw this
honourable avenue of escape from a cuttlefish, impenetrable behind the ink of his dissembling. He was sick of the rôle of policeman, and the Butler advised him on the heels of old Mr. Strang,
"Let the crab go back to the sea before his claws become too big."

Lonend was secretly pleased with this advice, which jumped
with his own wish. His greed of land would be gratified. He could
make good his taunts about the lobster-catcher, who, once
Lonend had withdrawn to his own half of the farm, had been left
high and dry on the manure heap, and was now forced to retreat
in a backwash of incompetence among the herring barrels of the
Quay. "Let him keep his 'tattie barrels for saut herrin'," Lonend
went to the length of saying to Lowrie, the banker.

The factor made no objection to the dissolution of partnership,
and agreed that Lonend should occupy and work Muirhead on
the terms of Galbraith's lease. Lonend, however, was ignorant
that the factor had been instigated to this course of action by
Gillespie, who had already paid that official a visit, and had
agreed, on being released from partnership with Lonend, to
rent the stores at the Quay, belonging to the Laird, which had
lain empty for several years.

Immediately Gillespie got the factor's consent he became extraordinarily active. In the forenoons of those days when the wind set to the sea he cunningly burned the heather in patches above the shore. The smoke was invisible from Lonend.

"Whatna bleeze is this?" asked the Fox.

"It's a bit fire for Lonen' to warm his temper at." The moor was scarcely cold when Sandy the Fox drove a large flock of black-faced sheep upon it. They felled saplings in the Planting in the early morning, and fenced every gap on the land, and hoarded every inch of manure in the farm-yard. Some year and a half previously Gillespie had introduced a strain of good rams among the sheep, and in this economical way had vastly improved his stock. He worked in silence, ignoring Lonend's gale of jests about his incapacity. The stock was now acclimatised, the death-rate low, and the fences gave the stock the appearance of contentedness.

Gillespie was now prepared to leave, and, choosing his time of year early in May, wrote to Lonend informing him that, in terms of old Mr. Strang's conversation, he was willing to hand over his share of the farm, and hoped that the arrangement could be come at by next month, as he was anxious to return to the town when the fishing season was entering on its best period. He had no love for farming; was losing money on the venture which he had undertaken chiefly on Lonend's invitation—here Gillespie sucked his pen, smirking—Morag would be better off in the town, and the like. He swithered over the signature, but finally wrote: "Your affect. son-in-law, Gillespie Strang."

Lonend, sneering at the title "son-in-law" instead of scrutinising the letter, swallowed the bait. He curtly replied, assenting. By return Gillespie asked for a meeting with the Laird's factor to complete the agreement. At the meeting each man made a show of friendliness, and it was finally agreed that Lonend should enter in full possession of the farm forthwith. As Lonend gathered up the reins in his hands—he always came in some pomp to the town—the factor, smiling shrewdly, hoped that Gillespie would leave no sting behind him. This random remark troubled Lonend on his homeward journey. He lashed the mare viciously with the whip, puzzling over the likelihood of his having fallen into a trap. Before he reached home he was persuaded that the factor and Gillespie were hand in glove to oust him from Muirhead.

At the end of May Gillespie wrote informing Lonend that he would move out in the first days of June; in the meanwhile he asked Lonend what price he was prepared to offer for the stock and farm-yard manure. Lonend, holding Gillespie for a simpleton, refused point-blank to take over a single head of sheep. He received a letter from McAskill, pointing out that he had concluded a written agreement to enter into possession of Muirhead Farm. The lawyer quoted from the terms of Galbraith's lease: "The tenant shall be bound to implement the following conditions, namely: (First) To reside on the said lands during the lease, and always to have a sufficient stocking thereon"—this last was underlined—"and whereas this is a special condition of the lease, it is expressly stipulated that if the tenant for the time being shall fail to implement this condition, excepting only owing to circumstances beyond his control, it shall so be in the power of the landlord at once to put an end to the lease."

McAskill pointed out that the stock belonged to the land, and that, in terms of the lease, "the landlord reserved power at any time during the lease to resume possession of such portions of the said lands as he may think proper." This also was underlined. McAskill hinted that the Laird would deprive him of the whole farm.

Lonend went hot and cold as he read. The words swam before his eyes, and he jumped to a false conclusion—here was the trick by which the factor and Gillespie would deprive him of the farm. By Goäd, he would show them! He would buy every hoof on the farm.

"(Second): The tenant shall not sell or dispose of any dung made on the said lands, but shall lay the whole dung on the farm in each year no less than twenty-five tons of good stable or byre manure, per imperial acre, and shall exhibit evidence thereof to the satisfaction of the landlord's factor at Whitsunday yearly."

Lonend gnashed his teeth. His suspicion was correct. In that moment he experienced a deep satisfaction in his foresight. Like another, he could have called out on his prophetic soul. Thus and thus would Gillespie cheat him out of the farm. No, by Goäd! In an impulse of fury he wrote a letter to McAskill, saying he would buy every sheep on the farm, and daringly made an obscene jest about the dung. Either the jest or the substance of the blind letter tickled Gillespie. "We've nailed him," he said, and patted McAskill on the shoulder, familiarly calling him Nathanael.

Arbiters were appointed. The farm-yard manure was valued at five shillings per cubic yard. Lonend, exultant, imagined he was baulking Gillespie in buying the manure. When they came to deal for the black-faced stock, the arbiters fought so bitterly that an oversman was appointed. Owing to the boundary-fences— cut by stealth from the Planting—the homing value of the sheep was recognised.

"Where can they stray tae?" Lonend demanded with heat; "is't to Lonen' or the sea?"

"Sheep are silly enough to have been drowned before now," the oversman answered drily. He pointed out that Gillespie had not neglected heather-burning, which had helped to keep down the death-rate. The sheep had plainly thrived on their native grazing. The oversman was nettled at Lonend's fiery and scornful interruptions, while Gillespie, on the other hand, kept his teeth on his tongue and courteously answered the oversman's queries for information.

Lonend recalled that he had been selling his cast ewes at thirteen shillings to seventeen shillings, whose lambs, with the shotts weeded out, had gone for ten shillings. The price finally fixed by the oversman, in conjunction with the arbiters, seeing it was early June, was £58 per clad score for ewes and lambs. There was a big head of stock on the farm.

"I'll tak' yeer cheque within three days for the manure an' sheep-stock," said Gillespie breezily, in the hearing of the oversman, "or chairge ye interest."

Lonend, speechless with mortification and rage, saw now that all along Gillespie had been determined to relinquish the partnership.

"Ye braxy beast," he spluttered; "did ye tak' to burnin' the heather when dacent fowk were in their bed?"

Of all the circumstances this was the one which galled him most, for he had not allowed such knowledge to Gillespie.

"Ou!" answered Gillespie, laughing good-humouredly and rubbing his hands; "Sanny an' me was makin' a lowe whiles by the licht o' the moon when ye were thrang in Brodie's backroom wi' your bit joke ower the lobster-catcher. I wush ye luck o' the ferm, Lonen'. I'm gey an' weel pleased to gang back to the lobsters. Ye ken I haena muckle skill o' fermin'."

Lonend's dark face was distorted with rage.

"Come awa'," he cried, "come awa', ye robber, an' I'll pey

ye the siller. Hector Logan o' the Lonen' can table penny for penny wi' the likes o' you."

"No, no, Lonen', that's no' business. Just pey the bit lawin' intae Mr. Lowrie in my name, an' I'll be obleeged to ye."

During the next two days Sandy the Fox and two hired men from Brieston dismantled Muirhead house. Once more the clocks were stopped, when Galbraith's furniture was put into carts. On the evening of the second day all the plenishing had been transported to the stores at the Quay. Morag went with the last cart, carrying the child at her breast, and sobbing bitterly, with her eyes riveted on the track across the brae leading to Lonend. She was being cut adrift from her last anchorage. The child gazed at her with those eyes of infinite depth which children have, full of a dumb unutterable expression. The next moment the child was attracted by the brush of the horse's tail, and stretched out its hands towards this new allure. The mother was left to sob in peace. Down the Barracks brae into the town the cart rumbled, and to the observer mother and child seemed part of Gillespie's goods and chattels. The descent of the brae had its peculiar significance for both husband and wife. For the one it was the descent to Avernus; for the other, a march towards the Alps and Italy.

It had been a depressing day. The wind, a high east, had darkened the town, which lay a huddled mass of roofs beneath a sour leaden sky. The far-off roar of the sea droned through the gloomy twilight; and as the cart halted at last at the end of its journey, on the eaves of the "Ghost" the sign-board jangled its rasping curfew, ushering in the close of that iron day with its hard light and a watery sun which, angry with the wind in its eye, scowled luridly in a wild, marly sky presaging storm.

To-morrow Lonend would send a grieve to occupy Muirhead Farm. To-night it was once more empty. Around its doors, in a rockery of Mrs. Galbraith's, glimmered the old-world wee white flowers of wood-ruff, haunting the dusk with their scent. The trees tossed and swayed, moaning beneath the sky, and sere leaves of ivy swirled upwards on the roof. A deep quiet reigned within the dark dwelling. It was housing silence, gleaning ghostly echoes, garnering retribution. Gillespie had carelessly left the kitchen door open. Suddenly it crashed to, racketing loudly through the echoing house at a snarl of the piratical east wind.

In the "Ghost" Gillespie's mother was dying of consumption. For two days she had been unable to speak, and had written on sheets of note-paper. Gillespie had carefully picked one of these up from the kitchen dresser, and read the pencilled words: "The doctor says I will not choke." He turned pale with fear.

She was choking now. At every gust of the wind, when the signboard without groaned and creaked, he felt her eyes following him in dumb dread through the room. Trembling, he left the kitchen and passed out into the night. Beneath the grinding signboard he stood and gazed across the bay at the dark loom of Lonend and Muirhead. Within Lonend a man sat in the empty kitchen at the table, his head between his hands, his eyes riveted on a sheet of paper spread out on the table. For the third time he slowly read the writing:

THIS HOUSE IS DEAD.
IT HAS BEEN MURDERED.
IT IS BURIED IN THE GRAVE OF A WOMAN'S
HEART.

"BE NOT DECEIVED; GOD IS NOT MOCKED: FOR WHATSOEVER A
MAN SOWETH, THAT SHALL HE ALSO REAP."

"It's God's shirra, God's shirra," he moaned. A deep groan broke the silence of the lonely room.

Some one touched Gillespie's arm. He turned, and saw his father silently beckoning to him, and followed him into the kitchen. Morag was standing with Eoghan in her arms, looking at the bed. His mother was gasping, her chin heaving up with every effort. Her lips were dabbled with a chalky froth. In the tense silence Gillespie heard his father whisper, "She is passing away." He heard a rattle and gurgle in her throat, and saw the whites of the eyes roll upwards. There was a gasp and a sigh; then infinite silence. His father stepped to the bed and leaned his ear down to her mouth. Then he straightened himself, turned from the bed, and, looking at his son, said, in a low, solemn voice, "She is gone."

Without, the signboard with the bloody dagger croaked to the night.

BOOK II

1

WHEN the plumber died Topsail Janet left the house in the Back Street and took a single room at the Old Quay, whose window looked into the rusty walls of the beetling Quarry. In the first year of her bereavement she hovered with a quick hunger about his grave; but every succeeding Sunday the grave grew deeper. She prayed that she, too, might die. She had to take to whelk-gathering, and rarely saw the sun within her room, for she went out at dawn and returned, wet and weary to the bone, at lamp-light. Carrying her bag of whelks she would creep cautiously from the village boys. "Topsail Janet! Topsail Janet!" they would shout mockingly, and careering against her would send her staggering forward. She wore her mother's tippet; and once, when it fluttered in the breeze, some one said "Topsail," and the name stuck to her. For a long time the name burned as a stigma; but habit made the brand cold.

There was a profound contrast between the parsimony of her life and the vastness of the sea, her daily companion. She waded at evening in gold-red pools, creeping over the russet tangle, scarce visible save for a fluttering drugget petticoat. At dawn she was a grey toiler on a grey isle, which the tide had given up for a little while, only to drive her shoreward with a gleam of flashing teeth. At times the shore-ice had to be broken; at times the squalls rushed up in black to her feet, and the rain rose along the sea swamping her in misery. To happy people she probably looked picturesque, wading in the salt-water pools or crawling about the rocks, as she plucked here and there a whelk and cast it into a rusty tin can.

She had her own bigness of heart. One day, as she stretched her tired back and gazed vacantly at the bare sea running in white flashes to the empty horizon, the north wind brought her a gift. High in the blue she saw a great rocking bird. It plunged downwards, sheered towards the cliffs, cannoned with a splash of feathers against the wall of stone, and fell among the sea-bent.

Often she had scurried for home, when, in the dusk, the whales arose out of the sea and fluked across the bay. Now she was more greatly scared as she watched the helpless flutter of wings. She divined the beating of the pinions to be death. With her heart choking within her she flew along the lonely shore, hearing the noise of the great wings, as if the shadow of death rustled at her heels. Once, round a sheltering point, she stopped, panting. In the silence she heard the labour of the wings slacken and cease. Her courage returned. The solan would be dead. The sea babbled plaintively on the shore. Everything in the stillness was as it had been. Suddenly there was a sharp scream, child-like with its load of pain. Her heart stood still. Again all was profoundly silent. She peered round the rock, and clutching at her bosom, stumbled forward, and saw a white inert mass. As she crept towards it the solan goose opened its bright eyes and beat the ground with one wing. This sign of life nerved her. She dropped on her knees and saw the white down dappled with blood. The hills began to spin slowly about her and the sea grow dark, when the wing beat again with a feeble spasmodic movement, and a low croak gurgled in the throat of the bird. She thought the sound came through running blood. A fierce wave of pity swept over her, and she put out her hand and touched the ruffled neck. At the touch the bird struggled on its side along the ground. She followed cautiously, wishing that her hands were less rough. The bird with the beautiful pinions became holy in her eyes. Taking off her shawl she wrapped the broken-winged solan in it, tenderly as a mother her first-born, and held the struggling bundle till it lay exhausted, her heart crying out at the terror of the bird. Leaving her bag, her whelks, her all, to the greedy tide she set off for home, wild with apprehension lest the bird die in her hands.

Dr. Maclean was called in. He had hurried at the summons of Topsail, wondering if she had caught pneumonia at last. When he was told that his patient was a bird he swore in relief, and bound up the mangled wing.

"Some day, Topsail, you'll fly too," he said, going out.

She looked at him open-mouthed.

"The Bible says that angels have wings. One of these days you'll fly out of the window and over the quarry there."

"Ach! away wi' ye, doctor."

"That's how you'll go to heaven."

Part of her small store went to the milk-cart. The sick bird refused the milk, even though she sweetened it with sugar. In deep anxiety she watched by it through the long evening, mending her fire with the best of her drift-wood, and making a nest for it with a blanket off the bed. In the morning she consulted Ned o' the Horn, who contemptuously kicked her saucer aside and ordered fresh herring. She went to the Quay to beg. The sharp eyes of the bird swung round, needle-like in their brightness at the smell of the fish, the long sinewy neck flashed out; in a vast wonder she saw the tail of the herring vanish. Croak! croak! came the low, glad note of thanks, going straight to her heart. Herring after herring vanished in the maw of the starving bird. She stared fascinated, and felt like a mother feeding her babe.

Now she had something to live for. Evening after evening she hastened home to the solace of her ministry, till one night the bird rose up with craning neck, its great wings sweeping the floor—her babe no longer, but a man grown restless for the outer world, as the strong rumour of the sea invaded its haven. With tears she recognised the end of the companionship.

She cut the cord on its feet and felt the bird lusty in her arms. She clung to it, her face whipped with the powerful wings, and staggered to the stair-head. The evening was high, clear, and calm. "Good-bye," she cried, and opened her arms. Up, up, in strong flight, squawking loudly; up into the clear heaven, standing out against the opal sky. Over the Planting into the north it flew, and the monstrous sky was empty.

She returned to her room and sat in the lampless dusk, and in the silence heard the phantom hobbled feet which would never, never more crackle and scrape on the floor. She had lost her second friend.

By the sea-edge, schooled to patience, her face became sadder, her eyes quieter. The silence of the sea, the solitude of the hills were part of her being. In the summer and part of the autumn she ceased from the shore and gathered the swathes behind the mowers. Her body was strong and supple, and she could work without great fatigue for a whole day. The work was a holiday, for it brought respite from solitude. Pleasant to her was the conversation at the dinner-hour in the shade of the hedges. "It's meat an' drink to be wi' folk whiles," she would say cheerily.

The iron of circumstance galled her soul so much now that

she began to dream of eternal rest. She wondered if she would rejoin the plumber. It was the dream of a more wonderful dawn than had ever broken upon her sight across the sea. When overcome with weariness there would steal across her, like music, the thought that rest could be gained at any time in the sepulchre of cool, shadowy darkness at her feet. Sitting on a rock, her whelk-can at her side, she would gaze into the sea beneath her, watching the shimmering green. It was a place unvisited by hunger, unvexed by toil. She whispered to herself that were it not for the kindly face of the land she would go. Fixing a wistful gaze on the wide sky and its sailing clouds, the green of the valleys and the old forests, the isles and the winding beaches, and the sea itself, hung with the shadows of woods as the walls of a room with paintings, she would whisper:

"It's as white and bonny as a waen's cairryin' clothes," and sighing, would bend to scraping again in the tangle. Penury was now disarmed. She went, accompanied by the secret thought of rest.

One morning she saw a dead man in the water beneath Barlaggan. Unafraid she dragged the body ashore; with her shawl dried the yellow-stained face, and in it wrapped the body. She found strength to be alone with the dead; and not till the policeman came that night and questioned her did she know fear. The look of the dead would not depart from her—the wet hair, the blue of the withered eyes, drained for ever of their moisture. "As blae as a berry" they were, she told the policeman.

The following morning she stopped at sight of the Barlaggan beach, suddenly afraid of the sea. Where would *she* have gone? Only now she thought of that. It was a cold, cruel beast, this sea. How its waters had plashed in the open, raw mouth and about the grey hair matted on the temples. What a poor thing *she* would have been bobbing in by the Perch, past the Island, through the herring-boats, till she came all tangled and ragged, with her boots full of water, to the mud beneath the shops—her tippet awry, her dress torn, her breasts wounded, lying on her back, her face up to the sky. The fishermen would carry her away, shaking their heads and whispering. They would not bury her beside the plumber, but in a lonely place, with a piece of wood at her head. No, God be thankit, she hadn't done it, and without looking so much as once, turned her back upon the sea and bade it farewell for ever. She saw the corn wave on Lonend, and a flood of happiness filled her heart. She stood listening to the birds in the wood, and hated death with a great hatred, and the sea, its regent. A long-broken string in the harp was mended. Her mind bloomed like a late winter flower, and people saw on her face a new content. She overtook some children on the road beyond the "Ghost." She did not, as she was used, furtively steal by, but walked behind them, greedy of ear for their babble. She seemed to herself to have suffered resurrection. Her mind was smoothed and folded down out of all asperity. She believed in the compassion of God, in the kindliness of man, and made up her mind—she would open a shop. No longer would she rake on that lonely shore, beside that cruel sea.

She turned in at the door of the Good Templars' Hall. In the ante-room upon a table, in a long black coffin, lay the stranger whom the sea had brought to her feet. To-morrow at noon he was to be buried. Timidly she stepped forward, drawing her shawl about her head, and peered. Something deep down stirred within her—a sense of the sadness and pathos which that strange still face gave to the room. The tears welled up in her eyes. She went forward on tip-toe, touched the cold brow with her hand, and closing her eyes, laid her lips upon the forehead.

With a swelling in her throat she hurried out, scuffled up the street, knocked at the postmaster's door, and asked him if he would rent to her the shop in MacCalman's Lane. Her renunciation was complete. She had triumphed over the sea.

2

FROM the beginning the shop was a failure. It was a little shop with a bell over the door to warn her of the entry of customers when she herself was in the back-room, for she was slightly deaf. At first she sold groceries, but the fishing was a failure; times got steadily worse: she had to give "tick" till her groceries were devoured. She took to sweets—toffee-balls which she made herself; packets of Epsom salts; black thread; Christmas cards; crockery; toys. Her best trade was in weekly journals for boys. The favourite was *The Boys of London and New York*—a pale,

113

green sheet; and, of course, "the penny horrible." Parents spoke to the Receiver of Wrecks, the pompous proprietor of the "Anchor Hotel," who was chairman of the School Board and of the Literary Association. He pulled a severe eyebrow, and said that such pernicious traffic ought to be put down. He was a fitting Oracle, being the father of a brood of children, while poor Topsail was childless. He spoke to Mr. Kennedy, the head master, who refused to interfere with lawful commerce, and uttered the heresy that such literature stimulated the imagination. The Receiver of Wrecks muttered something about men in their dotage, and high time he was retiring.

Topsail, oblivious of this civic wrangling, stood all day behind her counter, a little woman, visible from the shoulders upwards. She could not read. It was pathetic to watch her selling her books. Her face, brooding upon unflagging domestic sorrows, became wary and alert as soon as a boy entered. Her shrewd, persuasive eyes were upon him as she doggedly arranged her books of red-skins with the most cunning disorder. She had a curious air of literary familiarity as she recommended this and disparaged that, just as the coloured picture on the cover caught her fancy. She was especially pleased with careering horsemen. Did a boy hesitate, fingering two alluring volumes with a penny between his teeth, she fancied he had two months ago already perused one of them, and as she stooped to lift a fresh bundle from behind the deeps of the counter, a volume, not under dispute, was whipped into the boy's pocket. Foreign coins were passed upon her when these entered the town; so that the little shop, the solitary isle in the vast sea of her widowhood, was soon swamped. She vended sweets and literature, but scarce could purchase bread. She spent many nights in tears, and at last found refuge in an itinerant Jew who sold boots from a black oilskin pack. The pack carried away her household gods to the pawn-shops of Greenock and Glasgow. Thus, while the front shop glittered with toys and the bright covers of "penny dreadfuls," Topsail shivered in the bleak, denuded back-room. At last she was driven from this desolation to take comfort in the gauds of her shop. And the Jew came no more. Those precious things with which the plumber had lined their little nest were scattered through mean houses in the city of Glasgow; and Topsail, with eyes full of pain, turned the key in the door. She was a piteous spectacle as she shuffled along the pavement and hurriedly crossed the Square into the dazzling

114

light which fell upon her, streaming out from a wide entrance and from three large plateglass windows. Draggled, forlorn, abject, she paused at the brilliant entrance, quaking. She remembered Gillespie as a kind polite gentleman who had visited her husband on a business of pipes, rhones, and the like for Muirhead Farm. It was the remembrance of his kindness which lured her now to his imposing shop, into which she crept with furtive air, watching aghast the trail of muddy water which every step left behind on the clean floor. There was a pleasant air of warmth within. A barrel of apples was tilted up immediately inside the entrance against a stack of biscuits in tin boxes, which were surmounted by wooden boxes full of chocolates. Away on the left was a deep, dim interior, full of bales of cloth, ropes, glittering tin-ware; on the right, shelves were loaded with provisions of all sorts. Her eyes were riveted on a large half-cheese. The smell of the fruit gave a stinging sensation in her thin, dry nostrils, and she felt faint with hunger. She had not imagined there was so much food-stuff in the world as she gazed round the shop. No one was to be seen. Everything was strangely quiet. She heard a clock on the wall in front of her ticking. Uneasily she felt comfortable. The heat from a large oil-lamp beat on her face. Suddenly she heard some one behind her in the entrance stamping the rain from his boots. She turned and saw Gillespie filling the doorway, his large, red face full of soft laughter. He smiled at her and she felt at ease, and jerked a tremulous hand back from her bosom.

"It's a dirty night," he said, and walked slowly towards the counter. She followed like a prisoner.

"Ay," she faltered.

"And what's ado the nicht, Topsail?"

"I canna keep my shop open any longer." There was a hunted look in her eyes. The words burst out involuntarily as she strove to suppress a sob. Her teeth chattered violently.

"I could never understan' what you were doin' wi' a shop. Throwin' money away I'll go bound ye."

She hung her head, chidden.

"An' what's your wull wi' me, Topsail?"

He spoke so sympathetically that she took courage again.

"I'm a done wumman." Her mouth was still trembling so that she could scarce speak. The smell of the apples, pungent in her nostrils, made her faint. The dazzling light of the lamps was hurting her eyes.

"We're a' 'ill aff thae bad times," he said affably; "if I gied tick I'd sune hae to shut my shop lik' yersel'."

His eyes smiled down upon her, their light as oil upon the tumult of her breast.

"I thought ye might gie me a job in the store or at the guttin'." In press of business Gillespie hired the Back Street women, especially on days when there was a big herring fishing.

"It's a job ye're aifter. Weel, I'll gie that my conseederation." But his mind was made up. He needed a servant—one who could turn her hand to anything—in the shop, at the stores, in the house. His wife was become quite useless. He had forbidden her the shop. If he was any judge this woman would suit. On the brink of bankruptcy and starvation, she would be vastly content with bed and board.

"Hae you, Topsail, my wumman; put that in your pooch." He gave her an apple from the barrel. She was dimly conscious through her sudden tears of its red, sleek surface. Gillespie gauged well the effect of the obolus; and that night Topsail slept high up in the garret above the third storey over Gillespie's shop, on a little iron bed, in a room shaped like a coffin. On the morrow, the school-boys, having rushed down the Back Street lane in the ten minutes' interval at half-past-eleven, found her door blankly closed. Their place of commerce was gone, and Brieston became singularly empty, until, on the next day, they learned that a corner of one of Gillespie's counters was reserved for the vending of their literature. The camel had swallowed the gnat. Gillespie omitted to render an account of charge and discharge to Topsail. And she, happy in her asylum, forgot her tawdry books, her shiny toys, her little bundles of tape, black thread, and such-like fry. She was too busy. Deep in the night the flap, flap of her heelless slippers could be heard on the pavement as she scurried to draw sea-water for Gillespie's oysters. By candlelight she could be seen in the washing-house behind the house bending over a tub, and her cheery, nasal voice could be heard singing to the stars, "Last night there were four Mairies," and:

> "O! he sailed East, East,
> And he sailed West, West,
> He sailed unto a Turkish Quay"—

and in the afternoons, with Eoghan upon her knee, and a hungry light of motherhood in her eyes, crooning:

116

> "O love! it is pleasin',
>   O love! it is teasin',
> Love 'tis a pleasure, while it is new;
>   But as you grow older
>   The love it grows colder
> An' fades away like the morning dew"—

and, bubbling with laughter, she would hug and kiss the child, till her vehemence made it cry. Her mistress sat with her hands in her lap, and a wan smile on her face, looking out upon the harbour and its ships. She was thinner now than when at Muirhead, and more beautiful, with her fine face, like ivory, surmounted with its thick coil of raven-dark hair. Gillespie prided himself on the slave he had captured and then forgot all about her. She was another piece of his chattels—a profitable slave. Yet Rome fell by her slaves. Slave and mistress were comrades.

3

Topsail was ill at ease for two weeks because the house was so big. She was also puzzled by Gillespie. The idea slowly ebbed from her mind that he was a kind gentleman. Her mistress, afraid of Topsail's discovery of his ruthless character, tried to blind her. She had sunk to that hopeless level of a wife who, downtrodden, conceals her wound from the world by loyal defence of her husband. Topsail feigned ignorance, though in her heart she regarded her mistress as a child who sat half the day dreaming at the fireside, and telling her servant of the gay Edinburgh days she once had, or at the kitchen window gazing vacantly at the cats on the roof of the washing-house.

Gillespie had discovered the fact—in what way they could not divine—that they were pinching off the bread.

"I used to mand nine shaves off a loaf," he said one morning at the breakfast-table, as he stood, with protruding tongue, slicing down a loaf with a large ham-knife. "The loafs are surely growin' smaller noo-a-days." He cast a quick, suspicious glance at Topsail. "Aifter this I'll cut the loaf mysel'. I'm jaloosin' it's to Brodie's ye go whiles to buy the breid." The two women heard him in guilty silence. "We'll hae pitataes an' herrin' for the dinner," he said, and picking up the portion of the uncut loaf, put it inside the press in the wall. He asked Topsail if she had finished riddling the dross in the ree. She replied that she had. The two women, gazing dumbly at each other, listened till his heavy footsteps died away down the outside stone stair. The face of the mistress was blank with despair; that of Topsail comical in its puzzled, puckered wonderment.

"What'll we do now, Janet?"

Mrs. Strang's mouth drooped sorrowfully, like that of a child who, chidden for a petty fault, is on the brink of tears. Topsail's face was of that summer type that even disaster could not stamp with the mark of fatality. The sunshine of her smile would mitigate the direst stroke of calamity. Her mistress's mouth said—we are lost; Topsail's eyes—there is hope. Her timid, vacillating mistress looked at her with the child-appeal in her humid eyes which never failed of going home to Topsail's heart.

"I don't know what way to turn. Oh! dear me, Janet; to think that Gillespie would say such a thing. I don't know what's coming over him." The bracelet on her wrist rattled as her hand shook.

Topsail feigned to fill her eyes with the dust which her mistress had thrown.

"He's that thrang in the shop he doesna ken what he's sayin'." She flashed her white teeth, nodding her head and smiling. "He'll forget a' aboot it. The morn he'll be comin' runnin' tae ax if we've enough money for the hoose."

"Ye needna say anything about this outside. Lonend might hear about it," answered her mistress.

"Outside!" said Topsail in scorn; "I've mair tae do than be bletherin' tae a wheen women scartin' their heids a' day at the Pump." She spoke vehemently, convincingly.

Feminine artifice having smoothed the matter, the two women cast off the cloak of dissembling and immediately attacked reality.

"We'll just hae to hain off the breid in spite o' him."

In the indomitable light of her eyes victory was assured to the weakling, who looked at Topsail in vague wonder. This cunning Chancellor of the Exchequer opened up cheerful estimates of revenue and expenditure, and laughingly consented to starve herself. There was always one source of income upon which Gillespie could not lay piratical hands. At night in bed Topsail knitted little socks for Eoghan, and asked Gillespie for money to buy them at Mrs. Tosh's.

Yet sources of revenue were desperately limited. Their meagre household necessaries were sent up from that nefarious shop into which Mrs. Strang was not allowed, and where Topsail ventured only in the morning to wash the floor under the eye of Gillespie.

"We'll order a bottle o' the auld Apenty watter."

Mrs. Strang was smiling now. She had a charming, dreary smile.

"Ye'll need to drink a bottle every week for your stomach."

Mrs. Strang had been ordered Apenta water before the birth of Eoghan. Gillespie once took a mouthful and spat it out. "Soor wersch stuff to be spendin' the bawbees on," he said, and would never go back to it. Thereafter it was a safe place for whisky concealed behind the coloured label on the bottle. Topsail had soon become aware of this decanter.

That same afternoon Gillespie was informed by one woman that the other was sick.

"She'll need a bottle o' Apenty watter. She's never been right since she had Eoghan."

Gillespie was eating potatoes and salt herring. A pile of potato skins lay on the table. Topsail was emptying the last of the potatoes from a pot into a cracked plate.

"It's hersel' wanted Eoghan; no' me," he answered, his mouth full of food.

"I'll need three shullin's for breid an' three-an'-six for the Apenty watter." She had turned to the sink, and was rinsing out the pot.

"Whatna breid?"

She flouted him with a laugh. "Hear tae him! Whatna breid! Are we tae live on win'?"

"Hae ye bocht three shullings worth o' breid this week?" It was Friday afternoon.

"Three shullings worth. It wad hae been five shullings if I didna scrape an' sterve mysel' an' her." The pot rattled viciously in the sink. Topsail smiled into it as she thought how she was tickling him with this economic feather.

Gillespie laid down his knife and stretched out his legs beneath the table.

"Let me see the baker's accoont, Janet," he asked with a purr. Here were the methods of the shop being carried into illegitimate quarters of the household.

Topsail was nonplussed.

"Nae use o' fashin' wi' accoonts in the hoose; we're no' acquent wi' that."

"I doot no'," mused Gillespie; "if ye'd wrocht wi' your wee bits o' accoonts ye micht hae been in your wee shop yet."

"I haena a heid for thae things." She was becoming impatient, and rattled the fishpan away from the fireplace.

"It's because ye haena a heid for thae things, Topsail, my wumman, that I want to see the account frae the baker"—he hesitated a moment and rose—"an' frae Kyle the chemist," and with a gentle blistering smile he passed Topsail, giving her a playful clap on the shoulder.

Topsail was beginning to comprehend commerce and Gillespie.

"The cat," she said, looking towards the door out of which he had passed; "the big red cat." Thus she learned that a deeper craft was needed to outwit Gillespie. She would not confess defeat to her mistress. This was not because her mistress would be deprived of her cheering "wee drap in the mornin'." Oh, no! Topsail would see to that somehow; but she could not bear the look of vague alarm in the face of her mistress, and the spectacle of her eyes drowning in misery like kittens in the sea; and hear her pathetic attempts to "redd up" the misunderstanding with her husband. "Dearie me! I don't know what's comin' over Gillespie. He was aye the good man to me at Muirhead. Did I tell ye, Janet, o' the grand party he gave after we were married?" and the clinking of the bracelet would cease along the keys of the piano, and Topsail, with a fond smile upon her patient face, would listen to a tale that had been often told.

4

Dr. Maclean said that Gillespie had solved the problem of the British working woman. Certainly the folk who kept servants envied Gillespie his treasure. It seemed there was nothing which Topsail could not do. She could wield a shovel in the ree; gut and pack herring; harness and stable a horse—Gillespie sent a van now twice a week to the country. His dealings were mainly by barter. He preferred this way of getting fresh country eggs and butter for his shop. He taught Topsail the secret art of making one pound of butter into two by a process of mixing equal parts of butter and of milk, whipping them together in one dish which was placed within another containing hot water for a period sufficient to heat the mixture without allowing it to run to oil. It was then allowed to cool. He sold it a little cheaper than the rate in the other shops, and drew custom. He dared the law in this. He dared the law also in the matter of his scales, which were weighted. Lonend got wind of it, and lodged information with the Inspector of Weights and Measures at Bannerie, who warned Gillespie. Six months later Lonend insisted on the inspector taking action, as the matter had not been remedied. The inspector, arriving by steamer from Bannerie, took Campbell the policeman with him, and paid a surprise visit to the shop in the Square. Gillespie was summoned to appear in court at Bannerie; was fined, and bribed the editor of the local paper to suppress the news. Lonend gloated and told the story in Brodie's.

But Gillespie was impervious to the common tongue. He stripped the lead from his scales and instructed Topsail to commence rearing pigs and poultry; and after the episode of the baker's account to take to baking. She was indifferent in the art, never having had a chance to learn in the vigorous life of scraping the shore and the exacting one of vending literature. She summoned Mary Bunch; and after some mistakes and a little waste of flour and meal, which horrified her—for she was so careful as to husband scraps for two days and of them make a dinner on the third day—she became the most economical, and one of the nimblest and best bakers in the town. Mary Bunch retired, an emeritus-tutor, with a wallet of news for Mrs. Galbraith, the chief item of its contents being the fact that Morag had a penchant for "a glass," and was starved of her "crave" by Gillespie.

Topsail rose as a rule when she was wakened by the fishermen coming home towards the break of day, and dressed herself in a short drugget petticoat of black with a red stripe, and a pair of thick-soled boots which had been given her by Gillespie as wages. The house-work must be got through by the forenoon and the shop cleaned out, for Gillespie had always one or two little tasks of his own for her. Friday was her busiest day. On that day she polished the seven metal covers hanging in a row over the dresser; the two brass candlesticks; the pendulum disc of the wag-at-the-wa' that once told the time to Galbraith, and washed all the jugs, bowls, basins, and china on the shelves. The stairs were steep, and she stumbled under the weight of coals which she carried up from the cellar in the washing-house for the week-end. Then she lit her candle in the damp washing-house when the cats wrangled overhead on the slates, and went through the week's washing. She was afraid of the long-armed shadows swaying on the walls from the wind-shaken flame of the candle. They terrified her with their sombre suggestiveness of menace. She was glad of the feline snarling overhead, and joined in the babel with the "Four Mairies" and "Love, it is pleasin'." Her only taste of fresh air, except when she was hanging the washing over the little back plot which only the sparrows know, was when she blew out the candle, and scurried along the passage, and down to the mouth of the close. In the amenity of the night she felt a strange sense of alleviation, as the wind from the sea cooled her brow. The silence of the great spaces of blue-black darkness and of the shining sky touched the deeps of her soul. She would stand with her eyes upon the stars, watching them with awe, and puzzling dimly as to their life. She believed heaven lay behind those glittering eyes, and wondered if the immaculate plumber looked down in sorrow upon the travail of her life. Then she would scurry through the close and up the stair, tired to the bone, and so wearied that she could scarce sleep. She began to be afflicted with rheumatism in the knees, and there was a swelling about the knuckles of her left hand. Some nights in bed her body was bathed in flame. This was a legacy from her old life on the shore, aggravated by the cold of winter nights; for she had only one thin blanket on her bed. She covered herself with the drugget petticoat.

She was never heard to grumble. Willingness, which was her characteristic, robbed slavery of its thraldom. Even on the day of the annual Fair she was patient and cheerful, though she was worked to death. For the farmers who came to pay their accounts dinner had to be prepared in the front parlour. While the town was still asleep she was up, peering out at the solemn harbour, on which deep shadows from the hills lay like sheets of iron. The parlour was dusted. She never forgot to admire the green plumage of the stuffed parroquet in the glass case, and handled the mummy as if it were alive. The dinner dishes and cutlery were washed and set on the table, and part of the dinner prepared by the time that the organ of the hobby horses began to bray at nine o'clock. Gillespie always ordered "a sheep's inside" for the occasion. Topsail, with hands smeared with blood, cleaned it out; carried the head and trotters to the blacksmith to be singed; made black puddings with the blood supplied by the butcher. She served up the head and trotters with the black puddings and the liver. Gillespie saw it was the cheapest way to feed the farmers, who arrived in the afternoon with hunger in their big, red faces. The younger men nudged Topsail in passing, winking and leering at her, and inviting her to come out for her "fairing," passed their nasty jokes to each other across her face. Their boots were grey with mud. Their dogs followed them, sniffing around, and soiled the horse-hair furniture. "The more the merrier," cried Gillespie jovially at the stair-head. He was always in good form on the day of the Fair. While they were eating, Topsail herded the dogs to the washing-house and fed them there. As the day advanced a babel of noise filled the sea-shore street, thick now with people come from Mainsfoot to Bannerie. The Square in front of the house was crammed with horses. Strung around the harbour-front were the booths, the shows, the swings, the shooting-galleries, the ice-cream and fruit-stalls. The nickering of mares, the clatter of horses' hoofs, the cries of showmen jugglers; and the yelling of coopers, negroes, and men in charge of roulette-boards; the blasphemy of drunkards; and over all, the booming of the organ at the hobby horses rang in her ears all day; and she had scarcely leisure to look out on the welter. Long after the last naphtha light had gone out, she would stagger like one sleep-walking up the narrow, rickety stair to her iron bed in the Coffin, wondering where, in the morning, she would begin to attack the pile of dinner dishes. Gillespie always gave her a bag of painted sweets for her "fairing." These, when he got a little older, she always gave to Eoghan.

"That's my fairin' to you, my darlin'," she would say, with an access of tenderness, almost cheating herself into the belief that she had bought them for him. It never occurred to her that she *had* bought them at a price, though she had not purchased them for coin of the realm. It was the one gleam of comfort in that long, weary, harassing day that her gift would be ready for her darlin'. The light of angels' wings hovered about the paper bag in her bosom, and brought a tender smile to her face as it took the pillow in heavy sleep. At her second Fair a well-to-do farmer from Mainsfoot slipped a shilling into her hand as he was passing out. She had never received a tip before, and looked down at the coin in wonder, thinking the man had made some mistake. That night she slipped across the blazing Square to the dark lane at the Bank, and down through the Back Street to Brodie's. Within half-an-hour, with gleeful eyes and flashing teeth, she thrust her "fairing" upon her mistress.

It was the night of "wee Setterday," the last night of the year. The shops were open late; and Topsail was at the close-mouth. The lights of the town gleamed round the Harbour. Men and women, boys and girls moved briskly across the Square and up and down the streets. The stars overhead glittered in a brittle sky of frost. There was no one to speak to her. The loneliness of her life was extreme. The days of a happy childhood rushed back upon her; the happiness of being wooed and wed by the plumber. Then the veil of dreams within, which was her holy of holies, was rent by the hand of sorrow—the sorrow and emptiness of her later life, its bitter struggle, its childlessness, its penury, its chains. She sighed deeply as she timidly looked out on the thronged Square and the sea-shore street ablaze round the Harbour. She was about to creep up the close when she heard a thud, thud on the pavement that ran up from the corner of the house to the close-mouth. The one-legged man came nearer with a step now "forte" now "piano."

"It's a fine night," he said.

He was about to pass on; but something softer than ordinary in Topsail's voice stayed his wooden leg.

"Ay! a braw night, Jeck."

He leaned against the wall, took out and lit a cigarette. He was a lithe man, with red face and grey eyes, and a head that butted forward a little. In his youth he had been one of the crew in an American millionaire's yacht, which haunted the Mediterranean ports. He had seen Paris; had looked down the crater of Vesuvius; had visited the catacombs of Rome, following "the gentry" with rugs or lunch-basket, but in his own words he had "touched wood," meaning thereby that he had suffered a fall on a dark, windy night on deck, and come home with a wooden leg. Since then he had stood every day on the Quay, watching the commerce in coal and herring, and smoking cigarettes in a vast idle content. But cigarettes and a wooden leg being useless to appease hunger, he became the man of the Pier. Possessed of a large two-wheeled barrow, he transported luggage to the hotels; caught the steamer's lines; carried the baggage of "swells" aboard the steamer, and was the commercial travellers' man. Suave as an Oriental, he gently but firmly took their show cases and wheeled them from door to door of the shops, devouring cigarettes. He was known as "Jeck the Traiveller." In his slack hours he stood among the fishermen on the quay-head in the lee of the "Shipping Box," leading them with the most fabulous lies across Southern Europe. They were particularly interested in the doings of the American millionaire—his drinking-bouts, and of how, in his cups, he would descend and, for a wager, shovel coals with his own stokers; how, being a brawny man, he would fell them on the plates with his fist, and soothe the wound in the sober morning with a five-pound note. There was a rivalry to submit to the blows of this butcher. Jeck the Traiveller, always in a slipper and cigarettes, mimicked the American accent, pirouetting, cigarette in hand.

These Ulysses tales gave an itch to the young fishermen to seek adventure, crisp bank-notes, and wooden legs in Mediterranean yachts. Ah! he knew about ladies, this Jeck. When wheeling his traveller's kit through the Square to Gillespie's shop his tarry eye had fallen athwart the buxom Topsail, and we behold him about to coquette with the lady at the close-mouth on "wee Setterday." He opened in the orthodox way by casting an amorous glance upon her and inviting her to go for a walk. She laughed mirthfully.

"I dinna walk wi' wan-leggit men."

The experiences which Jeck the Traiveller's far-famed itineraries had harvested were not wide enough to meet this rebuff. He was baffled; not beaten.

"Have ye had your Hogmanay, Janet?"

She shook a smiling face in the glow of his cigarette. He offered to step round the corner into Gillespie's for the necessary poke. Topsail blithely accepted this manna of the night; and the talk veered from amorous trifles to the stern realities of life, as Topsail quietly munched the Hogmanay. Jeck gave her the news of the town and the Pier. The last thing he did was to carry up three scuttles full of coal against the morning. He felt that by these labours he had made an appreciable inroad upon her affections. And every Friday night we behold him whistling upon his wooden leg at the mouth of the close at nine o'clock; and, being an ardent and impatient wooer, sending her a communication by post. It was the first time that His Majesty's Postal Service had ever been employed on the affairs of Topsail Janet. The missive was a gaudy post-card which Topsail naturally delivered into Gillespie's hands. On the portion of one side was written "Janet Morgan"; on the other, "space for communication," these words—"God be with you till we meet again."

She received a rebuff or two every day from Gillespie. Soon she learned to expect nothing else, intermingled with sneers, covert or open. At first she had taken his jibes to heart, thinking him a kind man, and that the fault was hers. But quick to discover that her mistress was also the target of his mockery and rudeness, she found his jibes tolerable.

He held the post-card between his forefinger and thumb.

"Topsail," he cried, "hae ye a lover?"

"Ay," she replied.

"An' whaur is he, may I speir?"

"In heaven."

Gillespie was taken aback. "Nane sae bad an answer," he said, "frae the writin' that's here—'God be with you till we meet again.'"

A flame surged over Topsail's face, and her hands trembled. Could the dead send messages by the post from beyond the stars? Her mouth opened slowly upon Gillespie; her eyes filled with a vague alarm.

"Gie me that," she said, with a quaver in her voice.

Gillespie flicked it in front of her face. "I think I'll show't to the minister—the bonny bit sermon." Mockery darted from his eyes.

"I daur ye; I daur ye," she screamed, and darting out her hand snatched the sacred missive from desecration and fled up the stairs, up, up to her still Coffin, where she sat down on the bed and pored on the face of the cardboard. It was pale grey, with a border of gold, and gaudy with facsimile stamps at all angles. The position of each stamp was interpreted by a honeyed phrase beneath it. Long did Topsail gaze, till the gold edge round the card became a ribbon of stars in the blue, and the shining face of the stamps a patch of the spangled heavens. At last, in some mysterious way, the plumber had spoken. She repeated the words softly to herself, "God be with you till we meet again," and the tears sprang in her eyes. Fervently she kissed the jewels of the skies, and slipped the divine benediction within her bosom. With shining eyes and flushed face she descended to the kitchen. Her conversation with her mistress became voluble and a little wild—was heaven full of stars like ribbons of gold, and how did mortals transported thither send these pearls of Paradise to those upon this earth—on the wings of angels, was it? Her mistress, sunk in dreams—they had been more than ordinarily lucky at Brodie's that morning—nodded vaguely, and murmured that the kitchen was full of the drift of angels' wings. A bar of sunlight swarming with gnats had slanted into the gloom of the kitchen. To Topsail the air was full of a mighty throbbing. Her fingers stole into her bosom till they touched the post-card, and suddenly she burst out singing in a loud, harsh voice:

"God be with you till we meet again .
Till we me-ee-et"—

The thinner voice of her mistress quavered in unison:

"Till we me-ee-et,
Till we meet at Jesus' feet;
Till we me-ee-et,
Till we me-et,
God be with you till we meet again."

At the close of the hymn there was a long silence in the kitchen. The sunbeam and the motes died away, and Topsail stood gazing out of the window at the departing glory with her awed face lifted up to heaven.

That night she lay with the post-card beneath her cheek, and dreamed of bulwarks in the skies crusted with stars, over which the plumber leaned, picking them out and pasting them on to a letter. He beckoned to her with his hand and let the letter fall. As she ran beneath the heavens with her apron out, and caught the letter, a great glory of light struck upon her face, and with a gasp she opened her eyes to the broad day. She was late, and heard Gillespie shouting:

"Are ye in a trance, Topsail?"

"I'm comin', I'm comin'," she cried, leaping from bed. She thrust the post-card in her bosom and there, like a flower, she wore it all the morning. After dinner she had to go to the coal-ree. While riddling dross there behind the stable a horror of a great fear seized her. The plumber would be anxiously awaiting an answer. She hurried through her work and returned to her mistress, to whom she displayed the holy missive.

"This is a caird I got frae the plumber. Is he wantin' an answer?"

Her mistress, freed from the spell of dreams, turned a more alert face upon her.

"What plumber, Janet?"

"Him that's deid an' gone."

"Janet! Janet! what are you saying? The dead cannot send cards."

A look of misgiving came into Topsail's face, but she fought for the hope that was in her. "It's fu' o' wee stars."

Her mistress stretched out a languid hand. "Show me the post-card."

Topsail gave it up and devoured her mistress with her eyes.

"God be with you till we meet again."

"Ay! ay!" cried Topsail with irradiated face, taking an eager step forward.

"This is signed 'Jeck.' Who is Jeck?"

And in a flash Topsail understood. A single bright tear for the perished hope welled up on her eyelid.

"It's no' frae him, aifter a'," she sighed.

"It's from Jeck," answered her mistress, who had turned over the card and was now laughing.

"What is't?" Topsail's face was puzzled.

"It's the language of stamps."

"Whatna thing is that?" Sorrow was warring with curiosity.

"Here is one which says, 'Forget-me-not,'" her mistress read.

"The black-a-viced deevil," cried Topsail. "Forget him! It was only Friday night I saw him at the close-mouth."

"Answer at once," read her mistress, twisting the card round to the angle of the stamp.

"Answer! aw! I'll gie him his answer."

"Write to me as soon as possible."

" 'Clare tae God! Does he think I'm the school-maister?"

"Come soon."

"Aw! you bate I'll come wi' the brush in my hand."

"Do you remember me?"

"Aw! the timmer-leggit gomeril." Tears of mirth were now in Topsail's eyes.

128

"A kiss," went on her mistress.

"A kiss! is that on the caird? Aw! the fule, has he nae sense o' shame?"

"I love you: do you love me?"

Topsail gasped. "God keep us; the auld fule. Just you wait; just you wait, my man; puttin' a' thae havers through the post-office; the black-a-viced, timmer-leggit, tarry fule."

Jeck the Traiveller, emboldened by his amatory correspondence, whistled loud and boldly at the close-mouth and had not long to wait.

"Ye got the caird, Janet?" he asked anxiously.

"Ay! I got the caird, Jeck."

"The words o' the stamps is just what's in my he'rt." He came a step nearer.

"Then ye hae a geyan he'rt fu', Jeck."

"Janet! wad ye no' lik' to leave Gillespie's? There's nothing like a hoose o' your ain."

"Ay! your ain ribs is the best to rype."

He had piloted the wooden leg up alongside her.

"Janet! wad ye be willin' to tak' up hoose along wi'me?" Deftly his arm went around her waist.

She looked him full in the face for the fraction of a second, and the next smacked him where she had looked.

"I've a wheen pigs tae look aifter already; I dinna want anither."

And Jeck the Traiveller went on a blasphemous and hurried itinerary up the lane.

Topsail remained at the close-mouth watching him till he had stumped round the corner. Then her eyes gravely searched the stars and she sighed. The sigh was not for Jeck, but for the face lost for ever behind the cold glittering constellations.

5

But Topsail had a love upon earth that satisfied in the baulked mother the child-hunger which had burned like a fire in her bosom these ten years. Eoghan was her child in everything but the bearing of it, and was a constant source of wonder to her. She would sit by the hour with the baby on her knees, examining its body; and when she heard the sucking noise which the child made with its thumb in its mouth, she ached to undo her tawdry blouse and press that mouth to her breast. She conned its body and repeated to the listless mother all she noted—the dark, tiny hairs on its legs, the creases of fat on its shoulders and neck. Every smile of the baby called forth an answering smile from Topsail who, when it cooed, answered with chuckle after chuckle. If the child cried with colic, her heart would leap to her mouth in fear. The mother became jealous and, in a fit of passion, would snatch the baby into her arms and hug it to her breast.

On the whole it was a good child, though it showed on occasion signs of temper; but when it fell asleep this was forgotten, and all Topsail's being surged up out of the depths, choking her with tenderness. "Oh, the wee wean; the wee henny lamb;" and she would sit devouring it with her eyes, immobile as a statue for fear of wakening it. She was glad to hear its cry during the night, because Gillespie had once summoned her to nurse the child, calling his wife a "sleepy-heid." Now she would steal down the stairs and, picking up the wailing creature, would scurry to her own room and steal into bed, the baby in her arms.

It was about this time, when the child was some twelve months old, that Topsail conceived the idea that her mistress should bear another child. "I canna do withoot a wean," she said; but her mistress looked at her with lack-lustre eyes, and, wearily smiling, shook her head. It was about this time also that Jeck the Traiveller, who had discovered her passion for children, despoiled the wall of his mother's house, and presented Topsail with a faded steel engraving of Christ blessing little children, which she hung on the wall of the Coffin. She loved Christ for His love of little children; and often as she held the babe in her arms she would gaze up at His face in awe. She did not understand this Jesus, who lived far beyond the blue, and was seized with trembling when she remembered that He had been hanged upon a Cross; but her eyes would fill with tears as she gazed at Him surrounded by children. Once as she looked she heard the singing of invisible birds high up in the sky—a tumult of choragic larks. She peered out from her sloping window, holding the child's face up to the heavens, and thought that angels stirred in the sky. A strange peace filled her soul. "Och! Eoghan! Eoghan!

he's up there." It was the first time she had called the babe by its name as she thought of her husband in heaven. She wished to go to church. Gillespie acquiesced and suggested the Parish Church, because he was a deacon in the Free Church. It would do his trade no harm if one of his household were connected with the other church. She went for two Sundays, and was vastly disappointed in Mr. Stuart, who spoke too quickly. There was no stirring of angels in the heavens, no singing in the skies, and she returned famished to Jesus and the little children and her own babe. As she put off her widow's weeds she ardently wished she had been one of the mothers of Salem, and had seen His face on that wonderful day. Her heart beat strongly in her bosom at the thought. She felt faint, and cast her eyes down from the picture upon the floor in shame of her boldness. She hurried with her dressing, and hastened downstairs to the kitchen to set the dinner, but discovered that her mistress had neglected to prepare it as she had promised. She heard Gillespie's voice in the parlour angrily rating his wife. She very soon forgot her worries, however, because Eoghan had cut a tooth.

6

GILLESPIE was now a man in middle life, ruddy, weather-tanned, with lank hair streaked over a hard, intellectual forehead. His determined jaw ran like a streak of stone down to his tight trap mouth. He had the look of a man who would thrive in the midst of competition, and find something to pick up no matter where he was. He was becoming a man of standing in Brieston, and was asked to supper in other people's houses, through the influence of Lowrie the banker. Gillespie would have declined these invitations, but overcame his antipathy, because he spread thickly the butter which he had the keenest zest in eating at the tables of other men, took pride in his tactics, and brought them to his wife's observation with gusto. On returning from church he took from his pocket a fair-sized handful of sweets.

"I clean forgot them," he said to his wife, "till I felt them in my pooch the day." They had been handed round at the banker's with nuts during the previous Wednesday evening. Mrs. Strang, with a pleased look on her face, held out her hand.

"Put them in the bottle o' mixtures"—he had an air as of achieving something notable; "they'll sell to the weans lik' the rest."

"I never thought you could be so mean." With a look of disgust on her face she refused to handle the sweets. He thrust his head forward.

"Is't no' draps o' rain that fill the watter-barrel?" He took a keen pleasure in discoursing his prolegomena, "an' whiles a rain-barrel full is enough to mak' the fountain-heid o' a burn if ye start it in the right place; an' it's no' the first burn that has turned oot a braw river."

"Or a dirty one," she flashed.

"Hoots," he said softly; "I'm no' speakin' o' the burn at the Muirhead Ferm."

She flung up her head angrily.

"I'd rather be there with the right man, than stealin' sweeties from Lowrie the banker." Her cheeks flamed scarlet.

He was nettled.

"An' wha's the right man?"

"It's no' a sweety merchant, anyway."

"Sweety merchant!"—he tossed the sweets from one hand to the other—"is it no' the sweety merchant ye hae to thank that ye're no' milkin' coos an' forkin' dung frae morn till nicht?"

Traces of youthful pride still left in her flared up.

"I've you to thank for taking me away from plenty and decency at Lonend. Where's the tocher I brought ye? Didn't it set you on your feet? You were in rags when you came trapping the rabbits about Lonend. I'm ashamed when I think of what I left there."

The scene was uncommon. Usually his wife made no show of fight, but mournfully acquiesced in all that he did. Gillespie had begun by neglecting her. After the birth of Eoghan he ignored her. When he discovered that she drank he scrupulously kept her from his shop and despised her, grudging her her food. This course of action was more dangerous with her than with the ordinary run of women. As a girl she had dreamed of the intoxication of life. As a school-girl in Edinburgh she and other girls used to whisper with heads together about young men, and smuggled doubtful books into their rooms. *Sappho* had gone from hand to hand. They had witnessed it at the theatre, and had confessed disappointment with the presentation. This intoxication in life was denied her. She had long, idle dreams, and taking whisky at Eoghan's birth as medicine, grew fond of it. Gillespie was too much engrossed in the theory and practice of commerce to hold out to this passionate nature even crumbs. Rapidly they drove apart, each on a different gale of desire. Such a Sunday bickering was an angry signalling, as each drifted from the other, to seek out the satisfaction which life had to offer.

Gillespie passed through the kitchen with a flushed face, and descended the outside stone stair. Topsail heard him tramping along the back passage to the shop. He carried the sweets in his left hand. She scurried into the parlour. Her mistress was aimlessly turning over the boards of the album on the table.

"I met Mrs. Galbraith comin' from church"—her mistress looked up, smiling faintly—"she's axed ye to tea the morn's nicht at six o'clock."

Her mistress made no response.

"Ay," urged Topsail, her white teeth flashing in a grin.

"I wonder if she'll have any sweeties," her mistress said, musingly.

"Ach, sweeties!" Topsail blew contemptuously. "I told her she'd better hae a wee drap in."

7

But if his wife understood his greed, Brieston held Gillespie to be a rising man. The Banker, for reasons of his own, introduced him at supper parties to men of standing in the town. At one of these parties the question of the Poor Law Clerkship was discussed. It was vacant. No one was surprised when Gillespie received the appointment. It carried with it the post of Sub-collector of Taxes. "He's gettin' a big man," said Brieston with pride. He had a fair face and an obliging way with every one.

"Ay," said the Butler; "it's the like o' McAskill, a limb of the law, that speaks well o' him. It doesna do for corbies to pike oot corbies' een," and added with a sneer, "Souple Gillespie." The name stuck to him. "Souple Gillespie! I'm filled with nausea every time I see the cormorant."

Dr. Maclean, to whom he spoke, was a fair-minded man. "He has business capacity: his thrift is never done."

"Bah!" cried the Butler, "you don't know him; if every man in the place stuck a knife into him he wouldn't bleed."

But the fact is that the town looked on Gillespie as a public benefactor. Lucky had a good word for him at the Pump.

"He's mekin' a fortune oot o' kippered saithe. Ee noo in slack times he'll buy a box for a trifle an' sell them at two a penny smocked, or a dozen for sixpence. They're tasty fried wi' dreepin'. Mind you it's no' every sixpence worth 'ill go roond a family. I'm telt he's sellin' a pound's worth every day."

A benefactor indeed. Think of his plan of making one pound of butter into two. "All milk an' butter; no margareen aboot this." Think of how he cut out the smaller shopkeepers. If the men bought an ounce of tobacco and two boxes of matches he threw in a coarse clay pipe. Soon he had the tobacco trade of the fishing fleet. Oh! there was nothing in tobacco. But gradually he came to supply stores to the fleet. And what a way he had. On Monday mornings, when victualling the fleet, he would force ham and cheese upon the men.

"We hevna been in the habit o' eatin' ham at the fishin'."

"Just that," he answered. "Ye'd raither go to Brodie's wi' the money. Is ham no' better for ye than a pint o' raw grain wi' a touch o' pepper an' a drap o' saut watter in't? It's a wonder the tubes is no' burned oot o' ye. You try a pun' o' ham an' ye'll mand a dreg o' herrin' better the nicht. Good luck to ye, boys." As for payment he would humorously order the men out of the shop on the Saturday of a poor week's fishing.

"Hoots! boys! wait till ye hae a bundle o' notes." The money earned during the week was shared among the crew on a Saturday afternoon in the rooms of the public-houses. A share was laid aside for stores. Two men of the crew were delegated as paymasters. If it was a good week, when anything up to £200 fell to be shared among the eight men of the two "company" boats, Gillespie would turn up his books. He made up no detailed account.

"That will be four poun' ten shullin's, boys," or, "It'll run to seeven poun' fifteen shullin's."

The money was tabled; no receipt was asked or given; the

men never knew when they were "clear." All they knew was—and it was a prideful boast at the "Shipping Box"—that "on the Setterday o' a big fishin' Gillespie has a spale-basket behind the coonter to hold the pound notes." It was very far yet to the time when the common taunt was hurled at him. "It was the fishermen that made ye an' fed ye."

They had been a race of seafarers, father and son, since the town had had a name; in olden days trading salt herring with the smacks of France for cognac and silk. They were born to the sea—fishermen with shares in a boat or owning boats and gear—big boats too; smacks which sailed the western seas from the Mull of Cantyre to Stornoway.

From time immemorial they had used the drift-net: but while he was in Muirhead Gillespie saw that the day of the trawl-net was coming. It was the transition period. Government declared trawling to be illegal, and sent a cruiser to patrol the Loch. The Brieston men were the chief culprits. Drift-net work was tedious. They had to hang by the drift-net all night and "shot it" on the chance of getting herring. With the trawl-net it was different. They watched for signs of fish. The single "plout" of a herring would sometimes reveal a whole school of fish, and at once the trawl was out between the two "company" boats, and in again within two hours with sufficient fish in the bag of the net to fill half-a-dozen boats. The "fry" of the herring—the bubbles which they put up—was another sign; or when they rose to the surface to "play"; or the diving of solan geese; or in late summer and autumn the "stroke" of the herring in the water, that is, the trail of flame which it made when darting through the phosphorescent sea. A common practice on these occasions, on moonless autumnal nights, was to strike the anchor on the bow head as the skiff sailed along, and startle the fish, which darted away trailing fire. On such nights this loud noise of "crepping the anchors" could be heard over all the fleet.

But whatever the signs of fish were, anything up to two hundred boxes at a pound sterling a box might be had within a couple of hours. Not infrequently the Fishery Cruiser caught them in the act. The trawl was cut away and sunk. But what was a trawl when one lucky "shot" would bring them the price of half-a-dozen trawls? Was Gillespie not a benefactor? He supplied the trawls. It was only in reason, as the men were bound to recognise, that he raised the price of trawl-nets gradually—£35, £40, £45,

£50. Look at the risk he was taking. He was liable to fine and imprisonment like themselves at Ardmarkie. He sympathised with them on the loss of their nets. It was a shame that the officers and men of the cruiser were allowed with impunity to search the houses for trawl-nets—and on a Sunday, too, when the men were at church. Peggy More was arrested for attacking one of them with a stool. Yes; he had heard that she had given birth to a child in jail. It was horrible. But never give in, boys. The time of free trawling was coming. No one seemed to suspect that the Government men had accurate knowledge of the houses and lofts which concealed trawl-nets. It was impossible that an informer could live in Brieston—not even Gillespie had the taint of suspicion, even though he profited by the sales of trawl-nets. It is true that he was seen walking above the "Ghost" with a telescope in his hand, but that was only to see if there were any boats about with herring. For now there was no question whatever about Gillespie being a grand benefactor. He had turned herring buyer in a dramatic fashion. His had been a superb action. He saved hundreds of pounds worth of fish from destruction, and mounted to the zenith of popularity.

8

In foul weather Gillespie walked the wharves and quays, and nosing about among herring-boxes and fish-guts, would ask the fishermen and smacksmen news of the fishing. This was accounted to him for sociability. He entered into the interests of their trade and knew the baffling tides of their fortune, and picked up information, carelessly noting everything of importance that fell.

Especially he watched the methods of the herring buyers. These were two. Either out on the Loch in smacks which, when a full cargo was taken aboard, set sail for Glasgow. If there was no prospect of wind they offered a low price for the herring because of the risk of transport. On Saturday mornings the smacksmen refused to buy at all. Other buyers waited on the quays to which those fishermen came who found no market among the smacks. On the days of a "big fishing" the fishermen had sometimes to throw whole skiff-loads into the Harbour for want of a market.

The Quay buyers were meagre men. They rarely risked more than twenty boxes, which they sent to Glasgow by luggage steamer; other trifling boxes they bought on commission for merchants in Rothesay, Dunoon, and Helensburgh. Gillespie was soon master of their methods. He noticed they were a fraternity. If one of them happened to be a little earlier on the Quay than the others he bought up the fish—to share them later on with the slug-a-beds. Gillespie pointed out to the fishermen this heinous lack of competition.

He studied the flow and ebb of the Glasgow Fish Market, and keenly watched the Baltic ports as a haven for salt herring. He discovered that Manchester and Liverpool would take unlimited supplies of fresh herring packed in ice. And he waited patiently. No one knew that he had leased from the Laird the long row of stores and curing-sheds stretching along the shore road from the Quay. On a June morning of perfect calm, when ducks were swimming about in the Harbour, a skiff was seen coming in at the Perch, deep to the gunwales. The men on the beams were sitting on herring as they rowed. She was followed by a second, a third, a fourth, and a fifth, under clouds of gulls. The smacksmen had refused to buy. The half-dozen buyers on the Quay were in a flutter, running about like hens, sharing their empty stock. They bought some seventy boxes between them. There yet remained four and a half boats of herring. The fishermen were now offering these at any price—instead of being offered; at five shillings a box, four shillings, three, two, one. Standing on the Quay and looking down upon these fishermen in their loaded boats, one caught a look of pathos upon their rugged faces, tawny with sweat threshed out of them in a fifteen-mile pull in the teeth of the tide. Their tired eyes were grey like the sea, their blue shirts with short oilskin sleeves were laced with herring scales; and herring scales smeared the big fishing boots which come up over the knee; their hands were slippery with herring spawn; even their beards and pipes were whitened. Everywhere a flood of light poured down. It stiffened and blackened the blood of the bruised fish, and the heat brought up that tang of fish and that savour of brine which have almost an edge of pain, so sharp, haunting, and fascinating are they in the nostrils of men who have been bred as fishers and have lived upon the salt water. The spectacle was compelling in its beauty, in its suggestion of prodigal seas and of the tireless industry and cunning craft of man; and at the same time sad with the irony of circumstance—niggard dealers haggling, shuffling, sniffing in the background. The dotard buyers shook their heads, though their mouths watered. They could not cope with one hundredth part of the fish. It was too early in the season for curing. Besides, they had no empty stock. One of them, in slippers, with a narrow face and rheumy eyes, gave a doleful shake of his head. "No use, boys. It's the big market for them." The "big market" was the sea. What a heartbreaking task was there— to basket all these fish into the sea. These fishermen had laboured all the night and toiled home through the long, blazing morning. The fish were worth ten shillings a box in Glasgow. To basket herring up on the Quay and into the boxes—the music of chinking gold was in it; but into the Harbour—how green and still it was—that was hell.

A deep silence fell down the length of the Quay. One by one the fishermen, with dumb faces, sat down on the gunwales, the oars, or the beams, eyeing the load of fish. An old man seated on the stern beam of the second boat lifted a massive head slowly and took off his round bonnet. He seemed to be invoking Heaven. As they had come homewards in the break of day to the sweep of the oars, he was given the tiller, being too old for that long pull. As he leaned upon the tiller he had dreamed in the somnolent morning of the spending of money. The sun glanced and shone on his round, bald head. The streaks of grey hair were smeared with herring scales. He opened his mouth as if to speak, then closed it hopelessly in acquiescence of Fate. The frustrate words were more eloquent of despair than any rhetoric. Some one forward said "Ay! ay!" and sighed deeply. The old man bent and lifted a herring. He held it a moment aloft in the glittering sunlight; then he tossed it into the sea. It fell with a plout which seemed to crash in through the tremendous silence. Every eye followed it, wriggling down to the bottom. The old man nodded to the crews.

"Gull's meat, boys! gull's meat;" and he collapsed in the stern beam, huddled up, a piteous, forlorn wisp, stupidly nursing the old rusty round bonnet in his hands. An air of profound sorrow hung over the boat. She seemed chained in white, gleaming

138

manacles. It was not precious food that was aboard any longer but ballast.

The uneasy shuffling of men's feet on the causewayed Quay—all the idlers of the town had assembled—was now the only sound which broke the silence. In the clean face of bountiful heaven it was an indecency, a crime, to cast that bulk of food back to the sea, which lay with the patience and the sombre expectation of the grave on its sparkling face.

"Sanny, my man, hold up your pow." The words were spoken in a quiet penetrating voice. As if he were a child on a bench at school, the old man lifted his bowed head and looked into a red, jolly face. Every eye was turned with Sandy's upon Gillespie, who stood alone, leaning against the head pile of the Quay, with his baffling whimsical gaze steady on the old man's face.

"Ye've had a touch, Sanny." We call a real big haul "a touch."

"Ay! Gillespa', a bonny touch, tae feed the gulls."

Gillespie was broadly laughing without making any audible sound.

"That's no' work for a man that has been fifty years at the fishin', Sanny." Every one present had pricked ears. A subtle change had come into the atmosphere. It was indescribably charged with hope. The old man lifted up his bonnet and put it on his head. It was an act partly of reverence, partly signalising that a crisis had been past.

"Boys"—Gillespie's quick gaze swept round the boats and his voice rang out cheerily—"I'll buy the five boats at a shilling a box." An uneasy silence fell down the Quay. Men glanced at one another, and then stole an amazed look at Gillespie. A voice, like the crack of a whip on the still air, rang out from one of the boats. "By Goäd, but you're a man."

Andrew Rodgers padded softly in his slippers up to Gillespie, his slit eyes blinking as if he had arisen from sleep. He came of a race of fish-men. His father had cadged herring through Bute, buying them in a little lugsail. He was tacitly recognised as chief of the coterie of buyers, all of whom deferred to him. He lived in a house overlooking the Quay, and was accustomed to have the fishermen wait on him. They awakened him in the early morning by throwing mud and chuckies on his window-pane. He knew that Gillespie had "a big thing" in the stuff, but where was his empty stock? Besides, it was impossible to get the fish to Glasgow that day. The luggage steamer was gone. The next day at evening was the soonest the fish could reach the city. The market would then be closed. The stuff would have to lie on the Broomielaw till the following day. Three whole days in this heat. The bellies would be out of the fish. He smiled up in Gillespie's face sardonically.

"Fine, man, fine; is it manure for Muirhead ye're buyin'?" As he looked down on the shimmering bulk of fish his face was contorted with a spasm of hatred. He, the best buyer on the Quay, not so much as asked by your leave. The other buyers, the idlers, and fishermen looked on at the duel. Gillespie from his broad jovial height purred down on the acidulous little man.

"Hoots! Andy, I've gien ower the fermin': I'm goin' to try my hand at the buyin'."

"Ye'd better go to the school first an' learn a wee."

"I've bocht them at a shullin'. Can you buy them chaper?" A roar of laughter went up from the Quay. Gillespie, still smiling, said, "I'll stan' doon an' gie ye a chance yet, Andy."

"I winna tek' the damn lot at fivepence."

"No, man."

The withering words stung.

"Ye should learn to buy fish afore ye leave the back o' the coonter. Ye'll come doon heavily on this," snapped Andy.

The other buyers felt this was a just warning. The man was a fool to take all that perishable stuff on his hands.

"Andy, my man"—Gillespie spoke as if chiding a fractious child—"they're gran' herrin', are they no? worth half-a-soävrin' the box."

Andy's inane laugh cackled loudly over the Quay.

"Half-a-soävrin'!" The idea spurted out ribald laughter. He shuffled about in his slippers. "Up wi' your herrin', boys; Gillespie's goin' to fill them in sweetie boxes." All the buyers wheezed with foolish mirth; but old Sandy stood up in the stern with flashing eyes and whipped the carved tiller from the rudder head.

"If I was as near ye, Andy, as I'm far from ye, I'd mek' ye feel the wecht o' this." He swung the tiller about his head. "Gillespa's bocht the fish. That's more than ye could do, ye louse. Ye hevna the he'rt o' a pooked dooker."

In the midst of the laughter Andy roared:

"Away up to the shop in the Square, Sandy, an' cairry doon the sweetie boxes."

Gillespie laid a hand on his shoulder. "Come wi' me, Andy, an' I'll show ye my sweetie boxes." He turned to the boats, "You Ned, an' you Polly, an' you, an' you," —he pointed with his forefinger to the young men of the crews—"come an' cairry doon the sweetie boxes."

All the Quay and half the crews babbling followed Gillespie. He turned to the left, passed along the dike of the Square, above the Quay, stopped at the first of the doors in the long line of sheds and stores belonging to the Laird, and took a key out of his pocket.

"Are they your stores?" snapped Andy.

Gillespie nodded.

"Well, I'm damned, boys; an' never a word aboot it."

"This key's a wee roosty," answered Gillespie, and turning it gratingly pushed open with knee and hand the big red door. From ceiling to floor the store was packed with splinder-new herring barrels and boxes, tier upon tier. Quietly, unassumingly, Gillespie had had a score or so of these boxes and barrels brought down to him from Glasgow in every gabbart and puffer which had borne coal for his ree. The surprise of the rented stores was nothing to this.

"Goäd, boys," some one in the background shouted, "Gillespa' hes a forest o' barrels."

The crowd surged forward, peering at the miracle. Gillespie had forgotten Andy. That cheap sort of triumph had no appeal for him.

"Now, boys! now, boys!" he cried briskly, rubbing his hands; "doon wi' the boxes to the Quay. I'm in a hurry."

Andy was athirst. "Where in the name o' Goäd did ye steal the barrels?"

Gillespie shouldered past him. "Dae ye no' see I'm thrang, man?"—his tone was faintly irascible. "The bit sweetie boxes cam' frae the shop"; and with a jerk of his hand he brought the first tier of barrels to the floor.

"Hurry now, boys; I must catch the market." He kicked a barrel to the door. There was an air of capacity and mastery about the man.

"He'll likely hae a steamer in the other store." Andy's very eyes rolled with irony.

"When the herrin's filled I'll show ye the steamer. An' noo, Andy, ye'll hae to stan' aside. Ye're wastin' time;" and gently but firmly he shoved the waspish man from the doorway. Old Sandy suddenly stepped forward and took Andy's place. The shadow of the boxes darkened his wizened countenance. He held up his hand. "Wan meenut, boys." Gillespie straightened his back.

"Are ye goin' in for buyin', Gillespa'?"

Gillespie nodded impatiently.

"Boys? I've been a fisherman a' my days; an' no for fifty strucken years hae I seen what I saw the day. Thae men"—his condemning eyes swept over the buyers—"wad hae left us on oor backside. Never a tail that I fish will I sell to ony man noo but Gillespa' Strang as long's God leaves braith in my body." He smacked his palm with his clenched hand.

"Hear! hear! Hurrah! hurrah!"

From that moment Gillespie was the man of the fleet. The deep-throated hurrahing was the knell of the buyers. Some one in the crowd began to boo. "Way there, boys!" Gillespie appeared shouldering one of his brand-new boxes, followed by one of the crew with one box on his shoulder and trailing another by its bicket.

9

THE idle buyers lined the "Shipping Box" at the Quay, watching dourly as box after box was filled from the teeming cran baskets. The Quay rang under the iron-heeled sea-boots, stamping under the weight of the baskets. Gillespie, Sandy the Fox, and Jeck the Traiveller stood by the boxes. At midday three of the boats were discharged and had gone to anchor. Gillespie held a brief consultation with the fishermen, who ceased filling the boxes.

"By Goäd!" whispered Andy, "he's fed up."

"I'm no sae sure o' that," said Queebec, a fiery-faced buyer, and discerner of men, who in his youth had made a voyage to Quebec. He was discovering in himself a certain respect for Gillespie. They left the "Shipping Box" and joined the circle about Gillespie, who nodded cheerily to them. "Hot work this, boys," and went on speaking to the fishermen. "Ye understan' I'll send ye doon a gallon o' beer an' biscuits an' cheese."

"Did ye hear thon?" Andy whispered behind his hand; "beer an' cheese." The thing was unheard of.

"Right O!" cried young Polly; "we're your men every day." Above the Quay and adjacent to the stores was a large oblong Square, surrounded on three sides by a four-foot dike. The fourth side was partly built in with the dike, but a space was left to approach it from the Quay by a flight of three broad steps. Sandy the Fox, who had been hastily summoned from the coal-ree, entered the store, along with three fishermen. They re-appeared each at the corner of a huge tarpaulin, which they dragged into and spread out in the Square.

"He's rented the Square as weel frae the Laird," said Tamar Lusk, an active, bent, bow-legged man, who combined the buying of a meagre box of herring with the selling of ice-cream, vegetables, and newspapers. "There's nothin' ye can teach Gillespie." He meant to sting Andy, whom he hated with years of herring-buying hatred, because Andy cheated him like a fox. Andy, however, was too petrified to feel the jibe, and Tamar lunged again.

"Gillespie's the boy; he'll sweep us a' off the Quay in wan whup."

"The waff o' a newspaper 'ill sweep you off, ye bloomin' Eyetalian. What's the salt for, Ned?" he wheeled on a fisherman who was rolling a heavy, grinding barrel, its new wood tarnished with mud. The fisherman straightened his back, took out his clay from the top waistcoat pocket, and borrowed a match from Andy. He was a tall man, slow of speech, with a grave eye.

"Gillespie's goin' tae show you boys how to work wi' herrin'" —there was an accent of pity in his voice—"he's for roilin' them in salt."

"In salt! where did he get the salt?"

The grey eye smiled. "In the sweetie boxes behind the coonter," and was on its way again behind a puff of smoke.

Cran basket after cran basket was carried up the stone steps and poured on the tarpaulin. Gillespie and Sandy the Fox stood, each at one end of the growing pile, with a shallow tin plate in his left hand, with which he scooped up salt from a barrel, drew his right hand across the salt, and hailed it down on the fresh fish, as a sower sows seed. The Square was full of the tinkling sound of the falling salt. Jeck the Traiveller sat on an upturned herring box, and as every cran was emptied on the pile, the fishermen shouted "Tally!" "Tally oh!" answered Jeck, and dropped a herring into a small basket. In this way the count of the crans was kept.

Another of the boats was discharged. The fishermen, wet with sweat, drank their beer and ate their biscuits and cheese. They had never been fed before in discharging fish, and the last bolt in the doors of their heart was drawn. Andy had been whispering, "No wonder he was keen on your stuff at a shillin' a box wi' a' that stock. Catch him biddin' when they were at five shillin's."

For all that the fishermen esteemed Gillespie as a man of bowels, who had plucked their fish from the "big market." And where was his own market? And now beer and cheese. He was their comrade, the fisherman's friend.

"I hope to Goäd," cried old Sandy, as he drew the back of his hand across his mouth, "he'll get a pound a box. He's the best man in Brieston that Goäd ever put braith intae."

Work was begun again and the second boat discharged. The salted pile of fish gleamed high in the Square. Barrels were rolled from the store, and filled with shovels from the pile. Andy, putting on a supercilious face, went up the stairs leisurely, meaning to pick a sure bone at his ease. "Hey, Gillespa'! I thought ye were in a hurry?"

"A mile a meenut's the speed," came back the genial answer.

"Weel, I never saw herrin' roiled that wy before."

"No?"

"The wy it used tae be done was to fill the barrels, an' salt the herrin' as they were goin' frae the cran basket tae the barrel. Ye've been gien' yersel' double labour."

"Ye micht hae told me earlier," said Gillespie unabashed.

"Oh! ye think ye ken everything; I just let ye hev' your own wy."

"Weel! weel! a' that, Andy. I'll tell you something my faither's faither learned doon by the heids o' Ayr: aye roil them first ootside the barrels."

"Ay," came the sarcastic rejoinder.

"Ye see, Andy, when ye roil them in the barrels they sink terrible wi' the shakin' o' the steamers an' the trains, an' when they reach the mercat it's no' a fu' barrel ye're offerin'. The fish-merchants lik' a fu' barrel. An' the herrin' keep their bellies better this wy; but you'll ken best, Andy."

He was not only buying herring: he was teaching them something new about their business.

144

"Ye'll hae tae get up early in the morn wi' tackets in your boots afore ye get to windward o' Gillespie," wheezed the asthmatic Queebec.

"Ay! he's no' a scone o' yesterday's bakin'," Tamar Lusk gloated.

As each barrel was filled Gillespie covered it with a top of canvas cloth, nailing the cloth round with tacks.

"He can cooper as weel: I'll never leave the ice-cream shop again;" but Andy cursed Tamar for a fool.

The whitened tarpaulin lay empty in the sun; and the men, finishing their beer and cheese, eyed the three hundred odd barrels of fish—proud of their labour—and discussed the new order. On every one's tongue was a word of commendation or friendship for Gillespie. His action was heroic. He had stood gallantly in the breach of the sea.

"Does the damn fool think roiled herrin' 'ill keep in this weather?" Andy had again found a platform in Gillespie's inability to dispose of the fish—"An' what o' the fresh herrin' in the boxes?" he asked. "Manure! fair manure! they'll be stinkin' afore they get to the mercat."

"It's you has the black he'rt, Andy," roared old Sandy. "It's time your day was done on the Quay. Goäd be thankit, there's wan man that can buy fish, mercat or no mercat."

Precisely at that moment that one man was handing two telegrams across the counter of the Post Office—one to a Manchester firm, which ran: "Sending 330 barrels large herrings in salt." The other was to a merchant in the Glasgow Fish Market. "Sending 645 boxes large herrings by special steamer; arrive night." The Glasgow Fish Market would be closed before the hour of arrival, but early the following morning, Gillespie knew, a long line of lorries would be on the Broomielaw; the lumpers would be waiting. Gillespie's herring would be first in the market next day; at nine o'clock sharp the auctioneer would have them under his hammer, while the herring smacks would only be trailing round the Garroch Heads, six hours from market. Gillespie would have the market to himself.

"Manure! fair manure; he'll be fined for bringin' refuse into Glesca," sniped Andy.

"Weel, Andy, I was never so puzzled since the day I saw white poirpoises off Newfoundland." Queebec scratched his pow solemnly. At the old Quay, used for discharging coal, some four hundred yards further in the Harbour, lay a puffer, which had brought a cargo from Ardrossan for Gillespie's ree.

"Are ye dischairged?" Gillespie asked a black-bearded man who was drying his hairy arms in a rough towel.

"Naethin' left but fleas," was the succinct answer.

Gillespie lightly swung himself aboard forward.

"Where are ye for?"

"The Port."

"Goin' back light?"

The bearded man freed his face from the towel.

"As licht," he answered, "as a pauper's belly."

"I'll gie ye some ballast as far's the Broomielaw."

The bearded man's eyes twinkled. "Deid cats?" he inquired.

"Deid herrin'. Will ye mek' a run for me to Glesca?"

"Lik' hey-my-nanny," said the master mariner, becoming alert.

"Ye'd be burnin' your coal ony wy"—Gillespie was meditative —"You'll be gled o' the price o' the coal."

"I winna objec'."

"Twenty pound for the run."

The bearded man pulled a solemn face, though secretly he was glad of the found money. "Ye were goin' back licht," and, Gillespie added significantly, "I'll soon be wantin' another cargo o' coal if this fishin' continues."

"Streitch it to twenty-five."

Gillespie made a rapid calculation. For the number of boxes and barrels twenty-five pounds worked out at sixpence a package. The freight by luggage steamer was three shillings. He laid his hand on the jocose mariner's arm, and sucked in his breath. "You an' me 'ill no' quarrel ower a five-pun' note. I'll mak' it twenty-five pounds if ye drive her an' get up the night."

"I'll can do't in seeven 'oors, nate; the sewin' machine's in good order"; he jerked his thumb towards the engines.

"Get her doon to the Quay then; I'll get the fishermen to gie ye a hand wi' the stuff."

"Hae ye many?"

"Oh! a pickle, a pickle," cried Gillespie as he mounted the breast wall. He appeared in the Square with a large pile of labels, a box of tacks, and a hammer, and briskly instructed the fishermen to roll the barrels on to the Quay.

"Rowl them ower the Quay heid," shouted Andy, derisively; "it'll save them frae the dung-heap in Glesca."

Gillespie, who was standing beside the first barrel, imperturbably beckoned Andy with the hammer.

"Step ower, Andy, an' ye'll see their desteenation."

Gillespie tacked a large red label on the side of the barrel. The name and address of a fish salesman in Manchester was printed on the card in large, black type. He handed a label to Andy.

"It's a wee further than Glesca, Andy."

Andy flung the label in the mud, spat, and stamped on it.

"Dinna be sae wastefu' o' guid gear, Andy," said Gillespie, his mouth full of tacks; "I had to pay postage on thae labels a' the wy frae Manchester." Nimbly he went from barrel to barrel tacking on the labels. In the midst of this work a puffer came steaming down the Harbour. An ordinary sight, scarcely noticed. Suddenly a stentorian voice rang across the water. "The Quay ahoy! catch this line."

It was a common thing for such craft to put in at the Quay for oil or stores. No one surmised, and the puffer was warped up. Gillespie appeared with a bundle of slings from the store of the luggage steamer, which lay behind the "Shipping Box." The coal bucket of the puffer was unhooked from the end of the chain, and steam turned on the winch.

"Goäd! but he's chartered the puffer"—Queebec danced in excitement from one leg to the other—"He's fair bate us. I kent he'd something up his sleeve; he was that quate an' smilin'." The thing was so astonishing, so tremendous to these men who never bought more than twenty or thirty boxes at a time, that they could only stare in silence. To have a store crammed with stock; to have unlimited barrels of salt and have rented the Square—all that was nothing; but to have chartered a steamer! A dim conception of the bigness of this man and of his audacity began to impregnate their minds. He seemed no more than a boy, with his jovial red face and lithe swinging walk; yet he caused their trafficking in fish to appear to them a piece of shy, dawdling inefficiency. This man in one morning suddenly became gigantic, and these sparrows of Dothan saw that their day of hopping on the Quay was done. There was nothing to do but to retire from the shadow of an eagle.

"He'll hae the first o' the market the morn," wheezed Queebec, who in a dull way felt angry with Andy.

"Boys-a-boys, but he'll hev' the haul." The ice-cream vendor's mouth fairly watered.

"Every barrel 'ill be a pound in Manchester," cried Queebec.

The stem of Andy's pipe snapped between his teeth. He spat out the fragment and walking across the Quay accosted the black-bearded mariner.

"Where are ye goin'?" he asked bluntly.

"Yattin'."

The witticism stung Andy.

"Ye damn big fool; ye'll no' get the price o' paint for your rotten funnel oot o' Gillespa'." The black-bearded man, who had a wad of notes in his hand—the freight on the coal and the herring just paid by Gillespie—estimated Andy. A guffaw over at the "Shipping Box" caused a surge of dark-red blood to swamp his face; his bull-dog neck began to swell; his dark eyes to blaze beneath their bushy eyebrows.

"Ca' me a damn fool, div ye? me, Jock Borlan' o' Govan. I'll salt your whisker for ye an' tek' it to Glesca in a barrel for pickle pork, ye swine. See that"—he held up the wad of notes—"a bit praisint frae Gillespie Strang to my wife, by Jing!" Backhanded he swung the wad hard across Andy's cheek.

"That's Jock Borlan's wy, by Jing!"

Andy danced in front of him, screaming with rage.

"Get oot o' my way"—the mariner threatened Andy with the wad—"Wur ye ever at the thaieter? Whaur are ye for, div ye say? I'm for the Langlands Road tae tak' my wife to the thaieter the nicht." He walked ponderously down upon Andy, stamping at the slippered toes.

Andy leapt back, rubbing his cheek and screaming, "I'll pey ye, ye big Glesca keelie. I'll pey ye back for this."

"Ye'll never pey like Gillespie Strang," cried the bearded man, jocose again. "Gillespie Strang's pey"—he tapped the wad with a thick forefinger—"My wife an' me's gaun to the thaieter the nicht, by Jing!"

The eager song of the winch clanked over the Quay as tier after tier of the boxes was being slung aboard. At the same time the barrels were being rolled in on two planks. In an hour and a half the puffer cleared, the black-bearded sailorman roaring an invitation to Andy; "Ir ye comin' to the thaieter the nicht?"

Punctually to the minute at noon on Saturday Gillespie paid the fishermen in his shop.

"That's better than the big market, Sanny."

"Ay! you bate, Gillespa'; a full hairbour wad be a toom stomach for some o' us."

"Weel, boys," he said briskly, rubbing his hands; "I hope I'll pay ye ten times as much next Setterday." In this way Gillespie announced that buying would be a permanent part of his business. He retired to his back-shop and, seated at an aged black mahogany desk full of pigeon holes, made up his "returns":

	£	s.	d.
1020 boxes . . .	51	0	0
Freight Glasgow . .	25	0	0
„ Liverpool . .	39	16	3
Salt	5	0	0
Total . . .	120	16	3

His eyes had a profound look of regret. The Manchester herring had been a test and a risk, but fortunately the weather had been foul on the English coast. He had had a telegram from Manchester—twenty-two shillings a barrel. Yes! his eyes had a profound look of regret. He ought to have sent all the stuff to the English market—only it was a risk. He made his entry carefully:

	£	s.	d.
330 barrels @ 22s. . .	363	0	0
645 boxes @ 12s. 6d. . .	403	2	6

Balance £645 6s. 3d.

He chewed the end of the pen.

"Nane sae ill for a green hand;" he nodded, wiped the pen, put it behind his ear, carefully put the ledger away, and passed into the front shop, whistling softly between his teeth. He put a sweet in his mouth, passed to the door, and stood regarding the herring fleet, supine in the calm over their anchors. He had prestige. He had bowels of sympathy. He was the man of the town.

10

GILLESPIE'S coal-ree was large and flourishing; his places stored from cellar to roof. He bought up all the old iron in Brieston and the adjacent country, and had Sandy the Fox on the road with a pony and cart two days in the week collecting rags, hides, sheep-skins, rabbit-skins. "See an' lift half a ton o' woollens this week," were his instructions to the Fox on a Monday morning. These rags he obtained by barter, giving provisions from his shop in exchange. On two other days of the week, Wednesdays and Saturdays, the Fox went into the country with tinned meats, cloth, boots, sewing material, provisions, and bread. This Gillespie purchased in large quantities from the bakers, demanding a reduction in their retail price, or thirteen loaves to the dozen. For such stuff he got in exchange in the country fresh eggs, butter, cheese, and potatoes, which he exposed for sale in the shop. The bread he also sold to the fishermen. Nothing was too trivial for him. "Every mickle mak's a muckle," was his latest saw. He noticed a child kicking a piece of stale bread in the gutter; he chided the bairn, and said to McKelvie the mason-contractor, who was passing, "That doesna look lik' hungry Brieston." He became the gates of the town. None could go out or in except through him; and the town took offence at Lonend, because of his unsleeping enmity. Lonend was very sore, for having held Muirhead till the lease expired, and having asked for a renewal, he was fobbed off for half a year, and then given notice that a gentleman farmer was taking the farm. Lonend, forced to sell his stock at a lower figure than he had paid to Gillespie, was in retreat at his own farm, brooding on revenge, and against a day of reckoning had locked up the sheet of paper which Gillespie and he had found tacked on to the door of Muirhead farm-house.

It was December, and the fishing season being on the wane, Gillespie established his interests in new fields. On a raw, louring day of sleet Sandy the Fox and Jeck the Traiveller made a round of the town, leaving a rough cheap card at each door. The card, printed on both sides, agitated Brieston in its domestic nests, for it contained a gallant invitation:

Gillespie Strang begs to announce that he has opened a Rag, Rope and Metal Department.

And begs leave most respectfully to submit this card for your consideration, as the demand for White and Coloured Rags is more pressing than ever. He will Buy and Collect Rags of every description, such as old Dish-cloths, Velveteens, Sacking, Roping, Sheep-Netting, Carpeting, Dusters, or any kind of Rubbish made of Linen, Hemp, or Worsted; and though rotten as tinder, and only a pound or half a pound, look them up and bring them to Store No. IV at the Quay. Please do not forget that every piece of Rag helps to make a sheet of paper. Please to look them out of your coal-holes and back-places. All pieces of Rags that you have thrown to your back doors or into your soil holes or middens, wet or dry, clean or dirty, Linen or Woollen are wanted.

Be your own Friend and Pay Your Rent with Rags.

Please turn over.

Gillespie will buy and collect the above articles in this vicinity on Monday mornings, and from the country on Tuesdays and Thursdays by van at the highest ready-money prices. He also buys Old Coats, Waistcoats, Trousers, Gowns, Shawls, Night-Dresses, Pyjamas, or any Ladies' or Gent's left-off Wearing Apparel, Horse and Cow Hair, Old Ropes, Old Brass, Brass Candlesticks, Old Warming-Pans, Broken Spoons, Copper Kettles, Old Boilers, Metal Tea-Pots, Stew-Pans, Old Lead and Pewter, Cast and Wrought Iron, Metal, Copper, Old Carpets, Hammer-heads, Broken Guns, etc., etc.

He will be thankful to all persons who will look out the above articles, if only a handful. Gillespie Strang will give the best price and pay Ready Money.

Why have Middens when you can go to No. IV?

Furniture Bought, Sold, Hired, and Exchanged.

Best Prices given for Bones, Hare and Rabbit Skins.

No connection whatever with Hawkers, Collectors, or Jews.

Support Home Industries.

Business punctually attended to.

151

If Gillespie was a hero on the sea-front he reached the zenith of admiration at the hearth of Brieston, where it was conceived that in the bad winter times a gold-mine was opened at Store No. IV for a little scavenging. He was not a man, but a god, with his unlimited market, his fountains of beatitude. Mary Bunch had nerve at the Pump to utter discord. The card was in her hand.

"Dae ye ken what Mrs. Galbraith said? Sez she, 'It's the badge o' your shame.'"

"What's the badge o' your shame mean?" asked Black Jean, frowning.

"It means Gillespa's a fair bloodsucker; he'll sook the toon dry."

"Ach! wheest, Mary." Nan at Jock took her hand from beneath her apron and flaunted it in Mary Bunch's face.

"'Deed he will," continued Mary Bunch, ardently. "He's gettin' the big man noo, but I mind the day he opened the wee shop in the Back Street when he left Muirhead"—Gillespie took these temporary premises for some six months, till the house and shop in the Square were ready for him—"Losh! but he was the fly ane; he took thon shop in the old tiled hoose, for it had a lum ye could stand on when it was cold. When there was a big divide among the men on the Setterdays he wad stan' on the lum, watchin' the weemin goin' tae the shops doon in the front street; then he'd come doon off the lum an' kep them, an' get his debt oot o' them afore they'd a chance to get home." Her small dark head was nodding vigorously; her face flushed; her eyes bright like a bird's. "An' that wasna the only reason he had. It was awa' back frae the road to the Kirk. A bonny deacon him! Oh! but he had the gran' tred there on Sundays. It began wi' Floracs at Rob the Solan" (Flora, wife of Rob, nicknamed the Solan). "They said she was a witch. Hooivir, she cam' wan Sunday wi' a five-poun' noat—ye mind, there was a big fishin' in the Kyles. She'd a dram on the Setterday, an' took sixteen shullin's worth on the Sunday night. They cairrit three dozen o' ginger beer an' a whup o' pastry an' stuff ower to the Bairracks in a spale-basket." The Barracks sat tall and unlovely on the north road, where some of the Government men, who watched for the trawlers, had lodged. "An' what div ye think he did? 'Floracs, my wumman', sez he, 'I canna change that muckle money for ye on a Sunday.'

"'I'll get the change the morn,' sez Floracs.

"'Floracs,' sez he, 'there'll no pr'aps be another big fishin' for a whilie that'll ye hae five-pun' notes handy.'

" 'Ay! that's true.'

" 'Weel,' sez he, 'my wy o't wad be this. Just leave the money wi' me an' ye can tak' a run ower on Sundays for your ginger beer, till the money's feeneshed. It'll last ye langer that wy, Sunday money, than breakin' it up intae siller change. Ye ken hoo change slips awa' through your fingers.'

"Floracs said she wasna sae sure.

" 'Weel, this is the wy I look at it. If ye leave your money wi' me it's as safe as the bank; and on Sunday evenin' ye can slip oot withoot reingin' through the bowls in the dresser for't. That wad only mak' the Solan suspeecious; but this wy he'll never notiss. Dae ye see?' An' that's the wy Gillespie took to dale wi' weemin on the sly. Auld Strang cam' to hear o't. Auld Strang wad be doon on his knees in the 'Ghost' prayin' for his son. An' wan Sunday evening he drapped in instead o' goin' to the meetin', an' there was Gillespie an' Floracs at Rob the Solan hevin' a noise. The auld fella heard it a' frae the kitchen. Ye ken' the wy Gillespie did? He wadna open the shop door, but gied up a laidder, an' cut a hole in the loft above the shop an' went doon intae the shop by another laidder. An' there was the twa o' them argle-bargling awa'. Floracs cam' for a dozen o' ginger beer an' a dozen o' pastry for a wee tea-pairty on the Monday when her man wad be oot at the fishin'.

" 'Ye'll hae to pay this time, Floracs; your money's done.'

" 'Guidsakes! done already?'

" 'It's a' that.'

"An' then Floracs ca'd him for a' the thiefs an' blaiggarts frae here to Jonnie Groats, an' said she'd never put her fut inside his door again, an' wad expose his ongoin's.

" 'Dinna be sae hasty, Floracs; I dinna want to expose ye or any dacent wumman. Ye ken hoo it wad be if I cheep'd. Your man wadna be pleased to hear o' your tea-pairties wi' a' the Bairricks weemin when he's awa' at the fishin'.' An' clare tae Goäd Floracs got a wild fright an' began tae trummel in her shoes. That's the wy he got a grup o' them. It wasna shullin's he wanted, but soävrins an' half-soävrins, an' neither wan nor anuther kent when the money was done, but himsel'. He made more on a Sunday than the other shopkeepers made a' the week."

"An' what o' auld Strang?" Nan at Jock's voice piped eagerly.

"Weel! naebody kens the oots an' ins o' that; but there he was standin' in the kitchen when Gillespie cam' doon the laidder wi'

153

Floracs. She was that frichted she bolted. There was a big noise between faither an' son. Some say that auld Strang lifted his staff on Gillespie; an' some had it that Gillespie caught the auld man by the throat an' threw him on the bed. From that day till this Gillespie never showed face inside the 'Ghost.' "

"Ay," said Lucky, when the breathless narrative came to an end, "that was aye Gillespie's wy, makin' money a' the time, since he was a boy at the school."

"Onyway," said Mary Bunch, crisply, "there's noathin' good comes oot o' what Gillespie does. If ye just heard the curse Nanny at Baldy Murray put on his weddin'."

"I never h'ard," answered Nan at Jock for the others.

"Weel! weel!"—Mary Bunch's eyes were full of astonishment at such ignorance—"the night they were mairrit, but we'd the spree at Lonen'."

"Hoo were you there, Mary?" asked Lucky.

"Och! wheest, did I no' ca' on the bereavit when Galbraith slippit awa', an' Morag an' Gillespie was there?" She hesitated a moment. "Where was I? Ou! ay! but that was the jolly night. What a dose o' roasted hens on the table. Ye'd think ye were in a hen-hoose that gied on fire. Aunty Nanny, Aunty Kate, Aunty Mary, Jamaics Black an' my own faither were at the wee watch-maker's dancin'-school; an' och! but my faither was the dancer. He danced at the fushin' in the north through Skye on his stockin'-soles wi' the spree wi' Jamaics Black's faither. An' och! och! but he was the braw man, Jamaics. There wasna a better trump player in Argyllshire, an' he coorted Nanny Lang afore she took the sma'-pox an' lost the wan eye wi't, an' he said he'd tek' her though she was as blin' as a bat. Och! och! but that was the nicht. Weel, they say that Alastair Murray was talkin' aboot it tae himsel' in the church the next Sunday a' the time the minister was preachin'. Ye ken he went wrong in the mind, an' they had tae tek' him away tae the asylum up at Bannerie. Fine I mind the day. It was a Sunday, too—the Sunday Big Finla's wife had a wean. I mind afore they took him awa' his mother came tae me an' sez she, 'Are ye puttin' any odds on Alastair?'

" 'Nanny,' I sez, 'I put an odds on him. I aye hear him on the road lecterin' awa' tae hissel': an' he's aye goin' up tae the grave-yaird.' 'Weel,' sez she, 'it was Gillespie's weddin' began it on my poor Alastair. He got a crack on the heid, an' hesna been richt since. But mind what I'm tellin' you, Mary Bunch, my poor

154

Alastair's no' the only wan that'll go off his heid wi' Gillespie, whoever 'ill leeve tae see't'—She streitched oot her twa hands—'The duvvil in hell,' sez she, 'was at thon weddin'.'

" 'Wheest! wheest! Nanny,' I sez; 'dinna speak lik' that.'

" 'No! I'll no' wheest; just you wait. The curse that's on my Alastair 'ill be on him!' I catchit her by the airm.

" 'Dinna you curse him, Nanny, leave that tae the Almighty.'

"Weel, that brought her tae her senses.

" 'I'll say nae mair, Mary. My Alastair's tae be taen away come Sunday wi' Doctor Maclean. I hope tae Goäd I'll be deid afore then.' "

There was silence at the Pump. Something sinister and terrible seemed to brood over Gillespie and the opulence of Store No. IV.

"Dae ye believe, Mary, it was the spree at Lonen' that put Alastair off his head?" asked Black Jean in a low voice.

"Goäd kens," answered Mary Bunch; "but if anything comes ower Gillespie or his faimly, I'll mind o' Nanny's words."

She wrapped her shawl about her neck, and leaned a little to one side, ready to sheer off through the gathering night. "Goäd alone kens the wy things happen in this world."

The sound of their scurrying feet went down the cobbled road. At the foot of the Pump, one of Gillespie's advertisement cards was lying. Drip! drip! drip! the water fell on it, softening it, crumpling it, obliterating the writing of its gospel of commerce.

11

A STURDY, thick-set female figure walked slowly up the cart-road to Lonend. The head was alert, proudly poised, the dilated nostrils were eagerly drinking in deep gulps of the fragrance of the fields. It was Mrs. Galbraith, who had come to ask Lonend to be allowed to work at the harvest. He turned a shamefast face upon her.

"It's no' work for the likes o' you, Margaret."

"It's not for the money I want to work. I must live on a farm now and again or I'll go mad."

155

"Come as often as ye like an' welcome," he said eagerly, his face lightening.

"Thank you, Mr. Logan. I should like to stay for to-day and go just where I like."

She passed through a back gate, walked along a dike side, crossed at the top of a potato field, passed through another gate, and came on the harvesters. At the sight her step became light; her body swung free and rhythmically; her face was transfigured. It was a cloudless autumn day. The hush of fading things, of leaves dropping silently, lingered on the dew-drenched trees. The long valley below, in which lay Brieston, was grey with mist, and suggested a lake of amethyst, with here and there a lance of gold sinking into the soft billows. Light flooded the sky and drenched the earth. The wide sweeping view accentuated the curves of the country; and the light toned down its edges. The hills rose in yellowing slopes beyond Muirhead to the sky with wavering fires on their face. The slopes, billowing one into the other, appeared as if lifted by a mighty wind and arrested when their crests were about to break. Beyond all was high Beinn an Oir, assailing to the eye, towering up like something supernatural.

The plum-like bloom of autumn was mellow on the fields. A riot of bracken flamed on the hem of the wood; beyond, diamonds of dew hung on every bell of the heather; the hedges were ablaze with hips and haws; where the sun slanted through the leaves they looked like yellow flame; and overhead the sky was a blue lake of light. Dark bars of cloud in the south-west completed the image. They were fantastically shaped islands asleep in that vast hyacinth sea.

The reaping had been finished two days ago. The stooks were standing up like old bearded men. Mrs. Galbraith sat in the shadow of the wood gazing on the busy field. There was no sense here of life being an hostage to hard and wearisome labour, and the fruit of harvest depending on the many imperilling chances of the weather. The hopes that had been sown and ploughed into the ground in spring were realised, and the fears that attended the spring frosts and summer drought were at an end. It is an open-handed time, with an air of plenty encompassing fields alive with merry folk. There is no work on earth like harvest-work. It is a Bacchic time of song. The wine stands up to the bridles of the horses. And there is no time when master and servants mingle so much together in fellowship as at this sacrament of bounty.

"Dear God," she murmured, "it is good to be alive." None knows what freedom is like the man who, released from prison, stands without drinking great gulps of God's clean air, as he lets his sick eye rove over hill and field. Mrs. Galbraith felt this enlargement of life as she watched a group of children. The strenuous labour of ploughing, sowing, and harrowing is for men alone. The harvest is the children's hour. She watched them trot and gambol about, rosy as scarlet autumn flowers, and very much excited, as they rivalled each other in dragging the largest sheaves to the carts. The women chattered because they must, and, flushed and happy, shared each other's joy. In no hour do they know less of self. Mrs. Galbraith wandered among them, speaking a word to each, and was surprised at the respect they showed her. Lonend quietly joined her. It was a good harvest. He hoped she would come to the harvest home on next Wednesday; but she shook her head, smiling. "I do not care for these things, I prefer being here." Lonend knew from her tone and her smile that in some way he was forgiven.

Mrs. Galbraith crossed over to the carts where the men were at work. They saluted her, acknowledging her grave dignity where she stood stroking the glossy neck of the brown Clydesdale. The men worked with silent perseverance, tasting a slower joy than the children, a calmer pleasure than the women. Looking at their tanned faces and simple, incurious eyes she learned again the wisdom that is in healthful labour, and remembered the *orare ac laborare* of the monks. The very appearance of these men spoke to her of the deep, quiet things of earth. Their brown hands were stained with earth's very juice; ears of corn were in their hair and their beards and clung to their shirt sleeves. She felt the indescribable savour of the soil, sharp almost to an edge of pain, and the physical effects of its colour and scent pass into a realm of mystery, where that which is visible and tangible melts into a suggestion of something profound, baffling, haunting, which emanates from the bosom of mother earth. She turned away with a glorified face and joined the children.

She had eaten of Lonend's bread, and asked leave to take with her a bouquet of flowers when she went home. He turned in the direction of his garden, behind the farmhouse, but she checked him with a slight gesture of her hand.

"I wish to remain," she said, "till I see the lights come out in Brieston. If I may I will get the flowers then by myself."

The last sheaf was in the cart which rumbled across the field. The hush of twilight, of things that have been wrought with and are for ever finished, stole across the bare upland still heavy with fragrance. A few yellow leaves lay among the pale-gold of the stubble, whispering like ghosts in every eddy of the breeze. Rooks and starlings were busy gleaning, and as Mrs. Galbraith walked in the field, their black cloud rose with a tumultuous whirring of wings, and passing in thunder over her head, left her alone with that calm sanctification of evening in which there is nothing of man or of his works. The window of Muirhead, far off on the brae above the sea, turned to liquid conflagration as it caught the long level rays of the setting sun, and flamed in crimson fire. She watched the glow fade and pass as greyness crept down from Beinn an Oir. The trees around became spectres. A ghostly sibilation stirred in the dimness of the whispering wood where the chill wind stirred the leaves.

Sphinx-like, she stood regarding the field, which had a look of youth on its shorn face. It was beautiful and yet very sad, a marred face the sight of which, in the soft crepuscular light, provoked her to tears. "I am always destined," she thought sadly, "to be left alone in the stubble." Silence reigned through the sober hues; it was the solemn hour in which to be alone with broken hopes, with perished illusions, and fallen dreams. "And yet—and yet," she thought, "from this day that has been given me I can fashion fresh dreams and build up new hopes which may serve, in some measure, to relieve the gloomy background of coming winter, and light their candles in the darkness of life's inevitable vicissitudes." Happiness is not altogether vanished when unregretting memory can recall a golden hour of sorcery and colour, of mirth and magic; when it can send us into old valleys of light, and re-create a blue sky and a shining happy field. So simple it is to enter our Holy Land.

She sighed deeply as she turned towards the gate, for she was quitting the best that life held for her. As she gained a little crest, she saw the lights of Brieston shine around the bay, and long spears of gold search into the blue darkness of the harbour. Quietly she culled her flowers, and moved away down the cart-road. The figure of a man stood at the gate of Lonend in the shadow of a hawthorn hedge. He was watching his angelic guest

158

pass on into the night beneath the faintly breaking stars—a guest who had left behind a sense of pardon and peace, and a deep desire for revenge.

12

MRS. GALBRAITH'S room was skilfully arranged in a harmony of colour and foliage—blood-red rowan leaves, hips and haws, flaming gladioli, copper chrysanthemums, scarlet nasturtiums—a sensuous room of blood and wine; flowers and foliage which had gushed up from the heart of the earth in a blazonry of passion, in the blood of the martyrs. The flame of the portrait of a girl, over the mantelpiece, with a dark, oval face of honey—heavy languor, and eyes half-veiled beneath dark, heavy eyelids, was wreathed in the blood of virginia creeper.

Mrs. Strang, who had been invited to tea, came a little late. She was wearing a sealskin jacket, and her fingers were loaded with rings. From a thin gold chain round her neck hung a cameo set in gold. Mrs. Galbraith cast a piercing look out of her dark eyes on Mrs. Strang, who stood sniffing the heavy fragrance, and greedily drinking in the colour and the splendour with an amazed look.

"I have no longer a farm, Morag," she spoke with a grave, sweet air; "but the forests are here and the moor;" she touched a piece of purple heather in a china bowl on the mantelpiece. "I only need moss on the floor, and a hawk crying over the roof."

Mrs. Strang gazed pathetically at this image of her old life at Lonend. The subtle influence of the morning heather, wet with dew, the cool nooks of moss, the green patches of sward, the wealth of bracken, and bars of colour across the sky, were revived in her being. Her old gay, careless life at Lonend floated up in an enchanting mirage before her eyes, and she experienced a sense of pain and of loss. There was a sudden inspiration in the floral wreath of the room which saddened her. A reaction from her barren, penurious life of coal-dust and salt herring came upon her with intolerable force and pathos. Her eyes were as the eyes of a hungry, timid beast, stealing out of a wood. She saw in the glowing heather the seductive hopes that never had been fulfilled. She remembered her struggles growing fainter and fainter against a man of granite, on behalf of the unwearied passion which drove her from Lonend. Once she had imagined this passion to be inexhaustible, and that her life would burn eternal incense at its shrine. In the heart of these flowers she saw her secret raptures, her unspoken hopes, the aspirations whose flame lit the sordidness of her early married life. She felt exhausted in the midst of this riot of colour, and the despair attendant on unfulfilled hopes attacked her. Her hands hung loosely; vexations and rebellion swept over her, surging and ebbing, and leaving her utterly dispirited and wearied of existence. She was in that state of mind in which anything that may lend colour to life is grasped.

"Dear me," she said; "how bonnie it is! Oh, Margaret! I wish I was back at Lonend."

"I was there yesterday."

The simple statement appeared to petrify Mrs. Strang, who felt herself an outcast in an unknown country.

"Yesterday? What were you doing there?"

"They were leading-in. I went to see them. It's so beautiful and full of God." Mrs. Galbraith spoke in a subdued voice.

"I never go anywhere now." Mrs. Strang's face was like a mask. She looked vacantly round the room, and her gaze rested on a square wooden box, on a small table at the window. On one side of it was the figure of a dragon, on the other three sides the wood was unstained, showing that the poker-drawing was the work of Mrs. Galbraith. "An' I never do anything."

Mrs. Galbraith picked up the box. "I learned marquetry and poker-work at the Normal College. It is astonishing how the very smallest thing that we learn becomes of service to us," she said. "We are creatures made to conquer and beautify things." She then showed Mrs. Strang some crochet-work, a bedspread, which she was making to the order of the Laird's mother, for which she was to get twelve pounds when it was finished.

"I do it partly for a living and partly to divert my thoughts. I have no other manual work to do now. This is where I find men have resources which we are deprived of. For the vexations of life they find a solace in business, while women are often left with their thoughts."

Mrs. Strang felt the truth of this. "Yes," she said, wearily; "I sit all day looking at the fire."

Mrs. Galbraith smiled contemptuously. "I should go mad if I did that. I must keep grief at bay with my needle. The very fact that I have to preserve a watchful eye and a steady hand soothes my mind. I cannot give rein to the passion which consumes me while I am crocheting."

"What passion?" asked Mrs. Strang, with a kindling interest.

"Vengeance."

The word came like a gust; and a sudden fear of this proud, self-reliant woman gripped Mrs. Strang's heart. She herself was incapable of vengeance, the very thought of which terrified her hapless soul. Dark rings became visible beneath her large eyes, her face paled and her breathing quickened.

"Vengeance," she whispered; "what for?"

"For the treachery which drove me from my home. I felt it keenly yesterday." Sparks glowed in her dark eyes, like phosphorus in a night-sea. Mrs. Strang lifted a scared face. Her father, her husband, were threatened by this daring woman who was capable of anything. Mrs. Strang foretasted some horrible disaster, trembled before some irremediable misfortune. Her face flushed and paled; she was stifling, and felt herself giddy. An arm went about her waist with tender firmness, and drew her to a chair, from which she could only gasp "Margaret." Her bonnet was taken off; the cold edge of a tumbler was held to her chattering teeth as she laid her head back on the chair. Her face was like clay, and twitched in a nervous spasm; her hair a little disordered; beads of sweat oozed out on her forehead. She opened her eyes, beseeching peace and safety.

"Margaret," she whispered, "what a fright I got."

"Hush, Morag! don't think any more of what I said. I forgot myself. There, get off your jacket. We'll have tea, and then you'll be better." The slim neck was stretched out on the back of the chair, and the eyes closed. Mrs. Galbraith gazed down at her.

"There are two of us burning at a slow fire," she thought, as she turned to the table and made the room glad with the tinkle of cups and saucers.

At tea, Mrs. Galbraith gave an account of her visit to Lonend, and spoke warmly of the kindness of Mr. Logan. Mrs. Strang, relieved and happy, imagined that the vengeance spoken of meant nothing after all.

"You ought to visit Lonend, it is at its best just now." Mrs. Galbraith spoke with her accustomed air of decisiveness and authority.

Mrs. Strang's face became tearful.

"Gillespie wouldn't like it."

"You're a fool, Morag. You are suffering slow murder for a man who takes no notice of you." She spoke in a tone of acid irony, which would certainly have become insolent in Gillespie's presence. She began to knead the clay of Mrs. Strang's life. "He is pleasant to every one in Brieston but you." She poured forth the thoughts of long evenings at the lonely fireside—brooding which had gone far to spoil her fine nature. She had neglected her *Imitation* and her *In Memoriam*, and with the image of a murdered husband and a ruined home constantly before her had become cold, calculating—a machine of steel, constantly running. It was all poured out now in a jumble of invective, cunning, and pseudo-sympathy with Mrs. Strang, whose life, she said, was too solitary; the greed of her husband was blighting her nature. That dark, impenetrable man, Gillespie, who had no affinity of character, was freezing her life. Yesterday for Mrs. Strang was anguish; to-day, agony; and to-morrow would be torment, so long as she suffered herself to lie in silence beneath the thorns from which he alone culled the rose. Mrs. Strang, incapable of asking how Mrs. Galbraith became acquainted with these intimate facts, only understood the drift of denunciation, and saw herself a foolish, downtrodden creature, whom this superb woman advised to go her own way and live her own life, and leave Gillespie and his squabbles to look after themselves. Was she not a sad, loveless soul, drained of every pleasure which life had to offer? Every one had a festival at some time or another, and facilities for enjoying it, but she alone of all Brieston, the wife of one of its richest men, lived a grey and cloudy existence. What, perhaps, had greater effect on Mrs. Strang than anything else, was Mrs. Galbraith's advice to her to give over her tacit renunciation. She was sacrificing herself for one who was neither impressed nor grateful. Why did she fear him? An outbreak would not suit him now that his business was growing, and he was trying to curry favour with the country gentry. The very echo of quarrelling would injure his business, because the town regarded him

162

as a hero and benefactor, and he could not afford to have the
skeleton in his cupboard exposed. He would give blackmail
rather to satisfy her whims. She could have the whip-hand over
him. This cold, merciless logic sank into Mrs. Strang's mind, as
she listened with greedy ear to the stupendous Margaret. Yes!
she had nothing to fear; Gillespie's line was quietism, suavity.
Did they not call him "souple Gillespie"? He would have to keep
up the rôle; and Mrs. Strang could pursue her life with impunity.
Gillespie's wife, fascinated by this masterly plan of campaign,
felt herself lifted up and shaking the doors of secret, darling
dreams. Her flesh grew warm and her spirits ardent under the
dark, glowing eyes of this liberator, who she imagined was a
woman of mystery, of daring and romance. She sniffed the heavy,
sensuous odour of the flowers, and felt a new flow and torrent
of life for the first time since Eoghan was born. Her limbs were
no longer leaden, or her eyes bleached with staring at the kitchen
fire.

"Yes, Morag, all the penalty you are paying is for your foolish
acquiescence. Gillespie is intolerable. Even Mrs. Tosh speaks
of you as a hermit. 'She's become quite a hermit, really,' and you
know where she got that, from the minister's sister. Don't you
remember how you used to walk out in the evenings at Lonend?
You never walk out now. You are a woman no longer; you are
a victim."

Mrs. Strang, cypher of silent patience, had not the intellect to
combat such specious argument, but greedily accepted the word
of inducement which is sufficient to make a weak woman walk
in the path toward which she is hungering. "He is making you
contemptible before the whole town." Mrs. Galbraith drew a
sombre picture of a future of dark brooding taciturnity on Mrs.
Strang's part, and monstrous neglect on his. He would not even
give her clothes. Mrs. Strang remembered she had had none since
their wedding, and decided that to-morrow she would order
some from Mrs. Tosh. There would be ceaseless complainings
over trifles, constant domestic discontent; her children would
be alienated; she would not have even the dignity of a sphinx in
her misfortunes, but would become a mummy. The creepers
and weeds of existence would in such a lethargy stifle her life,
till she would be powerless, and have neither the strength nor
the resolution to ward off the pestering flies of circumstance.

The level rays of sunset streamed in on the flowers and foliage, and burned in pools of fire on the jewels on her fingers. The glory touched her face; the inner glow had ebbed from her body, leaving her sunk in dejection. Her head fell forward in abandon as she thought of her forlorn future—an animal that has long been coursed by hounds. She was hopelessly incompetent to wrestle with the problem of her fate; being a frail rudderless boat, tossed about on a dark night on a stormy sea. Yet one star burned brightly in the dark—she could take things in her own hands, and her husband, afraid of ruining his business, would be powerless to deny her. Neither Margaret nor she was aware that Gillespie would treat such conduct quite in another fashion—as he actually did treat it—by posing as a martyr, and out of his wife's errors gaining the capital of sympathy.

The setting light stung her eyes, and she bowed her head. "Out of all the days of your life, are you never to have one or two you can call your own?" said Mrs. Galbraith, rising and lifting a decanter from the dresser. "Topsail Janet told me to have in a dram for you," she smiled faintly; "but perhaps you're afraid Gillespie will know."

There was profound silence in the room. A leaf detached itself from a branch over Mrs. Strang's head, and fluttered down into her lap. She looked up with the blood-red leaf in her fingers.

"Thank you, Margaret," she answered, half sobbing, and took the tumbler in a trembling hand. Mrs. Galbraith watched with relentless eye. She felt herself begun on the task of sapping the foundations of the house of Gillespie Strang, murderer and benefactor of Brieston.

As Topsail Janet put her to bed that night her mistress babbled incoherently of a new dress from Mrs. Tosh, and of the bit of heather from Lonend, which Topsail had found awry in the button-hole of the sealskin jacket.

13

A CHANGE apparent to all had come over Mrs. Strang. She visited. Every afternoon it was fine she went, dressed in her sealskin jacket and wearing her rings, and gold chain about her neck, to

Lonend. Her health rapidly improved; her colour returned; she lost her thin, dry appearance; the magnificent coil of her hair became glossy, its raven darkness standing out against her white linen collar. Lonend, professedly glad to see her, engaged her in conversation about Mrs. Galbraith.

"She's a thoroughbred an' no mistake," said Lonend.

"I believe, father, you and she will make a match yet." Mrs. Strang's laugh had a girlish ring.

An idea which he could not express had for some time troubled Lonend, and he was amazed at its revelation by his daughter, whose face he keenly scrutinised. "Hoots, lassie! I might dae waur." From that hour Lonend had a new interest in life.

Two things befell Mrs. Strang on these expeditions. On returning from Lonend on her second visit, she put in at Mrs. Tosh's Emporium. That little, withered, spectacled woman got into a flutter; and when Mrs. Strang ordered a new dress and jacket, a new hat and gloves, she fawned upon the wife of the great Gillespie. Mrs. Strang, having tasted the sweets of power, walked home treading the air, and waited in impatience till the clothes were ready. Topsail demanded to be allowed to open the parcel, and at sight of the raiment fell into an ecstasy of admiration, insisted on Mrs. Strang undressing forthwith, and proceeded to clothe her in the new garments. She walked round her mistress, crooning her, patting her, open-mouthed with wonder and pleasure.

"Ye're a rale leddy noo," she exclaimed. "Gillespie 'ill tek' a second notion o' ye." Topsail herself was in coarse rags.

They were disappointed that on the next day grey sheets of rain swept across the Square. Mrs. Strang, however, did not sit gazing into the fire. "Janet," she said, "slip away down to Brodie's and get a bottle of whisky."

Topsail's rosy face was full of perplexity.

"There's nae money," she said.

"Never mind the money; tell Brodie to put it to Mr. Strang's account."

Topsail, thinking of the unexpected splendour of the new clothes, and that things came for the asking in the magical name of Gillespie, set out, and when she returned was rosier than ever and hilarious.

"What a drookin' "—she took off her shawl and shook it— "there's no even a spug left in the streets."

"Did you get the whisky?" asked her mistress.

"Ay, you bate!" said Topsail in glee, and not yet out of astonishment at the potency of the name Gillespie. "I could get the hale toon for the axin'."

The next day was grey and windless, and late in the afternoon Mrs. Strang set out for Lonend, dressed in her new clothes.

"A' ye need noo," said Topsail, at the head of the stair, "is a muff. A' the leddies cairry them."

Mrs. Strang entered the Emporium on her way, and asking for a muff, consulted jumpy Mrs. Tosh.

"Black will suit you best," said the lady; "black fox is worn just now."

The fact is that black fox furs were never seen within the Emporium; but a niece of Mr. Kennedy, the school-master, who was living in Edinburgh, was to be married in November, and he, preparing a charming wedding gift, had ordered through Mrs. Tosh a few sets of expensive furs, one of which he had chosen. The others were still with Mrs. Tosh, and about to be returned to Messrs. Stewart & Macdonald, Glasgow.

She led Mrs. Strang into her sanctum, in front of a long panel mirror set in a thin black frame, attached to one of the walls. The remaining part of the walls was covered with fashion-plates of tall, elegant ladies. Mrs. Tosh undid a large cardboard box, withdrew a fur boa, and with prim mouth and demure face of importance, hung it caressingly over Mrs. Strang's shoulders. Head to the side, like a bird, she glanced at the effect, hopping about. Mrs. Strang smiled rapturously at her image in the mirror.

"You suit black fox, my dear; it makes you so elegant, really." She returned to the cardboard box and withdrew a muff, which she gave to Mrs. Strang.

"Really, you do look sweet, Mrs. Strang. Every one will be quite jealous." Mrs. Strang, in this odour of flattery and furs, felt that she lived as she examined herself in the mirror. The effect was electrical. Buried in black shining fur, she seemed taller, more beautiful; her face flushed with health, her eyes sparkling, and the gold chain across the fur like a thread of fire.

"I think I'll just keep them on," she said, in a cooing voice; "they're lovely."

"You do look a picture, dear, really." Mrs. Tosh trotted after her into the front shop, arranging the furs. "Keep the fox-heads that way, so as to be seen; there now."

166

Mrs. Strang, with a fast-beating heart, went out into the timid sunshine, and took the road to Lonend. She had not inquired about the price of the furs. That was Gillespie's business.

14

THE road to Lonend was full of interest, having many happy twists and turnings. Mrs. Strang was walking fast, her heart beating as quickly, for she was anticipating her father's verdict on her appearance. At a sudden bend she came on a man who was looking through an opening between two rowan trees in the direction of West Brieston Loch, which lay, an eye of silver, beneath the tawny hills. His back was to her, and he leaned upon a walking-stick. Except Dr. Maclean, no one in these parts carried a walking-stick. In his right hand he held a pair of grey gloves. As Mrs. Strang came near he turned quickly round. She saw a look of surprised pleasure swiftly cross his face, and felt touched by the unpremeditated homage. He raised his hat, and bowing said:

"Am I by any chance on the right road to Lonend?"

Mrs. Strang was confused; should she say yes, and pass on?

"It's my father's farm," she stammered, and then blushed, feeling her answer to be stupid.

A quick, glad look leapt into the stranger's eyes.

"Ah!" he said; "you are perhaps on your road there?"

"Yes," she replied, putting her muff up to her burning cheek.

"May I be allowed to have the pleasure of accompanying you?" He gave a slight, deferential incline of his head forward.

"It's not very far." Her heart was beating so loudly she was sure he must hear it; but if he did, he made no sign. A strange exhilaration possessed her. She was glad she wore her furs. She had never walked with a man for years. She kept her eyes on the ground, and saw that he wore tan shoes—his trousers were turned up over them—and brown socks.

When he spoke again she was startled.

"Do you think Mr. Logan will take in a boarder?"

She glanced up at him. He had a clear-skinned, dark, clean-shaven face, and thick glossy dark hair. He seemed in age little more than a boy. He met her glance with a smile.

"I—I'm not sure; we never had boarders." She furiously hoped that her father would take him in.

"Oh, it's all right!" He flung his head up, and took a bigger stride. "I'd prefer to live out of town; that's why I've come to Lonend. I'm the new schoolmaster."

Mrs. Strang felt radiant at this confidence.

"I—I think father won't object."

"Ah!" he said, tossing his head, as a horse tosses its mane; "if I had you for my advocate, there would be no question about it."

Mr. Mowbray Campbell Rees Campion had been destined for the ministry of the Church of Scotland. His father, an Englishman, was in the cotton business of Manchester, and had taken to wife a woman of the Scottish hills, who desired to have a son in the Church. He was entered at Glasgow University, and proved himself an erratic, brilliant man, devoted to a fastidious course of reading. He soon discovered that to be a prizeman was to be a sponge. Soak in the lectures of the professor, pour them out on the examination book, and lo! you figured on the "distinguished list." "The yellow-backed examination book is jaundiced," he said, "with the ill-digested ideas of the professors, which the men who aim at lucrative posts in the professions splash in ink across its pages. It is all splash." He developed, as he said, "a fine taste for the wines of France," and took a degree with honours in English, because he fell under the spell of a tall, lank, stooping, dark-grey man with an eagle face, who made Shakespeare and the Elizabethans live and palpitate. Mr. Campion was a man destined for a career, if only he would apply himself; but with a reputation for force, fire, and originality in Union debates, he drifted into the Divinity Hall to idle. Alas! he found there neither the searching brilliance of the eagle-faced man nor his broad, tolerant humanity, but an atmosphere of parchments and portraits of Scottish divines upon the walls. The professor of divinity was droning, "We were discussing Schleiermacher yesterday," when Mr. Campion had a vision of a Man being led along a scorching road under a biting tree, one end of which was on the shoulder of a slave, mad with fear. A jeering mob surged about the Man. The slave, a negro out of Cyrenaica, glanced with bloodshot eyes for a chance of escape

168

from his maddened and maddening tormentors. The figure in front walked on, His pitying face to the skies.

"Schleiermacher, gentlemen, we saw, strove to do justice to the claims of both science and religion."

Mowbray C. R. Campion suffered agony of mind. At the close of the lecture he noticed the vicious snap with which the students closed their note-books, and went out and devoted himself to the wines of France.

The saintly professor of Church history, to whose charge he had been given from Manchester, walked with him for an hour and a half the following day in the Botanic Gardens. He accused Mr. Campion of nothing, but said that Saint Augustine, after spending a riotous youth, had enriched the world. Mowbray Campion was penitent; but he knew he was not destined for the Church. He left the Divinity Hall and its dull portraits of George Buchanan and Calvin, at heart sick of its futile, insipid life, which all spelled a "living." "The last place in Scotland where you will find the Cross so much as mentioned is in the Divinity Hall," was his farewell judgment.

Through the astonishing romance of life he came into contact with the Receiver of Wrecks of the "Anchor Hotel," who, unable to get rid of ancient, tottering Mr. Kennedy, had proposed the subtle plan to his colleagues on the Board of leaving the elementary department in the hands of the old teacher, and advertising for "a really good man, who will be up-to-date, from the University," to take charge of the Secondary Department, for which a two-storey building was nearing completion. Mr. Stuart, the minister, advised getting an honours-man; the Receiver of Wrecks acquiesced, without the least knowledge of who or what an honours-man might be. After some squabbling, the salary was fixed at one hundred and forty pounds a year, and Mr. Campion appointed.

"I'll do what I can," Mrs. Strang replied. She felt the flash of admiration in his eyes, and was sorry when, immediately, they came in sight of the crazy, wooden gate leading into the yard. They found Lonend superintending the building of a cornstack.

"This is my father," said Mrs. Strang, and hurried into the house.

Mr. Campion began to talk eagerly about the farm and the harvest, walking about everywhere, and asking innumerable questions. He had a curious, restless mind. He said he was the new schoolmaster—M. C. R. Campion. "I'm a man of initials;" his hearty laugh rang across the courtyard and up to Mrs. Strang, peeping at her old bedroom window. Her eyes devoured his face. He took off his hat. She saw a longish head with a large bump behind. How different he was from Gillespie—young, exuberant, well-dressed, courteous; and he asked such strange questions. Her father laughed heartily in explosive bursts as he listened to Mr. Campion touching off vividly the members of the School Board who had interviewed him. "Keen business men, I suppose?"

They disappeared round the cart-shed; and presently Mrs. Strang heard them come in at the front door.

"Step up this way. If the room 'ill suit ye, ye can have it; there's no one bidin' in't since my daughter got married."

She looked around for a place in which to conceal herself, and was discovered by Lonend, who was followed into the bedroom by Mr. Campion.

"Oh! I beg your pardon," he said, and turned to go out.

"Hoots! hae a look at it, seein' ye're here onyway. Morag, this is the new schoolmaster; he's wantin' to bide at Lonen'."

Morag flushed with her sense of guilty knowledge, and made no answer.

"I could not be happier, taking up your daughter's room." He bowed to her.

"That's a' richt; I'll be gled o' your company on winter nights. It's fell lonely here whiles."

Mr. Campion held out his hand to her and said goodbye. He gave her a firm hand-clasp. His hand was soft and warm.

He did not remain in the yard, but swung out through the gate and down the cart-road, slapping his walking-stick with his gloves, his head held buoyantly; his glance searching everywhere.

She remained standing at the window lost in thought. There was an air of gaiety and youth, of daring and romance about him; his black eyes were like Mrs. Galbraith's. "I should like to have another walk with him," she thought; and went downstairs to show her father the furs, and hear his opinion of Mr. Campion.

15

Mrs. Strang made a curious discovery that she was without courage to take any initiative of her own, except when she was under the domineering influence of Mrs. Galbraith. If she remained absent for more than two or three days from the house in the Back Street she lapsed into hopeless contemplation of the fire. The only thing which she persisted in was her visits to Lonend. Brodie had presented his account long before Mrs. Tosh, who had seen early in her business career that the people who buy fox furs do not like to have their account sent to them for some months. In respect of Brodie, Topsail and her mistress were faced with a difficulty. Once more Topsail had carried the magic name of Gillespie into the tavern, and was met with a flat refusal. The account had had its effect.

"No stuff," Brodie wheezed, "unless ye've a line frae Gillespa'."

They were in despair. Mrs. Strang had given all her time to Lonend, going out eagerly and returning listless. She had not seen Mrs. Galbraith for more than a fortnight. Topsail advised recourse to the Jew. He had thrived since the time when necessity had put up the shutters on her little shop; was grown broad and fat, and wore fine boots with patent toes, and a gold ring. Jeck the Traiveller was instructed to send him to the close at dark alone. It was a bad business for Topsail, for the Jew would name no price in the dark. He would have to examine the articles. Besides, the Jew knew intuitively that the business was clandestine. The first thing to go was Mrs. Strang's wedding-dress. Topsail wept. The dread of Gillespie made them cautious. In half the year the Jew had stripped these women. The unsophisticated Topsail had bound him to silence, and the Jew learned to threaten them with Gillespie. The jewellery alone was left; to which Mrs. Strang clung with pathetic insistence. She dreaded this lack of adornment when she went to Lonend to meet her lover.

Topsail and her mistress looked at each other in despair, when the servant returned with the news of Brodie's dire refusal.

Gillespie at this moment entered, asking for his dinner.

"Here's your letters," said his wife.

There was silence in the kitchen while he opened and read them.

"What in the name o' Goäd's this?" his voice was surly with rage, his face purple, the veins in his neck swollen.

"What is it, Gillespie?"

"What is it? What is it no'?" He slapped the blue paper with his fingers; "an account for twenty-nine pounds ten shillings frae Mrs. Tosh. Fox furs twenty-two pounds;" he could not suppress his rage, or read the other items. "Dae ye mean to ruin me, ye bauchle?" he shouted, striding up and down the room. "Fox furs, fox furs; whaur's the fox furs?" Half demented, his eyes danced about the room. "Goäd in heaven, but I hae the wife, ye drucken bauchle;" with flaming eyes he stepped towards her and clenched his fist. Topsail Janet flashed between them, in her hand a soup-ladle.

"Daur ye! daur ye strik' her? Deil roast ye, ye misert, it's time ye pey'd somethin' for her. Ye've never gien her a stitch since ye were mairrit. Div ye think she's dirt, Lonen's daughter? It's her is the leddy, wi' her muff, the bonniest cratur in the toon. We've done ower muckle for ye. Daur ye touch her an' I'll expose ye to the hale toon. It's me that told her tae get the muff."

Gillespie slowly unclenched his hand.

"It's you as told her?" he sneered. "Weel, I'll keep it off your wages."

"My wages! hear till him; my wages! I never got a brown penny frae the day I set fut in your hoose. Pey me my wages. Whaur's the price o' the toys an' books ye stole oot o' my shop? Ye robber! Wait you. I'll put a polissman on ye. Ye'll no' haud me doon the wy ye dae your wife, poor cratur."

Gillespie turned from her flaming face and sat down at the table.

"Weel, weel, Janet, we'll say nae mair aboot it. I'm hungry."

"Away an' mek' your ain meat then," she flashed. "You, ye misert, tae lift your nief on a puir wumman. See her greetin' her eyes oot."

"Gie me my dinner, Janet."

Custom was too strong for Topsail. The slave in her rose in obedience. She flashed the plates on the table, and spun down the clattering spoons.

"Dinna breck the crockery, Janet."

"Shut yeer mooth," she cried, "or I'll scad ye wi' the broth."
She filled his plate with broth. "Tek' your ain beef and potatoes,"
she said. "Come, Mrs. Strang, come awey an' leave the misert
tae say his ain grace tae the Almighty." And taking the arm of
Mrs. Strang, she led her out of the kitchen, into the front parlour.

"We needna go back tae Mrs. Tosh," said Topsail, grimly;
"he'll be there as soon as he fills his belly. Never mind," she said
cheerily, "I'll gie the Jew my wedding-ring the night."

"You mustn't do that, Janet;" her mistress was furtively
wiping her eyes.

"Ach! he telt me he'd gie me a brass imitation wan instead.
Naebody 'ill ken the differ; no' even Jeck;" she laughed merrily.

16

FEW in Brieston fathomed Gillespie. He had had the best of luck.
Times were good. There was no occasion for the wolf to cast its
sheep's clothing. He had cloaked his covetousness under the
guise of opening up new channels of commerce. The substantial
beginnings of a fortune in his hands, and the possibilities of its
ultimate attainment had sharpened his business faculty to a
monstrous degree. There was something hawk-like in the man,
as he hovered over the town spying out chances and occasions.
He had always been crafty, and had veiled his actions so adroitly
in hypocrisy, and was so cordial, even to his enemies, that he was
held as a first-rate man. When people have formed such an
opinion, and find it backed up by ostensibly beneficial public
acts they are tenacious, and ready to find reasons for any lapse
on the part of their idol. Thus, when Andrew Rodgers met his
death in the sea at Gillespie's store, the hero of the town at first
suffered no obloquy or disparagement. Every one remembered
Andy's unsleeping enmity; and he had in a moment of mad
frolic pushed his insolence, into the realm of terrorising, for
which he had suffered.

But as the affair was discussed, it began to take on a more
sinister aspect. Lonend went out of his way to insinuate the
depth of guile in Gillespie's heart, and Mrs. Galbraith expressed

herself to Mary Bunch as being deeply shocked. She could believe anything of the man. Gillespie, outwardly in the noontide of his glory, was now in the innermost heart of the people a man to be watched. "Who was informin' the Government men about your trawl-nets?" Lonend asked, and whipped them with scorn for their blindness. "Who was to profit on the loss of your nets, if it wasna Gillespie Strang?"

No man can be mixed up in a dire event and come out of it scathless, however much he may appear to have been the victim of circumstance. There is a voiceless, scrutinising, irresistible current of judgment, deep like a silently flowing river, about whose banks are whisperings and hints. It flows through humanity and influences the soul in a profound, inscrutable way, as a river quietly influences the country through which it flows. This is not public opinion, but is the solidarity of the human conscience, educated from time immemorial, and existing round the race as a moral atmosphere which, however corrupt public or individual life may be, cleanses the human race and preserves it in corporate righteousness. To this invisible influence is due the common anomaly of a man who, dishonest in private life, preserves an unflinching rectitude on a public board.

This deep wave of judgment flowed through Brieston. Outwardly, Gillespie had acted in fair play; but men, despite themselves, and even avowedly anxious to defend him, were haunted with sinister suspicions. Gillespie had been too swift and direct. Brieston was menaced by such a man. The banks of the river were full of whisperings.

The barrenness of the stores beyond the Quay was characteristic of their owner. They had lain in a dilapidated state for years, and except for putting new locks on the doors, and fettering the windows, Gillespie did nothing. The factor refused point-blank to spend a penny on their repair, and they remained bare, tumble-down, thick with grime. Corners were festooned with cobwebs; the floors were encumbered with rubbish—broken bottles, scraps of old iron, and rotten ropes. A daylight corner beside the door, which had once been rented from the Laird by a clog-maker, was heaped up with a sodden, yellowish mass of wood-chips and sawdust. In another corner had been stored part of the library of the doctor who had preceded Maclean. This library, laid to rest in a cemetery of boxes, had been plundered by fishermen and schoolboys. Gillespie had made use of the boxes; but a vast quantity of medical journals and papers lay scattered over the far-off end of the store.

At this end there was a door opening directly on the Harbour, on which the stores were built. Gillespie, who had begun to interest himself in the West Loch Brieston oysters, made use of this door for lowering his bags of oysters into the sea, to keep them fresh against the orders of customers. On the other door, by which ingress to the store was obtained, he had a notice inked in large letters:

"EVERYTHING OFF THE HOOK;
READY MONEY."

In mid-winter, when the herring-fishing season was over, the fishermen worked at "the small" and "the big lines," in crews of four men in open boats, some fifteen to twenty feet in length. A basket of small lines was baited with mussel; "the big" or deep sea lines with immature herring. They relied on the small lines for whiting, cod, and lithe; on the big lines—which they "shot" and left for a night and a day attached to buoys—for ling, eel, and skate.

"EVERYTHING OFF THE HOOK;
READY MONEY."

Thereafter followed a list of the different fish, and the prices, according to their length, Gillespie had learned from a Stornoway fish-buyer, who had visited Brieston on the chance of curing herring, that this was the method of buying fish which English buyers used in Barra. With ling, especially if they were under the length, Gillespie demanded a cod or a whiting to be thrown in to make up his price.

From the time of the herring-buying incident, Gillespie commanded all the fish caught. This was a severer blow to the clique of buyers on the Quay than the loss of their herring supply, for the herring market is risky, having glorious chances, but at the same time grave losses, while in respect of "white fish" it was different. The market was steady; they knew exactly what to pay for the fish on the Quay, and had found in this trafficking—especially in ling, eel, and skate—a steady source of income. Andrew Rodgers's rage was extreme at the deprivation. His small, yellow eyes had a wolfish glitter as he saw the fishermen sell their fish to Gillespie, though he offered the same money, and said that his silver was as white as Gillespie's.

"No, no, Andy; it's black, since the day ye told us tae go tae the big market."

Rage, however, will not go to market, and Andy himself was forced to take to "the lines," accompanied by Tamar Lusk and Queebec. They were lifting their second "shot" when that happened to them which had happened to Topsail Janet. The dead arose from the sea. The body was headless. Tamar, to whose line it was attached, fell backwards across the beam, and the line slowly sagged from his nerveless hands.

"What's wrong wi' ye, Tamar?" wheezed Queebec, from the other side of the boat.

"Hae ye a knife? I've brought up the Day o' Judgment."

The sight of Tamar's face roused Queebec. He made the line he was hauling on fast to the iron thole-pin, and began hauling on Tamar's line. Tamar caught Queebec's arm.

"Let go," he shouted, "let go; it's a man."

At the words, the familiar sea suddenly became horrible to these two men. An apparition of the dead floated up out of the dark-green depths, appallingly significant of the cold, stealthy, sinister deep. Tamar shivered and whined on Queebec to cut the line. Brick-red patches stood out on Queebec's high cheek-bones. Fear was taking him by the throat, but a spark of manhood flickered in him.

"We'll tek' him ashore an' gie him Christian beerial."

Tamar covered his face with his hands.

"No, no," he moaned; "I canna thole the look o' thon; there's no heid on it."

Andy, who had been silent at the stern, said coolly:

"I expect he got a skelp wi' a propeller on the neck. Tek' a turn roond the thole-pin, Queebec."

Queebec, with trembling hand, obeyed. He had no stomach, either, for a headless corpse.

Andy silently took a half-mutchkin bottle from his pocket and handed it to Queebec, who having drank, gave it to Tamar.

"No, no! I canna pree't wi'—wi' that anchor on to the boat."

The bottle went back to Andy, and was again passed to Queebec. They finished it between them.

"What's the maitter wi' ye, Tamar? Were ye never 'oot sweepin' for a deid body?" When a fisherman is drowned, long

176

lines of grappling-hooks are used to "sweep" for the body. "What's the differ between this body an' a fisherman's?" asked Andy in scorn.

"I don't care, I don't care; cut the line; we're no sweepin', we're fishin'."

Andy thrust forward his lean, dogged face.

"The big fella"—this was Gillespie's name on the Quay— "peys for everything off the hook, ready money. We'll gie him something for his money." Ah, Andy, the sea that returns the dead, will it not be avenged?

"Never since I saw white poirpoises off Newfoundland did I ever hear the like." The toughened mariner of the ports of the New World was not so squeamish as Tamar. He, too, had felt keenly the bite of Gillespie's claws; but there lingered in his mind a wholesome respect for Gillespie.

"It's the jyle he'll be gein' us," he said.

"Jyle be damned!" cried Andy fiercely; "are we no' tekin' the body ashore for beerial? Where wad we leave it but in the store? He's a damn coward, Gillespie. We'll mek' him the laughin'-stock o' Brieston." Andy began to pull on the line.

"For Goäd's sake don't tek' it up," screamed Tamar; "dae ye want the judgment o' Goäd on us?"

"Shut your mooth," yelped Andy, "or I'll heave ye over the side."

Tamar squirmed forward and buried his face in the bow-sheets, when he heard a splash in the water.

"Hold him by the shouther a meenut," he heard Andy say; "up wi' him noo." A scraping sound reached his ears as the body was hauled in and hastily thrown down in the boat. They buoyed the remainder of the lines and set sail. Queebec sat with his back to the body and faced Andy, who was at the tiller.

After a long silence Queebec spoke:

"I'm no' carin' for this work; we'll send word to Campbell the polissman."

"We'll do noäthin' o' the kind. We'll leave it in Gillespie's store an' send for him. Where's the hairm in that?"

Silence and the dusk fell on the boat, along which the sea mourned. Dark, long, and rakish, she had the appearance of a coffin.

Suddenly Tamar screamed.

"It's movin', my Goäd, it's movin'!"

"Shut up, you damn fool; dae ye want the hale toon to hear ye?" They were now in the Harbour mouth. The wind was westerly, dead in their teeth. They were on the windward tack, and when close inshore at the Pier Tamar, springing up in the bow, leapt overboard. The boat was about on the other tack. Andy jammed down the tiller; but the boat, with little way on her, came shivering up in the wind. In the silence they heard Tamar swimming, and presently he was scrambling up on the rocks.

"Hell scud him!" said Andy; "I thought he wad be drooned;" and put down the helm. When they reached the Quay night was come, and the stores were locked. They sent a boy to Gillespie to tell him there was fish at the Quay.

"We'll cairry this up to the door," said Andy. Queebec, now sober, refused at first the ugly task, and eased his conscience as he took the feet.

"Andy, you're just a duvvil."

"I'm no' the quate sookin duvvil Gillespie is. I'm for fightin' in the open; an' if I bate him, it's you an' Tamar an' a lot more o' ye that'll benefit." Andy always put a plausible face on his viciousness. He, indeed, differentiated his methods of attack from Gillespie's with some discernment. Andy leapt with flame in his eyes at a breach. Gillespie hated the sound of trumpets in his warfare, preferring poison and its arts to bullets and their butchery. The very appearance of the two antagonists was characteristic of their methods—the one lean and fiery, the other stout and cautious. Andy sought a present satisfaction, being more concerned with revenge than with any future advantage. Gillespie explored warily the human heart, and laid his strategy on the instability and gullibleness of men. He used men as his instruments, for every man could be useful to him in some way. It was not his policy to quarrel with men, and if on occasion he had to be servile, he extorted his price in the end. You will understand the weapons with which these men were about to meet.

"Any luck, boys?" Gillespie's cheery voice rang out.

"Oh! fairish, fairish."

"That you, Andy? Are ye no' for tryin' the mercat yersel'?" There was the faintest tinge of irony in the tone.

"I'm done wi' the buyin', Gillespie."

Gillespie unlocked the door of the store.

178

"All right, Andy; there's no a great dale in the fush ee noo, anyway. Just cairry them in." They brought in the fish, and then the body.

Gillespie lit one of the naphtha torches used at night on the Quay. It smoked, and cast huge, dancing shadows across the piles of empty herring-barrels, as if the wings of great flying bats darkened the air. When the fish were sold, Andy bent down and undid the wet sail.

"It's off the hook," he said, "an' inches weel."

Gillespie started at the apparition of horror, and his face paled visibly as he took a sudden step backwards. This brought him nearest the door. From his position he saw straight down between the shoulders of the headless trunk.

"Are ye mad, Andy?" he said in horror.

"It's you that'll soon be mad, by Goäd," and the venom of the man came out. "What are ye doin' wi' a corp in your store?" This sudden treachery took even Queebec by the throat.

"Did ye no' cairry it here?" answered Gillespie, who was plainly nonplussed.

"Not us; we're two to wan to sweir against ye; are we no', Queebec?"

Gillespie turned to Queebec.

"Will ye tek' an oath on Almighty Goäd that ye didna cairry that in here? Look at it, the twa o' ye. The very corp wad speak if it could. Look at it!"

As if Gillespie's index finger were a sign the trunk made a perceptible movement.

"What damn monkey tricks are ye up tae?" cried Andy passionately. "Stand back frae the corp."

Gillespie took a step towards the door.

"I hevna meddled it, Andy," he said, with quiet assurance. The great shadows hopped across the barrels; in the cold night wind, through the open door, the flame of the torch trembled and shook as if in sudden fear. Gillespie, with a backward jerk of his foot, flung the door shut with a clang that echoed through the cavernous store, locked it and put the key in his pocket. "No need for a' the world to see," he said.

Queebec stared fascinated. "God it's movin', see!"

Andy, who was standing at the foot of the body, jumped backwards. Gillespie, stepping to the barrels, lifted the torch. His shadow stood out solid and deep. He went back to his former position, and keenly scrutinised the trunk at the shoulders. At that moment the trunk gave a violent convulsion.

"Let me oot, o this, Gillespie; let me oot!" Queebec squealed. "It's Andy's work, I tell ye. Ask Tamar Lusk."

"The thing's no' canny, Queebec;" Gillespie took a measuring-tape from his pocket. His damp breath clouded the murky air. "But we've a bargain to mek', you an' me"—he nodded towards Andy; "it's inches weel, is it? Is it no' an inch or two short aboot the heid?"

Gillespie did not want to measure the body. He desired a pretext to get nearer it to verify his suspicion.

The wind suddenly went moaning through the empty barrels. Its cold wave passed as ice on the napes of their necks. Queebec raised his hand to his cheek with a nervous gesture. The hand suffered from a sea-boil, and was swathed in a dirty rag. He began gnawing the rag.

"Gillespie," he muttered sullenly, "gie me the key."

Gillespie turned on him a bland face.

"Are ye no' for your pey, Queebec? ye've had a touch the night." He bent down to the corpse and laid the brass edge of the tape on the neck. The frayed remnant of a dongaree jacket clothed it. As the tape touched the sodden flesh, a violent shudder went through the trunk, and a look of understanding passed quickly over Gillespie's face. He had discovered from his position at the head of the body what the others were unable to see.

"Here, Andy, my man, hold it quate; the thing's gey an' ill tae measure."

Andy, shrouded in the gloom, was making little sucking sounds, which froze Queebec's blood. An unseen terror lay behind the monstrous dancing shadows. Queebec slipped behind Gillespie, and began kicking the door with his big sea-boots.

"Nae use o' that, Queebec; there's no' a livin' sowl on the Quay a dark night lik' this." He rose to his feet, and stood directly between Queebec and the body. "Ay," he said, "it's the size o' a big conger nate; I winna cheat ye in the price o' this; no' for a' the world. Fower feet aucht an' a half. A fine, upstandin' man he must ha' been."

He pocketed the tape, took some silver coins from his pocket and counted them. Some he put back to his pocket, the others he held in his open palm.

"Here, boys! here's the blood money."

Queebec's voice rang out in a scream. "Gie me the key o' the door."

"Dinna be blate, Andy. Come and tek' the siller. See an' dinna drink it. Maybe ye'd better put it in the plate come Sunday. Eh! what was the minister on last Sunday, Queebec? Ou ay! I mind noo. Judas sellin' his Master. But ye sell a cauld corp as hevna' got the eyes to see ye. Look at it, Andy, look at it movin' again."

Queebec, enthralled by horror, turned his face from the door, and saw across the smoky glare a great shadow swooping like a thing of menace across the ceiling. Gillespie saw his terror-stricken eyes, the flash of their blood-shot whites; but was too late. The iron fist, hardened on the Spanish Main, swung like a hammer.

"Ye'll gie me the key noo."

Gillespie heard the maddened scream as he fell with a smothered groan across the dead body. His right hand shot out spasmodically; the torch flew from it in a downward curve, hit one of the barrels, and went out. The store was thick with inky darkness.

"Good Goäd! I've done for him."

Queebec staggered back against the pile of barrels which had been left in disorder since the day on which Gillespie had made advent as a buyer. It trembled and rocked; flattened out, and with a crash gave way. Losing this support to his back, Queebec fell. A hot, stabbing pain went through his head. He felt blood on his cheek. Then there was silence in the store, save for the sound of a barrel which was rolling down the gentle slope of the floor, rolling quietly, as if seeking furtively to escape from the confusion. When it ceased rolling, the sound of the sea along the walls broke in on the store with a hissing noise that died away into a feathery silence. Queebec rose to his feet, and stood like a block of granite, listening to hear Gillespie breathe, but he could hear nothing—nothing but the monotonous wash of the sea.

"Andy," he whispered into the dark. A water-rat that had been routed out of its corner by the fall of the barrels scuttled across the floor towards the corpse. Queebec, shivering and peering forward, cried, "Hiss——"

Suddenly there was a loud crash. Andy, creeping down the floor, had dislodged the remainder of the pile of barrels. Queebec put out his hands in front of his face.

"Is that you, Andy? Have you a match?"

"No;" the voice came from far away.

Queebec did not smoke. Andy had given his box of matches to Tamar Lusk in the line boat.

"Andy! can ye hear him breathin'?"

"Who?"

"Gillespie."

"Gillespie! where's Gillespie?" the voice quavered with fear.

"He's lyin' across thon thing. I gied him a clink on the temple. He wadna gie me the key." Queebec was hurriedly justifying himself, to stifle the terror that rose in his gorge. "Dae ye hear him movin'?"

There was no answer from Andy.

"Andy! Andy! Will ye no' speak?"

"Keep clear o' me," wailed Andy. "Ye've done for him. I'm no goin' to be hanged for you."

"No! no!" cried Queebec; "I didna mean anything. He wadna gie me the key; he wadna gie me the key. I dinna strik' him that hard. Where are ye, Andy?"

The silence was solid about them. Through the impenetrable gloom a faint noise came to their pricked-up ears. The thing was moving, moving.

"Oh! my Goäd, Andy, it's crawlin' to me!" Queebec screamed, and doubled up began to scurry towards the far end of the store.

Half running, he tripped and fell over Andy, who rose upon his knees, and in a blind fury caught Queebec by the throat. "I'll no' swing for you."

The two men, breathing hard, struggled in the darkness. Queebec, the more powerful, shook off Andy and pinned him by the two shoulders to the floor. His blood was on fire. His fist swung up and came down full on Andy's mouth with a sickening thud. "Ye bloody fool; wad ye throttle me?"

In the darkness there was a sound of blood gurgling.

Andy wriggled beneath the powerful hands. "Let me go, Queebec, ye're killin' me."

A wave of terror swept over Queebec. Was he to have another man's death at his door? With a groan he released Andy, who after a prolonged silence whispered:

"Queebec, we're a pair o' weans. Nobody saw us comin' in here. Dae ye no' see? If we get oot quietly they'll find Gillespie in the morn—alone wi'—wi'——"

"What o' Tamar?"

"Tamar be damned! He'll no' speak."

Queebec shivered with hope. "Hoo can we mand oot o' here?"

"Go an' rype him for the key," Andy whispered, and swallowed blood.

"I canna! I canna! I've done for him. Go on you."

"Me! Me! Touch thon; did ye no' hear it movin' in the dark?"

Again they listened, as from without came up the long sob of the sea. Andy gripped Queebec by the arm. "The back door," he whispered. "I clean forgot; the back door."

The plowter of the sea rose along the wall.

"The tide's in," said Queebec; "hear to it."

"I'll face twenty tides before thon thing. It can crawl, Queebec," and Queebec, with his blood curdling, began to wriggle to the far end of the store.

"Wait for me, Queebec;" the other followed and ran his head into a barrel. He leapt back, his nerves quivering; but terror of being left behind goaded him on. He rose to his feet and plunged head-foremost over the barrel, ploughing his wrist and arm on the concrete floor.

He backed into the clammy wall and crept upon some broken bottles. He was bleeding at the mouth, at the wrist and the hands. A cold wind suddenly blew on his face; the sea-draught from the door. He stood up, fumbling with both hands, found the sneck and jerked the door open. They saw the sky, placid with stars and the blue-black night, and gulped in great draughts of the brine-laden air.

"God in heaven, I'm seeck; let us get oot o' here," said Queebec. He sat down to take off his big sea-boots, and found the rope, which Gillespie had attached to a bag of oysters, steeping in the sea. Queebec took off his boots and jacket, gripped the rope, and swung himself over the edge.

"Queebec! Queebec! wait for me; I canna sweem."

Suddenly a barrel came crashing to the floor.

"Goäd Almighty, it's crawlin' among the barrels." Andy cast a look over his shoulder into the dark, then, holding his face between his hands, jumped feet first into the sea. Down! down! he sank. A black, thundering mass roared in his ears. His head was about to burst, when he shot gasping to the surface. Choking with blood and brine, he saw the peaceful stars glittering high overhead. Something gripped him by the hair; and the church clock began slowly booming through the night.

"Hold on to the rope, or ye'll droon," a voice was saying. The salt water was nipping his bleeding hands, but he gripped the rope and leaned hard against the wall.

"Are ye right?" he heard the voice again. He tried to speak, and nodded to the sea, which was rippling about his shoulders. He had never seen it that colour before—blue like steel in the starlight. A little wave splashed in his face, and stung his eyes. He swallowed some salt water.

"Are ye hearin' me, Andy?"

"Ay."

"Hae ye a good grup o' the rope?" the voice was somewhere above his head. He thought it was Queebec's, and would like to climb up to the voice, but his big sea-boots were heavy with water, and he had to keep swallowing salt water or blood, he did not know which. With the tip of his tongue he discovered that some of his teeth had disappeared.

"Ye've knocked my teeth doon my throat," he whispered to the water; and the little plashing waves mocked him, and licked his face. One bigger than the others took his breath away for a minute. He was feeling the cold boring into his bones, like a hot gimlet.

"Ye're sure ye've a good grup, Andy?"

"Ay," he said, to this pestering voice overhead. Then something that was holding him by the hair of the head let go, and he slipped down head beneath into the water. It was terribly black now and choking him. With a supreme effort he pulled himself up by the rope. The heel of his big sea-boot caught in an edge of the stone. He felt it supporting him. He tried with his other heel to find a corner in the wall; but the wall was smooth. There was a drumming sound in his ears. He thought it must be the church bell ringing; but the bell had ceased on the last stroke of midnight, and a vast silence covered the face of the sky.

"It's no high watter yet; we canna hing here a' night," the voice above him was saying; "they'll miss Gillespie an' come lookin' for him. The sooner we're oot o' here the better." Andy could not follow the voice. The thundering bells in his ears were drowning its nagging tones.

"Dae ye hear me, Andy? I'll sweem to the Quay an' come back wi' a punt. Hold on for your life noo. I'll be back in twenty meenuts. Don't let go, or ye'll droon."

There was no answer.

"Are ye hearin' me, Andy?" screamed Queebec, in fear.

Andy heard the words. They seemed to drop down on him from some height beneath the stars; and he was weary of this terrible voice.

"Ay, ay," he muttered, and closed his eyes. Something dark shot past him. He heard a splash in the water. The waves broke on his face, and blinded him. He swallowed more salt water. The salt still blinded his eyes, and he let his left hand go from the rope to rub them. This movement dislodged his heel from the protruding stone of the wall. He could not find it again. He was like a man being hung. The thought stirred some association in his brain. It was Queebec who was to be hung for killing Gillespie. Gillespie! He remembered and shivered in the water. He did not feel the cold now from the level, dark-blue sea that stretched away for miles. Far off across the water he saw a light burning in a window of the Barracks, and wished he was there. He moved his body, and at the movement thought some one was pouring water down the legs of his trousers. His legs were getting rigid like iron bars; his arms were terribly weary with the strain. Something cold was lap, lapping about his throat. He tried to pull himself up from it; and his legs swam away from under him. The weight was now pulling his arms out of their sockets. His eyes closed; he felt sleepy. Why was he clinging here, with such a sickening weight on his arms, and nothing beneath his rigid legs? That dark-blue mass at his chin was like a great, soft pillow. God! how he longed for his bed! His head was slowly turning round. It must be the rope that was twisting. The stars in front of his face above the hills were wheeling about in the sky like sparks stirred about in a big pot. He could not keep his eyes open. He was numb and wet and tired. God! to be in bed, and the soft, dark pillow below him! The head nodded to the stars, the mouth opened, the fingers relaxed. What a weight was off his arms! Slowly the hands slid down the rope, and with a gurgling sound the white, wet face disappeared in the dark silent water. There was a feeble beating of the hands for a moment, a fluttering towards the rope, one or two bubbles rose to the surface. . . .

A punt was being quietly sculled towards the rope. The sculler drew in his oar, and crept forward.

"Andy," he whispered.

There was no answer.

The bow of the punt drifted into the rope. Queebec stared upwards, following the length of the rope in the starlight till it disappeared over the edge at the door. He climbed up and shouted into the dark, terrible silence.

"Goäd in heaven, he's gone!"

Queebec, his hands on fire with their rush over the rope, pushed the punt away from the wall, and peered down into the dark water. He could see nothing. He kept staring at the water, paralysed with terror. Suddenly Andy's words hammered on his brain, "Nobody saw us comin' here."

"Nobody saw us, nobody saw us," he sobbed; jumped to the oar, and began sculling to the Quay.

17

BRIESTON was full of the wildest rumours. Gillespie had been found in the early morning by Jeck the Traiveller lying in the store beside a dead man, who had broken into the store and had felled Gillespie. Gillespie, in turn, had killed the man. All day crowds hung about the store, peering in through the key-hole, and craning their necks at the broken windows. All they could see was a litter of barrels on the floor. Excitement reached a pitch of frenzy when two boys, who had been scavenging along the seaweed of the walls of the store at low water for whelks, came running up the Quay with scared, white faces, crying, "There's a deid man on the shore; there's a deid man on the shore."

The agent of the luggage steamer, one of the porters, and three fishermen who were at the "Shipping Box" ran down the Quay. Willie Allan, who had a shop at the Quay, across the road from the "Shipping Box," hearing the hubbub, scurried to his door, and seeing men running down the Quay, shouted to the Fishery Officer whose office was next to his shop that somebody was drowning. Both set to running. Windows were flung up in the Quay tenements. The head of Andy's wife appeared with the others. The stairs sounded with the feet of hurrying men. The two boys ran up Harbour Street, shouting their news everywhere. In a quarter of an hour the shore was black with people around the body of Andy. He lay face upwards, with the head pointing in the direction of the Harbour mouth. Some of his teeth were missing. The thin, bleached face, and wet, wiry hair, the broken mouth and mauled hands, in the centre of this group of curious, healthy humanity, gave a sense of pathos to that forlorn shore and its burden, and silenced the babble of tongues in the inner ring of men. Those on the fringe were eagerly inquiring what was wrong, and pushing restlessly to the front to glut the eye.

"It's Andy Rodgers," went from mouth to mouth. The baulked fringe was determined on a sight of the body. The crowd heaved and swayed. Willie Allan flung his apron over his shoulder, and anger flashed in his eyes.

"Stop that shovin'!" he shouted; "did ye never see a deid man before?" The crowd became suddenly still. "One of you," he shouted, "go for Dr. Maclean, and tell the policeman."

Sandy the Fox pressed forward, staring down at Andy, and took another step beside the body. Willie Allan caught him by the shoulder and spun him round. "Here you, get out of this; let nobody touch the body till the doctor comes." The Fox showed his teeth, edged his way through the crowd, and hurried up the Quay.

Andy's wife, a large, buxom woman, was at the close, talking with two neighbours, and Andy's only son was hanging about near at hand.

"What's wrong, Sandy," he shouted, "doon at the Quay?"

Again Sandy the Fox showed his teeth, and glanced at the group of women.

"Your mother's a weeda," he snarled, and passed, loping.

Mrs. Rodgers put her left hand on her breast, and her face became as chalk. Her knees tottered. She swayed a little and lurched forward, gripping at the shoulder of her nearest neighbour. "Aw! Dhia! Dhia! tek' me home. Aw! Aw! Aw!"

They supported her in through the close and up the stair, and laid her on the kitchen bed.

Dr. Maclean had been roused through the night by Jeck the Traiveller, and had seen in Gillespie's store a sight which he would never forget. He had not gone back to bed, but sat till day whitened the window of his smoking-room. He had watched Gillespie as that man slowly came round to consciousness. "Queebec," Gillespie muttered, and lapsed into pertinacious silence. Maclean noticed that he betrayed no fear or horror of his ghastly companion of the night.

At eight o'clock in the morning, Maclean knocked at Queebec's door. He knew the house very well. Some five months before Queebec had come in the dead of night imploring Maclean to come and see his daughter. "She's in fair agony, doctor."

Maclean went downstairs, made up a medicine in the surgery, accompanied Queebec. When he reached the house, he found the youngest daughter in bed and her two sisters applying hot plates over the region of the stomach. A glance told Maclean what the trouble was, and he stood with his back to the fire, watching in silence for a few minutes the pathetic efforts of the sisters.

"Put the plate away, my girl," said Maclean; "you're doing more harm than good." Within two hours Maclean had delivered the girl of a child. He had not forgotten Queebec, nor had Queebec forgotten him, and was prepared to go through fire and water for the doctor.

It was a natural thing for him to find Queebec in bed at eight in the morning; not so natural that he should find Queebec ailing.

"I've a heavy cold lyin' on my chest, doctor," Queebec said, coughing.

Maclean watched him musingly for a moment. "You look as if you had seen a ghost," he said.

Queebec visibly trembled beneath the bed-clothes. Maclean stepped across the room, picked up a small mirror hanging over the sink, and coming back, handed it in silence to Queebec, who took one glance.

"My Goäd!" he moaned. His hair was white.

Maclean took the mirror out of the shaking hand and returned it to its place. "Take off the buttons," he said, "till I have a look at you."

Queebec's trembling hands could not lay hold of the buttons. Maclean undid them, rolled back the striped shirt and semet, and putting a forefinger on Queebec's chest, began to tap it with his other finger. In this way he traversed the chest.

"Turn over on your face." He rolled up Queebec's shirt and semet, and laid his ear in the region of the shoulder-blades.

"Take a deep breath," he commanded; "another." He pulled down the garments. "That'll do," he said.

Queebec rolled over and faced him. "Anything wrong, doctor?"

"You've got a complication, Queebec. I'll manage to cure part of it. There's some mischief at the base of the right lung." He tugged at his moustache, watching Queebec. "You've another trouble," he said.

"What is it, doctor?"

Maclean drew in a chair to the bedside. "I don't know," he answered; "it's left your hair white."

"Oh, doctor, doctor!" Queebec covered his face with his hands.

"Where were you last night? You've caught a bad cold."

Queebec's eyes stared at the doctor, beseeching mercy, pity, help. "I wasna to blame, Goäd knows. It was Andy Rodgers began it. Ask Tamar Lusk."

"Who struck Gillespie?" Maclean saw the sudden look of fear leap into Queebec's eyes—the look of a beast cowering as it waits the death-stroke. The man's face was agonised with terror.

"Don't be afraid, Queebec," said Maclean soothingly. "Gillespie's all right. Some one stunned him. He'll be up to-morrow."

A sudden glory irradiated the miserable man's face, and tears welled up in his grey eyes. He made an effort to speak as he gripped the doctor's hand.

"Doctor, doctor!" He took a long, deep breath. "Oh! I'm a new man."

After a little Maclean said, "Now, Queebec, tell me everything." And Queebec, concealing nothing, told the grim story of the past night. When it was ended, Maclean said:

"I can't go to Andy just now; I'll have to wait till I'm sent for." But he paid another visit to the store, examined the headless corpse, put his hand in at the hole where the head had been severed from the body, and caught something slippery. With an exclamation of disgust he pulled out a black eel, which had burrowed in through the sodden trunk, swung the serpent-fish by the tail, and brought its head crashing down on the concrete floor. It gave a convulsive movement down the length of its body, and lay still. With the toe of his boot, Maclean lifted it over beside the dead body, covered the body again with the sail, and glancing at the back door of the store, which stood open, and at

189

a pair of big sea-boots standing there, went out, and locked the door behind him. An observer would have noticed him glance up at Andy's window as he passed up Harbour Street homewards.

18

DR. MACLEAN had been summoned, and hurrying down Harbour Street, was met by the flying son of Andy. Periodically men, boys, and sometimes women, are seen running up the street. No one thinks of them as ungainly at such a time, because they may be racing with Death for a precious life. Especially terrible is the sound of running footsteps in the deserted streets at night. Maclean hurried to the help of Mrs. Rodgers, who was conscious again.

"Aw, Goäd peety me," she moaned.

"He died like a hero," said the doctor, "trying to save Queebec."

And that was all which the public ever heard from Dr. Maclean of the mystery of the store.

"Here's the doctor! here's the doctor!" The manner in which the crowd made way for him was their testimony to their faith.

Maclean did not so much as touch the body. "He's been dead for twelve hours," he said.

Brieston was in a ferment. Where was Gillespie? Who was the dead man in the store? Who had struck Andy on the mouth and sent him headlong out of the store into the water? No! it couldn't be that. His hands and his wrist were cut. From the Barracks to the "Shipping Box" groups of people lived with rumour; and slowly, pervasively, a sinister opinion of Gillespie began to take possession of men's minds. Why had he been in the store so late at night? Ugly rumours of his avaricious dealings with Galbraith of Muirhead got abroad. It was hinted that he had arrested the furniture of a small farmer in the country for debt without authority. The farmer had called him a thief, and Gillespie threatened the farmer with an action for libel unless he was paid fifty pounds. The unsophisticated man was ruined.

"It was a canty wee neeboorly through-gaen, but an' ben toon till he came," said Ned o' the Horn.

"You'll scratch me an' I'll scratch you sort o' toon," answered old Sandy, on the defensive for his hero. "We'd never ken oor ain faults if it wasna for the likes o' him. It's good whiles to hae a breeze."

"Weel," flashed Ned o' the Horn, to whom the opinions of the Pump were retailed by his better-half, Black Jean, "I lik' a breeze that's clean. No' thon wee yeuky eyes aye watchin' ye, an' his hand aye claut, claut, clautin'. You bate he dinna buy your herrin', Sandy, wi' his eyes shut. Poor Andy that's deid an' gone could hae bought them if he'd a store hotched wi' stock an' a puffer ready to mek' the run. He didna tell ye what they came oot at in Glesca."

Gillespie stood in bad odour. The Butler had an ill-omened story of Gillespie's dealings with Mirren Johnstone, when her father had died. Mary Bunch had it from Nan at Jock, and told Mrs. Galbraith. Campion, the new schoolmaster, had told the Butler, who did not know how Campion had got the story—very likely at Lonend. Mirren came into the shop with the stains of tears like blisters yet in the hollow of her cheeks, and asking for material for a black dress, burst into tears.

"What ails ye, Mirren?" asked Gillespie, picking up the measuring-yard.

"Faither's—deid."

"Ay! ay! that's a peety. I never heard he was so near his end."

"Och! och! no, no. He rose at the turn o' the nicht;" she bravely winked the tears away. "My mother cried me ben. She was frightened to be alone wi' him.

" 'Betty,' he sez tae my mither, "that's fine medicine the doctor's gien me this time.'

" 'Will ye no' tek' a wee drap spirits then, faither, seein' ye're up?' I sez, for mother was fair in the nerves.

" 'No,' sez he, 'I'm wantin' to sleep;' and he went back to bed." The girl burst out sobbing, "an'—oh—oh—he was deid afore he'd the clothes aboot him."

"Ay, ay!" Gillespie ran his finger along the yard; "it was a sudden call."

The girl dried her eyes with the corner of her apron.

"Mither an' me wad lik' some mournin's."

"How much did ye say?"

"Six an' a half yairds for me, an' seven for my mither."

"A black merino?" in suave inquiry.

The girl assented.

"Cloth's up ee noo, wi' the drought in Australyia." He swept the polished counter with his palm; "one shilling and tenpence the yard."

He scribbled on a coarse piece of paper. "That'll come oot at one pound four shillings and ninepence."

"I hevna the money," the girl faltered, shrinking back from the counter. All things must give way to the Angel of Death, they had thought in their misery, looking down on the Angel's marble-sculptured creation on the bed. The mines of Bonanza would surely unlock their treasures at the omnipotent sweep of its chiselling wings.

"I'm dootin', Mirren, I canna obleege ye; I'd like to fine, but thae traivellers frae Glesca is fair harasshin' me for money."

His voice was pleading with the girl who was stunned. She had not dreamed that any one could confront death with a denial. With a fleeting look of fear she swept his face, and shrank farther back, shame driving her to the door.

Gillespie recalled her. "Ye needna be in such a hurry, Mirren. Your faither an' me was good freends."

She faced him again with hesitant eyes.

"I mind o' him tellin' me he was insured."

The light of hope sprang in the girl's face.

"Ay! he was insured on fifty pounds."

"Was it fifty? I didna ken the amount. Come awa' ower to the other coonter."

This counter was at the back of the shop, away from the lane of customers, where Gillespie kept the "dry goods." He measured, cut, and made up the cloth in a parcel, the girl all this while answering his questions in low monosyllables.

"Was the rent all paid?"

"Were the rates an' taxes paid?"

Gillespie carried the parcel to the front counter and disappeared. Through a small glass window, which gave on the shop, she saw his head bowed over his desk. Presently he returned, and handed the girl an I O U with security on the insurance policy. A penny stamp was affixed at the bottom.

"Just run an' tell your mother to write her name there." He laid the point of the pen on the face of the effigy of the queen.

"Ye'll see I made it oot at 1s. 10d. I canna be lyin' oot my money, Mirren, wi' thae traivellers frae Grennock an' Glesca harasshin' me every Monday. An' I've just put in the penny for the stamp. Poor lassie! it's a peety o' ye lossin' your faither. It's kin' o' a wee thing alarmin', a sudden call lik' that. I'll miss him aboot the corner. Him an' me used to hae a crack whiles. Tell your mother I'll be at the funeral."

The story went through Brieston like wild-fire.

"Ay! that's the man," said Lonend; "thon corbie! thon white laugh!"

Brieston was baulked and angry. Watty Foster had brought the Fiscal from Ardmarkie; but no one was allowed into the store except the doctor, Gillespie—who passed down Harbour Street with a heavy, pondering look and pouched eyes—Tamar Lusk, Willie Allan, the Fishery Officer, the porter at the Quay, and Queebec. Queebec's appearance astonished the town. "He's as white's a sheep, an' hoastin' lik' an auld craw." The Quay head was dense with men. The clock in the parish church was booming the hour of two when the door of the store was reopened, and Gillespie came out alone. In a little he was followed by every one except the doctor and the Fiscal. Queebec and Tamar walked on together, speaking in a low voice. They refused to give any information, and Brieston gnawed ravenously on its curiosity. The Fiscal caught the mailcoach back to Ardmarkie, and Maclean drove to one of his cases in the country. The next day, being Sunday, the two ministers read an intimation requesting the people to attend a double funeral on Monday afternoon at three o'clock, one funeral to be from the Good Templars' Hall.

On the Saturday, when the door was locked, the Fiscal, directing attention to the unknown body, asked Gillespie how it came to be in his store. Gillespie shook his head. "Maybe," he said softly, "Queebec here can tell us." Queebec, with underlip trembling violently, looked hesitatingly at the doctor.

"Tell the Procurator Fiscal what you told me yesterday morning, Queebec. Keep nothing back."

"It will be as well," warned the Fiscal, "to make a clean breast of everything, my man."

With many stumblings, Queebec once more repeated the tale. The man looked so haggard and spent that in the midst of the narrative the Fiscal invited him to sit on a herring-box.

"An' that," ended the white-haired, broken man, on a sob, "that's the strucken truth; my hands tae Goäd." He lifted his palms upwards.

"I believe you, my man," said the Fiscal, who made no further comment, but questioned Willie Allan and the others as to the finding of Andy's body. He examined the back door and the rope, and noted Queebec's big sea-boots and jacket. The blackened torch stood out against a barrel as a funereal witness to the truth of these things.

"Have you anything to add?" the Fiscal turned sharply on Gillespie.

"Weel," he answered in an insinuating voice, and looking at Queebec; "I might hae a case for damages an' assault against this man."

"If you're wise you'll let that dead dog lie;" the Fiscal cast a withering look on Gillespie. "In my opinion the outcome of this unfortunate affair lies at your door."

"I don't a'thegeither see that," Gillespie answered smoothly.

"Come, come, my man," said the Fiscal, with a rising intonation; "you were here in this gloomy place"—he cast a glance round the store—"late at night with a locked door, and you saw the corpse moving. Do you tell me you weren't afraid?"

"No' me; it was Andy an' this man"—he pointed to Queebec—"brought it. I wasna feart. It was the Judgment o' Goäd on them." He frowned austerely like a Calvinistic divine.

"That's not the case, Mr. Strang," said Maclean. "You weren't afraid because you were standing at the head of the corpse."

"It had nae heid, doctor"—politely.

"Be careful, my man," warned the Fiscal; "you're in a court just now. Don't indulge in facetious expressions."

"Well, where the head should have been"—Maclean's tone was touchy—"and you saw the tail of the eel."

"What! what! what, doctor!" ejaculated Willie Allan.

"Silence!" commanded the Fiscal.

Maclean touched with his boot the dead fish, on which Queebec's eyes were riveted. "I found this inside the body, alive. Mr. Strang knew it was there. He ought to have told these men."

The Fiscal looked at Gillespie with a severe face.

"Do you hear, sir?"

Gillespie's ruddy face paled.

"It served them right," he said doggedly, "for their dirty

194

trick." He collected himself. "I was goin' to tell them when Queebec struck me."

"You were too late," said the Fiscal drily.

"Too late to bring the dead to life," Maclean said musingly.

The Fiscal addressed Gillespie.

"I cannot, sir, bring you under the penalty of the law for what you failed to do, but I have no words to express my sense of your vicious conduct. You wished to pose as a man of courage. You were an arrant coward, a bigger coward than this man who was afraid. In my opinion a man's death lies morally at your door. The law, unfortunately, cannot punish you. I leave you in the hands of God." The Fiscal spoke with a severe, unstudied simplicity, which deeply affected his hearers.

"Are ye feenished wi' me?" Gillespie asked with a veiled sneer. "I'm thrang the day, after being laid up yesterday wi' assault."

"I am, sir; and I hope I shall never have to do with you again."

"If you hae," answered Gillespie, unabashed, "I expec' Queebec 'ill be to blame again," and casting a venomous glance at the doctor, he turned and left the store. Little did Gillespie know under what terrible circumstances he would face the Procurator-Fiscal again.

"Well, gentlemen, we're finished. I thank you for your attendance. I need scarcely impress upon you the advisability of keeping silent about what we have heard. The death of Andrew Rodgers is due to misadventure. The death of this man"—the Fiscal stopped and regarded the headless trunk—"Alec"—he lifted his eyes to the doctor's face—"what do you think severed the head?"

Before the doctor could speak, Tamar Lusk quavered:

"I expec', my lord, he got a kick wi' the propeller."

"Ah, yes! I see. You'll incorporate that, Alec, in your report for his lordship."

The doctor nodded.

Willie Allan picked up the dead eel by the tail, and going to the back door, flung it far out into the sea.

The local weekly paper, on the following Saturday, had a paragraph headed in large type:

"THE MYSTERY OF THE BRIESTON CURING-SHED

'One of the strangest events which has happened within living memory, occurred at Brieston last Friday night. Some line fishermen, on lifting their lines, brought up the body of a man without a head, who is supposed to have fallen out of a Clyde steamer, and was decapitated by the propeller. In attempting to get their gruesome find into the curing-shed of Mr. Gillespie Strang, the well-known merchant, one of the fishermen, Mr. Andrew Rodgers, lost his balance and fell into the water. Before the other two men could get down to his rescue from the store the unfortunate man had disappeared. He was wearing big sea-boots at the time, which accounts for the swiftness with which he was drowned. The sad event has cast a gloom over all the town, of which Mr. Rodgers was an esteemed and highly respected native. He leaves a widow and a son, to whom the profoundest sympathy is extended. The two victims of the sea were buried yesterday. The funeral procession was a very large and impressive one.

"At the inquiry, which was held on Saturday by the Procurator-Fiscal in Brieston, Mr. Rodgers's death was found to be due to misadventure."

Brieston had at last got definite information. There was an unprecedented sale for the issue of the local weekly journal. Yet Brieston was not satisfied. Nothing had been said about the well-known fact that Gillespie had been found in the store in the early morning when he ought to have been in bed. A cloud of suspicion rested on Gillespie. Besides, it was known that he had left Brieston on the day after the funeral. Where had he gone?

Within a fortnight Gillespie was back in Brieston with a steamer. The idea of the steamer was monstrously simple. At the opening of the spring herring season, he meant to buy in her and "kill the smacks." He had been in negotiation for some time with a Glasgow firm of brokers, who were offering him a small steamer of some seventy tons, which had been built for the Duke of Sutherland in the deer-stalking seasons, for the transport of guests from one point to another. She had passed through various hands since then, till, like a broken-down race-horse, she had found an asylum in the Clyde. Gillespie was not at all impressed when he was told she had splendid cabin accommodation; but very much impressed when the broker pointed out that a single man below could fire her and work the engines. He had put off clinching the bargain, hoping to wear down the broker before the spring; but suddenly changed his mind and bought. For two reasons: he scented that his name was bandied about. He were best out of Brieston for the present. But chiefly because he determined to open up a new industry, the idea of which had obsessed his mind for some time. During the winter, fishermen had brought him not only whelks and cockles for sale, but frequently some one or two hundreds of oysters. He discovered that the fish-shops in Glasgow would sell these oysters at half-a-crown a dozen. They were large and excellent in quality. He entered on a brief, decisive calculation. He had gathered from the fishermen that oysters abounded in the Loch, and were neglected. In the deep of winter one or two whelk-gatherers collected what came to their hands. Gillespie went immediately to work, and through the Fishery Officer obtained a ninety-nine year lease of ground below high-water mark from the Government, "for the purpose of rearing shell-fish, and beginning what it is hoped will develop into a profitable industry on the west coast." So ran the words in a Blue Book report of the Fishery Board. A paternal Government gave him an easy lease—twenty-four pounds a year.

As soon as the fishing season was over, and the first skiffs drawn on the beach, Gillespie sent for a certain crew, who were in his debt for stores, and for a new trawl-net. He had had considerable hesitation, because he had determined to sink these men in debt to the value of their boats, but saw there was something more lucrative in the oysters. He told them he would give them a chance of working-off the debt during the winter. He had had a line boat conveyed by cart to West Loch, Brieston; they use it, and gather oysters with every tide. These oysters they would would deposit at an oyster-bed, which he had leased from the Government. He would pay them at the rate of four shillings a hundred; or rather would deduct a corresponding amount from the debt they owed him. Sandy the Fox would accompany them to keep count of the oysters.

The work had been carried on steadily for three months, and Gillespie laid the foundation of a fine oyster-bed. He saw with provocation that part of the spawn from this bed would inevitably float away on the waters of the Loch, and conceived a future scheme of building a wall round the bed, with sluices for the coming and going of the tides. In this way he would hoard all the spawn. He had gone to Glasgow to purchase the steamer, and to open a connection with a fish salesman there, who would dispose of his shell-fish. Narrow and battered, with high wooden bulwarks, and a lean, cream-coloured funnel, she looked the tormented ghost of a ship. The Butler facetiously named her the *Sudden Jerk*.

Gillespie now fawned on every one with a sort of angelic devilry. He offered a job as deck-hand to Andy Rodgers's son; spoke every man fair; made them feel more than they were. "I knew you for a man of that kind;" and again, "You're the open-handed fellow." His touch was a cat's with sheathed claw. He was like a man softly playing on a flute with his eye on the audience and an obsequious hat ready. His voice was demurring, soft—a song; and all the while his nostril whistled—whistled as a high wind which is blowing upon a trigger at full cock. He imagined that in the genial sun of this duplicity Brieston was again warming towards him. He reckoned on the gullibility of the public, and was about to prove his reckoning correct.

19

It was the beginning of the spring fishing season, when the herring leave the spawning banks on the Ayrshire coast and move north. News had reached Brieston that at last trawling had been legalised by Act of Parliament. A telegram conveying the momentous tidings had been sent from London by the member for the county to Gillespie, who had posted it up in his shop window. Few of the crews possessed trawl-nets, for prosecution had been severe, and heavy fines imposed, and many of the nets confiscated. The whole fleet would now procure nets—two hundred or thereby. Gillespie would reduce the fifty pounds figure he had levied when trawling had been illegal, and show himself a man of sacrifice to meet the new conditions. At thirty-five pounds he would still have a handsome profit. He sat poring over his ledger with a ready reckoner at his elbow, and after an interval of calculation, passed into the front shop, and with secret satisfaction displayed the telegram on the large plate-glass window.

The news gave unbounded satisfaction. The men talked of

nothing but their brighter prospects, mingling the note of hope with objurgations on the day of the blockade, when the Fishery Cruiser hovered like blight upon the waters of the Loch. They recalled times when knives had been drawn, and they had even been fired upon, and the trawl-nets, the title-deeds of the town, had been concealed in garrets, beneath beds, in sheds and hen-houses. Sunday was the chief day for searching by the Government men. Peggy More, exasperated, had attacked one of the marauders with a stool.

"Sparrow-hawk," she cried, "herryin' the nest;" and felled him with a blow on the head. When she was arrested, a hue-and-cry was raised that war was being waged on women. The business became more ominous when Watty Foster flung down his reins, and the news that Peggy More had given birth prematurely to a child in Ardmarkie jail. The news had gone like fire through straw. Men forgot to go home to eat, and in the greater feud lesser enmities were forgotten. The following Sunday a search was being made. The men came out of church about eight in the evening to find that the spring-tide, pushed by a sou'-east gale, was deep in Harbour Street. Wading in the water, they attacked the Government men, and women, incensed because of the fate of Peggy More, ran out, armed with pokers, stools, and the like, and joined the fight in the tide. The scrimmage became notorious. Wasps in the House of Commons stung the Government. The authorities in London, thinking the ill-feeling widespread and dangerous, and perplexed with other more vital concerns, restored peace by legalising trawling. Peggy More was released and given an ovation.

It got abroad—no one knew how—that Gillespie was at the bottom of these happier events, having made representations to the member for the county. Gillespie, again elevated to a pinnacle of prestige, walked down the middle of the street with high head.

Such pedestrianism was significant, for Gillespie had something in him of the animal which, when hurt or threatened, crouches out of sight. The circumstances attending the death of Andrew Rodgers were forgotten. The wilder public surmise is, the sooner does speculation cease, as flame blazes through tinder. The imagination of the public had been ill-fed on a garbled newspaper report; the reaction to which mental fatigue gives rise set in, and the mind of people, lying fallow through a winter of monotonous existence, was prepared to receive a sowing of new seed when Gillespie affixed the notable telegram to his shop window.

Eccentricities are a comic play-acting in life, offered by the fatuous or by men vainglorious of a cheap notoriety to a stultified or to a half-lethargic people, and are noticed as a wave is observed on a sea of immoderate calm; but in the beginning of new epochs personal idiosyncrasies are lost sight of, as the wave is indistinguishable in a sea lashed by tempest. Thus we find Gillespie come abroad from obscurity in his old eccentric walk in the middle of the street. Other men walked on the pavements, in the shadow of the houses. In the larger interests of legalised trawling his appearance was gratefully accepted. He had come out from a cloud, and took a larger place than ever in the eye of the town. Humanity is prone to steal omens anywhere, and Gillespie incited the men with hopes of a splendid season under the aegis of Government. They took fire, and became instant upon preparation. Trawl-nets were ordered, and crews of eight men to occupy the two "company" boats necessary for trawling operations were formed. For initiative and enterprise it was held that between the East Sea and West Sea of Scotland Gillespie had not his equal. His spirit moved the town, and his ill-fame suffered euthanasia in the sound of the scraper heard over all the beaches. The skiffs were being scraped, tarred, and varnished. Morning after morning the men came out of their deep-doored houses and made the beaches, the Quays, and the barking-houses loud and merry. A dead season gave up its ensigns of ballast, chains, ropes, sails, buoys, and oars, which littered the beaches and the foreshores. The town had a deserted appearance. The previous week the beaches were empty; the famous telegram came as with the snarl of trumpets, and the crunching of gravel on the beaches and the noise of the boat-scrapers were a Te Deum.

"There'll be many a cobweb brushed away this week," said Mary Bunch at the Pump. Forgotten now are moonless nights, and the ghostly snow-showers blinding the shores; blistered fingers and raw sea-wounds. There is a sound of singing—the sailing-songs of their sires—around the inlets and creeks and pleasant gardens of the sea. The boats are about to leave their gravelly nurseries for the blue balcony of the Harbour. Some of the men are painting the numbers on the bows of the skiffs— those deft of hand; others dragging nets in barrows from the hibernating stores of Gillespie; a rich savour of melting tar is in all the beaches, where the iron braziers are blazing with fire; sails and nets are being barked; oars, ballast, water-casks, cran baskets, anchors, chains, the big jib for fair weather, and the little jib for a reefed breeze all being stowed away. The traveller is greased against the mast; halyards are replaced, and sheet ropes spliced and tarred. Rattle, clink, roar of material; gust and ripple of talk; merriment and laughter; sea-boys coiling ropes; barrows and lorries butting each other, and irascible drivers vituperating in the vain language of the stable.

In the fulness of time the skiffs are ready, and laying their shoulders to the flanks and the curve of the stern, with a shout the men drive them down the glittering beach, and take them to their anchorage in the Harbour. On that night the sea-boys parade the town.

> "An' we are beatin' in the dark all up the Kerry shore,
> Mi boys,
> Where yon long seas do roar, mi boys,
> An' are white wi' dead men's bones———"

The song swells over the Harbour. Its like has been sung by many disciples of the sea, hardy men on famous ships: the song of daring mingled with sorrow for brave lives lost outside the harbours of the world, which all shipmen on all seas have known; and now brought home to this fag-end of a beach and bare sea-town, prepared to engage the seas on the strength of a message from London.

There falls upon the grey town at sunset a shining peace. A little wind blows in from the sea. The fleet, swung round into its eye, is peering out of the harbour mouth. The town from the Barracks to the "Shipping Box" is very quiet. A benign influence is abroad. Blue smoke slants up as from altars. The hills are ablaze with whin. The men stand looking out upon the boats, virgin yet of herring-scale, and smoke in silence. There is upon them a sense of hope about to be fulfilled; a sense of the replenishing and moving of the waters.

In the little wind from the sea the sign of the dagger at the "Ghost" is mournfully creaking. This wind cools the face of Gillespie. He had been delving into his books, and came on a note of a loan of hundreds of pounds received from his father, who had stupidly quarrelled with him over a business of selling on Sundays. Gillespie was not likely to be troubled about this loan. All day he had laboured at his books, entering in the long lists of nets, ropes, tar, and such-like gear, which he had sold, and stood now at the close-mouth beneath the stars in the cooling wind, looking at a forest of masts in the Harbour, raking in little drunken jerks across a patch of sky. On Monday the fleet would clear—"my fleet," he thought, with a faint smile of benevolence —and determined to have the *Sudden Jerk* prepared for sea on Monday. As he was about to turn up the close, he heard a familiar stump, stump, on the pavement. Traiveller Jeck appeared, and was about to speak, when, seeing he had made a mistake, he continued stumping. Gillespie detained him.

"You hae some skill o' boats, Jeck, my man."

"I was up the Mediterranean a dozen times."

"I'll gie ye a job on my herrin' steamer, if ye'll tek' it."

"Catch me refusing a loaf."

"Be doon then, brisk an' early wi' the morn's ebb, an' get her on the beach. Her bottom 'ill need a bit scrape. I want her oot by Monday."

Thus it was that on Saturday Brieston learned that the old days of depending on the buyers in the smacks were over. Gillespie was going to wait upon them with steam.

20

GILLESPIE could forecast many of the events which depended for their occurrence on the caprice or desires of men, but the mysterious workings of the laws of Nature were beyond his cunning. The herring fishing was a failure. The first week some few dozen boxes of small, immature herrings were fished; but since then barren night gave way to dreary morning, till—"I'm not goin' oot again," said old Sandy; "we reinged the bights a' last month, and never saw a scale."

This and that reason was alleged, till slowly it was borne in on the men that "trawling" was ruining the industry. Such constant raking of the Loch with large "trawls," had split up the great "eyes" of herring, just when they had come up from the spawning banks of Ayrshire, and had driven them back again.

"It stands to reason," said old Sandy, "wi' the drifts we lay quate a' night at anchor, an' the fish came into the shore, but noo wi' this trawlin', big boats an' nets hammerin' on the top o' the herrin' a' night long, no fish wad stand it."

"Hoo are ye, Sanny?" cried Gillespie, passing.

"My health's good, thank Goäd, but I'm in very reduced circumstances."

Soon the town began to feel the pinch.

"Boys," said the Bent Preen, at the "Shipping Box," "I've kent trouble. I've seen my faither, that's deid an' gone, greetin' wance in the middle o' the day; but thon was noathin' to this." Yet the Bent Preen had less cause for complaint than most, for he had no family, and his wife had said to him no later than that morning, when about to set out to a washing at the Banker's, "Mony's a bit turn a wumman can do that a man canna, an' win a shullin' thae hard times."

In more important quarters the matter was discussed. Willie Allan, Campion the schoolmaster, Dr. Maclean, the Banker, and Lonend's father, were seated in Brodie's back parlour. Brodie himself, Willie Allan, Dr. Maclean, and the Banker were members of the Parish Council. Campion had suggested that the Council might offer work to the more hardly hit.

"There's too much fuss," said the Butler, frowning, "far too much fuss made with this world—parish councils and school boards and football matches—an' no' half enough preparing for eternity." By which deliverance his cronies knew the Butler to be fairly deep in liquor. "No wonder there's hard times with a tea-drinking generation that bows down the knee to Gillespie Strang."

"How's that?" asked Maclean, laughing uproariously.

"They haven't got the stuff in them now-a-days, doctor, to go and look for herring. There was a day when every house in Brieston—and good thatch houses they were—was bursting with meat. We could lock the door, doctor, and no need to go out and buy anything but tobacco."

"And whisky," said Campion.

The Butler's eyes gleamed with silent laughter.

"Ay! of course, and whisky from our friend Brodie here. There's nothing like whisky for softening leather. But that's the way it was. The pig would be killed and the hams hanging from hooks; a barrel of braxy behind the door; a barrel at the window full of meal; another with flour; and a barrel o' salt herring an' a bag o' potatoes below the bed. The Arran smacks came in with cargoes of potatoes and coals, so cheap you were almost ashamed to buy. Now what is it?"

"A dark, misty day"—from Campion.

"Ay! ay! the weemin run to Gillespie for a pickle tea and sugar, an' steek their lug at the fire-end, waiting on the tea to mask, and sitting with a bowl in their hand, like the giraffes I saw in my travels with the Laird, stretching out their long necks to drink. No wonder the weemin's yellow in the face and Brieston's on the rocks. I tell ye," he roared, smacking the table with his fist, "it's tea, Gillespie's China tea, that's playing Old Harry with the town. Let the folk eat plenty o' braxy an' bannocks, porridge an' pease-meal, an' soor dook an' salt herring, an' I'll wager ye Gillespie can go for a living to Skye, an' every lassie will have two men running after her. Ach, Nellie! Nellie!" he shouted, "bring in a drink; I'm dry. Gillespie's name in my mouth always leaves me dry—the obnoxious rag; he's too cold and frosty a man for me."

"He's pretty near," said Campion.

"Ay," grunted the Butler, "it's my granddaughter can tell you that."

Campion coloured, and said nothing.

Nellie, Brodie's daughter, popped a tousled head in at the door. She had a half-knitted stocking in her hand, and stifling a yawn, shook her head at the Butler.

"No more," she said; "ten o'clock, gentlemen."

Brodie frowned. He hated ten o'clock when the company was good. They all disregarded Nellie, except by looks of menace.

Presently the door was again opened, and the voice thrust in upon them—a strident female, ranged with the law, against the comfort of the chief men of the town. "After ten o'clock, gentlemen."

"Ach! Nellie, ye bitch," wheezed Brodie, and they all knew then that they had to go from the "bien couthie" place and the warm talk.

They passed out into Harbour Street, into a thin, raw rain. Three men—James Murray and his two sons—passed to the house where Murray's mother lay dead, to see that all was well with the body for the night.

"They found her deid in bed," said Willie Allan, looking at the doctor.

Maclean's hand went up to his moustache. "Heart gave way; want of food," he said.

"Good God!" ejaculated Campion; "and look at that!"

A middle-aged man, with a scrub of dark-grey hair and eyebrows bunched in tufts, staggered over to Brodie's closed door and pounded it with his fists.

"Who's there?" came the well-known wheeze; "away home! it's aifter ten o'clock."

"It's me, Brodie, yeer freen' Jonnie."

"Oot o' there, ye tinkler, hooever ye are."

"Ye might let a freen' in a meenut; I'm only wantin' change for the plate the morn."

Willie Allan and his friends stood listening. Up the street a little, at the shoemaker's one-storey house, which stood by itself on the Harbour wall, a company of "Revivalists" was singing a hymn:

> "There were ninety and nine that safely lay
> In the shelter of the fold."

—the words drifted down the wind—blown through the rain to them.

"One dies of starvation," said Campion loudly, "and one has money in his hands, pushing in at the doors of hell; and ninety and nine are safe in the fold."

These doors at that moment received a vindictive kick. Presently one of the long, narrow leaves was flung open, and a purple face was thrust out. "Get oot o' here, ye blaiggart, or I'll knock the guts oot o' ye!" The man was violently shoved off the pavement, and the door was clapped to. After some circumnavigation with his mouth, he found the key-hole.

"That's the sort ye are, Brodie. Ye'll kiss oor backside afore ten o'clock an' kick it aifter."

The man lurched over to the group.

"As sure as my faither wore the tartan—I'sh—hic—join the Goo' Templsh—an'—hic—buy a plair—o'—gallush—A' grudged—hic—grudged 'em when I—wash—booze——"

"Blind and miserable, sick and naked. Oh, for God's sake, let's get away from here!" cried Campion.

They moved up the street in a body. At the shoe-maker's house, on the breast wall near the Square, which was blazing with light, stood the Revivalist meeting. A strange and moving sight met their glance. On the edge of the ring was Queebec, his white head bare to the rain, facing the Square and the fishermen assembled at "Gillespie's corner," and at the Medical Hall. In a loud, screeching voice, he was telling of his visitation by the Lord, and was warning all men against the evils of drink, of bad living, of revenge and greed. His eyes were flashing; long wisps of thin hair were blown about his face. Three men he openly denounced—the Receiver of Wrecks of the "Anchor Hotel," Brodie, and Gillespie Strang.

"Spawn of the devil they are, and Gillespie Strang is anti-Christ. Robbers and plunderers of the town they are." Zeal ate him up, as he shook the rain from his piteous white head, and uttered libel with glowing hatred.

"Too long I have been in the tents of sin," he cried, "and I have paid the price and the penalty; and now I warn you men of Brieston. Do you think the Lord is for ever going to give you herring to be drinking, and you giving it to a thief an' a robber like Gillespie Strang. I tell ye, the curse o' God fell on me. Look at my white head, all in a night." He tossed his head, and swung round from side to side, facing the three sides of the Square. "And it'll fall on Brieston too. Can ye expect to get herring to feed publicans and robbers?" He spread out his hands; his voice rose to a scream. "The sea that should feed you shall rot your boats. Blight and mildew shall devour them. God will make a worm to destroy them like Jonah's gourd." There was a gloomy grandeur in the appearance of the man. His eye burned with a prophetic light. "Woe! woe!! woe!!! I see it. Woe! woe!! woe!!! to this town, whoever will live to see it." Foaming and panting and hunched up at the shoulders, he fell back, and the silence was solemnly broken by a deep-throated Amen from a man in spectacles, who stepped forward to announce the hymn:

"Lo! He comes in clouds descending."

"He's right," said the Butler vehemently, "about Gillespie Strang and the Receiver of Wrecks. I don't know what I'm to think if I'm to be lost, and be in hell with folk I wouldn't speak to here—boozers an' scandal-mongers, an' liars, an' thieves, and all the riff-raff o' dirty livers an' rascals. My place is with gentlemen. Is it fair that I'm to be pitched in among folk I wouldn't nod to on the other side of the street, or give back an answer if they said it's a fine day or it's scoory weather?"

They turned across the Square in the direction of the Medical

Hall, whose large green and red bottles, a yard high in the window, relieved the greyness of the rainy night.

"Who is the preacher?" asked Campion, as they stood in front of the doors of the Medical Hall; "his face was like the face of a lost angel!"

"He is a man who will soon be mad," answered Dr. Maclean sadly. He saw Kyle, his chemist, beckoning to him from the shop, and nodded. "Gillespie's cup is filling up. Good-night, gentlemen." And entering the shop, he stood gravely listening to his chemist.

"What does the doctor mean?" asked Campion.

"He means what poor Queebec means, by God: ay! his cup is filling up." The Butler's voice boomed away into the blurred greyness of the weeping night.

Campion was distinctly uneasy. "Ugh!"—he shivered at the thought—"these Hielan' folk live and move and have their being in superstition. All the same, I don't like it. I'll cut her."

Thus Mrs. Strang lost her lover.

21

ALL the spring it blew persistently in easterly gales which darkened the land. To this, in turn, was attributed the failure of the herring fishing. There was hardly a day in which the men could put the bow of a boat over the Harbour mouth. At last the easterly gales died away; and summer suddenly blazed down from a sky of brass.

"This heat will bring the herring to the shore," it was said; but morning after morning the boats returned empty, till the conviction was forced upon Brieston that there was not a herring in that glassy, green, beautiful Loch. The firmament was laid in bands of blue steel. Inch by inch the awful heat crept up over the land, smiting it as with searing irons to brown, yellow, white, and in the end, when children began to die, to an appalling black.

The streams around Lonend and Muirhead shrunk. Lochan Dhu, in the hills, sobbed out its life to the water-lilies. The pools and marshes became black hollows, and the shallow head of

West Loch Brieston was leprous with dry salt. Far up the head streams, where the damp nests of green things are, the juniper fell in dry twigs, the heather was ablaze, and a great smoke hung on the hills. The grasses curled into wires; the mosses melted off the dikes; the stalks of the hardy sea-pinks wilted under their burden; the wild rosebushes were gaunt with thorns; and the roads and tracks on the hill-lands preserved, as if cast in iron, every mark.

The hillsides above the town lifted their bare rocks, quivering and grey, like bones in a fantastic body, and were deserted of birds which haunted the river-sides for frogs.

The tamer animals went back to a wilder nature. Pigs and dogs went rooting about, and the sheep fainted on the moor, which was whitened with the skeletons of birds, or lay down, a prey to flies and ravens, in the parched fields. The heron had wailed away in a stringing flight into the north, seeking the rains in the Hebrides. The only sound of bird-life was the moaning of wild doves in the gloom of the pines below Muirhead. The land was dumb save for that sound and the burden of the grasshopper, which spun the heat into a maddening noise as of wires.

The sea slouched in its oily calm, silent and glassy, until "the very deep did rot."

Dawn by dawn the sun flamed forth like a sword; the sky was a white-hot sheet of steel, raining down blistering fire. At night the big stars throbbed in the dark-blue vault, and reeled in their courses.

At last a lean blue gap of mud stretched across the head of West Loch Brieston, where the Brieston river used to run. The land shrunk; dust rose into the sun in the faint puffs of veering wind, till the crude glare was of brass. A furnace boiled in the sky at noon, as if the veil of the atmosphere had been rent away. The very shadows on the Brieston streets fled, as if seeking shelter from that dizzy glare.

Men, thin, white-faced, bleached, with swollen and cracked lips, scanned the heavens by day and searched the clear stars by night, when the tortured earth gave back its heat to the parched air. In the houses the children panted and moaned, and the women forbore at length, from weakness, to rub the sweat from their infants' faces.

The hills began swinging to the drone of the grasshoppers. The islands of the Loch rose up and floated in the air, cool with a long ecstasy of rippling water. Children began to die; women raved in the low-roofed houses of the Back Street; the men took turns at the Pump, standing in line waiting with the empty stoups sheltering their heads. In the adamant of the hills dwelt an unearthly silence, beneath the dry summer lightning which flickered from peak to peak. The thunder ran moaning and rumbling out to sea, and died away like the whimper of far trumpets.

The atmosphere went mad, rising and falling in a great wave beneath the furnace of the sky. The horizon was ringed with a hard red in the evenings, and twenty suns danced and slid over the sky.

The men no longer lifted their bleared eyes upwards. Their brains ached with the heat. The bones stood out on their bodies. They lay all day in a stupor till the tardy twilight came, and the sun sank in the sea like a great autumnal leaf falling on a loch.

One Sunday a derelict came in on the tide, struck end on at the Perch in the Harbour mouth, spun about in the tide-rip, sagged across to the Island, and drifted in a drunken fashion up the Harbour. She fell foul of one of the fishing-skiffs, cleared and crawled, a tall, mysterious, dark ship, up to the breast-wall in front of the Square. When the tide ebbed she careened over against the wall, her long, tapering masts stretching out upon the Square. On her broad stern-counter in faded letters of gold was the name *Flor Del Mar*. Her cordage was in rags; her foresail hung idly in the windless air; her deck was deserted. Gillespie and Rory Campbell, the policeman, boarded her. In the cabin they found a black-bearded man lying in a bunk dead. Lines of extreme pain were graved on his face, and his lips were drawn back from fine white teeth in a half grin, a half snarl. On the floor a dead boy lay twisted up. In the forecastle they found two others, who had plainly died in agony. In the cabin there was a large cage with two canaries. Gillespie looted the cabin, and established the birds, which were alive, in the shop.

Campbell crossed the Square for the doctor, who appeared in a white pith helmet. He looked at the silent occupants of the cabin. "Plague," he said.

The policeman's face went white.

"Constable," continued Maclean dispassionately, "go to Osborne the ironmonger, and get a charge of dynamite. Blow up the ship at once, or the graveyard will be the busiest place in Brieston."

Campbell sweated profusely.

"What ails ye, man?" asked Maclean irritably.

"I'm no likin' the chob at aal."

"Go home," said the doctor sternly, "and lock yourself in a cell; maybe you'll lock death out. I'll remember you from this day as a coward." The doctor pointed to the companionway. "Go!" The policeman slunk up the stair. The doctor shouted to Gillespie, who came down the companion-way whistling sharply in his nostrils. Maclean pointed to the black face grinning in the bunk. "There's a cloud of calamity hanging over Brieston. Go to Osborne's for dynamite, and help me to blow up this coffin."

Gillespie demurred. "There's a pickle salvage here," he said suavely.

"It will be gathered with a sickle," replied Maclean, "in the hands of the Angel of Death. The atmosphere is badly tainted. Your life is in far graver danger here than it was when Andy Rodgers and you met in the store." Maclean fixed Gillespie with a steady gaze, and saw him become livid. "I'll wait here till you get the dynamite."

"It's no' my business," muttered Gillespie; "the owners might sue for damages."

"It will have to be at the hands of the Almighty;" again Maclean pointed to the companion-way. "Go and lock yourself up in your house; p'r'aps you will lock out the plague."

Gillespie paused irresolute. Greed warred in him with fear.

"Do you believe in God?" asked Maclean quietly.

"You're jokin', doctor."

"No! I'm in earnest. This is His day, Sunday, and this is His message." He nodded to the dead huddled boy. "If you can't blow up the ship, go home and get on your knees."

Gillespie retreated, followed by the doctor. On the breast-wall he spoke to Maclean.

"Is there anything I can tak', doctor?" His knees trembled. He seemed in a state of collapse.

"Go home, man, go home, and get drunk on brandy."

For the first time since the night of his marriage, Gillespie drank in his own house. Towards evening, Topsail Janet purloined the half empty bottle; and that night Gillespie's wife lay by his side drunk.

Dr. Maclean told Osborne, a man with a large bald head and deep-sunken, smouldering eyes.

"It's best face to Greenock, this time, doctor," he said.

Preceded by Maclean, Osborne carried a keg of gun-powder through the Square. A crowd had gathered round the breast-wall, gaping on the silent ship.

"Back!" cried Maclean, in a ringing voice; "back out of here! There's a plague and death in this ship."

A bowed man with thin, white hair elbowed his way through the crowd, an open Bible in his hand. In rapid tones he began reading, his voice gradually rising to a scream. " 'The seed is rotten under their clods, the garners are laid desolate, the barns are broken down; for the corn is withered.' " In the still air, under the blazing sky, every word of Queebec's was clear as a bell. " 'How do the beasts groan! the herds of cattle are perplexed, because they have no pasture; yea, the flocks of sheep are made desolate.' " His flashing eyes swept the crowd. " 'The fire of heaven,' " he cried, " 'hath devoured the pastures, and the flame hath burned all the trees of the field.' " He shook the Bible aloft, chanting the words of terror over which he had pondered through the scorching weeks. " 'The beasts of the field cry also unto Thee; for the rivers of waters are dried up.' "

"He's mad," said Osborne to the doctor, who was holding out his arms to receive the keg of gunpowder.

"Ay," said Maclean, leaning forward with the keg in his hands, "God has made him mad."

" 'A day of darkness and of gloominess, a day of clouds and of thick darkness, as the morning spread upon the mountains.' " The lean arm was stretched out upon the fascinated crowd. " 'Run to and fro; death shall enter in at the windows like a thief.' "

"Shut up!" a deep voice of anger growled in the crowd, which began to sway in a great wave.

"You cannot shut up the voice of the Lord," screamed Queebec; "hear it: 'The earth shall quake, the heavens shall tremble; the sun and the moon shall be dark, and the stars shall withdraw their shining.' "

"Throw him into the Harbour!" a voice yelled. The crowd oscillated violently and surged forward.

"No, but throw Gillespie Strang and Brodie into the Harbour, the wolves of the town. 'Woe! woe! in the earth; blood and fire and pillars of smoke. The sun shall be turned into darkness, and the moon into blood——' "

A hand was suddenly clapped over Queebec's mouth, the Bible was torn from his grasp; a low-throated snarl burst from the crowd; it heaved forward, baying, and the white head went down in the rush.

Maclean appeared at the cabin door carrying the shoulders of a dead man. The crowd became still. The waves out of a vast, silent eternity washed over them. One, two, three, four, five bodies were brought ashore. Honour to the ironmonger. As for Maclean, it was his duty. "Back!" he roared, "back for your lives!" He leaped ashore, followed by Osborne. "Back, you men!" he shouted.

The people surged slowly backwards against the wall of Gillespie's house, the Bank, and the Medical Hall, where they waited in tense silence. Suddenly a scream was heard. "Look at him, the wolf!" Queebec's long arm pointed upwards. Just as the eyes of the crowd fell on Gillespie standing at his parlour window, a red tongue of flame stabbed the air. The ship rocked and heaved as if on a huge roller. A cloud of dark-greenish smoke, bathed in the heart with flame, rocked upwards in the midst of a deafening roar; splinters shot up into the air; the column of smoke curled lazily upwards, venomous with poison, and a belt of light spread along the breast-wall. There was a splitting of glass—the windows in Gillespie's shop and house were smashed. Silently they watched the wrecked ship blaze. The heat became intense. The crowd backed away into the lane at the Bank, and up the west brae towards the Post Office.

"Fire to burn and to cleanse," screamed Queebec; "fire to purge the sins of Gillespie." And many in the crowd in after days recalled those wild words of a madman.

"It'll maybe burn out the plague," Maclean said grimly to Osborne; "if not I shall never get my boots off;" and he entered his house, taking Queebec with him by the shoulder. A black fog hung over the Harbour all that day. On the morrow Campbell's wife was down with the plague. In two days she was dead, and her face turned black. Swiftly the plague ran its course. A curious circumstance was that children were immune. People refused to lay out and wash the dead, and Stuart denied them the last offices. The sailmaker and Queebec fearlessly took his place. A Sheriff-Officer from Ardmarkie, a man with a loud, booming voice, that could be heard far away in the stillness of that burned, plague-haunted town, came to bury the dead. The funeral procession was invariably composed of the same men— the Sheriff-Officer and the sailmaker, and Queebec walking ahead, bowed over an open Bible, Willie Allan and the Butler, Maclean, when he had the opportunity, and Stevenson the undertaker, a red, silent man. In that day of quiet heroes, none displayed such heroism as he. Over the door of his joiner's shed, to this day, can be seen the model of a coffin in oak, like a sign. He was young then, and of a shaggy, fierce appearance, taciturn, a hard worker, making as many as six coffins in a day of eighteen hours. He was like a shadow, slipping through the streets, hatless, in his shirt-sleeves, and bare of foot. He dragged the fallen off the streets, and coffined them afterwards. His wife haggled in grief-stricken homes for the coffin money, because of her husband's enormous expense for planks, till he lifted his gnarled hand upon her. The time came when he had to make a coffin for her also—taciturn then beyond his wont, and swearing at the wailing of her kinswomen. At all hours he was seen bearing a coffin, sometimes with the help of the sail-maker, sometimes with that of the Sheriff-Officer, passing on in the dawn after a night of toil to those to whom the dawn would never arise again. Most solemn he appeared then, beneath the scarlet arch of morning, uncertain whether the evening would find him on his feet. *Quid vesper vehat, incertum est.*

"The sea will never drown another man in Brieston," the Sheriff-Officer said to him one morning; "the plague will get them all."

"Who kens?" he answered, shaking his head, and looking at the row of masts which leaned over against the blank windows of the sleeping houses. The wind will blow again and the keels toss upwards to the stars, and the cordage be broken in the tempest. To-day the ships alone have security, and the undertaker passes on to meet the Black Death. Nothing can withstand him. In burning weather or in boisterous, he awaits all things. This usher to Eternity, this gleaner where the last sickle gleams and swings, is aware that if to-day the ballasted boats securely made an anchorage, to-morrow they shall enter into the storm—contemptible toys with their hard-won revenues spilled upon the waves, and their patrimony dismantled and devoured; and he, vigilant upon the shore, the wayfarer who goes to the grave-

213

mouth and returns, shall take the dead and bring them upon their last voyage into the haven, with their cares and vexations at an end, upon his rude, unrigged deal plank.

They passed through the town to the Quay. Willie Allan was dead. Stevenson did his offices silently. At noon they came to bury him.

"Good-bye, friend," said Stevenson, and screwed down the lid. In his shirt sleeves he helped to bear forth the coffin. They laid it at the door. There was no minister.

"Men, take off your hats," for he had none. He tapped the lid with his screw-driver.

"He's by wi't; he played the man." Then with simple assurance, "God has his soul;" and the sail-maker offered prayer. At the close, Stevenson signalled to them to bear away the coffin. He was not of the procession. Fog had delayed the luggage steamer with his pine planks. He went with a hatchet to the wood at West Loch Brieston for a serviceable tree. That night Stevenson stood shoeless and hatless at his door, like a famished eagle, wasted with fatigue and want of sleep. There was a white wheel about the moon, and trailing over her cold splendour a cloud scarce bigger than a man's hand, as if that luminary, wearied of her nightly torture of vision on the racked earth, had dragged up from the unrelenting deep one gleam of mercy. A little purging wind blew from the south-west. The undertaker held up his head and sniffed. "There's a smell of rain," he muttered; and he knew that his day was over, his destiny fulfilled. The end of death was for him the end of real life. Solemnly he contemplated the stars becoming dimmer in the skies, as the moist wind freshened, and he thought of Willie Allan and the strangeness of Fate. Only to-day he was buried; and to-night the rains were creeping in from the ocean.

Towards midnight the wind snapped and blew in fierce scurries, and thunder slowly rolled in the hills.

Zp-p! Zip! a flash tore across the vault, lambent, reddish; crash! came the answering roar. Queebec was at his door, telling mortals that God reigned, and His voice was riding the storm. A dumbness brooded over the earth as the last peal rolled away into the reverberate hills. The stifling air palpitated. Again a jagged bolt, red-hot, leapt out of the south-west, baring the firmament and spread in a blinding flame over Brieston, whose houses stood out sharp and pale along the Harbour front. Again the high artillery of the skies thundered and growled. The flash had opened the sluices of heaven. Slowly the rain began to fall in great burning drops, and the women crawled to their doors holding out famished hands.

The lightning winked; and heaven opened in a lake of flame. The earth shook; and a blind rush of rain ran in a white scurry along the streets, and reared a grey veil along the Harbour's face. Again and again the lightning lit the sky in splatches of blue and green and white. The rain rang out of the dark. Gusts leapt in thunder off the roofs.

In the morning it was still raining gently. Three rainbows were drawn against the sky. Over the wet windows a procession of drops of water passed. It was as the procession of those who had died of the Black Plague. They had come a moment upon the glass of Life and disappeared, some soiling the glass, others behind, cleansing it a little. The sun sparkled like silver upon the wet roofs.

You will not find Stevenson in Brieston now. He lived, a widower, alone, old, and forgotten, dreaming on winter nights of the days when the terror-stricken made way for him as for an emperor. His house was poor, and he shabby. Many families owed him a debt of honour for unpaid coffins. He lies not far from Maclean, and on his tombstone are these words:

"Here lies one who feared death as little as he loved his fellow-men greatly. He has entered into his rest."

22

EVERY one took heart when the rains broke, deeming the days of disaster to be over. Crews were formed again, for many who should have put to sea were now beyond all chances of fortune and mischances of storm. Gillespie had furnished the fleet with provisions. "There's nothing in the world like the joy o' teasin' tobacco again in your palm as ye sit on the gunwale, feelin' the big sea-boots in the crook o' the knee," said old Sandy. His faded eyes looked abroad, and saw two hundred brown sails towering on the Loch going north, south, and east to search the bights. Overhead the solans were sailing out of the north in the sharp, blue void, their pirate heads and yellow necks gleaming in the sun. Down all the shore the boats came to anchor till sunset, for there is a law against daylight fishing. In this peaceful hour of the evening watch, when tea was over, the drift smoke of the fleet hung aloft like another blue sea. The men were stretched out on the beams with that negligent grace which no landsman can wholly attain. Here and there one or two were busy on little jobs—putting a new piece of leather on an oar, splicing a rope, or mending their nets. Somewhere a blackbird fluted its evensong in the bushes. The mellow note died away and stillness gripped the woods, the beaches, and the darkling sea. Far off there was a soft sound of hill-waters running. The elder men dovered in the grey shadows.

Suddenly the snore of a sounding whale broke the silence. The anchors were lifted, and boat after boat stole out from the shadows. Every man was listening. It was in their blood to listen. The "plout" of one leaping herring might betray millions of its fellows swimming in the dark depths below. As the boats drew further out, the sails were hoisted to the gentle breeze, and one man in every boat stood up on the forecastle head the better to listen. There was something wolfishly intent in his tense body and pricked ears. He stood out a speck bending over the deep; a point of life scrutinising gigantic, imperturbable Nature, that had in its bosom the means of making the hearth bright and cheering the familiar things of the cot. The sea jealously guards her treasure; but always there is an armour joint which the sentinel speck finds. In the ambush of hope he waits vigilant till the unwary deep opens her guard, and in a flash the sword of his necessity is buried deep in her wealth.

The boats drifted south on the tide, moving like ghosts, and the little sentinel specks on the forecastle head vanished in the gloom, swallowed up of the vast brooding immensity of sea and sky.

The breeze from the south-west freshened, cresseting the sea, and faint voices were heard here and there from the phantom boats.

"We'll get a wettin' the night, boys; see thon sky. The tea's maskin' there for us."

"Ay," came the subdued answer, "it's dirty an' black-lookin'."

A louder voice called across the water: "There was a wheel last night about the moon."

In the silence which fell the moon rose stone-cold, and in its pale light they saw, far in the south, a long black line stretching from shore to shore. The line grew swiftly as they looked; came nearer in waves, like liquid lead, rising in fiery crests of white.

"Rattle! rattle!" in the south went the halyards of two boats.

"They're lowerin' to reef," came a voice.

"It'll be three reefs an' the wee jib soon," was answered back.

The black line on the sea galloped up, passed northward, foaming through the fleet, which it left in a grey smother. The Loch was now loud with the creaking of blocks, the whipping of cordage, the slatting of sails, and the hiss of brine along the forefoot.

"Scoury weather this."

"Ay! ay! an' it's no' the night only; this weather 'ill cairry this moon oot on its back. We'll pey noo for the long heat an' the calm." A grey driving shower, mingled of sleet and rain, slanted up like a wall. Leaden seas rolled up the Channel, filling the atmosphere beneath the heavy sagging clouds.

"It's Blanket Bay the night, boys," a stentorian voice rang through the screaming of the wind. These men were not fatalists; but generations of sea-faring had bequeathed to their blood a ready acquiescence in the moods of Nature. There was neither note nor murmur of rebellion as they ran reefed down to the Harbour, like brown little animals with ears laid back scuttering to their holes. They had encountered the "weemin's win'." The Harbour, lying deep between two forelands and sheltered by a long island running east and west, is immune from the fiercest sou'-east gales, so that, however vicious is the storm out of that airt on the Loch, the women know nothing but an inner silent Harbour, and are amazed to hear the boats coming in.

Like storm-beaten birds the fleet was in full flight from the south where the Loch was now one white smoke. The men, unable to discern the land, held high off, knowing they would find the Harbour mouth by the lights of Brieston, lying deep within. A piercing note rose over the moan of the wind and yelled in the cordage. The seas curled away like white paper. There was a greenish light upon the Loch, relieving the pitch darkness. At the tiller, at the pumps, at the sheet, they toiled as gloomy headland after headland opened out and swung behind the wet bows. The boats to windward were no more than a mast and sail lurching and sagging across a patch of sky. In a flock they drew in beneath the "Ghost"; flurries of the gale followed them; but the roar outside on the Loch died away. At the New Pier the oars were unshipped, and to their rhythmic sweep the boats stole in through the shadows of the Planting below Muirhead, past the Perch and the east end of the Island, till they anchored where the lights of Brieston sent their long quivering reflections into the dark silent water. The lunge of the anchors and the rattle of the chains sounded through the town.

"What's put the men in frae the fishin' a night lik' this?" said the Back Street women, the one to the other, feeling on their cheek but faint airs sighing down from the high hills.

"Ach, m'eudail," old Sandy was explaining to his grand-daughter who kept house for him, "thon's no' canny at the back-end o' the year, oot yonder, wi' the seas rollin' in glens, an' dark as the grave, an' a lee-shore on every side o' ye. I'm feart we're goin' to be in for a hard winter, mo thruaigh."

The wind veered to the nor'west the next day. The sky seemed torn in shreds which flew in the firmament. The rain-blackened houses stood out starkly in the hard gleaming light. The Harbour was full of bobbing punts. Every man was hurrying to give his boat all the chain in the locker. Each skiff was burying her nose in the smother, and rip, ripping, at her chain. The wind veered about from north to north-west. At every nor'west scurry the Harbour was darkened with sleet, and the spindrift flew in grey clouds. Once more the fishing fleet was bottled up.

23

THE terns left early, and gulls were scavenging inland. Autumn waded through a roaring equinox which blistered the fleet. The land was filled with the boom of rain-lashed gales. Old Sandy prophesied dire weather. "I saw three suns in the sky, an' the win's shifted oot o' too many airts." The brown nets on the poles along the Harbour were rotting, and could not be dried. The last birds to leave were the herons, which had watched on the shores in immobile gauntness as if carved out of grey rock. They flapped their heavy way like winged stone, leaving the Loch empty.

A savage nihilism of storms beat upon the town. They leapt off the hills upon the Harbour with the rushing sound of a great saw cutting wood. They were mingled with hail, and when the gust roared past it left the hills white to the sea, as if a mighty smearing hand had passed across their face. The water was hard, and black like iron; but at every snarl when the wind veered into the north-west it suddenly whitened, as iron in a furnace. Men said that they saw evil omens in the skies—the moon swimming upon the clouds like a great bat with wings outspread upon the earth. The gables rushed up black in the rain, giving the town a naked appearance, and every window in Harbour Street was white with salt. The grip of the storm was upon the wet, huddled seaport, whose stones stood out in the scourged street like teeth in a skull. There was something sinister in the aspect of the town when, with a steely hard look upon it, it lay black and drying from the twilight rains. This was the common time of respite. In the morning the unwearied blowing worried the town again with fresh venom! The beaches were loud and the streets resurgent with the noise and wash of the waters. The seas went up on the forelands as clouds of steam, and burst as snow. The men on the Quay head tasted salt, which parched and blistered as they watched the weather-worn squadron, rusty with the rains and bleached with spindrift. It froze during the night. In the morning a thawing wind was raw in the streets and whistled along the bases of the dripping hills. Sea-drift and rain beat upon a naked, shivering world.

The snows came and the sheeted hills stood up from the black edge of the sea as white marble on a black plinth. The birds perished in the frozen ditches. In the silence of the snow could be heard their last cheeping. The colossal magnificence of the garmented hills benumbed the minds of those who stared up from their low thresholds. Their leprous immensity deadened the souls of men. The horror of Nature was making them atheistic. Those monstrous hills appeared to swell as they gazed out, cowled across a grey sky of ice, above the bleating of mortals. Their passionless, unhungry strength sank down with crushing force on the race beneath, that was running its course with so many vicissitudes and pangs of disappointment, and on the salt-whitened skiffs riding out the winter.

Day and night in the lulls the men had hauled their nets and found them empty. The great autumnal moons arose, whitened the land and passed; and the potatoes and the bag of meal waned, and went swiftly down to their winter setting. The dripping lines slipped from nerveless hands in the heart of the night, when the breakers boomed on the veiled shores. The great ghost snow-showers stalked out of the glens; and when the long seas confused the morning-light, the men despaired of the glory of the Lord and any Galilean peace more. From the doors of their houses that shook in the tempest they heard the snapping of pines on the forelands, and knew that the raging sea would drive the herring eye into the unsounded deep. The land was sour with snow, bleached with spindrift, raw with rain. "The sky's worn spewin' snow and rain," said the Bent Preen to his wife, who was wasted with weeping. The children fretted day long. There were no marriages. Those which had been loveless became hell; those which had been of love meant a hell of anguish too. God seemed to hide His face behind the curtain of the snows. The men were in a fierce, morose temper. Some were inclined to believe in the ravings of Queebec. A judgment had befallen Brieston. They had suffered heat, plague, and tempest. Food was scarce. The school was deserted. The Jew stripped the Back Street and carried it in his pack to Glasgow. All the candles in the Back Street were burned, and it lay in darkness. Gillespie would give no credit. His eyes became flinty. Penury unmasked him. The bad state of trade gnawed like poison at his heart, and he came out into the open, militant. He taught his customers one sharp lesson, watching his opportunity. It was a Saturday night towards the close of the year, when the shop was full of women. One had asked for tea, sugar, butter, and cheese. As each parcel—made up in the leaves of medical journals rifled from the store—was laid on the counter, the woman hurriedly deposited it in a basket, and when the half-pound of butter—Gillespie's own make—was laid on the counter, he stood rubbing his hands, for the night was bitter cold. The woman leaned forward with discreet face, and whispered in a strained voice. These women had courage; they were out fighting for their children, privateering for their husbands.

"Mark it doon in the book, wull I?" Gillespie's voice rang out loudly. In the tense silence which followed, the sharp whistling in his nostrils was heard by every woman present, as he leaned

over the counter in turn and whipped everything out of the basket. His face was wolfish as the face of a looting Turk.

"I'm fair rooked gein tick!" and turning to the next customer,
babbled of the impudence of scum that drink "a' their money
and expec' me to feed them. Ye'd think I was Goäd Almighty
to look aifter the sparrows." These venomous and blasphemous
words made the women shiver. Three of them stole out of the
shop. His mood then suddenly changed. He had purged the
counter, and now relieved the situation by diverting attention to
the canaries he had stolen from the plague ship. Raising a cautioning hand he jocosely said, "Quate there wi' your feet; the hen's
havin' a bath." The customers awaited the pleasure of the lady-
bird, till she had hopped up with glancing eyes, preening herself
from the water.

"Noo, what dae ye want, mistress?" And as he cut the ham,
with the tip of his tongue protruding—"Isn't that cock a fair
whustler? He's the boy to waken the street in the mornin'. They
should pey me a penny a day for wakenin' them, the lubbers"—his
cheery voice rattled on—"I canna sell an alarm clock noo-a-days
for thae confounded birds"—his jovial face beamed on the
women—"I've a good mind to thraw their necks. Them sae
perjink to feed too"—The echo of his words was scarce dead—
"Ye'd think I was Goäd Almighty to look aifter the sparrows"—
He grinned at the silent faces—"A bonnie penny they cost, an'
a wastery o' good time. Topsail or Sanny don't ken when to
change their water. Useless folk! they just scar' thae birds oot
o' their wuts. Ask Topsail to fetch chick-weed, and it's night-
shade she'll bring, the murderer"—His rollicking laugh rang
through the shop. When business was finished for the night he
would hold up a playful finger—"You sharp-eyed devil! fine
you ken a' that's goin' on. Never mind, it's another penny in the
purse you're seein'." The cock mayhap would hop down and
splash in the water—"There you go, you knowin' deevil. May
ye never see Gillespie sterve. Some cat frae the Back Street wad
get a grup o' ye then," and he would poke cheerful-wise at the
bird with the point of a pen, till he realised he was wasting oil,
and hurriedly turned out the lights. At the close-mouth he would
stand gazing down the Square at Harbour Street smothered in
snow, or screaming with wind, with the air of one reckoning on
yet owning the street. The women who came to his shop resisted
him as little as they would resist a pirate beneath his guns. He

221

wanted the men in his power also, that he might possess the fleet, and tortured his brain, devising plan after plan to this end. He deemed that the elements were warring on his side. That very night Fate was to put a master plan in his grasp.

24

TIMES were so hard that Peter the jeweller closed his shop, and all his clocks were stopped. Every Saturday he used to wind the clock in the tower of the parish church with a big handle, climbing up among the droppings of windy birds to work at his inheritance; for his father, dead of an apoplexy while scaling the second flight of the narrow steep stair, had tamed Time there also within the gilt circle of the clock-face. Peter his son, having shut his shop, removed himself from the surging sea of the winds around the spire, and the clock by which Brieston set its time stopped. Men missed the solemn boom, and noticing the dead hands, concluded that religion, too, had perished in the blight that possessed Brieston. The gilt face of the clock in the turgid light was as the face of a corpse in candle-light. Men walked beneath it melancholy, bitter, darkened, morose, savage, without sanctuary, without hope. Old sorrows and old feuds were alike buried. People feared one thing—famine; watched one thing— the shop in the Square. Lowrie hinted to Gillespie that his shop would be looted.

"I'm ready for them any hour o' the day or night," and glancing up at the church he saw that the clock had stopped. He did not know the reason, for a certain tide of business still flowed in at his door, though it passed by the door of Peter the jeweller. Not even a queen can stave off grief with a necklace.

Despite the lifeless clock the hour came when the bottom of the meal barrel grinned up in irony in the face of Red Duncan. The men had scraped the very bottom of the Loch with sixty fathom string to the trawls. Heart-breaking work it was dragging them aboard empty from the ooze. No one from the Barracks to the "Ghost" had bought so much as a pennyworth of salt with which to cure the winter's herring, and they were burning heather in the Back Street. Kate of the Left Hand, Red Duncan's wife, went and bowed herself before Gillespie, who stood rubicund before her, with feet firmly planted on the floor. This woman was of one of those unfortunate families in which one commonly looks for signs of trouble. It would not surprise any one at any time to find one of its members running distractedly down the stair, wailing because of a death that had just taken place. Even in their gayest moments an air of fatality or a foreboding of ill hovers over their house. Red Duncan's family was such a target for sorrow. Of him it was a saying, "When the herring's south, Red Duncan's north." Several years previously his house had been burned, and in the conflagration his wife had lost her right hand. Dr. Maclean had amputated the charred stump. Her left hand, as she now stood before Gillespie, was empty.

"I've never wance compleened since I lost my all the night o' the fire. I'm stervin'."

"Thae rats! thae rats!"—it was alleged that rats eating into a box of matches had started the fire—"Is't no' wonderfu' hoo they beasties can herm us folk, ay?" Gillespie sighed.

"Wull ye gie me wan loaf, Maister Strang? it's no' for mysel'; my weans is greetin' wi' hunger."

"Breed's up the noo a haepenny. That'll be fowerpence."

"I haena seen fowerpence this fortnight."

"I'll aye be glad to sell ye a loaf when ye hae the money."

The woman's eyes were as those of one who is being crucified.

"Wull ye no help me?" she pleaded. "I'll pey ye when I can."

"I hear that story every day ee noo," he answered drily; "folk think I'm the Bank o' Scotland."

A thing too deep for tears was in the woman's face.

"Ye're a hard man," she said. "I've three weans at hame, an' I'm frichted to go back. I hope your weans, Maister Gillespie, will never ken the sufferin' o' mine."

Gillespie put on his spectacles, opened a ledger and shook his head.

"I'm fair weirin' my eyes oot wi' this rakin' through a book o' bad debts. I canna add more to 't or I'll be blin'." He turned his broad shoulder to her. Kate of the Left Hand, with her eyes upon that shoulder, deliberated. The house which had been burned belonged to Gillespie, and was the house in which he had had his first shop. He was found to be so rapacious that no tenant would live in it longer than a single term. It was alleged that he could still find his way into the garret, which he still used as a store, by the road of the trap which he had cut there in the days when he was engaged in Sunday trading. To burn the old shop and get the insurance money was a good way of ridding himself of the task of finding new tenants. Such sinister rumours were afloat at the time the house was burned.

Kate of the Left Hand drew her shawl about her head and her famished eyes swept round the well-stocked shop.

"Gillespie," she said fiercely, "tak' good care the rats dinna eat your matches here. Ye ken wha' fired the garret above me when I lost my all? A gey an' big grey rat."

He made a swift gesture of dismissal; "Ye needna open fire. I've heard a' that before."

She flashed round on him.

"It'll dae ye nae hairm to hear it again;" she snatched the shawl from her right shoulder, and exposed the pitiful stump. "Look at it," she cried; "an' ye'll no' gie me a loaf noo. You to say that ye're no Goäd Almighty to feed the sparrows an' the weans. Wait, man, wait, the Almighty's no' done wi' you yet. Ye're good at mekin' a bleeze. Maybe the next bleeze 'ill no please ye sae weel. I'll dree my own weird; but Goäd! I winna dree yours for a' the gold in Californy."

"Is't no' wonderfu'?" Gillespie thought, gazing up at the hams hanging from hooks on the ceiling, "the wy they ding doon a chap as soon as he begins to get on a wee in the world."

Kate of the Left Hand, darting out of the Square round the Bank corner, ran into Topsail Janet.

"What's wrong wi' ye, Kate?"

"The weans are stervin', an' Gillespie put me oot o' the shop."

Topsail pondered with a slack mouth of woe. "There's noäthing I can prig in the hoose. He's lik' a jyler noo-a-days wi' his keys, the misert. Come on," she flashed, "I'll mand ye something." She led Kate of the Left Hand to the ree, which was flanked by Gillespie's stable, whose door Topsail opened. A brown mare with a mangy hide stood in one of the stalls. Topsail lifted the lid of the box leaning against the wall.

"Hold your bratty," which, with a scoop, she filled with beans. "Thon misert," she jerked the scoop in the direction of the Square, "coonts the feed; but the mear can sterve for wan day. It'll be something for the weans to chow. There, noo," she patted

224

Kate maternally; "afore the beans is done, ye'll mand a bite somewhere. Try Lonend for a pickle auld potatoes."

Sulky night fell on the Back Street. The children, pinched and blue-veined, were huddled together asleep; husband and wife sat in stony silence. The last word of Red Duncan had been to rave at the keeper of the destinies of men. Misery like a beak was tearing his heart.

"The morn's Sunday," he said; "the Lord's Day," and lapsed into the silence of hopeless abandonment. The rusty gaping grate had the malevolence of an evil eye, watching these two figures of stone.

A wail came from the floor inside the wooden frame where the bed had been. The cold had wakened the children. The woman lifted her head. She had the appearance of a wild beast protecting its litter. The man eyed her fiercely.

"Noathin' to pawn?" he croaked.

"Noathin," she gasped; "an' I'm telt the Jew 'ill tek' nae mair stuff ony wy." His blood turned to water as the fretting wail became louder.

"Mither! oh, mither! gie's a piece; a wee bit; I'm stervin' wi' hunger."

"Wheest, son, your mither 'ill gie ye some more beans, an' ye'll hae a braw breakfast the morn."

"Will it be toast?"

"Ay, son! toast an' jeely."

She groped to the corner at the window; but the beans were finished. She groaned, and like a gaunt sibyl stretched out her bony hand to the darkening window.

"Goäd in heaven, wull ye no' hae peety?"

The children began to whimper; the mother to sob.

"Katie, my wumman, are ye greetin' at lang an' last?" The sound of his gnashing teeth like a dog's was terrible in the room. In a tone which he had not heard before—the tone of one who is on the brink of the Pit—she answered:

"Greetin'! ay, my breist's burnin', burnin'."

Then Red Duncan put on his cap and went out to steal.

Gillespie sat at the kitchen table over his ledger in a brown study. The bones of the impoverished town were his for the lifting, and he saw himself squeezing out their marrow. Topsail was cleaning up the supper dishes in the sink; his wife was seated in the corner at the fire with a pile of socks on her lap, for Topsail had insisted that she should be found of Gillespie on some active task. Mrs. Strang was darning in a desultory fashion, for she loathed the work. A dull noise was heard in the shop. Gillespie lifted his head alertly.

"Did ye hear a noise ablow?" he asked.

"It'll be a rat in the shop," and Topsail went on with her washing.

"Wheest, wull ye, wi' that clatter!" Topsail stopped. There was nothing to be heard but the beating of the rain on the window.

"Gie me my boots," he said sharply; "a man in his stockin' soles has no chance." He put them on and picked up the poker from the fender. He always carried the keys of the shop in his pocket. "Where's the candle?" Topsail glanced towards the dresser. He followed her glance and saw the candle.

"There's nae rats in my shop," he growled as he lifted the sneck.

He crept along the passage, unlocked the back door of the shop, and left it open as a way of retreat, for he had no stomach for an encounter in the dark. He stood in the back office breathing quickly and listening. A gust of wind snarling at the door made his heart jump, and a wave of heat spread over his head. Would he steal out and fetch the policeman? By that time the thief would be gone. He imagined some one ready to strike or spring at him. The drumming of the rain went on without in the thick night, and the wind whined through the passage. He took a stealthy step towards his desk against the wall beside the fireplace, laid down the poker on the desk, and struck a match. As it fluttered in the draught and went out he heard a brushing as of clothes touching something in the front shop, and his hand shook. He struck another match hurriedly, and lit the candle, sheltering the flame with his hand, as it died down, and struggled back to life. Fear of imminent peril crouching somewhere overcame him. At that moment he noticed the window. The glass had been broken at the catch, and the window was wide open. He shifted the candle to his left hand and picked up the poker.

"Come oot o' that, ye blaiggart!" he roared, his heart choking in his throat. A man stepped through the counter opening and stood in the doorway between the back office and the shop. Gillespie's amazement overcame him for a moment when he saw Red Duncan, meagre, thin with hunger, nerveless with detection.

At the sight of the man's confusion and hang-dog air, Gillespie's aplomb rushed back upon him, and for a moment he felt kindly disposed to the unlucky thief, for the relief his pusillanimous presence afforded. He walked up to Red Duncan, holding the candle between them.

"It's yersel', Donnachaidh."

The other made no answer.

"A wild night to be oot for a bit tobacco."

Red Duncan leaned against the counter and sobbed out: "I'm done for!"

"Ay! it's the jyle for ye, Donnachaidh."

"Mo thruaigh! mo thruaigh! I never stealt in my life before."

"Sixty days if it's a meenut. Ye'll be namely a' over Brieston."

"For Goäd's sake, gie's a chance. Man! man! if ye heard my weans greetin' the night. I'll do anything for ye. Gie's wan chance."

"Weel," Gillespie had laid down the poker and was smoothing his cheek with his hand; "I'm no that bad-he'rted I wad send any man to jyle."

"No! no!" Red Duncan quavered; "we a' ken that."

Gillespie, who had been keenly scrutinising him, suddenly extended to him the candle. "Hold the cannle. I'm goin' to trait ye better nor ye deserve, comin' alarmin' dacent folk in the deid o' night."

"If ye'd been in oor hoose the night ye'd ha' done the same," Red Duncan bleated.

Gillespie quietly surveyed the shop.

"An' what were ye thrang at when I spoiled the ploy?"

Red Duncan stepped backwards and pointed to the recess beneath the counter, in which three loaves, part of a ham, and a tin of salmon were lying.

"Ay! ay! nane sae bad, an' breid up an' Irish sae dear." He lifted the goods on to the counter, where they lay on the long polished surface, isolated, accusatory. Gillespie disappeared behind a pile of stuff in the midst of the floor, and returned with a basket.

"Noo, Donnachaidh"—he spoke briskly, and laid a hand on Red Duncan's shoulder as he passed—"I'll tek' peety on ye for the sake o' the wife an' weans. Ye'll no' can say I'm bad."

The man was exhausted and tears sprang in his eyes; the clear drops falling on the wiry red beard.

"I canna thank ye, Gillespie."

Gillespie walked to the butter kit.

"Hold the cannle here," he commanded. By force of habit Red Duncan went to the customer's side of the counter and leaned over, candle in hand.

"Come awa' roond, man; dinna be sae blate."

Gillespie scrupulously weighed 12 lb. of butter; cut a hunk of cheese and weighed it; sugar 12 lb.; tea 12 lb.; packed them up, and put them in the basket; weighed the ham, and put it with six loaves along with the other stuff. Neither man spoke a word till Gillespie took the candle from Red Duncan.

"Cairry ben the basket," he ordered. They went into the back office. Gillespie dropped some candle grease on the writing board of the desk, and struck the end of the candle in the grease.

"Noo," he said, "you'll tek' home thae vittels."

The one side of Red Duncan's face was deeply shadowed, the other was twitching in the candle-light. "I'll pey ye, Gillespie, I'll pey ye wi' the first fushin'."

"That's the talk, Donnachaidh. Ye're no' like a wheen o' thae blaiggarts that'll tek' an' tek' an' when they win a penny they're off to Brodie's."

"No! my hands to Goäd."

Gillespie interrupted him brusquely.

"Ye'll see I'm no' cheatin' ye." He drew a sheet of paper towards him and took up a pen.

		s.	d.				£	s.	d.
12 lb. sugar	@		$2\frac{1}{2}$	.	.	.		2	6
12 lb. cheese	@		10	.	.	.		10	0
12 lb. butter	@	1	4	.	.	.		16	0
12 lb. tea	@	1	8	.	.	.	1	0	0
$\frac{1}{2}$ doz. loaves	@		$3\frac{1}{2}$	.	.	.		1	9
7 lb. ham	@	1	2	.	.	.		8	2

He looked up smiling at Red Duncan. "Ye'll no' hae me at the expense o' the brocken winda'?"

Red Duncan nodded.

						s.	d.
1 pane glass	.	.	.	.	.	1	6
1 candle	.	.	.	.	.		1

"Let me see noo"—he was chewing the point of the pen, and

counting on his fingers—"that mek's three pounds nate. Is it no' astonishin' the wy it cam oot—nate the three poun'?" Red Duncan stared fascinated, Gillespie wheeled round in his chair—"You an' me 'ill mek' a bargain, Donnachaidh," he said. Gillespie was laughing silently at his victim—"I ken what it is to hae a stervin' wife an' weans." Red Duncan, still under the spell of fascination, blinked; "I'm goin' to show ye a wy to keep the wolf frae the door a' winter."

"I wish to Goäd I knew!" Red Duncan blurted.

"Weel, ye needna wait for the fushin' to pey me"—Gillespie was purring now; his eyes wheedling as well as his voice—"ye'll can pey me noo. That's the wy ony dacent man wad do."

"But I hevna a roost."

"Hoots, man!"—Gillespie jabbed him playfully with the point of his pen—"ye've a fourth share in the *Bella*—boat an' nets."

"Ay."

The *Bella* was a new caravel, built for trawling, and cost a hundred and ten pounds; the trawl-net cost thirty pounds. Anchor and chains, sails, and other gear forty pounds—a hundred and eighty pounds in all.

"Say we'll tek' thirty pounds off, seein' she's been oot a season. That mek's a hundred and fifty pounds. A fourth share is thirty-seven pounds ten shullin's."

"She's as good as new," said Red Duncan, suddenly awake. "The net hasna gone ower her side since she left the carpenter's shed."

"Weel! weel! say twenty pounds off. That leaves a hundred and sixty pounds—forty pounds a fourth share. Dinna argle-bargle a' night an' the waens greetin' wi' hunger. Noo you sign a bill to me for your share, an' I'll feed you an' yours a' the winter. Ye've gotten three pounds worth here in the basket."

"Can ye no' wait?" pleaded the dumbfounded man, who saw himself being enmeshed. "I'll can easy pey ye the three poun' wi' the first good fishin'."

"Man! I canna hev' my money lyin' oot that long thae bad times. I've to pey the traivellers. Ye don't ken what it is to hev' them girnin' in your face for money."

Red Duncan, unable to rebut this, was silent.

"Think o' your wife an' weans cryin' for breid a' the winter"—he grinned in Red Duncan's face. "It's no' as if Katie could go oot an' work. Wha'll gie work to a wan-airmed wumman?"

Red Duncan shifted from one foot to the other, and a fine sweat broke out on his forehead. "The other men 'ill ken," he said wretchedly.

Gillespie laughed scornfully.

"The other men 'ill be gey gled to do the same afore the spring. I canna tek' up the hale fleet. I'm gein ye your chance noo, Donnachaidh." His argument was persuasive.

"I canna! I canna!"

Gillespie's face hardened, and he rose ponderously to his feet.

"Ye gomeril," he said; "I'll nò' tek' ye to the jyle the nicht for shop-breakin'; but I'll gie ye in chairge the morn. Ye'll fin' oot the Shurrif in Ardmarkie 'ill no dale wi' ye lik' Gillespa' Strang."

Red Duncan was cowed. "If I hae the money I'll can buy my share back?" he asked.

"Ou! there's naethin' to hinder ye, Donnachaidh." The answer was airy; and he clapped Red Duncan on the shoulder. "Sign the bill noo an' be off wi' the basket afore it gets any later."

Red Duncan took up the pen in a shaky hand.

"Ay! there across the stamp; that's my he'rty; the date noo. It's no just the right kin' o' bill this; but ye'll step doon come Monday morn. I'll get the Spider to mek' oot a right wan." He scrupulously dried the wet ink with blotting-paper.

"Noo ye've paid your lawin' I'll gie ye a fill for a smoke on the road home." Gillespie passed into the shop and returned with about an inch of thin black tobacco. "Gie my compliments to your wife an' say she's no' to be blate aboot comin' for proveesions." Candle in hand Gillespie showed out Red Duncan with the basket on his shoulder.

"Good-night, Donnachaidh," Gillespie cried, shielding the candle from the wind and rain; "see an' send the boy doon wi' the basket on Monday."

Red Duncan passed in silence into the night, bearing his cross.

Gillespie returned to his desk chuckling. He owned the fourth share of a boat and net. The custom was to divide the price of a week's take of herring into five shares—one share for each of the four men of the crew, and one share for the boat and the net, after an allowance had been made for the week's stores. Gillespie would now draw his share for this boat and net, and Red Duncan would do the work for him, suffering the exposure and the peril. Gillespie reckoned that one month's good fishing would refund him in the amount he would extend on food to Red Duncan's

230

family. Thereafter his share in the boat would constitute a source of revenue season after season without burden. He looked forward to getting many of the boats in his possession in this way before the spring. He would choose the neediest crews, and point out how Red Duncan was comfortably passing the winter. These fishermen would become his servants. He had no intention of re-selling his share, either to Red Duncan or to any other gomeril. He took two black-striped balls from a long glass bottle and put one in his mouth. He always treated himself in this fashion after a good stroke of business. Then he barricaded the broken window, locked the door, and went upstairs. His wife lay on her back, mouth open, snoring. She awoke on his entrance.

"Who's that?" she asked, half sitting up in bed.

"It's me!" He crossed to the bedside, and put a black-striped ball between her lips. "Hae a sweety," he said. She looked at him with sleepy eyes. "I was kin' o' a wee lucky the night," he purred.

"What time is it?" she asked.

He examined a heavy silver watch.

"A quarter to one."

"Where have you been all this time?" She stretched out her neck towards him and yawned.

"Hoots! pookin a gull."

"Ye took your time to the job," she said, without understanding.

He flung off his coat and answered gaily:

"Never be in a hurry to lowse a stot frae a good pleugh."

25

The penury of Brieston became more and more galling to Gillespie, being a bit in the mouth of his progress. The feelings of humanity had seldom much claim upon him. If he took profit from his transactions, he esteemed as nothing the injury he was inflicting on others. His conduct now became venomous, his mind rancorous. Perhaps the fact that his folk were of another soil and blood blinded him to the hatred he was exciting. Gradually a considerable part of the fishing fleet had been pawned to him, and he conceived the sinister plan of getting possession of the whole fleet, and making the fishermen his servants. The people had passed now from suspicion to hostility, avowed and open. In times of sedition the smallest particulars are seized upon and given an exaggerated meaning. Ugly rumours of Gillespie's maltreatment of his wife were rife. He was of a Lowland breed. It was not only hardship but shame and dishonour that such an incomer should hold the reins of the town. Big Finla', who was the present occupant of Gillespie's house in the Back Street, complained of a smoking vent, and asked Gillespie to have it put right. Finlay's son was consumptive, and Maclean said that the smoke would be the death of the boy. Gillespie refused. The father, exasperated, swore he would have it done at his own expense, and Gillespie then ordered the plumber to "rig up a granny o' the very best on the lum, one that'll do a lifetime, an' chairge it on Finla'." The thing came out because Finlay when asked to pay refused.

Daily there were tales of Gillespie's greed, which went to swell the volume of gathering wrath. His bonds were not only drawn tightly across the town; he travelled among the farmers and encamped among the wool. Once a man was in his grip Gillespie was quietly savage, like frost. He had snared Dalrymple, a small farmer behind Lonend, loading his carts with stuff—meal, flour, potato seed, and fodder through the spring and blazing weather; and then jumped on his man.

"Gie's time, Gillespa'! I can dae naethin' wi' the grun'. It's soor wi' rain."

"Man, Dalrymple, dae ye want me to supply ye wi' weather too? What's the use o' a' your prayer-meetin's on Wednesday nights?" The farmer, a pious man, was shocked, but was forced to conceal his mortification. "My advice to ye"—Gillespie was smiling coldly—"is to redd up your ain hoose an' dung your bit parks, an' pey your debt afore ye put on a collar for the prayer-meetin', an' put siller in the kirk plate."

"Mr. Strang," replied the incensed man; "it's no' against me you're speakin': it's against God."

Gillespie waved an impatient hand. "Nae sermons! nae sermons! I'm needin' my money."

"I'll pey ye come the back-end. I don't ask this for mysel'. Ye wadna roup out my wife an' weans."

"Ay, ay! the same cry. Every wan o' ye run behind a petticoat."

Dalrymple was nettled. "It's no' for me to give way to anger, Mr. Strang, but I wad haud my tongue about petticoats. It'll p'raps be a gey ill day for ye yet that ye ever took up wi' Lonen's daughter, if a' accoonts be true."

Gillespie's face became sour.

"It's only a blaiggart that wad throw a man's ain dung at him," he cried; but in a moment the old coaxing returned to his voice. "I'll show ye I'm no' hard on any honest man wi' a faimly. I'll gie ye till the back-end to pey me."

Gillespie saw Dalrymple out of the shop, ruminating on the seven per cent. he had squeezed out of the farmer for the months of grace. Dalrymple was also ruminating. "Him to talk o' the prayer-meetin'. The fire an' sulphur o' Sodom and Gomorrah will devour him yet"—Dalrymple smiled grimly—"an' then I'll hae nae debt to pey him. The fire an' brimstone 'ill pey the lawin."

In his unimaginative, dogged way he clung tenaciously to the idea, and crossed over to Lonend in the afternoon to consult Logan about the seven per cent. He had a large simple faith in sturdy Lonend, whom he found bending over a tarnished look-ing-glass, and with moistened fingers carefully arranging wisps of hair over the bald spot on the crown of his head. Lonend, about to pay a visit to Mrs. Galbraith, was informed by Dalrymple of his visit to Gillespie.

"He's got ye nailed, Dalrymple," said Lonend. "I ken the breed an' seed o' him fine. I've eaten salt wi' him. Ye don't ken a man till ye've eaten a bushel o' salt thegither." The squat sturdy figure swung round on Dalrymple. "Ye're no' the only wan. Hide an' hair he's stripped Brieston. The toon's gettin' too small for him. He should hae been livin' wi' the tobacco lords o' the Trongate. There's some folk greet wi' evil an' spite, but ye can mek' noathin' o' him—thon deid calm. He's got the bulk o' the fleet in his grup."

"The vagabond," answered Dalrymple uneasily; "it's the fire an' brimstone o' Sodom an' Gomorrah that'll devour him yet. God will not be mocked."

Something in those familiar last words made Lonend shudder. Suddenly an idea seized him. The pupils of his eyes contracted and they glowed upon Dalrymple.

"By Goäd!" he said; "you've struck it, man. They're stupid doon by in Brieston about their boats. I hear they want to seize them. Fire! fire an' brimstone"—Lonend clenched his jaw—"he was fond enough o' fire when Red Duncan's wife nearly lost her life. Gie him his gutsfu' o't noo."

"Wheest! wheest! Lonen'," pleaded Dalrymple, terrified at the effect which his words produced. "Vengeance belongeth to the Lord; He will repay."

"You've struck it, man!" cried Lonend, carried away. "The bulk o' the fleet's Gillespie's. By the Lord! Dalrymple, but I'm gled ye cam' here the day. I'll back your seeven per cent. for this."

"Will ye?" asked Dalrymple, with snapping eyes.

"Ay! by Goäd! that will I, an' sign it by the lowe o' Gillespie's fleet."

That evening Lonend divulged certain things to Mrs. Galbraith, and sitting with his stumpy legs held wide, and his hands hanging loosely between them, asked her if she would marry him.

There was a tense silence in the room for a moment as Lonend raised his eyes furtively and riveted them on a mole on Mrs. Galbraith's cheek. Her full bosom rose and fell in short, quick pants. At last she turned her dark brilliant eyes on Lonend, making no attempt to conceal the expression of nausea on her face.

"Have you thought of Morag?" she asked, in a low stiff voice. "What will become of her if Mr. Strang loses the fleet by fire?"

"She's as ill-off as ever she'll be," he answered, dropping his eyes before her withering look.

When he raised them again, because of her continued silence, she held out her hand.

"Good-night," she said deliberately. "I shall marry you if you burn the boats which belong to Mr. Strang."

26

LONEND assiduously fomented ill-feeling against Gillespie. The Pump was up in arms.

"Souple, souple Gillespie," said Nan at Jock, whose son was

once more returned from the ends of the earth. "God be thankit. I'm no' in his raiverence. The slinkin' greedy face he has."

Mary Bunch craned her little dark head forward. "We'll soon a' be independent o' him. Ye ken I've a nesty bitter tongue, an' it'll no' do for me to open fire. But just wait you. Lonen' is the boy for him. There's goin' to be rippets. Petery McKinnon's sweirin' him terrible. He ca'ed his boy at the christinin' aifter Gillespie, thinkin' it wad soften him, for they're deep in his debt. An' what div ye think he said to Petery's wife?"

No answer was hazarded.

"Sez he, 'See that he mak's good use o' the name.'"

"Ach! ach! is he no' the mean scart?" said Black Jean; "it'll soon be a deserted toon wi' his ongoin's, an' no' a lum reekin'."

Lonend, more than any other, helped to bring about this moral earthquake. But the people, apart from Lonend's influence, were already deep in hatred. It leaked out that some of the men were mortgaging their shares in the boats to Gillespie. His avarice made them avaricious. They paid him as if coin were heart-blood. He bought by stealth and sold with consummate cunning; took in the day and gave in the dark. He was a busy moth in the decayed estates of the impoverished. Many were now actually afraid of his whistling nostril. The sibilant sound was likened by the Butler to the devil putting a whistle to his lips at the mouth of the Pit. The morning found him on the outposts of occasion as February came in; and at night he was a framer of traps, snares, and gins. In his eyes, the will of God was exercised in heaven only; the earth being purely a field of human activity— a theory as old as the human race. In practice Gillespie had a new mastery of this theory, as he bruised bees for their honey, and battered bald heads with a harp, giving no one a chance to smell powder. The rat McAskill was his right-hand man. Gillespie, however, was unaware that times occur in the history of nations and of communities when law is whirled away like a withered leaf in the tempest of a people's revolt. Such a time was coming to Brieston. What right had an interloper to seize the chief power in Brieston and enslave its folk? Red Duncan's family had now eaten the share of his boat; and Red Duncan was not chary of telling how he had been ensnared. Brieston was weary of its lot—burned with the heat, blistered with gales, and trapped by a pirate. The people were worn with vicissitude and savage at their impotence in being driven to sell their birthright for a mess at Gillespie's hands. They had imagined him a public benefactor, but recognised now that all along Lonend was right. In bitterness they formulated the axiom that many kings have ascended thrones only to tax the people. Lonend's denunciation had all the more force that his own daughter was married to Gillespie.

Distress had now in many families come to a head. Some of their members had gone to Glasgow, Clydebank, Port Glasgow, and Greenock, seeking work in the ship-building yards; but many of the hammers on Clydeside were silent and the yards half empty. Glasgow Harbour was full of idle ships. Tired of being sent from one gate to another of the yards, the men returned home dispirited and without money. They were goaded by ill-luck, blighting weather, the wretched state of their families, and the prospect of entering on the spring fishing season no longer their own masters. Some swore they would not lift an anchor, though it was pointed out that if they remained ashore they would starve. Others suggested seizing the boats and using them as if they were their own. Gillespie would baulk them in this, however, because he would withhold provisions and gear. Brieston was heaving in the throes of anarchy, and a low growl of despair like the snarl of a caged beast was heard. The people had reached that pitch when all that is needed is a leader to give them initiative.

It was said that a cat had been boiled and eaten in MacCalman's Lane. This turned the blood of Brieston to gall. Queebec at the time was preaching at the shoe-maker's shop on the breast wall to a deep sullen crowd. He raved of portents which he saw in the sky, and threatened the shop in the Square with outstretched hand which gripped a Bible.

"Let him come out and answer for his sins. It is the day of the Lord, a terrible day of vengeance. I see fire and blood." He spoke of cometary lights and blazing apparitions in the heavens, wizardry in the air, over a land that was a field of blood. "Let Judas be hanged in it!" he screamed; "Heaven will have no mercy till the blood of Andy is avenged." He heard a rushing mighty noise by night proclaiming woe. An angel armed with a sword was on the Loch. Funerals passed in the clouds, with long-maned black horses champing in the air. Apparitions appeared in the graveyard.

Horror stagnated in the faces of the men as they listened.

"Your churches will become empty: you will learn to rob each other. Gillespie has your very lives in pledge. He has taken a bond on the services of your wives and daughters for a dole of food. He has your very heart-blood. Woe, woe to you! Woe, woe to the despoiler and the vampire! Will you stand by any longer?" The man's eye flashed from end to end of the line of men. "To the Lodge! to the Lodge!" he screamed.

A guttural growl broke out—"To the Lodge!"

The next moment the black tide of men, headed by Queebec, was pouring down Harbour Street in the direction of the Good Templars' Hall.

27

EVERY public meeting was held within these walls. This meeting, ostensibly an inspiration, had in reality been convened by Lonend, who had heard of Red Duncan's escapade. Together they had concerted a plan for working up the people through Queebec's philippics. Lonend, with a packed jury in the Lodge, had as his chief concern the finding of a chairman for the meeting. There was one nicknamed Barnacles, a notability of the town, an undersized, podgy, middle-aged man of a good family, who had been rusticated in Brieston by his folk in the Borders, Peebles way. Stuart, the parish minister, received one pound per week, paid quarterly, for his board; and it was stipulated that on no account was his boarder to receive spirituous liquor of any kind. He was nicknamed Barnacles from the appearance of his face, which was covered with large, fiery pimples. He was a fluent speaker, and was in constant demand to act as chairman at concerts and public gatherings, where he always appeared in a Harris tweed suit. Except the Laird's gamekeepers he was the only man in Brieston who wore knickerbockers. He was fond of children— of whom he had often a following—was an accomplished German scholar, and sang German songs at the Banker's evening parties to his own accompaniment on the piano. At such entertainments it was a sight to see Stuart's sister languish on a couch, making eyes at Maclean as she said, "Oh! Mr. Elliot, do play us that charming thing of Beethoven's you played in the manse last night."

In the manse Miss Stuart treated him ill-favouredly. "You know one's house is not one's own with him about," she would say con-descendingly to Mrs. Tosh. Stuart treated him more decently, especially as on occasion Barnacles presented the minister with an excellent sermon, full of German philosophy and theology. He knew the Rhine as well as Brieston, and passed his life tramping about the country in which he had become a proficient Gaelic scholar. He knew every person's business, and boasted that after forty minutes reading of the *Glasgow Herald* he could answer any ques-tion on its contents. He spoke of politicians as if they were his intimates, and he was chairman of the local Liberal Club. He ought not to be Liberal, he said; but was disgusted with the landowners of the Borders—"a peevish, stupid class who bat-tened on the land." He was readily bribed with a bottle. So we find Red Duncan proposing him "for the chair," and the little fat Barnacles taking the platform in knickers. Commonly he was loquacious; to-night terse, for the bottle and the five-pound note which Lonend had promised him were awaiting him in the peace that lay beyond these voices. In virile language he pointed out the flagrant piracy of Mr. Strang. It was preposterous to think that the whole fleet was to ride at his command, and that he had hired the very services of their wives and children for the gutting season. Suppose that season were a good one, the cream of it would go to Gillespie, who would be enriched in idleness, while they bore the brunt. The Hall was packed to the door. Even women had fought for entry as if a new miracle of loaves and fishes was about to be performed.

"He supposes himself to be the saviour of the town in these hard times. Let him prove it now. Ask him to give up possession of the boats he holds on the promise that his money shall be repaid during the coming season. Put him to the test."

Barnacles ceased talking and looked around the sea of faces. "I call for the names of three men who will go to him now with this proposition."

Lonend's packed jury responded.

Peepin was one. He lived in a smack like an old Viking, and raked the Quay head among the fishermen asking for "old chows." This chewed tobacco he dried and smoked. He coughed incessantly, with a hacking sound, and was often to be seen very lonely, drawing his scavenging of the day in a barrow about the streets in the twilight—a melancholy spectacle which was a

238

résumé of the toil of humanity, labouring in the light beneath the sky and seeking a roof at eventide. The Solan was another, a notable free-thinker, who had sucked his opinions in his youth from Glasgow Green. He denied any sort of power in the heavens or upon the earth; and he had cause, said Maclean, for no power was of any avail to cure his chronic dyspepsia. The veterinary surgeon, a tall supple man, always accompanied with a following of dogs, had tested the Solan by offering him a leaf of an old Bible and a box of matches, with which to light his pipe. As the Solan contemptuously was about to make a spill of the leaf, his eye caught these words, underlined with ink—"I was betrayed in the house of my friends." His pinched, sickly face took on a greenish hue; his prominent red nose appeared to burn.

"Light it with your nose, Solan!" some one cried.

From that hour the god had feet of clay. The Solan was anxious to retrieve himself by doing something conspicuous for his fellow-men, and offered himself as a delegate with Peepin. Red Duncan made up the third of the trio.

They found Gillespie, who had heard there was an insurrection of the people, armed with a gun.

Barnacles sat in the chair, awaiting their return, and the boys in the gallery whiled away the time shouting songs:

> "Oh, Donal'! Oh, Donal'!
> Drink your gless, lad, and gang awa' hame,
> For if ye'll tarry langer ye'll get a bad name;
> So drink your gless, lad, an' fill yoursel' fou.
> The lang wud's sae dreary, but I'll see ye through."

The trio returned.

"I'll hae naethin' to do wi' the scum o' Brieston"—the Solan reported Gillespie to Barnacles, who sat smugly, his thick legs apart and arms, which seemed to grow out of his hip, akimbo. "Ye're just a' wheen blaiggarts that's runnin' your race for the jyle."

Barnacles rose to his feet, and waved a fat white hand.

"Gentlemen," he declaimed, "you have heard Mr. Strang bleat. His answer is of scoundrels and of the greed of dishonest men. I have no doubt he brought into play his famous smile of usury."

Barnacles got no further.

"The wolf! he would cast lots for the seamless garment,"

239

some one shouted at the back of the Hall. Few recognised that it was Campion's voice. Immediately there was a scene of confusion. Voices rang out over the Hall.

"He's only fit to be minched doon an' made bait for a lobster pot."

"He stealt oor boats frae us. He told us we needna compleen," a dark-a-vised foreign-looking man was shouting; "he said he'd gie us another boat, an' you bate he gied us wan. Dae ye ken what was in her?" he roared; "noathin' but rats; a fair riddle to droon men. A life is noathin' to thon man."

"By Goäd, we'll get to windward o' him noo; we'll put a clove hitch on him;" another voice was distinguished in the babel.

At that moment Red Duncan stepped on to the platform beside Barnacles, and the tumult suddenly ceased. "Boys," he shouted, "Gillespie is sitting up yonder wi' a gun in his hand. He'll no' yield an inch. 'They're my boats,' he said. 'Are ye for lettin' them be, boys?' He burned me oot o' hoose an' hame for the insurance money; he burned the airm off my wife. He threatened me wi' the jyle when she was stervin', an' then stole my share o' the *Bella*. He's good at burnin'."

Queebec arose in the midst of the Hall. "Vengeance! Vengeance! the sword o' the Lord an' Gideon. Burn the boats; it's the only way."

"Burn the boats! burn the fleet!" The hoarse cry, taken up by the whole Hall, pulsed far into the night, and the tumult was heard by Gillespie.

"Gentlemen"—Barnacles held up his hand—"is that your decision?"

"Ay! ay!" came the answering roar.

"Let the outer door be locked," rang out the voice of Barnacles. The sound of a grating key was heard.

"Now, men, this is a serious thing. If any man objects to this course let him stand up."

Old Sandy shuffled with his feet, half stood up, and sank down again on his seat.

"I must ask you now to swear an oath by Almighty God that no man here will divulge what has transpired, or give away the names of those who volunteer for the work. Remember that the crime of incendiarism is heavily punished by the law."

"To hell wi' the law; it'll no' feed us!" a voice shouted.

"Very well then, every one present hold up his right hand and swear." A sea of fierce malignant faces was turned up to Barnacles as he solemnly held up his right hand and said, "I swear by Almighty God."

The next moment a multitude of hands was·in the air, and "I swear by Almighty Goäd" rang deep and low through the Hall. The terrible curse of a whole community was called down on the head of Gillespie Strang, who at that moment was nursing a gun.

Barnacles called for volunteers. With fierce oaths every man offered. Six were chosen. Queebec clamoured to be one, but was rejected. Red Duncan was appointed leader.

"Let every man go home, and let no one move a step to-morrow night to save the fleet. 'Sow the wind and reap the whirlwind,' " said Barnacles solemnly, and descended from the platform. The scrunch of a key was heard unlocking the outer door. Some of the men passed out with frightened faces; some were elated; most had a hard, brooding look. Not a word was spoken till they had crowded through the ante-room and broke up in Harbour Street into knots and groups. In twenty minutes the street was empty, and the mourning of the sea arose in the dark along the Harbour wall.

28

THE next evening a strong gale of wind and rain blew the Butler down Harbour Street into Brodie's, where he found the Fishery Officer, a clean-limbed, alert man of some thirty years, with a sallow face and humorous twinkling eyes, who announced that he had had a telegram from Ardmarkie with the intelligence that the fleet there had opened the spring fishing season with a heavy fishing. It was time the Brieston men were getting ready. The Butler flared up.

"What are they to get ready for, with Gillespie sittin' like a hoodie craw on the riggin' of every boat? May the Lord look sideways on him."

Gillespie found a partisan in the Fishery Officer, who said

that Gillespie would make the fortune of the fleet with his steamer ready to buy their fish. No one could provision the fleet like him, or hold such a quantity of empty stock ready for emergencies. Why were the lazy Brieston men not preparing their boats?— By the irony of circumstance the Brieston men were at that very moment, under cloud of night, lifting the anchors of the skiffs and lashing them together, and soaking their fore-castles with paraffin supplied by Lonend—"Before they get out the Ardmarkie men will have fished hundreds of pounds' worth. There's a big eye moving up the Channel."

It took all Brodie's blustering tact to prevent a quarrel, and it was with a valedictory oath of camaraderie that he shut his front door upon them at ten o'clock. The Fishery Officer waspishly fell into step with the Butler and said: "We've drunk together."

"That's true," hiccoughed the Butler; "by the heave of your legs."

"We've told yarns together."

"You're never done, man—big ones."

"We've sang songs together."

"I've never heard ye, ye hoodie."

"Give me time; give me time, Butler; I'm gettin' it out now for what ye said to me in Brodie's. Sang songs, ay; but we haven't had a fight yet."

"Man," said the Butler blithely, "many's a spar I've had wi' the Laird wi' the gloves. Give me the wall for my back, and I'll tap claret."

Two shops in Harbour Street just at the point where they stood formed an acute angle. One was large, next indeed in importance to Gillespie's; the other a small greengrocer's, which had the appearance of leaning under and being crushed by the larger. Into this angle the Butler walked, and leaning against both walls, was dimly aware that the Fishery Officer was making certain strange gyratory movements in his vicinity.

"Hach," ejaculated the Butler peevishly, shot out his powerful hand, and caught his opponent on the shoulder. In this fashion they fell to, fell, and fell asleep. Some two hours later Campbell of Skye fell over a leg in the dark. Always eager for stripes, he flashed his bull's eye on the corner, and was in the article of arresting a house-breaker, when he glimpsed the Butler seated in the angle of the wall, blinking, with folded arms like an Indian god. The Fishery Officer had eloped with his respectability some time before, when the Butler, wandering through an indecent ballad, had awakened him. The Butler still sang.

"Wha-at iss this noise you are mekin'?"

"Noise!" said the Butler; "I'm singing."

"Maybe you iss; but move on at wance, or you'll be singin' in the chyle."

This was exactly the Butler's inability. An idea took the genial aristocrat that he would use the policeman as a valet.

"You don't know me, you surely don't know me, constable, or you wouldn't speak in that scurrilous fashion." He reclined on his right elbow. "You haven't been long enough in Brieston to hear of my trouble."

"Your trubble iss the dram; I'm tellin' you that, by Chove!"

"You afflict me, sir; you afflict me. What rascals do you move among to hear such low talk?"

"Rascals! move on at wance, or I'll hev' to took ye to the chyle."

"I tell you I won't move on. I defy you, sir, to lay your hand on me till I have explained to you my trouble. Extinguish your light. It is in my eyes." There was a click, followed by sudden darkness.

"Allow me, sir, to ask you to be seated by me."

"My backside on the wet; no fears."

"As you will; as you will. Observe then, constable, this is not the dram; it is a floating kidney. Have you ever heard of a floating kidney?"

"No, nor a flottin' puddin'. Chust you reise an' move on smert."

"I tell you I'm indisposed. Lay your hand on me at your peril." The Butler groaned and rubbed the small of his back. "Oh, constable! constable! it's here. If I could just get this kidney of mine anchored. It's an awful thing for a man to have a kidney sailing up and down inside him, like a yacht at a regatta." He groaned deeply: "Sometimes I feel it in the small of my back; the next minute—Oh! Oh!! Oh!!!—it's tacking away up my spine." His head fell on his arm. Campbell of Skye bent down an anxious face.

"Dhia!" he said, "iss this no' the state you're in; will I go for the doctor?"

"Maclean knows; Maclean knows," the inert mass moaned.

"There's nothing for it when it seizes me but to lie down if I can't get assistance. Big McCallum used to give me an arm home; and you talk of the jail. Do you want to drive me into an early grave, sir?"

Campbell's fat, red face was stupid with mystification and his eyes alarmed. "Since aal my days I neffer h'erd of a floatin' kidney through Skye."

"It's a new trouble, constable, a new trouble discovered by a German professor. Give me your hand now, officer; it's easier a little."

Campbell lifted him gently by the oxter, the Butler leaning heavily and stertorously upon the Law, and at every stagger groaning.

"It's pricking me, constable; pricking like a knife; my days are numbered."

"Dhia! if I wass in your boots I wad be gettin' some pooders from the doctor."

"Powders, sir, powders; I've had some to-night already; speaking powders they're called. Easy now at the brae." And the Butler informed Campbell of the shining qualities of his predecessor McCallum, on the brae and on the stair, which they were approaching. "He used to help me up and knock at the door. He's promoted since to Islay." The tone hinted that the promotion came from the Butler. Campbell, determined that in no wise would he come short of the serviceableness of his predecessor, panted up the stair with his ponderous burden and knocked at the door. A red-haired, small, white-faced woman opened it. She looked sleepy and fatigued.

"Here's the Butler," said Campbell.

She put out a hand and laid hold of her husband, a sad look creeping into her eyes.

"Ay! ay!" she said wearily; "it's always 'Here's the Butler.'" She accepted him from the policeman as a parcel, and closed the door.

"This iss no' the chob for me at aal, at aal," muttered Campbell of Skye, as he descended the stair; "tekin' home floatin' kidneys. The muschief iss in this toon."

When he gained the mouth of the close he saw that mischief indeed was in the town. Harbour Street shone in a pale glow, and Campbell ran down the brae. As he came into the Square a terrible sight met his gaze and petrified him. The fishing-fleet

244

was on fire. He heard the crackling and splintering of wood, and
the roar of wind-tormented flame.

"Dhia! Dhia! this is the Day of Chudgement," he muttered,
and ran across the Square, up the close and the stair, and was
thundering with his boots and hands on Gillespie's door.

"Who's there?" came a sharp voice.

"Reise! reise! the boats iss on fire!"

He continued hammering on the door till Gillespie had opened
it.

"What's that ye're sayin'?"

"I'm tellin' you; I'm tellin' you," he panted; "hell's lowsed
on the boats!"

29

A cool philosophy will recognise the necessity and worth of such
an upheaval as overtook Brieston, for there can be no redemption
without blood. War has its tremendous sanity, being a moral
earthquake in humanity. Because the primitive vices of violence,
cruelty, and revenge are always near the surface, men are drawn
into the vortex, and do things in the heart of a mob which they
bitterly repent of afterwards. So we find two of these men who
had volunteered to burn the fleet afraid to make the venture.
They had harnessed the boats together; had soaked here and
there a forecastle with paraffin, and now stood waiting in the
lee of the "Shipping Box" for the parish church bell to ring the
midnight hour. It was cold, dark, and stormy.

"Holy sailor, what a night!" said a subdued voice.

"Noo's the time," urged Red Duncan; "the breeze 'ill tek'
off wi' the ebb."

A crescent moon was sheering through the clouds like a
silvery fin slicing a phosphorescent sea. Dark-ribbed waves
slouched round the Quay head. A hurried step was heard coming
down Harbour Street beneath the police station dike.

"Scatter, boys," whispered Red Duncan. The men vanished
like shadows round the "Shipping Box" and down the Quay. So
strong is the sense of property that the most righteous aggression
upon it is not effected without qualms.

Red Duncan alone stood his ground, desirous to know who the intruder was. A squat, bulky form came round the corner of the "Shipping Box." It was Lonend. Immediately his eyes fell on Red Duncan he asked:

"Where's the rest o' the men?"

Red Duncan answered with a low whistle, and five shadowy forms crept back to the lee of the "Shipping Box." For the past hour Lonend had been watching from his farm door, and becoming impatient had set out to discover the cause of the delay. On the way he had nailed a certain paper on to the door of Gillespie's shop. One of the men who were now gathered round him muttered that it was an ugly job. It was all very well for Lonend to talk of burning boats. He was a farmer. The spring season was upon them. Where would they get boats for their work? And these boats! Lonend could not understand. They were old and precious. Their fathers had lived in them; they were haunted with memories. New and more daring sails might arise on the Loch; but never, never would they be such wings of beauty as those they knew. Every plank, every nail, every knot in the wood was familiar to them. To burn this heritage of associations was to commit sacrilege. They might as well fire the church or their own homes.

Lonend, having listened in silence, began to speak in a tone of contempt. Why did they not offer their objections at the meeting, and leave better men to the job? His voice, rising and falling in the dark, stung with sarcasm.

"Your boats! they're your boats no longer: ye'll only be galley-slaves in them."

"Maybe we'll mand to buy them back frae the big fella' wi' good times."

Lonend exploded in hard laughter. "I'll no' believe it while there's one bone o' me above the other. The devil maybe 'ill win back to heaven frae hell; but ye'll never buy the boats back. Gillespie's got the most o' ye pledge an' bond, an' noo ye've got him in your hand oot there. Are ye weans or not, by Goäd? Hae ye forgotten the black easterly win', an' the hunger, an' Gillespie wi' his wee papers wi' the stamp, an' McAskill blinkin' at his side? Hae ye forgotten the wolf, that ye're anxious to be his slaves? Gie me the torch." He plucked it from Red Duncan's hands, and appeared to swell with rage. His ruthless savagery beat upon them like blows. This was such a torch as they had used when they had got herring, and lit to attract the notice of the buyers. They were used to light it in happy times. The blessing of cot and hearth and Heaven was upon these torches! they were the light of the seas; the wells by which men lay; the stars of hope and home. To use one of them now to provoke hell—it was like giving their children poisoned bread.

"We canna! we canna burn oor boats."

"*Your* boats! *your* boats!" He shook the blackened torch in their faces; "you'll never sail them again as free men. What would the old Brieston men have said to you? They're Gillespie's boats, an' he'll wring oot your he'rt's blood in them."

"It's the Goäd Almighty's truth," rapped out Red Duncan; "it's me, boys, that kens Gillespie; he'll strangle ye lik' a wee bird. They're no' oor boats any longer. He stole the *Bella* frae me in the deid o' night in his back shop, an' noo in the deid o' night I'll tek' her frae him;" his voice shook with passion.

"Will ye hand them ower to the beast Gillespie to mak' his stable in?" urged Lonend.

"No! by the Lord! I'm wi' ye, Lonen'," Red Duncan rapped out.

"Awa' hame the rest o' ye; awa' hame to your wife an' weans, an' be Gillespie's slaves for ever. Burn them, men, burn them; better to burn them than be trampled on like dung."

The men still hesitated in sullen mood.

"Hame wi' ye, ye sheep. That'll no save the boats. Duncan an' me's for the crossing—awa' hame." He advanced on them as if to crowd them back.

"Who's goin' home?" a voice growled; "it's no' me." The fellow's temper was roused and raw.

"Be off, the rest o' ye, an' tell the weemin ye were frightened. They're watching roond the toon behind their windows. Ye'll be namely in Brieston the morn. Off wi' ye! I'll gang an' get men, no' a wheen o' Gillespie's weemin'."

"Shut your mouth, by Goäd, or I'll choke ye!" It was the voice of Big Finla'. "Are ye wantin' the hale toon aboot oor ears?"

"The hale toon"—Lonend's words fell like a thong on a raw wound—"the hale toon 'ill ca' ye cowards if ye dinna come. They're waitin' to see the bleeze"—his voice rose above the noise of wind and sea—"waitin' at the windas to see Gillespie's bonfire." His laugh exploded again as he stepped out from the lee of

247

the "Shipping Box" on to the Quay, and faced the houses curving round Harbour Street as if they were populous with fiery eyes— "to see Gillespie's bonfire." His mocking laughter burst out again—"Gillespie's comin' o' age the nicht." Big Finla' pushed roughly past Lonend, descended the steps at the head of the Quay, stepped aboard the punt and lifted an oar.

"Are ye comin', boys?"

The oar splashed in the water. There was a sound as of frenzy in the noise—sudden, startling, going home like a trumpet-call to the hearts of those men. The magic sound of the oar in their native element sent fire through their veins. It seemed an eternity since they had heard this music. For months they had had nothing to do but stand on the Quay head and watch the seas lift and break through the scurry of the rain.

"Put the oars on her, boys, to hell oot o' this!" rang out Red Duncan's voice. They trooped down the slippery steps and seized the oars. They were like men possessed; agonised with desire to bury the oar deep in the brine, and hear the slush of the water about the blade. There was a human sound in it. In wetting the parched oars they were slaking their long thirst for the deep. The wind came in sword-thrusts upon the punt as she spun round the Quay head. Lonend sat in the stern nursing the torch to his breast, and shielding it from the breaking seas. They plunged the blades deep into the sea, and set their teeth at every stroke. Their lust of battling with the storm made the punt rock and sheer through the waves. The water meeting the blade of the oar was too yielding, and spun away like smoke. They wished for something solid as iron to wrestle with. The fires of conflict consumed them. They had been robbed for long, weary months of their heritage, and now they were returned from an exile of hunger and blood, of iron, heat, and plague. They lashed the sea with the oars; no longer bound upon a mission of revenge, but ravenously satiating their hunger of the deep. Would that the storm were louder, the rollers deeper, to try them to the very citadel of their strength. The bow of the punt was forced under the head-seas. They were drenched. The wind sang riotously past; the sea chanted a battlecry. They were freed men out in the wide night beneath the heavens in a challenging gale, and freed men they would remain. A grim silence sank upon the tossing boat. Their fear had evaporated. They would have rowed into the heart of a cyclone. They felt their strength gigantic. The rowlocks in the bow oar snapped, and a man tumbled backwards over the beam. His oar was snatched away on a grey-backed comber. "My oar's gone to hell, boys; pull away."

In that moment they shot nose first into a skiff. The man at the bow rose and clutched at her gunwale.

Lonend leapt aboard crying, "My turn now." He crawled forward, swung himself down by the forward beam and disappeared. A light glimmered in the forecastle, wavered a moment and went out. It was followed by a strong flame. The torch was lit. Lonend heard a loud cry from Red Duncan. "It's—it's my faither's boat; the auld *Flora*, black wi' age."

A tongue of flame peered out of the fo'c'sle door as if spying upon the night, licked the dark with yellow tongue, and darted in again. Lonend in the forecastle saw the dark stain of the paraffin across the lower bunk—the bunk where many righteous men now dead had slept the sleep of the weary in wet clothes. He applied the torch. The flame ran along the oil with greedy swiftness. There was a crackling of wood.

"One for you, Calum Galbraith," he muttered; "that score is cleaned." He flung open the trap-door in the roof. The flame began to roar, and swooped upwards in a wavering wall. Lonend retreated to the punt. Thick smoke mingled with lances of fire poured out of the trap-door. The old *Flora* was ablaze. Red Duncan was sitting on the middle beam, an oar astraddle across his knee. In the lurid glare he saw the dark, determined face of Lonend, and his greenish cat eyes ablaze with lust of carnage.

"Go to hell, you devil, after the auld boat!" Red Duncan screamed, swinging aloft the oar. The punt wobbled with the jerk as he rose, and sent Lonend staggering backwards. The oar crashed down on the gunwale of the skiff and splintered. Red Duncan collapsed on the beam and turning his back on the blazing boat began to sob. Presently he leapt to his feet.

"Good-bye, the auld *Flora*," he cried; "ye'll hae company the nicht the wy ye go." He savagely shoved the punt off. The bow slewed sharply round with the wind, and plunged into another skiff.

"Gie me the torch!" Red Duncan roared; "the auld *Flora's* gone; an' my mither's furniture's gone in the Back Street bleeze; and my wife's airm. I'll settle my debt wi' Gillespa' Strang this night, by Goäd!"

He leapt aboard, and flung himself at the forecastle door.

"Noo ye are men!" cried Lonend. "Gillespie 'ill soon smell the fire. It'll burn his banknotes, an' his wee papers wi' the stamps. Ha! ha! ha!" Lonend's wild sardonic laughter mingled with the crackling of wood.

Fire broke out in the forecastle. Big Finla' leapt aboard—"I'll no' be behind-hand." He picked up the torch and jumped into the third boat, his figure gigantic in the light. The floor of this forecastle was soaked with paraffin. He dropped on his knees as if about to pray. A flame wriggled and ran along the wood. He backed out into the open, slid along the scuttle door on the roof and "Shove off!" he cried; "the work's done."

"Where's the torch?" demanded the insatiable Lonend.

"Helpin' the bleeze."

They pushed off the punt, and unshipped the remaining two oars. With wind and tide abaft she tore through the glowing water, the deepening roar of the fire behind them; and the sea ahead lit. Lonend plunged his hands into the salt water. They were badly burned. His eyes were fixed astern, where boat after boat appeared to rush up from a dark well into a scarlet heart. Lonend got a glimpse of Harbour Street glooming and glancing in the dissipating darkness.

"Beach her!" he cried; "beach her at once. Brieston will be as bright as day in five minutes."

Another glance curdled his blood. Conspiracy can never perfect its details. These men had overlooked the fact that some of the boats rode not to chains, but to ropes attached to their anchors. One of these ropes had been burned through; and a furnace was drifting through the Harbour. The property of the innocent would suffer. In the gale that was blowing nothing could be done to save the shipping of Brieston from a holocaust.

"The sooner we're ashore an' hame the better."

"Ay, Lonen'," answered Red Duncan, who was tugging at an oar; "ye're in as big a hurry to rin awa' as ye were to hurry to the ploy."

In that moment the bow of the punt grated on the beach. Lonend splashed ashore and set to running up the beach. The small patter of his feet was like an animal's. In that moment it had most vividly occurred to him that if Gillespie by any chance were awakened by the glare or roused by any one, he would instantly suspect the hand of Lonend in the destruction of the fleet. "It'll just be like the soor deevil to whup off to Lonen'."

Panting stertorously Lonend conceived the awkwardness of such a position. He would have difficulty in accounting for his absence from home. He reached Lonend, not passing through Harbour Street, but round the back of the town, and was relieved to find Campion fully dressed, standing at the gable end smoking as he watched the superb spectacle in the Harbour below.

"If the Biblical account is taken literally, Mr. Lonend, this is precisely how the angels above view the other place below."

In these words Lonend was taught his first great lesson in tact. He waited, however, for some allusion to his nocturnal wanderings. Instead this strange youth added—"I suppose the prince of devils in that lake of fire below there is Mr. Gillespie Strang. Wonder how he feels."

At that precise moment Gillespie had stopped dead in his trot at the foot of the street, which ran from the end of the Back Street into Harbour Street, where his eye had caught a solitary figure. He hurried across to beseech help, and looked into the grave eyes of Mrs. Galbraith.

"Marget!" he cried; and then suspiciously—"What are ye doin' here?"

"I came out to see your garden of red roses, and warm my hands at your fire."

His lower lip was bleeding. "God peety me! I hae fower thoosan' poun' on fire oot there," and then ran on.

The bitter anguish of his voice touched the woman's heart. She looked after him with pitying eyes.

"God pity us indeed," she thought; "we've both our price to pay for this night's work," and she turned home with drooping head, her heart filled with loathing as she thought of Lonend.

Harbour Street was empty, save for the trotting figure of Gillespie. It was a sinister solitude. Looking up at the windows flaring along the sea-front he saw them lined with faces as if steeped in blood. He stood between those faces and the flames, a man friendless, deserted, pitiable as a solitary figure in a vast empty city. Behind him he felt a heat which made him grow cold with horror, in front of him he sensed an inimical living wall. The horror behind pricked him to cast supplicating glances upwards.

"Will no one come an' gie me a hand to save the boats?"

The eyes of those faces were withdrawn from the Harbour and gazed down on him; but no one answered. Some of the eyes were cold; some malicious; some raining down hatred; others smiling. The smiling eyes made him shiver. They taught him to what a depth he had sunk in the estimation of the people. He passed along with his back to the sea, his face upturned to the windows, like a beggar beseeching alms, till he recognised he was running a gauntlet of eyes. There was something brutal, malevolent, fiendish in the spectacle of Gillespie in that lurid amphitheatre. Another man would have cried on the hills to cover him. Gillespie began walking between the houses and the breast-wall in a semicircle, like a mesmerised animal, and staggered as if drunk. A window was flung up; a woman's voice screamed—"Go an' save the boats; they're yours. Ye stealt them frae honest men. Away! away! ye thief. Thon's hell ye've set in a lowe. It's burnin' for ye oot yonder."

Gillespie did not hear her. He was walking now in a circle. His face looked demented. Suddenly he came to a halt as if baffled, his protruding eyes on the boats burning fiercely to the water's edge. He put up his hands to his throat, and fell prone on the street, upon the field of Armageddon.

30

A DENSE fire-smell was drifting across the town. The hills in the north-west were wrapped in thick smoke. The Harbour had the appearance of blazing oil. It seemed as if the wind blew in sheets of flame, over which a multitude of sparks danced grotesquely. The walls of the houses along the Quay were now hot. Fortunately the wind was south and by west blowing out of the Harbour. A new terror was added to the sublime panorama of fire. Boats whose anchor ropes were burnt were adrift and sagged, pillars of flame, down the Harbour. Right in their track ran out the long foreland beneath Muirhead Farm, clothed to the water's edge with fire. A blazing boat struck inside the point; another came down drunkenly upon her. The damp fir at first refused to take fire. Soon it was scorched with the fierce heat, and presently the firs on the edge of the water tossed tresses of fire to the night. In a short space of time a wall of scarlet fire stalked before the wind on the foreland. The fir wood spread left and right, and deeply ahead to the edge of the Laigh Park beneath Muirhead. It was in this direction the fire travelled. In the added glare the town was strung around the bay in naked outline, like a town built at the foot of the mountains of the moon, whose windows were molten gold. There was a blinding glare in the sky. The atmosphere was choking with a burning smell. It was at this point, when the fleet was ablaze and the shepherds and moorsmen beyond Beinn an Oir were disturbed by the glow in the heavens, that Gillespie fell in Harbour Street as he stood watching a splendid ladder of flame in the heart of the fleet. It had a rhythmic movement which fascinated the eye. Its flat, jagged head oscillated backwards and forwards slowly, like the head of a snake. This was the main sheet of flame, whose splendour and terror mesmerised. It took a hundred fantastic shapes—now like the chain mail of warriors tearing at each other with bloody hands in a cauldron; now like witches with streaming hair of flame; like ghosts in winding-sheets of Tophet; and again like a wall of beaten gold. In greater gusts of the wind the wall swayed, bellied, and broke, and great golden balloons hovered in the air. At the foot of this wall vicious tongues leapt out everywhere, seized the cordage, writhed about the masts, licking everything in their path; united and fanned upwards, they swooped across the golden wall as if fighting for life. The anchor chains were red hot; spars crackled like musketry and hissed in the sea. Stars seemed falling from heaven. The wall of flame swayed and bent, and fell across the boats like gigantic flowers. The Harbour was a sea of fire; the tide like blood. The wind veered to the north-west as the fire lapped up the anchor rope of one of its last victims. She drifted before the wind—a core of flame—up the Harbour. Burning fiercely she careened; her forefoot rose, a red tortured wound, and splitting with a roar she settled down by the stern with a loud hissing noise. A minor darkness fell across the house-fronts when she vanished. The appalling roar of fire surmounted the drone of the waves and terrified Brieston. The heat in Harbour Street became intense with the change of wind; and powdered with ashes, was hot as from the ovens of the Cyclops. Clouds of grey smoke rolled in upon the town. The hills surged up out of the golden lake, alone immune beneath a bluish mist. A strong perfume exuded from the pines, as if they were giving up their life in the parched atmosphere. Some titanic maleficent power was abroad. This was no longer vengeance upon Gillespie but supernatural terror. The red foam of hell was being brewed upon the tortured face of the night.

With the north-west wind came the rain, falling in fiery spears. It lashed upon Gillespie, who opened his eyes and felt as if a mountain lay upon his breast. He began to pant and gasp for air, and rolling on his side saw the house-fronts pallid, naked, and solemn in the broad glare. A flight of screaming birds drove over his head. The maddened beating and rush of their wings was terrifying. Tongues of flame appeared to him to be playing about the windows; and his eyeballs burned at the sight. He thought Brieston was on fire beneath a volcanic cloud of smoke. He staggered to his feet and faced the Square. Scarlet rain was falling across the rigging of his house. This made the night more terrible than it was from all the mad beating of wings, the screaming of sea-fowl, the roar of fire, the crackling of wood, and the hissing in the sea like steam. His tall house was threatened and his shop. Gillespie threw up his head, and ran at the top of his speed towards his home. With a sob of relief he found he had been the victim of an hallucination, and quaked with nerves unstrung at this strange experience. Gillespie for the first time in his life had encountered something beyond the realm of the material. He went into the house and searched for whisky. Topsail Janet and his wife were cowering in the front parlour. At sight of his face his wife rose, her own face like ashes, her eyes suddenly enlarged with terror, her breath coming in short, quick pants.

"Whusky!" he gasped. His knees were bowed, his shoulders hunched forward. Topsail jerked round her head, her mouth wide open, upon her mistress, and slowly rose and shuffled out of the room. She descended the stair, trailed along the passage to the washing-house, and unearthed a half-mutchkin bottle quarter full, where it was concealed among the house coal in the washing-house. She hurried back with it to Gillespie. As he drank dawn broke sullenly over a rainy sea. The boats were burned. The rain had extinguished the last of the flames. The planting below Muirhead was smouldering, and a sour smoke oozing upwards. The rocks were blackened like cold lava; the trees stretched out bare black boughs. The wood had a crucified look. Harried ribs and charred spars were floating over the Harbour seeking for a sanctuary or a grave. A saturnine silence lay upon the smoke-blackened town. Dead gulls lay on the shore street, their plumage covered with fine soot, their beaks yellowed with smoke. The wind mourned in the skeletons of the boats.

Gillespie stood looking at the charred embers bobbing on the waves with ironic jerk. Benighted, he was sinking in a sea of profound misery. He could not understand why he had been visited with wrath. He lived over his life again in that searching half-hour. He did not summon it; it appeared as a picture before his eyes, standing against the wall of this strange supernatural visitation which had afflicted him. He saw above the wall a line of menacing, silent faces, and hedged around it a reinless fire. Suddenly his life shrunk. In the face of those mighty forces it became pinched, acerb, ill-directed; puny in the face of a power beyond his control, a vast demoniac force which he had despised. His soul was frizzled as by a baleful cometary rush through it. He stood gazing at his blackened altar, like the priests of Baal when the controversy was summarily finished on Carmel by the fire of heaven licking up their obscene sacrifices.

But Gillespie in that hour had no qualms about Divine judgment. He had been hemmed in with fire and hatred, and in physical weakness had experienced an hallucination. He laid his account to the mob. The people he had considered a carcass set down for his prey; and lo! the carcass had developed a brain and an eye of raging malice. He had no sense of awe in his ostracism. His was not a lofty sorrow. He had made no daring aggression upon Fate, had woven no splendid purple pall over the dead body of an exalted hope. The corpse of avarice was swathed in rags. The little breasts of his mate, greed, could never have become pregnant with great life. The avaricious are held in some measure of esteem so long as they are not ruthless; for the most part of humanity is engaged in laying up goods; but there is a stronger sense in humanity than that of possession—the sense of justice. Gillespie was punished because he had derided the permanent things in life, which humanity have learned to prize through centuries of the discipline of immitigable sorrow, vicissitude, and blood. To deride those permanent things is to flout the hope and ideals which in the breast of mankind have borne privation, suffering, and death with fortitude and patience. For innocence, youth, laughter, friendship, natural ties, and even death Gillespie had had neither bowels of sympathy nor compassion. He had been self-centred in rearing his house of life and filling it with his own peculiar idols. The precious things of man's soul outraged took their inevitable revenge. Gillespie had not denied the deity; he had committed the sin of the fallen angels; and before his assault upon what is eternal in the breast of humanity, he had encountered the grim judicial award gained by those who would usurp the function and authority of God. The penalty visited him unerringly, and Gillespie wizened in the slow wrath of God. The menacing dictum of the ancient Hebrew prophets that Jehovah is a just paymaster was fulfilled upon his head.

The mob had struck him a crushing blow. He admitted so much as he saw the solans flying northwards across the morning moon. He watched their flight pondering. Not for months had they visited the Loch. The herring "eye" was surely moving. His mouth closed in a grim line.

"They'll come on their knees to me yet," he said aloud; "best face to Greenock noo. I'll show them the stuff that's in Gillespa' Strang." He determined to go down and open the shop.

Fine ashes drifted in the Square. The whole town after the rain glistened, slate and window.

Gillespie had been like an open oyster, fancying he had been swallowing the ocean, whereas he was but a fragile thing in the shadow of iron rocks, liable to battering and disaster from the unquiet waves of his creek, which are but the hoarse lips of the titanic deep. The oyster, nevertheless, will not believe otherwise than that the whole ocean is its world. So a look of decision came into his haggard face, making rigid the lines about his mouth as he took the shop keys from his jacket pocket. There was something napoleonic in his attitude. He imagined he had acquired wisdom from calamity, whereas he had only learned a deeper cunning. Disaster was schooling him in a prudence of which he had more than sufficient already. It was not teaching him contrition or righteousness. With tightened mouth he began to order his life anew for another bout with Fate. Nothing worse could occur to him, he thought. He did not dream that a more grievous thing than the loss of a fleet could be laid up in the treasury of Heaven's wrath. He was ignorant of the doom which had haunted his mother's life with dread and horror. He set his face as he descended the stair to retrieve his fortune. He would be more wary, more deft, a deeper watcher of occasions, a spy upon this land of giants, as he plucked the grapes. With the most vigilant scrupulousness he would trim his sails, and pull his claws further within their sheath to pad among men more noise-

256

lessly. Men, he saw, cannot be mocked without limit; but they can be cajoled. The bitterness of these late months had caused him to overreach himself. The rabble was a vast capricious engine which can sweat for you or ravin upon you. He would exercise a more watchful eye upon the fly-wheel in future. It must not break loose again in chaos. He would cunningly guide it in the groove of service.

He was about to insert the large polished steel key in the hole of the front door of the shop when his eye fell upon a placard nailed to the door. The writing was in large letters of ink. A dim recollection of having seen this placard before stirred in the chambers of memory. Ah! he remembered. It was on the door of Galbraith's farm at Muirhead. Slowly he read the missive, and as he read a sudden trembling seized him. He had a feeling in that moment of being dogged by unseen, implacable vindictiveness.

THIS HOUSE IS DEAD.
IT HAS BEEN MURDERED.
IT IS BURIED IN THE GRAVE OF A WOMAN'S
HEART.

"BE NOT DECEIVED; GOD IS NOT MOCKED: FOR WHATSOEVER A MAN
SOWETH, THAT SHALL HE ALSO REAP."

He smiled sourly. "Oot o' your reckonin'; oot o' your reckonin' this time, Marget. There's nae wumman." He had forgotten that piece of chattels, his wife. "I'll mak' short work o't this time," he muttered vindictively, and tearing the placard off the door, scattered on the pavement the fragments on which the drift soot of the wrecked fleet fell. He wheeled about, gazing at the cold face of Brieston, the fragments of the placard beneath his heel. Pale and dry as clay with vigil, and haggard with shock, he presented a piteous spectacle beneath the overarching solemnity and loneliness of the dawn. And the sun shone upon the skeleton of his fleet.

BOOK III

1

THE burn divides Brieston, in respect of its armies—the Barracks Boys north and west of the burn; the Quay Boys south and east.

The legions drilled, one at the old Castle behind the Quay, the other at the Barracks. Their swords were laths which the luggage steamer brought in bundles for Toddle Peter, slater and plasterer, himself a lath of a man.

The Captain of the Quay army had little appearance of a warrior, being small, thin-faced, pale, meagre in look, long-haired. His eyes were arresting: quick and sharp, they burned with internal fires. The spey-wife, whose husband, a MacCann from Ardmarkie, had deserted her and three children, and who made a living by selling cockles gathered in West Loch Brieston to Gillespie, observed the boy's eyes upon her as she counted her cockles in the store.

"He's got an eye like a traivellin' rat," she said to Gillespie, with one of MacCann's Irish oaths.

"A chip o' the auld block," Gillespie answered.

The boy, secretly pleased, from that moment practised the battery of his eyes in drilling and in fighting, because he had an itch to excel.

Gillespie was at the back of the store searching for a bag to hold the cockles, and the boy heard the cockle-wife sigh as she straightened her back. She saw compassion in his eyes.

"Ay! Tam's taen up wi' another wumman in Ardmarkie, an' the ault mear's left to bear the burden." She told him to be good to his mother. Another sorrow was added to the boy's life. He was finding that in the world there is much cruelty and heartache, and because he could not analyse the causes of things, and his lively imagination fed superficially on what he saw, he wasted an enormous amount of pity, and was tortured in the silence of his breast. Only last week he had suffered in another fashion. On

258

his way to school he had been cajoled into his father's slaughter-house. It was a back yard littered with empty boxes and straw behind MacCalman's Lane where Gillespie housed the country vans. Big Jumbo the butcher was standing in the midst of the yard lighting a blackened cutty, his hairy arms naked and rusty with gore. Having lit his pipe he led out from the shed a famished beast, brick-red, with fallen flanks, and broken-kneed. Its coat was muddy, its tail worn, its horns stumps—"one of Gillespie's beasts." It stumbled and stopped, sniffing among the straw, and was dragged forward by a rope twisted about its stubby horns. Suddenly it cried. It was not a bellow, not a bleat, but a half-human cry, as if knowledge of its doom had come upon it. It was trailed forward with its fore-knees raking the ground. The bovine wail reached the heart of the boy, who in that moment recalling what he had read in the Bible—"He can send legions of angels"—prayed silently for these angels of flame to come and blast this devil, who, coolly smoking, was trussing up the beast's feet. It lay on its flanks, its cheek flat on the straw, the weight of its head pressing on the stubbed horn. The great brown eyes, the boy imagined, were looking into his with a liquid sob of fear. They gnawed him in mute appeal; they were as darkened windows out of which gloomed the horror of a great gulf of darkness. The muddied flank, with the hollow in the side, so pitiably shrunken, was heaving and falling with deep pants, and the tail whisking feebly, like the hand of a little child beating gently as it falls asleep. The boy wanted to cry out for mercy; it was his father's cow, let the butcher spare it. But there was a crowd gathered. He was afraid of crowds, afraid they would see his quivering body.

"Any one like to try his hand wi' the hammer?" this fiend was saying; "a tap is a' she needs."

As the boy turned his eyes away from the terrified innocence at his feet, he felt something hard thrust into his hand, and looking down saw the blackened polished haft of the slender hammer.

"Here, young 'un; now's the time to learn."

He felt petrified: the haft dropped weakly from his hand.

"No muckle o' Gillespa' aboot you." The boy blushed at the insolence. The butcher spat in his hands; and Eoghan, Gillespie's son, turned his head away and closed his eyes. He heard a dull thud. When he opened them again a black moist muzzle pointed skywards, and a glaze like thin grey mud was gathering over the brown eyes. Something beautiful had been ruthlessly stamped out there. A flame of anger surged over him. Big Jumbo was bending over the dying beast. Running up to him Eoghan swung his leg viciously, and blindly kicking the butcher on the ankle, turned and fled through the yard. As he gained the entrance gate he felt the air suddenly blow icily cold about his cheek, and almost instantaneously the hammer-head crashed on the gable wall in front of him. With his blood on fire now he swerved, and picking up the hammer fled down MacCalman's Lane, past the Bank, and through the Square to the breast-wall, where, planting his feet with his back to the sea, and whirling the hammer around his head as he had seen athletes do at the Regatta Sports, he swung it out in a flying curve into the Harbour. A thrill went through him at the "plout" with which it took the sea, and his eyes danced at the jet of foam it flung up. Lust and cruelty, rapine and crime, were buried in the cool oblivion of the cleansing water, which closed down over the horror of pain, darkness, and death which he had seen through the fathomless windows of a cow's eyes.

At four o'clock he crept home quaking with his bundle of books. At the tea-hour Gillespie stood tweaking his ear.

"Let him be, Gillespie," pleaded his mother.

Gillespie frowned on her. "I'm no' goin' to alloo such wastery."

The boy made no external sign that he was suffering even when he thought his father would tear the ear from his head. His thin face turned the colour of clay.

Gillespie suddenly pushed him violently against a chair.

"Ye'll tak' to the wulks every day the school comes out, an' on Setturdays, till ye mak' up the price o' the hammer."

The boy, devouring his mother's face with his eyes, felt himself strangling for the pain that he saw there. He made no answer to his father.

"Do ye hear me, Eoghan?"

"Ay."

"Weel, keep guid mind o't. Lonen's no deid when you're leevin'; gang noo an' greet behind your mother's bratty."

"I winna greet for anything ye can do," the boy shouted, and bolted from the kitchen.

He was stubborn enough then, and hardy enough to command an army by a brain fired with the stuff of books. Gillespie's business had expanded so rapidly that Topsail Janet's "penny dreadfuls" had been jettisoned into a corner. The boy's grandmother would have trembled to have seen him devour those romances, as he lay in the warm heather and fashioned phalanxes going out to war. Another clog-maker had inhabited a corner of one of the stores, and Gillespie, for reasons of thrift, ordered a pair of clogs for his son. The steel-shod soles rang loudly on the pavements, and the boy conceived a cavalry regiment, each member of which, shod in clogs, was a mighty charger. The regiment thus armed marched on a bleared evening, stepping quietly to encounter the Barracks troops. Waving a lath above his head the boy yelled out "Charge!" and thirty pairs of clogs thundered along the pavements of the Square. At the clamorous onset the Barracks troops became a panic-stricken rout, and a notable victory was achieved.

The chiefs of his army he then led to the dungeon beneath the Castle—a thirty-foot cavern, with a low roof arched with black stone, slimed with lime, and hanging with stalactites. A dim light was admitted at the low end by a thin slit in its two-foot wall. He told them, gathered round a candle, of mediaeval prisoners who had groaned and suffered the last extremity there, of brownies on the braes without, whom his grandmother from the "Ghost" had chased with a graip when she was digging potatoes, and of maleficent beings in the quarry beneath them behind the Quay, of whom there was a song:

> "Did ye ever see the devil,
>   Wi' his cock-a-bandy shovel,
>   Howkin' in the Quarry for potatoes?
> He washed them in a well,
>   An' he roasted them in h—l."

Try as he might, he could never find a rhyme for his last line. But there was a tale which came from beyond Knapdale with his grandmother—he did not know it was part of the drift-lore of Europe as far as Hungary—of a piper who had entered the dungeon, and by a secret passage now lost had crossed beneath the Harbour to the caves of Beinn an Oir, where he had been devoured by rats. On still nights a plaintive music of bag-pipes arises out of the sea. And Nelson! He sang of that sea-hero thundering at the gates of bleached Spanish towns, and of men naked to the waist and black with powder, fighting ankle-deep in the blood of the scuppers. Nor could he forget Bruce, the walls of whose Castle rose frowning above the dungeon, and remembering the strategy at Bannockburn he proposed to use rabbit-traps—of which there was an abundance at the "Ghost"—and lure the Barracks army into this snare.

Night after night he lay awake planning strategy and fighting again ancient battles. Solemnities, obsequies, mourning for the dead seized upon his imagination, and he came to fashion the Red Burial. Once he had seen a vault opened and shuddered at the yellow rain-waters within. It would be no such place for his dead, but a mausoleum set in a grove of trees with a clear water in the midst. In the Bible he had read of pillars of cedar wood, columns of brass and beaten gold. The walls would be wrought of marble, adorned with ivory, and a blazing stone on the head of the tomb—the Eye of Light.

He prepared his chiefs to carry out the obsequies of the only son of a widow—he was influenced here by the narrative of the widow of Nain—whom they must carry forth by torch-light when in the valley the muskets would flash, the trumpets cry among the rocks, and the bag-pipes wail in the hills. Trembling, and the eyes in the thin face ablaze in the candle-light, he told of the splendour of the gems upon the tomb, and of how with swords sloped they would enter upon that funeral march from the Quay, while the salvoes rolled in the dark hills over their war-chant for the dead. They sang and sang again the requiem; and those appointed to the drums, which were large tin cans, laboured at the rehearsal till the rites were known.

The V-shaped flights of birds which pass over the town had flown westward in the twilight when the band assembled on the Quay head, in the teeth of a hungry wind, which went wailing in the shrouds of the ships and gloomed upon the town. The hills stood out clear-cut in the last of the hard dry light.

The regiment drawn up awaited the signal when the shop-lights should break out along the sea-front. It was that hour of greyness before lamplight when men come home from their labours and the birds have left the sky, and eye after eye the first stars begin the life of the night—the hour of waiting on the earth.

Suddenly the entrance to Gillespie's shop and its plate-glass windows stood out warm and bright towards the Harbour, and the regiment became restive.

"Steady! steady there!" the command rang out.

The large green and red bottles shone in the window of the

Medical Hall. One by one around Harbour Street the lights broke out in a curve of gold.

"Ready!"

At the command the lanterns were lit.

"By the right, quick march!"

Shoulder to shoulder the boy-army passed up the street of the old sea-town in silence. In the Square they wheeled and fronted the shops. Some of the fishermen had followed them from the Quay head; others joined them on the way and stood now along the Medical Hall and the Bank. The coffin—it had once contained ginger-beer bottles—was laid on the ground, and the lanterns were raised and lowered in the manner of signalling. A second time they were raised and held aloft, and a low, mournful chanting came from the bearers of the dead, and mingled with the sobbing of the sea around the Harbour wall:

> "Carry up a soldier, carry up a soldier,
> Carry up a soldier to the old churchyard."

The appointed bearers lugubriously waved their lanterns in slow passes.

"It's Gillespa's son," some one said. The fishermen had ceased talking; windows were thrown open; the Banker and his wife were on the doorstep; Kyle the chemist, who was always so busy that he was rarely seen at his door, was out in his apron; the Butler on the road to Brodie's was at the foot of the brae where it runs into the Square, a man of amazement; Pat, the doctor's driver, retreated from the Square which he had intended to cross to the ironmonger's. Brieston waited and watched.

The black box was again shouldered high, and the legion wheeled and headed for MacCalman's Lane. With a crash of drums the chant broke out again above the wash of the sea:

> "Hear his mother weeping, hear his mother weeping,
> Hear his mother weeping near the old churchyard."

The music wailed along MacCalman's Lane into the Back Street, trailing away to the right into the dark empty road leading to the churchyard.

To the Captain the air was full of grief and wailing. He had forgotten he was in MacCalman's Lane and that a horde of boys was at his back, as he crouched forward into the darkness of the graveyard road. Terror was about him—an unknown form of fear bestriding the dark, a monstrous danger, the flapping of carrion wings on a battlefield, a rushing in the air as of death. He repressed his sobs as he walked by the coffin, ahead of the long steel-shod tramp which rolled behind him as the noise of battle. He heard the shock of armies, and saw their onset in the thick of night; and when the drums crashed out again and the dirge rose 'plaining:

"Hear the trumpets wailing, hear the trumpets wailing,
Hear the trumpets wailing in the old churchyard."

he ground his fists in his eyes, for he saw ahead the gates of the graveyard, and, passing on in imagination down the avenue between the yew-trees dripping in the dark, came on the widow mother weeping upon the mould, and heard the sound of wailing women among the rocks behind the grave. It was no mausoleum; but a hole in the ground of damp yellow clay shining out like dull gold:

"See the rifles flashing, see the rifles flashing,
See the rifles flashing in the old churchyard."

Away towards the loom of the hills he saw the gun-flashes, and the dark above the graveyard streaked with lines of fire. Around him the threnody rose and fell, full of the abandoned weeping of the mother. The mouth of the night opened like an inferno; the hills were full of red artillery. Spit! spit! Crack! crack! and the dead lay so solemn still through it all. The slow tramp, tramp behind him was pushing him on to a place of tears, woe, and horror; it was deepening into a sullen roar of doom. In another minute he would not be able to stem that tide of savage sound, and would be swept forward through the big wide gates of the graveyard, which led to that yellow damp hole in the ground. He was moving now in a trance; changing into stone; a heavy sleep was falling on his limbs; but his mind saw vividly the night ahead fearful with rifle-fire, snarling with trumpets, and stormy with the wailing of distraught women. A burning picture surged up before him of the dishevelled mother, her face stamped with a pale unearthly radiance upon the background of the night. It was his mother's face. It floated in the dark, essaying to rise, but could not for the weight of its sorrow. It was far away, flat like a picture on a dark wall. The eyes were upon him, full of unuttered pain and dim with ineffable tenderness.

264

"See the muskets flashing in the old churchyard." The rifle-fire poured out like red rain, and fell like shooting stars over the pale face framed on the wall of the night; streaming over her it washed her face in blood. He heard her moan wandering on the wind.

The beating of his heart was stifling him, and the feet behind hounding him on. With a groan he shook off the fascination of the face, the mesmerism of the feet, and wheeling, fled swiftly as from an accursed place. Behind his back the night opened flash upon flash as the guns spat over the grave. . . .

He burst in upon his mother and Topsail Janet, who cried out at his ghastly appearance.

"What ails the laddie? Hae ye seen a ghost?"

"I'm feart, mither, I'm feart; they're buryin' a sodger in the kirkyard."

His mother lifted her head from gazing at the fire and let it droop again.

"Dinna bother your mither the nicht, laddie, wi' your nonsense; she's no' feelin' weel," wheedled Topsail.

The boy crouched on the fender, and now and again cast a hungry eye upon his mother's face.

2

His sanctuary in the aisles of the derelict smacks was desecrated for ever by the sad incursion of fact. There he had passed the most marvellous hours, sailing in shining ships down the wind, through purple seas, past grey navies, into ocean harbours beyond the flower-like isles of the deep. As he gazed up at the high, carved sterns and broken bulwarks, the thought of the strange lands these black ships had sailed to moved him strangely. On Saturdays he had aboard a press-gang, whom he set to the task of warping out a slaver for the Caribbees, or a Viking to foray in the High Hebrides. Himself stood on the poop, a pilot of pirates, shouting the most incongruous sea-terms—Full speed ahead! Stand by the winch! and the like. A cloud of long ships of war sailed in his wake—keen battle-hawks harrying the sea-board of the west. He fought to the death against great odds, his battered fleet rolling sullenly in the gales, and his dead on the deck with their faces to the moon. His ships vanished in spindrift with the dim grandeur of death upon them, past lonely coasts till they huddled in the last harbours upon the rim of the world.

Those fond sea-fights gave place to strife in reality, and the boy suddenly emerged into the vicissitudes of a too early youth. He had quietly stolen into the Butler's shop with a message from Lonend, about whose farm he loved to wander. Brodie and Maclean were there, with some others whom he knew only by name. He withdrew into a shy corner and waited till the Butler should notice him.

"They put in four new elders. They'd my name among twenty. Duncan the shoemaker told me"—the Butler was speaking.

"You wouldn't stand," wheezed Brodie.

"There's plenty devils there already. Thomson, a bell-mouthed man; he'd tell the fleas he catches in his shirt. The tide-waiter, wi' the dropsy in his eyes, blinkin' like a hoodie standing on a stone. Might as well have Peepin with his crooked nose. Sinclair, a cat! but he's better since he married again. Now on Sundays he wears four different rigs; his lum hat in the afternoon; that's what put him in. And Gillespie. Well! well! there's aye a Judas. He'd lift the kirk away on his back if he could manage it, the thief."

At that moment the Butler lifted his head and looked into Eoghan's eyes. He gazed for a second, and his eyes fell before the boy's. Eoghan had a sharpness of intuition which, through a loose word or an unwary look, touched the pulse of men's minds. He sensed an inimical atmosphere and that the Butler's eyes had fallen nonplussed. He crept like one beaten out of the shop. It was the tea-hour when he reached home. His father was standing at the table cutting a loaf. His jacket shone, elbow and sleeves; his wristbands were frayed; a battered sailor's cap was a-rake on his head; the tip of his tongue protruded.

"I used to mand ten shaves off a loaf; noo there's only nine. That baker's fair robber." He flung off his cap and sat down to table. Eoghan, with his slice of bread ready buttered and cut in two, was lifting his hand when he overturned the cup. The tea drenched the bread and scalded his leg. He sat like a stone, the yellowish sodden mass before him. His father glanced at him and went on eating. Eoghan was hungry, but dared not stretch out his

266

hand for another piece of bread. Furtively his mother pushed her slice to him across the oil-cloth.

"Just so, auld wife, spoil him. Ye'll keep the other slice an' gie 't to him the morn for his breakfast. Mind, noo."

Eoghan, with eyes bent on the veined oil-cloth, rose from the table, gulping back hot tears of anger.

"Whaur hae ye been the day?" asked his father.

"Nowhere."

"Nowhere! it's time ye were oot the school. When I was your age I'd my ain basket o' lines an' money in the bank. Idlin' your time. Ye'll tek' the lines an' go oot to the banks the morn an' try for whiteys. They're shullin's the stone ee noo." Gillespie rubbed the back of an eczema-blotched hand across his mouth. His father's imperviousness maddened Eoghan. To breathe the least of his youth's ambitions would be to drink bitterness; and he felt that a prophecy of something signal in life was upon his brow.

"I'm no' goin' to be a fisherman," he said stubbornly, defending his prophecy.

"An' what is my gentleman goin' to be?"

"Mr. Kennedy asked me if I would like to go to the University." This request had changed the current of the boy's life and gave him a land of dreams. McAskill had shown him a photograph of Glasgow University, over whose stately edifice he had pored by the hour.

"Let the schoolmaister pey for your coallegin', then," Gillespie answered tartly, and left the room.

The boy, much troubled, accosted Topsail Janet that evening. "I heard them in the Butler's shop call my father a thief."

"Wheest! wheest! Eoghan; it's no' for thae trash to speak o' him. He keepit a wheen o' them through many a hungry winter. Ye should be prood o' your faither. He's the richest man in Brieston; an' it's no' for you to be heedin' thae kiss-ma-futs. Your faither's a savin' man for us a'. It's everything in the world to hae a good faither. Ye'll get your he'rt crackit noo an' again in the world, but that's naethin' if ye hae a gude hame. An' it's your faither that's battlin' wi' the world to keep the roof ower a' oor heids."

Still troubled, Eoghan walked through the Square and down Harbour Street on his way to the "Ghost." Was he wrong, after all, to accept the Butler's opinion of his father, and was not Topsail right? Early and late his father slaved—watching for the

267

boats before dawn; behind the counter all day; and wrestling with his ledgers at night. There was a murky light in the store, and he peered in at the window. He saw his father stooping over a bag, counting oysters. A guttering torch splayed the interior with great shadows and patches of smoke. The store was draughty and slushy; cold, cheerless, damp. The patient figure within went on rising and stooping at its lonely toil. Eoghan recalled the eczema on his father's hands. It would never heal with such raw work. The tears welled up in his eyes; he wanted to go in and help; but was too sensitive. What excuse could he offer? He turned away and hurried home.

"Mother," he said, "you'll no' quarrel wi' father the night?" Those quarrels were frequent.

"No! I'll no' quarrel," she answered wearniedly.

Towards ten o' clock Gillespie came in. He unlaced his boots and straightened his back.

"I'm fashed wi' rheumatics in my shouther," he said; and laid his hand on his shoulder-blade.

"Late again at your books"—Eoghan burned with mortification as he heard his mother's querulous voice—"ye'd think you hadn't a wife."

"Bonnie wife," he growled; "she does a' the compleenin' an' I dae a' the work." In a moment the quarrel was full-pitched. Eoghan held his mother a traitor who had broken the peace incontinent. He looked savagely at her, and went off to bed without saying good-night.

In the morning he poured some syrup on a spoon for his porridge—Gillespie allowed no milk—and sullenly traced out golden curves with viscous stuff across the half-cold slab of meal. His mother poured him out a cup of tea.

"There's no bread in the house," she said with an abstracted air.

Eoghan, looking up, saw crumbs only on the bread-plate, and a pang shot to his heart, a sudden fear of penury.

"No bread?"

"No."

"Has my faither no money?"

She smiled faintly. "He has plenty in the bank."

He felt relieved; but was puzzled. His mother looked very pale; there were thin blue veins on her trembling hands. A vague fear assailed him. He searched for his cap and stole away to school full of pity and dread.

268

He found no respite that day from his torment. Passing on his road to school at the dinner-hour he loitered at the end of the Back Street, where certain women were baiting the lines. It was a raw day.

"Cold work?" he said.

Black Jean could not resist a jibe and snarled:

"Ay! an' a' for Gillespa's son."

Nan at Jock saw the pained look on the boy's flushed face.

"Never heed her, Eoghan; her bark's worse nor her bite. Think shame, Jean, speakin' that wy."

As Eoghan walked away with bent head he heard Nan at Jock's angry voice. "Let the boy alone, wi' his mother puttin' up blood as black as coomb," and the angrier retort—"No wonder; thon slasher o' a man aye huntin' her the wy the boys hunt wee cuddies at the Quay."

Eoghan was now full of the wildest apprehensions. At four o'clock he went to the shop to ask his father what Black Jean meant. A smack had arrived with a cargo of coal from Ardrossan. The rawness of the afternoon had turned to rain. The Square was rutted with the frequent passage of carts to the ree, black with coal-dust, and deep in mud; and the coal itself was sodden and foul. Gillespie, wearing an apron, and a pen in the left ear, was standing at his shop door watching the carters.

Eoghan told him what he had heard.

"She said that, did she?" he interrogated with a grin. "I'm gled she minds she's in my debt. She'll hae to shell a wheen mair mussels afore she'll pey me the last boll o' meal I gied her. Tak' that cairt," he roared across the Square, "up to Stuart."

The little bow-legged man ran to the head of the horse, jerked the reins, and wheeled the beast round to the brae. A word from Gillespie had galvanised him. Eoghan felt himself dismissed. There was something ruthless, despotic in his father.

"Mother," he said, throwing down his books, "are ye no' feeling well?"

"I'm bothered with my breath." Her face was pale.

"Will I go for the doctor?" His voice was trembling; he felt sick.

She shook her head.

"The doctor told me long ago to take a little drop of spirits. It gives me ease."

He started forward eagerly.

269

"I'll go for some."

"I've no money, Eoghan: your father doesn't allow it."

Rage choked him. He clenched his hands as he stood looking at her, and a wave of devouring tenderness surged over him.

"Don't you fret, mother. I'll get money."

He returned to the Square. On carting days he knew that at intervals his father hurried from the shop to the ree. For an hour he stood sentinel. Sandy the Fox was again coming up the street by the horse's head, and Gillespie appeared at the door, crossed the Square, and accompanied Sandy into MacCalman's Lane to the ree. Immediately the cart jolted round the Bank corner, Eoghan slipped into the shop, scurried round the counter, opened the till, and drew out a handful of coins. Stuffing them into his pocket, he darted into the office and out by the back door.

When gloaming fell he roused Brodie from his perusal of the *Glasgow Herald*, and bought a bottle of whisky.

3

GILLESPIE had taken down his shutters precisely at seven o'clock on the morning on which his boats had been burned in the Harbour—earlier by an hour than his usual time—and with partially frozen water washed the large plate-glass windows, as he had done for sixteen years. Scores of curious eyes were upon his methodical movements. It was the day for the country van. He went to the coal-ree, summoned the Fox, and helped him to load the cart with sacks of flour and meal, and with provisions, exactly as he had done last week. The Fox, afraid to lift his eyes to Gillespie's face, scurried about in silence, and at last gathered up the reins with the feeling of a prisoner leaving jail. He breathed a larger air as he took the west brae. He had felt that he was on the crater of a dormant volcano. Gillespie had given him final instructions in an even voice, advising him of the amount of butter, eggs and cheese he was to bring back from the country. Then at the shop door, in the face of the Square and of Harbour Street, he placidly shook his apron free of the particles of flour. He was waving a flag in the teeth of Brieston. The sight caused Kyle, a rooted Calvinist, to shiver. To the Chemist it was the flouting of Heaven by an unrepentant demon-soul.

As the day passed the usual events occurred. The Ardmarkie mail-coach thundered down the brae at noon, and Maclean and Watty Foster walked down the street to Brodie's. The mail steamer from Glasgow arrived up to Government time, and carried back intelligence unofficial but weighty, to be sown along astonished ports of call. The town in its afternoon languor stood in knots at the Quay head, at the Barracks, at the hotel corners. The Square alone was deserted. Stuart on that day was to have sold doves in the temple; but four women only came to the jumble sale. Brieston coughed discreetly behind its hand, wondering how soon Gillespie would take action and the dynamite explode. It was rumoured that he had turned Campbell the policeman out of the shop with a flea in his ear. The town was standing over a loaded mine. Chrystal Logan said he could hear the fuse spluttering.

No one was seen to enter Gillespie's shop that day.

"He has a face lik' the wrath o' Goäd," some one had said in the morning. Towards evening it was reported that Gillespie had not turned a hair. The town, robbed of a spectacle, was murmurous. Brieston thought Gillespie was intimidated and hid his face.

"Let him cairry on the glory noo," boasted Red Duncan openly. "He'll ken whether me or him has the strongest back stays. I've got to windward o' him at last; an' I'll keep my weather eye on him." Some said Gillespie was resigned; others that he was leaving Brieston; none saw in him a gaunt tree stripped by a gale of all its branches, yet standing up again unflinchingly to the ruthless sky.

On the morrow Gillespie made no sign that the *débâcle* had caused him to lose an hour's sleep, and the Quay received a shock. The Fishery Officer walked across from his office bareheaded, a telegram in his hand. The Loch was full of herring; the Ardmarkie men with new trawls were filling their boats. He had been to Gillespie. There was a man of iron nerve. He was going out in the *Sudden Jerk* to buy Ardmarkie herring. "It'll take a bigger flame than you men can light for him to play the moth at. He says you've cut your own throats. The one half o' ye have neither boats nor gear."

That portion of the fleet—some thirty-five boats—which had not been mortgaged to Gillespie, and which had not perished in the fire, was hurriedly got ready and put to sea. In the midst of the brown sails moving down the Harbour could be seen the lean, cream-coloured funnel of the *Sudden Jerk*.

The next day two boats came back full of herring. Whether it was because the sea had been so niggard for almost a year or not, the men could not tell; but herring was not only plentiful— "Fair boiling in the watter," said one of the crews—but of excellent quality; large and firm. The *Sudden Jerk* had gone to Glasgow loaded to the funnel, and Gillespie, unable to carry more, had sent these two boats to Brieston with instructions for Sandy the Fox to see that they were "roiled in saut an' gutted." A list of the gutters' names was handed to the Fox—the names of certain women who had pledged their services to Gillespie in return for food during the winter—the debt to be paid off at the rate of ninepence a barrel.

The men whose boats had been burned looked on with hungry eye. The Loch beyond the Harbour mouth boiled with fine herring; they had neither boats nor nets; and Gillespie was in Glasgow. The town was empty in his absence. Two crews were formed, which put to sea with old drift-nets in two line boats. The rest of the men stood at the "Shipping Box" with their hands in their pockets. And the sun shone on the charred remains of their fleet. As they looked in the revealing light a closed carriage rolled up the north brae. They scarcely glanced at it across the empty Harbour. It contained Dr. Maclean, who sat opposite Queebec, beside whom was Campbell the policeman. On Queebec's thin red wrists were a pair of handcuffs. The other evening he had entered Gillespie's shop and attempted to set it on fire, and later attempted his life with a razor. Maclean was taking Queebec to the asylum at Bannerie. On passing through the Square a spasm of passion contorted Queebec's face; he wished to get out and burn the shop. Maclean in some way had become his enemy; he must get rid of Maclean. A look of cunning came into his eyes as he leaned forward.

"Doctor," he whispered, beckoning, "come here; I've something to tell ye." Maclean inclined his head, and the next moment two hands were madly grappling about his throat. The carriage rocked and swayed as the two men fought, Queebec clinging on with a madman's strength. Pat leapt from the dickey before the horses had pulled up, and as he wrenched the door open saw his master put up his knee and jab violently into Queebec's abdomen. The lunatic relaxed his grip and fell backwards foaming. Maclean leapt on him and pinioned him down.

"Drive to the police station, Pat," he ordered. Thus Queebec, his mission on earth accomplished, went to the asylum in Bannerie with handcuffs on his wrists.

The fishermen on the Quay head, however, scarcely noted the carriage, for they were watching the herring gutters. There is nothing which gives to one ashore such a profound impression of the riches of the sea as a herring-gutting scene. The wings of angels hover upon the silvery mass as one looks abroad over a field of fish in many boats. Those beautiful fish, silk-shot with a greenish-blue through the scales, are the strongest hostages against penury. From the cold deep they have come to brighten the hearth; fashioned in silver in the dark, as diamonds in the bowels of the earth. The burnishing of knives was a labour of love in the Back Street. What a sight it was to see again the big fishing-boats laced with scales and the shining pile in the Square. The women sat on empty herring boxes by the pile, their arms bared and dappled with blood. They worked in pairs, one gutting, the other salting and packing in the barrels. Every hour or so they exchanged duties, for it is wearing on the back constantly to be stooping over a barrel, and wearying to the wrist and fingers unceasingly to be tearing out the guts of fish and jerking it on to the red heap of offal. When the dusk came the work was continued within the store, whose interior, lit with torches, presented a weird spectacle. Beneath the glare of the torches mingled with smoke, the gutters with blood-stained hands sat around, their faces starting out of the reek in the murky light and falling again into shadow. The pile of herring smouldered in pools of dull gold. There was a sense of happiness in the atmosphere. The moving of the waters, for which they had so long waited, had come, and tongues went as fast as knives. What would the men do who had no boats? they had been fools to burn them. The big guttings of former days were recalled when the splendid fishing lured gutters from Stornoway and Peterhead to Brieston. Old times were restored; the old dead were resurrected; the aged were seen as young.

"Many's the guttin' ye hae sang at noo, Flory;" and as the

torches flicker and the knives grow idle, and the weary hands are at rest a moment, a sweet treble voice sings the Scottish ballad:

> "Last night there were four Maries,
> To-night they'll be but three,"

and fifty women take up the haunting air, making it swell beyond the rafters and the roof to the night and the stars. In that song the hungry days are ended, and the sorrows of the sea.

Daily the gutting went on, and Gillespie moved briskly through the town. The men without boats, eaten up with mortification, watched the business at first with rage, and then, as news came in of big fishings, with despair. The carpenters would not risk the big undertaking of building boats for bankrupts.

"Ye're weirin' your clothes oot against the 'Shippin' Box,' boys, an' the Ardmarkie men mekin' a fortune," cried Gillespie, with the cheeriest voice in the world, as he passed to the gutting shed. "I'd seeven hunner boxes o' fine big herrin' this week for Glesca."

It was Red Duncan who answered:

"We hevna a plank to float on, or a mesh to wet."

"Ay! boys," said Gillespie, "fire's no' a chancy thing;" and that was the single reference which he made to what had come to be known as the "Night of the Big Burning."

He invited those who wished to fit out boats to meet him that afternoon in his office at the shop—one man to represent each crew. Every crew sent a representative. Gillespie, with ledger open, reminded them of the mortgages on the old boats. Some were bonded full value: others three-fourths; others again one-half. Were the men willing to let the bond lie? They were fools to go idle with such a fishing; but he had no desire to press them; he had sufficient on his hands, what with buying herring, and gutting and provisioning the existing Brieston fleet. He hated, however, to see the men idle with such good prospects. Did they agree?

Fast enough—Red Duncan was the spokesman; but they wanted to get to the fishing immediately. It would take months to build a fleet. By that time the best of the fishing would be over.

"Surely, Donnacaidh, you don't think I'm such a gomeril as a' that. I hae at this meenut a boat for every wan that was burned."

The men's faces expressed their incredulity.

"I hae reinged everywhere, frae the Heids o' Ayr to Stornoway, and bocht up a' the boats I could hear tell o'. I hae them lyin' up at Greenack ready."

Incredulity now gave place to unbounded admiration, and then to vague alarm. They became afraid of this man's tenacity of purpose and his gigantic enterprise. They were pawns in his stupendous game. "Of course," he went on, "you boys needna tek' ower the boats; I'm no' forcin' ye. I'll can get crews for them a' frae Kerry an' Bannerie an' Ardmarkie; an', as you say, Donnacaidh, the carpenters 'ill tek' months to beeld ye new boats. An' whaur are ye to get the money? Lowrie 'ill no' advance ye a ha'penny." Gillespie had made sure of this.

"Noo, boys, are ye on, or are ye no'?" He spoke briskly, rubbing his hands.

"There's noathin' else we can do; we're on oor beam ends," muttered Red Duncan.

"Weel! weel! that's common sense at last. Noo, I'll gie ye an account o' what the boats cost me." The name of each boat was mentioned, was assigned to a crew, and then her price shown, the receipt being displayed. The first thing they would have to do would be to pay Gillespie back the price of each boat. His capital had lain out for a considerable time in the purchase of these boats. Had they taken a bill on the bank to build a new fleet, Lowrie would have charged them interest at five per cent. He, Gillespie, would charge only four and a half per cent.

Till the principal and interest were paid he would look on the boats as his own. Thereafter the old bond on them given for provisions would remain, and on the bond Gillespie would claim his share of the profits. The boats would still remain his to the extent to which they had been pledged by the bond—some few of them his wholly; others to the extent of three-fourths; others again to one-half.

"That's my proposeetion, boys; tak' it or leave it. If ye don't agree, there's noathin' for it but to gang back to the 'Shipping Box,' and watch the other Brieston men mekin' a fortune. I'll easily mand to get crews oot o' Kerry an' Bannerie;" his voice was insinuating, deprecating. Wrath now mingled with their fear—wrath at their own impotence, for they were tied hand and foot. He had turned the flames of the lost fleet upon themselves. They cursed the ravings of Queebec, but he had found an asylum from their wrath; and blaspheming the name of Lonend, asked what had moved that farmer to mix himself up with the affairs of the fishermen. When each man had signed, Gillespie instructed them to gather their crews on Monday morning and go by luggage steamer to Greenock, bring the fleet to Brieston, and get it provisioned. He laughingly told the men as they trooped out that they would require to furnish the boats with a considerable amount of new gear, and of course trawl-nets. They went away humbled.

"Thon bit bleeze is the best thing that ever happened to Gillespa' Strang," he informed the canary, as he tickled the bird with the point of a pen. He stood to make a huge profit out of the fire. The women were paying off their arrears at the gutting; he would get four and a half per cent on his capital; would rake in his share money on the takings of the men; and there would fall to be sold a considerable quantity of new gear.

But in the matter of gear Gillespie had over-estimated human nature, and the indecency of some of the men betrayed itself. Nets, sails, oars, water-casks, chains, tackle, began to see the light from the obscurity of lofts, outhouses, and from beneath beds. This enraged those men who had been loyal to the conspiracy. All was to have been burned. This did not prevent many, however, from sneaking nets and gear out of the doomed boats under cover of night. It was hellish, said the honest men; they had been betrayed and overreached in their own camp. Bitterness was gendered which caused enmity between some of the men for life. A section took up arms for Gillespie, and even turned informers, so that Gillespie had the culprits under his thumb.

"I could clap ye in jyle the morn," he said to Red Duncan.

"Ye can clap Lonen' along wi' me then," flung back the fisherman.

"Ay! ay!" answered Gillespie softly; "I jaloosed the win' blew oot o' that dirty airt."

The fire had strengthened Gillespie's hands all round, and he was induced to believe in the justice of Heaven visited upon the unrighteous. He made his counter a pulpit, from which he preached softly of the wrath of God upon the iniquitous, and sedulously attended church. After a week he omitted his sanctimonious discourses, being immersed body and soul in the glittering pursuit of gain. Brieston stood in wholesome fear of him, though they nagged at his name. One example will suffice.

Tamar Lusk, by reason of his position as a vendor of fripperies, had a seat on the Parish Council.

"If some o' you boys were wi' me roond the green cloth"—he was standing on the edge of his boot soles—"up gyards an' at them: it's a' for the good o' the place I'm aifter; but since Gillespie came on the Council"—Gillespie was Poor Law Clerk—"ye'll no even get a bottle o' oatmeal stout at the meetin'. It used to be a cheery place wi' the bottle on the green cloth an' the crack goin' back an' forrut. Now everything's that clean cut, there's no' even dreepin'. It's no pleasure noo, but back-bitin' an' business, an' business an' back-bitin'."

Tamar's deep-sea cap was rakishly askew, his left eye closed, his right shining beneath a white eyebrow stiff as pig-bristles. He beat time to his philippic with his left foot.

"Ay! he came an' axed for my furniture for a wee debt o' mine"—this was an old piracy of Gillespie's. Tamar's thick neck swelled with rage; his face was turkey-red, in midst of which his fiery little tongue clapped—"Boys! I'd a noise wi' him. I'm a sergeant o' the Volunteers"—the left eye opened and closed; he appeared to be sighting a monster gun—"ready for any Keeng an' country any time. But no quarter wi' him. He's a Rooshian. Shoved his backside to the door an' axed for the furniture lik' a drink o' watter. An' it didna gie him a red face. But I'll get to windward o' him. Doon yonder at the Quay it's fair sweemin' wi' muck an' herrin'-guts. Ye canna steer wi' barrels an' deevilment an' dirt. See if I don't speak to the Laird. Heavens! boys! am I no' a Pairish Cooncillor? I fought for't, an' my rival had a heap o' votes. I got a noise frae the Receiver o' Wrecks aboot the fish-guts. Of course he'd a right to speak to me, me being on the Board; but no' thon wy o' attackin' me lik' a pickpocket. I told him gey smert who he belonged to, an' to go an' compleen to Gillespie. They need the hems on them, the hale jeeng-bang o' them."

"Is that me you're speakin' aboot, Tamar?" came the well-known sibilant voice, as Gillespie came round the corner of the "Shipping Box," cran basket in hand.

"Ay! an' I was just sayin' to the boys that the Receiver o' Wrecks yocked on me yesterday in my capaceety as Pairish Cooncillor aboot the herrin'-guts at the Quay. You bate, Gillespie, I gied him his coffee. You'd think us poor boys could catch herrin' withoot guts to hear the wy he goes on."

277

"Just speak a word in his ear, Tamar," answered the peace-maker; "that we're thrang cairtin' the guts ower the Quay heid. It'll feed the stanelacs."

"It'll no' gie him that satisfaction, Gillespie"—the eye closed down valiantly beneath the spear-serried bristles—"he should be thankfu' to see the pickle guts. It's no' every day there's a big fishin', an' he'll get his own wheck on Setterday when the boys share."

"I hope, Tamar, the fishin's taen a turn for the better. It's badly needit," answered Gillespie.

"Ay! ay! Gillespie," Tamar cried to the bulky retreating figure. "I wish I saw ye up to the eyes in herrin'-guts frae noo to Neerday."

Gillespie, walking towards the store, heard a roar of laughter behind him.

"Tamar! Tamar!" the Bent Preen was saying, "ye'll need to go back to the Volunteers an' learn to face the enemy."

Tamar stared after Gillespie, and his head righted from its valorous list.

"He's a crool man, thon; it's no' chancy comin' in his rai-verence; but he'll hear more o' his muck when I put in my oar roond the green cloth. Just you wait."

"Keep your oar," said Big Finla', "for the next haul at Bar-laggan."

Thus Gillespie was hated and feared in secret; but the salutary lesson of the "Big Burning" left him immune from any further open attack. He thought himself invincible, invulnerable.

4

"Nae use peyin' a man when I hae a son for the work." In this summary fashion Iain, Gillespie's eldest son, was taken from the "Ghost" and made to share Eoghan's room. He was a tall, spare lad of twenty or about, with a dark complexion and a thin dark moustache. His face in repose had a mournful look. He was inclined to be taciturn, and would sit by the hour at the fireside in the "Ghost" humming songs or playing upon the flute. He was of a saving disposition—"a canny easy-goin' Scot"—it was said of

278

him—"wha kens to keep his mouth an' his neif shut." He evinced the keenest interest in out-of-the-way characters, and with his dark eyes lit with fun made the shrewdest observations upon their doings. On these occasions he fell into sudden unsophisticated laughter which, for all his parsimonious disposition, betrayed a careless side to his nature. He was sterlingly honest, had saved the bulk of the money he had earned, and was ill-dressed. He had noticed that poor people get little consideration in the world. "The best freend is a pickle money o' your own, young fella," he would say to Eoghan, raining affection out of his dark eyes upon his thin-faced, elfin brother. But he had none of the greed of his father who, unable now to attend to his business ashore and to his herring buying, put Iain aboard the *Sudden Jerk*. The son was already skilled in the sea and very hardy; he endured fatigue and danger without talking about it.

It was Saturday when Iain had rest from the *Sudden Jerk*, and Eoghan had pleaded with him to go on a nutting expedition. On the road at the head of West Loch Brieston, they met the spey-wife, whose husband was a tinsmith. She wore a shepherd tartan shawl and big heavy boots, and in her left hand she carried a shepherd's crook; on her right arm a bundle of shining jangling cans. Round her neck she wore a long chain, composed of the small silver coins of many nations. Iain laughingly accosted her. "Fine day, old lady."

The spey-wife rubbed a rheumy substance from her eyes and peered at Eoghan.

"What's your name, my bonny boy?"

"Eoghan Strang."

She put out a hooked skinny forefinger.

"Ay! ye hae the spunk o' the Logans. I can tell it by your e'e. It's a peety o' the Strangs."

"A peety, old lot?" Iain asked, good-humouredly.

"Ay! while there's water to droon, or fire to burn, or poison to mak' an' end, a Strang 'ill no' die easy in bed."

Iain's fine white teeth flashed beneath his moustache as he burst out laughing.

"Well, that's ripe, old party."

The spey-wife sighed and looked at the younger brother.

"One o' ye 'ill mind my words when ye're liftin' the other oot o' the water." She mouthed at Eoghan, jingled her chain of foreign coins, and added, "We can nane o' us help but dree oor weird," and tramped heavily up the road towards Brieston, her tin cans jangling loudly on the still morning air.

The brothers walked on for a little in silence. Eoghan shivered as he spoke.

"The blatter o' her cans made me think o' the sign at the 'Ghost' on windy nights."

"She's a queer old card;" Iain's eyes were full of merriment.

It was dusk as they came out of the hazel wood with their pillow-slips full of nuts and, too hungry and tired for conversation, trudged on in silence. When they came to the head of the brae beneath the church, Eoghan stopped in his walk to shift his pillow-slip from one shoulder to the other.

"Iain, I've a queer feelin' that the spey-wife is right. It came to me in the wood, and I got frightened. The wood was full o' eyes watchin' me."

Iain's face was long and mournful.

"You're needin' your tea, young fella," he answered; "you're tired; gie me your pillow-slip." Iain's face remained mournful as he walked down the brae, and he began to whistle softly with his mouth very wide, and his eyes fixed ahead on the Harbour. Eoghan felt a weary weight of inexpressible sorrow at the sight of his brother's face, and was so fatigued and miserable that he went down the brae in a little blind trot. As he pushed open the front door at the head of the stairs he heard his mother in the kitchen singing plaintively a ballad of old-time sorrow in the West Countree. This intensified his melancholy. The kitchen was gloomy, for the wick of the lamp was smoking. As was usual on Saturdays tea was late. He felt faint, and the droning of his mother irritated him.

"I wish, mother," he said irascibly, "you would stop that singin' an' get the tea; I'm hungry."

"Janet's away down to the shop for butter," she answered; "she'll be back in a minute"—she smiled at him dreamily. "I haven't felt so well for ages. I took a wee drop out of the bottle you gave me. What would I do without you and Margaret? You're the only friends I have." She passed her left hand slowly across her forehead and pushed her fingers among her hair.

"Is Mr. Campion teaching you Latin yet?" she asked. He was surprised at the question, because she rarely referred to his work at school.

"What makes you ask, mother?"

"He said you were going to the University."

"Who? Mr. Campion?"

She made no answer. Cheeks on her hands and elbows on her knees, she gazed into the fire.

"Where did you see Mr. Campion, mother?" His decisive loud tone was meant to summon her attention, for Topsail's heavy foot was on the stair. "Where?"

"I see him sometimes when I go to Lonend." She spoke falteringly with a flushed face.

Topsail entered with a loaf in one hand and some butter on a plate in the other. "Iain's awa' doon to the 'Ghost' for his tea," she announced.

That night Eoghan lay in bed reading. A storm, which had arisen at nightfall, was blowing in fierce gusts. The scurry of the rain on the window was like the fingers of wild wandering things of the night trying to get in from the wind, which sounded like a gigantic steel saw ripping up the dark. The hoarse sea plunged upon the Harbour wall like a monstrous blind thing in pain seeking rest. "What a night! it frightens me. I wish Iain hadn't gone to the 'Ghost,' " he thought. His active brain gave him no respite. "The air is full of flying things. I wonder what men are doing out at sea to-night."

Was that the sneck of the outside door? He listened intently. Somebody was groping to lift it from the outside. It was of peculiar construction. In the wood of the door was cut out a circular hole, into which a finger when pushed came in contact with an iron circular disc, which lifted the sneck within. "It's Iain come home to sleep after all," he thought, with a sense of relief. Presently he heard his father in his stocking soles pad, padding along the passage from the kitchen.

"Whaur hae ye been straivigin' to this time o' the nicht?"

"It's my mother;" the thought shot through him with sudden, unaccountable fear.

"Am I to be keepin' the lamp burnin' a' nicht for ye? If ye'd another man it's kicked oot ye'd be."

Eoghan jumped up to a sitting posture in bed, as a skirl of laughter broke on his ear—shrill, defiant, inane laughter. "But ye're the angry man, Gillespie; it's no' that often I take a jaunt."

"Come in wi' ye!" he heard his father snarl. The bed shook

beneath Eoghan with his agitation. His heart was beating violently against his ribs. A step stumbled in the passage; his father's footfall shuffled past, soft as an animal's; there was a dull sound of a door being shut, followed by silence. He breathed easier now. Where could she have been so late on such a night? She must be soaked to the skin. His alert ear was listening for what was beyond the closed doors. Vague soft voices purred in the distance as if caressing each other; a mouse scuttled behind the wall, and once more there was silence, through which he heard the tick! tack! tick! tack! of the death-watch, like a small, invincible voice riding the storm. Suddenly there was a crash somewhere in the kitchen. Again he sat bolt upright. The kitchen door opened, and in the draught from the outside stair it snapped to with a whip-like crack that echoed through the house. "What is going on? what is going on?" The beating of his heart was stifling him, and he crouched forward on his knees. Softly, as if a ghost were seeking entrance, his own door was pushed open; slowly, inch by inch, and at every inch a drop of blood seemed to ooze from his heart. His eyes dilated with fear when his mother appeared in the doorway in a white nightdress open at the neck, her long black hair tumbled on her shoulders. Her breathing was rapid, and her eyes, brilliant as with fever, had a hard, bovine stare. There were brick-red patches on her cheek-bones. In her right hand she held a heavy lamp by a long, slender pillar. The sight of her hectic, disordered appearance made Eoghan feel faint. Her eyes, stupidly searching round the room, fell on the crouching form of her son.

"Eoghan! Eoghan! will ye no' take me into bed?"

The words were the frightened wail of a child, and pierced his heart. The fainting seizure passed from him; he felt himself endued with marvellous strength, and leapt from the bed. She was swaying like a tree in a gale; her face full of profound sorrow. The swaying ceased, and the body began to sag backwards and forwards. The heavy lamp took a list in her hand, and the funnel smoked. He jumped forward and caught the pillar.

"Mother," he cried, "ye'll put the house on fire."

They looked at each other in silence. All at once he trembled, and a horrified look came into his face as the dreadful truth flashed upon him. Afraid that the lamp which he held in his shaking hand would fall, he staggered to the dressing-table where a candle was burning, and with his two hands placed down the lamp. She followed him, sobbing.

"Let me in, Eoghan; your father has put me out of his bed."
With arms rigid by her sides she swayed, dry sobs shaking her
body, and her tearless eyes were drenched with a piteous look.

"You'll catch your death of cold standing there," he moaned.

"Little does he heed: he put me out of bed." She lurched forward and gripped the iron poster; took another step, her arms out
before her as if she were blind. He was afraid she was about to
fall, and jumping forward caught her arm. She lurched heavily
against him, so that it took all his strength to support her. The
tears began to well up from what was choking him. He slipped
his arm round her waist.

"Is he no' the terrible man, puttin' me out o' bed . . . out o'
bed in the deid o' night?" she murmured wearily. " 'I wish you
were deid an' in your grave,' he said. What did he say that for? I
was only in Margaret's. He cheated her out o' the farm . . . I
canna mind now . . . I'm light-headed, Eoghan . . . I cried all
evening wi' a pain in my head . . . an' when I told him what
Marget said he tried to choke me . . . God forgive him. . . ."

"Lie down, mother, lie down;" his voice was hoarse with anguish. He put his two arms about her; but his left hand touched
her breast, and he hastily withdrew it, as if it had been burned.
He placed her sitting on the bed, and holding her round the
shoulders with one arm, flung back the bed-clothes with the
other. Her hot breath, sour with the fumes of alcohol, rose up in
his face. She fell back sideways across the pillows, moaning as if
in pain. Solid walls of darkness surged up before him; the room
was unaccountably stifling. He raged with anger against his
father, who no doubt was asleep as if nothing had happened. He
would have turned her out like a piece of cork into the storm.
With face averted he gathered his arm beneath her knees, slung
her feet into the bed, pulled up the clothes and wrapped her in.
A ferment of horror was working in his brain. His soul was
lacerated as with thorns. He envied his father's placidity, his
brother's repose. "We are unsheltered, unsheltered, she and I"—
thought like fire devoured his brain.

"I thought when we got married he would take me to London
to see the sights . . ."—her shining eyes were fixed upwards—
"the crown jewels . . . when I was in school in Edinburgh some
one told me about them . . . I canna mind her name . . . He has
plenty of money . . . he never took me anywhere . . . he kept me
slavin' on the farm . . . he put me . . . put . . . out o' bed;" the

voice trailed away to a whisper; the head fell slackly to the side; she began to snore heavily. As Eoghan watched her, Topsail Janet crept down from the Coffin and came candle in hand to the door. A spasm of rage contorted Eoghan's features. He glared at Topsail wolfishly, his pale face betraying the intensest hatred. "Be off!" he hissed; "be off, you hag; my mother is ill." He took a threatening step toward her.

"I'll tak' her up the stair to my bed," pleaded Topsail, big-eyed, open-mouthed.

With a savage look he picked up the book he had been reading and hurled it straight at Topsail. It took her between the eyes. Too late she put up her hands in defence. With a bound he followed the book and slammed the door in her face.

The sweat oozed in beads upon his forehead as a new thought seized him and made him cold and pale as a corpse. Had any one seen her coming home? We shall stand now in the harlotry of the town's mind. He groaned, and began pacing up and down the room, tortured by his ignorance and his impotence. Suddenly he stopped and, folding his arms, gazed down at her. "Wrecked . . . wrecked . . . among the breakers," he muttered.

"Let me in, laddie, let me in," a voice whined at the door. Stealthily he went to the door, jerked it open, and saw a face looming out of the darkness, with blood trickling from one of the eyes like tears.

"Be off, I tell you, or I'll murder you," he groaned out, and again slammed the door in the face of a wounded angel.

He returned to the bed and stood gazing down at his mother. Her breathing was gentler, more regular, and the hectic flush had crept over her cheeks. A sense of her beauty suddenly struck him. He recalled her as he had seen her years ago. The picture was imprinted vividly on his memory. She wore a linen collar, and at a looking-glass, tress by tress, was combing out her long hair. In imagination he had fancied her like Mary Queen of Scots. Oh, that he could arm the stars or fire the town to safeguard her now from prying eyes and slanderous tongues! Since that time he had not seen her long black hair on her shoulders. He was amazed at the beauty of her face as he pored upon her. "The belle o' the ball! the belle o' the ball!"—the phrase rang through his brain. The wildest thoughts chased each other through his mind. "The eye of some curse has searched out the reins of our house." His mother's intelligence, goodness, generosity, tenderness, where were they gone? "I am sorry for her;" and the mental whips lashed him. "Where does that sorrow go? Does it escape me like an unfulfilled wish, and melt away in the air? It does not help her. It did not help Iain to-day. What is the use of it all? God"—he cried aloud—"I am going mad!" He walked to the mirror and gazed at his blanched face, staring into his eyes as if to probe his very soul. He imagined that another face, grey with dry sweat, was looking back at him fixedly from the glass. It made him recoil, for in another minute he felt this face would make him judge her. He went back to the bed and gazed upon the face there, which in sleep had assumed an expression of utter weariness. It assailed him with great compassion. "She is the author of this divine pity, and I am the author of her wretchedness; I stole to give her the whisky." And then he thought fiercely of his father. "He is the cause. Is there justice anywhere existing on earth?" Being young he was not sure. "Oh, what sorrow! what sorrow is in that face! and Iain's face—it looked so woeful to-day with the bewildered mouth hanging open." He began walking to and fro in the room, a thousand miseries besieging his mind; then ceased abruptly in his walk, and stood with limp hanging arms, a prey to despair. "Does God permit him to live to torture her?" and the ghastly thought came to him—"P'raps there is no God." His face grew hard; his eyes gleamed like a madman's. "If not, I cannot permit him to live;" but the next moment his sorrow-smitten heart rose up and condemned the thought of his tortured brain. "Yes! Yes! He lives. Great God! what am I to do?" He looked down at her, apostrophising her: "You are one of the world's suffering creatures." He saw light and eagerly grasped it. " 'God looks not on your sin but on your suffering.' How does it go? how does it go?" He strove desperately to recall the words— " 'Neither do I condemn thee; go and sin no more.' " Sin no more; and if to-morrow, and to-morrow, and to-morrow she sinned, what must he do? "It is impossible. Can she be fond of vice? Is she debauched? It cannot be. She is not a low woman without education." This mental excitation maddened him. "If so, better for her and me to be drowned." He grew cold with a great horror, remembering the words of the spey-wife. "It's me . . . it's me she meant." His pale, thin face was lit up with an unearthly light; the bluish-grey eyes were on fire. "Shame or the sea—it is the fate of our house—a grave in the sea." His breast heaved and fell rapidly with the stress of emotion. His brain began to swim in a vortex. A gloomy look came into his face. He was seized with vertigo. The light of the lamp began slowly to become blurred. He looked about for water, wetting his parched lips with his tongue. The cold made him shiver, and falling on his knees beside the bed, he buried his face in his hands, and remained prostrate before his broken altar. He arose muttering, "He is a vampire; I could kill him now in bed"—and going to the door, opened it. Without, with her back to the wall, sat Topsail Janet, her head sunk forward on her breast. He shook her by the shoulder.

"Wake up," he said, "and go and take care of my mother." He passed wearily up the narrow wooden stair to the Coffin and fell heavily into Topsail's bed.

5

A SEA-GRAVE for the house of Strang, or poison, or fire—that was what the witch said. This was his last thought as he fell into a fevered sleep and wandered into a horror of dreams. The spey-wife had manacled his wrists with a chain of foreign coins, and led him to the breast-wall over a sea black as ink, in which there were little lights as of sparks from the swords of men fighting in the dark. At first he feared the sea was on fire, and that he had made the discovery. It would blaze up ruddy as blood upon the windows of Brieston as once he had seen it when the boats in the Harbour were on fire. The fishermen were laughing and talking at the corners. How could they jest on the hem of a volcanic lake? Their boats would go up again in a blaze and the flames lick up the town. He stared fascinated: then wanted to run home and save his mother by escaping to the hills. But she would smile and tell him he was a foolish boy. "Mother, mother, it's on fire! it will set the land on fire! we'll be burned!" but he could not see his mother's face. Then he learned that the fire did not leave the sea. He tempted it, gathering up stones in his manacled hands and casting them into the water. At each splash a cascade of green flame darted up and paled on the dark waters. A new fear assailed him—this burning sea was waiting for him. Some night it would

286

gather him into the heart of its fire and he would be no more. His hands trembled so much that the chain of coins rang out like the shaken bridles of horses. He glanced over his shoulder for the comfort of the lights of the town and encountered the baleful eyes of the witch. The wind began to moan in the rigging of the boats and made the sea rise in waves of multitudinous red. He was fascinated and crept down the slip, drawn by an evil magic he could not resist. Why were the lamps of the town unlit, and the big green and red bottles in the chemist's shop not shining? Little dark town, you will break my heart; the wild eyes of fire are watching, watching your forlorn sea-front, and will smother me in a foam of flame. Those restless eyes were slanting like rain; leaping elfinly, sparkling blue like clicking swords; shining like the eyes of tigers in the night; beady as snakes coiling all around the sea-wall. They were strangling infants. Gluck! Gluck! how the children were sobbing with fear! Some night they will strangle him too; some night when he is sobbing like that, and the water is muttering and moaning, and the boats are twisting about, and the beaches are scraped as with the hoofs of horses, and the slates are rattling like pebbles on the roof.

How the little town huddles back dripping and lonely and dark! How dismal the houses are, all run together in one dark mass in the gloom! How still they are, like a man whose heart stops beating when a serpent is about to strike at him.

The wind began to scream in the cordage of the boats, and the sign at the "Ghost" to rattle like a kettle-drum. The water leapt at his feet and fell in chains of flame. He was wet with red brine. The sullen roar of the wind went over the roofs, and all the madness in the heart of the sea rose in a snarl of wind. Spindrift drenched him; the fangs of wild beasts gaped upon him, breathing fire. He broke away in terror, stumbled up the slip, and saw the town in front of him black and silent as the graveyard. The eyes of the spey-witch drove his face again to the sea, and he saw all the boats vanish away through the dark gale like ghosts beneath a sky ringing as with cymbals. He screamed at the spey-wife, gnashed his teeth upon her and began to run. He knew why he was running—it was to make the most of the murky twilight which the sea-fires cast upon the air. The stars, he knew, would not come out. They fought, choking in an inky sea above. Faster and faster he ran through Harbour Street, past the Quay, his heart hammering on his ribs. He swerved in a blind little trot to the "Ghost," and heard its mournful sign. It was all unlit and its door closed. Sobbing, he trotted on. What a piteous little bleat his feet made on the road as he came down to its end where the old Crimea guns stare out to sea! A white sheet of flame was upon the Loch, as if a giant hand were raining fire mingled with snow. Fanwise it spread, to vanish in chains of fire into smoky mist. The strangled stars of heaven dropped in great clots of blood, and to his horror he saw the falling stars burst in the midst of the chains of fire and devour the sea, licking it up in smokeless heat. All the cold dead, all the friendless who had found in the salt water their ultimate refuge—some with babies in their arms— were returning through the shallowing gulfs like homing birds to the limits of the land, their weary eyes and sorrow-laden faces upturned piteously in hope of rest from the tossing deep. Iain led the way, his mouth pitifully open and wet with salt. The mangled breasts of women were hidden with their hair, and they, remembering the old, happy years on land, held up their babes in tears, arising through the thinning foam pale as snow, cold as dew; but with lips so pure from their long cleansing sepulchre that naught might come from them but beseechings and blessings and holy songs. He understood now the old anguish-note and keening of the sea. It had been loaded with all their pain and grief, their weariness of death and the fathomless sighs of those outcasts from light and the mould—a vast, pale army who have lain unburied and sleepless, stricken with dreams of hearth and cot and home. In the cold fountains of the bitter sea their faces have been so marred with scalding tears that the brine of the oceans cannot cleanse the furrows of their grief. Up from the glens and hollows where the sea was all burned they trooped, and the noise of their feet was as the rushing of many waters through the skies, and their eyelids glowed upon the land with hunger. With eager feet they passed on through the narrow mouth of the steep place of the ocean-bed, and climbed up the cliffs to the shore. He could not help them for his manacled hands; but they needed no help. He followed them up the road and saw them go as dark, fluttering shadows on the windy, vacant streets. A charred town stood around wrecked by the stars. The doors were desolate, the lintels fallen, the roofs broken; and this was a misery above all the miseries which they had suffered in the sea; and such a wailing broke forth as made the darkness quiver like a curtain, and the fire-blackened walls rock and fling the echoes shrilling into the hollows of the dried-up sea, where they rumbled through the gorges and mingled with the dry whistle of the wind in the eye-sockets of the skulls of murderers who would never, never rise. He heard the soft passage of the resurrected as they prowled, weeping. Full of the memory of things of old, they touched the empty doorways and charred walls as if with healing fingers; and ever their muffled cry went hollow through the gloom. At this unassuaged grief came one stately in white, with inviolable eyes that looked upon Christ in pure love. "Come," she cried; "you have suffered for your children's sake or for mother or sister or brother. Christ's compassion knows and His love understands all. He will pardon those who have loved much. He will forgive Morag Strang too. He knows her to be gentle and tender and to have suffered. You were all worthy that He should die for you. His kingdom is prepared at the end of the world and He has raised you from the sea." And as the Magdalene spoke all their unlit life flamed again in their parched veins. She stooped and touched each one gently as she passed, naming a name to each of olden, secret love that moved them deeply—the name of their dreams, the name which had haunted and tortured them with its fragrance in the hold of the deep. She moved among them, a bridal woman of joy, with her evangel. And then she commanded that each return to the bed of the vanished sea and take therefrom the mangled bodies of dissolute men, of murderers and suicides and harlots, and bring them to rest in the graves of those by whom they were beloved, the son by the mother, the wife by the husband. In the splendour of her face they turned back, moving slowly, unwilling to leave her glorious eyes. They moved like a sightless army down the silent streets to the end of the road, where he came and sat again, and saw them go down into the glens and hollows of the bowels of the earth, gleaning the grey bones of the maimed, and taking them up to the red earth in the west. There flowers sprang up, tall, pale lilies, Madonna-wise, with a new tender light which filled the world. As the Magdalene went by she touched him on the shoulder and said to him, with a face so piteous that it quenched the shining of its glory: "Your hands are bound; you are no longer free. Sorrow and madness will come upon you for one that shall be a sinner too, and we shall gather up your broken body." She bowed her head as to Fate, and he felt her tears fall upon his upturned face. He held up his chained wrists to her. "It is not for me to unbind you," and she passed away as a shadow upon the wall of gloom. Mournfully he sat gazing into the ravine where the ocean waters had flowed, and saw a woman, the last of the pale army, come up over the rocks with her eyes intent upon the derelict walls of the "Ghost." The face was full of inexpressible sorrow; her eyes were deep wells of pain. It was his mother, tottering beneath a dead body which she had rescued from the bed of the sea. As she came upon the road with the body gathered up in her arms he saw that its face was Iain's.

"Mother! mother!" he screamed, leaping towards her.

He found himself in the midst of Topsail Janet's room. His knees gave way and he sank down upon the floor. The horror of the dream mingled with that of the hours he had spent with his mother rushed upon him, intensified by the cold, silent, impassioned dawn.

6

MR. COLIN KENNEDY, A.M., the parochial schoolmaster, one of the last of his race, was shrunken, tottering, white-haired, with the eyes of an aged man, dim and waiting. In the school-house set in a garden of trees he was engaged upon *A Book of the Dead*, in which no names were to appear. That was matter for history proper, biography or autobiography. It would be an epic of the obscure dead, whose faded hands he saw upon the living, whose ghosts haunted all the centuries, whose feet guided us, and the eloquence of whose dust blossomed anew upon our lips. This eternal alchemy of the vanished wrought anew in the workshop of the world. He saw in procession, as well as Caesar and Hannibal, Plato and Demosthenes, Sophocles and Virgil, Paul and Mahomet, Michelangelo and Leonardo da Vinci, Shakespeare and Beethoven, a phantasmal crowd—some scanning the stars, some pounding in a mortar, some telling their wounds, others peering at the compass on pitch-black nights; others, again, the mistresses of kings, dancing in palaces—men and women, fierce and tender, brooding and plotting, mangled and torn; and over all the wind of the Great Spirit whirling the chaff into chaos, and leaving the grain behind to spring up anew in the living generations. He had finished Chapter V, "The Fortuitous in Life," and was begun on Chapter VI, "The Note on Destiny—a Hidden Factor." He saw the unknown human legions rise up on the earth and sink again into her breast. "What dust! what multitudinous dust!" he would murmur; and the mournful tenure of life, its indefinable yearning, its fierce ambitions, its baulked endeavours, would rise up before him like a hill of sorrow, and the vague flight of the clouds of mortality would sweep before his eyes, drifting into the undiscoverable leagues of eternal silence. In the peace of his garden beneath the stars he would gaze down on the nestling town, its grey huddle of roofs and the shadow-fleet all enfolded beneath the wings of the dusk; and the voices and rumour of men would come up in his ears like small shot peppering something brittle. He imagined the people beneath projected on the face of the sky as if from a gigantic magic-lantern. The figures capered grotesquely upon the clouds, their antic gestures inspired and controlled by some passionless conjurer. "*Umbra sumus*," he would murmur sadly, "my book will never be finished;" and the relentless clock, the unerring pilot of Time, would solemnly boom out on the hill that another hour had passed away into eternity.

He was of that sort of men who have a look of home in their faces; from whom Eoghan in the depth of his distress sought comfort and advice. Eoghan told him all, including what was the innermost fear of his being: "I can't bear it, Mr. Kennedy; the whispers of the town will stab me; their eyes will burn me; they will cough at me behind their hands as I go by."

The schoolmaster made no sign that he disapproved this blatant egoism of youth, or was horrified by its moral cowardice.

"It takes one half of our life," he said, "to know how to live the other half. You have yet to learn. You are too imaginative, too highly-strung"—he smiled gently; "too—thin-skinned. Those who were great were undeterred"—he lapsed into dreams of his book—"they held far-off communion with the goal, and let the gnats sting them. They did not imagine the slander of others. Ignore the scoff and the jeer. Do not writhe like a trampled worm. Watch over her tenderly; guard her gently; lead her by love. Cowards stand around and scoff; but love is at the foot of the Cross, watching in silence. Do not rage or blaspheme. In suffering silence we best come to our haven. The birds of evening do not sing when flying to their nests. This is Sunday. Go to-day in silence to God and pray to Him. You know that when scholars exhaust their learning the poor man turns to the Bible." He cast a sorrowful glance at Eoghan, as if reading his vacillating character.

"I can't heal myself with such philosophy," cried Eoghan, "when I walk through the streets to-morrow."

"Do not carry such thoughts of shame with you. Brooding increases misery with compound interest. Put it in the fire and burn it. It is smoke."

"It is I who burn—all last night."

"You are stricken"—he laid his thin, shaky hand on Eoghan's shoulder—"and being young you are in despair. You will not believe if I tell you that suffering is good. We are torches lit to that wind; at least the best of us. Look at Marshall the baker. He never paid a fee to Maclean all his life; he's seventy, and rich as a Jew. His daughters are well married and bearing healthy children. His sons have good positions. I taught them all. They were sly and some of them rogues; but they flourish"—the old man spread out his fine, fragile hands as if blessing him— "Eoghan, my son, Marshall is to be pitied. God is letting him drift."

"Maybe," answered Eoghan, not daring to gaze at the visionary face of the old man; "but my wound is raw."

He touched Eoghan delicately on the shoulder, stooping towards him. "Though you were in many ways a clever scholar I caned you." He smiled fondly at Eoghan. "It was fine to thrash you because you were so clever. The cane was a trowel. I was laying manhood on you at every stroke. This sorrow of yours is the first touch of God's trowel"—he peered at Eoghan's face— "if you have not brought this trouble on yourself. Many a cross is a cross of folly." The words appeared to rise up from a deep well of sorrow. "If the trouble is not of your own making, fear nothing. The human heart is proof against all. When the worst comes to the worst the soul sits within at the storm-centre looking out in profound calm. We fear life too much. Come," he added in a brisker tone, "together we'll go to church for knowledge and wisdom. There are the bells"—and seeing the hesitant look on Eoghan's face—"It is Maurice from Ardmarkie who is preaching to-day. He is a good man. You are tired, my son," he ended with infinite tact; "come and rest in the house of God."

"I never go to church; I don't see the use of it."

"Perhaps you will to-day. Religion is never an ecstasy, a hope, or a promise to those whose lives run smoothly."

Reluctantly and shamefacedly Eoghan accompanied him down the garden path, dreading the encounter with the church-goers. Harbour Street was populous with men and women in black. The world in that hour seemed to have no poor, no sick, no afflicted. The old folk wore those indefatigable clothes which would never be replaced. On the brae they met Maclean, who shook hands with the schoolmaster and nodded to Eoghan.

"For church, doctor?" asked Mr. Kennedy.

"Ay! the last shot in the locker."

Eoghan was startled. Did Maclean know anything? What did he mean by referring to church as the last resort? The blood rushed to his head; his knees began to tremble. He stole a glance at the doctor; but he was looking unconcernedly ahead as he talked to Mr. Kennedy. "Maurice is a pious man and a good preacher. I hope he left a dram for Stuart in Ardmarkie Manse." His deep, hearty laugh rang with exquisite comfort to Eoghan's heart. If the doctor knew anything he would not have spoken about a dram in that careless fashion. Eoghan entered the church with a sense of relief.

He was startled when the preacher gave out the text. His subject was the Magdalene. " 'Seest thou this woman?' This poor pariah," the preacher went on, "was nameless. Haunting the nests of vice and walking the mean streets of Jerusalem, would she desire a name? Was not her name reft from her, as convicts to-day have their names taken from them and are given a number instead? But once pardoned she will forsake her old haunts, she will establish that which is dear to every woman's heart, a home, and take her name again, the name of childhood, which came blowing its fragrance and its innocence across the weary years." The preacher's earnest voice, in which was a hint of tears, seemed to Eoghan to be sobbing through the building. He sat spell-bound. "The Pharisees and wolves who had preyed upon her would sneer now, and hint and whisper"—Eoghan felt as if a cord were being tightened about his heart, and breathed with difficulty—"but repentant sorrow is proof against contumely. The storms of life and its passion have broken her, and only one thing on earth can mend her. The white flower of chivalry will not strike a fallen one. Mercy sees only the suffering heart, and mercy makes self-righteousness blush for itself. Ah, the nameless fragrance of that mercy! She dares wipe His feet, dares let herself dwell on the thought of His love. She has found her haven from the ruthlessness of the world. A memory is left to her that will never perish, that will never recur to her without evoking scorching tears. This woman makes us know what unabashed faith is, what is the love that knows neither shame, suspicion, nor fear." Eoghan half rose to his feet, his eyes riveted on the transfigured face of the preacher. A hand gently drew him back. "In her we see the tenderness and devotion that can transform a woman who has returned from the doors of hell to the gates of heaven. In her we see the Man of Sorrows both as the Star and Haven, the giver of noble thoughts, the gladness of the future, the restorer of what is broken, the endower of the heart with fortitude to rise after defeat and wear out the most relentless foe. One hour with Him wipes out all—past sorrows, past brooding, past despair. These are now so many bonds by which the soul is tied to its Redeemer." Eoghan thought the burning eyes of the preacher were riveted on his face. "The nails of your cross He plucks out, and they are driven into His own hands and feet." A mist swam before Eoghan's face; the blood was drumming in his ears. He had lost some of the golden words from the pulpit. "If you cannot help such, leave them alone at least. Don't play the part of the Pharisee with your jibes and your jeers. . . . Once she was nameless. The angels now know her name, the new name by which her holy love was called in that fearless day when, penetrating to the home of the Pharisee, she, with the hair of her head, dried her own scalding tears, which had fallen upon those feet soon to be doomed to the nails by those who were her own tormenters."

A deep silence bound the congregation as the preacher ended. For a moment Eoghan felt an insane desire to burst into laughter. His mouth and jaws were working convulsively in an effort to repress the welling sobs.

"Let us pray"—clear like a bell the words rang out. Eoghan dropped down on his knees, the only kneeling figure in the church, and buried his head in his arms.

"Thou who watchest over the fall of a sparrow and numberest the hairs of our head art the unceasing guardian of the children of men. Thou hast given us the highest pledge possible of Thy love in the death of Jesus Christ. Wilt Thou not along with Him freely give unto us all things? This, O God of Mercy, is our simple faith. We need this trust. We have but a brief day, lightened a little by happiness, broken by grief, burdened with care, soiled by sin. We are but shadows upon the background of eternity. Children we are, groping and stumbling till our day decline and wearily we seek our rest. Shine upon our vicissitudes, O Thou infinite strength; break, break upon our hazardous career, O Thou immortal light. When a deeper yearning falls upon us for the good, the true, the lovely, the things of excellent report, let naught of mischance or evil quench the God within us seeking out the God that is Thee. And when all is done—a little well, perhaps, by Thy grace, and much that is feeble, wayward, and ill—may we also, leaning upon Thy compassion which knows, Thy love which understands all, be brave to say, 'Lord, Thou knowest all things; Thou knowest that I love Thee, O Jesus Christ, my Lord.' "

Involuntarily the compelling Amen rang out on Eoghan's lips. Maclean glanced at him, and began tugging fiercely at his moustache. Eoghan rose off his knees, chastened, uplifted, redeemed. The wings of the cherubim were adrift in the church.

"A humane prayer," Maclean whispered, staring at the minister. With a swelling heart of gratitude Eoghan also looked at the man, who somehow he felt had left him in the hollow of God's hand. The preacher announced the hundred and third psalm, and slowly read through the verses to be sung.

" 'He will not chide continually.' " The words lingered, charged with a spirit of redemption. They began singing:

> "Such pity as a father hath
> Unto his children dear."

The doctor was singing in a tuneless, rasping voice—singing as if all his soul were coming up into his mouth, and all the people with mighty fervency. "Kilmarnock" rolled and swelled in waves of triumphant sound. Angels were ascending and descending on a ladder of light. "They are grasping the hem of Christ's garment. God is here! God is here!" Eoghan wanted to cry it aloud:

> "Like pity shows the Lord to such."

His bosom was heaving and falling with emotion; he could sing no more for choking sobs; the tears freely ran down his cheeks.

He walked down the street without fear or a sense of shame. At the foot of the brae Maclean abruptly addressed Mr. Kennedy:

"Damn it, Kennedy, Maurice has done me good the day. I'll ask the Laird to send him a brace of pheasants."

"Come and see me to-night, Eoghan," said Mr. Kennedy.

"Thank you, sir;" they shook hands—rather lingeringly Maclean thought—and the two men watched him cross the Square.

"We'll make the lad a minister," said Maclean.

The schoolmaster gave him no answer.

In the presence of his father Eoghan dared not ask Topsail Janet for news of his mother, who was not at dinner. Gillespie asked his son if he had been to church. With the schoolmaster and the doctor! Imphm! Trade was surely bad when Maclean was there. And was the Laird present? Gillespie wanted to know if the Laird, with whom he had business, was at home. The collectorship of harbour and passenger dues at the Pier was about to become vacant. The present man, Gillespie had wormed out of the factor, was paying in rent one hundred pounds per annum. The Laird had no notion of what the business was worth. The steamship dues alone paid the rent; the passenger dues—which in the summer were considerable—stood a clear profit, and must run to hundreds of pounds. Gillespie meant privately to make an offer to the Laird over the present man's head of one hundred and twenty pounds per annum, and use his son as a catspaw. He was a dwaibly, fushionless body, good enough at books, but useless for hard work. Such a post the Laird must see would be the very thing for his son. This would knock the colleging scheme of that old rogue the schoolmaster on the head, and at the same time bring in a handsome income.

"Ye didna see the Laird, did ye no'? Maybe noo ye werena keekin'."

"I wasn't," answered Eoghan doggedly; "I was looking at the minister."

"That'll please Stuart," Gillespie said merrily.

"It wasn't Mr. Stuart."

"An' who was it?" Gillespie was picking his teeth with a fork, and spoke absently.

"It was Mr. Maurice from Ardmarkie."

"Eh! who! Mr. Maurice? Ane o' the hallelujah boys."

His father's nonchalant, disinterested air had been irritating Eoghan, and now a wave of anger surged over him at the indecent libel. Instantaneously his mind was projected forward and he saw what would happen—his own blazing face and his father's surprise. Even as he jumped to his feet he saw his action take being to meet what his imagination had already forecast. He snatched up a dinner spoon.

"Another word against Mr. Maurice," he yelled, "and"— fear for an instant gripped his throat; he overleapt it with fierce joy—"and I'll brain you——" He swung his arm back, and brought the spoon crashing down on the table. His legs quivered so much that he was scarcely able to push back his chair. He rocked giddily out of the kitchen and, bursting into his own room, locked the door and flung his trembling form on the bed, where he lay face down, biting the clothes with his teeth. Hour after hour passed. He became afraid of his father, and determined to leave the house. Fear passed into defiance; defiance into cynicism. As he lay brooding, the words of the preacher came back to him without any conscious effort to recall them; they stole into his soul with solace and balm. Again he heard the gracious prayer, and felt how a vision of angels had swept through the church. He arose and, searching for his Bible, passed out of his room into the kitchen. It was empty. Topsail Janet was aloft in the Coffin, scrutinising the face of Jesus in the picture on the wall. Gillespie was gone in search of the Laird's factor. Eoghan passed through the kitchen to his mother's room and saw her dark form on the bed.

"Is that you, mother?"

He heard a deep sigh: "Where have ye been all day, Eoghan?"

"At church."

There was silence. Again she sighed deeply.

"Are you not feeling well?" His voice betrayed anxiety.

"Oh, I'm sick! sick!" she answered, "sick of my life; oh, Eoghan, my temples are throbbing like to burst!"

He knew that if he did not say it now his courage would ooze away, and his heart began to beat rapidly.

"Mother"—he spoke in a low voice—"I had a strange dream last night about you——"

"What was it, Eoghan?" she asked, in a faint, listless tone.

"I saw you and myself and Mary Magdalene——"

An exclamation of horror from the bed interrupted him.

"—and Mr. Maurice was preaching to-day about Mary Magdalene."

"It's no' canny, Eoghan, your dream." She was half sitting up in bed now, gazing large-eyed at her son.

297

"There's something strange about it, mother." His face was full of gloom and his voice broken as he said: "Mother, I would like to read about Mary Magdalene to you."

"Ay," she answered, "it's Sabbath. I haven't read the Bible since I left Lonend. You'll need a light, Eoghan."

He returned to the kitchen, found a lamp on the mantelpiece, and carried it into the bedroom. His mother was sitting up in bed. He lingered over the lamp, afraid now to begin. The untrimmed wick was smoking. He opened the Bible, rustling the leaves loudly.

"Can't ye find the place, Eoghan? I don't remember where it is."

"It's in Luke," he muttered; "I forget the chapter."

At that moment his eye lighted on the passage. He tried to begin, but the words would not come. He wetted his lips with his tongue.

"I've found the place," he said.

"Will you give me a drink of water, Eoghan?"

Again he passed into the kitchen, from which he heard his mother's weary sigh. She took the glass from him with shaking hand. He bent his head over the Bible till she drank. When the gurgling sounds ceased, he glanced up and saw her sitting, tumbler in hand, her head drooping like one who is a prey to dejection, her eyes fixed on the coverlet. She seemed to have forgotten him. In a strained voice he began to read:

" '*And one of the Pharisees desired Him that He would eat with him.*' "

"What's that you're saying, Eoghan?"

He looked up and saw her bewildered eyes upon him.

"I'm reading about Mary Magdalene."

"Mary Magdalene!" The bewilderment of her eyes was now in her voice.

A strangling tightness in his chest prevented him from continuing.

"Eoghan"—her querulous voice seemed to come from an infinite distance—"will you tell Janet I want to speak to her?"

"Oh, mother! mother! let me read the Bible first"—he was unconscious that he screamed the words—"it did me so much good to-day."

"Ay! ay!" she repeated mechanically, "read the Bible; this is the Sabbath day."

" '*And, behold, a woman in the city, which was a sinner, when she knew that Jesus sat at meat in the Pharisee's house, brought an alabaster box of ointment*'"—his throat was bursting. It cost an immense effort to articulate the words. His mother had fallen back on the bed; her eyes were fixed upward with a glassy stare on the ceiling—" '*and stood at His feet behind Him weeping, and began to wash His feet with tears, and did wipe them with the hairs of her head, and kissed His feet, and anointed them with the ointment*——' " Emotion overcame him. The lines were all blurred. He blinked rapidly and the print swam up clear again, and he went on reading: " '*Now when the Pharisee which had bidden Him saw it, he spake within himself, saying, This man, if he were a prophet, would have known who and what manner of woman this is that toucheth Him: for she is a sinner.*' "

He glanced at his mother; her eyes were closed.

"Mother, are you listening?"

"God peety me!" There was a distracted look on her face which terrified him. He jumped to his feet and the Bible fell to the floor.

"Mother! mother! what's wrong wi' ye?"

Her head swayed to and fro on the pillow; a low, moaning sound escaped her lips.

"Oh, Eoghan! Eoghan! my temples are throbbing: my head's burstin'. Oh! Oh! Oh! it's on fire! Will ye no' tell Janet to come?"

He ran into the kitchen.

"Janet! Janet!" he yelled, "mother's ill; come quick!" He heard Topsail moving on the stair and ran back to the room. His mother was again sitting up in bed, the light of fever in her eyes, and scarlet patches on her cheeks. Topsail came in panting.

"Away, you," she commanded in a firm voice, "away an' tek' a breath o' fresh air. I ken what to do."

He felt a sudden sense of relief at Topsail's quiet confidence and mastery, and hurriedly left the room. On the stairhead he stood pondering. How easily the minister had that day affected him, and how futile had been his own effort to bring his mother to the Ultimate Refuge of men from the whips of existence. He remembered his Bible, and hurried back to pick it up. As he gained the threshold of the bedroom he saw Topsail Janet standing with her back to him, and the whisky bottle which himself had bought in her left hand. His mother was drinking. He heard the tumbler clink against her teeth.

"There noo; that'll do ye good."

Eoghan felt suddenly whipped, defeated, a spy. The devouring eagerness with which his mother drank, pressing the tumbler with both hands to her chattering mouth, revolted him. He crept backwards and stole through the kitchen; and in the darkness of his own room became a prey to misery. The picture of his mother sitting up dishevelled in bed ran before his eyes in lines of fire upon the darkness. He closed his eyes to banish it; but it would not leave him. He went about groping for his cap, seeing his mother's haunting face before him. He put out his hands in front of him as he went down the stair. "Good God! Good God!" he kept muttering. "Good God! what's to become o' us now?" and he passed out into the night.

7

A VAST, jet-black cloud trailed upon the sea, with a clear white rift in its eastward portion wedged in between sea and sky. The waves ran fiercely beneath this cloud. It was an ominous sight to the crew of the *Sudden Jerk*, which was making bad weather of it with Iain Strang at the wheel. A small, lumpy man in sou'-wester and oilskins was forward, peering over the windward gunwale at a marly sky which glared and bled as with wounds. The engineer, huddled against the engine-room casing, was patching a hole in the bottom of the bowl of an old clay with a piece of cod-skin. He was doing this to keep a grip of his nerve. He had just shouted to Iain, "Let her away for Ardrossan; there's no' a bucketful o' coal in the bunkers." From where he sat the wind appeared to be pinning Iain to the large wooden wheel.

After every flash of spindrift heads jerked up over the Ardrossan breakwater to watch a little steamer with a wisp of an ochreish funnel sheer through the spume, loom out of it, and vanish again in a cloud like the phantasmagoria of a dream. Inch by inch she lunged nearer, warring with the waste. They saw her peaked black nose rise and plunge like a thing in agony; then she wriggled down into the trough and rolled to her gunwales. They heard the soggy clank, clink of her wearied engines fitfully through the screaming of the wind and the roar of the water—clattering and wheezing, and tearing herself in every swipe of the cross seas. The harbour master was dancing on the breakwater, yelling through a speaking-trumpet and waving off the labouring steamer. It blew hard from the sou'-east; the sky was changing its appearance at every few minutes; it was impossible to open the dock gates in face of the tremendous seas.

"There's nothing for it but to run," Iain yelled over his shoulders, and heaved himself upon the wheel.

The engineer rose and went below to nurse his coal. "The harbour mud 'ill get washed off the flukes the night," he muttered, and flung the old clay into the heart of a grey comber.

They ran before the gale, sweeping past a tramp steamer and a large blue-funnelled liner hove to. They dared not broach her now. The stern lay low on the water, and the frightsome following twin seas curled up on either hand as high as the funnel, threatening momentarily to swoop upon the stern. It was necessary to steam her hardest to out-race that pursuing wall of water. A slackness at the wheel, the variation of a foot, and the *Sudden Jerk* would sink like a stone. Grey sheets of spindrift rose off the water and fell like sleet across the decks. To port, to starboard, and ahead nothing was visible but leagues of spindrift, out of which suddenly loomed phantom-like a lonely grey ship-of-war, smoking through the seas, the black snout of a long gun pointing through the spray. She had a faded, drenched appearance, yet looked fierce as the sea she warred with, and hungry against the naked sky-line as war itself. Her funnels belched flame.

"Rule, Britannia!" yelled the engineer; "wish we'd a ton o' your steam-coal."

High off the north end of Arran, where the wind shrilled down the glens with a tormented sound, they met the cross seas of the two channels.

"There's nothing for it but Brieston Harbour," yelled Iain.

"By hedges, it's blowin'!" the engineer answered, roaring into the wall of wind, with the words flung back in his teeth. There was a sob of fear in his voice. He swung round the ventilator.

"Here's a Goäd Almighty sea comin'," screamed the man at the wheel with Iain. A ghostly grey-back swooped up and shouldered aboard forward; the ventilator melted away beneath the engineer's hand, and he recovered breath sitting in a river of·water in the corner made by the engine-room casing and the foot of the bridge. The br·ge ladder was gone. She was half filled forward.

"Let it go by the gangway," shouted Iain.

The lumpy man in oilskins crawled aft and began wrestling with the gangway door, which refused to yield. Iain swung himself over the bridge railing and dropped on the slanting deck. He crawled aft, disappeared down the engine-room, to reappear with a large hammer. Gauging her plunge, he staggered forward. Crash! crash! came the hammer-head; the gangway door swung open; the torrent of salt water hissed out. Iain, caught in the suction, saved himself by dropping the hammer and clutching a stanchion. The *Sudden Jerk* heaved up, relieved from the weight of water, and righted herself. The gangway door swung to and caught Iain on the leg. It snapped like matchwood. He fell, pinned as in a vice. The lumpy man yelled on the engineer. Together they extricated Iain, whose face was drawn with pain, and bore him to shelter in the lee of the casing beneath the bridge.

From where he lay he instructed them to work the *Sudden Jerk* into the Loch, hugging the east shore. The wind was howling from end to end of the Loch at the same time, and the whole body of the storm leapt in dense black squalls. Lightning flickered and darted among the clouds bastioned on the southeast horizon.

Gillespie was about to be punished for his greed. The coal was done. They burned the platform of the hold and fired her with herring boxes. The steam-gauge was emptying with ominous rapidity. With a list to port she was now swept by the seas clean as a table. Her head broached away constantly. She began to wallow. The engineer came up for the last time from the bowels of the ship. His teeth clicked as he tried to articulate the words.

"The fire's—oot——" He turned from the sick son and began to curse the father. "No'—even a rag—o' a sail——" Gillespie had refused to supply them with a mizzen. He was not the man to provide both sail and steam.

The dark fell. She drove now, beam on, shaking under every impact of the solid water.

The engineer peered into the engine-room and heard water washing on the plates.

"It's no' a steamer," he muttered, "it's a mill; she's chokin';" he was on the verge of madness through terror.

302

Slowly she sagged towards an iron coast. The lumpy man crawled out of the forecastle, and came aft hand over fist along the starboard gunwale.

The engineer eyed him vaguely.

"Whaur's the cook?" he asked.

"He's forrut, greetin'."

The deck-hand, dressed in his best clothes and wearing a collar and tie, spoke apologetically:

"I'm no' goin' to be picked up in dongarees."

"Dressed for your funeral, by hedges," the engineer laughed hysterically.

"Let go—the anchor—it may—hold," Iain, dazed with pain, was whispering. No one paid him any attention. He lay listening to the boom along the shore mingling with the steady scream of the wind.

"Another ton o' coal an' we'd have made the Hairbour," the engineer's words were a roar of despair. A small sickly moon, hoar-white, sheered out of the clouds.

Iain opened his eyes.

"She was right—the spey-wife," he muttered; "it's comin'; it's no' the wee fellow after all—thank God—one of you will find the other." His face became inexpressibly sad. His mouth was open, miserable, hanging loosely, dejected. For a moment he heard a triumphing scream in the rush of the wind, felt the drunken swaying of the ship as if she were being butted by an enormous ram; then a great vacancy stretched away before his eyes. He was oppressed by an intolerable heartache which divorced all sorrow, pain, and desire. There was nothing left but infinite vacancy stretching away far beyond the roaring of the sea, and the hills, the moor and the hoar-white moon. With incredible swiftness an age of a thousand years out of a remote past rolled up before him, and he felt himself swimming into this vast peace of eternity. He opened his eyes to see if the world were real, and across the gunwale saw through a cleft on the foreland in the scud of the moon the tall, harled gables of the pallid "Ghost" as of a thing he had never beheld before. The next moment the *Sudden Jerk* crashed and shivered through her length; there was a grinding, ripping, tearing sound; a rending of wood and iron that was swallowed up as an enormous sea rose and broke over her stern. A sickening sensation stole over Iain. He closed his eyes, as he felt himself being lifted and torn away into the darkness. . . .

Her nose rose slowly in the air, and a huge sea hurled her forward. There was a loud explosion as she burst amidships. The after part vanished; the water boiled where it disappeared; then broke into its turbulent race shoreward.

Nothing but the stem of a broken ship and the water sculptured gigantically by the gale to tell that brave lives had been cast away through the insensate greed of a man.

Behind the window in the "Ghost," which Iain's dazed eyes had glimpsed as he passed away from it for ever, sat two persons: old Mr. Strang on a hard wooden chair placed against the great four-poster bed tented with red curtains, in which generations had been born and died. Opposite was the big fire-place with white-washed jambs. Between the fire-place and the dresser in a corner was a cushioned box, on which Eoghan sat. The racks of the dresser were full of willow-pattern plates and, beneath, old punch-bowls lying on their sides. A long shelf above the fire-place was sacred with relics—some of them far-fetched articles brought home by the old man's brother, who had made many foreign voyages and was buried in an unknown place abroad; the long-necked champagne bottle which had been opened at Mr. Strang's wedding; a crystal christening bowl. These were silent orisons in glass; things of eld on which a moss of affection grew; monuments of old happiness and sorrow. Over them all the hundred-year-old wag-at-the-wa' ticked still in tune and time, and in a corner by the meal-barrel was a mouldered spinning-wheel, which the hands of many women now dead had used. It was a room heavy with the odour of antiquity, and to Eoghan transforming what had been the reality of the past into a romance in the present, haunting him with a certain wistfulness, a tender note of mournfulness for those dear ones who had lived, suffered, aspired, and passed into the unknown. He felt very strongly Iain's absence to-night, as he listened to the arid patter of the rain on the window like the hard hoofs of little animals. He was oppressed by a sense of disaster; but dreaded to speak his fear, lest he divert his grandfather's mind also to a sorrowful contemplation of danger.

Part of a ham hung from an iron hook in the ceiling. The old man stood on a chair and took it down to cut some for their tea. "It'll put by the winter," he said, sighing; "your faither said I'll be glad to go an' beg frae him yet. God be thankit! I'll no' be brocht to that. I'm in no man's debt." He pushed back a thick, black, curling lock behind his ear. "I've aye peyed my way. Iain, God bless him, he never failed me for my feu duty and taxes frae the day he gied aboard a boat. What wad I do withoot him? He's better to me than twenty sons. Och! och! I bocht a shop for Gillespie an' gied him curing-sheds wi' a' I saved frae the fishin', an' I'm left bitin' my nails noo. How could I help it when he wad come greetin' on my face sayin' his business was goin' back? Ay! I gied Iain the cheque to go to the bank, an' I swithered too, for I was leavin' mysel' bare in my old age. Och! och! an' Iain said, 'He's your son, grandfaither.' It was Iain knew hoo greedy he was then, though I didna. An' it was Iain's own name wi' mine that was on the deposit receipt, for it was to him it was to go. Weel, Gillespie got it an' made a big sicht o' money, and then I askit my ain back.

"'What's an auld man lik' you needin' a' that money for?'

"'Gillespie,' I said; 'you're weel off noo; gie me the siller I lent you; it's no' for mysel', it's for Iain.'

"'Iain! Iain's a young man; let him face the world an' mak' his own wy lik' me.'

"'God forbid,' I said.

"'Don't be nesty noo ower a wee pickle siller'—that's your faither's way, Eoghan, to turn the faut on every one but himsel'. I could maist greet to think that his mither's son had siccan a black he'rt."

"'I canna sterve,' I said to him.

"'Hoots, I'll no' see ye bate for bite or sup.'

"'Dinna fash, Gillespie. God has never seen me go wantin'. I'll mand for a' the time I hae to leeve. If ye'll no' can gie me my ain, pay me seven pounds noo for your mither's coffin.' Och! och! poor granny!" The old man's body shook pitiably. Eoghan was swallowing back the choking sobs.

"'I haena any ready money by me; thae traivellers are aye on the top o' me; there's no leevin' wi' them, faither,' that's what he said." The muscles on the old man's face became rigid.

"'Faither! did ye say? Never ca' me that again as long as ye leeve. Ye're nae mair a son o' mine. The curse o' God Almighty 'ill visit ye yet for this. Some day ye'll darken my door when the hand o' God lies sore on ye—ay, some day. If ye winna pey me, ye'll pey Him. He's His ain judgment bidin'.'

Even as he spoke the judgment was begun: the foundations of

the house of Gillespie Strang were being sapped. Iain his son lay with a broken leg in the lee of the engine-room casing. This as a privation would not have been momentous to Gillespie had he known; but what would have troubled him would have been the knowledge that the skilled hand was departed from the wheel, and his uninsured craft was exposed to imminent peril.

Eoghan, saddened by the recital, sat with a look of hopeless misery, the incarnation of a recent description of him: "Ye ay expect him to be greetin' wi' thon face."

The great seas thundered on the beach without. The wind was now as stallions maddened by demon riders and screaming in pain; now in a lull as eagles from eyrie headlands, whose great wings rustled fiercely as they swept past. The door opened with a rush of the wind. The visitor had to force it shut with his shoulder. He came in stooping, dripping wet, a thin, pale-faced, white-haired man, round-shouldered, a little, with small eyes which, when they rested on old Mr. Strang, melted with tenderness. It was James the sailmaker, who lived in a loft among the rats, and who often in his evening walk visited Mr. Strang. To-night, however, he came on a mission.

"It's tempestuous wild, Jamie," said old Mr. Strang.

The sailmaker pulled down the collar of his jacket and took a seat.

"I'm anxious," he said. "Gillespie wouldn't allow a mizzen or foresail on his steamer."

The old man rose to his feet, then sat down, and his dark, massive head fell forward. He knew the way of the sea. Presently he raised his head, and going to the outside door opened it. Those within heard him moan two words twice over, "Mo thruaigh! mo thruaigh!" He wrestled with the door and returned to the kitchen.

"It's sou'-east," he said, and the leonine head sunk on the breast; "Iain—Iain—granny's boy——"

The sailmaker rose, and looking at Eoghan said in a low voice: "Bring down the Books."

Eoghan gave him his grandfather's Bible, a broad book with large type.

"Let us sing together the twentieth psalm."

The wind raved without; the firmament seemed to be huddling along in a dark madness.

> "Jehovah hear thee in the day
> When trouble He doth send;
> And let the name of Jacob's God
> Thee from all ill defend."

The sailmaker's head was thrown back, his eyes were on the ceiling with a rapt look, his voice rang out full, resonant, appealing above the storm. The old man sat with his head buried in his hands. Eoghan's eyes were fixed intently on the sailmaker, the intercessor who, he was persuaded, was in that moment in communion with the Almighty. Strong and compelling the sailmaker's voice soared, as if he were summoning legions of angels from the throne of Heaven.

The psalm was finished and he announced in a loud voice: "Let us read in the hundred and seventh psalm."

Eoghan waited upon the rustling of the leaves as if Fate were stealing a march ahead. The sailmaker cast up his eyes to the ceiling in silent invocation and began to read:

" '*They go down to the sea in ships,*' "—("and meet with lightning, snow, and tempest,")—the words were arising involuntarily in Eoghan's mind—" '*they mount up to heaven, they go down again to the depths,*' "—("It's sou'-east, sou'east, the shelterless wind;" an overmastering desire came upon Eoghan to scream out the words)—" '*their soul is melted because of trouble.*' " Eoghan had a sudden vision of Iain, his mouth open, drooping, wretched; his sorrow-smitten face—"Ye'll mind my words when one o' ye finds the other"—the spey-wife's malicious face rose before him, symbolical of doom. His knees quaked and shook together. In that moment he knew his brother was lost. " '*Then are they glad because they be quiet: so He bringeth them to their desired haven——*' "

"No! no! no! Iain! Iain! Drowned among the lightning and the storm; no more, no more."

The sailmaker looked up wonderingly at the wild cry.

"Wheest!" he chided, "it is still his haven; he shall be glad because he is quiet." The sign without clattered as with the jangling sound of the spey-wife's tins.

Down on their knees they went, his grandfather's boots scraping on the floor. The fervent voice of the sailmaker rose in appeal to the Maker of the heavens and the earth to safeguard him who that night was tossing upon the stormy deep. The clamour of the wind could not drown the voice; in sobbing tones it pleaded with

307

Jesus of Galilee to intercede at the right hand of God, and in simple, burning words life and destiny were committed to the care of the Great, All-Seeing Father. The old man rose with difficulty from his knees, with tears upon his face. The house shook to the onset of the gale; the seas tore and clawed upon the beach. A gigantic comber burst in thunder, and its spindrift whipped across the window-pane. This was part of that long wall of water which, smashing upon the stern of the *Sudden Jerk*, had lifted Iain away into the vast darkness and the desired haven where there is quiet.

Eoghan had trotted down this road from the "Ghost" to the Crimea gun before—blindly as now. He remembered—it was in that awful dream. The wind tore at him as he stood clinging with his arms cast about the muzzle of the gun, and staring into the blinding waste seaward. The rollers burst with loud reports on the concrete fragments of the Pier at the end of the road, and the spray flew in sheets, soaking him to the skin. He felt nothing, heard nothing, as he strained out across the wild wash and roar of the night. He had been capricious, sensitive to affront, quick-tempered, secretive, full of pride, obsessed with dreams and hopes of future distinction. Probably had he lived and been tutored by circumstance he would have developed into a more human being, less selfish, brooding and capricious, and in old age have become a tender, pious man. But hauteur, secrecy, brooding, gave way at the moment to hopeless, incurable grief. Like all sensitive souls he was paying the price for his gift of imagination. His soul was flayed.

"Shame is sitting at the fire, and sorrow looking in at the window from the sea. I wish I were dead too." Iain's mournful face swam up before him. He saw the whites of the eyes turned up and open, pitiable mouth all wet. "I slept with him. I stole sweeties out of the shop and passed them to him on Sundays." He clenched his fist, sinking his nails into his palm. He was feeling the answering squeeze of his brother's fingers. He remembered a clear-shining night and a rising moon, and the sails of fishing-boats shimmering against tall dark hills, and Iain wrapping him in a great-coat as they stood on the bridge at the wheel. For a long Iain had refused to allow him aboard the *Sudden Jerk*.

"You're far better in your bed at home, young fellow. Thon life's no' for you." The fact is that Iain never trusted the *Sudden Jerk*;

but in fine midsummer weather he had yielded, and by the wheel on the bridge had taught Eoghan to steer by compass and read the mariner's stars. Eoghan remembered now how in the cold wind of the dawn Iain with tender solicitude had sent him with eyes heavy on sleep to bunk, and on the next day had commanded him home in one of the herring-skiffs.

"Sonny, you're not built for this work; take my tip and quit." Eoghan saw again the white teeth flashing as he laughed. And now that mouth of laughter, those radiant dark eyes, were drenched in the brine. He felt his heart was breaking, and leaning his head upon the gun burst into a paroxysm of sobbing—another tragic echo of humanity's ancient heart-break cry for what is irretrievably lost.

"Oh, dear God! how I loved to hear him laugh—cold, cold in a sea-grave——"

8

IN a sea-town which harbours a fishing-fleet these are the foot-steps of the men in the night which the women know—the trudge which tells of bleak shores and empty boats; the joyous ring of the steel-shod heels with which the younger men dent the pavements, crying aloud of herring; and another step—ominous, slow, shuffling, as men creep silently home. Women strain their ears, for the step may not stop at their door; and if it does not—why, there shall no longer be the big sea-boots to clean. On that step at the threshold hangs life and death; will it go by or enter in? The families who have given tithe of their folk to the sea have heard it pass away up the lane into a silence which, louder than trumpetings, they shall never forget. What a moment is that when the step comes to the door and it is opened and "Oh, is it you?" cries the wife or daughter, and, overcome with joy, drags in the wearied man! In another house the wife is lying staring into the dark waiting, waiting for the feet that will never come.

Such a step would never come to Gillespie's door; only the footstep of Eoghan, who passed into the kitchen, drenched to the skin, and looked in silence upon his father, who was bending over a ledger opened on the table.

"How's the wind?" he asked without glancing up.

Eoghan shuddered.

"Sou'-east," he answered.

"No fishin' the nicht," Gillespie grunted in a dissatisfied tone; "Iain 'ill be playin' the f'ute to the Ardrossan keelies."

"You'll never hear his step upon the stair again." Eoghan wondered why he said that, and how dispassionately he uttered it. The clock ticked on through a minute's silence. "Never again! never again!" it was rapping out. Gillespie laid down his pen in the cleft of the book and slowly lifted his head.

"What's that ye're sayin'?"

"Iain has found his desired haven."

Gillespie stretched out his hand for the pen. "Ay! he'll hae a' the tinklers o' Sautcoats listenin' to him in the fo'c'sle."

"That's not the haven;" Eoghan spoke calmly, as if wrapt in a far-off dream. The hand of Gillespie was arrested on its way to the pen.

"Whatna hairbour?" he asked sharply.

"Heaven, I hope."

The hand slowly slid backwards and fell off the table, and Gillespie rose to his feet, supporting himself by gripping the edge of the table. His eyes were dilated upon his son.

"Eoghan"—his voice shook—"what dae ye mean? Wha told ye?"

"Iain's drowned and I'll find him. The spey-wife told me."

Gillespie's mouth slowly opened. In a flash Eoghan saw its resemblance to that of Iain in its slack, dejected droop.

"Drooned! Hoo can that be an' him in Ardrossan Hairbour a nicht lik' this?"

"They're at the bottom of the sea, steamer and all."

Gillespie sank limply into his chair and stared fixedly before him. "Drooned! drooned! a nicht lik' this. I thocht he had some skill o' the sea, an' was playin' his f'ute to the Ardrossan keelies; drooned! an' the steamer no' insured——" Gillespie was ignorant that he was alone in the kitchen. For the first time in his life his ledger was as ashes.

To the sorrow which death brings it was a grievous addition in the minds of maritime nations that their dead should by mischance lie weltering in the ooze. We have that noblest of laments by Propertius, giving poignant utterance to this feeling in words full of the complaint and roar of the sea:

"And now thou hast the whole Carpathian Sea for a grave."

Men whose labours are in the deep abhor its vastness for a sepulchre, whether it be in the great South Seas or within sight of the lights of home.

So new "sweeps" had to be prepared for dragging the Loch when they discovered the bow of the *Sudden Jerk* pointing skyward among the rocks—a lonely, pathetic memorial to the drowned. The old "sweeps," the property of the town, had last been seen in the sailmaker's loft. Some said they had been sent to Ardmarkie when a fishing-skiff had sunk there in the first of the great gales which arose after the plague ship had come. Brieston was prepared to have new "sweeps" made at the public cost when, contrary to expectation, Gillespie sent the hanks of rope, the twine, and the hooks to the Good Templars' Hall, where the fishermen had gathered.

"Boat an' son lost; the birch is on his back," it was said, when Sandy the Fox deposited the material in the Hall.

Eoghan could not endure the house, which had suddenly become too big. The sight of his brother's clothes in their room was intolerable, and he heard his mother weeping in the kitchen. The shop was closed; every one was idle; a cloud of inertness lay on the town. Stocks and stones and living beings gazed dumbly upon each other. He crept to the Good Templars' Hall, which he found half full of men scattered over the forms. Each man had a pile of gleaming hooks at his side. Old Sandy was teaching a younger fisherman how the thing was done.

"Put a clove hitch on't—see, like that." The old man twisted the thin twine at one end twice round the index finger, ran the other end through the double loop thus made, placed the ends of three hooks together, inserted these ends within the loops, tightened the loops upon the butt of the triple hook by pulling the end of the twine, and then wound a thinner piece of string tightly along the diminutive grappling anchor thus made. To this anchor of hooks a yard of string was attached, and hundreds of these so constructed were fastened, each by this yard of string, to a long, stout back-rope at intervals of about half a fathom. With this apparatus the bed of the Loch was to be swept. As Eoghan watched, the glittering hooks became like snakes. They would find Iain; would sink into his face, tear out his eyes . . . Dizziness came over him; the Hall and its figures grew blurred. He felt himself about to fall, and groping to a form sank down on it. He saw his father walking about among the men, his face drawn and haggard. Not wishing to be seen by Gillespie he swayed upon his feet and stole out. He saw the blinds drawn in the shop in the Square and in the house. Harbour Street was empty save for a large black dog, which lay with its head on its paws and its amber eyes fixed on the door of the Hall, and further along towards the Square the town scavenger with his barrow. He shuddered at the bleak aspect, and mechanically turned in the direction of the "Ghost." On the Pier Road people passed him with pitying glances. A woman dressed in furs and carrying a small paper parcel halted and spoke to him. He cast a forlorn look at her and hurried on. He passed the "Ghost" with bent head, hoping he was unnoticed. In that hour of bitterness he could not face his grandfather, who he knew would be sitting on the chair against the bed, his elbows on his knees, reading the Bible. At the end of the shore-road, a little beyond the guns, he climbed a fence that ran down into the sea, and stumbled along among boulders and bracken. A long grey foreland rested upon the sea in front of him like a gigantic whale asleep. He climbed out of the valley of bracken up the face of the foreland. The same benumbed calmness now possessed him, as he was about to gain the ridge, which he had experienced last night when talking to his father. He knew what the shore held beyond that ridge. Presently he was on the top, and below him saw the thing —a sharp bow projecting over a rock, tilted upwards and pointing straight at him. A piece of rope hung over the bow and swayed in the breeze. The thin foremast, displaced by the shock, leaned away with a deep rake from the bow, as if in dissension with that part of the ship which had led it to this death-trap. The only thing of man's handiwork on that long grey shore, it looked, in its battered blackness, full of profound pathos—melancholy, solitary, empty, dead. Eoghan gazed down in awe. The sinister calm which is in the heart of a cyclone possessed him. He had passed beyond tears to unutterable pain. The emptiness of the broken boat, the silence of the sea, piled upon him a world-weight of heartache. Like a blind man he groped down the hill-side. Above the shore the russet hazel wood was thick with nuts, through which glanced the streak of a squirrel. With a rush the

312

memory came upon him of their last visit to a hazel wood, and the ominous prophecy of the spey-wife. He stood on the edge of the water and peered out beyond the broken thing on the rocks into the blue-black depths, profound, silent, oily.

"Down there, down there," he groaned.

The water had a silky movement, a lazy, noiseless motion; its dark, blind, restless face looked up at him ironically. There was something insatiable in its depths, inscrutable in its calm, stealthy and padding as a beast coming out of a wood in its gluck upon the rocks. It watched him with fixed, glassy eye—an eye void of intellect and passion, but baleful, hard, and cold. Beneath the eye it was a long, black, polished wall down which men slipped—the Lazaruses of the sea. He looked abroad upon the flat, unwinking face of the deep with growing terror. He recalled his old fear of it as a boy—fear of its eyes of fire—terrible eyes that watched and waited for him. A chill struck upon his heart. The silence around him had become monstrous. It lay like a great dark-green wing against the face of the hill. Menace was materialising. The naked rocks jutting out of the heather had a savage look. He was in the presence of loneliness, in the presence of death animated by terror. The sea became glassy like the eyes of the dead, and fearful as if such eyes were to wink. The silence was now a material thing—shutters of iron pressing in upon his brain. He turned sharply and saw a face of horror upon the wood. It, too, was full of eyes watching him. Menace surrounded him— eyes in the forest and nemesis in the sea. He heard his heart beat loudly in the stillness. A gull flapped past with a carrion stroke of its wings, accentuating the blasting solitude. The smoke of the haven drifting up across the foreland seemed far-off and homely. One of these surges of the ground swell that roll in on the calmest days struck the shore, and the broken boat made a harsh, grinding noise. It reminded him of the sinister power of the sea. Fear gripped him. He was chained to the spot, listening to his beating heart. The wood was listening in all its blood-red leaves as with a million ears, till on his last heart-beat it would toss its branches aloft in fiendish glee; and the sea was watching with its cold, merciless eyes. With a mighty effort he wrenched himself as by the roots from the spot and fled towards the foreland. A thing invisible in the wood jeered behind his back. He swerved up towards the hills, fighting his way through man-high bracken. The trees cut off his route, and he plunged down towards the

313

shore, determined to crawl across the sloping snout of the foreland, which was his shortest way. His right side was red-hot with pain. Twice he slipped on the smooth stone as he crossed it, and his teeth clicked together as he heard the gurgle of the black water in the caves below. Its sullen plunge was the knocking of the Angel of Death at the door of his life. He lay face downwards on the sloping rock, his nails dug into its cracks and wrinkles, and with eyes averted from the sea crawled across the gigantic stone nose. The ground was more open here; in a few minutes he was across the valley and over the fence, and flung himself down on a grassy plateau above the guns. His body was quivering from head to foot like a doll that is danced on springs. He buried his face in the cool turf, drank in deep draughts of the fragrance of the soil, and his panic oozed out of him into the profound breast of mother earth. Ah! if he could but have sunk into her vast bosom then, deep in the place of forgetfulness and rest, and taken upon him the dreamless sleep of the ages. . . . When he raised his head he saw, across the old Crimea cannon and the low, flat roofs of the powder magazines, his grandfather standing at the door of the "Ghost" gazing out upon the Loch. Above the old man's head the inn sign gently stirred in the sea-wind. It was like a leaf of autumn swaying and about to fall. Then he thought it a moribund hand beckoning to him from the rigging of a house of mourning and calamity.

They worked till the light failed in the Hall, speaking of the dead with commiseration. Whatever Gillespie was, his son had been a staunch comrade, a quiet fellow, jolly at times, without pride, and it was noted always with a special word for the old people. They mourned his untimely death, and rejoiced that they were privileged to labour a little in order to do him the last service. The rain was upon the roof at dusk when Mr. Maurice, who was still in Brieston, entered the Hall and inquired for Gillespie. The two entered into close conversation. Presently Mr. Maurice walked down to the front of the Hall, faced the men and uncovered. The wind was rising in sudden gusts which drove the rain in showering cascades on the windows. The men followed the example of the minister, took off their caps, rose, and bowed their heads. "Remember them, O Lord, that go down to the sea in ships." The beating rain drowned his voice, and fragments only were heard " . . . that are swallowed up to await the restitu-

314

tion of all things. . . . Thy way is in the sea, Thy path in the great waters. . . . O Lord God, have pity when there is a noise of a cry from the fish-gate, and the thresholds are desolate for the sorrow that is in the sea . . . unto Thee at whose face the waters are afraid, till there shall be no more sea . . . unto Thee who art the Resurrection and the Life for ever and ever. Amen."

At the Amen old Sandy lifted his white head and face to the ceiling, and his solemn petition rang out in a lull of the wind to every corner of the Hall. "May Goäd Almighty make the morrow calm."

Without, a dry moon was lying on her back—a sign, said the old men, of good weather.

9

HER mistress had lost her head, and kept on saying, "Thank God it's no' Eoghan." Janet had managed to soothe her, as if she were a child, when she started up, exclaiming:

"Oh, Janet! Janet! I wish the Almighty would burn up the sea." Topsail was amazed at any one thinking the sea could burn. Then the secret of her mistress's fear was revealed.

"He'll put poor Eoghan into the boats, an' he'll be drowned next." A great deep sigh burst from the pale lips. Her eyes stared mechanically like the fixed glass eyes of a doll.

"There! there! dinna tak' on noo; we'll no' allow Eoghan into the boats; he's goin' to the Coallege."

Her mistress wiped her eyes and made a gesture of despair. "I wish He would burn it to the bone. I mind when Eoghan was a boy he was scared o' the sea." A troubled look came into her eyes; her head fell slackly on the back of the chair.

"Come an' lie doon a wee whilie." Topsail took her arm and oxtered her to bed.

Topsail returned to the kitchen, and as she laid the table for breakfast there was a hunted expression in her eyes. "Och! och! the sea! that weary sea!" She shook her fist in the direction of the Harbour. The astringency and callousness of the sea had indeed invaded the house of Gillespie.

He looked crumpled as he sat at the table. His hair, now shot with silver, had wasted away from the high forehead. In that hour he looked old. The silence of the meal was broken only by the canaries' crack, crackling of their seed. He had transferred the birds from the shop because they had attracted mice. Eoghan came in, dressed in a jersey and a black silk muffler round his neck.

Gillespie looked up. Eoghan remarked that his father's face had a wilted appearance. "Are ye for the sweeps?" he asked.

"Yes."

Gillespie lapsed into silence.

"Och! no! it's no' the place for you," coaxed Topsail, alarmed at the effect this would have on her mistress. "Was it no' enough for poor Iain to be at the sea? Many a sore trial he had on thae weary boats——"

"Hold your tongue, wumman," Gillespie snarled.

"Och! then just bide at hame," she wheedled.

"You fool! they'll never find Iain without me."

Topsail smiled, as if the insult were a blandishment.

Gillespie gloomed upon his son with a hint of fear in his eyes. He opened his mouth to speak, closed it without saying anything, and went on with his breakfast.

"Is my mother not up yet?" Eoghan fixed Topsail with a sharp glance.

"She never slept a wink a' nicht, an' has been vomitin' a' mornin'."

Gillespie's chair scrunched on the floor. He rose sharply to his feet.

"Did the spey-wife tell ye thon?"

"What?"

"That ye'd find Iain."

The peculiar sensation again affected Eoghan as of speaking out of a dream. He felt impassive, immune from either sorrow or fear, and his answer came as from an oracle.

"She said one would be drowned, and would be found by the other."

Gillespie contemplated him gloomily. "Old wife's noänsense," he muttered.

"It's prophecy." Eoghan felt detached from the world; a voice that was not of him was speaking; he was in an environment half familiar, half strange. He was listening again to a tale of his grandfather's; but it was not his grandfather's voice; it was a dim, ancestral voice. The wind of ancient days shook his soul, and a spirit of remote times passed upon him.

"It's prophecy; always has been prophecy; a prophecy of doom upon our house; a curse that shall never be removed till murder is done; the hands of the son shall be in the blood of his parents."

He was drawing slowly, then more swiftly out of a vague immensity, hurrying at frightful velocity out of a realm of shadows. He was dimly aware that in a moment he would awaken from this hallucination. He found himself shivering in the midst of the kitchen floor, with his father's hand on his shoulder. What immediately occurred to him was the simple thought that his father since childhood had never touched his person. He heard his father's voice full of sorrow:

"Are ye sleep-walkin', Eoghan?"

He shook himself slightly. "I think I was in a trance," he said, with a puzzled look. He became afraid as he went slowly down the stair—afraid because he had seen fear for a moment pass into his father's eyes.

In a stupor he took his place in one of the boats. There were seven in all to work the "sweeps." He was on the instant of saying, "This is the boat that will find the body," but checked himself. What had he said to terrify his father? He groped for the dim, elusive words. Their meaning hovered a moment on the confines of memory and then vanished, leaving him baffled. Why was he here, impelled by a power not himself? If he had refused to come they would have discovered Iain without his help. Perhaps, on the other hand, they would never find the body.

Fragments of the conversation in the boat impinged upon his consciousness; but conveyed no meaning:

"Poor Iain has got the auld grey nurse to rock him asleep. He was the dacent quiet fellow . . . ay, but Eoghan's her he'rt laddie; she'd lay her hair about his feet . . . It must hev been a cruel night, boys. There was an eclipse o' the sun an' new moon the same day. I don't wonder wi' thae eclipses at folk gettin' drooned . . . it's butivul weather." He was now aware that some one was addressing him, and roused himself. It was old Sandy. The varnished skiffs ahead of him flashed in the sun. Over the villas on the Pier Road blue smoke hung like foliage in the air; the bells of milk carts, taught of Gillespie, were ringing blithely in Brieston, and cocks shrilled lustily all round the horse-shoe Harbour, proclaiming the blandness of the morning. A barque, two-masted, with every sail set, was floating out tall and stately on the tide, as if mermaids' hands were pulling her from beneath. Quiet fish were leaping inshore where the blue shoaled to green; ducks paddled around like floating masses of snow; a multitude of birds sang among the bushes.

As they cleared the outer Harbour to the rhythmic sweep of the oars there opened up a distant clear and blue prospect. The morning was faintly misty, and the sunlight quivered through a shimmering veil. Blue promontory, lazy curving bight, the sweep of bays, flashing beaches, a panorama of forest, bracken, and grey lichened rock filled the eye with tranquil aspect. The shadows of rocks and trees hung motionless in the water, and one could scarce discern where shore ended and sea began. About the solemn fleet of boats with barked sails reddened in the light the sea was soiled with the scum and tangle that appear after a gale.

They drifted south, and the men, touched to taciturnity and vague melancholy by their traffic on lonely waters, were unusually silent, because of the solemnity with which their mission was fraught. The shadows of gulls flitted over the rocks; other shadows trembled in the shore-shallows, and looked like faint waves. A dolphin's razor back cut through the surface of the water; and far off on the empty southern horizon stood up the sail of an invisible boat—an aimless, solitary thing blown out to sea. Beyond it a cloud of snowflakes drifted seaward. It was a great flight of solan geese glittering in the sun.

They rounded the foreland across which Eoghan had crawled, and an imposing spectacle met their gaze. In the soft light all things looked far away, floating up out of a dream country. In the south-east sky bars of purple were changing rapidly to violet, to pink, to cinnabar; here and there were nooks of delicate sea-shell tints and traceries of gold. In the deepest sky was a fret-work of flame, which changed to cloud cataracts of golden fire. Stark against those swaying, gorgeous sky-flowers was the black mast of the broken ship, pricked out in unrelieved desolation, and the bow rearing up impotent and sombre against the magic and splendour of multitudinous pools and lines of fire. She was bathed in a baptism of flame, heeling into the long dream-glory of the lingering morning. The southern isles swam up in mirage into the atmosphere, and became diaphanous

318

apparitions in the midst of vast sea-spaces—cloud-crowned islands floating in light, transient and melting as in a thoroughfare of sea-dreams. "Boys, it bates a' the artists"—old Sandy's face quickened as he gazed on the spectacle of ineffable beauty. Eoghan raised his head and looked across the gunwale. In the heart of the glowing sky pain was seated. Pathos and poignancy rested upon that elusive vanishing glory. It was full of sadness, this ethereal tapestry of light, woven of angels' jewelled hands, and spread by them over the dead in his cold, dark grave. Eoghan groaned within himself. This splendour mocked him with its irony; its beauty made him faint with heartache. Cold, passionless, terrible painting! The bars of gold across the sky lay upon his soul in that moment as metals heated in a furnace.

The boats were now strung out in a long line and the "sweeps" let down into the sea. Each boat was attached by a sixty-fathom line to the long back-rope, from which hung the grappling hooks. They began to row, trailing the "sweeps." Now and again a man shouted; the line was drawn in; the back-rope appeared; and beneath, attached to the hooks, a mass of tangle, which was torn off the "sweeps" sunk once more. Once a dog-fish was hooked. Eoghan shuddered as he saw the grey serpent fish wriggling in the water, with its baleful pale-blue eyes fixed upon him full of malice. The faces of the men were channelled with sweat. Some one in the fourth boat off shouted, "It's no' seaweed this time!" The men in this boat began hauling gently. A bald head shot above the water. The sun struck on it, glittering on its wetness. Immediately on the next grappling a dark shoulder surged through the water, as if the man were swimming. These were the bodies of the engineer and the deck-hand, who had gone down together.

Again the work of mercy went on. The men in Eoghan's boat discussed the drift of the tides, the probable position of the body, its chances of being wedged in among boulders. Eoghan all this time was gazing intently into the face of the sea, as if he could divine the secrets which lurked in its smiling face. His mind was far from the reality of the present. He was picturing Iain alive. He saw his white teeth flashing beneath his moustache; saw him cock his head with a characteristic gesture; heard his slow, measured speech. The face grew beneath him out of the water, mysterious, twilit, strong with life. The mouth was about to speak to him; the eyes swam mistily with all their old tenderness;

the laugh, scarce more than a smile, that always got home to his heart—the low laugh of pride on the day when Eoghan had carried a silver medal home from school.

"You're a brick; you're small, youngster, but the medal's bright." That was all; but it was a world. He could hear the words now, as he beheld that dear lost face gazing up sorrowfully from the salt grey waves. It was full of that solicitude which he had discovered in it on that windy dawn when he had sent him below from the bridge. Dimly in his sleep he knew some one was covering him in the bunk with a horse-blanket—some one who, in the broad morning as he was preparing to go aboard the skiff that was to bring him home, said, "You quit the sea, youngster, an' stick to your books"—there was a world of regret in these words—"for once she gets you she keeps you till the end." Till the end!

He laid his hand with startling suddenness on the heaving line. "Iain's here!" he said. Again he was speaking out of a dreamland words not his own.

"Easy there, boys!" old Sandy shouted.

Eoghan was hauling on the line. "She keeps you till the end" was echoing in his brain. An opaque face in the grey water was looking up at him piteously. He was making swallowing sounds in his throat. Oh, face swimming up in the salt sea!

"Easy aft! easy aft!"

The wet face slid into darkness as the strain on the back-rope from the other boats was relaxed. "Pull a touch!" rang out the command with strained intensity. Old Sandy was about to take the line from Eoghan's hand when the expression on the lad's face stayed him. Out of the dreamland beyond Time and Space that face was growing again into his vision—the mouth was slackly gaping; wavelets playing over the forehead and stirring the thick dark hair; the eyes utterly dead, their light quenched, their smile gone. They had a strange callous stare; they looked like balls of granite, on which the brine streamed like tears. The flesh was sodden and of a greenish-yellow. An arm clothed in rags was piteously stretched out to him.

"Iain! Iain!" he whispered, and leaning down over the gunwale put his hands beneath the head. It gently swam up to him, as if suddenly alive at his touch.

"Oh, Iain! Iain!" The piercing cry was heard in all the boats. "Easy there!" yelled old Sandy angrily; "don't lift the heid oot o' the watter." From old experience he knew that the head might come away from the trunk. Eoghan did not hear him. He slipped his arm around the shoulders, embracing the body and sobbing, "Come home! come home, Iain!" The shoulders lurched up; he leaned far over the gunwale, drew the face upwards and placed his mouth on the clammy lips, on the moustache, on the brow. Old Sandy deftly slipped the bight of a rope beneath the shoulders, and to disengage Eoghan put the end of the rope into his hands. Other ropes were slipped down to the middle, the thighs, the feet. The nearest boat came up and closed in on the other side. In the quadruple sling they lifted the dripping body out of the water, tenderly as if it were gossamer. The broken leg hung limply. Old Sandy nodded to the men in the other boat, then glanced at Eoghan. They lifted the body into this boat, which drew apart.

Eoghan sat in the bow, his eyes fixed on the boat ahead, seeing the dripping face that lay now covered with a jib. The world was full of light, and a very little was denied those eyes. Nothing will restore to them their smile. He closed his own eyes wearily. "I shall never, never hear him speak again," he thought, and cried out:

"Oh, Sandy! Sandy! I wish I were dead."

"Ay," answered the old man, looking sadly up to the hills; "but He doesna tek' us when we want." The little ball of wool on the top of his round bonnet nodded ludicrously. "He keeps us to thole an' to learn." There was a profound look of sorrow on his wrinkled, sea-tanned face.

Within the hour they found the cook. Of all the crew the seaboy was the only one whom the dog-fish had touched—Andy Rodgers's son, and his mother was a widow. "An ill day for Andy an' his faimly that they ever saw Gillespa'," muttered Ned o' the Horn, as he covered the boy's mangled face.

The boats went home in a silent, funereal procession through a faint mist. Off the "Ghost" Eoghan asked the men to bring Iain's body ashore there. Four of them bore it in a sail to the house. Fog had gathered thick from seaward. Eoghan followed behind with drooping head. Old Strang stood beneath the sign over the door awaiting them. He lifted his feet heavily on the stone flags, going in before them, and with shaking hands placed chairs in the midst of the kitchen floor. There they laid the body, and tenderly himself the old man set straight the broken limb which was lying awry. When all was finished he contemplated the upturned face.

"More than a son to me," came the mournful words. He swayed like a flower in a gale. "God kens it was hard enough wi' the oar in his hand a' nicht; but he didna compleen; no, he didna compleen. I'll no' be lang after him. The kirkyaird 'll be hoose an' hame to me noo. I'm but leevin' on borrowed ground. But the Lord has been kind to me thae weary years wi' Iain. Thank the Lord for His lovingkindness." The swaying of the body ceased. It became rigid. The silence was broken by the drip, drip of water on the stone flags.

"I'm a broken auld man, an' my son herrit my hoose; but that's noathin'; I'm a forlorn object." The sorrowing tones pierced the hearts of the listeners.

"Dinna tek' on, Dick," old Sandy said pityingly.

Mr. Strang lifted his gaze from the dead; his withered eyes were searching around for the one who spoke.

"No! no!" he cried, making a gesture with his hands. "I'm no' fashin'; what for wad an auld man wi' a rookit hoose be fashin'? .... There was a day when I could sing a ballat; but no' noo; no' noo. . . . I wish I might be beggin' at Gillespie's düre wi' my bare heid in the rain than that this had come aboot. . . . A broken leg forby! . . . He was as bricht as the lown morn when he played his flute at the fire-en'! . . . Am I no' the fair object? . . . noathin' to do but to bring him to mind." He was now unconscious of his audience. "Iain was his granny's boy. . . . 'It's growin' dark, Richard,' she said to me; 'are the blinds doon?' but the blinds werena doon, an' the lamp was burnin'; 'then I'm goin' fast.' . . . It's growin' dark—growin' dark." He sat down heavily on the single chair at the bed, and buried his face in his hands.

Without in the fog the sign had ceased from its strangling cry. The half-obliterated face of the man holding the dagger looked down as if brooding upon the fate of the house of Strang, and the sign was at rest. Death had brought it reverie and peace. Out of the illimitable grey on the Loch came the boom of a steamer's siren. It wandered away in the vast, as if with wings growing feebler in the baffling gloom, a wailing phantom seeking a lost land of holy quiet. It was answered by the mournful croak of a heron somewhere on the shore below Muirhead Farm. Eoghan was at the door. He had started out to seek Mary Bunch or another who would minister to the dead. As the wailing cry

on the opposite shore died away, and the heavy blanketin
silence closed down again, his eyes strained to seaward, and ou
of the far land of dreams beyond the fog and the sorrow of th
sea, beyond the weariness of watching woods and demon forest
and little sea-towns besieged by the melancholy of waves, an
mournful with the noise of rains, a drift-music like soft bell;
invincible, balmy, dividing asunder the joints and marrov
reached him.

> "They are all at rest,
> They are all at rest,
> Far over that summer sea."

BOOK IV

1

Rob's daughter was coming. The news moved Eoghan deeply. How well he remembered Rob when every winter that hero put in at Brieston in a large two-masted smack which had come from "the North"—a land of enchantment, where for many months he had cured herring for a salesman in the Glasgow Fish Market, and on the way home touched at Brieston. When the Strang family had broken up in Ayrshire his grandfather's brother had shipped before the mast in a Cape Horner, leaving his wife and two young children in Ayr. Three times he came back like a resurrected man from the great South Seas, the last time clothed in a blanket, having been robbed and plundered in the Vennel at Greenock. Once more he shipped, and old Mr. Strang thought him buried somewhere behind the Great Barrier Reef, this luckless Archie. Of his family one, a girl, was married, and kept a fruiterer's shop in Port Glasgow. The other was Rob. Just as sure as the sun would rise would a cran basket full of unused provisions be brought by two of the smack's crew to the "Ghost." Eoghan remembered that among other things it would contain ketchup, which was never on Gillespie's table, and just as sure also would the basket be followed by Rob. His grandfather would be restless all evening, going frequently to the front door to peer up the road to the wharf; then return to his Bible or to patching his clothes, and when the door would at last open he was on his feet saying, "I got the proveesions, Rob," and Rob would laugh with flashing teeth and "How are ye, Richard?" he would cry. He had such big white teeth, and a light golden beard and blue eyes filled with liquid laughter. Then he would sit down on a chair at the bed—it was always the same chair—and in a minute they were deep in conversation about the North fishing. How the strange names rang in Eoghan's ears like a song—Kylleakin, Loch Broom, Loch Hourn, Stornoway; and Rob's teeth flashing bare to the gums and his blue eyes dancing madly in his head. Up and up he would hitch his trousers, till their folds were almost at his knees.

"And how's Gillespie?" he would cry; "makin' money as usual?" and would not wait till the old man gave an answer. It was long afterwards that Eoghan wondered how so hearty a fellow as Rob could be so delicate as to save the old man from replying.

About nine o'clock Rob would take out of his pocket a bottle which came all the way from Skye, and stamping his trousers back over his ankles he would leave it on the table, shake hands with the old man, and say as he was going out of the door, "The boys 'll leave you the herrin' the morn"—a barrel of cured herring specially pickled by Rob.

On the morrow he was gone, trailing the savour of his wondrous Northland, and leaving his gifts and ketchup behind. Only once did he take particular notice of Eoghan, who was seated with the back of his chair against the press door beneath the wag-at-the-wa', at the little round mahogany table, working at mathematics.

"Hullo!" he cried, "what's the professor doin'?" and he looked over Eoghan's shrinking shoulder.

"Algebra," Eoghan answered shyly.

"Algebra! your faither could beat us a' at the coontin'. You'll have your faither's heid for arithmetic."

"He's goin' to be a scholar," said the old man; "but his faither 'll no' gie him money for books."

Eoghan felt humiliated, and his face became crimson.

"I'll no' see him bate, Richard;" and Eoghan saw a big, shining half-crown lying in the midst of his hot palm. He could not look up at Rob for the shame and the wild joy that was in him; but gulped over his book and clenched the coin till it burned his palm.

All that evening he watched Rob, furtively stealing hungry glances at his sea-tanned face. He was unable to understand this being who tossed half-crowns to boys to buy books, and forget it all the next moment. He belonged to another world—the enchanted land of Skye and the North. He could have fallen down and worshipped this hero. And the years passed and Rob came no more.

"Is Rob no' comin' back from the North any more, grandfaither?"

"No more."

The dark, massive head dropped on the frail hands.

Eoghan's heart stood still with sudden fear as in a flash he guessed. The tears rushed into his eyes.

"Grandfather, is Rob dead?"

"No more; no more," was the answer.

Deep, dim, and lost for ever within the enchanted land beyond the magic of Loch Hourn and the wondrous Isle of Skye lay Rob, the big, cheery laugh stilled for ever in a land of far distances. Rob had been snatched away by some envious power. No more the two tapering masts and the tall smack filling the Harbour. The world was blank and grey. It was Eoghan's second loss.

And now his daughter was coming.

"Is she to stay long, grandfather?"

"She's no' goin' back. Och! och! this is a gurt empty hoose since Iain was drooned." After a moment's silence he added, "We'll be kind to the lassie."

"Ay, grandfather." He wished Rob could hear him, now a man grown, vowing defence and protection of his girl—ah, that the gallant could hear him! but the deep, silent North was shrouded in the twilight of eternal sleep, and Rob lay on the shining sands where only the seals come.

After Iain's burial Mrs. Strang began to lose strength, and Topsail Janet could hear, mingled with her coughing in the night, the boom of Gillespie's grumbling that his sleep was being broken. Topsail was deceived in the spots of red which burned on the cheek-bones of her mistress. She simply thought they made her look very young, while her eyes shone brightly. Maclean recommended a change, to which Gillespie agreed for reasons of his own. Through the chatter of his household he had picked up the information that Barbara, Rob's daughter, was expected at the "Ghost." He knew that Rob had had considerable property in Dunoon, and had no doubt that his own father was constituted the girl's guardian. The business of getting into touch with her had exercised him for some days, and he now instructed his wife that she must go for a change to Dunoon and form acquaintance with Barbara. Topsail was up before daybreak preparing the clothes of her mistress. Her feet could be heard crinkling through the leaves in the back green at dawn. Gillespie gave his wife five pounds, and Topsail added many injunctions—

that she was to put on her goloshes; to be sure and remember her toddy before going to bed—one teaspoonful of sugar; to take good charge of her umbrella; and God forgive her if she would allow herself to get run over with horses in the big streets. "Hurry back; good-bye, good-bye." Topsail hastened to the parlour window, watched the ascent of her mistress into the 'bus at the "George Hotel," and stood waving a duster as the 'bus racketed down Harbour Street and vanished beyond the police station at the Quay.

The afternoon wore on long as a December night. Eoghan spent most of his time at the "Ghost." The house was singularly dreary and still as the grave. Topsail heard all the clocks ticking. "Weary fa' that Dunoon," she muttered for the twentieth time that evening, and lay awake all night. At dawn she stripped the kitchen, and at breakfast-time Gillespie found chaos, in the midst of which Topsail abated the fever of her mind by standing on the top of a table, with a towel wrapped about her head, and whitewashing the ceiling.

"Ye're thrang," observed Gillespie.

Yes, she was sweeping away the cobwebs when the chance offered. Gillespie, plunged in thought, now and again eyed Topsail, whose face was speckled with whitewash and ochre. She demanded that the canaries be taken back to the shop.

When Gillespie came in that evening at nine o'clock the kitchen shone like a star. Topsail proposed to redd out the parlour to-morrow, and dreamt that night of rescuing her mistress from the feet of horses, which she beat off with a whitewash brush.

In the morning Gillespie had important news for her. Her mistress had sent him a telegram which Topsail eagerly scanned.

"Ay," she nodded briskly, "I ken her hand o' write."

Gillespie, who did not trouble himself to rectify this mistake, announced that her mistress and Barbara were returning home.

Topsail was overjoyed at this news. "What wad she dae in yon gurt toon, sweemin' lik' a cuddie among a' thae folk? I kenna what's comin' ower the doctor sendin' her away frae the caller air amang coomb an' reek." Maclean had suffered a loss of prestige in her eyes. Gillespie, however, had something of moment to tell her. In his hand he held a letter, the product of long and anxious consideration. He had determined to act as Barbara's guardian, hoping that the signature Strang would be sufficient for the girl who, ignorant of the relations of father and son, would not differentiate between the signature Richard Strang and Gillespie Strang. The thing would come out, of course, when the girl reached Brieston; but by that time the affair would be on the road to completion, and Gillespie would then point out that his father was too old to undertake the duties of trustee. Gillespie chiefly reckoned on the first step, concerning which he had written a letter, and which if carried out would put the reins in his hands. He had thought at first of posting the letter; but two reasons weighed against this course—if he dispatched it by the hand of the family servant it would carry more weight, and the post was uncertain, for they might leave Dunoon at any time. He had come to the determination of disposing of Barbara's property in Dunoon. He had heard that a steamer which was something of a white elephant to the owners was to be put on the market. Her boiler had blown out once or twice and was leaking; freights were low; the debt on the steamer amounted now almost to as much as she was worth; the owner would be glad to be rid of her. Gillespie knew she would be a profitable boat for herring-buying, but was now afraid of risks at sea, and chary of sinking his own money in the venture. He would transfer Barbara's capital in property at Dunoon to this new investment, and in the letter would give his father's authority for the step. When the affair came out he reckoned on his father's scrupulousness for the family name to shield him. Besides, he had a right to some such action, for his father had had all the profit out of Iain, and now in Iain's place was obtaining a housekeeper in the person of Barbara. The facts which Barbara had to learn were contained in the letter—that the value of property was depreciating; that feu duty, rates and taxes and the cost of wear and tear were becoming onerous; now that she was leaving Dunoon a factor's percentage would eat away the rents. On all accounts it would be better to sell the property on the basis of a twenty years' purchase. This was the usual thing, and would bring in about a thousand pounds, which would be invested in a more advantageous way in Brieston. He impressed on the girl the importance of mastering these details and laying them before the lawyer who was to conduct the case. "Thae lawyers are a set of tinklers," he wrote. In point of fact he furnished these technicalities to divert any suspicion which the lawyer might entertain; but on second thoughts he would send out his own lawyer—a step that would save her trouble and expense. "Your father spoke to me more than once

as regards this, and my own father at the 'Ghost' gave me orders
to write to ye, as he is too old for a pen, and I think it is best for
all concerned. Your own father thought this a needcessity, and
it is not convenient for you to have that property in Dunoon when
you will be in Brieston. Topsail Janet will meet ye in Dunoon
and give ye this letter, and you can tell Mr. McAskill the lawyer
that he can be looking out for a good buyer with *ready money*"—
the last two words were underlined. "We are all enjoying good
health, hopping this will find you all enjoying the same Blessing.
My father joins me in saying we will do our best for you, in-
vesting your money and settling your affairs. If you will take
my advice settle it at once and don't delay. Hopping this will
find you well,

Your affectionate friend,
"G. Strang."

There was no express reference to his wife in the communication.

"Topsail," he said; "ye hevna had a holiday since ye cam' into
my service."

"Are ye for puttin' me away, Gillespie?" She stood like a
child, looking down at her raw red hands, waiting for the word
which would cast her into the street. She knew Gillespie's suave
way of stabbing people, and was not so unsophisticated as to
believe that he gave gifts of holidays. Ah! little shop, old sacred
spot, thou wert a roof indeed now; but a shoemaker sits there
driving sparables. She had revisited that shrine once, with boots
to be mended. It was dingy and stank of leather. Where could she
go? Jeck the Traiveller. No, she would not be unfaithful to the
plumber. Her mind became a grey blank.

"Hae ye the toothache, Janet?"

Cruel jester! she wished she was beside the plumber beneath
the sod.

"I've nae toothache."

"What ails ye, then?"

"I hae neither freen' nor hame to gang to."

"Never mind freend or hame; ye'll gang to Dunoon the morn
for a bit jaunt."

She suddenly swam out of the deep of one emotion into a
greater.

"Oh, I was never on a jaunt a' my days! I. don't ken the wy."
The earth was being torn up from its settled foundations.

"The wy's easy enough; ye'll tak' the steamer the morn."

"No! no!" She wrung her hands. "An auld roosty craw lik' me. What'll become o' the hoose?"

"Huts! the hoose 'ill no' gang oot on the tide for a day." Gillespie, tolerant so far, now proceeded briskly to instruct Topsail.

"Ye'll tak' the steamer the morn an' gang to Dunoon wi' her; dae ye unnerstan'?" He spoke slowly, as teaching a lesson.

"Ay! ay!" she answered out of a nightmare.

"Here, then, tak' this." He handed her the letter and a slip of paper. On the slip of paper was written:

"Barbara Strang,
27 Clyde Street."

"Show the bit paper to the man at the Pier an' ax him to direct ye to this hoose"—he tapped the paper with his forefinger—"an' when ye win there gie this letter"—another tap with the forefinger—"to Barbara."

"Are ye fo-ollowin' me?"

He repeated his instruction *da capo*. "There, noo; dae ye understan'?"

"Am I to be in Dunoon wi' the mistress?"

"Ye are," answered this strange maker of gorgeous events.

Topsail's face was suffused with joy. She was about to embark for the Hesperides or the Morning Star.

Though the hour of the steamer's departure was two o'clock she, after a sleepless night, was up betimes, for there was a thing which troubled her, concerning which she wished to consult Gillespie. At seven o'clock she sat at the parlour window in her bonnet, wearing black cotton gloves and tenaciously gripping a heavy umbrella, to which Gillespie was wont to attach himself when he honoured the dead by attending their obsequies. She had polished her square-toed boots by candle-light. The last time she had worn them was when she had ventured to church. She watched the light steal upon a Harbour grey as glass; heard on the Quay-road pattering footsteps, and saw the baker appear with the collar of his jacket up to his ears. This melancholy man had always a foreboding that at such a still hour of drawn blinds there was no money in the town, and all labour of man was vain. He vanished with hanging head in a close-mouth. A yellow dog

330

trotted across the Square and Topsail, vaguely wondering to whom the dog belonged, sighed:

"It's gey an' gled I'll be this nicht for a sicht o' the beast." She turned away from the fires of dawn in the Harbour mouth, and the morning acclamation of sea-fowl on the skerries and on the net-poles. The adventure was becoming terribly imminent. She stripped off her finery, for she had overlooked breakfast; but forgot her bonnet, on which dust settled in grey clouds as she raked out the ashes in the grate.

At breakfast she feared to broach her trouble to Gillespie, and in the interval to the one o'clock dinner wandered from room to room with a blanched face, and her eyes constantly riveted upon the clock. At dinner she could eat nothing.

"What ails ye, wumman?" Gillespie asked, in a far-off voice.

"Och! och! dinna fash me; this is the greatest trial since the plumber died. My inside feels fou o' wee jaggin' preens."

Gillespie appeared to be deaf.

A pathetic look of defiance came into her eyes. "If I'm gaun to Dunoon"—her voice quavered upon tears—"I'm gaun respectable."

"Eh! wha-at's that ye're sayin'?"

"I'm a dacent weeda wumman." The agonised brooding of a feverish night was out; she swayed a little, feeling faint.

Gillespie looked up critically from among the fish bones.

"Ye're nane sae ill put on," he said, and resumed his steady attack on the boiled cod.

"I tell ye, Gillespie, I'm gaun respectable, wi' my wee black tin box. A'body that's dacent tak's their luggage. Ye're no' gaun to shove me aff to Dunoon lik' a moonlicht flittin' wi' naethin' to my name. If my mither's wee black box doesna go, I'll bide at hame." She was on the verge of tears.

"Hoots! dinna get intae the nerves, wumman."

"Jeck'll be here in a meenut or two"—she glanced at the clock whose dial she could not read—"an' me wi' noathin' for him to cairry; him that's accustomed to the pockmanty's o' the nabbery. Nan at Jock an' Mary Bunch an' Lucky 'll be keekin' doon Mac-Calman's Lane to watch me gang across the Square. 'An' there's she's off,' they'll be sayin', 'off to Dunoon lik' a pookit hen. I'll be fair affrontit." She gasped as if for air.

"Where's your box, wumman?"

"It's ablow the bed up the stair."

"What hev' ye in it?"

"Noathin'," answered Topsail wearily, "but a broken he'rt."

She fled up to the Coffin, and presently returned with the sacred relic, whose empty interior shone like a mirror.

"It's gey toom," sneered Gillespie; "ye'll gang fàst on the road wi' an empty kist." He pushed back his plate and rose to his feet, took some coins from his pocket, counted them, and gave them to Topsail.

"There's twa shullin's an' ninepence; that's the price o' a ticket to Dunoon wi' the steerage; Barbara 'll pey your fare hame." He kicked the tin box, and said jocularly:

"Put in your tooth-brush an' your nicht-dress, Janet; that's what the big fowk cairry."

"I've nane," sighed Topsail, without shame.

Halfway down the stair Gillespie shouted, "It's no' every day ye gang on a jaunt, Janet. Bide a meenut." Gillespie returned, a little brown bag in his hand. "Hae," he cried, "there's a poke o' black strippit balls for your box." Topsail solemnly added this contribution to her treasury. Gillespie completed his instructions and said it was time she took the road. He could not afford her threepence for her 'bus-fare to the Pier. She picked up her box and hastily retreated to the Coffin. She took a battered book off the brace, and reverently laid it within the box. It was her mother's Bible. Then glancing furtively at the door she plunged her hand beneath the mattress, deftly whipped out a half mutch-kin bottle wrapped in brown paper, and laid it beside the Bible.

"Goäd only kens if she got a drap frae the day she left home," she whispered to Gillespie's poke of sweeties and her mother's Bible.

2

ONLY the poor sail from the Quay by luggage steamer, on which you embark leisurely, picking your way among sacks of flour, barrels of herring and the like. Sometimes you slip on the bottle-green causey stones or sprawl over a rope, and away you go like the boys on a slide at the Barracks brae. You tell the fishermen where you are going and why, and joke with the porters—a cosy, easy, old wife. Once aboard with your little tin box you find the crew have leisure to gossip, and so keep at bay all manner of sickness—sea-sickness, home-sickness, and poverty-sickness. They know everything in Brieston, as if they were paid to find out—a surprising thing in men who are always sailing. They tell your astonished face that some one is always coming and going with bits of news.

They are putting cattle on board, whose sterns little boys are flicking with switches. Standing near the Captain in his pilot jacket you are filled with unholy joy to see how difficult it is—the boys are yelling; one of the porters is twisting the tail of the foremost beast, another is dragging it by a rope round its horns; men are belabouring it with sticks towards the gangway. The Captain, very angry, has an enormous silver watch in his hand. The boat will be fearfully late and she may take the ground. His face is very red as he swears and shouts:

"Thresh the coo; twist the bitch's tail; she's as dour as Lonen' himsel'."

What a hubbub of bleating sheep going away to the Low Country for the wintering, barking of collies, bellowing of cattle, yelling of men and boys, and the shopkeepers in their doors in shirt sleeves watching the ploy. The horses are the worst. They stand on their hind legs as if they were at the circus on fair day. There is nothing for it but to put them in a loose-box and swing them aboard. They look so funny snorting up there with terror, their heads against the sky. And there is Kate the Hawker cursing mankind with her Irish brogue because one of the porters, pushing a fast barrow, knocked her down on the top of her crate of hens which she bought in Islay. It is rich sailing from the Quay; but just because the Captain never knows when he can start most people sail from the Pier away down near the "Ghost." It needs a nerve and genteel clothes to take steamer there. The thing is to fly down on the 'bus if you have no carriage of your own, and have Jeck the Traiveller carry your luggage aboard where, in the twinkling of an eye, you are swallowed up in a crowd of strangers. The Captain, high up in a glittering place all alone, would no more think of asking after your health than he would of swearing or smoking or pulling a rope. He speaks to a man standing beside a little brass wheel which you think makes the boat go. And the hands wear collars, and have some writing across their breasts on their jerseys. What an awful crowd!

and you glued in the midst on the deck like a limpet on a rock. They are all gabbing even on and laughing and glowering with spy-glasses at Brieston, and reading books with covers like the covers of the red-skin books you sold long ago. You check a sigh, afraid of its being heard among these people with such fine clothes. The children play around you as if you were a post, and you feel yourself in the way, so that when a skemp in gold and brass buttons comes up and says, "Ticket, please," you wish you could sink through the floor. They have no tickets on the luggage steamer, and are glad to see your half-crown. All trummlin' you take out the little black purse. It was a wedding gift. It is battered; the clasp is broken; it is bound about with thread. Like yourself it is gone far on the way of life; yet you hold it dear as a regiment treasures an old flag. You try to hide its rags; nor are you going to show that inside you have a little photograph of Eoghan taken at the fair, which you carried away from the Coffin for safety, in case the house should go on fire while you are absent. The skemp tells you to walk ever so far down among all those swells to a box where you may buy a ticket. The floor is so clean you are ashamed of your big boots. Every one is staring at you because you have no ticket. You feel hunted, and stand with your fingers in your bonnet-strings. Oh, oh, here he comes again! You know your face is flushed. Shame overwhelms you. The skemp is in front of you, pulling at a little moustache the colour of straw. He offers to lead the way. Does he think you haven't the money? You put up your hand in the black cotton glove as if to keep off a blow and follow him, your eyes on the floor, walking as lightly as possible lest your sparables mark the wood. You bump into a fat lady all spread out with silk, and look up beseechingly into gold specs. How she smiles, as if it were her fault! She must be some princess. You could almost weep for vexation after that as you dodge the folk. Then you have to explain about your ticket; you are going to the mistress and Barbara. The man at the window laughs, and you tell him no more. You have more pride before strangers, Goäd be thankit!

You turn to put the ticket in the black tin box, and suddenly the heavens and the earth become just as black. You have left it behind in your hurry! What a state of nerves you are in as you hurry back, your feet going as fast as your heart, and that goes if anything faster when you find the box is gone—gone with the black-strippit balls, and a new silk hanky Jeck slipped into your

hand, and the wee brown paper parcel, and your mother's Bible.
Her name was on it. The tears are in your eyes, making the
water, that is rushing by like a sea in a dream, and the hills all
blurred. Life has suddenly become cruel; the world very big,
very empty; you wish you could die.

"Hullo, Janet, whither bound?"

You fairly jump at that warm, hearty voice, and your heart
jumps too. It is Nan at Jock's son home again from foreign pairts,
dressed like the best of them, with a collar and white shirt and
smoking a cigar. His face is not white like other folks. He is tall
and thin, and his eyes are looking about as if the boat belonged
to him.

"Oh, Jamie! Jamie!" is all you can say, twittering. The next
moment you are telling him all your trouble. He leads you to a
seat, bids you bide there and is gone, to come back in a minute
with one of the men who have writing on their jerseys. How angry
Jamie is as he speaks to the man! caring not, though you tell him
to wheest, if all the ladies hear. They go off together, and you see
Jamie giving the man a cigar. He comes back carrying the tin
box. How your fingers close round it! and you nurse it on your
knee as once long ago you nursed Eoghan. The hills are pleasant
again; how the children laugh as they breenge about! and only
when Jamie, carrying the box, leads you down a braw big stair
into the longest room you ever saw in your life do you begin to
get afraid once more. Such a sight of mirrors and furniture.
Gillespie's house is nothing to it: it will bate the Laird's castle.
You don't know how it comes about, but a wee man in a white
shirt has placed a cup of tea before you and Jamie. You don't
know yet how you managed to drink it; but it did you a world of
good. Jamie is saying he is giving up going foreign, and has got
a second mate's job on the Clyde shipping, and lucky, too, for
there's as many Skye men looking for jobs as would carry the
ships of Clyde on their shoulders. You don't hear one half he is
saying, for you want to tell him—there it is out—that you are
going on a jaunt to your mistress at Dunoon. But out of pure
vexation you could never have told him had the wee black tin
box been lost.

And when you look at your glove after Jamie has shaken hands
with you at the gangway at Dunoon Pier, you see a big white five-
shilling piece looking up at you like a flower. You turn round to
thank Jamie, but he is gone.

3

SHE stood a forlorn figure on the Pier, with her back to the town,
waving to Jamie. She watched his face growing smaller and
vanishing; watched till his handkerchief vanished also and nothing was left but a gigantic steamer moving beneath a cloud of
smoke. She turned and faced the town, alone on the threshold of
the world.

"What a wecht o' hooses!" she murmured. Lights were springing up along the sea-front in a bewildering blaze as she went up
the Pier, her bonnet nodding cheerfully to Dunoon. She had a
bunched-up appearance in her severe black clothes, and felt
fatigued, and was faint from her long fast. The stony gaze of the
unknown town left her sick at heart. Yet it was a smiling face
which accosted the young lady at the turnstile—a face pathetically small buried in its bonnet.

"Will ye kindly direct me to Barbara's hoose, miss?" Her bonnet bobbed and curtsied.

"Who is Barbara?" The young lady was petulant; her figure
stiff as a tree. It was tea-time, and the last steamer gone for the
day. She was pulling on a glove.

"She's a freen o' Gillespie's. I cam ee noo wi' the boat frae
Brieston."

"I'm afraid I don't know anything about your friend." The
tone was icily polite. "Twopence, please." The young lady
drummed impatiently on the ledge with gloved fingers.

"Gillespie told me they wad direct me at the Quay to Barbara's. I'm to bide there the nicht."

She was coldly, incisively interrupted:

"You have to pay twopence, please."

"Whatna tuppence?"

"To get out."

Light broke in upon Topsail. "Is this a jyle?" she asked.

The young lady reddened. "If you don't pay you will be left
here all night."

"Och! och! ye needna be sae hasty. Jamie gied me a
croon——'

336

"Oh, do hurry! I can't wait here all night hearing about your friends."

Topsail tabled the five-shilling piece with lingering fingers. The young lady was humming disdainfully.

"Have you no change?"

"That's a' I hae in the world." The bowed face was concealed beneath the nodding bonnet. "It's a peety if I'll no' can fin' oot Barbara an' the mistress."

"Sorry," was the tart answer, "I can't help you. There's your change;" and the little window was slammed down. Topsail's gaze wandered around helplessly, looking for an exit; she tapped on the window, but got no response. Suddenly the light within was extinguished. A step was heard outside and Topsail saw the form of the girl walking away from her.

"Dinna leave me here!" she cried; "I canna win oot."

Something frail and wizened in the older woman's appearance moved the girl to compunction and she retraced her steps. "Push!" she commanded, and at the same time pulled the turnstile. Topsail was amazed to find herself slowly wheeling out to freedom. "This whutteruck o' a whirlmaleerie's like Lonend's mill-wheel." The girl's equanimity being restored, she suggested that Topsail should apply to the police for information. Topsail, searching her pockets, discovered that she had left behind her the slip of paper with Barbara's name and address. Gillespie's excessive caution had prevented him from addressing the envelope containing the letter destined for Barbara. The girl, whose patience had given out during the search, was disgusted with such stupid provincialism, and, saying good-night, rapidly walked away. A thin grey rain began to fall. Topsail drew in to a street lamp and searched her black box. It contained no paper of Gillespie's. She felt weary and old and afraid of homelessness as she began to walk down the street. Dishevelled and rain-draggled, she presented a drunken appearance. She met a man who turned his head to look at her as she passed; then two girls in macintoshes who giggled as they hurried by. There was a gnawing in the pit of her stomach. The noise of the waves breaking on the shore in the dark scared her. Her feet were dragging heavily. She moved off the road, put her box on the ground, and sank upon it. It buckled beneath her weight. The rain became heavier. She closed her eyes and began to shiver. She was feeling light in the head. A tag of an old nursing-song occurred to her; the words involuntarily forming themselves in her brain to the swing of the sea. She had repeated the first two lines:

> "Oh, love it is pleasin',
> Love! it is teasin',"

when she heard a shriek out in the night. It was a liner's siren. She jumped to her feet, snatched up her box and scurried along the street. Presently another street opened on the left where a bright light shone in a large window, and reminded her of Gillespie's shop. It was a baker's. When she entered she saw a man with a white beard behind the counter, and thought he was like Lonend's billy-goat looking over a hedge. She undid the black thread on her purse and poured her money on the counter.

"I'll be obleeged to ye for a scone."

The billy-goat gave her a large milk-scone and asking for twopence put out a plump white hand for the money, and observed it was a wet night.

"Ay! I've got a drookin'," she answered. The smell of the hot scone made her faint, and she began to eat ravenously. The baker, eyeing her, asked if she had come far. "Yes, from Brieston. I've been stravaigin' the toon the last 'oor lookin' for Barbara an' the mistress."

The billy-goat baker, a benevolent man, was touched, and soon had from Topsail her miserable story. He invited her up to "the missis"—a little elderly woman with a round, merry face and an abundance of soft brown hair. She was darning, and wore spectacles. The baker informed her of Topsail's plight. He desired to shelter Topsail for the night, but was timid in suggesting this to his wife. "The poor wumman canna go back to the street a night like this, Erchie." He nodded, with an expression on his face which conveyed "of course, I know that."

"Dinna stand glowerin' there. Put on the kettle an' go back to the shop before it'll be robbit." The baker ceased nursing his magnificent beard and became active. His wife waddled with solicitude about the kitchen. As she laid out cups and saucers it occurred to her that the stranger was wet. She must change. Topsail hung her head, and confessed that the box contained her mother's Bible.

The baker, having shut his shop, sat down at the head of the table, his stiff beard over his tea-cup, and said grace. Blind man! he did not notice that the meagre stranger was swamped in an

338

amplitude of skirt. Topsail praised the scones. "Ye maun gie me the recate for thae scones, Erchie," she said. Erchie, forsooth! What else would she call him? and you may be sure Erchie promised. If there was a better flute player in the wet length and soaked breadth of Dunoon that night I should like to have heard him. Erchie sat in the low wicker armchair, unslippered and in socks with pink stripes, tootling away on a wee hole lost in the beautiful white beard, till the room rang like a wood on a summer's morning. Topsail commended him in no uncertain way:

"Man, man, Erchie! ye're the braw hand ca'in' awa' at the f'ute! I canna keep my feet stiddy for a meenut. Just you wait till I win hame an' get started on a pair o' warm socks for ye the winter." Topsail was thoroughly happy, for she had conceived a new work, of charity; yet sorrow came upon her for the flautist evoked a poignant memory. She thought on the dead Iain and his music. "It minds me o' poor Iain that's deid an' gone."

"Who was Iain?" asked the baker's wife, and as Topsail told the sad story light came to the brain of the musician.

"Did ye say the name was Strang?"

"Ay," Topsail nodded.

"It'll be Strang's Land ye're wantin' —Barbara Strang."

Topsail nodded again; her eyes shone.

"Is that no' great?" ejaculated the baker; "we found her out wi' the flute."

To Topsail's amazement the next morning she found Mr. Mc-Askill with Barbara and her mistress, and he at once asked for the letter, which Topsail handed over to the girl. During the time Barbara was reading it the lawyer invited the baker into another room; told him that Miss Strang was removing to Brieston; that Mr. Strang, her guardian there, was anxious to dispose of her property in Dunoon, and he, the lawyer, would be under an obligation if the baker could give him the names of any likely purchasers in the town. Mr. Strang did not want any publicity in the matter. The baker pondered, looking down the line of his beard, and saying he would consult his wife, arranged to meet the lawyer on that evening at Miss Strang's house.

McAskill, secretly anxious to have the way clear, postponed the meeting with the baker till the following evening, dismissed him, and then informed the ladies that there was no necessity for them to delay longer in Dunoon. Miss Strang could make her preparations to-day, with Topsail's assistance, and leave for Brieston tomorrow morning. He asked Miss Strang for Gillespie's letter, because he must show his authority for effecting the sale of the property. McAskill's eyes gleamed upon the letter as his hawk-like hand closed over documentary evidence of felony. Topsail, on her departure, asked McAskill to remember and get from Erchie the receipt for the scones. A smile hovered over the thin, compressed lips of the lawyer as he promised to attend to the matter.

4

TOPSAIL JANET was at her wits' end. Her mistress was going from bad to worse, and there was a nameless fear upon the house. Once or twice she found a man lurking about the close at night. Jeck the Traiveller had hinted that such on-goings were the talk of the town, and that her mistress was too often in the Back Street among scum, with that Galbraith woman who was to marry Lonend at the New Year. A bonnie stepmother indeed! Topsail took the news with disquieting silence. She was thinking of Eoghan, who seemed to live in the "Ghost" now and had a grey, hunted look on his face, and had become very thin—the stamp of soul-famine. Topsail commended mother and son to God as she listened to the stump, stump of her departing lover, and turned her eyes to the ancient lights of the sky in whose august processional march to-night she found no balm. Trouble brooded upon the house of Gillespie. She could not fathom all that was going on, nor find armour against this stealthy danger. She crawled to the Coffin loaded with anxiety. Since her return from Dunoon she had had very little sleep, because her mistress was often late, and Topsail would pace the floor of the Coffin in her stocking soles, one ear alert for her mistress on the stair, the other for sounds from Eoghan's room. As soon as the step was heard on the outside stair she was down to the kitchen, cautioning her mistress to silence and assisting her to the Coffin. Her mistress was querulous and rude on these occasions, but Topsail took no affront as she swiftly undressed her and put her to bed. Gillespie had long ago discovered this retreat and was without concern at the absence of his partner from his side. Once in the morning he had said to Topsail, letting the cat out of the bag, "Stravaigin' as usual; some night she'll walk over the breist wa' into the Hairbour—a good riddance."

Topsail became stupid for want of sleep, and did not manage to get through her work. No one appeared to take any notice. Gillespie frequently had his meals in his office. The kitchen became slovenly and Topsail troubled at first; then became resigned. The apathy of her mistress had fallen upon her, entangling her in its mesh.

"A' thing's tapsalteerie in the hoose," she complained to the Traiveller, who put a timid hand on her sleeve.

"Janet," he said hoarsely, "will ye no' come home to my mother's? She's gettin' blin'. I'm doin' noane sae bad noo at the Quay." He had a large barrow now which helped him greatly with the luggage, and was earning a steady seven-and sixpence a week for "catchin' the steamer's lines at the Quay an' the Pier," and for tending the gangways. "The auld ane's no' fit for work."

Topsail withdrew from his touch not unkindly.

"Ye're a good man, Jeck; but I winna leave the missis ee noo for a widger." Such are the intuitions and promptings of the heart of man that Jeck stumped home strangely elated, feeling the hard, raw hand of this woman yet warm within his own.

Topsail's mind was numb as she gazed at the vivid veins standing up on the neck of her mistress, who was watching the cats sporting themselves on the slates of the washing-house. Mrs. Strang was become an automaton of appetite, frozen by her husband's negligence to a sphinx whose lustreless eyes looked out with appalling apathy upon the desert of life. She had sought elsewhere what had been legitimately denied to her passion; and now passion degraded to debauchery was revenging itself mercilessly upon her, and she succumbed, a tragic figure played upon by the wiles and beaten upon by the rage of men. She had at first found easy access to the slaking of desire through the house of Mrs. Galbraith, when she found messages from Mr. Campion left for her there. He had been introduced at Lonend to Mrs. Galbraith, who admired him for his intellectual ability, and hoped that he might yet turn out a poet. It did not take her very long to discover from Mrs. Strang that some sort of intimacy existed betwixt Mr. Campion and Gillespie's wife. Mrs. Galbraith, estimating that on the burning of his fleet Gillespie's fall was imminent, was almost in despair at his wiry prosperity. Memories of her lost husband and home provoking her, she nursed her hatred and atrophied her conscience. She was about to contract a distasteful union with Lonend, hoping that in this way she would find fresh opportunity to trouble Gillespie. In the meanwhile she would strike at him through the infamy of his wife. The better sort would soon give the cold shoulder to a man whose wife was not only a common prostitute, but who had been driven to those vile courses through her husband's cruelty. Mrs. Galbraith had no compunction for Lonend, and did not disguise from herself the fact that he had had a chief hand in evicting her from Muirhead. She betrayed as little compunction for a woman who had, she was convinced, already committed herself with the new schoolmaster. Remorse seized her sometimes at night; but before the puling face of remorse she conjured up the grey, dead face of her husband, strong in its compulsion, from the unsleeping grave.

Topsail Janet paid her a furtive visit on one of those rare evenings when Gillespie was at supper at the Banker's. He was chagrined to find himself attacked there by Mr. Kennedy on the subject of Eoghan, whom Gillespie designed for the receipt of custom at the Pier; but much to his mortification the Laird had refused to rent the Pier, and installed there one of his own men. Mr. Kennedy observed that Eoghan was unfit for manual work and had talent; he was getting on in years and time was passing. Gillespie admitted so much, but objected to the cost of a University education.

"Money is nothing; your son's happiness everything."

"Noathin'!"—Gillespie glanced slyly at the Banker—"maybe ye leeve on the wun'. I hevna come across anything in the world that'll bate it."

"Money is tyranny; and tyranny is impotence."

"It's a minister ye should be, Mr. Kennedy." This jest masked the rage in his heart, for he felt he was being trapped in public.

"Make your son one. Ministers are the true aristocrats of the earth;" and Mr. Kennedy promised to coach Eoghan for the preliminary examination.

Gillespie sneered openly. "Thon's an expense—playin' the cairds wi' young swells an' boozin' in the theeayters." He had heard of such University wildness. "The jib halyard wad soon be blown oot o' the pin at thon rate." Such talk was typical of Gillespie now. The pessimism of age was finding him out. He was constantly whining, and had become lachrymose. His money was engaged in dubious enterprises; he made no secret of the drain his wife was upon him; she made money go like snow off off a dyke. He could hardly sell a barrel of salt herring now-a-days —him that had sent thousands to Rooshia. Even the Banker was bored, and changed the subject by asking his frivolous wife to play some music. The clatter of the piano drowned Gillespie's querulous boom.

Topsail heard this rattle and tinkle as she crept through MacCalman's Lane to visit Mrs. Galbraith, to whom she signified by a gesture of unutterable weariness all her misery. Mrs. Galbraith easily pumped her, and was enraged to discover the stoicism of Gillespie.

"Nothing but the wrath of God will break his heart," she said in such a fierce tone that it scared Topsail, who was profoundly amazed. She thought that all people were glad to remain at peace, so long as they had a roof and got a bite. She offered to help Mrs. Galbraith against Gillespie so long as her mistress was safe-guarded, and pleaded that Mrs. Galbraith would deny her house to the mistress. It was the futile challenge of unsophisticated innocence to sin. Mrs. Galbraith, sane enough not to be angry with Topsail, saw that this simple mind might easily become the still, small voice that is louder than thunder, and soothed Topsail's fears, assuring her that Jeck the Traiveller was absolutely wrong, and that her mistress came to no harm in the Back Street. In a sudden flash of inspiration she advised Topsail to inform Eoghan of her suspicion concerning the men who haunted Gillespie's close. Topsail trembled at the idea, and shook in all her body. She was afraid of this woman, and intuitively felt herself in the presence of danger. Drawing her dark-green shawl over her head, she slipped out, a defeated angel. She presented a piteous spectacle as she scurried in the shadow of the low thatched houses, tripping and stumbling over the causey-stones, and fluttered like a lapwing across the lit Square. Terrible in God's sight are the tears of a defeated angel.

5

"AM I not a terrific swell, grandad?" Barbara shouted merrily,
tears of laughter running down her cheeks. "Listen to the shoes
creaking; they're crying out that they are on loan." Her incongruous dress accentuated her beauty. Miss Barbara Strang was
some twenty-three years old. Her figure was tapering, firm, and
trim. She had a fine poise and grace of head, which was covered
with a cloud of soft brown hair; and a column-like magnificence
of neck. Her present attire brought out the bold curves of her
hips. Her brown eyes were swimming in liquid laughter as
Eoghan gazed from the threshold, conscious of a flower-fragrance
in her face and fire upon her parted lips. His grandfather, leaning
back in the old-fashioned armchair with the high, carved wooden
back, was purring in laughter. He wore his silver chain in his
oxter. The girl was dressed in a tartan shawl whose fringes came
to the knee. Between the top of her stocking and the fringe of the
shawl was a span of white leg. Rabbit skins were wrapped about
her boots; a piece of white rug hung from her middle as a sporran; inside the rope which girt this sporran to her person was a
bread-knife, and projecting from the top of the stocking his eye
caught the handle of another knife—the skene dhu. She was holding a tile hat in her hand, and as he watched her glowing face she
put up her leg on the whitewashed jamb of the fireplace, made a
bow to the old man, and said with a mimicking simper, "How
d'ye like a kiltie for a lass, grandad?" The old man's expression,
changing from merriment to recognition, made her suddenly
wheel like a startled fawn. With an exclamation of horror she
jerked down her leg, dropped the tile hat, and stooping, with the
shawl fringe held over her knees, ran past Eoghan and bounded
up the stair. He got one glimpse of wild, shy eyes lit with mischief and horrified with shame, and in that fleeting look his heart
descended to infinite depths, and the next moment swam up to
the surface drenched in love.

"Is she no' the diversion?" his grandfather was saying. "She
made me put away the Bible and dressed me." His eye sought the
silver chain apologetically. "She was curling my hair before you
came in."

344

Eoghan made no answer except to ask if she was Rob's daughter. The "Ghost" had become wondrously festal and young. He was about to ask how the caper of the kilt had come about when he heard her descend the stair. She entered with drooping eyes and suffused face, approaching him slowly and, smiling faintly, held out her hand. "How do you do?" she asked. He rose from his seat, shook hands, and sat down in confusion. She thought him brusque and rude, and turning, addressed to the old man a question about the Castle overlooking the Harbour which she had seen from the steamer's deck. Eoghan stole a furtive look. She wore a low broad white collar over the neck of a black silk blouse. She had something of the Quakeress in her appearance. Her attitude breathed purity and innocence. His gaze rested on her face as upon a happy home. She had fine brown eyes; there was a light on her brow, a white star on her forehead. The old man nodded across the hearth.

"Eoghan there 'll tell ye; he's a scholar."

Eoghan had a speaking eye, a compelling force of countenance when his emotions were aroused, and his eye fell burning upon the girl as she turned. She slipped her fingers inside the low wide collar, ran them round till they met on her throat, and then, smoothing the fringes of the collar on her breast with a white, rather fragile, hand, vividly blue-veined, swept over Eoghan's face a quick, dewy look. Immediately he began to pour out the history of the Castle. Her lips were parted; her eyes now lustrous, now wide, as she listened. They brimmed over with laughter as he told the story of the key of the dungeon where the Bruce once locked in his English prisoners. The Bent Preen came one day to Gillespie and displayed to him a ponderous key about a foot in length, alleging that he had discovered it in the dungeon of the Castle. Gillespie brought the treasure-trove for a shilling, and made conspicuous display of the antique in his shop window. On a placard was printed, "The Key of King Robert the Bruce's dungeon." It attracted crowds, who were convulsed with laughter, for the Bent Preen had let out the secret. The key was part of the scrap-iron gathered by the Fox in his country journeys, and was discovered by the Bent Preen lying on the heap at the Quay, waiting for the luggage steamer. Eoghan was glad that he had made her laugh so merrily. She asked if it was true that he was going to College. His heart leapt within him—she must have been talking about him. His volatile spirit rose like a flame. Yes;

in three weeks' time. And what was he going to be? "A minister," the old man piped out. Oh! oh! she would be afraid of him then, and confessed she had made grandad stop reading his Bible to watch her pranks. She stopped suddenly and blushed furiously, and put her hands lightly behind her back. This gave her figure a willowy, supple appearance. Himself confused and his heart beating tumultuously he offered to show her the Castle, where he had played truant as a boy, hiding in the Douglas dining-room.

His sleep was broken that night with dreams of a peerless presence, whose radiance stood out sharply against the background of his mother's life. In his sleep her face floated before him, hovering, a vision of light, upon a wilderness. It was a holy harbour for his misery. Her soul was the guest of heaven. When he awoke in the morning the rain was whispering on the windowpane. The sound of her voice returned singing the haunting Gaelic air of last night. It mingled with the voice of the rain in the fragrance of the wet dayspring; it bridged the years of heartache and weariness, and led him into a valley of dreams. The melody was a gladness dripping out of her being upon him in balm. He was perhaps never so happy as on that morning. Again he heard the song; again saw the light upon her brow; her eyes like a deer's, soft and limpid with gentle fire. She had had a red rose in the cleft of her breasts. Last night, as he had watched its rise and fall, its scent mingled with the frankincense of her hair.

Day followed day, bringing to him the torture and secret joy of love. One day he saw her in Harbour Street; watched the swing of her lithe figure, the flutter of her dress till she disappeared beyond the police station. Something ineffable went with her; and when she faded off the street he saw nothing but dreariness, backed by grey cold hills and a sullen sea. A golden light had vanished across bald Brieston. He rarely spoke to her. When he did address her, things of the least significance became enlarged. He was under a spell in her presence, and his heart would leap up when she spoke to him even casually. He felt his answers flat, his language stupid. On the other hand, he remembered her words and phrases which would recur to him involuntarily and at the strangest times. He wrote secret verses. His first effort was to paint in words the meshed sunlight in her hair. He used the most stilted epithets—cherry lips, snowy neck, and the like. Once or twice he felt he began well with a line or even a couplet, but could go no farther—as on the occasion when he sang of a gold cross which she wore suspended by a thin gold chain around her neck. His emotions were beating as with manacled hands against an adamantine wall of expression, out of which he could not carve the fine jewels of words. But he found a lively pleasure in being thus to himself a pedlar of dreams.

He was troubled at the swiftness with which the days passed. He had shown her West Loch Brieston and its glen, the vista of the Loch beyond Muirhead Farm, and that terrible shore beyond the "Ghost" where Iain had been drowned. The tears welled in her eyes, and she put her hand in his as with the appeal of a child. The timid fragility of her face took his heart by storm. They walked home to the "Ghost" hand in hand in silence, their full hearts beating against each other, and unutterable yearning stirring in the dusk as with angels' wings, and weaving around them a holy spell. On that night Barbara discovered that the thought of him had been constantly with her, lying upon her heart like a dew-drop on the petal of a flower, and waiting for the dawn to open the flower. Noiselessly like dew he had slipped in, and she found him seated in the heart of her being she knew not how.

The following day he took her to the Castle. They had come up from wandering idly in the aisles of derelict ships upon the beach, where in this sea-cathedral each had dreamed of love, and in which Eoghan had felt blow upon him that spirit of our youth which breaks in with its haunting face upon the sudden clear window of consciousness. The savour of reaped things was in the air. Schoolboys tramped in from the country laden with brambles and pillow-slips full of nuts, and gave to the town an atmosphere of mellow things. The sight of all this saddened Eoghan, because it recalled Iain, with whose loss was mingled a sense of the pitiableness of his mother's life. He sat plucking mournfully at the grass beneath the Castle wall.

"What's wrong, Eoghan?" she asked tenderly.

He said that the beauty of the autumn evening cast a spell of sadness upon him; it brought back Iain and old nutting days.

"Is there not sadness at the heart of everything, Eoghan? I think, when I look at grandad's eyes, that life is built upon sorrow." His hand sought hers, and held it. "I remember a friend of mine in Dunoon telling me of the feeling she had when she sent her wee boy to school. In her dreams she used to hear him con his lessons."

"What is it?" he asked.

"I don't understand it quite, but I think I know. She told me it gave her heartache. It was the beginning of the weary struggle in life in which the mother can't help."

"In so young a thing!" he answered bitterly. "If this is the way from the beginning, is God not playing with us?" He felt a sense of shame as soon as he had spoken. He was a traitor to Mr. Kennedy, and added hurriedly that he must introduce her to that silver old man.

"No," she said earnestly, ignoring his offer. "He is not playing with us. Grandad says it is because He has a big reward in store for us." Her eyes shone.

"Ah, Barbara!"—he caressed her hand—"I believe you."

"But don't you believe more than me, Eoghan, dear?"

He thrilled at the evangelist's endearing word.

"I can't say." The moment's mood of despondence left his face. "God chooses the beautiful and the good for His revelation." Reverently he kissed her hand. Nearer and nearer those two souls were drawing, as out of a vast deep. Their eyes rested tenderly upon each other; they ceased speaking; their lips smiled. The evening smoke hung in the windless air upon the roofs of the town below, and on the Muirhead road across the Harbour the telegraph wires ran like gold in the evening light. A sound of larks behind them in the south-west fell in a cascade of song. The bleating of flocks died away on the hill. It aroused to a sudden enraptured thrill a single bird, whose melody mingled with the 'plaining of faint shore-water, and the lowing of homeward cattle in Muirhead across the Harbour.

"How quiet and serene it is!" she murmured. She felt herself in a house not made with hands. By mental telepathy this feeling was dimly conveyed to him. He leaned towards her, gazing deeply into the darkening wells of her eyes.

"I love you, Barbara." Again the old sensation rushed over him that he was speaking out of a far dream with a voice not his own, as on the night when he told his father that Iain was drowned. Her face swam up before him, inexpressibly precious. Hands tender and compelling out of that dreamland were upon him, and he put out his arms, gathered her to himself, and kissed her upturned mouth again and again. From his eyelids he saw the down glimmering on her cheek and neck, and, leaning down, kissed her neck beneath the chin-bone. She answered with a crooning

348

sound and an upward look full of incommunicable tenderness—the look of one who had found a pillow and peace after long wayfaring. Aloft in the grey church on the hill a liquid bell rang the hour. The booming sounds were young as with the vigour of new love. High up in the still evening air the sound carolled, pealing its long lin-lan-lone, drifting over the roofs to the old grey Castle like angels' feathers falling upon them, celestial snowflakes drifting down in soothing waves of rest. Its pulsing in unison with his heart seemed to stir her hair and weave a fragrance about her. His mind became tinged with sadness; he heard the music whispering to him. "Oh, sea-bells of magic foam; Oh, land-bells of golden dreams, how often have you called to me with the tongue of a young twilight spirit, speaking across the sorrow and the lost effort and the illusion of the years, mysterious, yet familiar, burdened with the beatitude and the grief of love. Is there not sadness at the heart of everything? Ring on, ring on for ever, lest the magic fade and the dream-light die, and the sorrow come. . . ." The last lullaby note melted away in the darkening sky, dying, as if love were bleeding out its life and the drops were falling, falling. . . . Her face was childishly wan and small against his shoulder; her gaze dumb upon his face. She seemed about to cry; her lips quivered and trembled. He tightened his clasp about her in an anguish of solicitude, and she nestled, lamb-like. The birds flitted to their nests in the ivy of the Castle; silence flowed down like a grey river; the two heads leaned to each other; the faces caressed each other; the two mouths met in a lingering kiss; and the silent music of love beat around them as from white birds singing in their breasts. She looked up smiling with bedewed eyes.

"The pain has gone from your eyes, dear," she whispered like a mother, and the maternal note nigh broke his heart. Hand in hand they arose. Eastward above them towered the looming masonry, its huge black bulk silhouetted against the moon-whitened sky. In the west the church spire soared over Brieston, and was pricked out needle-wise against a clear background of amber. Beneath the first faint stars they walked across the reaped fields, the multitudinous wings of silver-grey doves brooding around them. And out of the dungeon and the Douglas dining-room her heart was crying, the old, old baby brownies and little folk were stealing to play their pranks in the moon and dance upon the green grass where they had been sitting. He was chanting:

349

> "Far away beyond the sunset skies,
>   Where the true love never, never dies . . . "

She looked up timidly. His eyes were fixed on the deep crepus-cular west with a rapt look. The peace of that over-arching im-mensity of colour had entered his soul, dissipating the fever of life. From the height of a glowing third heaven he was gazing down at life's turmoil, its sadness, its darkness, its evil. Suddenly he turned and looked back at the lofty bastioned wall dark against the sky. It endured. Its makers had gone empty-handed into the unknown.

"Barbara, what is the meaning of life?" he asked, in a mourn-ful tone.

"To love and be loved," she replied, with glad quickness.

The answer cleared his troubled mind. Had there been love and to spare those fire-blackened walls behind had never been built. The fibre of his spirit responded to the eternal truth of the answer, and the girl saw tears in the corners of his eyes. Her look became a gaze of worship.

She wanted her grandfather to know that she was loved; yet for to-night she would cherish her secret as a peculiar treasure in the recesses of her heart. When she dismissed Eoghan at the door of the "Ghost" he strode along as if walking on air. The salt and pungency of happy youth rioted in his veins; the touch of her hand was tingling in his palm; the tones of her voice flowed about him in enveloping sweetness. He felt infinite power seething through him. The leaves of the trees beyond the "Ghost" on the burn-side were tossed up in fevered drifts of vague magnificence in the night wind, and fell with a jibbering sound on the decks of the derelicts lying on the beach beneath the "Ghost." To him they were fingers of commiseration touching the broken bin-nacles, as the delicate fingers of a loving woman would rest upon the blind eyes of her lover. This multitudinous gold spread enfolding wings across the shattered decks which shall no more go out beneath the steering stars.

The villas on the beach-road stood out white and sharp in the moon, and over them the leaves whirled in joyous mad mirth. He saw the gables and roofs climb up in the dim whiteness to a bacchic place in the clouds. A cathedral, vast and dim, took the air amidst chiming bells and a dream-drift of burnished leaves. Beneath his feet the fret of leaves was like the motion of the wounded feet of naked children shuffling along trailing blood. But what was that to him? His blood was a flood of fire. He ground his heels into the road as he danced along, swung his arms tempestuously, and had to throttle a mad desire to shout aloud. He brought down his fist upon the door of a wooden shed, exulting in the pain, and clenched his hands till the hot blood was about to ooze from his finger-nails. He laughed exultingly, and flung wide his arms to enclose her in a deathless embrace. A man passed him. He ground his teeth. "Fool, fool; I wonder if he heard." He walked forward vehemently, and as he careered through the Square he thought: "It is great, great; what a girl! what love!" and so stormed home on the crest of a fiercely-rushing wave, thinking of how he had taken her face between his hands, peered down into her eyes, and kissed her on the mouth.

Hitherto when Barbara awoke in the morning she remembered her sense of dependence, and that she was an orphan. Now when she opened her eyes comfort came to her with the sun, as she brought forth the jewel of her love from its casket. She subscribed to the public library, and read the love poems of the English language.

"On such a night . . ." she rolled the witching words on her tongue. In church she surreptitiously read the Song of Solomon, while overhead Stuart denounced sins of omission and commission; and the face of her lover floated before her. She lay on the burn-side at the "Ghost" on sunny days waiting for Eoghan, and watching the placid sea from her eyelids as she wandered into a lotus land rich with humming hives of Hibyla honey. He and she were content, and held the world as content along with them. Steeped in their new rapture, their eyes raining happiness on each other, they saw naught else, saw not that his mother was sinking deeper into her shadowland. Each of them, mother and lovers, clutched at shadows, strove at the bolts of the doors behind which lay the glory of life—that dim, grey Never-Neverland whose guardian doors so many stain with the blood of their heart.

It was two days before he was to leave for Glasgow to sit at the entrance examination to the University. She stood in the door of the "Ghost," her hair blown upon her forehead, and watched him disappear up the road. Presently she entered the kitchen, her cheeks glowing from the frosty air. The old man was seated in the big chair at the fire, half sunk in the gloom and dancing shadows.

"Grandad!"

"Is that you, m'eudail?" He roused himself from his reverie. She stepped over to him, taking off her hat.

"Have you been lonely?"

"No, mo chdridhe." He had picked up those Gaelic phrases of tenderness and pronounced them with a Lowland accent. She sat down on the edge of the chair, her fingers playing nervously with her hat. The old man roused himself.

"Hae ye been up by?"

"No, grandad, I've been with Eoghan;" and suddenly she put her arms round his neck.

"Oh, grandad, I'm so very, very glad you brought me here! —I—I want to tell you," she stammered, "to tell you I love you so. He—he kissed me——" She buried her cheek in the thick, dark, curly hair of his head. Reticence between them was at an end. For a long minute there was silence, broken only by the wheeze of the sign without. Then he spoke in a prayer:

"The lovingkindness of the Lord is very great."

The girl was inexpressibly touched. Youth the heritor of life and age the bequeather sat united. A profound sigh rose through the deepening shadows. Who was it from—age or youth; age which remembers, and whose old distresses, lying like dry tinder, flare up at the spark of the kinship of joy and sorrow which a word can bring to birth; or youth, the flood of whose ripe experiences disarms the pangs of yesterday, and makes it tremble before the haunting possibilities of to-morrow? The sigh that is born in the shadows—is it from age or from youth? The girl rose hurriedly and lit the lamp in the window.

6

EOGHAN refused to go into the shop though his father cajoled: "Ye'll hae the business some day."

"I would not take it though it was a hundred times as valuable."

This blow paralysed Gillespie, who imagined his son was bewitched by that snuff-taking dotard the schoolmaster. Gillespie, having reached that period in life when men of property or affairs consider the making of their will, was agitated by vague fears. What would become of his business when he died? He lashed out at an elusiveness which baffled him. Had he founded a house after all upon sand? The dupe of a subtlety which ensnared him, he went to consult his wife, whom he found dovering at the fire, her eyes deep with melancholy, and eased his wrath by arraigning her on the sole evidence of an empty glass.

"It's no' enough appearingly that you spend the siller boozin' your eyes blin'; but here's Eoghan noo wantin' to go to Coallege, an' him ready to step into the business."

Her hands wandered aimlessly over her lap. "I'm a weary wife; a weary, weary wife. I was in the College in Edinbro'; but noo I've a deep, deep water to wade."

"Muckle good the College did ye," sneered Gillespie; "ye can neither gang to kirk or mercat noo;" and he flung out of the kitchen, imagining that his wife was in the conspiracy to baulk him. There was only one way to keep his face with his son, and that was to let him go.

"You an' me, Eoghan, hae to redd up things a wee," he said, and thrust some gold into his son's hands. "Tak' guid care o' the bawbees," he cried jocularly, but with a twinge at the heart.

Eoghan gazed on the sovereigns glittering in his palm.

"What's this for?"

"It's for your collegin'."

"I thought you refused to let me go."

"Huts!" he cried, "your daft mither's fair set on havin' her son College bred."

Even to a soul-hardened Scotsman College is a land of wonder and romance, and Gillespie had his own quiet pride in the venture. Eoghan, however, thinking of his mother, hoped that his College career would stimulate her interest anew in life. She was failing in health, was lack-lustre and dispirited; she let things drift, and had a passion for wandering about the house, aimlessly rummaging among things of old time, whose history she would recite with infinite repetitions in a half-maudlin way, weeping over treasures brought from Lonend, especially faded photographs of the dead, some of whom she imagined to be alive. The furniture of the parlour was that of her wedding-day, and she recalled her glory as a bride, and peopled the room with the faces that had been there. She would ramble on, talking loosely and vaguely, beginning a remark and finishing in the middle of a half-expressed idea. Eoghan pored on her expressionless face, which to him was like a worn effigy on a coin. Her aimless hand at her hair accentuated her listlessness to an intolerable degree. If his departure for College would deepen her interest in life, that in itself would be sufficient to drive him as with whips to the University. A wild hope seized him that here, perhaps, the doors of redemption would open. She would not dishonour her College-bred son. Mr. Kennedy had advised him in one or two ways. "You must find the money for her yourself; bring her in the stuff if need be, and keep her at home." At home! was she not always at home? Alas! the eyes that looked on Barbara saw naught else. But Mr. Kennedy was mad to advise him so. Instead, he watched to rob her, and every chance copper he picked up. He had now about a pound and did not know what to do with the hoard. "It will soon amount to thirty pieces of silver," he thought sadly. A torrent of wild words burst out of him as he told Mr. Kennedy of the money. He had been brought into the world without being questioned; had he not the right to save himself from this shameful connection by going to one of the colonies? "But what can you do there? you have neither trade nor profession, and you are unfit for the hard manual labour of these parts." And Eoghan, cursed with an unbalanced imagination, saw himself creep up from the foreign quays into vast streets of stone, full of strange faces—pitched headlong into the roaring wheels of modern civilisation with its cynicism and selfishness. It was a dreary fatality. He saw himself an unimportant speck tossed about for a little, his pride congealed into pain. If he escaped his environment, could he escape the shame? That was indestructible, and would become gigantic on a foreign soil. "I here, and she there, the greater castaway;" and with shame rigged as a dogged pack upon his back, his mournful face would vanish in the sea of isolation, and the chariot-wheels of life would roar over the head of a wanderer irrecoverably lost.

"Never cast a woman over; if you fall, fall together." The eyes of the schoolmaster looked out upon him, eyes of hungry sorrow, transfigured in that moment by the tenderness of forty silent of soul famine. Eoghan felt he was in the presence of another sufferer; and born of the whirlwind and the furnace of grief came the note of purging pain and expiatory wisdom. "If you fall, fall together." But the schoolmaster had perhaps been at fault. Eoghan's mother certainly was; and he answered sullenly, "I have done nothing wrong." The sword of justice was in his hand, facing foursquare to guard the Eden of his life; but with the schoolmaster's eyes upon him the sword wheeled upon himself, lambent with wrath. Beneath those penetrating eyes he felt he was making an effort to defend himself; and to make an effort has not in it the large serenity of the pure at heart, who stand before Pilate. Rage and writhe as he would, the scorch of the brandished sword was shrivelling up his selfishness, and blinding him with its radiance. Lacerated, the caitiff in him moaned doggedly his apologia: "I've done nothing wrong; am I to suffer?" And the schoolmaster's one smiting word, plucked from the mouth of Pilate, fell like a hammer blow upon his soul: " 'This Man hath done nothing amiss; I find no fault in the Man;' " and in front of the face of the evoked Christ—a face hewn with the chisel of grief, yet glowing with an eternal assurance—Eoghan began to sink in an immensity of despair. His wail rang through the open window across the silence of the leaves: "I cannot suffer the shame. Oh, we are lost, lost!"

The schoolmaster touched him lovingly. "Child! child! you have made your grief too big for you." And this old man, who for a sin of his own youth had walked through hell and was homeless upon earth, watched with a new speechless misery the anguish of the boy, and saw no hope for either in the world. "I can suffer for my own fault, but how can he pay the penalty for another's?" was his weary thought, going round and round in his brain as a horse goes round a circus-ring, as the night passed silently before his window, and the Morning Star arose upon the pictured face of the dead woman of his dreams. Wretched man! he had been to the boy a schoolmaster to the very end, and he shuddered when he recalled the boy's words: "I'll only have peace when I hold her dead body in my arms."

Here at last was the solution of the problem which had baffled them. "Your mither's fair set on hevin' her son College bred." Gillespie's lie, spoken to save his face, was hugged closely by his son, who divined the news to be a door of redemption, and one which, so close to the heart of the old scholar, would be as welcome to Mr. Kennedy as to himself. He must go and tell him. He had already said good-bye, but all the same he would go. Besides, he had promised to introduce Barbara, and it must be done this evening. She responded eagerly, and they set out behind Brieston by the way of the Castle. The moon was like a taper in the sky when they entered, by three moss-grown stone steps, the large garden which surrounded the school-house. The lights of Brieston twinkled below, and the moon was on the Loch, a long bar of silver. As they walked over the grass beneath the fruit trees they heard a window being pushed up. Firelight alone glowed within the room.

Mr. Kennedy, pondering upon the dead in his book, had heard a voice, deep-toned and vibrant, calling these words as from infinite distance: "Thy brother shall rise again." He lifted an alert head, and raising the window listened; but the silence of the garden and the fragrant night remained unbroken. "Strange, that," he murmured; "the only person who ever said it was Jesus." He peered through the trees where the moonlight glimmered among the trunks with a grey sheen. An Unseen Presence passed among the leaves, going upon the tops like a gentle wind. Suddenly the watchers beneath saw a white head leaning out and a pallid face turned upwards to the skies, and two hands were stretched out in supplication. The girl felt ashamed, as if she were spying on something sacred. "Let us go, dear," she whispered, and clung to Eoghan; but before he could answer these mournful words fell on their ears: "Hast thou called? O Thou who walkest the darkness like light and movest as the wind before morning in Thy breathing, pardon my sin, sanctify my life, make me pure, and grant me Thy peace." The hands remained outstretched. To the watchers a halo shone around the saintly face. "O great Spirit of the stars and the sea, of the earth and the soul of man, be with him who is as my son. Rend the darkness about his feet; suffer him not to lose hope; amplify his aspirations; protect his place; safeguard his destiny."

Eoghan shook like the column of water on a fall. The Spirit of the Unseen passed as breathing upon the face of the night, and the tree-tops trembled and were still. Far off towards the isles the sea murmured an antiphone, and an influence of heaven rained down from the velvet depths of the sky.

The girl's lips quivered as her hand stole into Eoghan's. "Amen, dear, Amen," she whispered.

Eoghan, who felt himself sinking through a great deep into

immortal peace, was unable to answer. The heart of the night had ceased its beating, the stars their wanderings; there was a vast listening void. Far off through the gloom there arose the sob of the sea made majestic by its unutterable meaning; and as its plangent note melted away the white head was withdrawn and the window was closed. An emeritus angel had vanished from their sight, and they awakened as if they had stepped back on to the grass from the vestibule of heaven.

Eoghan shook himself. "Let us go in."

"No! no! no!" she whispered. "*I have met him.* Oh, Eoghan, Eoghan, I wish I were good like that old man."

"O Thou that walkest the darkness like light, make her pure and grant her Thy peace." He was praying earnestly in silence for his mother, as the children of love's wondrous morning, saddened and sublimated, passed away from that lonely house, and from one who within stood gazing in the firelight at the photograph of a girl. He turned from the photograph, and closed the MS. in which he had lived with the noble obscure dead.

"I am too sad to read to-night," he sighed. It was always the same book—of Dante and his Beatrice. The dead poet and he had a tragedy in common in the name Beatrice. "I shall send in my resignation to-morrow," he muttered. A shadow passed across his face as he thought of this house which he would have to leave. The Board were anxious to give it to Mr. Campion. "This sense of oppression is making me stupid," he spoke again, and began pottering at the fire with the poker. The fire-light leapt on the covers of his books as if giving them a soul. He sank into his arm-chair amidst the shadows which were gathering between the fire and his bookcase. In a few minutes he was asleep. The head of snow fell away; the breathing, deep at first, became easy and gentle, and a long sigh quavered through the room, which was rapidly growing dark beyond the fire-light. In the flickering light his thin, worn face looked beautiful and serene in its marmoreal calm. A little noise of air expelled from his lungs broke the silence, and the slack figure in the chair stiffened. A deep hush lay upon the house and the garden. A little scurry of sea-wind sobbed in the boughs without; a patter of leaves on the path; a flame hissed and darted up in the coals; the tick of a clock sounded loudly in the hall; the flame perished in the grate; darkness and shadows fell upon the old man. In a little while the

357

great, solemn, autumnal moon stole in at the window and touched the silent face and kissed the head of snow.

Beneath that moon the lovers were leaning upon the cannon beyond the "Ghost," and Eoghan was telling Barbara how Mr. Kennedy had said good-bye. "Don't be impulsive"—Barbara felt the wisdom of that—"work steadily; think more of truth than of the laurel; be frugal, and don't worry. Never be mean or unkind or cruel; and read a portion of the gospel every night: it is the greatest book in the world. If ever you are in a difficulty, use me. I have some money I don't need. May a rich blessing attend upon you." He went up the path, stumbling slightly, his hands clasped behind him, his head sunk forward on his breast, making his lean shoulder-blades to stand out. An autumn leaf fell upon him as he passed. Eoghan, watching the drooping white head, saw the leaf slide off to the ground. He thought of blood upon the silver breast of a dove.

They took a fond farewell of each other that night at the door of the "Ghost" rather than to-morrow in the broad day.

"Tell me again," she pleaded, "before you go."

"I love you, Barbara, beyond all women."

She smiled bravely. "I wanted to hear it again before you left. Good-bye; good-bye." She flung her arms around his neck: "Good-night; good-bye till my eyes cannot see you," and kissing him fiercely she pushed him away and vanished indoors. Presently she re-appeared and watched his figure go up the road in the moon, till it disappeared where the road bends round to the Pier. She stood gazing at the lunar light upon the empty road.

7

Mrs. Strang had acquired the habit of "stravaigin'." She visited the shops and ordered unlimited quantities of goods, saying she had abundance of money in the bank, and jewels at home as fine as the crown jewels of London. At first she used to drift home with an armful of parcels, but Gillespie promptly returned the stuff. Thenceforth the shopkeepers took her orders but did not fulfil them. Some of them pitied her, some joked behind her back. Topsail went out to search for her, chiefly that Eoghan might be spared the sight of his mother in such a condition. When Topsail was piloting her mistress home, cajoling and coaxing her by turns, she would interpose her own person betwixt her mistress and "the men" at the corners, and betrayed none of that stupidity which one feels in steering a drunken person in the street.

But Topsail was busy to-night, revelling in a welter of socks and shirts, the choicest of which she laid aside with the eye of a hawk, along with pots of jam, fresh butter, and other delicacies from the shop which she had demanded for Eoghan's bag. These rites were being performed within the holy place of the Coffin. To College, among the professors! She conceived them as gods, among whom none save men of great learning and nerve would venture.

Jeck the Traiveller was pressed into service. "It's me 'ill be in the bonnie pickle, an a' night sortin' his clothes," she said to him gleefully at the close-mouth, with her arms full of clothes taken from the back green. "I've to iron them, yet."

Jeck made no response and Topsail was irritated.

"Look, ye gomeril"—she nodded to the top of the bundle—"that shirt's goin' to the College."

Jeck stared, ignorant of etiquette.

"Hev' ye noathin' to say, Jeck? It's goin' to the Coallege where they learn to be doctors and ministers."

Jeck saluted the garment with phlegm.

"Ach!" she cried, "it's easy to see the lik' o' you never had a Coallege eddication, ye dumbfoondered stirk."

"Thank God!" he ejaculated fervently; "what wad a man wi' a wudden leg want wi' a College eddication? I couldna sclim the pulpit stairs."

Topsail's wrath evaporated.

"I'll bate ye a thoosan' poun', Jeck, when the wean's a minister, he'll preach that bubbly Jock Stuart blin'."

Jeck acquiesced, and she of her grace informed him that on the morrow he would be privileged to carry the wonderful bag to the Pier. She had twenty commendations, and a final warning—if anything came over the bag he need never show his face again.

In the meanwhile her unguarded mistress appeared at Mrs.

Galbraith's door, after having visited several shops and houses. She had two red carnations in the hand with which she knocked.

"I've brought ye a bunch o' flowers, Marget." Her head had a stupid, listless angle.

With eyes of contempt Mrs. Galbraith took the flowers. "If Mr. Strang has robbed me of my garden I'm glad to see his wife makes up for it."

This was a new tone for Mrs. Galbraith, who had no longer any use for this broken instrument. To understand this it is necessary to trace the mental development or rather the retrogression of this arrogant, strong-willed woman. She was in some respects a tragic figure, with her fine intellect prostituted to plans of cunning, and to a perversity which, afflicting her with a moral nausea in its early stages, was founded on loyalty to her husband's memory, which she continued to revere, and which had proved an insuperable barrier to Lonend's matrimonial schemes. The memory of him kept her chaste as though he were alive. He had found release; she was in a prison cell, enduring pain and agony mingled with an intense brooding upon and yearning for revenge. She was racked with remorse that that vengeance yet went hungry. In spite of her rash promise to marry Lonend she swore to herself in the secrecy of night never to marry again. Men had brought upon her all the suffering she endured. They were rank egotists, ruthless liars, perjurers, murderers, who, in spite of Christianity, made slaves of women, beginning in slight, insinuating ways, seizing every advantage of woman's pity and sympathy, and relying on her mercy, till they had her beneath their heel. She read anew into the original attitude of Jesus Christ towards women. The half of His ethic was a championing of their cause and claims. More than half the ignominy, the disgrace and shame of the world they bore, and often in secret, for the sake of their name, their family, and their home. They compromised themselves, not out of vice, but simply to please men, who take advantage of the ease with which they succumb to the male influence. Man had taught woman bestiality and then visited her sins pitilessly upon her, while he demanded tacitly or professedly for himself the greatest latitude. He had not eradicated from his nature the disposition of his savage ancestors to regard woman as a piece of chattels. She recognised that woman was capricious, prone to trifling iniquities, petty falsehood, and little acts of vindictiveness, due to the predominance of the child

360

in her nature; but she had rarely the courage to attempt a great crime. In such enormities she simply yielded to the suggestions of men, was instigated by fear or terror, or blinded by love. Woman adhered with a criminal, dog-like devotion to men, refusing to betray their most brutal secrets, even if this would rid her of an existence of persecution. This is because of her desperate loyalty to honour, a virtue which is a toy in the hands of most men. A woman will sacrifice everything, even life itself, which often is a slow martyrdom, to satisfy the claims of her family. The law, which is made by men and administered by them, had no understanding of, or sympathy for, her position. The prisons were full of women martyrs.

Again and again she had resolved these thoughts, and towered up strong in pride that she was the sworn antagonist of the worst man in Brieston, whom to destroy was to stamp out a leprosy that was gnawing on the vitals of the town. She was the militant defender of her sex; the avenger of her fallen house. Till Gillespie was buried beneath the broken lintel-stone of that house she would have no peace of soul, no absolution for an unfruitful widowhood. She would gloat in that day when she could carve Gillespie's shameful epitaph upon the recumbent lintel-stone of Muirhead farmhouse. Though of late she had confided in Lonend, she would trust no one but herself as she ruthlessly demoralised Mrs. Strang, in the hope of striking at her impervious husband through the ruins of his wife. She grudged Lonend the least grain of that revenge which it was her constant dream she would evoke upon Gillespie Strang. In all this she was capable of the deepest sentiments of tenderness and charity, and was a chief favourite with the barefooted children of the Back Street. On Sundays her kitchen was a private school, in which she taught churchless bairns the Bible, and induced them to learn by offering to the cleverest a monthly prize of a toy or a little illustrated book.

Enraged that Gillespie Strang yet stood immune, she did not perceive that she herself indulged in a vile crime at the instigation of a man dead in his grave, and was committing greater folly than that of the unfortunate of her sex whose offences were inspired by living men. This judge of men imagined herself the protectress of her sex by waging war on one man over the battlefield of his wife's body and soul. Her personality dominated Mrs. Strang to such a degree that she believed she could induce Gillespie's wife to poison him; but her spirit quailed before that, and at this period of her life revolted from such a consummation. She had gloated for years over the idea of vengeance, which had passed from being a stern duty to an exquisite pleasure. As she had given it birth she nursed it as a babe, and it became a companion, a solace, a fierce joy. Were Gillespie to die, were he even to be murdered, her life would be robbed of its most agreeable passion, and her imperious temper would have detested the conqueror death. She preferred a species of slow torture for Gillespie. Her ideal was to see him come forth from prison begging in rags at her door. She imagined a scene in which in that hour she fed a starving dog in the rain, but with a sneer shut her door in the face of a Gillespie worn out with hunger, cold, and misery.

By no means featherheaded, she had reached that mental state in which her joy was not full unless she could disclose her idea of revenge to some other. She made a confidant of Lonend, who at once informed her of Gillespie's transaction in Dunoon and of the letter which McAskill held as proof of his guilt. Old Mr. Strang or Barbara would have to take action against the pirate.

"It's no' at the boil yet," said Lonend, his eyes gleaming with the hidden lust to destroy; "he'll be up before the Shirra on another chairge as weel; he's embezzlin' the Poor Rates." Last year he, Lonend, had supplied money to six poor people of Brieston unaccustomed hitherto to pay these rates, offering them as much again when they had paid this money to Gillespie as rates and taxes. They had been given no receipt. "It's been goin' on wi' others for years," laughed Lonend. "A' we want is a squint o' his books. McAskill's workin' the oracle. We'll hae the blood-sucker up on twa coonts. It's the jyle for him this time, an' then good-bye to Gillespie Strang when he wins oot. The old men o' Brieston that hae noäthin' to do but tek' a walk 'ill hoast at him when he comes oot o' jyle wi' his hair cut."

Lonend's excitement impregnated Mrs. Galbraith's blood, who saw her dream about to be realised. Yet she feared Gillespie's cunning. "He's as slippery as an eel," she said doubtfully.

"He'll no' can wriggle oot o' this, by Goäd—sheer embezzlement an' fraud. I've pleughed lang an harrowed lang, an' noo, by the Lord, the scythe's ready for the hairst."

Thus Mrs. Galbraith had no need any longer for the broken instrument at her door who was saying, with a furtive air of confidence: "I just took a run up for a wee whilie, Marget."

"I'm very sorry, Mrs. Strang," answered Mrs. Galbraith coldly, opposing the bulk of her form in the door, "but you can't come in here in this disgraceful state. I'm reading an interesting book, the philosophy of Lotze, and can't be disturbed just now. Is it not time you were home to milk the cows at Muirhead? You know your husband stole it from me." There was a cynical smile on Mrs. Galbraith's face as she shut the door.

Mrs. Strang looked at the inimical wooden wall with eyes full of vague wonder. "Dearie me!" she murmured, "I'm gettin' to be a fair outcast."

The veil of kindly night shrouded this shameful spectacle, and she reached the door of Mrs. Tosh as the taper light of the moon lit the sky. When Mrs. Tosh also refused her asylum, vaguely the words "Muirhead Farm" entered into her consciousness, and she trailed wearily up the north road as the moon grew upon the bay. As for Mrs. Galbraith, she thrust the carnations to her nostrils, sniffed them greedily, and placed them in a thin vase with water.

"Another trophy from Carthage," she ejaculated, and resumed her book with a smile of satisfaction. "They all come to my door," she thought. "Topsail; Mrs. Strang; the next will be Gillespie."

8

WHEN Eoghan left Barbara he hurried home to pack his books on mathematics, a subject to which he meant to give a final revision in Glasgow on the evening before the day of the mathematics examination. The town, white as snow beneath the moon, lay strung around the bay so still that he heard the burn run into the sea, and the dying drip of oars in the Harbour mouth. Ahead of him at the Quay he saw the figure of a woman, walking slowly and heavily. It was his mother. Half-way to Muirhead Farm she had retraced her steps, coming to a sudden determination to visit the "Ghost," and discover for herself if Iain were in prison. Then she remembered he was on the sea in Gillespie's steamer, and turned homeward. Eoghan saw her trailing like a ship, with frayed cordage, that sways and sags across a wintry sea. The shame was now abroad in the eyes of men. He crouched back in the shadow of the police station wall and halted. Her weak feet tottered with silly little lurches, and the frill of a white petticoat trailed in the mud of the herring guts—the refuse cast of the furnace from which Gillespie drew molten gold. The street was empty. The church bell rang the hour of eleven as he watched her sway up the pavement, hirpling like a wounded duck. The beating of his heart was stifling him, for the college door of redemption he recognised would never open. He became weary of existence. Two men came out of a close and began walking rapidly towards the Quay. Eoghan was forced to hide behind a pile of tree-trunks on the breast wall that awaited shipment to become railway sleepers. As the men passed he heard one of them in the still night say:

"It's Gillespie's wife, a gey cauld bed she's makin o't."

Eoghan knew the man, a tailor. His companion answered:

"She'd sook whisky oot o' a dirty cloot," and called her by an offensive name.

They passed on, laughing. The blood tingled in Eoghan's veins. That name! surely not that! He felt himself going mad. The whole town knew, and spoke that obscene name concerning her. He felt like a watch-dog before his father's door that can only whine. No! he could not believe in that name; it was only the loose talk of a fool. But why should he say it? Distraught with fear and shame he crept from his shelter, and spying up and down the road, hurried on, a wave of anger surging over him. He wished she would die. He saw her crossing from the Bank into the Square, in the midst of which a large black dog lay in the moonlight, as if it were cut out of marble. She sheered across to the dog and addressed it. He was now in agony lest the Banker's folk see her. Suddenly she attempted to kick the retriever, which gathered itself up and trotted away. Hitherto he had conceived her as keeping the house in her orgies, which, indeed, so far as they came under his observation, had been of rare occurrence. He had pitied her, numbering her in her poor state of health with frail old maids with sad faces, who sit at home with shawls about their shoulders. Now she was flaunting her degradation in the eye of Heaven. She laughed mirthlessly at the dog, and trailed across to the close, where he found her, standing in its mouth, swaying like a stripped tree in a winter's gale, and saw with horror that in a drab, swollen face she had a practised, soliciting eye.

"Get home!" he said; "get home, for God's sake, out of here!" and pushed her roughly by the shoulder.

She gave him a glance of hatred and slouched away. Panting upstairs, she complained of a pain in her back. In the midst of the kitchen floor, with a child's toy in her hand, she gazed round furtively. "Ye didn't notice a sixpence?" she asked; "I thought I put it in the blue bowl. It was your granny's bowl."

The blood was singing in his ears, and leaving his sight murky. "Why don't you stop drinking?" he cried; "you are a disgrace." He could not look at her. Instead of accepting his challenge she simply acquiesced.

"What for?" There was a world of weariness in her voice. "Where's my sixpence? My inside's burnin' like a fire; it's rats that's eatin' me. I wish I were dead."

"Death's maybe at the door, mother," he answered bitterly.

The word "mother" aroused her, and her eyes searched his face hungrily. "I carena if it come ben to my fire en'," she said.

He felt raw, scorched. "Oh, mother! mother! I can never look man or woman in the face again."

As he wailed these words she appeared to take cognisance of him, and the anguish in his voice pierced her consciousness. "Who's got any right to meddle ye?" A cunning leer passed over her face. "Let them redd up their ain hearthstone first." Her lapse into the coarse dialect of Back Street marked for him a further descent in one who had always been scrupulous about the book English, learned in the Edinburgh school.

"Have you no pity for me?" he cried, rage breaking into his voice. "I can't walk in the streets for shame."

Her haggard eyes searched his face with a blink of understanding. "Ay! ay!" Her body shook as if a sudden wind had blown upon it. "I'm just an auld hanky fou o' snotters; it's long since my dancin' days were done." She folded her hands resignedly, as if awaiting the last stone from the slingers of Destiny.

Rage deepened within him at her intense egoism, and a threatening look came into his eyes. "You're killing me by inches," he cried out.

She was dimly conscious of his anger. "Dinna flyte on me; dinna be angry," she cajoled.

"Angry!" he shouted, losing control of himself, and striding up and down before her; "what pity have you got for me? Between you and my father we're the byword of the place."

365

The mention of "father" started a new train of ideas in her mind. "Your father's a bad man an' a thief. Have I no' a friend in a' the world that I can get to live in peace?" In that moment she suspected her son of being in alliance with her husband against her, and the idea became fixed in her mind. Her voice went on monotonously: "I'm better dead; far better. I was sair trachled a' my days between ye a'; farmin' for him, slavin', hainin'; aye keepit frae my ain; fair trachled to death. Am I no' the bonnie ticket?"

His rage ebbed away. The sight of her misery unmanned him —her glassy sunken eyes, her hair prematurely grey, the crow's feet and wrinkles under her eyelids like furrows of grief. He thought, "What a wreck!"

"Will you not give over drinking, mother?" he pleaded. "You're breakin' your own heart as well as mine."

"My time for vexin' ye a' will süne be by," she answered rather cynically, and lurched from him across the kitchen into her bedroom. He heard her fumbling in the dark and stood baulked, hopelessly at bay. He would pack no books on mathematics. What was the use of it all? He heard Topsail in the Coffin wheezing some stupid ballad. Why didn't she shut her mouth, or if she did open it, lament? His father came in, tired from a late hour in the office, where he had been dealing with returns from the first of his cured herring for the season. They had turned out badly, because of a heavy fishing all along the East Coast. He betrayed his annoyance in his surly face and voice.

"Whaur's a' thae bitches?" he snarled; "can a man no' get a bite o' supper?"

At the sound of his voice his wife came into the kitchen.

"I'm busy ironin' Eoghan's hankies," she said softly; "he's going to College."

"Whaur hae ye been stravaigin' the nicht?" said Gillespie in a harsh voice, noting her appearance.

"I've no more mind than them in the grave," she answered. "I'm Lonen's daughter; a respectable woman." She was leaning against the meal barrel. Topsail had been baking some bannocks for Eoghan, of which he was extemely fond; and the lid of the barrel, ill-placed, fell on the floor.

"There's granny's barrel. I used to be the grand baker o' scadit scones."

Gillespie absolutely ignored her, and produced a letter from

366

his inside pocket puckered his brow over its contents. He had read it several times during the day. It was from McAskill, and offered to sell to Gillespie his own letter of instructions to Barbara concerning the Dunoon property if they could agree on the price. Gillespie was afraid of McAskill; but relied on his own father taking no action, and determined to visit old Mr. Strang. He pondered the letter with drawn brows, the tip of his tongue protruding, and fell into a brown study. He was raking up McAskill's past, seeking for a joint in the lawyer's armour.

"I dinna bake now-a-days; there's nothing to bake with. Oh, dearie me! I daurna go near the shop; and Janet compleens she canna get me howkit oot o' the fire en'; but I dinna compleen." She cast a wary glance at her husband. "We've been married over twenty years an' I've scarcely left his hip yet." She nodded over her domestic revelations and smiled at her impassive husband. The smile was like the last flicker of a dying fire, the faint perfume exhaling from a crushed and soiled flower. "He promised to take me to see the crown jewels. . . ."

"Oh, God! this is awful!" groaned the miserable Eoghan.

"Ye needna sweir, Gillespie," droned the whining voice, as she sank heavily into a chair. "I've tholed for more than twenty years." She took a red cotton handkerchief from her pocket and dabbed her nose. "He's aye greetin' in his sleep, Gillespie"— her voice became high-pitched and sharp—"greetin' even on till I soothe him wi' my hands. 'Dinna be doin' that, Eoghan,' I cry an' cry. I can hear him greetin' noo; an' his legs goin' that way"— she kicked out spasmodically. She was plainly recalling scenes of his boyhood—"an' his mouth a' twitchin'. An' when I touch him, poor wean, he catches me wi' a death-grup, sayin' he's fleein' away in the air. Oh, my poor, poor laddie"—she rocked herself in the chair—"my heid's a' wrong wi' him." She put her hand to her head, and her eye caught the vivid red handkerchief. "It was my granny's; I took it out o' the kist. They were the braw big folk in Islay." Her shining eyes searched round the room. "I'm feart he'll go wrong in the mind. Do ye think, Gillespie, it's a lassie?" The tears trickled down her wrinkled cheeks. "If I only kent her I would go on my bended knees to her."

"For God's sake, father, look at her! she's going mad!" Eoghan screamed.

Gillespie looked across at his wife in a long, steadfast gaze.

"What ails ye, that ye glower at me like that, man?" she

367

asked in an angry tone. "I haven't another tocher for ye to steal."

"Ay," Gillespie said heavily, "she's been on the spree wance too often; it'll soon feenish her, the rate she's goin' on."

A greater horror fell upon Eoghan—horror of his father's judicial, dispassionate attitude. The world was huddling away into an arctic night of desolation and woe.

"What are we to do?" he cried in despair.

"Och! och! my heid's dizzy; it's gettin' dark."

Eoghan leapt to her side. Her hands made a groping movement towards him; her breathing became deep and heavy like a snore; little beads of sweat oozed out of her forehead.

"What is it, mother?" He put his arm around her shoulder.

Her eyes turned up at his voice. "It's one o' my black—turns." She fainted in his arm.

He screamed on his father, who rose leisurely, frowning, filled a cup with water and splashed it on her face.

"Dinna be scarred," he said; "she'll come to." He went to the door and shouted on Topsail, who came scurrying down, a sock in her hand. Her mistress was again conscious.

Topsail cast a spiteful glance at Gillespie and said to Eoghan: "Tak' an oxter wi' me intae the room."

Between them Mrs. Strang was borne to bed, and Topsail assured Eoghan that his mother was now quite recovered. As he was leaving the room he heard his mother say: "I have these glasses since Glasgow Exhibition wi' my name on them. They were never used before now."

He staggered as if stricken with blindness into the kitchen, his eyes blazing on his imperturbable father.

"You sit there like a stone!" he screamed. "She's mad! mad! I'm weary of misery and heartache; my mother is lost. Oh, thank God I'm going away tomorrow!"

As day after day had passed Gillespie was more and more convinced that his name hung upon his son, and that its future was in his hands. His son was become a desperate necessity to him, and being a necessity and the centre of his forethought now, was the chief object of his solicitude. His life had been given to the mastery of Brieston; he had neglected almost every obligation within his own doors. His married life had been one of sheer disregard of the claims of the home, which was not for him a sacred place, but a shelter, and more recently a kennel. He despised its interests, evaded its necessary cares, refused except in the most niggard fashion to maintain its life. Insufficient and bad food—the scraps of the shop—and neglect began the mischief; and what had a worse effect on Mrs. Strang was the denial to her of all forms of recreation and pleasure, which were a sort of moral oxygen for her existence. She began to suffer from insomnia, and resorted more deeply to drink. As her body gradually became emaciated and her strength enfeebled periods of bewilderment fell upon her like a cloud, and gave rise in her mind to fears and apprehension. After a period of revolt—instigated by Mrs. Galbraith—in which Gillespie finally threatened violence, she sank into an apathetic acceptance of her position, lost all interest in her home, then in herself, became loose in her behaviour, and was bordering on a state of collapse when the daily stream of her misery burst its dam, and spread abroad in a turbulent sea of insanity.

Gillespie was anxious to defend himself, for he knew that if his wife's condition was laid by his son to his charge, this would make a mortal enemy of the only being in the world for whom he had any affection, and would rob his life of its one redeeming hope. He was increased with goods, but Fate was beginning to expose to him the barrenness of things. He must cling to his son at all costs; and so he put on a martyr air now. "Ay! you're young at it," he answered, in a tone of commiseration, "an' it gies ye a red face. I've kept it in my he'rt thae twenty years."

"Twenty years!" Eoghan was aghast.

"Ay! since ye were born, Eoghan. Twenty stricken years, withoot a word o' complaint. It's me that kens the weary coont o' them—twenty to the pound"—Eoghan was stupefied at this stupendous, silent warfare—"but the dogs," went on his father's pathetic voice, "the dogs that sniffed at her I hae broken, an' sterved their weans."

Gillespie, pleased at this magnificent finesse, which made of his greed a rapier over her defenceless head, aimed at the heart of her slanderers, smiled softly.

The thought of such a dumb, titanic contest bewildered Eoghan. But his grandfather! the old, lonely, despoiled man in the "Ghost," bending over his consoling Bible—this bare tree—had Gillespie struck at him also in his wife's defence? Eoghan recalled the gnarled hands of his grandfather—their thin, twisted veins, the knuckles swollen with rheumatism, turning over the leaves of the Bible like a marooned mariner consulting a chart—hands that had toiled at the oar, and were in their old age ruthlessly plundered. Hunger and thirst, death and anguish of the sea he had endured with patience; but the separation from his family was slowly killing him. Eoghan swallowed a sob.

"What about my grandfather?" he blurted out.

"I needit amuneetion for the fight."

"His money is all gone in his old age."

"Hoots!" answered Gillespie lightly. "the old man 'ill no sterve, ye know that. Ye canna aye keep your ain folk in your pooch."

"It's a lie, a lie," rang in Eoghan's brain; "greed has slain its own, father and wife." The thought smote on his brain like a hammer on an anvil; and as he moved to the door he flung a look full of contempt at his father: "Then your pocket is a worse hell than my mother's;" and he went out in wrath before his father.

The next morning he went by luggage steamer to Glasgow without saying good-bye to his father. He had started so early that he missed the intelligence which circulated through Brieston at noon—that Mr. Kennedy had retired from his office. Mr. Campion found him stiff and cold in his armchair.

9

EOGHAN lived in part in a vertigo of waking, in part in that dream state with which he had been familiar in boyhood, and before him constantly were the callous eyes of his father and the wild, denunciatory laughter of his mother, a figure of fury swooning into stone. His own face was petrified, his stare fixed, as he roused himself with difficulty at the banal sounds of the street, and the harsh rumour of a commercial people. "If I could sit on here, sit on for ever," he thought. His text-book on mathematics lay open on the table, where he had placed it to defend himself from the intrusions of his landlord, a fiery-faced man in stocking soles, who last night had curled himself up in a horse-hair armchair and recounted to the lodger his personal history. He had seen the Queen in Glasgow twice; his son had been driven "silly" by the police, who had held him as a marked man, and had mauled him on a Saturday night. His son now spent his time hanging over the window, and shrinking back when he saw a uniform. Now and again he would flap his arms and say: "If I were a wee spug I would flee awa' frae the poliss." Eoghan had been invited into the kitchen overlooking Byres Road to see the "silly," who mouthed at him and made noises like an animal. His landlord and he filed out again, as if they had been in a zoological garden or a museum, the red-faced mason whispering that it was all up with a man when the poliss took a spite to him.

Eoghan had that day sat the paper in English, and determined to revise his trigonometry after tea. Rousing himself, he lit the gas and sat down to a chapter on the solution of triangles. He read the first page without any conception of its meaning. Weariness, hopelessness, fell upon him as a curse, and he got up in despair. His eye caught an oleograph of Gladstone on the wall, showing a young pink-and-white complexion and a cherubic smile. He shook himself with an effort from this mood of detachment. "What am I doing? Nothing; nothing," he thought, overcome with vexation. His misery was irredeemable. Aimlessly he picked up the examination paper in English, headed Glasgow University Preliminary Examination. By an enormous effort of will he had that day tackled the questions which were all, he thought, so utterly divorced from life. What had they to do with the horror of his existence? Mechanically he read them once more. "Give, in your own words, the substance of the following passage" (the lines swam before his eyes):

> "No voice divine the storm allayed,
>   No light propitious shone;
>   We perished each alone,
>   And I . . .
>   And whelmed in deeper gulfs than he."

"Poor devil! poor mad devil," he muttered. He read, on stultified:

" Characterise the style of the following passages:

" (a) 'But the iniquity of oblivion blindly scattereth her poppy, and deals with the memory of men without distinction to merit of perpetuity.

" (b) 'Till the day break and the shadows flee away.'

" (c) 'Through the sad heart of Ruth when, sick for home,
        She stood in tears amid the alien corn;

The same that ofttimes hath
Charm'd magic casements opening on the foam
Of perilous seas in faëry lands forlorn——' "

The examination paper fluttered in his shaking hand. Beyond the
walls he saw the spindrift rising behind dim isles of the west,
upon the rigging of a gaunt, lonely house smothered in clouds
of snow, and heard the sign of a dagger jangling above the door.
Pale dreams of a sombre sea-land drifted up and vanished, leaving unappeasable pain and sadness behind. He read on:

" (d) 'Oh, eloquent, just and mightie Death! whom none could
advise thou hast persuaded; what none hath dared thou hast done,
and whom all the world hath flattered thou only hast cast out of the
world and despised. Thou hast drawn together all the farre stretched
greatness, all the pride, crueltie, and ambition of man, and covered it
all over with these two narrow words—*Hic Jacet!*' "

What fiendish torture! What infinite malice to torment him
with those words! The babbling of the "silly" in the next room
broke the silence. He was whining for his mother to protect him
from the poliss. What a world of devils and of geniuses! Eoghan
crushed the examination paper into a ball and threw it on the
fire. The thought of returning to the text-book on trigonometry
filled him with nausea, and picking up his cap he went into the
street and walked up University Avenue, away from the crowd
in Byres Road, like one in a dream. He was startled by the
University clock booming the half-hour as he hurried down the
brae of Gibson Street. In Woodlands Road the crowd was
thicker; but he thought them morose, alien to the feelings of
pity or terror, and untouched by any great trial. They moved as
a cloud. He retraced his steps, plunging blindly, and his level
stare distinguishing no face in front of him.

Within his room he felt safer and calmer. The clear light, the
bright fire, made the place an asylum from the great callous city.
Determined to resign himself to the hazards of the future, he
would seize an omen from to-morrow's examination paper. If
it suited the course of his studies he would pursue his way
through a College career relentlessly, with his back for ever
turned upon Brieston and its shame. He went to bed in a com-
paratively tranquil state of mind.

The morning was dark with fog, out of which, as he passed
along Dumbarton Road, he saw a funeral loom, the hearse gigantic

in the gloom. He shuddered. At this time in the morning! He took his chair at the square, black table—No. 104—in the Bute Hall, and having written his name on the examination book, sat gnawing the end of the pen. As something far off in a dream he heard the rustling of papers all over the hall, and the uneasy shuffling of feet. It was no use—his youth was despoiled; he saw that now. The armour of last night's resignation was only cardboard. A cloud of anguish brooded on his mind. He would have to live in a house whose blinds were eternally drawn, within which sat a dishevelled woman with a face of stone, who only roused herself to commit acts of shame, and to return from her orgies trembling and white as a sheet, her glassy eyes pools of madness. He gave way to the direst suspicions, recalling the obscene name he had heard the tailor use, and seeing once more the desert emptiness of a moonlit street, and its blind, blanched house-fronts crudely staring down on a dark, ugly figure reeling along to the accompaniment of inane laughter. He saw the great dog slouch away in fear, and heard her childish skirl rise over the fevered scraping of hundreds of pens, wielded by young men who were racing with each other against time for a place on the Bursary List. There had been in Brieston Harbour a yacht's anchor-light which had a wobbling movement like hers. From the degradation of this woman proceeded a flame that was devouring him. She, sordid and derelict, was become the arbiter of his fate and he the puppet. Pitiably ignorant of her debauchery, she was Olympian over him in menace, her dishevelled head towering among lightnings. The cleanness of his life was an ineptitude before her vileness; his ambitions and hopes lay strangled in the coils of her obscenity. As long as she was above earth he would be a target for the jibes and whisperings of men who could think of nothing but the weather and the fishing. What use to carry College laurels back to the mire of Brieston? His quivering, secretive, proud heart was bleeding as he thought of his darling dreams shattered by a malign and sordid despotism. He gazed around in anguish at the hundreds of young men with heads bent over the little square, black tables in the large, silent hall, and felt himself an outcast. He had chewed the end of his pen to pulp, and his chair was scrunching on the hard wooden floor. His fellow-examinee at the next table looked angrily across at him, and Eoghan bent his eyes on his examination book and began to write, he knew not what. After a little he glanced at the

373

examination paper, but, unable to discern the algebraic symbols, threw down his pen and pushed back his chair. The pen rolled off the table on to the floor. He stood a moment swaying on his feet. The student beside him looked up and was about to speak, but at the sight of the shocking appearance of Eoghan's face went on again with his writing. Eoghan walked rapidly down the matted passage towards the door. Some one shouted, and turning he saw the superintendent of the examination, a thin, wiry man, with dark, piercing eyes, relieved by a humorous, tolerant smile. His gown was floating out behind him like a cloud. Eoghan awaited him with a fixed smile and set jaws, as he would a blood-hound on his slot.

"Have you finished your algebra?"

Eoghan felt angered at the cool, self-sufficient darkness of this man, at his malignant politeness and immaculate get-up—neatly curled black moustache, superb linen cuffs, high, snowy collar, a dim blue stone in his tie-pin, his thick, curly hair neatly cropped.

"I've done all the algebra I'll ever do." He felt at bay and revengeful.

"If you want to leave the hall at this hour you must leave the examination paper behind."

"I have no paper." Eoghan bowed ironically and turned on his heel. The superintendent stared after him, betraying well-bred surprise; then strolled to the vacant table and curiously read the name on the yellow cover of the examination book. He opened it at the first page. It contained no algebra, but:

"Oh, eloquent, just and mightie Death, so early in the fog.',

A little beneath it in a large, sprawling hand:

"No voice divine the storm allayed,
  On perilous seas in faëry lands forlorn."

And further down, in a more ragged hand:

"The gown has yielded to infamy; the eternal lamp of learning is quenched because there was whisky for oil in the bowl."

"Life is a page of Punch, with the letterpress by Sterne and Rabelais. *Vae victis*."

The whimsical smile faded out of the black, piercing eyes as they rested for a long time on the scribbled writing. "The incoherence of talent. I ought to have detained him;" and the super-intendent picked up the book as a trophy for his wife's careless hour, and went back to his duty of patrolling the hall.

Everything looked as simple as before—the long frontage of the Infirmary; the red-flannelled patients taking the air; the West-end Park with its trees, its sinuous walks, its muddy river; the cabs and cars rattling along Dumbarton Road; the squat little uniformed porter at the gate of the Infirmary, keeping official watch upon the living and the dead—and yet all was changed. It was hateful, inimical, leaping suddenly out of a state of sun-drenched quiescence into an amazing busyness, wrought of the hand of ambition, hung with dreams and hopes, ripe with achievement, and accusing him as he crept along with his infinitesimal pain of vacillation, cowardice, and puerile despair. The sight of the Infirmary and University was hideous, and he hastened to get down to the street, where were men of affairs like his father. He had formed an idea of escape from an accusing conscience—he would return to Brieston and engage himself in the business of his father. He flung back a look of hatred at the long front of the University. It was a big, grey cage. He had no tender resignation, but a spirit of sombre revolt against this seat of the monopoly of haughty intelligence. He had the super-intendent in his mind's eye, and ground his teeth as he thought of that dark official, who had smiled like a god upon his disquiet. He had spoken with a lisp and a supercilious curl of dark eye-brows, a play of white fingers and manicured nails. Simpering fool in the swaddling bands of fine linen! The drone of Glasgow's traffic came up to him. What did that academic ass, that dry surd know of all this—the life of the great grimy servant beneath, who keeps a door in the house of the world—his eyes swept around to the Infirmary—or of that carbuncle on the back of the city? Does he know anything of the poor devils who are glad to creep in there out of ships?—Iain, broken on a reeling deck in the midst of a gale, was in his mind—out of factories, out of the big offices, out of the wee homes. Ay! out of the wee homes. "Bethes-da! Bethesda!" he muttered. The sun struck along the noble front of the edifice. He remembered the crowd he had seen yesterday standing at its gates. How fine it looked with its trees and lawns! but that silent crowd, with their bunches of flowers, their drawn faces, their bleeding hearts waiting at the gates of the grim resolver of all their fears. He nodded to the grey pile—how quiet it was!—death is quiet—and the windows, hundreds of them, watching and waiting. A siren screamed on the river. Though the fog had lifted from the heights of Gilmorehill it clung in shreds about the Clyde. Why do these seamen blare so in the very doors of pain? Do people ever think what is behind that long face of stone with its watching windows, where the pigeons flutter in the silent sunshine—a knife perhaps going this very moment into a girl's body? He shuddered. Then, recollecting himself, he rose from off the railing on which he had been leaning, and gazed down on the roofs of Glasgow. Life was going on there, big and palpitating, breeding and bleeding, sowing and reaping, founding and building, hewing and banking. There should be a Chair of Life founded in this University—he lapsed again into meditation—but where would they find a professor? He was eager to escape into the streets, having succeeded in pouring an anodyne upon his conscience. The University is an artificial rose planted in the midst of a field in which men are toiling and sweating. The rose for ever blows, rain or sun, and young fools learn to carry away from it beautiful artificial petals. With this specious idea, which was his apology to his conscience for his retreat, he passed out of the University gate into the turbulence of Dumbarton Road. An incubus of grey stone, a meaningless network of mathematical figures and quotations from the classics was behind him. A blind man, anchored to a dog by the gate, was reading aloud from a Braille book. The latter-day fear of life gripped Eoghan at the sight; and rattling some coppers in the blind man's tin he hurried on in the direction of Partick. He wandered without sense of direction, and felt jaded and his mind empty. In a little while he asked aloud, "Why am I here? I've made an ugly mess of things. What will Mr. Kennedy think?" His brain burned with the consciousness that he was like an animal caught in the toils. Twice he stopped gazing around, feeling terribly lonely, and hungering for the sight of a known face. In Great Western Road, not far from the Botanic Gardens, he asked a policeman to direct him to Byres Road. He asked this to have an opportunity of speaking to some one, for he felt in this monstrous isolation that he must scream aloud. He found his landlady out. His limbs were heavy like metal as he sat down in company of the "silly." He felt languid and depressed. His companion turned large eyes of fear upon him, and crouched into a corner. Neither spoke a word. After an hour of this inanition, feeling refreshed by his rest, he picked up his cap and went out. Grey evening was brooding on the streets of Partick, along which the "black squad" was hurrying home for tea. He remembered he had eaten nothing since breakfast, and walked along on the look-out for an eating-house. In Kelvinhaugh he entered a dairy, drank two glasses of milk and ate a scone. His eye caught a play-bill on the wall, and he asked the girl behind the counter by what streets to reach the theatre. He lost his way, and paid a street urchin to act as guide; but the boy, proving too loquacious, was dismissed. In the theatre he felt a sense of isolation, and suffered from the happiness of those about him. His neighbour, a stout, short man with a clear, healthy complexion, was deep in talk with his fellow about a bowling tournament somewhere in Langside, with which the season was to be closed. The tournament was to be followed by a whist drive. The little stout man spoke wittily, and incensed Eoghan. The play, a gross travesty of life, teemed with skipping girls, a naval officer smoking cigarettes, in a splendid uniform, who sang a bombastic sea-song in a rich baritone, and a wizened little man in grey side-whiskers and spats, the rich father of a willowy girl, who was in love with the baritone. The father posed in attitudes of grief as he reviled the officer and his wilful daughter to a ringletted woman who was once nurse to the daughter. What tawdry banality! The scene overwhelmed him with mournfulness. The fat witty man at his side was whispering innuendoes behind his programme, and scrutinising the painted girls as if they were cattle. Eoghan left the theatre, weary of its tinsel, sick of its cardboard life and stucco characters. He would go home, yes, home; Barbara would bring out her fiddle and they would make a night of it. He went down Renfield street and bought his ticket at the Central Station. In Argyll Street he boarded a car for Partick. The beards of middle-aged men hung over the buttoned-up collars of their coats as they leaned attentively towards the women, and with an air of responsibility searched for the necessary coins in their pockets. Every one was silent except an old, stout man, grey like a lichened rock. A young girl tripped in, leaving a legacy of laughter behind her to some friend or lover. She wore neither furs, veil, nor gloves, was all in white, and filled the car with breeziness, spontaneity, joyousness, a sense of health. On her entrance convention paled, and every one began to talk. Eoghan thought of Barbara, and saw as in a dream the face of the morning hills

377

rise in a bland air above a tranquil sea; the "Ghost" laved almost by the tide, and sea-birds flying over its roof. At its door an old man with expectant face watched the road. He glanced timidly at the girl. Feeling his eyes upon her she returned the glance. In confusion he looked out of the car and saw a woman of the street, her neck foreshortened in the depth of imitation sable furs, dallying at the window of a music-seller's shop to evade the police till the music-hall across the street disgorged the devotees of an empty art.

At Finnieston a couple entered. One a wisp of a man who sat down hat in hand. A white tie marked him as a wedding guest. He ran his fingers through his hair and babbled of his recent revelry to the woman, who was enormously fat and sat legs astride. Her flesh quivered with the movements of the vehicle. She had a paunch of a bosom on which lay droppings of food. Her hat was awry. She began to recount the history of a quarrel at the wedding feast. Her eyes were bleary with drink; she rolled in her seat, grunting, and presented a sordid spectacle. A woman in bangles and furs beside Eoghan murmured "How disgusting!" The female leviathan belched and, angry at the man for monopolising the conversation, plucked a rabbit fur from her neck and stuffed it in the man's mouth. He threatened her with his fist, and the conductor of the car intervened. Eoghan was sickened, and the silver vision of home vanished. He saw his mother in this slavering, foul-mouthed woman. He rose hurriedly, left the car, and found himself at the gates of the West-end Park. A tall, thin, dark woman with a child's hand in hers stopped singing to beseech alms of a young man and girl who approached the gates arm in arm. She said they had had nothing to eat that day. The girl was leaning towards her lover with her shining eyes upon him, and they did not so much as glance at the starving mother and child. The woman sighed deeply, and looked down in pity at the babe. What a relentless world! He thrust a handful of coins into the woman's hand and dived into the darkness of the Park. He had noticed a falling-in about the woman's temples. He heard the girl ahead of him laughing, and was filled with rage. He walked rapidly till he came to a vacant seat. Above him the massed gloom of the University pile made him shudder—gigantic under a dark night-sky, inhospitable, and yet harbouring in its scrupulous aloofness a thousand thousand dreams—the home and asylum of all the talents which yet ground individual sorrow and grief into dust. He took no notice of the chance couples who passed him, clinging to each other's arms. What was he to do? He attempted to count his money. There was seven pounds in notes. The loose money he had given to the woman at the gate. He would go to some strange town and rid him of the incubus of the University and his mother—Dundee, Aberdeen, Perth, Edinburgh, Ayr, Dumfries, London; he conned name after name—Oxford. "What folly is this?" he cried aloud, half bewildered; "I must go home and live it down; Barbara at least will be glad to see me." The University bell boomed out solemnly. He counted the heavy strokes. Twelve o'clock. He jumped to his feet as the last stroke died away. It was the farewell of the University to one of her lost children.

He recognised when he reached his lodgings that Brieston was a retreat which would expose him to humiliation, and which was big with unnamed fear. He sat down with an abandoned air, his arms hanging loosely. The fire was out, and he began to shiver with the cold. He was unable to think. If only he could go and hide somewhere. The tears oozed into his eyes, and when he angrily shook them away his eyes became fixed like stones. Suddenly he saw his mother before him—she was in her nightdress, her hair on her shoulders, a lamp in her hand, and she besought him mutely, with a face of fear and hunger. He jumped to his feet, full of alarm, and a scream rang from his lips. It awakened him to reality. The vision had vanished, the room was horribly empty, and life also empty of everything dear that it possessed—faith, aspiration, effort. He felt himself rising up with the floor and sinking down. "She needs me! she needs me!" he moaned. The room began slowly to spin about; but he was unable to lift his head, which felt numb and hard like a block of iron. He tottered to the mirror and gazed at his face. It was drawn and like clay.

"I am going to be ill," he whispered in a strained, tense voice. He thought he heard some one moving in the next room, but was not sure, for a loud buzzing sang in his ears. He staggered back towards the chair and felt himself sliding into an enormous space. The room had ceased spinning, and was receding from him swiftly, as if winged. He flung up his two arms and sank into the black void. The door was opened cautiously an inch or so; a red-whiskered face peered in, and two slits of eyes, blinking with sleep.

379

"Is anything wrang wi' ye?"

There was no answer.

It was not till the seventeenth day after that the Partick doctor allowed Eoghan to rise from a bed of low fever and influenza to go home. The doctor advised him to take a thorough rest, and if possible go on a holiday that would give him a complete change. Above all, he was on no account to worry. Eoghan set out for Brieston, after having sent a telegram to Barbara from the Central Station.

10

TOPSAIL wore a clean apron, and had dinner ready for him in the parlour. She had dusted the box of birds' eggs, collected when he was at school, and set it in a conspicuous place beside the stuffed parrot in the glass case. Her work finished, she became shy; and this feeling grew as it came nearer noon, at which hour the steamer was due. What would she call him—Eoghan or Mr. Strang? She could not decide. "Mr." was cold and strange. A distant rumble was heard, and she ran to the parlour window. "There's the coaches; there's the coaches frae the steamer," she shouted excitedly to her mistress. She watched the coach stop at the "George Hotel" and the bareheaded proprietor scurry out of doors. There was a cloud of steam above the horses' ears. The driver jumped down, whip in hand, and his bandy legs twinkled round to the nose of his horses. Three passengers descended and entered the Hotel. The driver climbed up again to the box and laid his whip across the flanks of his team. Topsail's eyes widened; her hands fell listlessly to her side. The Square and the front of the Hotel became desolatingly empty. She blamed the driver for this and hated him. Mechanically she picked up the case of eggs, wiped the glass with her apron and looked round the room—the bright fire, the first since Iain's funeral, ordered that day by Gillespie, and the table with its snowy cloth. A phantom presence that had come there with strong familiar solicitations had crept away again. She felt widowed afresh. Again she moved to the window. No! Yes! it was he. She wiped the tears from her eyes and craned her neck. Wearing gloves, too, and walking up the street with Maclean. The dear doctor! pulling away at his moustache and watching Eoghan with his keen eyes. But what a face the laddie had—white as a sheet!

"Come over to-morrow and have breakfast with me." Oh, the dear, dear doctor. Just listen to his big, cheery voice.

"Oh, he's here! he's here! Do ye think he'd come up wi' the coaches? The folk winna see him. He walked up wi' the doctor." She gripped her mistress by the arm and shouted in her ear:

"He's gotten a moustache; I saw 't frae the winda; a wee black moustache." An ecstatic joy irradiated Topsail's face. Her mistress gloomed up at her from lowering eyebrows, and made no response.

Gillespie was standing in the front door of the shop. He was now past middle age; his neck, straight and massive, was so red that flame seemed to be smouldering beneath the skin. His skull was immense; its frontal part polished like an ivory ball; and his hair turning silver. A pleasant, almost patriarchal man to look at, were it not for the quick eyes, which darted with the weasel's cunning and flash. He had a ponderous, saturnine, half meditative air as he watched his son.

"An' hoo are ye?" he hailed cheerily, while Eoghan was some two yards off. With a glad light in his greenish eyes, whose moistness gave the impression that they had been sucking something succulent, he scanned his son.

"A wee thing thinner; ye're at the studyin' ower much." Eoghan was moved by the solicitude in his father's voice and look.

"Oh, I'm all right!" He brushed past his father into the shop from the gaze of the Square—Lowrie in linen at his window; Kyle, with his withering smile, at his door.

Gillespie followed, and when they were within the shop, held out an almost timid hand, and with a hungry look at his son said: "Shake hands, Eoghan."

They shook hands in silence.

That face, pale as the dead, the listless air, the slack hands, the weary voice, found out Gillespie in the very centre of his being.

"Ye're home for a holiday." He spoke with desperate cheerfulness.

No! he had failed in his examination; he had been ill in Glasgow. "I've come back to go into the business as you wished":

then he turned his back, and stood spent and motionless, the lines of his body quivering into rigidity. In that bowed figure Gillespie divined that there was more than the effect of failure in examination, for which, indeed, Gillespie was glad. He refrained from questioning his son about his prolonged absence and how he had spent the "siller." The stark figure troubled Gillespie, who was ready to make sacrifices now that Eoghan was prepared to go into the business. His son's decision removed a deep, secret trouble. Final attainment in life was now possible. He would leave a "braw pickle siller" to his son, who would prolong his name and carry on his works. He knew the smouldering hostility of Brieston; the implacable enmity of Lonend; Mrs. Galbraith's unsleeping desire of vengeance; but trampled on these in sheer contempt. A balance at the bank was invulnerable armour, and nothing could touch him now in face of those words: "I've come to go into the business"—nothing except that ghostly face consumed with woe. It filled him with a growing uneasiness.

"Is there anything wrang wi' ye by ordinar, Eoghan?"

"I've come back to the slave-hulks," was the answer.

Gillespie was non-plussed. He determined to make a bargain with his son that any man would jump at, for the wounds taken in life's vicissitudes could all be healed by bargains. "Dinna tak' on aboot thae examinations; I'll soon be gein' up business; I feel gey an' düne whiles in the mornin's: ye'll hae a braw sittin' doon; naethin' in a' Brieston like it. I've wrocht lang an' late an' early; the tocher 'ill a' be yours, Eoghan. There's seeven thoosan' in dry money in the bank; an' eight hunner good in shares in shippin'; an' a score o' fishin'-boats; an' a' the stores and the business; an' I'm insured on a thoosan' wi' profits when I'm sixty-five."

To Eoghan his father was enumerating the results of a life of oppression, dishonesty, and theft.

"Step ben the office an' we'll look ower the books an' papers; it's as weel for ye to ken whaur ye stan'."

Eoghan turned and confronted his father. "Don't insult me any longer with your offer of plunder. You make me feel a rogue. The more the thousands the deeper your guilt."

The cold, merciless tones smote Gillespie like a sword. He saw himself baulked, his life defeated and closed up without avenue of escape, his wealth ashes, and nemesis in his path. If his son denied him, what lay ahead of him but a dreary existence of aimlessly amassing money? It would go through his wife—who seemed to be as wiry as a cat—to Lonend, who was to be married to Mrs. Galbraith at the New Year. The thought was gall to him. What could he do with his possessions? The profile of nemesis now was turned full face upon him—to have laboured for Lonend and Calum Galbraith's widow. More than ever was the anchor of his hope cast in his son. Gillespie turned harrowed eyes upon him, and in that glance, resting on the silent figure of grief which already had begun to haunt the father, he felt how impotent he was.

"What dae ye mean, Eoghan? Ye canna go intae a business noo-a-days withoot capital."

"Do you know what I did with the money you gave me when I went to Glasgow? I paid my landlady and the doctor."

"Of coorse; of coorse. I hope ye werena skimped."

"The rest I gave to the poor," Eoghan went on pitilessly. Gillespie winced, and sternness crept into his eyes; his nostrils whistled with suppressed anger. "If you want me to work along with you pay back the money you have plundered."

"To wha?"

"To the fishermen; to my grandfather; to my mother."

At this signal of menace covetousness gripped Gillespie's heart.

"To your mother," he sneered; "bonny lik' thing, to squander it in drink."

"That fault is yours. You have denied her all her life; you have made my grandfather weep tears of blood; your greed has been the means of drowning my brother."

"Ay! ay! blame me for Goäd Almighty's storms."

"No!" The boy's face was blanched with passion. "I blame you for a rotten, ill-founded, under-manned boat. The heap of your gold is the heap of your iniquity. Remember when you come to die that I told you so."

Gillespie trembled before the fierceness of the accusation. The solid ground was gone from his feet. "Is that what ye cam' back frae the Coallege to tell me?" The feeble light of a last hope fluttered in his breast—his son had spoken at the first of entering the business without those terrible stipulations. "Will ye no' tak' up the pleugh-stilts, Eoghan, an' no heed thae noänsense? Ye're tired oot the noo. Bide till ye get a chack o' dinner."

"I warn you I will give your money away to its rightful owners."

Fear and greed made Gillespie abject. He moaned the death of Iain. Where could he turn now? He had slaved all his life and was this the end, the thanks? Was he to carry his white hairs to the street a beggar, and begin the fight again empty-handed? Brieston would fling glaur on him. Had his son no bowels of mercy? Was he to see a' his money an' gear slippin' into the hands o' Lonen', his dour enemy?

He spent his last word and stood waiting, beseeching an answer. Eoghan's back was still turned. "Goäd in heaven! I canna thole to see my money gang to Lonen': it wad gie me the grue in my grave."

"If there's no other way, then take it with you to the grave."

The words fell on Gillespie loaded with doom. One minute, two, three of terrific silence. It was broken by a gush of song from one of the canaries. In the midst of the raining melody Eoghan began to walk out of the shop. "I will return as your partner when you have paid back what you have taken unjustly, and restored to my mother her proper position as your wife."

Gillespie did not hear. The blaze of bird-music drowned every other sound. He raised a stupefied face to the canary. "Wheest, wheest ee noo wi' your blatter; wheest, I tell ye; hae I no' enough to thole?"

He felt stifling, and walked heavily to the door for air. His son was walking rapidly across the Square. He watched him go down Harbour Street, on the way to the "Ghost." For a long time Gillespie pondered, and at last retired and addressed the twittering canary. "There's only ae thing noo—get him mairrit on Barbara. She'll haud a grup o' the siller."

11

SOME ten days previous to this scene Gillespie had paid a furtive visit to the "Ghost"—the first since he had removed to the Square, and the following morning at breakfast old Mr. Strang spoke of the visit to Barbara. He fidgeted a good deal and finally said:

"He's stealt your money, Barbara."

The girl's bosom rose and fell quickly.

"Have we no money, grandad?"

"Yours is gone, lassie—the thief, thief"—those words were wrung out of him.

Barbara was overcome with horror. Life, threatened with penury, suddenly assumed titanic proportions.

"What are we to do, grandad?"

"McAskill, the lawyer, advises ye to go to law." He spoke without looking up. She thought of Eoghan and her face became tender, compassionate.

"Oh, no! no! not that."

He groaned. "We maun nurse oor sorrow an' oor shame. The wolf! the wolf! needit the money for a steamer."

He lifted his eyes upon her out of tearless depths, and the pathos of something once beautiful and now mangled in that face stirred the girl to a wave of motherhood. She ran to him and flung her arms around his neck. "Never mind, grandad; we've always got each other."

"Ay, God's good to me . . . Gillespie doesna believe in God. It's a terrible thing, the wrath o' the livin' God." The voice rang out loudly. The girl gazed at him in fear. "Your granny was feared o' a curse. What am I sayin'!" he broke off abruptly; "a wheen noansense o' the olden times——"

Barbara listened wide-eyed. Something of horror in the backward life of this house overshadowed them, and her glamorous beauty faded away into an aged look, as that of one who has watched a battle, and has seen the ruin of war conceal the face of one beloved.

But her fear of penury, her horror of the unknown curse were now forgotten. Eoghan was coming to-day, and great prison walls crumbled to dust. Fire licked up the grey shadows upon the world. There were tongues and voices everywhere. She consulted the telegram again and again, flung open the window, and drank in breath after breath of the cool air. Frost whitened the grass and hedges; the road was like iron; diamonds flashed in the sea. Life was glory, and she ascended her mount of transfiguration and saw the heavens open. The scents of the shore; salt of the sea; its sparkle and glitter and crooning; the fleece-clouds in the blue; the imperial blaze on the windows of Muirhead Farm; the wheeling of the gulls; a tawny fisher sail leaning on the gentle north wind—all entered through eye and ear into her blood, intoxicating her. She opened wide her arms and murmured his name. Her eyes, like frosty stars, shone along the road to Brieston.

The sight of her was at once a solvent of his trouble. As he became aware of the marvellous fragrance of her face, the tender, shy glance of her eyes, the eagerness and joy of her whole being, he ascended out of his misery into another plane of being. She blushed before his long, ardent look, and came towards him, her two hands out, her youth full of alluring grace, speaking his name breathlessly. As he kissed her he saw in the shadow of her hat a magnificent lustre in her eyes. Then they walked by the seaside, where the Loch was a great pearl, bordered along the shore as with green iridescent glass. She called his attention to the insignificant things of the wayside for sheer joy of talking to him, jested about his moustache, which she caressed with pouts of laughter. "What torment my life has been since you went away; but now—Oh, Eoghan! Eoghan! I love you better than God."

"Hush! you mustn't say that."

"Oh, but it's true! it's true!"

Her eyes were shining as if she beheld an unearthly vision. "Oh! Eoghan! Eoghan! you've come; you've come back at last." She edged between his arms, and hungrily gazing on his face, leaned her head on his shoulder and began to sob softly. A bird was calling, calling upon the hill, where the grey little wind was purfling among the trees. The song of the bird became a pain to him.

"Barbara, dear! what is wrong?"

"I thought you were never, never going to come ... it's terrible .... I don't know what has come over grandad ... I wish, oh, I wish he could cry!"

He ceased walking.

"What is it?" He had a premonition of disaster.

"That lawyer came—I shudder yet when I think of him: he's so like an eel—and then, dear, your father. Grandad hasn't been the same since. He doesn't seem to hear when I speak to him; but keeps on muttering about grandmother and some sort of doom. He says the sign over the door must come down." Her lips were pale, and they stood hand in hand, looking in at each other's eyes in dread. "When I read the telegram you sent he said you must not step below the sign again." From where they stood the sign was visible. Swaying in the little grey wind, its hand that held the dripping dagger shook as with frenzy. Its

386

mournful sound came to their ears, cold-blooded, croaking. In a puff of the wind it snarled as if in rage. The girl shivered as a cloud went over the sun.

"I wonder what my father was doing there——" He checked himself; he felt something sinister and unfathomable gathering on his life, and thought of his mother. "Were you there when my father came?" he asked abruptly.

"I was upstairs . . . I think they were quarrelling."

She was withholding something, he felt.

"Barbara, tell me what you heard."

She lifted candid, trustful, yet frightened eyes to him. "Grandad said to him, 'No! I'll hae nocht to do wi' lawyers. I leave ye in the hands of God.'"

"And then?"

"Your father answered, 'I'll tak' the risk o' that.'"

"Ah! what a devil! what a devil!" by a prodigious effort of will he recovered his calm. "Come," he went on, "come with me to the 'Ghost.'" He took her hand and led her down the braeside above the burn, which they crossed, walked along a fence, and came out through a little gate at the back of the "Ghost," at the outhouse where Gillespie used to keep his snares. They passed round the gable-end, along the gable wall, to the corner of the house. A flurry of wind blew in their faces, and the girl bent her head; but Eoghan's eyes were riveted on a sight that made the blood drain away from his heart. Against the wall of the house was a ladder, which his grandfather, hammer in hand, was climbing. His shoulders were rounded into a hoop; his hair had grown grey; his head was bare; the long grey locks were tossed about by the wind. The girl lifted her eyes and shrieked:

"Grandfather, grandfather, you'll be killed!"

The old man continued to climb up, his eyes fixed on the sign above, his mouth open, the blue-veined hand clutching the hammer. The Bent Preen drifted up from nowhere and stood, pricked out against the grey sea, in a new pair of brown checked trousers, surveying the scene. The old man never once withdrew his gaze from the sign; but crept up as if he were on some clandestine business. His earnestness emptied the heavens, the earth, and the sea of all interest to the watchers; and the tremendous silence was broken by the hammer ringing out on the sign. The Bent Preen waved his arm. "Smash it down; it's the flag o' the devil." His mocking laugh rivalled the sound of the hammer.

"Ha, ha, ha! Dick, I'd sook whisky oot o' a dirty cloot; but I'm damned if I'd touch that thing for a' the gold in the mint." Again the metallic sound leapt out sharply—the sound of brass or bronze. It appeared to enrage the old man, for the blows now fell thickly, as if he were beating a tocsin. The gulls screamed and flew out to sea. The old man's energy was amazing. His head was thrown up, an expression of the intensest hatred was on his face, and his lips, curled back, gave him a savage appearance. The light glittered on the sign where he had struck it; it was like a wound on a negro's face. The wound seemed to outrage, to defy the old man, who struck with redoubled fury, aiming blow after blow at the painted dagger, till the hillside rang with the clashing sounds. Those beneath heard his laboured breathing—stertorous, panting in hot, quick sounds. The girl's face, terror-stricken, was buried in her hands. Something abysmal surrounded Eoghan. The sound of those blows was coming out of a chasm of dead men's bones, which rattled fiercely. He looked at Barbara, and thought that his grandfather and she shared some secret horror. He had a feeling of desolation, a sense of ruin. An exhalation of the accursed drifted about the place.

"Oh, please, please, Eoghan, stop him! take him down! The sounds; oh, they are bursting through my ears!"

The old man's wrath was now demoniacal. He was hewing, not at brass, but at some sombre fatality as he gnashed his teeth and muttered between the short pants of his breathing. The sweat dripped from over a pair of blazing eyes. Eoghan swallowed his saliva, as if he was swallowing cinders. "He'll kill me with that hammer if I go up." He leapt at the ladder, and began to run up on all fours, shouting, "Come down! come down!" but his voice was swamped in the gulf of sound. The rhythmical movement of the arm went on like a smith's at the anvil. As the arm fell at a blow Eoghan shot out his hand and gripped the wrist of the old man, who glared down a look of malevolence. Again the hammer swung up. Eoghan saw the steel head glinting in the sun, and jerked his body across the ladder out of its track. It crashed down on a rung. There was a splintering of wood; the hammer fell to the ground; the ladder violently jerked; swayed like a boat on the sea; began to slide along the wall, slowly, then with accelerated motion; and the next moment they were hurled to the ground, the ladder astraddle across their bodies. Eoghan felt something sharp and burning sting his forehead; sucked something hot and salt, and knew it was blood. He opened his mouth to drink again the pungent liquid, and slid into a chasm of darkness, with a torrent of water roaring in his ears. The weight of a mountain lay across his chest. . . . Something cold and soft was on his forehead; but his eyes were sealed with molten lead. He put up his hand, and it was caught and held. What an intolerable time it took to open his eyes! He was drawing light up into them out of eternity. At last they sucked up the light from the abyss, and he saw Barbara's face.

"I fell off the ladder," he said. He moved his head, and a pain shot through it. Suddenly he remembered. "Grandfather?"

"Hush! Eoghan dear; you've cut your head and must lie quiet."

"Grandfather?" he asked querulously.

"Dr. Maclean is in . . . grandfather is in bed . . ."

The room began to wheel round. "I'm dizzy, Barbara." He put his hand in hers, and, like a tired child, closed his eyes. He was wrestling with some untoward phantom on a mountain peak. The dream deepened, the face of the phantom became sharply outlined; he was struggling in a death-grip with the superintendent of the examination on the spire of the University.

12

ON the day after the accident Mrs. Galbraith came to the "Ghost" and offered her services as nurse. "Mr. Strang and I are old friends," she said, and her charming smile immediately won Barbara's heart. Mrs. Galbraith was not only a capable woman within doors and an excellent cook, but she read the Bible to old Mr. Strang, and the poets to Eoghan, the wound in whose head rapidly healed. Mrs. Galbraith and he had long discussions on philosophy and theology, and she induced him to read his own verses to her—mostly scraps and fragments. Mrs. Galbraith fell in love with the boy—an affection rather of the head than of the heart. She revered him for his gift and for his intellectual attainments, would sit big-bosomed at the bedside holding his hand, and in the morning, when she entered his room, would frankly kiss him on the forehead. When the wound in his head was healed, he set out to visit his mother, and determined on the way to call on Mr. Kennedy. With a sense of shame he walked up the dark avenue to the schoolmaster's house. Mr. Campion, with a familiar air of possession, and smoking a cigarette, opened the door. Eoghan, suspicious of strangers, felt the teacher's presence an intrusion, and abruptly asked for Mr. Kennedy. The teacher withdrew the cigarette from his mouth in amazement.

"Have you not heard? Mr. Kennedy is dead."

Eoghan felt suddenly faint, and leaned against the jamb of the door, unable to speak.

"Come in for a moment and rest."

Eoghan shook his head, and put out his foot, feeling for the step. He was stunned and blinded. Having groped his way to the walk he turned, and asked in a low voice: "When did he die?"

Mr. Campion considered. "About a month ago."

Eoghan felt suddenly overtaken by disaster, and, casting a look of fear at the looming house, crept out of the garden. Anxious to avoid public gaze, he passed along the Back Street and down MacCalman's Lane, at the end of which, at the corner of the Bank, the usual crowd of fishermen were assembled. He hesitated and stopped, timid of the passage into the fierce light of the Square. Their conversation was about his accident and that of his grandfather. Alert, he crouched against the wall. They were talking now of his father—who would be glad if the old man died; he would get his hands on the "Ghost"; he meant to lock up his wife there. Every cruel, careless word of scandal burned in Eoghan's brain. "She's senseless wi' the booze. The Revivalists started a new kind o' preachin' aboot the Judgment Day comin' soon, an' she put on the white dress she was mairrit in to be pure, an' threw hersel' into the Harbour. She was floatin' away singin' in a wee crackit voice when Ned o' the Horn jumpit in; an' what dae ye think Gillespa' said to poor Ned? 'Your breeks were in need o' a cleanin', Ned; ye can thank my wife for that at your leisure.' "

There was a boisterous outburst of laughter.

"It's as weel Ned's mairrit, or he'd soon get a lass."

The blood was drumming loudly in Eoghan's ears. He recalled what he had overheard the tailor name his mother. It was true, then; Oh, God, it was true. She was the byword of the corners. He trembled so much that he was afraid he would fall.

"She's only an auld bauchle o' a whüre."

Again the devilish, inane laughter. He had to suppress a scream as he crept backwards along the wall.

"Unclean! unclean!" The words rang in his brain as he crept in the gloaming along the Back Street, up the brae past the school, and cast himself face down in MacCalman's Park, digging his nails into the soil. "While there's water to drown an' steel to wound, a Strang 'ill no' die in bed." Where had he heard those words? he could not remember. The face of the speaker loomed bafflingly in a mist. "I must kill her; I must kill her; it's the only way." Why had he not thought of this long ago? Then a cunning thought came to him—he would watch and seize her in her sin. The day had been dark, with east wind; the night was now gloomy as he staggered wearily to his feet. In the Back Street a thin rain fell on him, and on the herring gutters of Gillespie, as they trudged homeward. The chemist's shop was closed; the blinds were drawn in his father's shop; the Square was in semi-darkness; and the moonless Harbour was like a slab of black granite. Eoghan loped across the Square, ran through the close, and up the stair into the kitchen. It was empty, and searched from corner to corner by the shadowless light of the lamp. He heard his father moving about in the shop below. Topsail, the pack-horse, was evidently on some business of her master. It was Gillespie's custom, when the Fox was gone into the country with the horse, to dispatch Topsail with goods ordered by his customers during the day. Horror left Eoghan faint. He had determined to kill his mother; but how? "I shall stand no longer in the horses' dung in the streets, our name a common reproach," he thought. The empty kitchen testified to her baseness. How long had she carried on her nefarious trade? "We are disgraced, disgraced; I can never walk in the streets again. Better for me to perish too." He was in the midst of these maddening thoughts when his mother entered, with a shawl about her head. Her face was flushed; her eyes hot and brilliant. He walked straight up to her.

"Where have you been?"

She took the shawl from her head, and replied with a weary gesture:

"Dearie me! nobody heeds me noo; Marget wouldn't open the door."

"Mrs Galbraith is at the 'Ghost,' " he replied fiercely.

Her delicate head swayed forward on her thin neck.

"What is she doing there?" she leered at him.

"Grandfather fell off a ladder and has taken a shock."

"Och! och! I've seen the shadow o' death. It passed me by last night." These words, spoken in a mournful tone, almost unmanned her son. She walked, shawl in hand, to the dresser, turned her back on him, and slipped a shilling in behind a large toddy bowl standing upright in the corner. Eoghan, watching her closely, heard the coin clink against the delf. He took a stride forward; but before he could reach her she snatched up the coin. He gripped her closed hand and opened it, displaying a silver coin, slightly tarnished.

"Where did you get it?" He pointed with his forefinger.

She laughed shrilly. "It might be frae ane o' thae weary men." A cunning look came into her face and eyes—the egomaniac's desire of confession, mingled with the woman's fear of detection. "But Gillespie winna jaloose that I got it out o' the till."

He knew that she lied. The hunted look on her face betrayed her. A surge of madness swept over him.

"God Almighty! but this is the bonny pickle." He snatched the coin from her. She pounced upon it with a snarl, and missed it; her face became bewildered, bleak, and pinched.

"I'll melt it," he cried, in mad rage. "I'll cut the cross on it and melt it, and give it to my father to drink. He doesn't like whisky."

She put the shawl up to her face, and peered at him over its edge. "Ye winna clype on me."

He spat on the coin, rubbed it on the sleeve of his jacket, and held it up.

"Did ye ever see a leper? Jesus Christ cleansed them"—the surge of madness was blinding him; and his words became guttural as his voice thickened—"Jesus Christ cleansed them——" He swayed upon his feet, his eyes burning on her face. "Oh, God! my heart's broken." The wail rang through the kitchen like a child's.

"What's wrong wi' ye?" She stretched out a thin hand and moved towards him. He flung out his arm to ward her off. His temples were ready to burst with the throbbing of blood, and, recoiling from her against the dresser, his arm slouched across the toddy bowl, which rolled over and crashed in fragments at his feet. He pawed blindly in the ruin.

"The b'ue bowl broken; that's no' chancy; it was granny's. I'm feart something's goin' to happen."

He was appalled at this terrible detachment of mind. She insisted on the triviality, making it gigantic. "It's a peety the bowl's broken; granny gied it to me in a marriage-present."

All the world, time, and space stood still for him in that moment of utter hopelessness and despair. He stared in stupor at this woman, who was his mother no longer, but some one sprung from the loins of the gods of malice, sent to torment him. She did not know what fear or shame was, because such gods would rend the firmament between their hands as paper, and smile down upon the terror of mortals. Grief and panic leave them passionless, and they sup upon woe. She was their daughter. He heard her voice as of some one far away, and could not connect her words. Her face before him was dark, sinister, full of cunning—the face of a sphinx that has looked out across a thousand battle-fields and calmly watched the vultures plunge their hot beaks in dripping flesh. He believed in incarnate evil.

"When I cam' to him frae the Lonen' I'd a bonnie tocher; he stealt that. I'm the daughter o' Lonen'. I was in the College for young ladies. Mr. Campion was in the College too; an' my son Iain's in the College. He's to be a minister, wi' a' the fowk that quate sittin' lookin' up at him. I can't stand Gillespie Strang. He won't allow the minister to come an' see me." A dazed look came over her face; she seemed to be staring at something invisible. "Dearie me! I haven't seen a minister for three years."

What was she saying? What right had a Sphinx to have such bleary eyes? How stupidly her head sagged! Why had such a graven image froth at the corners of her mouth?

"Oh, my head, my head! it's liftin' off." She put her hands up across her temples, pressing her fingers hard on the top of her skull, and rocking her body with pain, "I canna stand it; my head! my head! Will ye no' take my life an' put me oot o' torture?"

Ha! her life! was he not there for that? but who could slay such a daughter of malice? He watched her mouth working constantly, as if she were gnawing on something. The muscles of her face seemed to be jerked from the inside by a concealed string, and a line of chalky white edged her lips. She steadied herself by a hand on the sink, and went backwards, collapsing on the stool at the fire, leaving her hollow eyes absolutely expressionless.

393

Those homes of tenderness and love were dead—blackened embers of a lost fire. They gazed out upon the world without a sense of pain or intelligence. They were petrified in a face of stone. The hands alone possessed life, as they plucked at her lap. This Sphinx began rocking slowly to and fro, her knees twitching to the tune:

> "O love, it is pleasin', love, it is teasin',
> O love 'tis a pleasure when it is new———"

Hark to the voice of the ages singing, the voice that was locked in eternal frost, the voice that would not scare the ravenging vultures from the slain. He laughed out aloud, and she lifted sullen eyes.

"My voice is crackit. I used to be the best singer in the Free Kirk."

He felt he was in a nightmare, and would waken anon.

> "But as it grows older, the love it grows colder———"

She broke off. Every fuddled word was a dagger raw in his heart. This must end. He approached her stealthily, and suddenly displayed the shilling.

"Tell me," he snarled, shaking her by the shoulder, "who gave it to you?"

She felt she was listening to a deadly enemy, and stared at him fixedly to imprint the lineaments of the face of her foe on her memory. Then she screwed her face into an innocent look. "It's you, Eoghan; you broke the b'ue bowl. It's a bad sign. Granny said it was in the faimly since the Flood, an' something no' chancy wad happen if it got brocken." Her forehead was seamed with wrinkles; a chiding frown sat on her eyebrows.

"Tell me quick, by God!"—his voice broke with rage and hatred—"tell me, till I kill him!"

Her face darkened with a surge of blood upon this implacable enemy, and she attempted to struggle to her feet. His hand caught in her hair, which tumbled on her shoulders. This gave to her head a wild appearance; and her breath stank in his face. "Oh, but I'm the bonny ane, Lonen's daughter, among ye a'." She lurched across the floor into the bedroom, sighing heavily. He heard her fumbling in the dark. Presently she returned to the threshold of the kitchen, and, watching her son with a sly look, complained of a heavy, sickening smell in the room, and babbled

394

of poisoned lilies which she had eaten in Marget's. Again she retreated to the bedroom; and he heard the plunk of a cork. A mist grew before his eyes. His heart was about to burst in his breast. He followed her almost at a run. She was standing immediately inside the threshold, where she could have her eye on the kitchen, her figure ghostly in the stream of the lamplight. A half mutchkin bottle was in her hand; her head was tilted back; and one eye, raging with demoniac light, was on the doorway. Despair paralysed him. The Sphinx face, smileless and bloodless, with cruelty in its stony flesh and a hawk-like craftiness in the single wild, wary eye, was devilish with its faint glitter of pleasure, and fed with the damnable fiery liquid, which he heard gurgling, gurgling. An insensate desire possessed him to strangle that mocking glitter of the roving eye, to stamp out for ever the evil in that grey, debauched face. He leapt forward and swung his clenched fist. She saw the danger, and, before he could avoid it, the whisky bottle crashed between his eyes. He was stung, temporarily blinded and maddened with the pain. The fist continued its curve through the air as he reeled back; he felt its impact upon bone, and a dirl go up his arm. He had struck her on the side of the head. He swung his arm a second time, but there was no evil eye, no sinister face before him. The stench of the spilled whisky, pungent in his nostrils, restored him completely to reality. With heaving breast he stood looking down at her; listened to her low moaning, and realised that she was alive. He heaved a sob of relief, and got down on his knees beside her, unconscious of the scalding of the whisky in his eyes. Tears mingled with the alcohol. He became the victim of unbounded remorse; and his knees quivered so much that he was forced to sit upon the floor by her side. The silence of the room was now as the silence of death. The voice of the sea rose up hungrily across the Square and entered the room. Its voice was as the voice of one who had seen and cried aloud that there are things which cannot be kept out of the most secret place. He murmured her name; at first in anguished accents, then, as her eyelids quivered and her eyes opened, in caressing tones. He lifted her head upon his knees, stroked her raven hair, and watched with hungry gaze every movement of her eyes. They were leaden and dull, and her lips were bloodless. She seemed deaf to his entreaties. The lines of pain and debauchery, which had vanished from her face, gradually crept back again, as by stealth. Her mouth was pathetically

395

open, like a babe's, and she began to speak a meaningless jumble, in which the names Campion and Marget recurred. "How did I do it? how did I do it?" played like a shuttle of flame through his brain. "I am almost a murderer." Horror shook him like a leaf in the blast. The darkness and the world without were full of stern, watchful eyes. She may die yet. A cold sweat broke out on his forehead. He scanned her face with a famished look. She was babbling of the strangest things in a whispering voice; a spate of broken images ravaged her brain. She was going to London to see the crown jewels. Would Campion not give her a peacock's feather for her hat to go to church? "I haven't seen the minister for three years." Iain was in prison; she was milking cows at Lonend; she was gathering flowers in the meadows there for Marget's room. He bent over her, consumed with pity. Suddenly she began to weep, complaining of pain in her back. He tried to relieve her by easing her position; and at this juncture Topsail appeared, breathless from her hurry. With a sense of unspeakable relief, he shouted, "My poor mother has fallen and hurt herself." Topsail snatched up the kitchen lamp.

"Mercy me, laddie; your face is a' ower wi' blood."

"Never mind me; get her to bed, quick."

They lifted her on to the bed, and Topsail, unlacing her boots, ordered him from the room. "It's no' a place for you," she said, with a kind pitying glance; "she's in wan o' her black turns."

He waited in the dark kitchen till his patience was exhausted, and, returning to the room, found Topsail sitting in the bed behind his mother, who lay, with her knees hunched up to her chin, between Topsail's legs. In the night-dress she looked gaunt and wasted to the bone; her face like clay, her head hung limply to one side. Pain had engraved its lines once more on her face, and the deeply sunk eyes looked out at him above the lantern jaws strangely, as if she were a being of another race from a remote world. The lower teeth protruded on the upper lip, giving to the mouth a slack, cadaverous expression. She had the appearance of a famished animal. On her hand, stretched along the coverlet, he could trace the line of the bone whitening along the back of the wrist. He seemed to be looking upon a skeleton, and shook with fear—a skeleton that was moaning. "I never thocht I'd come to this—a sair, sair bed."

"My God!" he whispered hopelessly, "is she going to die?"

Topsail shook her head, indicating her hopelessness. "We're

396

a' puir things when it comes to this—puir things in a Higher Hand."

"Ay! rub me there below the shoulders. Oh! Oh! it gangs through me like a knife!" He fell on his knees at the bedside and took her hand, which was icy cold. "Will the Almighty no' gie me peace one hour, that I'll can win a wee sleep?"

"I'll go for Maclean." He jumped to his feet.

Topsail shook her head. "It's wan o' the black turns. Gie her wan o' thae white pooders." She directed him where to find them. "She's no' to get ower many, the doctor said, in case she sleeps awa'."

He prepared the powder, and held the tumbler to her lips.

"Oh! Oh! it's goin' through me like lances, something's teirin' inside me." She swallowed the liquid, gasping over it. "Rub me, rub me." Topsail leaned back and began rubbing her between the shoulder-blades. "Oh, the drouth, the drouth! my tongue's like leather."

He hurried and brought her water. Finding it cool at her lips, she raised her deep, sunken eyes and, gripping the tumbler, mouthed it in her eagerness, and drank ravenously. He turned his eyes from the sickening sight, and heard her make little sounds of gladness at each gulp.

"Take a little more, mother."

"No, no! I've drank what wad do the hale toon. Oh! Oh! I feel as if I'm drawn separate. If the Almighty wad only gie me one wee hour. I haven't asked muckle o' Him a' my days——"

She now lay silent, belching wind; then moaning again: "Och, och! the sweat; the caul sweat's lashin' ower me." Her head fell a little more awry against Topsail's knee; her breathing became regular. In a little she opened her eyes and gazed vacantly round the room.

"Dearie me! lyin' sae muckle on my heid, I'm losin' my memory," she said.

Topsail nodded to him, smiling cheerily. "She's got ower 't, puir sowl." The white powder had done its work. His mother was fast asleep between the legs of her faithful slave.

13

THAT night Eoghan was crushed by anxiety, and existed in a saturnalia of horror. The curtains of the window could not keep out the choking night or the gloom of old haunted forests which was in the room. A foreboding of evil was every moment about to be realised—a misshapen thing of fear about to rise up before him in vindictive, inexorable rage. His anguish became frenzied. He was like a man in a desert surrounded in the night by prowling beasts, whose sinister roar was every moment about to burst on his ear. He shuddered as he thought of the bewildering depths to which human nature can sink. His mother's face swam up before him—a marble face in which the only sign of life was the pain-drenched eyes. His hatred and his loathing were gone, along with the desire to slay her, and his heart, heavy within him, pitied her. At last, overcome by fatigue, he fell asleep, and dreamed that his mother and he were gathering flowers in the meadows of Lonend. He brought the flowers in armfuls—lilies, and lilies of the valley, and wild violets, wet with dew—and strawed them on her dressing-table, on the floor, on the bed; everywhere he filled her room with their perfume; and the canaries sang from the ceiling; and the sanctity of the fragrance, and the richness of the bird-song defended her, and kept her feet from wandering in the night. Then he saw her lying in a coffin, with the flowers he had gathered heaped about her—pale lilies in her hair, lilies of the valley on her breast, and the canaries stunned and mute in their cages. She smiled up at him with the assured smile of death, with the peace that laughs at shame, and which the gloomy sound of the sea shall never break. The noise of the sea—surely it was loud in his ears . . . He was awake, bathed in sweat. For a moment he lay supine within the doors of the dream, hoping it was true—that outrage, indecency, shame, oppression were for ever at an end, that the trump of God had sounded and the supreme hour had come. Beneath his window a drunken voice was singing:

> "Oh, Donal'! Oh, Donal'!
> Drink your gless, lad, an' gang awa' hame,
> For if you tarry langer ye'll get a bad name;
> Ye'll get a bad name, sae fill yersel' fou'.
> The lang wud's sae dreary, but I'll see you through."

He groaned. Nothing was changed. Another day of weariness and horror had broken.

She was up at the breakfast-table along with Topsail. He was astonished at his mother's hardiness. She seemed to smile at misfortune and defy prostration. Her face, though unbroken, had the appearance of being scarred. Earlier that morning her moods had bewildered Topsail. She had come into the kitchen, her hair adorned with a bright artificial flower, which she had discovered while rummaging in the parlour, and, getting down on her knees, began to wash the floor. Topsail protested, but her mistress informed her that it was by the doctor's orders. Half-way through her task she desisted, feigning a vomiting. She had forgotten the tawdry decoration nodding grotesquely in her hair, and Topsail snatched it away when she heard Eoghan's footsteps in the passage.

His mother, who sat by the fire at the head of the table, with a spent look, seemed to have forgotten the incident of the previous night. She wakened up to say to Eoghan that he ought to marry Barbara. Her voice was hoarse, probably the effect of her wandering about in all sorts of weather. He was amazed, and, flushing deeply, asked her her reason for this exhortation; but she had lapsed again into silence. The fact is she had conceived that Mr. Campion was in love with Barbara, and a blind rage against Eoghan, who did not express instant willingness to marry the girl, possessed her. She arose, and suddenly snatching the kettle from the hob, poured some of its boiling water on Eoghan's hand. He jumped up, smarting with pain and convulsed with rage, but was unable to utter a word at sight of his mother's apathetic face. She appeared to be unconscious of her treacherous deed. Topsail hastened with soap and a cloth.

"I'm going for Maclean," he said; "she's mad."

At the mention of the doctor's name she became highly cunning, protesting that her health was good. Eoghan showed her his bandaged hand, and taxed her with her folly. She lied audaciously, and battered down irrefragable proof. In fact, she was not so much guilty of lying, as that the memory of her crimes became rapidly dim. Eoghan was aghast, and, hurrying across the Square, asked Kyle to send the doctor to examine his mother. When Maclean arrived in the afternoon, she was openly perspicacious. He instructed Topsail that her mistress was not to be allowed out at night, and must constantly be watched. He was no sooner gone than, in a violent fit of passion, Mrs. Strang smashed a pot with the poker, attempted to tear off her clothes, and accused her son of inducing the doctor to perform a highly dangerous operation on her person, with a view to taking away her life. She now conceived an intense hatred for Eoghan, and cloaked it by informing Topsail that he was seriously ill, and could not live very long. She spoke these words in a whisper, creeping stealthily to Topsail's ear, exhibiting every sign of sorrow and beginning to weep. Topsail, to console her, scouted the idea, and her mistress, desiring Topsail to kiss her, suddenly bit the servant on the neck. Her countenance was perturbed and her eyes wild, as she retreated to the stool at the fire, where she sunk into a state of gloomy torpor, and preserved this obstinate taciturnity for the rest of the afternoon, rousing herself only to complain of intense thirst, and opening her mouth to show Topsail how hard and dry were her palate and her tongue. She screamed out in her servant's face that she was being strangled, and Topsail, beside herself, appeased her by giving her a large quantity of whisky.

When Gillespie came upstairs for tea—he had reverted to the practice of taking his meals in the house since the return of Eoghan—he asked Topsail to fetch his spectacles from the bedroom. He wore these now in the evenings when poring over his books. Topsail returned without the spectacle case. The events of the day had left her stupid.

"I saw a licht like the licht o' a can'le dancin' on the bed. It gied wan blink an' went oot," she said, with awe.

"Noäne o' thae noänsense in my hoose." Gillespie's voice was louder than usual, and he jerked Topsail by the arm into a chair. "Sit doon, will ye; ye're doitered."

"Wheest, Gillespie." His wife touched him on the sleeve. "Is it no' a warnin'? I dreamt last night that the hoose was in confusion an' granny's b'ue bowl was broken. Eoghan's no' lookin' weel." She trailed away, wringing her hands, and passed into the next room, where they heard her searching with frantic hands about the bed. Gillespie rose with horrible quietness, his upper lip slightly drawn up in a snarl, walked round the table, his head butting forward, and, tip-toeing towards Topsail, clenched his fist. Neither spoke a word. As if turned to stone Topsail awaited the blow. Looking down into her mute, uplifted eyes, he struck her full on the face. Without sound or moan her head fell across the back of the chair, and blood oozed from her mouth. Gillespie raised his clenched hand a second time; but his wife appeared from the room crying shrilly, "I hear the death-watch tick, tick, tickin'."

Slowly the clenched fist opened; the arm dropped heavily to the side, and at the voice of her mistress Topsail opened her eyes, which fell full on Gillespie.

"Janet," he said slowly, "my he'rt's roasted for Eoghan." Topsail's eyes smiled faintly. "I owe ye twa—three years' wages;" and turning on his heel, he rapidly walked away to relieve Sandy the Fox, custodian of the shop.

His son was standing in the shop in the scud of the light, gazing into nothingness, and Gillespie, with a fierce heart-hunger, furtively watched him. The face was deplorably thin and white and full of sorrow.

"I dinna think ye're as weel as ye micht be, Eoghan." Gillespie deprecated this interest with a soft laugh. "Gang an' pack your pockmanty an' off to Edinboro' the morn for a jaunt."

"It's too late for that." The mournful words troubled Gillespie.

"Are ye no' feeling weel?" A deep tide, long throttled, was rising up within Gillespie. "Ye'd better gang, Eoghan; dinna heed for siller."

Eoghan shuddered. "Keep your money."

The tone in which those words were uttered brought a sense of guilt home to Gillespie. It is from the top of the hill of iniquity that the mountain of righteousness is best discerned. Gillespie saw that peak all the more glorious, that it was receding for ever.

"Here I stay till death gives me release." The words burst out of his son's breast in despair, and Gillespie became terrified, feeling his world melting away beneath the dews of death. He thrust his face nearer his son's. What he saw there made him recoil.

"Son! son!"

At this cry of misery the son gazed at the father with all his broken heart in his eyes, and moaning, "Oh, God! I am weary," staggered against the counter—that altar where so many hearts had been broken. A draught from the back door swirled through the shop. Mrs. Strang appeared. It was years since she had been there. While seated in the kitchen she had suddenly fancied that

401

her husband's business was going to ruin for want of her help and supervision.

"What's wrang noo?" The tone was full of petulance, and she nodded, as if in answer to an unheard voice, as she reeled forward between father and son. "Maggie Shaw has a baby"—there was a whimpering smile on her face. Gillespie made a hard, swallowing sound, and looked over her shoulder at his son.

"I'm coaxing Eoghan to tak' a jaunt to Edinboro'," he said, wetting his lips with his tongue.

"Dearie me! dearie me! I was at school there."

"He's no' lookin' ower herty on't."

"Poor Eoghan! poor Eoghan!" She began to weep. "He's no' himsel' at a'. He'll soon be by wi't. Ay! it's a bonnie place, Edinboro'." She smiled with infinite cunning at her husband.

"Mother and me will go," sobbed the boy.

"Weel! weel!" Gillespie's face shone. "If ye want your mother we'll manage till you win back."

"It'll be a long journey, mother." He left the counter—another heart had been laid upon that altar—and passed behind her out of the shop. Gillespie gripped his wife by the shoulder. "Get him to gang wi' ye, an' I'll gie ye a new dress." She leered, licking her bluey lips. "Dae ye hear, wumman,"—he shook her violently—"my life's scaddit every time I look at his face." She cowered away from his hand, and made a mocking sound and a sardonic grimace.

14

WHEN Mrs. Strang's head was very bad she complained of deafening thunder, and one afternoon awoke out of her lethargic state and mourned that the Square was full of bleating sheep, which she insisted on herding to the folds of Lonend. She spat in Topsail's face when her servant laid a restraining hand upon her, and then attempted to lick the spittle. Topsail Janet was bewildered, for that afternoon her mistress had evinced deep concern for her servant's rheumatism, which was very painful with the winter sleet. Mrs. Strang suggested a dozen cures, and would not be hindered from rubbing Topsail's knuckles with turpentine and tying on bandages of flannel. Topsail was thoroughly happy at this. "Hoo can I get through my work wi' thae cloots on my hand?" she cried merrily.

"There's no work, Janet, wi' Iain in the jyle."

Topsail, alarmed at the answer, submitted to the ministrations in silence; and her mistress wept for her servant's suffering. "You've more to thole than me, Janet, far more; you've burnin' nettles on your hands," and almost as she looked pityingly at her servant her talk became very loose, and was accompanied by silly grimaces. It turned on her marriage and on sexual things. Her colour ran high; she became excited, and began to search the rooms. Eoghan, coming up the stair—he seldom went out now by day—heard her in a hoarse voice telling Topsail that Mr. Campion was concealed somewhere in the house. The name of this gentleman was frequently on his mother's lips, but speculation as to the reason was cut short by the tragic spectacle of his mother's distress. She was wandering through the house wringing her hands, and moaning that the breath of dogs was on her face—would no one give her a hatchet to kill them?—and there was fire in the sleet.

"Good God! this is terrible!" he groaned to Topsail.

"Ay! ay! she's fair distractit. Goäd keep her."

Mrs. Strang backed away from her bedroom, complaining of an offensive smell there, due, she repeated over and over, to a dead rat. Topsail tried to coax her with a cup of tea, but she refused it, saying there was no taste in food. She tottered as she walked, fell in the passage as she was making for the parlour, and betrayed no sign of pain. She caught Topsail's hands when they lifted her up and laid them on her breast. "Oh, Janet! Janet! my heart is as heavy as lead, an' my breasts are like ice." Topsail led her to the kitchen stool, where she began to babble of her husband's business. It would fall to pieces without her control; for want of her ministrations the cattle in the byre at Lonend were dying. She got up and, passing to her room, began to rummage in the drawers. "Iain's starvin' o' cold in the jyle; he hasna a stitch to put on." She turned out a welter of old things, sat in their midst, staring fatuously, and played with a piece of black ribbon as a child amuses itself with a toy.

Eoghan, seated at the kitchen fire, was faint with palpitation. The unspeakable calamity which he was witnessing was slowly killing him. He felt as if red-hot chains bound his body, which the next moment became icy cold. His mother reappeared in the kitchen, a distraught look on her face, and catching sight of the sleet on the roof of the washing-house, moaned:

"Ring the bell, Janet; ring the bell an' tell me when the snow is gone; it's full o' fire." She harped on this with weary iteration, till Eoghan, groaning and gnawing on his lip, ran through the kitchen and to the ree, and asked Sandy the Fox to go and sweep the coating of snow from the washing-house roof. By this time his mother had forgotten her terror of the snow, and attempted to rise from her chair. "I can't go, Janet: my legs are as heavy as lead." Topsail took her by the arm. "No! no! my body's swelled so big; I can't get through the door." She planted her feet firmly and refused to move.

So it went on day by day. Her will power had ceased to operate. Wandering in shadows, and seeing as through clouds, she was completely indifferent to the moral necessity in human nature. Repulsive deeds exercised a peculiar fascination over her. Topsail Janet caught her one day perfectly naked descending the outside stair. Sleet was falling and melting on her skin; but she seemed impervious to the rawness of the atmosphere. She contracted a cold, which shook her in spasms of coughing, and she began to spit blood. She became rapacious for drink, which Maclean had strictly forbidden. She resorted to the most cunning methods, sending messages to the driver of the mail-coach to bring whisky from Ardmarkie. The bottle she concealed among the dross in the coal cellar in the washing-house. Her violent outbursts scared Topsail, whom she terrorised into procuring whisky, declaring she would burn down the house. On her knees Topsail implored her mistress, promising her anything in the world. She looked at Topsail Janet maliciously, and suddenly jerked her head forward attempting to fasten her teeth in Topsail's throat. The servant, beside herself, gripped the maniac by the arms, forced her back in her seat, and held her there till the rigidity of her body relaxed, and she wilted up into a pitiable huddle. The two women, breathing fast, gazed in at each other's eyes; Mrs. Strang, with a look of hatred at Topsail, whose face was bleached with fear. Her mistress, pointing a malicious forefinger, burst into sardonic laughter, which was cut short by a severe fit of coughing. This poor creature was a spectacle of pity for all eyes, human and divine.

The next day she poured forth a torrent of calumny against her servant, her husband, and her son, and watching her opportunity, when Topsail was in the coal cellar, stole across the Square to Kyle's shop. Eyeing him furtively she asked for poison. She could not remember the name of any specific poison, but said it was for rats. Kyle gave her a bottle of water coloured with cochineal, which she concealed in her pocket. Extremely affable to Topsail, she despatched her to the bedroom for a comb, and immediately emptied the contents of the bottle into a pot of potato soup. At the dinner-hour she feigned sickness, and sat watching narrowly her husband and son as they ate, and she chattered so incessantly and rationally that Eoghan thought the cloud had lifted from her mind. After dinner she kept whispering to Topsail that her husband and son looked to be in a wretched state of health, and that they could not live long. She showed no surprise at finding them still alive the next day. She imagined that poison could not destroy them.

The horror of his life banished sleep from Eoghan. The grey light of the dawn would find him wide-eyed, snatching back his mother's words, gestures, looks, and magnifying them till she became a grotesque, gibbering apparition of dread. He trembled at the light of the morning, and the pitiableness of his life made him bury his face in the pillow in a fury of despair. He envied Topsail when he heard her ryping out the ashes in the kitchen grate in the grey dawn. His mother, so hopelessly incompetent, debauched, and now mad, was a power embattled overwhelmingly against him. He had given up his darling dreams of the cloisters; his ideals were smeared as with the slime of a serpent; chains were loaded upon him. He leapt from bed. A blue mist lay on the Harbour, which was brittle and still as glass. Everything in the mist had a dim, indescribable softness, and the boats were but half seen through the veil as in a magic land. A garment of hoar-frost clothed the hills. The still beauty of the morning, hanging as from the heavens, took him by the throat. A robin with bold, flamboyant breast lit on the window-sill, and cocked up a bright eye at him. He went to the kitchen for crumbs to feed the tiny life, and watched with pity the blood-red breast swell and flit away.

He had not visited the "Ghost" for days. He would go now, before Brieston was astir. His grandfather was totally paralysed on the right side, and mumbled so thickly that no one could

405

understand him. Maclean had warned Mrs. Galbraith that the shock was likely at any time to be followed by another, which would probably prove fatal. Mrs. Galbraith and Barbara, on alternate nights, sat up with the old man.

Barbara admitted him. They looked at each other sorrowfully as he took her in his arms. She was parched with vigil.

"He's had a peaceful night," she said, in a heavy voice, and, turning aside to the window, added: "Look, Eoghan dear, the day is breaking over the hills."

"Yes, breaking; breaking in eternal pain," he answered mournfully.

There was no talk of love between them whom suffering and grief had united as man and woman. Hand in hand they stood at the window, and saw the trees near the house on the burnside shiver in the dawn-wind, and the great hills march on at the head of the Loch, mile upon mile of imperturbable majesty, to meet the kindling light. The spectacle wrung a profound sigh from the depths of his breast—the purity, the peace, the strength, the beauty and calm of the high places of God. He turned to the girl and tenderly dismissed her. "Go to bed, Barbara, you're worn out. I'll wait for Mrs. Galbraith."

She held up her mouth, as a child, to be kissed. Hour after hour she had sat attentive upon the grey face sunk in the pillow, and her soul was one incessant prayer to the God of life and death. He had housed her as a dove in a nest; had named to her the names of goodness, purity, and love. The days he had made gentle for her with a solicitude that was almost maternal. His hand had been upon her, a refuge and a support, from the hour in which death had darkened her home. She had lived in happiness and peace in the shadow of his age. With great sorrow she recognised that something noble and sweet, redemptive, solacing, and protective, was passing away from her for ever in lonely, unuttered agony. Often she retired to the foot of the bed to weep silently there. Her body became sapless; her hair dry and brittle, her face grievously wasted and pale. In the watches of the night she felt that old, sullen death was creeping stealthily towards the bed. A granite mass of despair crushed her, and sinking on her knees she would lay her face on the coverlet with an unuttered poignant cry: "Grandad! Grandad! my heart is breaking!" and the eyes that were inflexible upon the ceiling would sweep tenderly upon the bowed head; but sorrow, prostrate upon its altar, would lose

406

the benediction. Prone beneath the talons of anguish, she would miss the holy breathing of those eyes.

She turned from Eoghan and, approaching the bed, put her arms gently beneath the old man's head, and kissing him on the brow and cheek, said, "Good-bye, grandad, for a wee whilie." The eyes, having followed her hungrily to the door, returned to their vigil on the ceiling. Eoghan sat by the bed; but the old man never attempted to move or speak. He seemed plunged in profound, unclouded dreams. The eyes had the upward, unwavering look that belongs to the dead. Day will mingle with the twilight and night roll into the morning; but nothing on earth will evoke the voice already summoned into silence, or restore from the dusk to those grey eyes the light which had gone out thence in a wild sunset. The bitterness of Eoghan's cup was full. He scarce heard Mrs. Galbraith when she came down at seven o'clock and began the day by reading to the old man the mighty words, " '*Who shall separate us from the love of Christ? Shall tribulation, or distress, or persecution, or famine, or nakedness, or peril, or sword——?*' " and when she had finished the sublime passage in a voice broken by emotion: " '*For I am persuaded that neither death, nor life, nor angels, nor principalities, nor powers, nor things to come, nor height, nor depth, nor any other creature, shall be able to separate us from the love of God, which is in Christ Jesus our Lord,*' " the old man moved his left arm off the coverlet and muttered unintelligibly with a despairing force of energy. Eoghan thought that his heart would burst in his breast and, unable to control himself, ran out of the room.

15

GILLESPIE slept now in the parlour, because he was disturbed by his wife, who would get up either to search the room for vermin or to look for dead babies. Topsail Janet had the greatest difficulty in understanding what she said. She complained of bells ringing in her head, and that she saw the faces of the dead following her about; but chiefly that she was spied upon by her husband and son, who meant to take her life for her crimes. Some dark night they were going to throw her into the Harbour. This was now her constant dread. "In two weeks I'll be drowned," she whispered to Topsail Janet. She determined that her enemies must be put out of the way. She was unable to endure their persecution any longer.

For the past two days she had been sunk in a stupor, in which she had spoken once, in a refusal to go to bed, on which lay a dead child to which she had given birth. Eoghan had heard her say this, and was almost mad himself when she stuttered, "Is Mr. Campion no' comin' to see his baby?"

The words kept repeating themselves in his brain. He thought nothing now of the scandal that seethed and blistered at the corners and the "Shipping Box"—"Gillespie's wife's makin' a caul' bed o't." He had passed beyond that—Brieston and its malevolent eyes, and its malice hissing into his life. For him the throne of the Deity had receded into an abyss, and a stony God gloomed down from the height of eternity, on whose marmoreal breast there was a hollow, where He had leaned over His eyrie from the ages of the ages. Of late he had ceased to think of or hope in the Deity. His soul was broken up in a vast ruin. He saw a large, impassive, determinate hand in the heavens shaking a dagger, beneath which the accurst, the tainted, and the innocent alike were driven. " 'The gods of wrath are in the sun——'Good God!" he cried out, "I'm laughin', I'm laughin'; I'm goin' mad." He ran to the mirror and stared at his face. It was drained to a livid whiteness, and subtly underwent a transformation. He was looking in upon the very lair of life. "That's not me," he whispered in fear. "Eoghan! oh, Eoghan!"

Completely exhausted from want of food that day, want of sleep and the torment of thought, he fell back on the bed, hoping that he might die in his sleep. It was now the grey dusk of the last day of the year. At first he slept as if in lead, so utterly wearied he was, and was disturbed by dream after dream. He was being carried off on wild horses with cometary manes threshing the heavens. He began to babble of gibbets which he saw, and chains of lightning frozen by a supernatural cold, and a multitude of priests droning of hell. He fell sheer down one cavern of smooth black walls into another fiery with waves of flame. The flames lit up axes with bloody edges hanging from a ceiling. Like a stone he dropped through the running flames into a thick dark river which, to his horror, he found was black, clotted blood. A loud booming arose out of this bottomless world, and a rain of bloody sweat from the Gethsemane of humanity fell thick on the black river and congealed. Cries of the damned ascended in sulphurous clouds. Rain! blood! disease! contagion! flame! and he screamed out in answer: "Oh, naked soul, this is a wild place!"

He was sitting up in bed, his heart hammering violently against his ribs, having forgotten for the moment where he was. The day had been sunless and stormy, and the thick, solemn night had fallen as if it were the last night in the world. The wind leapt with quick claps over the Harbour, and its noise was upon the Quays, the Harbour wall, the streets, the house. It whined away over the hills, dying beyond human confines. He suddenly remembered what awaited him, his vigil and his anguish, and was filled with a mournful sense of the vastness and futility of life, and a great inscrutable Presence standing over it, calm as the dead. In a flash he saw the tall policeman in Argyll Street directing the traffic of Glasgow, and flower girls in the blue, greasy mud of the city, blind men groping with their dogs, ambulance vans hurrying, strange women hovering at the doors of theatres. Why did these things come to him? Was he going mad? And Mr. Kennedy's face, grave and white, shining out of clouds; and swinging high up in the dark the red cross of the ambulance vans, and beneath the cross, over an incarnadined world, the pierced feet of the Redeemer, august in His torment. Wave upon wave of darkness swept over his soul. A vast shutter opened on a gulf; an ebon wall rolled out of this gulf on silent wheels; and as it was about to whelm him, with a crest of jet foam it suddenly contracted into a cone-shape which, entering his body, spread fanwise over his soul, smothering him in an inky cloud. He began to weep softly. The titanic wall of pitch rolled from his shoulders over the stump of a pier, to sink into the sea like a black mist. Again the shutters of the dark moved swiftly, pulled upwards by an invisible hand, and another inky wall stalked up from the abyss, rolling on wheels of dense smoke. He felt blinded. The wheels of smoke rolled down upon him with slow, roaring ponderousness. Would the Eternal Mercy never relieve the gloom? Those wheels would crush him into pulp. The sea over the stump of pier sent up peal after peal of demoniac laughter. It had waited for him, ever waited, with its horrible eyes of fire, since he was a boy. He was running from it past the "Ghost." He had run this way before, when his mother had gathered up Iain beneath the eyes of the Magdalene out of the hollow deep. A lightning flash blinded him, and he opened his eyes. Good God! he was dreaming again; and, sitting up in bed, he shook himself like a dog bewildered. Thunder suddenly roared about the house. He jumped from bed and ran into the parlour. The Square was brilliantly lit, and loud with the roystering voices of the "first foots" preparing to bring in New Year. It was Hogmanay night, or "wee Setterday," and the shops would be open late. Even children, undismayed by the growling heavens, were singing the swan-song of the year. Their voices floated up to him from the Square:

> "Hogmanay, Hogmanay;
> If ye'll no' gie's oor Hogmanay
> We'll break your door before the day."

He, too, had sung that song from door to door for a piece of bun or an orange.

> "Rise up, auld wife, an' shake your feathers,
> Dinna think that we are beggars.
> We are only boys an' girls
> Come to seek our Hogmanay."

Tears blinded him. It seemed only yesterday that he had struck the tents of boyhood. The childish voices became unbearable:

> "This is wee Setterday,
> Next day's cock-a-law."

Never, never more, his breaking heart was crying; those voices were tearing at his heart:

> "We'll come back on Monday
> An' gie ye a' a ca'———"

Shrill and gleeful rang the carolling through the Square. Again the unappeasable yearning to mingle with them, to be a boy again! Ah! little children, you, the begetters of dreams, who turn men's hearts to water as they listen, and flood the bare trees of age with green, what anguish your joyance and innocence can cause to those burdened with remorse! What a sense of estrangement you bring to men, with your wonderful immunity from life and its vicissitudes! What despair you can cause as you tramp out of the Square, careless of the thundering skies, and

410

leave one stripped of all hope, staring across the lights of the Square into the gulf of the night, with a deeper gulf of darkness surrounding his soul.

The kitchen was empty. He shook with dread at the discovery. "She must be with Janet; she must be with Janet," he thought. He was about to discover something quite different. That morning Topsail had been at the wash-tub. She had steeped the things the day before, and towards noon had hung out the clothes in the back green where the cats congregate, and as the north wind ruffled her hair she dreamt beneath the line of a merry baker taking in the New Year, playing upon a flute. She saw Maclean pass up the stair. What a man he was! Pat, his driver, had told Jeck the Traiveller how he had gone in the face of a snowstorm to a case of childbirth.

"Two lives depending on us; give the mare hell an' get her through." He had to crawl through the snow-drifts to the shepherd's door.

Topsail gazed with adoring eyes at the man who went through the snow to bring babies into the world. He came out again with Gillespie, and stood on the stairhead, looking so stern that Topsail trembled.

"Is she failin' that sair?" she heard Gillespie ask.

Maclean, who had found her pulse feeble and rapid, made no answer. He pulled out his watch and looked at the dial. He was still looking when Topsail heard him say, "The spring flowers will be growing over her head."

Topsail felt her knees giving way beneath her, and saw the top of the house rising and falling upon a suddenly darkened sky.

"God keep us a'; an' Ne'er Day the morn. A sair, sair Ne'er Day it'll be," she moaned.

In the afternoon Sandy the Fox and she carried in the clothes, because it was unlucky to leave them out over the last night of the year. The Fox informed her that after tea she must go with a basket of things to West Loch Brieston. This was in spite of Maclean's instructions to Gillespie that his wife must be narrowly watched. It was after eight o'clock before Topsail Janet was able to set out obscurely by the Back Street. As soon as she had left, her mistress, who had not spoken all day, passed swiftly down the stair and along the passage to the coal cellar in the washing-house where, among the coal-dross, she was in the habit of concealing her whisky bottle. McAskill, the lawyer, was on the watch for her. He had given Lonend's money to six of the poor of Brieston for the last two years, that they might pay the Poor Rates. They had received no receipt from Gillespie. In order to have absolute proof of Gillespie's guilt it was necessary to see his books; and there was no other way than by bribing his wife.

Eoghan, who had come out to the stair-head, heard a man's querulous voice at the end of the passage. It froze his blood. He could not distinguish what was being said, and began to tremble violently. At last! what devilish infamy and shame! Did these hounds not know that his poor mother was insane? Wide-eyed, open-mouthed with horror, he clung to the railing. His faintness had left him; a river of fire was in his veins; and he saw in the air streaks like blood. A great stone seemed to hang suspended aloft, ready to drop and crash through the monstrous silence. He thought he distinguished his mother's voice—a voice full of unutterable weariness, the voice of one mercilessly beaten upon her knees—and he began to gnaw on his lower lip, seeing the twin doors of hell flung wide open, and the sheeted dead arising out of their graves beneath the church on the hill.

He began to creep down the stairs.

"Listen—what's that?" He heard the sibilant words distinctly; it was the voice of the serpent lawyer. Eoghan drew in a deep breath, filling his lungs, and, dropping on all fours, started crawling along the passage.

"You'll get the money on Monday—a pound." The words came of a seething pit, and set his brain on fire as with hot pincers. A wild laugh broke the silence—his mother's terrible laugh.

"Shut up, can't you? or I'll be off. I'm here long enough already."

A fiend seemed to pin Eoghan to the causey for a moment; the next he rose up like one in a dream, and the great stone suspended in the heavens crashed down. It was his own yell. "Eoghan's here, mother! Eoghan's here!" and his hot breath was in the lawyer's face. "Oh, hell! hell! hell! and all its devils." He had blindly gripped the lawyer by the hair, and was sinking his teeth in the lobe of an ear, chewing and gnawing upon it in blind rage, as he felt for the lawyer's throat.

"Good God! you're murdering me; let me go!" McAskill screamed, as he twisted and writhed. Maddened with pain, he

412

jerked up his head, tore his ear from Eoghan's grip, dashed his two hands in Eoghan's face, and broke away down the passage. The mind of the lawyer was actively at work as he ran—this madman would pursue them through the Square; and the Square on Hogmanay night is ablaze with light and choked with wives out in their gee-gaws. What a sorry spectacle he would present, flying across the Square, hunted by a comet of wrath!

The passage continued along the whole length of the buildings to the back door of the shop. At the foot of the stair leading to the kitchen, the close ran off the passage at right angles. The lawyer darted into the close, brought himself up smartly, and crouched against the wall. The next moment a dark figure, growling in a manner which made the lawyer's blood run cold, tore past him down the close. The lawyer slipped round the corner to the right, scurried down the passage and, without ceremony, turned the handle of the door and stepped into the back shop. It was empty. He walked to the door leading to the shop, and saw Gillespie handing over the counter to Topsail Janet a large basket, giving her at the same time instructions which the lawyer could not catch. He heard Topsail cackling, "Ye micht gie me a poke o' sweeties for my Hogmanay."

Gillespie was reaching forth his hand to a box of cheap confectionery when he saw the lawyer beckoning him from the entrance to the back shop. Dismissing Topsail Janet with a suggestive jerk of his head, he walked swiftly round the counter to the lawyer.

"Hoo did ye win in here, laawer?" he asked tartly.

"A drunken fool at Brodie's knocked my cap into the mud. I take six seven-eighths."

Gillespie smoothed out his face.

"Light or dark?"

"Dark."

While Gillespie was fetching some caps the lawyer determined on his line of action. He concluded that Eoghan had overheard the conversation which he had had with Mrs. Strang, and that the son would doubtless inform the father. All Brieston knew from Gillespie's own mouth that the son had given up the idea of the University to enter his father's business. It would be as well for the lawyer to be beforehand with his own story. When Gillespie returned with an armful of caps McAskill, having retreated to the back shop, asked:

413

"Have ye half-an-hour to spare, Mr. Strang? Ye might close the door." McAskill licked his lips with his tongue.

Gillespie, pushing the door to, interrogated the lawyer with a look.

"I'm thrang the nicht; is it pressin'?"

McAskill nodded. "I'll mention no names, you know; but there's one or two folk not exactly your friends in the town."

"That's news."

"And to make a long story short they suspect you're not keeping your books right."

"Whatna books?"

"As Poor Law Clerk."

The single ferrety eye of the lawyer saw Gillespie's brow cloud and his eyes widen with apprehension. It did not need the sharp whistle in Gillespie's nostrils to confirm the lawyer. "By the Lord," he almost breathed the words aloud, "it's true." But when Gillespie scanned the lawyer's face, the eye of the lawyer was bent upon the floor. Burly, almost genial, the healthy tan now restored to his face, his chin tilted up in a characteristic way, Gillespie appeared as if he were the accuser, and the weak-kneed, thin-shanked, furtive McAskill the accused. "If he's innocent he'll order me out of the shop," McAskill was thinking at that moment when Gillespie said:

"The books are passed every year."

"We all know that, Mr. Strang."

"What are they sookin' at then?"

"Well," answered McAskill, "the moneys you enter in the books are passed; but they suspect these are not all the moneys" —a watery smile played round the thin, cruel lips—"and that's what I've come to see you about."

"Sit doon, laawer; sit doon." Gillespie re-entered the shop. He was gone some time, having searched for the Fox to take charge of the counter. When he returned he seated himself at his desk, and picking up a pen, nodded across at McAskill.

"Noo, oot wi't." His tone was that of a judge.

McAskill shuffled about on his chair, and began: "One or two gentlemen called at my office and asked me if I would like to get your job—collecting the rates, Registrar, and all that." The lawyer waved his hand. "I thought you had resigned, and said I would be delighted."

As Gillespie made no answer, the lawyer went on: "You see,

there's so many of the poor have got off paying their rates that it's difficult to know who pays. The word of Mr. Strang has simply to be taken that so-and-so is relieved of his rates, while, in point of fact, so-and-so has paid. This is their argument, you understand."

"Ay! man."

"So, for the last year and this year they have given the amount of their rates to half-a-dozen men who have never paid taxes in their lives—none of your friends either, I'll warrant you—and put them up to the job of paying their rates."

"Imphm!" The ejaculation was ground out of the listener. "And they are of opinion, not to mention any names, that you haven't credited these sums with the names in your official accounts and statements." McAskill came to a breathless halt, like a diver risen from a deep plunge.

"I'm follo—in'—ye."

These words had the effect on McAskill of a physical blow, and he cringed. "So they bribed me with the offer of your job to get hold of your books."

"Ye've come for them, nae doot?"

"I was to get them another way."

"Steal them lik'?"

The lawyer deprecated with a thin smile. "Oh, no; for a little consideration, honorarium." He coughed in his hand. "Your wife was to hand them over."

Gillespie slowly rose to his feet, and the lawyer blinking, imitated, as if dragged up.

"I'm no' a violent man by ordinar, laawer; but ca' canny. Ye'll no' be the first furrit o' Lonen's that was trampit on."

Gillespie ponderously resumed his seat, and McAskill slunk on to his chair.

"But I've come here to tell you, Mr. Strang," he whined; "surely that's proof of my good intentions and honesty."

"Ay! man, your honesty's a thing that canna be proved; it's too often rowed up in a dirty cloot. What gars ye bring it oot noo?"

McAskill, ruffled, drew a hand over his smooth mouth.

"Oh! that they'll not get your books, now that I've warned you."

"I'm dootin' no'." Gillespie laughed sardonically.

"Do you not think, Mr. Strang, it would be just as well to credit the rates to those who have paid them?"

415

This sudden spurt of malice did not appear at all sinister to Gillespie. "That's my business, laawer."

"You see you didn't happen to give them receipts—Oh! a slight neglect, I'm sure. No doubt you can produce their names and the amounts paid last year if called for by a chartered accountant."

There was a profound silence. Gillespie put the pen behind his ear, and gazed meditatively on the floor.

"What coorse are ye on, laawer?"

An evil smile flickered about the thin, sucking lips. "I know the names of the men and the amounts paid. Quite easy to let each man have his receipt, and credit the amount in your statement of moneys received. There are only six names in dispute. For any others"—McAskill shot a keen glance at Gillespie—"it doesn't matter."

"It's no' for noäthin' they say you're a smert ane, Mr Mc-Askill." Gillespie had become amazingly suave and affected cordiality. "You an' me 'ill hae to mak' a bargain."

"That's exactly what I've come for. Had I stayed away you'd have been ruined."

Gillespie was stung in the seat of his pride by these words. Many things of late had tried his temper—Maclean's interference in the matter of his wife; Barbara's money; above all, the mysterious attitude of his son.

"Ruined! Gillespie Strang ruined by a sook o' a laawer, an' a wheen kiss-ma-futs. Ye've come to the wrang shop."

Again Gillespie rose to his feet, but this time McAskill remained seated. "There's no need to get angry," he said softly.

"Ondootedly; it's no' my practice; but keep a ceevil tongue in your heid." Gillespie again sat down.

"It'll be so much a name." McAskill leered horribly.

"I winna gie a pun' note for the hale jing-bang o' the scum."

"The names will be worth more than that to the Parish Council."

"An' hoo muckle dae ye mak' oot they're worth to Mr. McAskill?"

Gillespie sneered broadly in the lawyer's face.

"Shall we say five pound a head?"

"Ye mean a five pun' note for a' the tinklers."

McAskill laughed mirthlessly.

"Ye're he'rty on it, laawer; what preceesly is the bit joke?"

416

"Oh! I thought for the moment we were buying and selling slaves. I imagined myself on the coast of Zanzibar."

"I'm jaloosin"—Gillespie frowned—"that it would be female slaves the likes o' you wad be bargainin' for."

McAskill flushed and drummed with his taper fingers on the chair. "Let us come to business," he rapped out.

"I'm willin'. It's yersel' stairted in amang the slaves."

McAskill pondered. He was a vindictive man. Revenge for this insult, and for many wrongs which he had suffered smilingly at the hands of Gillespie, would be sweet. He would get paid for those names; but at the same time would not by any means throw away Gillespie's job, which he now held in his hands. Gillespie, self-confessedly, had cooked his accounts. McAskill hoped the defalcation was large.

"Well, how much do you propose to pay for each man?" he asked.

"Hoo dae I ken the thing's no' a story o' your ain mak'-up?"

"It's a story I can make gospel pretty quick if I take to preaching in the sheriff court at Ardmarkie."

"Weel! weel! ye said five pun' a heid; that's ower muckle for swine."

"I'm willing to say four."

"No, no, laawer; we'll split the differ an' say three."

McAskill knew from experience that he had reached the limit. Besides it was near ten o'clock, and he had business with Brodie. He assented.

"Hand me ower the names noo." Gillespie's face was nonchalant, his tone careless.

"I am forced to admit that I admire your acting, Mr. Strang. You would be an ornament to any profession but the Church."

These words made Gillespie afraid more than anything McAskill had said. The lawyer had never before dared be so personal. This sleek rogue had always been a poltroon, a toady, and a constant dog at heel. Where he glided, Gillespie knew, his shadow was disastrous. To have him show his teeth now was ominous. Gillespie had often seen him at his backstairs tricks, and knew what a scoundrel he was. There was more in his flagrant insolence than merely an attempt at bleeding a victim. The penumbra of eclipse touched Gillespie cold. Through the instrumentality of this fellow Gillespie had once "downed" Lonend. Was the unsleeping hand of Lonend behind McAskill's effrontery? If this matter of the Poor Rates were pushed home he would be in a fix. He had not forgotten the Procurator-Fiscal. He was a fool to have riled that man. It was doubtful what Eoghan would do with the estate if the Procurator-Fiscal got his claws on him. Had this angel of evil, McAskill, only postponed his visit for a year, for six months even, till Eoghan had worked himself into the business, and it had become safe in his hands. What a cursed miscarriage! His own flesh and blood was in league against him. For a moment Gillespie's face was distorted with passion; but with a superb effort he recovered his calm—he must follow warily the lawyer's lead. Though his mind was in a fever the only sign of uneasiness which he betrayed was a puckering of his brows, as he looked up swiftly at the rat eye which was watching him with a mocking smile. If he could only wrest the secret of this oily hound or win this grinning shadow of the law to his side! To be niggard now was to invite defeat and disgrace. Gillespie trembled, not for himself, but for his idols.

"What dae ye mean, Mr. McAskill? Surely ye can trust a freen'."

"I mean that I'm not Galbraith or Lonend or a simple fisherman."

"Then ye dinna trust me, aifter a' we've been through the-gither?"

"I don't believe there is honour among thieves."

The words stung Gillespie like nettles. Mercilessly they revealed to him his plight. Goaded as he was, he felt impotent before this extortioner and liar. By devils are devils heartlessly condemned. The pure shudder to pronounce woe. Gillespie ground the stump of the pen between his strong teeth, and the air whistled sharply in his nostrils.

"Surely I maun hae the goods afore I pey ye, man." He was unable fully to repress his anger.

"I want to see the colour of your money. I will give you name number one for three pounds."

"Hoots! hoots! dinna be sae hasty. Ye'll find Gillespie Strang's no' that slack wi' a pun' here or there among freen's. I'll mak' it five pun' if ye dale wi' me fair an' square; there, that's an offer."

McAskill leaned forward, with a smile of blandishment, in the strong, hard face of his prey.

"Double your five, Mr. Strang, and I'll put ye on the track of your enemies."

Gillespie, who felt his fetters fall off at these unexpected words, opened a long narrow drawer in his desk and took out a cheque-book. "I'll mak' oot a cheque for sixty poun' in your favour."

There was a tense silence for a moment, and McAskill crooked his mouth to restrain a wild desire for laughter.

"I'll give you six names, Mr. Strang, and the amount paid by each for Poor Rates. You can enter them into your books. Then let Lonend lay a charge of defalcation against you, and you can have an action against him for libel."

This cunning veneer and plausible gracefulness turned the tables. A demon of revenge, the reaction from his state of desperate fear, seized and blinded Gillespie.

"Mak' oot your list, by Goäd!" he breathed. Suddenly one of the canaries in the shop burst into song.

"A fine whistler, that bird," said the lawyer, with austere politeness.

Gillespie reared his massive head to listen. The stolen bird's requiem as suddenly stopped.

"I never heard the boy so late at e'en before." He turned to McAskill, cheque in hand. "Ye can sell me the slaves noo," he said jocularly. Through sheer force of habit Gillespie had assumed his jocose counter manners. McAskill dived into his pocket and took out a longish slip of paper. It was Brodie's account, rendered at the end of a quarter for "goods." The lawyer was now come to the climax of his daring game. So many hundreds of people pay the Poor Rate. Could Gillespie particularise any six names in which, up till now, he had had no interest? McAskill determined to furnish six names other than those in question. If Gillespie accepted them he would soon be in jail, and McAskill Clerk to the Poor in his shoes. On the first name hung the issue. McAskill asked for pen and paper; then—Angus Cameron, fisherman, the Barracks. He called out the name like an usher in court, and waited for a challenge. There was none. The lawyer squeezed his knees together in repressed exultation. The giant of business was trapped in the snare of forgotten details. McAskill thrilled in writing down the two words, for he was writing the doom of Gillespie at the rate of ten pounds a name. No sound broke the stillness now but the scraping of the pen, whose shrill music was that of the *Dies Irae*. The lawyer had a neat hand, and was making out the bill of indictment, not with a pen, but with a dagger. Gillespie's eyes gloated on the paper, which was the winding-sheet of his honour. Scratch! scratch! scratch! The profound silence was suddenly broken by the sound of a dull thud overhead.

"What's that?" asked the lawyer, without looking up. His eager hand was at the fourth name.

"Oh! it'll be the missis lookin' for the books." Gillespie's tame sneer was lost on McAskill, who wrote the fifth name; and the Christian name of the sixth was completed when a louder thud shook the ceiling. McAskill peered up at Gillespie, his pen hovering in midair. They heard a faint moan.

"Something wrong up there"—the end of the pen was jerked towards the ceiling.

"Oh! I expect the missis is bringin' in Ne'er Day."

The pen swooped on the paper and finished the writing of the name. Had McAskill only known it, his duplicity was in vain. In that sound overhead nemesis had already done for him all that his treacherous soul had sought. The woman, whom an hour ago he had attempted to bribe, and who had answered him strangely by asking what he had done with the dead baby, lay above prone upon the floor, and her body, dethroning the house of Strang, became the stepping-stone for the lawyer to his official seat among the revenues. With the Judas money which he had wrung from Gillespie he had paid his bill at Brodie's, and jovially ordered a fresh supply of whisky for the New Year.

As for Gillespie Strang, he went and talked of important matters concerning Lonend to his canaries. As he talked he made a sudden hissing sound in his nostrils. He had omitted to charge McAskill two shillings for the dark cap.

16

BAFFLED, and with the aspect of a beaten hound, Eoghan returned from the darkened and locked office of the lawyer, and took refuge in the mouth of the close from the driving rain, as he sought to recover his thoughts. A gale was screaming with high-pitched note through the Square. The shop lights drizzled against the dreariness of the wet night; the wind whistled as upon the

edge of knives in the rigging of the fishing-fleet; the greedy tide
lapped over the breast wall; the slates rattled like musketry. A
night in the dying year for wrecks.

"My sorrow is upon you, little town," he groaned, as his eye
swept the deserted, sea-beleaguered street. He scarce could climb
the stair, because of a fierce pain low down in his left side.
Greenish sparks of light whirled before his eyes in orgiacal gambol, like a cloud of wasps. He had been in the vertigo of hell, out
of which he floated into a lake of eternal darkness. Rage had given
place to inexpressible weariness, and weariness to terror of the
mysterious forces which surround human life. When he reached
the head of the stair he heard a cough—hard and hollow, and an
icy hand gripped at his heart at the sound. The convulsive swelling in his breast recommenced, and a sense of imminent danger,
murky as the night, seized his mind. That little cough, blatant
and callous, challenged and defied him. It made a blood-freezing
sound. Faint with dread, he leaned heavily upon the stair railing
to ease the tumult of his heart, as he sought for some light in his
darkness. This child of dreams and the plaything of circumstance
was learning to gnaw upon vicissitude and withstand the arrows
of Fate. Had he turned then and gone to the "Ghost," as he had
almost determined, the course of this history would have been
changed, and Eoghan Strang would probably have emerged from
the conflict with his soul welded in its fires, as into a sword
sharper than Fate, and able to withstand Destiny; but in that
moment he heard a tremulous wire-drawn voice begin to sing:

> "Last night there were four Maries,
> To-night there'll be but three."

Back beyond this night of wrath and fear, the words bore him to
the havens of childhood across the miles of angels, and he saw his
dear mother, young and beautiful, as once he had beheld her at
the shop door, wearing a linen collar, and the black coil of her
hair stately upon her head, and her smile ineffable and half wistful upon the fishermen who passed, doffing their caps. The tears
smarted in his eyes. One effort, yes, by God! one effort, and he
would save her yet; he would tear her away from this place of
infamy and shame.

She was seated at the fire, nursing a whisky bottle in her lap
as it were a babe. Her clothing was drenched with rain; her face
was ghastly with the cold. She fixed her eyes upon him as upon a

stranger, and with stealthy cunning whipped the bottle out of sight under a cloud of babble, her mouth and knees violently twitching and jerking. She looked as if she had been cruelly beaten. Her eyes were glazed and exhausted, and were fixed on her son with wide, horrible calm. She recognised him now—this dogged spy.

"Give me a drink of water," she said, with a wrinkled leer, and in a wheedling tone. Immediately he had turned to the dresser for a cup her face assumed an intensely virile appearance. She jumped to her feet, and casting the look of a warder upon him, broke into a little blind trot to her room, where she went down on all fours and searched beneath the bed for the instrument of liberty which she had concealed there, Gillespie's razor, and which she whipped into her skirt pocket. It made a dull sound against the bottle. She returned to the kitchen, refused the water with a sulky look, and sat down at the fire. Without the storm tore across the Harbour, and every snarl drove the smoke from the chimney in clouds into the kitchen. After a fit of coughing she watched, from the corners of her eyes, the movements of her son, who took off his wet jacket and soaked collar. She conceived him watching for an opportunity to rob her of the concealed treasure in her pocket, which she had brought up from the washing-house. He was a spy of Gillespie's. Why were they constantly watching her, as if she were a thief or a dog? They would not allow Mr. Campion to come and see the dead baby in the bed.

"What were you doing in the bedroom, mother?"

He knew, then, of the dead baby there, and would steal that away too. An intense hatred of him possessed her, and she gnashed with her teeth. He stepped to the table against the wall next to the bedroom and turned down the wick of the lamp, which was blackening the funnel. He moved mechanically, for his mind was in a whirl. He wished to tell her of the strange dream, in which he saw her lying among flowers in a coffin—a dream that might come true very soon if she did not give over this drinking. What a cough she had! Yet if he told her it might leave her panic-stricken with fear. His heart bled for her. He wished Topsail were here to put her to bed. She would catch her death of cold in those soaked clothes. Or would he demand outright an explanation of her business with the lawyer? His emotions deprived him of the power of clear thought; he moved like an automaton; his hand shook violently as he turned the screw of the lamp. The gale shook the house with a sudden clap, and a torrent of smoke rushed from the fire. The light of the lamp went down too far, and the kitchen was buried in semi-gloom.

The rage to drink was burning her. She looked upon him from her eyelids. Would he seize the bottle? They all robbed her. She must drink, for her head was mad with pain, her mouth was parched, her lips were on fire. He adjusted the flame of the lamp, and turning, saw her greedily drink.

"Oh! mother, mother, it's drawing to the end o' the Year; will ye no' try in the New Year to give it up? You'll try, mother; we'll go away from here together." The anguished pleading choked him.

"Ay! ay! the weary end o' the clock. My baby's dead an' ta'en awa'. Did ye hear the cocks o' the Muirheid crawin'?"

The horrible hopelessness of her life seized him. He seemed hardly to breathe.

"Do you believe in the judgment of God, in hell?" he asked.

Another would have been moved by those words, coming from his corpse-like lips; but she, seizing on the word "hell," whispered in a sane moment the stupendous secret of her shipwreck.

"Gillespie Strang is hell." These were the last words she ever spoke. They revealed to him all the agony of her life, rising up in a flame of atrocious suffering—a life of loneliness and slavery, of neglect and extreme misery, overshadowed by terror, sullen hatred, and fear. Her colourless, down-trodden life rose up before his eyes, sublime in its resignation to tyranny and cruelty. Her soul had been battered to death. Had he himself done his duty? He drove his nails into his palms. The happy hours and days spent with Barbara rose up as damning witnesses before this self-set tribunal, and he bitterly denounced himself: "We have all been reposing on hope—I on Barbara'a love, my father on gold—while she, miserable, has drifted in the dark." He gazed mournfully upon the profile of his mother, upon her figure, sunk and steeped in immobility, a statue of tragic despair. Devouring her appalling stillness with eyes anguished with remorse, he made a movement of his arms as if to clasp her in a shielding embrace. The gesture expressed the poignant depths of his suffering. Stooping, he sank on his knees and began crawling towards the draggled hem of her skirt, and spread out his arms in supplication, as if he were nailed upon a cross.

Her hard, glittering eye was riveted unwaveringly upon him—this hound, who had scented out her secret and in a moment would snatch the bottle from her and discover the razor. Her eyes darted round the room in a quick, stealthy glance. They were alone. She had brooded upon this chance for weeks. Now she would be rid for ever of this loathed adversary, who meant to cast her into the Harbour. Her left hand lay open, palm upwards, on her lap. With the right she made a restless jerky movement. Her eyes, cunningly upon him, were blazing with the immensity of her savage hatred, and the devouring lust to see this dogged spy struck down. He rose upon his knees at her feet to beseech the living God to give him absolution for his neglect, and break the blight of his mother's face with His light.

"Oh, Jesus Christ, lead her sorrow and her woe into my breast," he cried. The chimney suddenly belched smoke. Her gloomy face lightened with a fierce expression of joy, and with incredible swiftness she half arose, seized him by the hair, jerked his head back savagely, and drew the glittering blade of the razor across his throat. A tiny artery spurted upon her hand. The hot blood drove her crazy. She tightened her knees upon him as with a vice, and deepened her clutch in his hair. Profound astonishment paralysed him. His head was viciously wrung back again, and in a horrible silence she, with the savage strength of a demoniac, slashed his throat open through the muscles, till the razor scraped on the surface of the bones of the neck. A huge gout of arterial blood spouted on her face, blinding her, and pumped far across the room, splashing on the wall. He glimpsed the stained blade in her hand as, with a superhuman effort, he heaved himself up. The chair toppled; she crashed backwards; the thud of her head on the back of the fender mingled with the brittle sound of the broken whisky bottle. She rolled over on her side, her face smeared with his blood, and in her right hand the dripping razor. Neither had spoken a word.

Astonishment, incredulity, anger swept rapidly over him, and gave way to deep-seated fear, to horror unspeakable. A dark steady stream poured and poured down his neck and shirt. This is death, he thought; my life is pouring out of me. His body burned and became cold. He clapped his hands to his throat and staggered up on his feet. From the cut windpipe a mound of bloody froth hissed and crackled. He strove to cry out for help. There were bands of light appearing and disappearing before his eyes. He swayed upon his feet, fainting into an enormous region of darkness; crashed down on the floor and lay like dead in a pool of blood. He was aware of a vast terrible silence, which isolate him from humanity. Panic-stricken, he got up again and lurched to the sink, turned on the tap, and attempted to wash his neck. Again he fell on the floor in a pool of red and dark blood . . . Nailed on the sky above were the heads of malefactors, whose blood fell on the earth like rain. It ran on his face and throat; God Almighty, it was his own blood. . . . Again he got to his feet, stumbled to the kitchen door, his face like dough, reeled through the passage into his own room, where again he crashed on the floor, face downwards, and lay still in a sea of blood, his pupils wide and staring into a damnable abyss of horror.

17

"WEE Setterday," the last day of the year, was drawing to an end. The lights went out one by one in the shops of Harbour Street, and the wind-besieged night took possession of Brieston. Gillespie Strang blew out the lights and locked up his shop. He was revolving the business which the lawyer had disclosed, and cherished the hope that his son would begin the New Year by entering into partnership with him. For a moment he stopped at the front door after he had locked it, and listened to the howling of the gale, which blew from the nor'-west with blinding sheets of rain. He was alone in the Square. "The auld year's being blawn away like hey-my-nanny," he muttered; "the new ane 'ill be no sae pleesant for some folk." He was thinking of Lonend.

Gillespie was tired, and shambled round the corner of the house, his head bowed to the storm—tall, broad, ponderous, alone. He was buffeted in the draughty close, and clung to the iron hand-rail of the stair. Fatigue had subdued him. The kitchen door stood wide open in the passage; the lamp had gone out; a single red spark glimmered in the ashes of the fire. An oppressive quiet reigned within the house.

"Janet!" he called sharply up the narrow stair to the Coffin. Topsail was at West Loch Brieston, persuaded by the storm and Angus Carmichael, to whom she had carried certain goods, "to stay and bring in New Year."

"Janet, are ye deif?"

Nothing but silence and darkness on the stair leading to the Coffin, and the moan of the storm. "A cauld lik' New Year," he sneered, and pushed into the kitchen. The shop keys jangled in his hand—the instruments with which he had locked life out of his existence. He put them in his jacket pocket.

"Are ye there, Morag?" He cast his voice in the direction of the bedroom. The house shook under the impact of the gale, and a gust went whining through the Square into MacCalman's Lane.

"Bonny lik' nicht to be oot stravaigin'. She'll be bringin' in Ne'er Day wi' her freens."

He began to sniff like a terrier on the scent, casting his head round to every point of the compass. He was puzzled. Along with the pungent odour of whisky mingled another smell which baffled him. It was the acrid smell of his son's blood.

"Just so," he muttered wearily; "she's forgotten her wean; she'll hae plenty whaur she is." A grim smile hardened round his lips as he remembered Maclean's words that the spring flowers would be growing over her. Then he would be rid of the burden. She might, any of those dark nights, wander over the Harbour wall—perhaps tonight in the darkness. Yet those thoughts made him gloomy, and he searched for matches in his waistcoat pocket. Outside on the slates of the washing-house the startled wail of a wandered cat rose up on the wind; the lonely cry of pain seemed to wrestle with the storm. As the second meowh quavered piteously like an infant greeting, he felt there was an unaccustomed silence in the house. Where were they all? Eoghan would be at the "Ghost." Why was Topsail not returned? He passed heavily into the bedroom, sat down on the edge of the bed, and began unlacing his boots.

"Oot stravaigin' to a' oors." He spoke bitterly. "I micht as well be a weedaoor. Weel, well, it's a kin' o' caul' hame-comin' at Ne'er Day for Gillespie Strang." He meant that such an one, with all his wealth, ought to be able to buy or achieve some welcome or happiness. He was proud of his loneliness. One by one the boots fell on the floor with a loud thud. He groped on the dressing-table for matches and put his hand to a drawer. It was already open—the drawer in which he kept his razor. It contained no matches. He thought of the kitchen mantelpiece and retreated thither. His right foot came down heavily on a splinter of broken bottle and was deeply pierced. It was the whisky bottle which his

426

wife had brought forth from concealment in the rubbish heap of the washing-house. Gillespie Strang, with an exclamation of annoyance, hopped back, lifted up his leg, and making a wry face pressed his hand to the sole of his foot. Hop back as fast as he could, he did not hop back quickly enough. Gillespie had touched death in the dark.

He was forced at last to seek for matches in the shop, in the pigeon-hole of his desk, where he always kept a box since the night of the attempted robbery. He also brought back with him a candle. When he entered the kitchen he struck a match. The yellow light flared and went out; and he fumbled for another. Drip! drip! drip! the water from the tap fell with clammy insistence in the sink. Without the cat still wailed, as if crying for mercy from the inclement night. The fretting noise broke irritatingly upon his consciousness.

"Deil tak' the beast, greetin' awa' there lik' a wean."

He sheltered the feeble flare of the match in the hollow of his hand and lit the candle. He turned at once to the dresser, for the sole of his foot was smarting. "Whaur will I get a bit cloot?" he said mechanically, and opened one drawer after another. He found a piece of bath-brick; soiled pieces of rag; an empty cocoa-tin; a photograph. He held up the photograph to the candle-light. It was that of Eoghan, concealed there by Topsail Janet. Gazing at it with ardent face, Gillespie forgot his wounded foot, and turning with a deep sigh, the candle in one hand and the photograph in the other, he saw his wife. She was lying at the far end of the fender on her side, face downwards. In the badly-lit room he did not notice the blood-splashed wall or the dark-red pools at the sink. Shadows danced on the ceiling and half across the wall—danced elvishly, mockingly. Drunk, of course, and her bed anywhere.

"So ye're hame, auld fugie wife; in blanket bay wi' a' your regimentals on." Getting no answer, he added sarcastically, "Brocht in Ne'er Day in guid time." The wild wind shook the window. The gable was in its teeth, and Gillespie stood a moment listening to the booming sound as of guns in the chimney. On such a night was Iain drowned. As he listened the clock in the church spire began to strike twelve. The sounds came now faint, now clear and strong, as if they were being worried by the wind. The grey warden of the years upon the hill had given notice. At the third stroke remembrance came to him.

427

"Guid New Year to ye, Mrs. Strang," he cried mockingly, "an' guid New Year to Lonen', your faither;" and putting down the candle and the photograph of his son on the table beside the dead lamp, and taking out a large silver watch, he began to wind it. A deep gust shook the house.

"It's loud enough to wauken the deid." He glanced at his wife, expecting to see the dark head stir. "Hae! rise up, auld wife, an' shake your feathers, it's Ne'er Day;" and in that moment, with a sudden rush, as if a supernatural wind had blown in upon his spirit, he felt that death was there, nursing his wife at the blind fire-end. He was across the floor in two strides, leaving a small pool of blood on the floor where he had been standing. He slithered over a dark-red pool, and then saw the blood on her cheek.

He staggered back with terror in his eyes, crept to one side to bring her face into full view, saw her glassy eyes and the rigid, yawning mouth—which seemed to have taken in a breath and never expelled it again—and the blood. A cold sweat broke out on his forehead.

"My first fut, my first fut," he cackled; "this . . ."

Beneath the thunder of the wind there was an uncanny silence in the kitchen. The missile rain, crashing upon the panes, roused him out of his stupor. With a backward glance he lurched out of the room, slipping on the blood, and put out his hands at Eoghan's door.

"Waken, waken, Eoghan! the kitchen's like a slachter-hoose; your mother's cut her throat."

He heard nothing but the beating of his own heart as he waited for an answer.

"Waken, Eoghan, waken. Do ye hear me?"

The bedroom, which was towards the front, was filled with the dark plowter of the sea and its half-strangled cry. He groped forward, catching the iron end of the bedstead, and put his hands into the bed to shake the sleeping body. They fell on empty space. A clear water dribbled from the corners of his mouth, and he uttered a deep groan.

"Good Goäd, the hoose is empty!"

He backed away, a prey to fear, shot a look of terror in through the kitchen door, and half ran through the passage to the stair. In his shirt sleeves and stocking-soles he bolted into a night hoarse with the sea and maddened with the wind, and casting

428

one fearful glance over his shoulder at the dark pile of his dwelling looming down upon him, ran across the Square to Maclean's house, whose night-bell he sent jangling all through the house. A window was thrust up; in the rush of the wind Gillespie could not distinguish what was said. Presently a bolt was drawn, a key rasped, the big door opened, and the maid invited Gillespie into the hall. The red night-light on the oaken table, the unconcerned face of the maid, the homely sounds of the doctor moving above, restored his courage to Gillespie. With the access of calm, his fears gave place to a more pleasing outlook. Affairs were moving beneath the stars in his favour; Lonend would soon be in the hollow of his hand in a court of justice; his wife would trouble him no more. His star was steadily rising upon the evening of his life. Maclean's descent broke in upon his rumination. Under the doctor's keen scrutiny, Gillespie recognised that he was in his shirt sleeves and stocking-soles.

"You, Mr. Strang; what is wrong?"

"Come away quick, doctor; the missis's stravaigin' days are done."

"What do you mean?"

"She's lyin' yonder on the flure a caul' corp, up to the bridles in blood."

Maclean darted past him, and when Gillespie stepped to the door he heard the doctor running across the Square. When next he saw Maclean, the doctor was stooping over the dead body of his wife.

"Hold the candle here, sir," was the peremptory demand.

Gillespie, candle in hand, went prying and sniffing about the cold clay, his face impassive. To have grown grey in greed and iniquity was nothing in its monstrosity in comparison to this silent jubilee. The horror of death appeared to leave him invincible. Chafing at Maclean's long investigation, he stooped forward, pointing at the corpse, and was about to speak when Maclean seized his hand, and rising abruptly to his feet, gazed sternly into Gillespie's face.

"There has been murder here."

Gillespie threw up his left hand as if to evade a blow. It carried the candle upwards till it singed his eyebrows. In the silence was heard the sound of the singeing, whose acrid odour permeated the room. Maclean was keenly watching him.

"Murder!" Gillespie gasped, paling to the lips, the full signifi-

429

cance of the terrible word slowly breaking in upon him. Since the Night of the Big Burning he had assiduously built up on the ashes of his fleet the goodwill of the people. He expected to be made a Justice of the Peace, and consolidate his power and wealth. This talk about murder would land him on his beam-ends. It was an ugly thing to have in one's house. In her lifetime he had seldom been angry with his wife. Insolence, contempt, scorn, neglect, had been his weapons. Rage against the impotent clay that was threatening his edifice now possessed him, and he ground his teeth.

"I've aye had to thole for her, an' noo to the bitter end," he blurted out. "It was aye me, an' noo she's by wi't, it'll be 'Gillespa', the brute,' an' 'I telt ye it wad come to this. Is Gillespa' no' the rag, the scum, the vaigabond?' " The muscles of his neck swelled, his face became purple; wrath made him terrible to look at, vindictive and lowering over the dead body of his wife.

Maclean rapped out a sharp question.

"Where is Topsail?"

"Goäd kens; I sent her to the West Loch wi' a pickle messages."

"At this time of night?"

"She gied awa' at the back o' nine o'clock."

"Where's Eoghan?"

The ring of suspicion in Maclean's voice sent the blood to Gillespie's head in a rush, and his breathing became stertorous.

"Ye dinna mean to say it was me?" In spite of a superhuman effort at self-control his voice broke.

Maclean shook his head, and said in a grave voice: "I make no accusation; it is not to me you will have to explain, Mr. Strang."

Gillespie trembled. The suspicion of crime would stick to him; he would have to prove innocency of hands.

"Whatna judgment's fa'en on my hoose the nicht?" he cried, his beady eyes widening dumbly upon the doctor in panic.

Maclean pointed his forefinger at the blood-splashed wall.

"There is the handwriting of the judgment," he said.

The high, pitiless blood seemed to blind Gillespie, who looked helplessly from it down to his wife, and back again at the wall.

"It is not hers," said Maclean, in a solemn voice. "Let us finish our work."

The doctor was convinced. It had not taken him many minutes to discover that the blood was not Mrs. Strang's. He had also found in her right hand, upon which she lay, the blood-smeared razor. He wished to be convinced that Gillespie had not had a hand in the business. Having ascertained this, he pitied the man. He guessed that Mrs. Strang, in a fit of frenzy, had cut some one's throat; he thought it must be poor Topsail's, simply because of her absence at this time of the morning. He beckoned to Gillespie to follow him with the candle; tracked the blood to the sink, through the kitchen door, and across the passage. At that moment a step was heard on the outside stair—heavy and slow. Maclean halted, listening.

"Who's there?" screamed Gillespie in nervous fear.

The next moment the outer door was pushed open, and the wet, rosy, smiling face of Topsail appeared.

"Good God, you!" cried Maclean, in horror. His face took a sudden bleached aspect, as he turned and looked at Gillespie in profound pity.

Topsail stood gazing at the two men, and the smile slowly faded from her face. She let go the door, which swung to, in the fierce draught, with a crash which went echoing through the house. Plucking nervously at her skirt she chirped:

"A happy New Year."

Gillespie flung on her a scorching, malignant look.

"Hush, woman," Maclean said sternly; "stand where you are." He beckoned to Gillespie to bring forward the candle. They were on the threshold of Eoghan's room.

"Mr. Strang, I warn you that we may find a terrible sight here."

The hand that held the candle shook violently, and the breath in Gillespie's nostrils whistled loudly. Maclean led the way. Beyond the bed in the midst of the floor Eoghan lay, face downwards. Gillespie gripped the end of the bedstead, leaned heavily forward, panting, and shook like a dog. His figure became rigid, his eyes protruded in their stare, and he began to moan like a stricken ox. Maclean stooped and turned over the body. The face lay in a pool of dark blood. The nose was flat with the pressure. A large, gaping wound was in the throat, the face was red to the hair on the forehead, and the shirt soaked in blood.

"Jesus Christ in heaven! he's near cut the heid off hissel'!"

Gillespie's awful cry rang out to the ears of Topsail in the passage. She hastened to the door, and the next moment a woman's scream rang out above the noise of the gale, and

Topsail Janet, covering her eyes with her hand, reeled backwards and sank in a heap on the threshold.

The miserable Gillespie hovered a moment about the ghastly body, his hands twitching, his face working convulsively. Maclean arose, wiped his forehead, and gently took the candle from Gillespie.

Death, the black beagle, had hunted Gillespie to earth. The sight of his murdered son tore his dark soul into his baited eyes, and in one awful glimpse reduced his life to the lees. In that blood Gillespie foundered. In a state of swoon, baulked, defeated, broken, he whined like a sick child: "Doctor! doctor! tak' me awa' oot o' here."

Maclean led him from the room, and locked up the house. Topsail Janet, walking like the blind and sobbing hysterically, followed them like a dog to the doctor's home. Two o'clock of the New Year boomed down on dark Brieston as Maclean set off to arouse the policeman.

18

GILLESPIE had again encountered the Procurator-Fiscal, and wilted under his naked examination. The legal formalities were ended, and it was the time of the coffining. The countryside was rigid as iron, as white as salt. The Butler was in the shop, dressed in the famous sealskin waistcoat. For the first time in many years he had omitted to have his photograph taken at Rothesay.

"Hard weather, Gillespie!" His tone was cordial and open; a little boisterous to conceal his rugged pity.

"Ay! blae lik' an' cauld." Gillespie was pouring seed from a paper bag into the canary's feed-box. Nothing was audible but the hissing of the seed.

"This bird o' mine was stervin'," he said, not daring to raise his eyes. His voice trailed away into a quaver. His hand shook so violently that the seed spilled over on the floor. The Butler contemplated the spilled seed, poked at it with his stick, and spoke in a slow, burring voice.

"Gillespie, you an' me didn't pull; but that's a' bye."

The seed rained on the floor, rained. Gillespie raised his massive head, and nodded, gulping hard. A sense of the immensity of his loss came over him again at the Butler's tone of condolence. He stood in a shaft of the wintry sunlight, with a scared look on his face. The bird burst into song, flooding the lance of the sun with melody. Gillespie raised a tremulous face and tear-twinkling eyes to the bird.

"It's a clean sweep, Chrystal," he groaned. "Aw! thon sicht, thon gash sicht!" The Butler, with downcast eyes, was ploughing a feverish staff-point among the seed. "My hert's brocken; there's nane sae much as left to watch the deid. Goäd Almichty! this is a forsaken hoose." In the gloom of the shop, whose front door was locked, he turned a piteous face on the Butler.

"Wait here till I come back. I'll go for Lonend and Mr. Stuart."

Gillespie shook his head.

"Lonen' 'ill no' come."

The Butler brought the point of his stick down upon the floor. "Hector will come. Get on your blacks and a white shirt." Did the Laird's old valet speak there, or a man of tender sympathy, offering to grief something to do?

Topsail Janet and Sandy the Fox were in charge of the house. Gillespie, taking no notice of them, entered his room and glanced at the long rigid outline beneath the sheet, and the pallid, impassive face. This deathly stillness isolated him from all the world. The atmosphere seemed charged with minute particles of lead, whose load rested oppressively on his chest. The room had a profound depth, a silence that flowed out and mingled with immensity, and haunting him at his shoulder was that eternal calm on the bed.

He turned out his best clothes and a white shirt, scrupulously obeying the Butler's directions. He had a difficulty with one of his fine boots, for the wound on the sole of his right foot was angry.

Dusk was falling when he had finished dressing. With haggard face he passed out in silence before his servants, and sought the parlour to watch for Lonend. Aimlessly he shuffled about, touching this and that with nerveless hands, till he sat down at the window in the grey light of the sea and tried to think. Nothing but the most trivial things occurred to him. He remembered the sleek face of the lawyer, and his thin-lipped, menacing leer, as of something which he had seen years ago. He put his hand idly in his pocket and discovered there a pound note. He knew at the touch it was money. He could not remember how it came to be there. It was money possessed by his wife, which Eoghan had picked up in coppers and small silver coin, and which, when it had amounted to one pound sterling, Eoghan had converted into a pound note, and in a spirit of tragic irony had for safety banked with his father. Gillespie pulled a frowning brow of perplexity as his fingers closed over the crinkly parchment. Suddenly, with terrible clearness, the dead face of his son rose up from its recumbent place upon the bedroom floor, and swam before him in the gloom. He put his hand over his eyes. It held the pound note. The tragedy of the lives of father, mother, and son met and were centred in that piece of paper-money, which could not shut out the appalling vision. His son was in the room confronting him; there was blood upon the face; a great, ragged, red hole gaped in the throat; a frozen stare in his abysmal eyes; eyes mute, and yet, by the might and majesty of death, resurgent with condemning tongues. Gillespie crouched on the chair, congealed with fear, and strove in vain to cry out, but his dry tongue was glued to his palate. A vapourish flame wavered in the direction of the door, and the room became dark with night. The pound note fell from his paralysed fingers, lay a moment on his knee; its twitching sent it slowly down. He was startled at the little sibilant noise, as the paper fluttered to his pained foot, and rustled on to the floor. He arose, breathing deeply and steadying himself vainly from taking a giddy plunge, lurched into a table. There was a crash of glass on the floor. It was Eoghan's case of birds' eggs. The splintering sound sent Gillespie's heart drumming into his throat, and he recoiled sideways.

"Good Goäd!" he breathed; "a' things goin' to wrack an' ruin?" In speechless panic he stumbled out of the parlour, hands spread out in front of him. The judgment of silence had found him.

This silence of the house unmanned him, and he trailed down the stair and passed into the back shop, where he lit a candle. Mechanically he began to turn over the papers in his desk. His eye fell on a yellowish piece of printed paper folded in two. It was a cutting from the local newspaper. He picked up his spectacles, and at the first glance horror seized him. He remembered it now, long forgotten in the dust of a pigeon-hole.

"From the results just published of the Examination held by

the Governors of the Trust for education in the Highlands and Islands, we notice with pleasure that one of their bursaries has been awarded to Mr. Eoghan Strang, a pupil of Brieston Public School, who stood third in the list for the County. We heartily congratulate Mr. Strang on his success. The bursary is tenable for three years, and enables the Bursar to proceed to the University. Mr. Strang, who is a young lad of great promise, is a son of Mr. Gillespie Strang, a well-known merchant and fish curer of Brieston, whose other son, it will be remembered, was drowned under exceptionally sad circumstances."

Gillespie remembered how, on a Saturday night, this newspaper had been handed to him across the counter by Carmichael, from West Loch Brieston, and how, when the shop was closed, he had secretly cut out the notice and hoarded it like a treasure. He had felt kindly disposed ever since to the West Loch Brieston man, and counted it no inconvenience to have sent Topsail to his house with a basket on that fatal Hogmanay night. Regularly Eoghan had handed over to him moieties of that bursary in endorsed cheques—money which had gone into the gluttonous business. A clear globe of water splashed down on the bleached newspaper-cutting, and the sorrow of Gillespie's soul was heard in that forlorn chamber of commerce.

"Och! och! I had the bonny penny hained for him."

He was roused from his Gethsemane by the deep voice of the Butler.

"Are ye there, Gillespie?"

He hastily thrust the cutting into his waistcoat pocket, and blowing out the candle, went out and followed the Butler.

On the stair-head, at the entrance to the passage, lit by a lamp on the wall to show the way for the undertaker, Gillespie faced Lonend, bull-headed, truculent. All that day Lonend had been in a blind rage which, since the death of his daughter, had alternated with his grief.

"Whaur is my daughter?" he snarled.

Gillespie made a gesture of despair.

"By Goäd! a bonny mess you've made o' her!"

"I'm a lonely man, Lonen', let me be."

Lonend flung on him a look of devilish hatred, curling back his lips in a grimace. "Ye'll no' be richt lonely till ye're in hell." He watched in thick-set malice to see the effect of this sting; but upon Gillespie, confessing himself as "lonely" to an enemy, such

435

barbarous words were powerless to hurt. His eyes simply blinked; and Lonend, sick with rancour, and a sour cloud on his face, strode from him muttering a curse, to digest his spleen in the solemn presence of his dead daughter.

The Apostle James, the sailmaker, the companion of rats in his windy loft, to whom Gillespie had flung now and again an alms of work, crept up the stair and appeared at the entrance, white-haired, rheumy-eyed, famished of face, painfully thin and shrunken, and held out his hand to Gillespie. "May the Lord be gracious to you and comfort you;" and he, too, passed into the kitchen, a poor, simple man, with hope in God large in his soul.

Gillespie stood alone in the dimly-lit passage, his mind foundered in a grey blank. He was only conscious that other men were preparing Eoghan for the grave,. and were going to take him away from his sight for ever. Could this thing be? His strength ebbed from him at the thought. Those terrible events were moving with irresistible, impetuous speed. His shoulders drooped, he bowed his massive head upon his breast, under a load of intolerable weariness.

Tramp! tramp! shuffle! shuffle! the slow, measured footsteps sounded hollow in the close, and scraped at the foot of the stair. A cold chill ran down Gillespie's spine, and he shivered as if with ague. The sound of voices reached him; the clatter of feet upon the stair. Royal death had given all men the right of free entry. Surging out of the darkness on the stair-head, Gillespie saw the end of a coffin, and put out impotent hands to ward off the sight. The emaciated, tired face of Stevenson the joiner, with its wiry, straggling beard, rose up on the stair-head out of the darkness, like a face arising out of the sea. Gillespie's huge bulk blocked the passage, but the joiner, who did not see him across the coffin, pushed on with protruding tongue. The coffin hit Gillespie on the shoulder and sent him staggering back against the wall, pushed unceremoniously out of the way. The sallow, unhealthy face of the undertaker's man appeared at the other end of the coffin. Gillespie heard him panting. The coffin went past him as if sailing in the air with a life of its own. His eyes, level with its top, saw the glitter of the name-plate. The undertaker's man, on Gillespie's side of the passage, encountered him, nodded and whispered with a lisp: "The thecond ith comin' behind."

The second! a world of coffins!

Gillespie could not tolerate the sight, and stealing back to the shop, locked the door. Ignorant that man knows not himself, he had received at last some specific knowledge of his soul, from the sight of a coffin. Careless always and, finally, utterly neglectful of providing for his wife, he was forced now to provide for her this extreme shelter. He was learning that things outside himself were greater than he. Of the other coffin for his son, yet invisible, he did not learn; he felt, felt that he stood barefoot on the red-hot lava which had destroyed his house. The trumpets were dumb, and would never be blown again. The edifice of marble and gold, which he had so painfully reared, would be uninhabited, and for ever silent—a house of clay doomed soon to annihilation; though the fates decree that the deeds by which it was achieved will remain indestructible—the back of to-day being tied with the burden of all the yesterdays. Though in that hour Gillespie Strang would, to an observer, have appeared cold and calculating, yet it was the coldness of snow covering a volcano. As he saw the pride of his life take wing and vanish in a whirlwind, mortality made him acutely conscious that his will was yet to be made. He was in the pitiable position of a man whose life has been one long crime to make a fortune of which, now that he is childless and friendless, he does not know how to dispose. He used to be imperturbable and, so Brieston thought on the morning when his fleet was in ashes, of iron mould. Only there are hurricanes which destroy more things than fleets. Did he think of it, we can fancy him smiling now at his career of scheming, chicanery, and lubricity—but what a smile. He had trimmed his sail to every wind, and found a lee-shore. His fate deserves some pity. He stumbled upon it reluctantly, in the height of his ambition, when he was about to satisfy his pride by wreaking vengeance, through a tool of a lawyer, upon the head of his implacable enemy. He had been great in his activities, and in another sphere would have played a large part, and affected much more than the destinies of a little town. But in such a theatre his fall could not have been greater. A giant, perishing in a mean hovel, is a more pitiable sight than that of the same man dying upon the stage of the world. The arrow of destiny rankled in Gillespie's breast as much as if he were expiring with a crown on his head, not because his dark genius had suffered defeat, but because he was now forced to make a will over the dead body of his son. Whoever has sympathy will recognise that he had a certain earnestness and vision, no matter the dark ways that he travelled, and that many things

437

depended on him, and if he shook Brieston, it was with single hand. Beneath his tarnish was a lamentable and even a wistful love. Over the fierce lightnings that play upon his ruin somehow there fall the dews of pity.

Seated at his desk by candle-light he summoned that lamentable love, as he pored upon the photograph of his son, and chewed the stump of a pen that had written much in blood and tears. Mr. Kennedy had been proud of the boy; even the gluttonous Stuart had babbled of him. Dumbly, Gillespie stared at the photograph. The haunting smile of the face, like a wavering flame of the spirit, caught him by the throat. He had never seen that smile on the face of the original. On that thin face it had a strange elusiveness—beseeching, fleeting, yearning; and suddenly, as by a dagger struck home, Gillespie knew the smile—it had shone on his own mother's face. The discovery of this elfish trick of heredity came with a shock, and he watched the photograph with that strange sense of expectancy that we experience in gazing upon the picture of beloved ones who are dead, or vanished from our ken. The eyes smiled out on Gillespie's woe. With this son by his side he would cheerfully have faced the world; but now he was against the wall facing that world—the world that had always hated him—the jeering, keeking, whispering, dodging world. A pitiless people would crucify him on the cross of obloquy. He had led men, had cajoled, trapped, sold, beaten them, and now for the first time in his life he wished for a friend. He thought of Maclean—the only man in Brieston who would not brook his double-dealing, and yet treated him frankly man to man. But Gillespie discovered that he feared the doctor, and with the discovery an immensity of future pain opened and shut on his mental vision, as a turbulent sea on a dark night is bared by the lightning and vanishes again. Deep within his breast there stirred a feeling he had never before experienced; it was remote, vague, yet insistent, in which he felt comfort. The flinty heart of Gillespie was struck by the rod of Heaven; the Angel of Death had passed in the night through the land, and finding no blood of sacrifice, in a long life, upon the lintel of his door, had entered and taken away his son; but deep beneath it all was this vague sense of comfort. Gillespie's heart was stirring to feel after the compassion of God, as over his head he heard the muffled sounds of other men putting his son into a coffin. He addressed himself to making his will, to making at last his sacrifice.

Mrs. Galbraith, in the company of Topsail Janet, who was weeping softly, visited the chambers of the dead, and with deft tenderness cut a strand of Eoghan's dark, lanky hair. She returned to her house in the Back Street, and opening the big family Bible, laid the wisp of hair as the offering of a broken heart upon the verse: "*Be not deceived; God is not mocked: for whatsoever a man soweth, that shall he also reap.*" Hour after hour she sat in sackcloth by that altar, knowing she had been bewitched, and that to God alone belongeth vengeance. Again and again, in tears, she passionately kissed the hair.

She saw no one. The grey, sorrowing days passed till, on an afternoon of gentle rain, she heard the tramp of men passing down the street. They had crossed the Square and come up MacCalman's Lane. The flags of the coasting-steamers in the Harbour were at half-mast; the shops closed; the blinds drawn in the houses; Harbour Street was empty. Brieston looked on in silence; children hung on the flanks of the large procession; Maclean walked at the very tail-end, chewing savagely at his moustache. He was in an ill-fitting black coat, and wore a coloured tie. His face was grey and lined.

Mrs. Galbraith heard them coming in the gentle rain, and turning from her attitude of sentinel at the window, flung herself on a chair face downwards on the Bible opened on a table, her forehead pressed on the lock of hair. The sounds of the muffled feet beat as hammers on her brain, and she put her fingers in her ears and ground her face on the Bible. The head of the procession appeared—Gillespie, Lonend, and Chrystal Logan walking ahead; and the coffins on the stretchers slowly filed past the window. Their shadow fell upon her room, darkening it as with eclipse—an image of the gloom that was come upon her soul. Her body was absolutely motionless and rigid. Then the shadow passed away from her room. But over Mrs. Galbraith's soul was spread a night more desolating and grievous than any shadow or external darkness.

19

GILLESPIE limped down Harbour Street in his Sunday clothes, past the police station to the Quay head, in a gauntlet of eyes.

"He's thrang wi' coffins noo," sneered Tamar Lusk.

"Look at the face o' him," nudged the vicious Bent Preen.

"Damn ye," roared old Sandy, "hae ye no' peety for that leakin' boat?"

Gillespie was now abreast of the Quay head, and Old Sandy, quitting the group of men, crossed the road and held out his hand.

The Quay head watched in breathless silence.

"It's a gran' day, Mr. Strang."

"Ay! it's a' that, Sanny." But his heart said, "A gran' day; but my son is dead."

"Ye've got your ain trouble to thole this day, Gillespie; I'm sorry for ye."

Gillespie took the blue-veined, wrinkled hand.

"Thank ye kindly, Sanny, thank ye;" and Gillespie walked on, rocking slightly as he went. Brieston or its Quay head had no power to sting. Gillespie was beyond that. He was stripped bare of all entanglements, and those idols of a day with which his hands had been hampered. He looked upon Brieston as upon a desert, with vacant, unseeing eyes. Death had resolved all things for the dead, and also for Gillespie, this—the value that is in things. He was broken, clay upon the potter's wheel, and wished to see his father and be reconciled. After that he would deal with Lonend.

As he drew near to the "Ghost" he put up his hand to his black tie, futilely arranging it, and cleared his throat every few yards he travelled. He looked up at the windows, but they were all vacant; and noted that the harled wall was rusty. The house had a gaunt aspect; sea-bleached and solitary to the beach; raising its rugged front to the whistling winds, and looking out blindly upon the grey, empty sea. A house of no resort; a house of silence, save for the jangling of the sign over the door. A faint smile came over Gillespie's face as he recognised the sign. The smile redeemed his face, for, like the house, his aspect was wizened and gaunt. The old familiar creak over the door awakened the past out of its sleep, and he became afraid of meeting his father. Like a stranger he knocked at the door, and stood facing the green-painted wood, waiting. Barbara was in her room at the window, in the gable-end on the top-floor, staring out on a grey sea full of unrest. Its movements were sinuous and stealthy, like those of a great snake uncoiling. She watched the quick-changing shadows of the clouds on the face of the water as if they were phenomena of another world. The empty hills beyond, the sleeping fishing-boats, with their masts all pointing the one way, the distant trees, the strip of road that lost itself behind Muirhead Farm, as if it had dived down in the hurry of some discovery, the cows wandering on the hillside towards Lonend among a patchwork of green, and the dark whin—all these things she saw as in a transmagoria. Her world of reality lay beyond the apparent, enclosed within the walls of profound grief. Something barbaric in league with death had wrecked her life. These were not really cloud-shadows which she beheld, but the gloom of a fatality which had ushered her into that land of sorrow where men and women wander seeking peace, and are given the bitter gift of undying remembrance. She was sick of thought, and yet her mind went round and round about one thing. As if she had been breathed upon by the spirit of the Recording Angel, she felt that all the horror of ruin and disaster was due to her uncle. She had seen him trail down the road to the "Ghost," and shuddered as she would at a murderer, who had been drawn to gaze once more on the fatal spot of his crime. She dared not look upon his face within the house. She had seen it from the window, and his appearance shocked her—he was hollow-eyed and haggard, and for all his size and stoutness, had a strange, withered look. The firmness had gone from his flesh; his cheeks were flabby; and over his countenance there reigned the mournful air of a disastrous battlefield which, once a smiling champagne, had been scorched and fire-blackened. Something had gone from him—his alert decisiveness, his air of initiative, boldness, and expectation. His leonine head was held low, and he stood at the door like a great beech blasted by lightning.

No one came to answer his knock. Poignant misery stabbed him to the heart as he put his hand on the handle and found it turn in his slack grasp. Surely the son of the house might enter unchallenged. So he was used to open this door when his mother was alive. Mechanically he hung up his hat as if he had come to stay. In that corner in the dark of the kitchen-door he used to keep his hand-lines; the place met him as with a blow. He remembered how his wife used to plead with him to take her to this house with Eoghan in her arms, that the breach might be healed; but the five hundred pounds loomed up, an insurmountable barrier. He had never repaid that money. Now she was dead, and Eoghan was dead; his father lay sick of a "stroke"; and he had fifty times five hundred pounds. All that was worth striving for was gone. Ah, no! his father was left. He was here for that. If medical skill, the best in Glasgow, could help, his money would be freely given. This thought brightened Gillespie, and he began ascending the stair. His right foot felt on fire. He had been shivering all over since the funeral, and thought he must have caught a chill at the grave. It had made his neck stiff. "My face feels as hard as airn," he had said to Topsail that morning. He noticed some difficulty in swallowing. Certainly his mouth looked hard and set, with an unwonted stiffness about its angles. And now, as he ascended the stair, his right foot felt on fire.

On the landing, at the top of the stair, a carved tiller was suspended by a brown cord against the wall. He had carved that tiller under his father's directions, and with it had learned to steer a boat, under his father's eye. Beneath the stars it had guided the boat home, when his father would wrap his own oilskin-coat about him against the dawn-wind. He, miserable, had never wrapped Eoghan against the cold; but had sent him beneath the smacks, when the tide had ebbed, to scavenge for the fragments of coal fallen from the buckets; had sent him on Saturdays and holidays to glean among freezing rocks for whelks; had loaded his head with heavy baskets of goods to be delivered to customers, and had quarrelled with his wife when she pleaded for the boy. He had sent him to College, and sneered at book-learning as he sent him. It all came back now like revenge. He brought it back, and found the pain sweet.

Beneath the tiller was a deal table. He opened its drawer, an old action which he had by rote. All were there—thole-pins, a dog-collar, rabbit-snares. He was unable to look upon the ghost of unsullied youth, with the slow wrath of outraged manhood upon him. The atmosphere of the house was terribly charged with an old-world tenderness. He could almost believe his patient, uncomplaining mother yet to be in the kitchen, knitting those long grey stockings up over the knee for her fisherman-husband. Nemesis drew him on, limping to the end of the passage, where there was a narrow stair of bare wood leading to a low, long room beneath the roof—his room, half workshop, half store. Slowly he ascended his Via Dolorosa, and came upon the door wide open—the sign of utter neglect—betraying at the first glance the model of a yacht lying on its side, careened for ever, its sails green-mouldered, and an open knife beside this other wreck, as he had flung it down. It was black-red with rust.

He leaned hard against the wall, whose dust smudged his coat. The overmastering silence which had oppressed him in the presence of his dead wife settled again upon his soul. Gillespie, in despair, had no tears to shed, and could not pray. His heart was withered, and was slowly cracking. This room was a grave. Gillespie went out, and slowly descended his Via Dolorosa on the way to his cross.

When he was mid-way down the stair Barbara came out of a room on the right. Her colour was gone; her eyes were large and dark-ringed; her hair was drawn tight over her forehead. She looked old—this nun of grief—and her face was full of sorrow. She was startled at sight of him, and glancing away said, in a cold voice of scorn:

"You have come at last!"

Gillespie, with sunken head, descended the three remaining steps, and lifted upon her his drawn face and terrible eyes of pain.

The girl screamed at the sight: "Uncle! uncle! you are ill?"

"Is there where he is?" Mournfully he indicated the room from which she had stepped.

"No," she replied, her lips trembling convulsively; "he's in the room downstairs off the kitchen."

Gillespie knew that his father had taken a "stroke"; not that it had been followed by another. He took a step towards the stair-head.

"Would you like to see him, uncle?"

He turned, beseeching pity of the girl in a look. She spoke as if his father were a stranger. His tortured eyes rested upon her thin, shaking shoulders. Her attitude was one of abandonment to grief. To Gillespie the atmosphere was charged with dread. He was suddenly plunged in a bath of flame. A string seemed sharply drawn across his breast and cutting into his heart. He feared he was about to die. He tried to breathe deeply, and could scarcely open his mouth, which seemed to be clamped. Beads of sweat started out on his forehead. The shivering seized him again, and an icy coldness crept over his body.

"Is he no' any better?" He ground out the words.

"He'll—he'll—not live very long—the doctor says."

In the profound silence that followed, the rasping of the sign upon the rigging of the house mingled with the hard, dry sobbing of the girl, and were followed by Gillespie's spasmodic cry of woe, as Barbara burst into a fit of uncontrollable sobbing.

"Barbara! Barbara! there's nobody left but me!" and the heart of Gillespie Strang broke. He gazed at her a moment as if bewildered at her tears, and turning, his body rigid like a steel wire stretched to snapping point, painfully scrambled down the stair to the room off the kitchen.

For the second time within a week he looked on a long, white form, marmoreal in its stillness, stretched out on the bed—a fragile outline, stiff as if in death, beneath the clothes. At the sight, Gillespie felt himself sinking into the depths of an unknown condemnation. An invisible power of reproach was emanating from that stark form and still, unaccusing face, so thin and worn that Gillespie scarce recognised it. The cluster of thick grey hair was swept back from the fine forehead; the mouth, all awry, seemed to have collided with lightning, and one hanging eyelid, tainted with blood, to have been torn with a claw. There was no sign of life on the bed. The eyes were fixed in a glassy stare on the ceiling. Gillespie, making strange strangling sounds in his throat, approached the bed.

"Faither."

The eyes slowly came down from the ceiling and swung round on the face of the son.

Gillespie was breathing in quick, little gasps.

"Faither, I meant to pey ye back wi' interest at five per cent."

The face in the pillow remained immobile, and fixed in a deep, inviolable calm.

Gillespie put out his hand in a beseeching gesture.

"Are ye hearin' me, faither? It's me, Gillespie, your son."

There was no response. The vast deep of affliction there remained still and unruffled. It was beyond the power of mortal to break that profound quiet. Its judgment, the judgment of unearthly silence, had again found Gillespie, ringing with a mighty

444

anvil-stroke of doom upon his soul the words, "Too late! too late!" He tottered from the bed, casting one long look of anguish upon the wearied face sunk in the pillows. In that moment he would have given gold and house and gear, if only one glimmer of tender recognition would divinely light those eyes and sweep across that face, which had so often hovered upon him like an angel's, beneath the stars in the open boat upon the sea. But they were staring upwards, upwards unswervingly, with glazed look upon the ceiling—gazing past Gillespie and the world, into the archives that are stored for ever beneath the Great White Throne. Gillespie's face was the face of one who had seen undying fear. He took a sharp intake of the breath, deep, rending, convulsive; his arms jerked upwards spasmodically, and he fell prone on the floor, his body contorted in a spasm. The crash brought Barbara and Mrs. Galbraith running. They found Gillespie with his teeth firmly clenched, the muscles of his neck standing out in high tension, the body half bent like a bow. He had lockjaw contracted when he had stepped on the broken whisky-bottle which his wife had brought from its place of concealment in the refuse heap of the washing-house.

The spasm was of short duration. The help of fishermen, who were passing, was summoned, and Gillespie was carried to the bed in the kitchen, where his mother had died. Maclean was sent for. Gillespie spoke only once, when, with haggard eyes sunk in pits of pain, he summoned Mrs. Galbraith, and slowly, with enormous difficulty, ground out each word: "Tell—Lowrie—to—pey—five hunner—to—my—faither—at—five—per cent.—for—twenty—year—to-day—today——" His eyes were agonised with entreaty. The effort cost him another spasm.

Maclean ordered the room to be darkened, and that no one was to speak to Gillespie or make the slightest noise. Barbara was prohibited the room. Gillespie was now left in absolute silence, in an atmosphere of semi-gloom, in the twilight of approaching death, with Mrs. Galbraith, the tenderest nurse in the world; and beneath the croaking of the sign of the dagger, father and son took the Last Journey, the one as in a dream, the other in unspeakable torment.

On the second day Gillespie lay dead, his teeth broken, black swellings on his limbs, his eyeballs fixed, glassy, and staring as into a damnable abyss. His lips were purple and stained with blood-froth.

Mrs. Galbraith stood at the window, her terrible vigil done, her heart purged and purified, with her back to the bed. Across the Harbour she could see in the clear, frosty day a ploughman ploughing in the Laigh Park of the farm which Galbraith and his people had tenanted for generations. The squawking of a cloud of gulls behind the plough floated across the Harbour on the still air. At the sound which, perhaps, stirred some memory of the sea, the glazed eyes of old Mr. Strang turned from the ceiling to the window. His wife was dead; dead was his son in the kitchen; dead were his grandchildren; and he, as borne on a tide of sleep, was slipping into the shadows. The sign above the door was at peace in the windless air. Passion and greed, love and dreams, lust and madness, were all vanquished, were all vanished; grief and shame, yearning and hope, were all at rest; faces had faded away; things dissolved; nothing was left but the earth, about to renew life at the hands of another transitory ploughman. With a long, deep sigh old Mr. Strang closed his eyes in the House of Ghosts, to meet the everlasting silence, and look into the things of eternal rest. The sunset flamed along the sea and hung out banners in the heavens. It flooded the "Ghost" with golden light. It shone upon the features of Gillespie, exposed in a ghastly grin. It irradiated the still, white face of old Mr. Strang.

"Earth to earth, dust to dust," murmured Mrs. Galbraith, as she shook the tears from her eyes. The ploughman on Muirhead Farm went on ploughing the lea, ministering to the faith that is imperishable in the breast of man.

GLOSSARY

Acquent wi: acquainted with, accustomed to
afore: before
ain: own
airn: iron
airt: point of the compass, direction
aloo: allow
argle-bargling: arguing
a'thegeither: altogether
a'thing: everything
aucht: anything
auld: old
awa': away

Bairn: child
bate: beat
bate: bet
bauchle: slipper, down at the heel slipper
bawbee: penny
beerit: buried
ben: in, indoors
bien: in comfortable circumstances, comfortable
bide: stay
black-a-viced: dark of complexion
blae: blue
blaiggart: blackguard
blate: shy
blethers: chatter, nonsense
bocht: bought
brae: hillside, declivity
brak: break
bratty: apron
braxy: sheep that has died, flesh of a sheep that has died
breengin': darting
brig: bridge
brocht: brought
broo: brow
buirdly: well set up

Cairryin' clothes: grave clothes
caller: fresh
canna: cannot
canty: cheery
chack: a bite, a slight repast taken hastily
claut: clutch, rake in
clishmaclaiver: gossip, pointless talk
cloot: an old cloth
clype: tell tales on
cock-a-bandy: fir cone
coo: cow
coomb: small coal
corby: crow
corp: corpse
couthie: snug, cosy
creish: grease
crepping: knocking (Gaelic *cnap*)

Dae: do
dale: deal
daleins, dailins: dealings
Dhia: God (Gaelic)
ding: strike, knock
dinna: don't
div: do
doitered: stupid in a senile way
Donnachaidh: Duncan (Gaelic)
dooker: guillemot
dour: stubborn, unyielding, mulish
dourly: stubbornly
dreg: haul
dreich: dull, wearisome
drookin': soaking
drouth: dryness, parched state
drucken: drunken
dumbfoondered: taken aback, overwhelmed by surprise
duvvil: devil

Een: eyes
eenoo: at present, just now

447

efter: after
en': end

Fairing: money or a gift given at the time of a fair
fash: bother
fashed: bothered
faut: fault, blame
feart: afraid
feegur: figure
flyte on: scold, jeer at
foozy: soft looking, blurred
fou: full
fowk: folk
frae: from
freen: relation
frichted: frightened
fugle, fugleman: funk
furrit: ferret
fushionless: pithless, useless
fut: foot

Galluses (gallush): braces
gang: go
gash: ghastly
gether: gather
gey, geyan: very
gie: give
gied: gave
gien: given
girn: whine, make whining complaints
glaur: mud
Glesca: Glasgow
gloamin': dusk
gomeril: rascal
gravat: neck-scarf
greet: weep
grue: shudder, have a sensation of revulsion
grup: grip
gurt: great
gyard: guard

Hae: have
hain: save
hale: whole
haud: hold

havers: nonsensical talk
heid: head
henny: darling
herry: plunder
hoastin': coughing
hoo: how
hoodie: crow
hoose: house
horo-yalleh: a to do (Gaelic *hóro-gheallaidh*)
howk: dig

Jaloose: guess
jant: jaunt
jyle: gaol

Keeking: peeping
ken: know
kep: catch
kirn: churn
kittlin': tickling

Laggery: lumber, rubbish
leeshins: licence
leeve: live
leevin': living
lowe: blaze
lown: placid, quiet
lowse: set loose, cast off
lum hat, lummer: top hat

Mair: more
maist: most, almost
male: meal
mand: manage
maun: must
mercat: market
m'eudail: my darling (Gaelic)
minch: mince
mo chridhe: my heart (Gaelic)
mool: clod
morn: the morrow *The morn:* tomorrow
mo thruaigh: my pity (Gaelic)
muckle: much

Ne'erday: New Year's Day
nesty: nasty
nief: fist

448

nock: clock
nyaf: an insignificant scoundrel

Onyway: anyway
oor: hour
ower: over
oxter: armpit
oxtered: led on linked arms

Perjink: finical, pernickety
pickle: a fair quantity
pleugh: plough
ploy: frolic, exploit
pooder: powder
pook: pluck
pooked: plucked, moulting
pree: taste, take
preen: pin
prig: haggle, importune
punt: rowing-boat

Quate: quiet

Redd up: put to rights, clear up
ree: coal-dump, enclosure
reinge: search
reingin': searching
rippets: uproar
roost: coin
roosty: rusty
roup: auction
rype: poke out a fire

Saut: salt
scad: scald
scaddit: scalded
scarred: scared
scart: cormorant
scartin': scratching
scoory, scoury: overcast and blowy, bad (of weather)
sculduddery: grossness, obscenity
seeck: sick
seegar: cigar
shirra: sheriff
sib: related
siccan: such
sillar: silver, money
skemp: scamp

smock: smoke
smocked: smoked
snog: snug
snowkit: snuffed, smelled
sook: suck
soor dook: buttermilk
souple: cunning
spale-basket: a large shallow basket
speir: ask
steek: to fix, set
stot: a young bull
stoup: water-bucket, a vessel
stravaig: roam, wander
sweert: unwilling

Tapsalteerie: upside down
telt: told
thaieter, theeayter: theatre
thegither: together
thocht: thought
thole: endure
thon: yon, that
thrang: busy
thrang wi': far in with
thrawn: stubborn
through-gaen: active
timmin': emptying
tocher: dowry
toom: empty
trachle: bother, trouble, exertion
trachled: worn out
tred: trade
trokin': having truck with

Waff: draught, waft
wag-at-the-wa': a wall clock with pendulum
wan: one
wance: once
waur: worse
wean: child
wecht: weight
weeda: widow
weedaoor: widower
weemin: women *The weemin's win':* the women's wind, the south-east wind
wersch: insipid, flat tasting
wescut: waistcoat

449

wheck: share
wheen: a lot
whesel: weasel
whigmaleerie: gimcrack
whutteruck: contraption
wice-lik': sensible
wrunkled: wrinkled, entangled

wud: wood
wulk: whelk

Yeuky: itchy, eager
yin: one
yock on: attack verbally, find fault with